To Rick!

Remember – well-behaved women seldom make history!

:)

Martha's Mirror

A Novel by

Sheree Zielke

A pleasure to know you!

Please pass your books along to other readers so I can always replace them!

Creeping Ivy Publishing House
Suite 329, 9768-170 Street
Edmonton, Alberta T5T-5L4

This novel is a work of fiction. Names, characters, places, and incidents either are products of the author's imagination or are used fictitiously. Any resemblance to actual events or locales or persons, living or dead, is entirely coincidental.

First Edition

COVER ART BY FRED SANFILIPO

ISBN: 978-0-9866437-3-6

Martha's Mirror

"...logic clearly dictates that the needs of the many...
outweigh the needs of the few."
(Mr. Spock, Star Trek II: the Wrath of Khan, 1982)

***

"Oh, how I wish I had wings like a dove;
Then I would fly away and rest!
I would fly far away to the quiet of the wilderness.
How quickly I would escape—
Far away from this wild storm of hatred."
(Psalm 55: 6-8, New Living Translation Bible)

***

"Don't let the floods overwhelm me,
or the deep waters swallow me,
or the pit of death devour me."
(Psalm 69:15, NLT Bible)

***

"In your strength, I can crush an army."
(Psalm 18:29, NLT Bible)

Martha's Mirror

For my eldest daughter, Rienna.
May your daughters become mirrors of your strength.

***

For my husband, David.
My best friend, the love of my life.

Martha's Mirror

Logo designed and adopted by The Man, a self-proclaimed biker king who draws motorcycle clubs together in a post-apocalyptic Alberta.

Art mercenary, tattoo artist, and co-owner of
Black Market Tattoos, Edmonton, Alberta, Canada

Acknowledgments

WHOM DO I INCLUDE? Whom do I leave out? That question plagued me for many weeks as I reached the end of the writing and editing of *Martha's Mirror*. Even at the writing of this, I am still not sure I have gotten it quite right. So, with sincerest apologies to anyone I might have overlooked (and please know it was unintentional), I shall make a run at this...

First, I must thank those closest to me, the ones who have seen me through the good times and the bad times: my husband, David Thiel, and my very close friend and editor, Robert Christman.

Then I want to thank my friend, Susan Estes Smith, who was a reader on the first book, but who morphed into a very talented editor on this book.

Thanks to Paula Sorken and Paul Birkitt who guessed the title of this book and won the right to read and comment on a third draft of *Martha's Mirror*. Terrific edits!

I want to thank my on-location crew—those who have accompanied me on multiple book signings—good friends like Wonda Phillip, Denise King, and Marilyn Ferrett. You girls are so terrific. Thanks also to Kevin and Jason Phillip, Ashley Jones (for getting the room for the "Coming Out" party), Asheena Phillip (for the celebration cake), Sylvia Labelle and Guhdar Ali (for taking photos during signing sessions), my daughter Rienna Nagel (for her enthusiasm—she knew about *Martha's Vine* more than fifteen years ago), and to my son Ryan Zielke (for his fantastic support during the book launch).

Thanks to my supporters who have never failed to be there for me with uplifting words of encouragement like Stuart and Grace Hellis (a special thanks to Stuart for wearing a tuxedo to the signings!), and my sweet friend Lauri Latour.

Then there are my faraway friends whose encouragement and support has been fantastic: Arlene Blades, Jenny Gandert, Alan Shapiro, Gina Pearson, Aaron Winters, Andy Birkitt, Claudio Alejandro Mufarrege, Sharon Young, Kirsten Bowers, Dave Hilditch, Laurie Dirkx, Lindsay Truman, Bruce Seltenright, Terri Burks, and Sunny Deuber Carney.

My thanks to the bookstore managers like Angel Ilnicki at Chapters and Indigo. Thank you for giving me shelf space and for the signing dates.

Thanks to my Indy buddy, Bud Tymko, for his engine advice.

Thanks to tattoo artist, Conrad Plews, for designing the *Apocalypse Archangels* logo matching the one described in *Martha's Vine*.

Thanks also to my dear long-time friend, Eveline Garneau, for her fantastic signage. She is one of the most amazing women I have ever known. When this woman says she's building a house, she means she is building a house, from scratch, with hammer in hand. I want to be with Eveline should the world go sideways.

And a huge thank you to all my readers, both current and new. Without you, Martha's world would be nothing more than a mass of black ink on paper or a bunch of symbols in cyber space.

God bless all of you.

~~~

"Think about it. Tight knit groups survive in chaos.
What's tighter, better organized, and more disciplined than a motorcycle club?"
Virgil, Martha's Mirror, 2011
~~~

Table of Contents

Synopsis

Martha's Vine: Book One

NOBODY WORRIED much when the lights went out—at first. People had been through power outages before; they knew the power would be back; it always came back. Even when two days passed, and the power had still not returned, they remained calm. A day or two off work irritated the workaholics chasing deadlines, but the impromptu holiday was welcomed by most of the population. Fridges and cupboards were still bulging with food; gas stations (via generators) still sold fuel; candles were in abundance; computer and cell phone batteries were fully powered; and emergency generators had kicked in—just as they were expected to do. People grumbled a little, but they believed in the system, reminding each other that the power would be back "any time now."

It wasn't until the fifth day without power, that people began to question. Things they had taken for granted like phone service, groceries, and gasoline had begun to disappear. Most cell phones had quit working because the signal tower backup batteries had died. Replenishing food after the last glass of milk was drunk and the final egg was scrambled, via a trip to the grocery store, was useless because fresh produce was largely gone. Long lines at the gas pumps, and EMPTY signs hung on gas station doors, made many a brow furrow and a temper flare. The people began to suspect that something was amiss, but still they had faith. Like eager children anticipating a Christmas morning of ripped wrapping paper and new toys, they still expected the power to return.

However, after the seventh day without power, bewilderment set in, followed by a cold fear that started in the belly and swept upwards like a sudden icy breeze. After the seventh day, the people knew they were in trouble. But by then, for most of the population—it was too late.

Except for Martha and her family.

Except for Matthew (the Gatekeeper) and his people.

Except for The Man and his army of bikers.

Except for the Crazies.

~ ~ ~

CHARLES DARWIN had been right. When the Change lumbered in, a great, stupid beast unmindful of the pitiful creatures beneath its leaden feet, only the strongest, the fittest, the fastest, and the smartest survived. As for the rest—a community that had put its faith into computers, the Internet, and the power grid—they stood impotently by as the snow fell, trapping them in their suburban prisons and their inner city apartment cells—without heat, without light, without food, and without hope.

The harsh Alberta climate with its frigid temperatures and heavy snowfall caused many deaths—of urbanites, mostly. City people, so used to convenience—picking up a perfectly roasted chicken from a grocery store for Sunday dinner, a latte at the corner coffee shop, a tank of gas at the neighborhood gas station, or hot water at the turn of a tap and heat at the flick of a tiny switch—those people didn't survive. They couldn't survive. So used to legislated fairness, a five-day workweek, and a fast food existence, the majority of city folk were not prepared for the perfunctory and dismissive inequality of the Change.

At first, age-old habit and reliance upon the normal, the mundane, the expected—what was...and what would be again soon—kept people in their homes, in anticipation. Just a few more hours, just a few more minutes—and it would be time—time for the power to come back on, time for things to go back to the way they had been. Then everything would be good and wonderful. Just like before.

It didn't happen that way.

After several days of no light, no heat, no operating ATMs, people discovered a baseness in themselves, a cutthroat coarseness they never knew they had. Cash exchanged hands—politely, at first. Soon the cash ran out. Courtesy, like an old shirt at the back of a closet, was demoted to the bottom of societal priorities. That's when the looting started, and the madness took hold. Guns made an appearance, and the killings began.

Police, the military, and other officials tried to keep the peace. However, hunger has a way of triumphing. At first, food and water handouts were plentiful, and people waited obediently in line. But when the handouts turned into paltry rations, well-behaved citizens morphed into angry mobs. A growing panic, fueled by desperation, replaced respect and any fear of authority. As their casualties grew in number, police and soldiers began to defect, in favor of their own families, their own needs, and their own survival.

But how did it happen? How did the power just disappear? Nobody knew. But they had their suspicions.

Rumors erupted like mold on warm cheese. And, like cheese, the speculations came in many flavors—everyone had their favorite explanation, their favorite *truth* for what had happened—and what would happen next. However, the only *true* truth was that civilization was in trouble—the power was not coming back on. New plans had to be made and old ways retired. Those who understood *that* truth were the ones who adapted; they were the ones who were ready when the early snowstorm hit.

The late autumn snow drifted down, unapologetically covering an already desolate world with even greater bleakness. The heavy wet mass congested city streets, making them impossible for the average vehicle to traverse. Many still tried—shoveling as far as they and their neighbors could go—but fell down exhausted, thwarted, and very angry when their shovels reached a major artery and they realized that without a snowplow, they weren't going any further. They trudged back to their homes and did what they could to wait out the storm; the realists did what they could to wait out the *winter*.

Seniors, the disabled, and those still hospitalized were among the first to die. Caregivers chose between their professional ethics and their families—with their families taking priority. For those empathetic souls who remained behind, a lack of food, scant fuel, no heat, frozen water pipes, and an innate sense of self-preservation soon sent them—albeit, reluctantly, and with several backward glances—in search of survival, leaving their patients to starve or freeze to death. Some patients, upon learning of their fate, threw back their covers, crawled from their beds, scavenged up warm clothes and boots, and joined the race for survival on the streets.

Martha's friend, Amanda, had done just that. The feisty older woman had ripped the intravenous tubes from her arms, kicked over a table laden with pill bottles, and turned her back on cancer. She returned to her home, and made the best of the Change—thriving, and not just surviving. Amanda was one of the rare ones. Resourceful and clever, she had surprised and delighted Martha by revealing what was hidden in her handbag—a brick that neatly took down a drunken Crazy outside a church. A brave act that had saved their lives.

For the most part, only those who had done some survival planning before the Change hit, those who owned RVs, and those willing to walk away from their homes in favor of the countryside—only those people survived the devastation of heavy winter snows and -50 wind chills. The ones with snowmobiles parked in their garages had an edge, too. Especially the ones with jerry cans filled with stabilized fuel. However, with the blessing came a curse—the battle between the *Haves* and the *Have-nots*. The Haves soon learned that *the having* necessitated a constant state of alertness. Fighting. Running. Or dying.

Martha's family had been prepared. An RV stocked with food, fuel, and weapons awaited them in an RV trailer park just outside Edmonton. Their first thought, however, was to leave their acreage and get to a cosmopolitan center, like Edmonton—a big city where emergency services would be in full swing. After all, if power were to be restored, it would happen in a big city first.

Or so they had surmised.

Martha, her husband Josef, and ten other family members, left their acreages and headed east to Edmonton. They pulled into a Holiday Inn on the west side where, surprisingly, rooms were still being rented, at a discount, but cash was the only payment being accepted. They pooled their money and took five rooms. They settled in. Grocery stores, gas stations, and malls surrounded them. A Walmart was only steps away. They would be fine.

At first, they waited patiently for the power to return. However, after several weeks of no power, after several weeks of watching people scream and quarrel, claw and punch in their quest for food and fuel, after nights filled with the screams of those who had tapped out—those who had allowed endless struggle and hopelessness to take their minds, after days of seeing despair in the eyes of mothers and fathers as they cradled their starving children, after several weeks of that—Martha's family deserted the city.

A crowd of people greeted them when they pulled into their campsite; some they recognized, some they did not. They breathed a collective sigh of relief when they saw their possessions—their fuel and their food stores—were still intact; nothing had been damaged or stolen. So, cramped inside their RV, their new life began.

Weeks later, during a family meeting, Martha questioned the decision to remain on the campground. After much debate, they decided to hold out until the spring melt. They knew they would have to replenish their food stores by hunting or by scavenging. Every chance they got, when the weather would break and the snow would melt sufficiently, they would get into their 4X4 and drive to nearby small towns. Deserted convenience stores and private homes yielded up a wealth of foodstuffs and fuel, enough to keep them comfortable. But Josef kicked himself for not buying a snowmobile; he wanted to use it to hunt deer. It wasn't long before fate supplied one.

Late in December, the sound of buzzing engines made them run for their guns. Everyone had learned to fear the "Crazies"—renegade bullies who ruled the urban areas from the backs of their motorcycles. As the months passed, their control spread into the suburban areas and acreages, but now they rode snowmobiles. The nickname came easily and instantly to people's lips as a cover-all name for the wild men who showed up, firing rifles, killing, and stealing what they could.

The campers staved off the first attacks—scare tactics mostly—but the attacks became more frequent as the weeks wore on. And more violent. After a midnight raid on the campground and the loss of two more campers and several full cans of gasoline, a watch was set up. This time, the campers were ready. This time the Crazies lost—not only their power toboggans, but their lives, too.

All members had been trained to use guns, they were always armed, and it was agreed that killing the men had been necessary. Nevertheless, the killing sickened Martha, and while she accepted that other humans had to die in their quest to stay alive, she vowed never to shoot a person herself. She had kept that promise...for a while.

When late March arrived, the snow on the roadways had melted sufficiently, and the threat of more snowstorms had passed, Martha's family packed up their unit and pulled out onto the highway. Their inaugural drive took them around hundreds of abandoned vehicles. The trip went very slowly because each car or truck was checked for fuel and other valuables. After siphoning gasoline into jerry cans, they would move on.

Nearer to the city, they began seeing the devastation. Small groups of humans shuffled along in dark masses of despair—their clothes were filthy, their bodies were filthy, and their eyes were hollow and vacant. Sometimes, they looked up and then plodded onward like cows with no destination in mind, other than to find a morsel of edible food, and a safe haven.

The family had become very good at surviving; they had honed it to a fine art. Their little scooters helped them get around the towns and cities quicker and more efficiently, and enabled them to carry bigger loads of scavenged goods. They had added to their group: two orphaned children, an autistic boy named Reggie, and a baby named Moses. They had even been able to check up on old friends, like Amanda. She joined them on their scavenging runs. It was on one of those scavenging runs that Martha crossed the line of her convictions—

Never to kill another human...

A Recap of Martha's Vine

MARTHA'S MIRROR is the continuing story of Martha, a middle-aged Albertan woman, struggling to survive in a post-apocalyptic society following the *Change*: a total loss of the power grid. No computers, no lights, no heat, and a shutdown of the infrastructure results in chaos, starvation, disease, civilian brutality, the emergence of murderous biker gangs, and hundreds of thousands of deaths across North America. However, under Martha's gritty leadership, she and her family survive long enough to unite with another strong leader: Matthew, the Gatekeeper.

Matthew is a survivalist who established his compound years before the Change. He has a symbiotic relationship with a nearby Hutterite farm; he provides protection from attackers, and the Hutterites provide fresh produce, milk, eggs, and meat.

He is selective about who he allows into his compound and resists when Martha and her family, including Reggie—an adopted autistic boy—first arrive. Matthew refuses them entry to his camp, but Martha knows her family's days of outrunning biker gangs—the *Crazies*—are numbered, so she persists. She emphasizes her value as a medic, that her family members are all strong, trained in the use of weapons, and that the younger women can bear children. Matthew relents and the thirteen members of Martha's group join Matthew's survival compound.

The rest of her family slip into their new environment with ease, but Martha is used to being a leader and finds it very difficult to accept Matthew's male-driven society, his laws, and his...*Discipline Committee.* She butts heads instantly with two of Matthew's men, Vince and Brad, who head up the *Morals and Ethics Committee.* Even after being reminded that she has no place in the running of the compound, she can't keep still and voices her disdain for their judicial system.

Martha repeatedly questions Matthew's decisions, and refuses to partake in gun practice, saying she could never kill another human. However, it's not true; she has killed—in cold blood—to save her family from danger. The memory haunts her.

In addition, a primal rush of attraction for Matthew takes her by surprise since she is happily married to Josef, who establishes a strong bond with Matthew and the two become close friends.

Meanwhile, another force, *The Man*, a self-proclaimed motorcycle club sovereign, with plans to amass a huge army of bikers, and take control of the new world, sets his sights on Matthew's compound, and subsequently on Martha and Josef. He has help from a traitor in Matthew's camp: Brad.

Brad provides The Man with inside information about the camp, and even arranges secret midnight visits. One visit ends with Josef and Martha being wounded. They wind up in the compound's medical building—Josef recovering from a beating and a heart attack, and Martha recovering from knife wounds to her leg and hand. They don't know who attacked them since the men wore hoods. They later find out that one of the men was Brad.

Several new members join the camp including fifteen pregnant girls abandoned by their biker boyfriends. Matthew consults with Martha for the first time when deciding whether to allow the girls into the camp. They agree to do so, and Martha prepares for midwife duties, along with her daughter, Ruth, and one of the pregnant girls, Anna.

Martha is cold to Anna at first, but she grudgingly comes to respect and love the girl after Anna saves her life. Anna employs medical knowledge gleaned from assisting her late father, a veterinarian.

Matthew met Anna before, but he keeps their past relationship a secret. The truth of their relationship comes to light when Anna can't birth her own baby, and Martha prepares to perform a C-section that may kill Anna. Matthew steps forward as the father; he tells Martha that babies in his family have big heads, and to give Anna a chance. Anna gives birth to Gordon, a healthy baby boy. Martha is both shocked and unhappy that Matthew has fathered a child with young Anna.

Day-to-day living still embraces some of the comforts of a mechanized world, so scavenging trips are a must. It's during scavenging trips that Martha encounters most of her troubles, including a blue-eyed man—fun-loving and seemingly amoral, Meteor. Martha once more finds herself attracted to another man besides her husband. Meteor is attracted to her, too, and has no qualms about her being married.

However, Martha soon becomes widowed when Josef is kidnapped, tortured, and killed by Brad—under orders from The Man, as a message of strength to Matthew. Martha collapses and enters into a long grief and guilt-filled period. At the time of Josef's murder, she was involved intimately with Meteor during an overnight stay on their way back from a scavenging mission to Hinton.

Josef's murder sets off a war between Matthew's people and The Man's forces, led by a new general, Virgil—a military man, who turns out to be Matthew's ex-friend. Virgil puts together a special team that he hopes will defeat Matthew's men quickly, but this is not to be.

After getting word that they can finally get to Brad, Matthew rallies his forces and then faces-off with The Man. Matthew is taken captive, but luckily, he has an ally amongst The Man's people: Meteor. Earlier, after a falling out with Matthew, Meteor was evicted by Matthew, but he didn't desert the Gatekeeper's people. His love for Martha keeps him loyal. Instead, he goes undercover into The Man's camp, endures flesh-searing torture, and continues to report to Matthew. When Matthew is kidnapped, Meteor sees to his well-being without giving away his subterfuge until Matthew's men can respond.

Matthew's men devise a plot whereby Virgil's forces are taken out with rocket launchers stolen from The Man. The weapons were stolen along with The Man's woman, Cammy. Against her will, she is taken to Matthew's camp where she enters into a relationship with happy-go-lucky Trojan—a former member of The Man's camp. Cammy soon learns that The Man has ordered her execution and she voluntarily joins Matthew's people.

A few peaceful months pass while The Man rebuilds his forces. In the meantime, Martha works on her relationship with Matthew. After several disappointments and another intimate encounter with Meteor, Martha makes her choice clear: she loves Matthew and she will wait for him to love her. Meteor is hurt by her decision, but he secretly loves her, and will do all he can to protect her.

Meteor continues to glean information about The Man's forces from friendly contacts, and he creates his own army of independents who have managed to survive without any allegiances—cowboys, First Nations peoples, and farmers. Meteor convinces them that for the good of all, they would be better off helping Matthew. They set up camp near Matthew's compound with plans to assist Matthew when needed.

Meanwhile, Martha and Matthew work toward a peace and finally a love affair that quickly results in an impromptu marriage, attended only by themselves and God. However, the honeymoon is very short as they discover their camp is about to be attacked.

The Man, in consultation with Virgil, makes his move on Matthew's compound. He is after the compound's winter supplies, access to fresh foods from the Hutterites, and Matthew's oil reserves. The Man's attack comes in the middle of the night when most of Matthew's men have been deployed to a secret second camp, the one with the oil reserves. Only a small group of men is left behind to protect the women and children at the first camp, because most of the remainder of Matthew's men has been sent off to guard the Hutterites' property.

Brad leads the attack on the compound, and soon the women and children are taken hostage and locked inside both of the women's bunkhouses. Except for Martha. Something wakes her and she escapes before being captured. She meets with Matthew's soldiers at the Hutterites farm, before making her decision to go back to the camp and rescue the women and children.

She is discovered and attacked by Brad and his men, who brutally rape her and leave her in the Meeting House, naked and bleeding. She manages to get back to her cabin, where she cleans herself up and makes plans to distract the men guarding one of the bunkhouses—the one with a secret exit. She plans the women and children's escape. Anna and baby Gordon, Martha's two adult daughters—Ruth and Elizabeth—and Martha's grandchildren—Samuel and Mary—are among the escapees.

Martha's plan works and the women and children from the first bunkhouse escape into the woods. In the meantime, Meteor has mobilized his army and they are advancing on the compound with plans to save the women. Miles away from the second camp, Matthew and his men have tricked Virgil and his forces into a crossfire. Trojan and Cammy are part of the plan; they've even provided a truckload of The Man's weapons, originally bound for Virgil.

Virgil believes he has captured Matthew, but he soon realizes he is trapped. He surrenders and asks to be killed. Meanwhile, Martha asks for a meeting with Brad; she intends to kill him. She holds Brad at gunpoint and manages to lock his guards in the women's bunkhouse. She raises her gun to kill Brad, but she falters. Instead, Brad shoots her. Martha collapses. More gunfire. Brad watches as dark shapes converge on the compound. He raises his gun and fires once more. Then he runs.

A young woman with a baby on her hip stops walking. She studies the line of women and children snaking their way through the forest, glowing as they pass through patches of moonlight, winding and wending their way to safety...like a vine...*Martha's Vine*. She stops following the fleeing women and turns back to the compound. Where she feels she belongs. Where she feels she is needed.

Meanwhile, a big man rushes into the camp. He finds Martha unconscious and bleeding. He scoops her up and retreats into a nearby cornfield. The young woman joins him, and they examine Martha, who is barely alive. A quick examination of Martha's gunshot wound gives them hope. However, they must get Martha and themselves out of the battle zone.

Amidst the sounds of gunfire, they rush into the darkness of the surrounding forest...to a place of safety...

Prologue

A Clean White Page

MARTHA PUSHED silvery bangs from her eyes. She gazed at the pistol on the table where it lay nestled in a stiffened shroud of blood-encrusted fabric. She picked up a thick, green pen and pressed its cool barrel to her cheek. She knew it wouldn't bear his scent, not like his turtleneck sweater did—the one she had tied around her shoulders. She pressed her nose into a sleeve and inhaled. He was with her, if only in this small way. Her scar twinged and she used the pen's rounded bottom to massage the rough, ribbed skin between her breasts.

She pulled a notepad toward her and flipped it open. She recognized his handwriting. It made her smile. Her tears started again, but she swiped them away. Crying wouldn't get it done, and somebody had to write it all down. Somebody had to tell. She wasn't a writer, had never been one. Her words would never find their way into print—she knew that—but she still needed to write the story.

If only for herself.

If only to help her heart find its way.

She stared at the notepad. She turned to a clean, white page. She willed the words to come to her. Her scar twinged again.

Brad.

The rape and then the bullet to her chest...she didn't relish writing about Brad, but he was a big part of the story, too. She buried her face in the sweater again and breathed deeply.

She uncapped the pen and placed its nib on the paper. She wrote:

"The Change" happened so suddenly. One night, we went to bed with power. The next morning, it was gone. Just like that. Poof. No power. No morning coffee. No morning emails. No heat. That was the really bad part since it was fall and we were headed into winter—an Alberta winter. Six-foot snow drifts and -50 temps with wind chill. Alberta is no place to be in winter—without heat. But that's exactly what happened.

We all complained and grumbled at first. We waited for the power company to flip a switch. But after a few days, we got suspicious. Our faith in the system was being tested, and our faith was running thin. Suspicion led to uneasiness, and then finally to terror. That's when runs on the banks started, riots at the grocery stores, and the line-ups at the pumps. Oh, Lord—what a mess! It was really scary. But that was nothing compared to what was headed our way...

Martha stopped writing. She capped the pen, and laid it carefully next to the notebook. She rose from the chair.

She glanced out the cabin window. It was getting late. There were other things to do—camp life was calling. She turned and stared at the clothing hanging on the wall hooks, at his flannel shirt, at his jacket showered in golden sunlight. Her heart clenched. Tears burned her eyes again.

She couldn't leave. The room was not going to let her leave. Not just yet.

Martha sank back into the chair. Life outside the door could wait. She picked up his pen again, relishing the silken smoothness of the barrel as she rolled it between her fingers.

Memories—bittersweet recollections of him—tumbled through her mind, as soft and as flitting as downy feathers. They would not be denied—they wanted to be remembered. No matter how painful.

She pulled his sweater tighter around her shoulders as she leaned forward, and continued to write:

...Now I'm here in your room, surrounded by your things—familiar things. I know I'll never see you again. And that breaks my heart. I wish I could tell you just one more time how much you mean to me—I wish so much...so very much...

Chapter One

Surgery on the Run

THE YOUNG WOMAN panted as she ran alongside the big man, a baby bouncing up and down on her hip. She watched the man struggle under the weight of a woman clasped to his chest. The woman's mouth hung open, her eyes were closed, and her head lolled back and forth against the man's shoulder. She was older, mid-forties, with medium length hair. Her long white dress glowed under the moonlight. One arm swung loosely at her side, its fingers trailing dark smears over burdock leaves beneath them; her other arm was tucked between her chest and the chest of the man who carried her. Finally, the young woman called out in a desperate whisper, "Meteor, wait! If I don't stop the bleeding, she'll die."

The big man stopped. He turned to face her. The woman in his arms, moaned. "Shhh, Martha," he said, and repositioned the woman so her head would fall back into the hollow between his shoulder and his chest. A large amoeba-like stain on the front of his coat shimmered in the moonlight. "It's too dark, Anna. You can't see. We've gotta get her out of here." Without waiting for Anna's response, he strode away.

"Wait!" Anna sprinted after him. "I have a flashlight." Anna rummaged with one hand inside her shoulder bag. The baby on her hip whined. His mother's voice and her movements had disturbed his slumber. She kissed the top of his head, suddenly terrified he would awaken and his wails would bring their enemies down on them. She found the flashlight and pulled it from her bag. "Look— I have it. Please stop. Let me work on her."

Meteor hesitated. He turned and glanced around. The pair stood in silence, listening to the sounds coming from the campground. Guns rattled and popped. Men cried out. He lowered Martha to the ground. "Hurry..." he said, pulling at the sleeves of his jacket.

"Thank God," Anna said with a rush of breath. She got down on her knees. She lifted the baby from her hip—little Gordon had fallen back to sleep. She laid him on the ground. She pulled at her scarf and scrunched it into a pillow. She raised Gordon's head and pushed it underneath. He squirmed and whined, but did not awaken.

Meteor and Anna were deep in the tangled woods that surrounded the Gatekeeper's compound. They were several hundred feet on the other side of the compound's perimeter. Shadows were velvety thick, but the moonlight added a jeweled glow, just enough for them to see each other. Meteor had pulled off his jacket. Now, he laid it on the ground. He gathered Martha into his arms and gently set her on the jacket.

Anna glanced at him. "You're going to be cold," she said.

Meteor ignored her and dropped to his knees. Anna watched as he folded back one of the jacket's arms to cushion Martha's head. He hesitated...then he touched Martha's face, sweeping stray hairs from her cheeks. His brows furrowed. He drew back his hand and turned to Anna. His eyes were bright with anger. "What the hell happened to her face?"

Anna stared at Martha's face, bruised and puffy. "I don't know...exactly. It was like that when she snuck into the bunkhouse to get us." Meteor's eyes narrowed and his face tightened. He waited, apparently expecting more in spite of what she had just said. Anna sputtered on, "Sh-sh-she wouldn't tell us what happened. But little Mary told us that she saw Martha in the Meeting House with Brad and some of his Crazies. She said Brad was 'being mean' to her."

"Brad? Being mean to her? How?"

"I don't know...Mary didn't say." Anna rummaged in her shoulder bag and pulled out rolls of gauze and a baby's diaper changing pad. She spread it out on the ground near her knees. She set the rolls of gauze on top of it.

"They were in the Meeting House? How long ago?"

"Late afternoon— Yesterday..."

A small growl emerged from Meteor's throat. "That bastard shot her." Meteor began to rise. "He's got to be nearby."

"Wait...calm down." Anna reached out and rested her hand on the big man's shoulder.

Meteor stared at the small hand restraining him. A long moment, as hard and cold as compacted snow, passed between them. Her hand slipped from his shoulder, and she shrank back. Her eyes were earnest, her tone pleading, as she spoke.

"Help me take care of her. There'll be lots of time to go after Brad...later. But right now... *help me*. Or Martha *will* die."

Meteor settled back down, his eyes fixed on the unconscious woman. He reached to touch Martha's face once more. He spoke again, but this time his voice was soft and low.

"When this is over, I'll find Brad. And I... *will... kill him*." He adjusted the makeshift pillow under Martha's head as he added, "But not before I make him hurt."

Meteor turned and stared at Anna. His blue eyes, bright orbs, glinted in the dim light. Anna returned his stare.

"But right now..." she started to say.

Meteor pursed his mouth and breathed in through his nose—a long, determined sound. He let it out, slowly and deliberately.

"Tell me what you want me to do."

BRAD HUNKERED down near a group of trucks in the parking lot, just outside the Gatekeeper's compound. He twisted his head around at the sound of approaching footsteps, but he stayed low. He raised his pistol and pointed it into the gloom. With his other hand, he touched his nose. His fingers came away slippery with dark blood. "Damn her," he said under his breath. He searched for a rag in his pockets, and finding none, he used the front edge of his flannel shirt to wipe blood from his nose and lips. He froze as two men crept through the shadows toward him. They spoke in low, raspy whispers.

"It's so damn dark. It's hard to tell who to shoot."

"Just shoot. Ask questions later," said the taller figure, his voice a deep, gravelly whisper caused by years of ravaging his vocal chords with cigarette smoke.

"Oh, that's a good plan." Both men laughed, but stopped when they heard a voice call out to them from the shadows.

"Guys... Over here." Brad had recognized the men, both bikers who represented *The Man*, a strategist whose goal was to unite all splintered motorcycle clubs and their wild, undisciplined men, the *Crazies*—regardless of colors or creed—into a massive army. The Man dubbed his new alliance the *Apocalypse Archangels*—a hard-fisted, weapon-toting membership of bullies and sociopaths, modern day pirates that took what they wanted. These men were bona fide members.

They dropped to their knees, guns pointed forward. "Who's that?" asked one man.

"It's me— Brad."

"Brad? Where the fuck did you get to?" asked the taller figure. He wore a thick winter jacket, dark green, with a hood. A black leather vest was pulled atop the jacket, but it hung open, unable to close over his expansive belly. Bare spots in the shapes of old club patches patterned the vest; the shiny areas caught the moonlight as he moved. It was one of The Man's laws: all old MC patches had to be removed and destroyed. All tattoos had to be destroyed, too—burned away—and subsequently replaced with a new tattoo, a more primitive design created by the blistering heat of a metal spoon held into flames. An evil-looking oval patch of ripped and ruggedly scarred crimson flesh was their new tattoo. All three men had the new tattoo because each one had gone through the color-cleansing many months before. The biker squatted down beside Brad. He grunted and farted from the exertion of dropping his large belly onto his knees.

Brad grimaced and waved at the noxious air. "Geez!"

"Ain't you our leader now?" The man chuckled good-naturedly.

Brad met the pleasant sound with a hard glare of annoyance, both at the jesting and at the fact that he had failed The Man: he had lost control of the compound. Because of a woman.

One goddamned woman: Martha.

Brad growled hatred under his breath and checked his watch. He pressed the button to make its face glow.

Was it really only twenty-four hours ago?

The compound was one of The Man's targets. His biker troops, led by Matthew's ex-friend, Virgil, had wrested it away from the former Gatekeeper. Matthew had deployed his men elsewhere, leaving the compound without adequate protection. Virgil's men raided it in the middle of the night, killing anyone who resisted their takeover. Virgil then handed control of the compound over to Brad before he left to do battle with Matthew's troops at a second, more secret campsite. So, Brad became the *new* Gatekeeper.

It was all part of the plan, The Man's master plan to take over Matthew's well-run compound, his winter supplies, and his pipeline to fresh food from the Hutterites down the way. But not just that...The Man wanted Matthew's females, too—*all* his females including the little girls. He was stockpiling women, *clean* women, women free of sexual diseases, and the younger, the better in terms of the prices they would fetch when bartering for other necessities like food and fuel. All the women and children were roused from their beds, rounded up like a flock of sheep, and locked into the two women's bunkhouses. Brad grimaced again. He knew one group of women and children had already fled the camp, assisted in their escape by the same woman he had shot: Martha.

"I hope she's dead," he said in a barely audible mumble through gritted teeth. He was roused from his thoughts as the other biker slipped down beside him.

"What the hell?" the man asked. He wore a hunter's cap; its flaps were down, but they stuck out like small wings from the sides of his head. "What happened? I thought we had the compound locked down."

"We did," said Brad. "But there was a surprise attack. We weren't ready for it."

"Where in hell are the guards?" asked the second man, pointing toward a far rectangular building. His thick hand was encased in a leather work glove. His fingertips poked through raw-edged fabric where the glove's fingers had been cut away. "Last I saw, they were boozing it up out front."

"They were locked up in there—in the women's bunkhouse," Brad said, pointing with his gun.

"What?" The second man showed genuine amazement. "I thought we had the women and children locked in there."

"We did, but they got away."

"What? How the f—?"

Brad cut the man off. "We've got a second group locked up in the other bunkhouse." Brad turned away as he spoke. He studied the gun in his hand, the one he had fired at Martha. He wondered if she was dead. He mentally chided himself for not waiting, for not putting a second bullet into her.

Into her head.

But the swarm of dark shapes coming through the trees and the whizzing bullets had changed his priorities. Brad fired his gun at them and ran, stumbling down the wooden steps, and racing into the safety of the darkness. Now, he shook his head and muttered under his breath.

"The Man's gonna be pissed," the first man said. "He's gonna take it out on somebody." Brad ignored him. "Anything from Virgil?" the man continued.

"Nope."

"The Man?"

"Nope."

"Well, what the hell—?"

"Shut up," Brad said. "You're talking too loud."

A bullet whistled over their heads and ricocheted off something metallic. The pinging sound made the men duck lower.

"So, who the hell are we fighting now?" the first man whispered. "I thought we got all the Gatekeeper's guys."

"Yeah, I thought—" Brad began to answer. Another bullet, and then another whizzed over their heads. Brad ducked. "Must be Meteor's *army*," he said sarcastically.

"Meteor? An army? What the hell is that all about? Thought he was one of us."

"He isn't...he wasn't. Now he's running his own show," Brad added with bitterness cracking his voice.

"Can't see anything moving," the second man observed. "Wonder where Virgil and his boys are."

"Don't know. Dead, maybe," Brad replied.

"This is stupid," the man in the hunter's cap whined. He slumped to the ground. "I'm tired. I'm hungry. I'm sick of this. I'm ready to quit this whole damn—"

"And then what?" Brad hissed. "Then what will you do?"

The man sighed. "Aw, shit." He propped his elbows up on his knees, pushed his hat back, and rubbed one hand over his face, letting his gun dangle from his other hand, between his legs.

"Listen, I have a plan," Brad said. "I think we can fix this mess."

"How?" the gloved man asked as he turned to face Brad. A moonbeam played across Brad's face. The sight caused the man to snort in surprise. "What the hell happened to you?"

Brad touched his nose—it was still sticky and encrusted with blood. "I went hand-to-hand with one of Matthew's guys," he lied.

The other man made a sound of disgust. "I hope you gave him as good as he gave you."

"I shot him." Brad said simply and looked away. An image of Martha's body lying on the landing at the top of the stairs just outside the bunkhouse door swam into his mind. He wondered once more if the bullet had done its job. A ferocious anger erupted inside him as he remembered her shoving him down the bunkhouse steps. And then her standing near the bunkhouse door with her gun pointed down at him. But she never pulled the trigger.

Why hadn't she shot him?

He shrugged his shoulders and studied something in the distance.

"So, what's your plan?" the gloved man asked again. He pulled a small metal flask from an inside pocket, unscrewed the cap, took a drink, wiped his sleeve across his mouth, and then offered the small bottle to Brad. "Want some?" Brad shook his head. "Suit yourself." The man took another swallow, recapped the bottle, and returned it to his pocket. He farted again.

The man in the hunter's cap gave the gloved man a pained look. "Hey, what about me?"

"Get your own, asshole." The gloved man turned back to Brad. "So? Your plan involve food? My stomach's really bitching at me."

"Food... no. But cooking... yes," Brad said.

The corners of his mouth curled up into a thin smile. He raised his pistol and pointed toward the hulking dark shape of another rectangular wooden building just off to their left.

ANNA LEANED over Martha's body. She panned the flashlight across Martha's chest, shielding the lens with her hand to constrain the bright light. She gasped when she saw the front of the white dress—the bloodstain was large and dark. It shimmered under the yellow beam. "Hold this," she said, passing the flashlight to Meteor. Meteor didn't respond. He was staring down at Martha. "Meteor!" Anna said urgently.

Meteor raised his head. "Can you fix her?" The question was asked softly, a near whisper.

Anna responded with a small, soft smile. "Yes."

She thrust the flashlight into Meteor's hand. He accepted it, and shielded the beam while Anna pulled Martha's dress open. Martha made a small sound and Anna froze. She held her breath. Martha went still, but her breathing was ragged. Anna released her own breath. "Help me get this thing off her."

The pair pulled the dress from Martha's arms, revealing a flak vest. The noise of the Velcro straps pulling away echoed in the dark woods. Meteor trained the flashlight on Martha's chest as Anna pulled the vest up over Martha's head. She tossed it to the ground.

Meteor drew in a sharp breath. "That bastard..."

Anna snatched up a roll of white gauze. She unrolled a mass and used it to wipe away the blood. "There's the hole," she said excitedly. "It's very small."

Meteor picked up the discarded vest and studied it. He waved the flashlight over the dark material. The light revealed a small hole surrounded by frayed fabric. “The bullet went through.”

“At least the vest slowed it—reduced the impact.” Anna looked back at Meteor. “I need that light.”

She motioned for Meteor to train the light back onto Martha’s chest. She wiped more blood away as she studied the bullet wound—a long, narrow slit weeping blood.

“It hit her breastbone,” she said excitedly. “A shield...”

“Her sternum acted like a trauma plate. Thank God.” Meteor paused. “Josef would be happy. She hated wearing that vest.”

Anna wiped Martha’s blood from her hands. “The slug slid sideways. I’ll have to pull it out. The pain might wake her.” She glanced up at Meteor. His face was a mask of deep shadows. He was nodding.

“I’ll keep her quiet.” He knelt closer to Martha’s head and gently placed his hand over her mouth. He scowled. “Why is she dressed like this? Like she was going to a party...”

“It was part of her plan, I guess.” Anna shrugged. “To lure away the guards.”

Meteor lifted the crystal necklace, now spattered with blood. He sighed softly. “Some soldiers wear grease paint... Martha wears jewelry.” He gently laid the necklace back down onto Martha’s neck. The chatter of machine gun fire drew his attention, for a moment. He jerked back to Anna. “Hurry up.”

Anna nodded. She reached once more into her bag and pulled out a pair of small forceps and a bottle of alcohol. She opened the bottle and doused the tip of the forceps. She hesitated with the silver instrument aloft in her hand.

“Go on,” Meteor coaxed. “You can do this.”

Anna took a loud breath and grimaced. “Oh, God,” she prayed aloud. “Don’t let it be too deep.”

Martha moaned again, but Meteor kept the sound muffled. Anna continued to probe.

“I found it,” she said. “Oh, damn. It’s stuck... just to the edge of the bone.” She withdrew the forceps and glanced up at Meteor. “I’m afraid of pushing it in further.”

More gunfire. Meteor glanced over his shoulder.

Anna winced. “I need to open the wound a bit more.” She waited for Meteor’s reaction.

"Do whatever you think is best. They could be here at any minute. You've got to hurry, Anna."

Anna removed a narrow, hard plastic case from her bag. She opened it and pulled out a scalpel. She rinsed that with alcohol, too. "Just a small cut. That should do it." She pushed the blade into Martha's flesh. Fresh blood spurted from the wound. "More light. I need more light." Meteor redirected the light, causing Anna's hand to cast a shadow over the wound. "No! The other side." Meteor tilted the flashlight. "There it is," Anna cried in an excited whisper. "I see it. I can get it." She used the forceps, and after a few seconds of grasping with no results, the bullet came free. She held it up for Meteor to see. They exchanged small grins of relief.

"Good job, Anna." Meteor glanced back over his shoulder again. "Finish up."

"It'll take me a minute to slow this bleeding. I'll wash the wound and stitch it."

Anna unrolled another mass of fresh gauze and pressed it down on the gaping wound. After a moment, she lifted the gauze. "That's better." She motioned to the bottle of alcohol. "Can you lift her? Turn her to her side. I'll irrigate the wound."

Meteor did as she requested. Alcohol tinted in red flowed down Martha's side.

"That should do it," Anna said. She reached once more into her bag and pulled out a small leather pouch. She opened it to display a series of curved needles and coiled waxy, black thread.

Meteor watched the woman's fingers work. Anna didn't speak as she deftly used the needle to pick up one side of the wound and then the other, stitching the raw edges together and knotting the thread ends as she went.

Martha gave a small breathy cry. Meteor cupped his hand back over Martha's mouth. He leaned next to her ear. "Shhh... hang on, girl. It's gonna be okay..."

Finally, Anna sat back. "I'll bandage her now."

Meteor held the flashlight as Anna continued to minister to Martha. "Did Ruth take everyone to the bunker?" he asked.

Anna nodded. "Except for the women and kids stuck in the other bunkhouse. I don't know what happened to them."

"My guys were sent in to check all the buildings. They'll find them. They'll get 'em out."

"Glad to hear that."

In a few moments, a mound of fresh gauze pads secured by surgical tape covered the wound. Anna drew back. She touched Martha's bloodied dress; the fabric had stiffened where the blood had congealed and dried. "We've got to keep her warm somehow. She's in shock."

"Cut away the wet part of her dress," Meteor said. "Just leave the sleeves. I'll wrap her in my coat." Anna nodded. She picked up the scissors and cut through the blood-soaked material. With the bloody front of the dress removed, the pair wrestled Martha's arms back into her sleeves. Martha cried out.

"Shhh," whispered Meteor into Martha's ear. "It's okay." Martha quieted.

Meteor tugged his jacket around the unconscious woman who was still breathing, but so quietly, that he stopped to check. He reached out and touched Martha's cheek, as white as alabaster in the moonlight. "C'mon, sweetheart. Don't you leave us now. You're a tough girl. Hang on."

Martha shuddered as though in response to Meteor's gruffly whispered words.

Anna finished cleaning and re-packing her equipment. She got up from the ground and then stooped to pick up Gordon; he was soundly asleep. She used her scarf to create a sling across her chest. With Gordon's bottom secured in the scarf, her hands were free. The baby snuffled and nestled into his mother's chest. Anna picked up her shoulder bag. "Okay," she said. "Now where?"

Meteor gathered Martha to him. He grunted as he struggled to his knees. "Damn," he said.

"What's wrong?"

"My leg still hurts from the old gunshot wound. It gets stiff." Anna reached out to him, but he shrugged off her hand. "I'll be fine." Anna waited while Meteor balanced Martha's weight against his chest; her head once more nestled against his shoulder. "Okay, I'm good. Let's go."

"Where are we going?"

"We've set up camp about an hour from here. It's a place Matthew and I use for our meetings."

"Oh." Anna gave Meteor a puzzled glance. "I... um... it'll be a long walk. Especially in the dark. Will you be okay?"

"What choice do I have?"

The pair laden with their human burdens slipped deeper into the forest gloom.

RICHARD STUMBLED over dead bodies hidden in the shadows. He cursed as he tripped and fell, and then picked himself up. The tall native man with dark braids was a member of Meteor's impromptu army. The eight men with him waited patiently.

"What now?" one of the men asked. The man's face was fully whiskered—tendrils of wispy hair poked out from under his ball cap. "Where'd Meteor get to?"

Richard shook his head. "Last I saw him he was carrying a woman away from the far bunkhouse."

"A woman? Who?"

Richard shrugged. "Don't know."

"Where did he go?"

"Into the cornfield."

"Should we try to find him?"

"No."

The man shrugged. "What should we do then?"

Richard breathed heavily. "We've got to take back this camp."

"It's so dark."

"Yeah, but there's enough moonlight."

"For what?"

"For picking off The Man's people," Richard said.

"But without connecting with our other guys, we don't know how many are left."

"Sure we do."

"How's that?"

"A lot less return gunfire," Richard said.

"We should pull back. Find out where we're at."

"What about the women and kids?" Richard asked. He stooped and hovered on his haunches. The other man hunkered down, too. "We've got to find them."

"I disagree. We'll wind up getting ourselves shot. Besides, maybe somebody has already rescued them."

Richard shook his head. "No. I don't think so. Look, Meteor gave us a job. We're going to do that job." He unfolded the hand-drawn map that Meteor had sketched earlier. He pulled out a tiny flashlight and turned it on, dimming the ray with his hand. He pointed to the map. "Let's check inside both the women's bunkhouses. After that, we'll check out this Meeting House." He tapped the map as he spoke.

A bullet whined overhead. The men ducked down. Another bullet whizzed by.

"Stay low," Richard warned.

"Ya think?" the whiskered man said as the men stooped and ran through the darkness.

~~~

BRAD CHECKED his watch again. Another hour had passed. The time had ticked by with no signs of the enemy in their immediate vicinity. Gunfire was sporadic, but constant. Their attempts to get to the bunkhouse to free the guards locked inside, were constantly thwarted by random sprays of bullets. He switched his pistol to his other hand and flexed his cramped fingers. He turned to the two men beside him. The man in the hunter's cap was lounging against a tree; he looked half-asleep. The gloved man took another swig from his flask. Brad peered out into the darkness again.

"So? Are you going to tell us, or not? What's the plan?" the gloved man asked impatiently.

"Burn it."

"What?" The gloved man swiveled around to face Brad. His eyes glittered brightly under scraggly eyebrows. "Burn what?"

"Burn the other bunkhouse. It's gonna be light in a few hours. Burn it. Now...while it's still dark."

The gloved man jerked back so hard that he banged his head against a tree. "What're you saying?" he asked, rubbing his head. "Burn women and children? That's your plan?"

The man in the hunter's cap remained silent.

"Grab some gas cans, soak the perimeter, light a match, and it's done," Brad instructed.

"You're *serious*?" the gloved man asked, his voice squeaking in disbelief.

"Look," Brad continued. "It'll draw out Matthew's people. When they come to put out the fire, we'll kill them."

"No!" The gloved man pushed himself to his feet. "It's bad enough we did the Gatekeeper's wife—" He backed away. "I'm done with this bullshit. Not kids... I won't be a part of this."

"No...you're right," Brad said, raising his pistol. A sharp crack, a stream of fire as the bullet left the barrel, and the gloved man collapsed to the ground. "You won't be a part of this."

Brad turned to the second biker who was up on his knees, his mouth hanging open in surprise. He was fully alert now. "And you?" Brad asked. "Can you be part of this?"
~~~

The man in the hunter's cap shrugged his shoulders. "No problems here, boss."

"Good." Brad rifled the gloved man's body, claiming weapons and ammunition. With a glance around, the pair slipped into the shadows.

A few minutes later, the gloved man regained consciousness. He groaned. He pushed himself up, gasped for breath, and struggled to reach the radio on his belt. He wrenched it off and fell back to the ground. He raised the radio to his mouth and pressed the *send* button.

"Lost...fighting more...camp lost...Brad shot...burn women..."

A short, quick gasp and the radio tumbled from the man's lifeless fingers.

~~~

A Change in Plans

A CONVOY of half-ton trucks raced up the main highway. The Man and his personal guards were in the lead vehicle. They were headed toward the Gatekeeper's first camp, with plans for visiting his second camp, too. There had been no word from The Man's general, Virgil, so it was assumed he had done his job—that he had vanquished the Gatekeeper's forces and had taken over both camps. Behind them sat a woman. Her reedy body was hunched over. She stared at her manicured fingernails, and listened while her "brother" laid out his plans.

The truck's driver glanced into the rearview mirror. The woman looked up. He caught her eye and shot her a leering grin. She stared back at him, her face as pale as her blond hair, her eyes unblinking. With one broad finger, he tapped the brim of his ball cap in greeting—the cap was tattered, greasy, and worn, but a large gold ring, surrounded by a collection of diamonds, sparkled with newness on his finger. The life of a Crazy under The Man's rule had been good to him.

"Where we taking her?" the driver asked.

"First camp," The Man said. "We'll leave her there. We'll drop reinforcements there, too. Then the rest of us will hit the second camp. Hopefully, hook up with Virgil along the way." The Man turned back to the woman. "Won't that be nice, Marion? To see Virgil?"

Marion's eyes widened with shock.

"Didn't think I knew?" The Man chuckled. "You underestimated me, sister." He narrowed his eyes. "I told you to stay away from him."
~~~

Marion involuntarily clutched at her jacket and pulled it tightly to her chest.

The driver rubbed his chin. "Might be a plan to check in with one of our radio relays, you know...just in case something's changed. I haven't been able to raise him on the radio."

"Do so."

A few miles up, the driver pulled the truck onto a side road. In front of a combination gas station and RV park, he turned off the engine. The rest of the trucks followed. The Man grasped the door handle and then turned to Marion. "Stay here."

Marion remained silent.

The men bounded from the vehicles.

"What's up?" one of the other drivers called out.

"Checking the relay," the first driver said.

The Man strode through the station's door. The glass door was surprisingly still intact—a rare thing to see since the Change; glass doors were the first things to go during scavenging runs.

"Where are you?" The Man demanded.

No answer.

"Where the hell are you?"

A frenzy of movement and a mumbled reply came from a back room. The Man walked forward and motioned to the closed door. The driver kicked it open. A woman shrieked and clutched a coat to her body. By the light of a camp lantern, the men could see that she was naked from the waist down. A man, his belly hanging low over his genitals, jumped up from the couch where the woman sat; he grabbed at his unbuckled pants that had collected around his knees.

"I'm coming," the man said, puffing with exertion as he tried to pull up his jeans and walk at the same time.

The driver snickered.

"Get your ass out here. Now!" The Man said.

"Okay, okay..." The fat man pulled at his pant legs—shoving his feet into his boots, and buckling his belt as he obeyed. The men escorted him out the door.

The fat man stopped near a bank of radio equipment. The radios were numbered and identified with masking tape and felt pen. "It's been quiet..." he said. "Picked up some communications earlier...about the weapons being delivered to Virgil."

"And?"

"And then...nothing. Quiet."

"No word from Brad?"

"Well..." the fat man said. "Except for one garbled message. It came in a little while ago. It was hard to make out and I don't know who was talking—but it sounded like the Gatekeeper has taken back the first camp."

The Man stared at the fat man. "And you didn't think that was a message worth relaying back to me?"

The Man's fist rose and connected. In an instant, the fat man lay on the floor.

The driver kicked at him. "Get up, idiot!"

The fat man clambered to his feet. He rubbed his jaw. "I wasn't sure it was a real message. That's all." He stepped back, out of The Man's fist range. "I didn't want to pass on a message that meant nothing."

The Man stepped forward. He picked up a radio and shoved it at the fat man. "Call the first camp."

The man did as he was bidden. No response. He called again. This time there was a crackle and a male voice came back.

"Need help. We've lost the camp. Meteor's army here. Lots dead. Don't know where Brad is. Over."

The Man smashed his hand palm-down on a nearby countertop. Pens jumped in a glass jar. "Son-of-a-bitch."

"What now?" the driver asked.

"Ah, hell...tell our men to get out of there. Get to the South Camps."

The driver took the radio and relayed the message.

The Man turned to the fat man once again. "Absolutely no word from Virgil? Or have you screwed that up, too?" he demanded.

The fat man gave his head a speedy shake. "No—that's it. That's everything."

The Man strode to the door. He pointed to the truck. "Get her."

Two men near the door rushed out. In a moment, they were back, with Marion in their grasp. They shoved her toward The Man, so hard, that she stumbled against him. The Man reached out and gripped Marion's shoulders. He gave her a quick appraisal. He smiled at the terror shining in her eyes.

"Well, sister...I promise we won't do any lasting damage to that pretty face—"

"What?" Confusion clouded Marion's eyes, but then realization set in. "No, Hezekiah—you can't mean that." She began to cry. The men nearby gave The Man a puzzled look at her mention of the strange name.

"It's time to return the favor. To earn your keep. I've taken good care of you. Now you're going to do something for me," The Man said.

"No!" Marion backed away. "You call me your sister."

"Yes—and this is family business." He grabbed her by the hair and pulled her face close to his. "And I don't like to be disobeyed." He gave her a shove and she stumbled backwards against an empty chocolate bar merchandising rack. He stood over her, his face pressed in close to hers. "You're going to get into that camp and send back all the information you can. Understand?"

"I can do that. But you don't have to hurt me. Please...be reasonable."

The Man turned back to the fat man. "When these guys are done with her, give her a radio, fully powered."

The fat man agreed.

"You boys—" he said nodding to Marion, "—No broken bones. And go easy on that face." He walked over to Marion, pulled her to her feet, and pushed her toward the waiting men. "Remember what I said—mess her up, but no permanent damage." The Man pinched her cheek and gave it a little shake. "It's the least I can do for my sister."

"Open-hand..." the driver volunteered.

Marion cried out. "Don't do this. I'll do what you say. Please don't do this."

"Marion...my sweet, sultry sister...we're dropping you at the Gatekeeper's camp. And you simply must look the part. Matthew likes rescuing abused women. You know—useless whores—like you." He gave her another push.

"You bastard!" she shrieked. "I've never done anything to hurt you."

The Man turned and gave final instructions to the fat man, while the two guards hauled a screaming Marion outside. The Man glanced at the door and then turned away when he heard the first blows fall. He turned back to the fat man who was nervously hitching up his jeans.

"You understand?" The Man said. "Give her a fully charged radio, extra batteries, and sometime over the next few days dump her up the road from Matthew's camp."

"How far away?"

"A mile or so. The walk will cool her off...bring her down off her high horse."

The fat man nodded and began checking the radios again.

The driver came over. "So, what do we do now?"

"The battle's over. Time for a change in plans. We don't have what we need to survive the winter. We'll make like the birds and head south. Lots of business down there to attend to anyway."

The driver and The Man walked to the truck. They passed by Marion who was slumped in a heap on the ground. She was groaning and crying.

"Is she really your sister?" the driver asked.

The Man reached the truck and yanked the door open. "Once upon a time." He got into the seat and pointed to the steering wheel. "Drive."

In a few minutes, the trucks were headed back to Edmonton. The fat man watched them drive away; then he turned back to the weeping woman. He bent over Marion and helped her to her feet. The woman from the backroom was beside him. She helped to steady Marion. She grimaced as she pushed Marion's hair aside to reveal a cut lip and a blackening eye. Marion groaned and began to cry anew—her face constricted and huge tears rolled off the tip of her nose.

"What did she do?" the woman asked.

The fat man shrugged. "She was his sister."

Sheree Zielke

Chapter Two

The Kid with the Orange Hair

MATTHEW YAWNED, arched his back, and stretched out his legs. He was seated on a folded sleeping bag on the ground, near one of the trucks. A plate of food sat abandoned near his thigh. Untouched. He dropped his ball cap, and raked his fingers through his hair. It was stiff and sticky with sweat. He yawned again, and tried to remember the last time he had slept.

A day ago? Two days ago? Or was it three?

He wanted to sleep, but each time he would drift off, guilt would jolt him awake.

The women. The kids. Martha.

He gazed across the makeshift campground. A plump harvest moon, when it wasn't obscured by a gauzy cloud, glowed overhead, frosting the hard-packed ground with its blue light. Matthew heaved a tired sigh. At least one battle was over—the battle with Virgil and his troops. Now they were set up in a farmyard near the battle site, resting before the next confrontation—the one he hoped would free the captive women and kids.

Matthew studied the men around him. Some snored, their chins on their chests, emitting soft purrs of air at regular intervals. Others lay on their stomachs on the ground, cocooned in sleeping bags, rattling the dirt with their nasal roars. Some were stretched out on their sides, their fronts cuddled to a blazing fire. Some stared blearily ahead in a stupor of exhaustion and hopeless worry. Matthew looked beyond the fire pit toward a line of heavy fir trees where more men stood, sprawled, or slept. There was no laughter. Only subdued exchanges. He understood. They knew their wives, their children, their sisters, and their mothers had been captured and were being held hostage by Brad back at the first camp. Guilt grabbed at his gut and Matthew grimaced. He tried to push the memory away, but it persisted.

In all his wisdom, and in spite of all his experience, he had misjudged The Man. He gambled the enemy would first go after the second camp with its oil reserves, but instead they went after the main camp. Matthew clenched his fists, remembering a trusted captain's misgivings when he announced the deployment of the troops. The captain felt that not enough men were being left behind to protect the camp, but Matthew had brushed his fears aside. All the women and children, including his wife, Martha, were now hostages. At least he hoped they were hostages, because that meant they were still alive.

Matthew ran a hand over his eyes. Fatigue made his head feel woozy and heavy, but his heart was heavier still. He stared at his gloved hands; he curled and uncurled his fingers. The cream-colored deerskin gloves were soft and supple. He remembered the day he found them on Martha's bed, a surprise for him that she had earned by killing and plucking chickens for the Hutterites. He had married her that day. Only Martha, himself, and God were present. He allowed himself a quick smile and a pang of heartache as he remembered his new wife of only a few weeks—her blue eyes, her soft smile, and her easy laughter. He drew a long breath.

Please, God...let her be okay. Please don't make her pay for my mistake.

Tears formed in his eyes. He gave his head a sharp shake. He gazed once more at the sleeping men.

Another man sat on the other side of the fire, apart from the group. He was slender with long legs and medium-length, silver-gray hair. A ball cap was pulled low on his face. He rested up against a tree. He slumbered fitfully, jerking in his sleep. Matthew looked away.

What time was it?

He glanced down at his arm and pulled up his sleeve. He squinted as he read his wristwatch's face by the light of the flickering flames—almost 1:00 AM.

Matthew looked across at the lone man again—Virgil's head lolled from side to side, and then snapped up, falling once more to one side. Matthew searched inside himself; he still wasn't sure how to feel about this foe, this ex-friend, this man who only hours before had nearly killed him.

Matthew leaned forward, his head in his hands, his elbows dug into his knees. His mind flickered back to a few hours before.

Why didn't I kill him? He would have killed me. He would have killed Martha.

He remembered the electricity that had zipped up his arm as he held his gun on Virgil...

...Virgil's eyes had gone dark, November dead in defeat. He stood quietly, accepting his fate, that he was about to die. At the hands of an old friend. He stared ahead and waited. The men at Matthew's side hummed with anticipation. They wanted this man, this general—dead. They could return to their compound, rescue their women and children, and resume their normal lives.

"Kill him, Matthew," Trojan said. "Shoot the bastard."

"No," Matthew said. The word fell from his mouth like a bag of wet sand—heavy and inert. He lowered the gun to his side, turned, and walked away.

Virgil kept silent.

Trojan and the rest of the men stared at Matthew's back. It was Cammy, the only female in the group, who asked the question. "Why don't you shoot him?" And then, "He'd shoot you."

Matthew turned. "No, I don't think he would. We were friends for far too long to just murder one another." He looked back at Virgil. "Am I right?"

Virgil maintained his silence.

Matthew gave the word to imprison all Virgil's men. After that, they set up camp in the farmyard crowded with silos, farm implements, and piles of wood. Someone else had previously hollowed out a giant fire pit; blackened and brittle remnants of logs lay corpse-like in a soft bed of dark ashes. The men found kindling in a wood chest near the farmhouse. It wasn't long before a fire was blazing. There was no need to be cautious with the resulting firelight; their enemy was within arm's reach and was no longer a threat since Virgil's surviving troops had chosen to join Matthew's men.

Matthew replayed that conversation in his mind...

..."They'll join you, Matthew, on the strength of my word. They're good men." Virgil shook his head in earnest. "Spare them... Kill me, but spare them."

Matthew had stood silently. He heard the muted rumblings and grumblings of his own men in response to Virgil's plea. He knew they wanted no part of Virgil's men, many of whom were bikers—Crazies—the same men who had made compound life so miserable in the past.

A man dressed in a pair of overalls and a black toque with *Arctic Cat* emblazoned on its side spoke up:

"What are you waiting for? Kill them. We can't trust them to side with us. They've been with The Man. They're snakes, Matthew. Kill—"

"No." Matthew held up a hand.

The pony-tailed captain came alongside. He stood near Matthew. "We know allegiances can switch," the captain said. "It happened with Meteor. And with Trojan."

"Yeah..." Trojan said. He shook his head. "But I was never really with The Man. Neither was Meteor. These guys work for him. I don't trust them."

Matthew regarded Trojan for a moment, and then he turned his eyes back on Virgil. "I can't kill you and I can't let you go. You know that. As for your men, they understand there's no shame in surrendering to strength."

"I—" Virgil began to speak, but Matthew interrupted him.

"Our women and children are in trouble. What The Man has planned for them is wrong. I think you guys know it." Matthew waved his hand over the captives in front of him. "I suspect many of you are family men, too. Do you accept what The Man is doing? What kind of men are you? Can you stand to follow a man like that? What about honor? What about integrity? These are women and children we're talking about." Matthew paused, allowing his words to sink in. "We are going back in to get them. I am giving you a choice. You can help us—honorably—or... You can die here."

Virgil studied his men as they glanced back and forth at one another, and then back to their leader, awaiting his response. Virgil looked back at Matthew. "What about the bad blood between you and me?"

"You and I can work out our differences, man-to-man, alone and apart from this mess. We were friends for a long time. That counts for something. Right now, I'm going to do what's best for all of us. Talk to your guys. If they're ready to join us, they'll live. If not, I'll give the order to execute them."

Angry words erupted among Matthew's men, but in the end, they accepted the surrender of Virgil's men—all his men, who had quickly voted against death, many muttering that The Man wasn't worth it.

Tensions between the former enemies soon eased once talk turned to the imprisoned women. Suspicion merged into hesitant acceptance when the new brothers-in-arms exhibited empathy...and even an eagerness to help Matthew's men rescue their loved ones.

Matthew breathed deeply as he stared in the blackness. The fire had gotten smaller, its light diminished. He used a small penlight to check his watch again. A few hours of rest, a little daylight, and he and his new army would take back the compound.

But most importantly, he thought with a rush of fury, *they would take back their women and kids.*

His anger was followed by a shot of shame.

I should have listened to Thomas. He was right. I made a mistake...a big mistake.

He glanced at his watch again.

But I can make it right, he consoled himself. *In a few hours, I'll make it right.*

METEOR AND ANNA reached the secret campground. Meteor was sweating and breathing heavily. Two men rushed up to meet them.

"Who's she?" asked a blond man with scraggly muttonchops.

"Matthew's wife," Meteor said. "She's hurt. Which tent?"

"Over there," the blond man said, pointing to a large blue tent several feet away. "Let me help you."

"No!" Meteor's eyes glittered.

The blond man drew back in surprise. "I was—"

"Uh—sorry, buddy," Meteor said, his tone softening. "It's okay. I've got her."

The blond man strode toward the tent. Meteor followed him. Anna, with Gordon jouncing in the scarf sling, trotted along behind them.

"Where's Richard?" Meteor asked.

"Don't know for sure, but none of his men have come back yet," the man answered, pulling the tent flap aside. Small camp lanterns glowed from small bedside tables. Two camp cots were set up on either side of the small space. Anna rushed forward and opened a sleeping bag. Meteor bent and laid Martha on the cot, easing her head from his shoulder to the bed. He grimaced as he stood.

"You doing okay?" Anna asked. She got no response. The blond man spoke:

"Can I talk to you Meteor? Outside?"

Meteor nodded. "Can you handle things from here, Anna?"

"Yes. Go." Anna gave the big man an encouraging smile.

Meteor smiled back. “You’re pretty amazing.”

Anna blushed and turned back to Martha.

Both men left the tent.

“Bring me up to speed,” Meteor said, once they had made their way over to one of the campfires. He groaned as he sat down, stretching out his leg in front of him.

“I’ll get you some coffee.”

With coffee cups in hand, the two men chatted. “We’ve lost a lot of men, Meteor. Not sure of the number yet. Since we haven’t heard anything from Richard’s group. You didn’t see Richard?”

“No. We split up.”

“Lots of confusion.” The blond man shook his head.

“I’ll go back in, but I had to get Martha out of there first.” Meteor scrubbed his face with his palms. “Tired.”

“I’ll bet. You carried that woman for miles.” The man clapped Meteor on the back. “Matthew will be pleased.”

Meteor sighed deeply. “If he’s still alive.”

“Nothing from him either?”

“No.”

“I’ll gather the guys that are here—we’ll go back with you.”

Meteor drank the last of his coffee and handed the cup to the blond man. “Thanks. But maybe that won’t be necessary. Send out a scout to find Richard. Tell Richard to come back to camp.”

“Okay.”

Meteor rose, groaned, rubbed his leg, and limped back to the tent.

THE KID sprang out of the shadows. Brad jumped back. The man in the hunter’s cap raised his pistol. Suddenly, they recognized the kid as the one who had been feeding them information on Matthew’s camp all along. The one who had a hate-on for Matthew. The kid with the orange hair.

“Hi,” the boy said. His eyes were bright and his smile wide.

“I could have shot you, kid,” Brad said. “Where did you come from?”

“I have hiding places around here. I figured I’d lie low until all the shooting stopped. I’ve been watching people move around.”

“Yeah? So what can you tell us?”

“There’s more guys coming in from the far side of the compound. They’re moving in pretty quick.”

“Tell you what kid...we could use your help.”

"I'm your man, Brad." The kid gave Brad another wide smile. Brad didn't smile back.

"A bunch of our men are locked up in the bunkhouse over there." Brad pointed. "Sneak over and unlock the door. Send the guys here to me. Can you do that?"

The orange-haired kid puffed out his chest. He beamed his large toothy smile. "Sure, I can— 'cause I know where the secret entrance is."

"Secret entrance? I didn't know— Never mind. Go."

The kid scampered off. In a moment, he had disappeared into the darkness.

The biker next to Brad spoke. "He could get himself killed."

Brad shrugged. "Better him than me. But I think he knows his shit. He'll be fine." Brad stared across the compound. He shrugged and spoke again. "Let's cause a distraction. Time to burn the other bunkhouse. Find some fuel and start soaking the ground."

The biker ran to one of the sheds. In a few minutes, he returned with red jerry cans in either hand. "Full," he said.

"Good," Brad said. "Go."

RICHARD DROPPED to the ground. He leaned heavily against a tree. He and his men had continued their creeping exploration around the compound for hours, but the darkness made identifying friend from foe a difficult task. It was the middle of the night and they were tired. He wrinkled his forehead as he tilted his head back and sniffed the air.

Wood smoke.

It had his immediate attention. He scanned the gloom. Small patches of glowing ash danced upwards above the fir trees, flitting like fireflies across the murky sky. He jumped to his feet when he saw the first small fiery tongues licking the darkness. Their bright glow, contrasted against the black expanse of the night, made his heart beat faster.

"What's that?" one of the men asked.

"Fire."

"I know, but what's burning?"

Richard looked perplexed. He pulled out his flashlight and studied the map again. "I think it's one of the women's bunkhouses," he said, mashing the map into a smaller size and shoving it into his backpack.

"Good God," the other man said. "Do you think there're people still in there?"

"Let's find out."

Richard's men sprinted forward. Bullets zinged over their heads, but they continued their dash around the cabins toward the smoking bunkhouse. Flames licked eagerly at the wood—crackling, sizzling, hissing, spitting. Screams came from inside the building. Somebody smashed a window.

"Help! Help us!" a chorus of female voices screamed.

Richard pointed to one man. "Come with me. We'll go in through the front door. The rest of you— Cover us."

Under a volley of bullets, Richard and the other man rushed through the mounting flames and up the steps to the door. It was locked.

"An axe! We need an axe!" Richard cried. "The shed. There's a woodshed. Over there."

"Got one." A third man pounded up the steps with a small hatchet in his hand. A bullet smacked into the wooden step beneath his feet. Another one crunched into the doorframe.

"Get back!" Richard yelled to the women inside. "Get down. We'll get you out."

Gunfire rattled around them. The men ducked, as the man swung the hatchet, sending a flurry of wood chips spiraling into the air. The door was stubborn, but they broke through, wrenching the door from its hinges. Women and children poured through the opening, crying and screaming. They made their maddened escape down the steps, as the flames grew hotter. Another shot rang out. Richard watched a woman fall.

"Damn." He scooped the woman into his arms and raced across the yard after the fleeing figures. Soon, they disappeared into the cover of forest lining the perimeter of the compound.

BRAD CROUCHED low in the shadows, his pistol pointed forward. Then he swore. "Goddammit!"

He scowled as men he didn't recognize converged on the burning bunkhouse, rescuing the women and children inside. He watched the line of escapees snake away from the compound and into the distant woods. He swore again. The building was now fully ablaze—a wall of dancing orange flames that seared the sky.

Maybe it would attract Matthew, if Matthew were still alive. Maybe not. He shrugged. *Not all was lost.*

The distraction had helped to free his imprisoned guards from the other bunkhouse. The kid had been true to his word. Now, the bleary-eyed guards stood near him, grumbling, and awaiting his orders. He regarded them.

Losers.

"I know... I know where—"

"What?" Brad said sharply. He turned his attention to the nattering boy at his side.

"—a secret bunker is," the boy said without missing a beat.

Brad gave the kid his full attention. He smiled at the inside information that spilled from the boy's mouth. He chuckled. He was starting to like this kid...this kid with the orange hair.

"A secret bunker? Of course. That makes sense. Wait a minute..." Brad raised an eyebrow. "How do you know about it?"

The kid gave Brad a wide grin, one filled with unbrushed, dirty teeth edged in a green growth. "Duh-h-h... I used to sneak around there all the time. I know most everything about this camp. The women have gone there. I'm pretty sure." His head bobbed enthusiastically.

Brad re-holstered his gun and motioned to the men huddled beside him. These men had been given the task of keeping the women and children imprisoned, but they had gotten over-confident. And sloppy. And drunk. Martha had hoodwinked them and then locked them inside the bunkhouse.

They were sober now...and very willing to make amends.

"We're not done yet," Brad said, addressing the men. "The kid knows where the other women went." He thumbed toward the boy.

"How long to get there?" one of the men asked.

"About three hours," the kid answered.

"Let's go get 'em." The other men agreed.

"It's a long walk. I made a map," the boy said brightly. He held up a wide rectangular piece of paper.

"Hm," Brad said, taking the map. "Thanks, kid."

"Can I go with you?"

"No, it'll be better if you stay here. Keep an eye on things. Radio us if you find out anything."

"I don't have a radio."

"There's a dead dude back near the gas tanks. He's got one. Take his," Brad said, dismissing the boy with a wave of his hand in the direction of the man he had killed earlier.

"Thanks. I will." The kid grinned. "I won't let you down, Brad," he said with his signature *Aw, shucks* zeal.

Brad motioned to the men near him and they slunk back into the woods behind them. They made their way around the compound in the direction of the bunker.

RICHARD HUSTLED his charges forward toward the temporary camp he shared with Meteor and the rest of Meteor's army.

"What now?" a man asked. The older man was limping, but was keeping pace with Richard.

"We'll get these women and kids out of here and then hope for the best. Maybe this war is over."

"I wonder who started the fire. I don't even want to think about what would have happened if we weren't there to save them."

"Neither do I. But we got them."

"What about Meteor? Should we try calling him?"

"No. We have no idea where The Man is or what Virgil is up to. No sense risking them hearing what we're doing. We'll regroup at the camp, get some rest, and then go from there."

Conversation up ahead caught his attention. A boy in his late teens broke through the crowd of women and ran up to them.

"Richard," he yelled. He sucked in a lungful of air and continued. "Meteor's already back at the camp. He has Matthew's wife. She's hurt. Shot. By some guy called Brad."

"She gonna be okay?"

"Don't know. One of their medics is with her—a woman who didn't leave with the rest of the women."

"Leave? With the rest of the women?" Richard cocked his head.

"Yeah, a group got free and headed to a bunker a few miles from here." The boy gasped for air again.

"Should we try to find them?" asked the limping man.

"How long ago?" Richard asked.

"Around midnight."

"That was three hours ago."

"Should we go after them?" the limping man asked again.

"Meteor said to tell you to come back to the camp," the boy interjected.

"Go back. Meteor might be worried by the smoke." Richard pointed behind him. "Tell him that we freed a group of women and kids from the bunkhouse. Before it burned. Tell him I left men behind. They'll contain the fire. Matthew will have a home when he gets back. Minus one bunkhouse...but he'll have the rest of his compound."

"You heard from Matthew?" asked the boy.

"No. You guys?" The boy shook his head. "Okay, get out of here. We'll get there as soon as we can, but these little guys are pretty slow,"

Richard said, bumping his chin toward a couple of toddlers being hauled along by their mothers.

Meteor's messenger ran off.

The limping man picked up a little boy who had tripped and fallen. The child cried out in surprise and began to wail. The man handed him back to his mother. "Sorry. Just trying to help." The woman smiled with gratitude.

The kid with the orange hair smiled, too.

He had caught up to Richard's group and was now running parallel to them. He had been privy to their conversation. Now he stood still. He lifted the radio to his mouth, the radio he had found on the gloved man's dead body, and pressed the *send* button. Twice. Then he held it down and spoke:

"Brad? She's alive you know." His tone was rich with the brazen smugness of youth. "You didn't kill her."

~ ~ ~

The Regrouping

INKY DARKNESS surrounded the parking lot, but the area out front of the clubhouse was lit with massive construction lights powered by generators. One by one, the trucks pulled up, parking in every available space: the lot, the front street, and in business parking lots across the street. Soon the area was crammed with trucks. Men jumped out. They had followed The Man back to the main clubhouse without knowing why he had turned back. They gathered outside the front door. Now they demanded to know the reason.

"What are we doing?" asked a man in torn jeans and a khaki hunter's jacket.

The Man got out and climbed into his truck bed. He addressed the men. "Something went wrong at the first camp. Brad and his team lost it."

"Shitheads!"

"You all remember Meteor?"

Nods and mumbles of agreement.

"He never left the Gatekeeper."

"I never trusted that asshole," said a large man with a patch over one eye. "Me, neither," added a small man next to him. Other bikers joined in. The Man held up a hand.

"He had the smarts to come up with his own army, too—a bunch of farmers. I'm guessing he's the reason Brad lost the camp."

"So, let's take it back!" yelled the man with the eye-patch.

The Man shook his head. "No—we're done here."

The men began to protest. The Man held up his hand again.

"For ***now****—we're done here—for* ***now****." He paused. "It's not a retreat, so much as it's a regrouping. We were counting on taking the Gatekeeper's camps and his winter supplies. That's not going to happen now. But our South Camps are in good shape. We control the Calgary area. We'll go back there. Build up our troops and come after the Gatekeeper's camps in the spring. Or in the summer. We'll be even stronger by then...he won't know what hit him. As for Meteor—and his army of farmers—he won't be a factor." The Man smiled—a thin, grim smile. "We'll take him down* ***first****."*

The men shouted and clapped.

"Go to your homes, gather up your old ladies, your supplies, and meet me at the South Camps. Go soon. Don't chance an early snowstorm."

"What about our friends? Virgil and his guys? Shouldn't we go looking for them?" called out a man from the back of the crowd.

"Virgil can take care of himself. If he's not already dead." The Man paused. "If any of you want to go after friends...then go ahead. But I suspect you'll find them dead...and you'll end up dead, too. The rest of you...we have work to do. I want to be out of this city in a few hours. I'm not taking a chance that the Gatekeeper's men are headed here. We can stay and fight...or we can fall back. Regroup...like I said."

Some men moved immediately toward the clubhouse, while a few leapt onto motorcycles and roared away. The Man watched them leave.

"That's probably the last we'll see of them. Anyone else leaving?"

The remaining men stood silently.

"Good. You single guys— I'll break you into teams. Take the bigger trucks and clean out our main clubhouses. Take what you think is valuable. Leave the rest behind. It'll be there for us when we come back next year."

"What about the grow op?" asked a tall man near the truck.

"What about it?" asked The Man. "Leave it."

"Weapons?" asked the man in the khaki coat.

"Help yourselves. Just make sure we don't leave any ammo behind—not a single shell."

The Man motioned to his driver. "Head up the crew that cleans this clubhouse." The driver nodded. "I want everything from my office. We leave as soon as you're finished."

"Should we relay a message that we're coming?"

"Not right now."

"You got it." The driver shouted to a group of men. "You guys—come with me." They shuffled obediently into the clubhouse.

The Man turned to one of the guards that had accompanied him earlier. "Get our communications equipment. All of it. I want it in my truck."

"Sir?" The Man turned to a short man dressed in full biker gear. "What about the women in the hothouses?"

"We're not leaving them behind. Far too valuable." The Man nodded his head in the direction of a pair of long cargo vans parked on a lot across the street at a semi dealership. "Those will do. Load 'em up. And haul them down."

The biker gave The Man a puzzled look. "That'll be a rough ride. What'll they sit on?"

The Man shot him a warning look. "This is not rocket science. But I'll help you...just this once. Show the truck to the women, tell them it's their ride, and let them figure it out." The biker grunted, but it was clear he was having trouble with the concept. The Man gave an exaggerated sigh, and added patiently, "Line the sides with couches. They'll ride like queens."

The biker called out to several men leaving the clubhouse, boxes in their hands. "When you're done there, I need two drivers. To haul the women."

The Man spoke again: "No harm comes to those women, understand?"

"Yes, sir."

"They'll be our currency someday soon."

The Man climbed out of the truck box and walked to the clubhouse. He passed men who scurried back and forth like a procession of busy ants, their hands piled high with boxes. He followed one group into his office where several men had already begun to box his possessions. Some were dumping papers, books, and knickknacks into rubber tubs with lids.

The Man reached down and stopped a man who had opened a desk drawer. "I'll do that," he said. He reached in and drew out a plastic container filled with colored objects. He lifted the lid and touched a finger to a cheery Mickey Mouse figurine staring up at him.

"Whatcha got there?" the man clearing his desk asked. The Man jammed the lid back onto the plastic box. He dropped the container into the open drawer, and slammed it shut.

He called out to another man who was clearing books from a shelf. "Wait." The Man walked over and pulled down a bedraggled hardcover copy of Hitler's ***Mein Kampf****. He tucked it under his arm.*

"What about this?" asked another man pointing to a heavy floor safe.

The Man gave a wave of his hand. "I'll do it." He twirled the dial and pulled on the safe's heavy door. He grabbed an empty box and filled it with the safe's contents. A journal was the last thing to go into the box. He changed his mind and picked it up. He took a pen from inside the safe. He walked to the side of the room, near the window. He flipped the journal open and turned pages till he was satisfied. He ran his finger across the page and then made a single motion with his pen. He shoved the pen into his coat pocket and studied what he had done.

~~***Marion.***~~

"You ready?" His driver had come up behind him.

The Man snapped the journal closed. He strode over and dropped it into the box. A large Persian cat jumped up and padded across the desk. "Nearly forgot about you." The Man retrieved a fabric pet carrier from a shelf. He grabbed the cat, shoved it into the carrier, and zippered the case closed. "That's enough from in here. Let's go."

The men stopped opening drawers and clearing shelves. Everyone grabbed a box or a tub and the procession line headed out to the parking lot. The Man deposited his box into the truck box and jumped into the cab next to his driver. The cat carrier sat between them.

The Man thought a moment and then lowered his window and leaned out. He motioned to one of the men, whose arms were still laden with boxes. "Blow it up," he said.

"What?" the man asked. He dumped his boxes into the back of a truck bed and turned back to The Man. "I thought you said—.

"Blow it. No sense leaving a perfectly good clubhouse for someone else to use."

"Okay," the biker agreed. He motioned to two men with dark hair and beards. Both were dressed in black leather from head to toe. "He wants us to blow it." The two men nodded back. He looked back at The Man. "Done."

The Man closed his window and stared ahead, tapping his fingers on the cat carrier. The cat gave a low meow. The Man lifted the carrier onto his lap, and poked a finger through the mesh.

"What's your problem?" he asked, his voice a high falsetto. "You're going to a new home."

"Maybe he's hungry," the driver suggested. He looked at The Man, expectantly.

The Man pointed to the street.

Sheree Zielke

Chapter Three

Feeding of the Mob

RUTH LED the women and children through the trees. The winding path was known to her. She had walked it many times before in preparation for walking it tonight. Matthew had planned their escape, should something go wrong. And it *had* gone wrong. Very wrong. Ruth held up her arm, and pressed a finger to the side of her watch; the watch face illuminated. "We should almost be there," she said to a redheaded woman next to her.

The woman turned to face her. "Sounds like the gunfire has slowed down."

"It's dark," Ruth said. "They can't see very well. And we're a couple of miles away from the compound now." The redhead nodded, stumbled, caught herself, and walked on.

They rounded another bend. A wire fence greeted them. Ruth took a small path to the right; it ran parallel to the fence. She soon found a small gate. It was locked—a combination lock. She twirled the numbers— right, left, right—the lock popped open. She pushed at the gate, and then motioned for the shadowy band of figures to follow her. The women spoke in low voices as they shushed whiny children and whispered congratulations to them on having walked so far.

An older woman lagged behind. She was trying to keep a little boy moving along. He was nine years old, and he lived in his own world.

"Hurry, Reggie."

"Need some help?" Ruth called.

"No, I've got it," Hannah replied.

Reggie's didn't speak in words; he spoke in sounds: hushed unintelligible whispers, grunts, and high-pitched shrieks. He would stop and study something on a bush, something on the path, something on his shoe, on his finger, on Hannah's face—yelp with excitement or giggle— and then flit down the path. Hannah's face registered terror with each outburst.

"Reggie," she said in a tone laced with exasperation and exhaustion. "Shush. You can't yell." She grabbed him by the hand, and tugged him along beside her.

"Weggie," the little boy whispered to the dark woods. "Weggie."

Ahead of them, sat a domed bunker. It was difficult to spot because of the heavy camouflage of tree branches and military netting, but Ruth had seen it before. It was a secret shared by only a few members of Matthew's camp. Ruth thought about her mother.

Martha knew about this place; she was privy to the secret, too. However, she hadn't come with them. She had stayed behind to keep Brad and his drunken guards from stopping their escape. A vision of Martha's face came into her mind. Bruised cheek and bright blue eyes.

Is she alive? Is my mother still alive?

Fear rose in Ruth's belly, creeping upwards to her heart, but she drew a deep breath and forced it away.

She's alive. I know she's alive. And Matthew? What of Matthew? And Peter? And Simon? And Jonah?

Ruth allowed the faces of her loved ones to appear and slide across her mind. But Peter's face remained. Fear gripped her again. Peter had gone with Jonah to protect the Hutterites.

Was he alive? He had to be. He just had to be. He's a smart man, she reminded herself. *And a good soldier. He's alive.*

The creeping fear abated and she turned to a woman who had come up beside her. The young woman's thick dark hair was pulled back in a ponytail. A green knitted tam sat low on her head, partially covering the tops of her ears.

"There're quite a few of us missing," said Elizabeth.

Ruth's sister was a little taller, and stockier, but the pair shared the same muted, olive green, almond-shaped eyes framed in dark lashes.

"I know," Ruth said. "But without a secret entrance in the other women's bunkhouse, Mom couldn't help them— Just us."

Elizabeth stared ahead. "I have friends in that other bunkhouse."

Ruth put her arm around her sister's shoulders. "Me, too. Let's get the kids into the bunker. Would you run a team to set up beds? I'll put someone in charge of doling out food and water."

"Okay. Just don't make me babysit the kids. I am very short on patience."

"Aren't you always short on patience when it comes to kids?" Elizabeth shot Ruth a sour look. "Well, you are," Ruth said.

The observation wasn't meant to be unkind; it was merely factual. Elizabeth had no tolerance for children. She didn't have any children of her own, and didn't want any either. She abided her niece and nephews, but only because they were blood. Other children from the compound either avoided her or loved teasing her. Several had gotten a sharp smack from Elizabeth when their teasing had pushed her beyond her limits, and they had not run fast enough to escape her blow.

"C'mon," Elizabeth called out to the women and children huddled in groups near her, and then she ushered them toward the bunker.

Ruth pulled aside a large wall of camouflage netting and twirled the dial of another larger combination padlock. The lock clicked. Ruth pulled it off, lifted the hatch, and opened the door.

"Camp lanterns are on a shelf to your right," Ruth said. "Use them wisely. We don't know how long we'll be here. And the propane is limited."

The high wail of coyotes or wild dogs rose through the darkness, stopping her words. Like fingers of early morning light, the ethereal canine notes curled through the trees, dissecting the darkness. The children cowered against their caregivers. Ruth herded her charges into the bunker. She glanced back over her shoulder.

Where's Mom?

Fear squirmed inside her. Again she shoved it away.

A soft bump against her side caught Ruth's attention. She looked down. Her youngest child—her five-year old daughter, Mary—was staring up at her, eyes wide. Ruth smiled.

"Go on," she said. "Go into the bunker with everyone else."

The little girl didn't move. "Where's my nana?"

"She had something to do. You'll see her in a little while." Ruth crouched down and took her daughter's chin in her fingers. "It's okay. Don't worry. Nana will be okay."

I think.

"I miss Wilbert." Mary's pet cat had been left behind in their hurried escape from the camp. "He's gonna be hungry."

"He'll be fine. You'll see him later, too." Ruth stood and placed her hands on her daughter's shoulders, pushing her toward the open doorway now spilling a pool of yellow light onto the dark ground. "Go."

Mary obeyed and joined the line of women and children filing into the bunker. Ruth followed. Once inside, Ruth drew the door shut and slid a bolt into place.

"If you have to go to the bathroom, use an indoor potty for now," Ruth said.

Soft cries rose from the group: "That's gross," and "It's gonna stink in here," and "I want to go potty now."

Ruth sighed. "We can't run the risk of having you go outside. We don't know if we were followed."

More grumbles and mumbles, and cranky complaints.

One woman called out, "How long do we have to stay here? I want to know about my husband."

Ruth began to answer, but she was interrupted by more questions. The assembled women and children had no idea of the whereabouts of their husbands, their fathers, their brothers, or their sons. Or, even if they were still alive. No one had heard from any of the men in many hours.

"I don't know," Ruth said. She held her hands open, in a helpless gesture. "I just don't know." Ruth hung her head.

Elizabeth stepped back beside her sister. "You okay?"

"Yeah, but I miss Peter. I'm worried about him."

Ruth thought again about Peter defending the Hutterites' farmland. There was bound to be plenty of gunfire. Once more, she assured herself that he was alive.

"He'll be fine. He always is," Elizabeth said brightly.

"I know. God will take care of him."

"The kids are really hungry," complained one of the mothers, struggling with a set of twin boys in her arms.

Ruth motioned toward rectangular, lidded plastic tubs that were neatly piled against a far wall. "Everything you need is over there." The woman followed Ruth's nod. "Olive oil and jars of popping corn. And salt."

"What? You want us to feed them—"

"Popcorn," Ruth confirmed. "It's fast to make and it'll tide them over until we can make a real meal."

The woman studied Ruth for a moment, and then shot Elizabeth a questioning glance, but Elizabeth pursed her mouth and nodded toward the tubs, too.

"Should we build a fire?" the woman asked.

"No, we can't run the risk of a campfire. Too much smoke. Use the propane hotplates." Ruth pointed to long, narrow shelving lining the wall near the plastic tubs. "Over there. Lots of them."

The woman made a face at the twins that were now babbling and twisting in her arms. "Arrrrgh. These little devils." She hiked both up onto either hip, turned, and walked away.

"I'll see about getting everyone some bedding now," Elizabeth said.

Ruth laid her hand on her sister's arm. "Thanks."

Elizabeth hesitated. "I—I wonder how Mom is doing..."

Ruth bit her lower lip and shook her head. "We won't think about that right now." Suddenly, she pushed her eyebrows together in puzzlement. "Where's Anna? And Gordon?"

Elizabeth glanced around. "I don't know." She moved into the middle of the group of women and raised her voice. "Has anyone seen Anna and Gordon?"

A soft mumbling of *nos* and *uh-uhs* emanated from the group.

"That's strange," Ruth said. "I wonder if she went back."

"With her baby? That's crazy," Elizabeth said.

"Anna's not stupid. She must have had some sort of plan." Ruth watched as the women set up the propane hotplates. "Can't worry about her right now. We have this lot to take care of."

Elizabeth nodded. "Right... where's all the bedding?"

Ruth pointed toward the far left side of the giant hut. "Over there." Then she turned and studied a dark patch of flooring near the corner. "I'll set up a watch team and equip them with guns." She looked up to see if her sister had heard her, but Elizabeth had already walked away.

Ruth grabbed the arm of a tall blond woman passing near her. "Get somebody to help you. Grab some plastic jugs and fill them with water from the cistern. It's to the right of the bunker."

The blond scurried off.

Ruth walked to the dark rectangle, reached down, grasped a thick metal ring, and pulled upwards. The door opened with a screech. Metal stairs led down into a small room dug into the earth. Ruth lowered a lantern. The walls were lined with shelves filled with guns and boxes of ammunition. The sound of hardened kernels of corn hitting metal echoed through the hut, and the scent of freshly popped corn made Ruth's stomach whine. A woman with short brown hair came over. Ruth waited.

"The babies... They need to be changed. We need warm water. And diapers."

"I've already sent someone for water. There are plastic tubs in the storage cabinet over there." Ruth pointed. The woman's eyes followed her finger. "Go easy on the water." The woman nodded. "Diapers are in the same cabinet." The woman hurried off.

Ruth turned back to the steps and began her descent. She stood on the earthen floor, shivering slightly as a chill crept up through the soles of her boots. Her eyes swept the walls and the shelves lined with weapons of all shapes and sizes. Her stomach whined again and she pressed her fist into her belly to quiet the hunger pangs. It didn't help. However, food would have to wait—guards needed to be armed and shifts assigned—then food. Ruth gave a loud sigh.

Where's Mom? This is her thing. Not mine.

She twisted her face into an angry grimace, one that quickly faded into a stony resolve. She made her selections.

I'll take the first shift, she decided.

Ruth climbed the stairs.

MATTHEW STRUGGLED against the concrete forming in his head. He wanted to think, needed to think. His body was exhausted. He hadn't slept in nearly forty-eight hours. His eyes would close, and he'd begin to drift, hovering just on the edge of sleep, when his troubled mind would snap him back into consciousness.

Where had it all gone wrong? So many mistakes. Would the men trust him after this?

His stomach growled. He considered the food on the plate beside him, but instead he fumbled in his pack. He found a small plastic bag with four oatmeal cookies studded with chocolate chips. He held the pack without opening it. Martha had made them. His mind conjured up his wife's face, how she looked on the day he had married her—in his old bedroom—only a few weeks ago. They had eaten chocolate chips that day, too.

Where was she? Dead? Alive? Hurt? Was she one of the women taken captive by Brad's men?

He removed a cookie and bit down. He chewed and swallowed, but in spite of the sweet chocolate, it was tasteless to him. He leaned back against a rolled sleeping bag, and let his thoughts drift. The fire crackled nearby, sending bright sparks into the dark sky above. An unfinished cookie fell to the ground as Matthew finally yielded to sleep.

ELIZABETH SCANNED the food on the shelves: dried beans, peas, lentils, a variety of grains and flours, oatmeal, muesli, a huge variety of rice, and bags and bags of pasta lined an upper shelf. She grinned at the army of mute and deadly sentries that surrounded the dry goods; mousetraps ensured that human food *remained* human food. She picked up one of the traps. Sure enough, a large gray-brown body was trapped in its jaws; jelled, dark blood stuck to its mouth and whiskers. "Ugh!" She carried the trap and its stiffened corpse toward the door. She met Ruth on her way out. She held up the trap.

"Did we lose any food?" Ruth asked, eyeing the big mouse.

"No, I don't think so. Only one mouse in the traps."

"Good. I'll be out for the next two hours. I've made a schedule. I posted it on the wall near the entrance. You aren't on duty till tomorrow afternoon."

Ruth shrugged the long gun on her shoulder into a more comfortable position. "Oh—since I'm working, can you plan some meals?"

Elizabeth's response was bitter. "Of course— What did you expect? Just because you're telling everyone else what to do, doesn't mean that I need to be told, too."

Elizabeth's curt reply caught Ruth off guard. She looked hurt.

"I didn't mean it like that," Ruth said, her voice rising an octave. "Why talk to me like that? I didn't ask to be the leader of this group. But somebody has to do it."

Why don't you do it? Ruth thought. It was a petty, unkind thought and Ruth knew it, but it felt good to think it all the same.

"Stay awake," Elizabeth said, pulling the bunker door open and then shutting it behind her.

Ruth sighed. She stooped to pick up a canvas shoulder bag. The sight of the gray bag made her sad—it was the same kind of bag her father had once carried. She remembered the day they learned of his murder. And that Brad had been his killer. Rage and hate rose up inside her.

Brad.

Brad was the reason she and all the others were now in a bunker—in the middle of a forest—instead of nestled in their warm beds back on the compound. She gritted her teeth and roughly re-shouldered the gun. She checked her side weapon.

Brad will get his. Some day.

Angry tears burned her eyes. She swiped them away.

Ruth left the bunker and strode down the path where a half dozen other women awaited her instructions. Her mother flitted across her mind again.

Martha loved running a show. Loved? Loves?

She swiped at another tear, and set her jaw. For the time being, at least—leadership would be on her shoulders.

METEOR SANK to the ground beside the lone man. Richard's long, dark hair was secured tightly into two thick braids. He was seated on an upturned pail as he poked at crackling logs in a small fire pit. He was roasting something on a stick. He turned away from the fire to greet his friend. Meteor's blue eyes sparkled with warmth as he clapped Richard on the back.

"Tough night, buddy. I heard what you did. I'm proud of you."

Richard smiled—a small one, a tired one, but it was grateful. "Thanks. But it's because of you that we were in the right place...at the right time."

"You done great, Richard. There'll be a bunch of guys who're gonna want to say *thanks* to you."

Richard smiled again. He turned the stick in his hand. Meteor could see it was some sort of ground meat squished into a cylindrical shape around the stick. Meat juices spattered and hissed as they hit the burning logs.

"I saw you carry a woman away from the bunkhouse. Was that Matthew's wife?" Richard asked.

Surprise and something guarded shone in Meteor's eyes. "Matthew's wife? Yes... Martha."

"Matthew's...wife." Richard said again, but with a tiny lift at the end of his sentence. "Martha..."

Meteor looked away.

"You know her pretty well?" Richard prodded. He continued turning his roasting stick. Some of the meat had scorched slightly.

Meteor looked back at his friend. "Yes."

Richard pushed out his chin, and tilted his head slightly. "Too well... Maybe?" It was said carefully, tactfully. He stared at Meteor, but the big man remained silent. A few moments passed. "I see..." Richard said. "How's she doing?"

"Barely alive. Gunshot wound to the chest. Anna got the bullet out and stitched her up. She should have died, but her sternum deflected the slug."

"You must be glad of that."

Meteor said nothing. A few moments of silence passed. The sound of a squalling toddler drew the men's attention.

"Who's that?" Richard asked.

"Gordon, I think. Anna's kid."

"Well, he's got lots of company now."

"Yeah. Hope the rest are doing okay?" Meteor said.

"Who's missing?"

"According to one of the older women—about a hundred and fifty others—including Martha's daughters...and her grandkids."

"Oh— Sorry to hear that."

"But her daughters—Ruth and Elizabeth—are smart like their mother," Meteor said. "They aren't as feisty as she is, but they're tough."

"Like Martha?" Richard asked rhetorically. "Can I ask you something?"

"Why do people ask that?" Meteor flipped a hot coal with a stick. "No."

"How long—?"

"Too long. Too damn long."

"Sorry." Richard rotated the stick. Juices dripped and sizzled.

"Me, too."

"Does he know?"

"I'm not sure. I think so."

Richard placed a hand on Meteor's shoulder. "Not much I can say."

"No need. I'll survive. Just glad she's here."

"What about Matthew? Should we take a truck and go looking for him?"

"Wait till it's light. We'll figure out what to do then."

Richard gave his friend a warm look. "It's only gonna get harder, ya know?" Meteor got up, grabbed at his thigh, gave it a brisk rub, and left the fire. "You've always got a place with me," Richard called after him.

Meteor didn't respond.

THE BUNKER was quiet, now that the younger children were tucked into camp cots and sleeping bags. Some of the babies still fussed, but for the most part, a sleepy silence prevailed. Elizabeth yawned. The nutty scent of popcorn still hung in the air. She had not gotten any and she was hungry. She made her way back to the food storage area. A number of women were poking through shelves, wondering aloud as to the immense variety of foods, the well-equipped bunker, and the fact that most of them had no idea the sanctuary existed. A woman turned to Elizabeth.

"I knew there was a safe place for us, but—"

"No— Very few of us knew about this bunker. Matthew and Martha wanted it that way. Only trusted people were told. We didn't want Brad or one of The Man's people finding out. This way, we should be safe."

"What about the rest of the women and children? In the other bunkhouse?"

The question made the women within earshot go silent while they awaited a response.

"Who knows—" Elizabeth said, trying to stifle another yawn. "Mom might have found a way to get them to safety, too."

"I so wish that's true," the woman next to her replied. "My cousins are in that other bunkhouse...along with their new babies. It's a good thing that mothers and kids were allowed to stay together." She hugged the toddler in her arms.

Elizabeth changed the subject. "We need to make a meal. Popcorn is a good snack, but it's not a meal."

The women returned to examining the shelves. One younger woman with spiky black hair picked up a jar filled with thin, pink slices.

"What's this?"

"Pickled ginger," said an older woman standing to her right.

"Yuck." The younger woman looked up. "Why are there so many jars? Who wants to eat this stuff?"

Elizabeth responded. "It's food," she said flatly. "If you're hungry enough, you'll eat it."

"You like this stuff?"

Elizabeth examined the jar she was handed. "Hm, you might have a point there." She returned the jar to the shelf. She pushed at a can of stewed tomatoes, picked up a can of creamed corn, considered it, and set it back on the shelf. She groaned. "I don't know," she said, her tone short and irritated. "Anyone have any ideas for supper?"

A slight woman wearing a peasant dress, a long sweater, and a kerchief wrapped around dark curls spoke up:

"I have an idea. Somebody heat some pans. Here," she said, handing tins of luncheon meat to one of the younger women. "Cube this up. And you..." she said, pointing to the woman with the spiky black hair, "...Bring a jar of that ginger."

Soon cast iron pans were warming on several of the propane stoves. The slight woman continued to give orders. "Get some beef lard out of the suet buckets. A tablespoon or two in each of the pans."

The younger woman with the dark hair once again grimaced. She was one of the newer arrivals at the compound. "We used to give that guck to our chickadees."

"Yes," the slight woman answered. "And they ate it, right? So, it must be a good thing."

"Yeah, sure. If you say so, Sarah." The dark-haired woman paused. "How come you know so much?"

Sarah smiled. "I was taught by Martha."

An older woman laughed. "Yeah, that's for sure. How's the sex life, Sarah?"

"Shut up, you old cow. Martha gave good advice. And you're here because of her. Remember that!"

The woman's laughter ended abruptly.

"Now peel some onions. We need at least two onions per pan—diced small." The women did not move. "Do you want to eat... or not?"

"We can make our own food," challenged another woman.

"Not tonight," Sarah said. She straightened and her eyes sparked with determination. "Tonight, we cook for everyone and we will all eat the same meal. You got that?" She made a small move toward the woman who had begun the rebellion. "You—got—that?" she repeated. The woman was now silent. Sarah pointed at the chains of braided Spanish onions hanging from the rafters. "Onions. Peel. Now!" The woman did as she commanded. However, not without grumbling. Sarah shrugged and turned back to the stoves.

Pale lard sputtered in the pans. "Turn down the heat," Sarah instructed. "You'll burn the onions."

The women obeyed. After a few minutes of stirring, the smell of browned, caramelized onions filled the large building. Stomachs growled in primal response.

"Now, add the meat." While one woman stirred, other women added ingredients.

"What do we do with the pickled ginger?" the dark-haired woman asked. She was now an active participant in the culinary event.

"Drain off the brine," Sarah said.

"The brine?"

The juice... the pickling juice." The woman turned to leave. "Use a slop bucket," Sarah warned. "Don't pour it outside. It'll attract animals." The dark-haired woman nodded.

A few minutes later, the meat cubes were browned. Worcestershire sauce, maple balsamic vinegar, and a large spoonful of pickled ginger joined the meat and onions. Sarah sniffed the air and smiled.

"Smells good," Elizabeth said. She picked up a piece of the fried luncheon meat and popped it into her mouth. "Hm, delicious."

"You've come a long way," said an older woman; it was Hannah. "I remember when you couldn't even peel an apple." Hannah winked. "Martha would be proud."

"I hope she's okay," Sarah said very softly. "I said a prayer."

"Me, too," Hannah replied. "But if anyone can get out of that mess, she can. Right, Elizabeth?"

Elizabeth looked up, but said nothing. She sniffed the impromptu concoction again. "I think this is ready. Do we have any takers?"

Sarah motioned toward picnic tables laid out with colored dishes and plastic cutlery. Women and older children sat obediently, expectantly.

"Let's feed this mob," Elizabeth said.

~ ~ ~

The Alliteration

THE MEN wended their way through the trees, following the map the kid with the orange hair had sketched for them. The darkness made traversing the thick forest difficult. The men complained as they stumbled and fell, barking their shins, and scraping their hands on rugged deadfall.

"Son-of-a-bitch," complained the biker who had kept pace with Brad for over an hour. He tripped again. He wiped fresh blood from a cut on his hand. "Women and kids walked through this?"

"I think we must be off the track." Brad shook out the map and held it up to his flashlight. The radio on his belt crackled. He extracted it from his belt, and waited. In a moment, he heard a voice. The final words buzzed in his ears:

"You didn't kill her."

So, Martha was still alive. The thought made his hands clench and unclench. "Damn." He kicked a small branch out of his way. "That bitch."

"Why are we going after those broads anyway?" asked one of the guards who had been imprisoned in the bunkhouse. Brad turned on him—displaced anger found an easy mark.

"Listen, asshole...if you had done **your** *job, we would be enjoying a nice warm fire. Quit complaining— I'm saving your butt." Brad tripped, but caught himself. "Getting those women and kids back might just make The Man overlook your stupid fuck-ups."*

"How long do we have to walk?" the man in the hunter's cap asked.

"Till we get there, idiot," Brad snapped.

Another man ran up. He held up a radio. "I found a channel. I got through. The contact in Winterburn has arranged for the buses." He was out of breath. "He said he'll try to have four buses on the road nearest to the bunker. About five to six hours from now. But only if he can get the drivers."

"Why can't he get drivers?" Brad asked as he continued to walk. The man ran alongside.

"No one to drive. The Man pulled everyone back."

"What?" Brad halted. "What?" he repeated. Spittle flew from his mouth as he spoke, landing squarely on the lips of the man with the radio, causing the man to instinctively swipe at his mouth with his sleeve.

"The Man...they were on their way, but they stopped at the relay station in Winterburn. The guy there told him he'd gotten a message saying that we'd lost the camp. So, The Man turned around and went back to Edmonton."

"Just like that? He went back to Edmonton?" Brad made a sound of disgust.

"Not just Edmonton. He's pulling everyone back to Calgary—the South Camps."

"Nice of him to do that," Brad said. He swore and kicked at another branch in his way.

"Yeah—nice of him," the guard echoed. "Leaves us to crawl around this friggin' fuckin' forest in the middle of the night."

"Ooh...ah...wow...alliteration," quipped the biker who was nursing the cut on his hand.

"What's that?"

"A literary device you mutilated monkey moron."

"Oh."

Brad scowled. "Who would have told him we'd lost the camp? Did you hear anything about us—what they were going to do about the rest of us?"

"No," the man with the radio said. "And no one knows where Virgil is either. The last they heard was that the messenger with the truckload of weapons had contacted Virgil. So he must have delivered the extra guns."

"Yeah, I heard that idiot call Virgil. Virgil gave him hell," Brad said. "Okay, let's get moving."

The whiny guard growled. "What the fuck? The Man took off on us. And we're still going after a bunch of broads and their brats?" He kicked at a small tree stump.

Brad grabbed the man by the collar. "Look...It's your goddamned fault that those women and kids got away." He gave the guard a push. The man fell to the ground with a loud exhalation of air.

"Yeah, but we went into the bunkhouse and let that old broad lock us in just to save your sorry ass." The guard was not quick enough to dodge Brad's boot. A second later, blood trickled from a split lip.

Brad stood over him. "If I tell The Man about how you let a bunch of women and kids escape, he'll shoot you on sight. Don't forget that. So, shut the fuck up." Brad kicked again and the guard let out a squeal of pain.

"Okay!" The guard scuttled away to avoid another blow. "But don't get mad at me. Get mad at Martha. Make that bitch pay."

"She will," Brad said. He touched his sore nose. "Her daughters and her grandkids were in that bunkhouse."

Brad smiled.

"She'll pay."

Chapter Four

A Fateful Conversation

MARTHA AWOKE and struggled to sit up. "The pumpkins—" She fought with the woolen blankets covering her, twisted free, and fell from her cot to the tent floor with a loud thud.

"What—?" Anna sat up, bewildered; she had been sleeping in the cot near the opposite wall. They were still sharing one of the larger tents belonging to Meteor's men. She threw her sleeping bag to the floor and scrambled over to Martha, who lay still on the ground. Anna's eyes grew wide. She reached out to touch the fallen woman. She held her breath.

Was she dead?

Anna touched Martha's cheek. It was hot.

She's burning up.

Anna studied Martha's chest, looking for the familiar rise and fall. When she couldn't see any movement, she leaned her ear toward Martha's mouth. She gave a soft sigh of relief as warm breath touched her flesh. Martha gasped. Anna jumped back with a little shriek.

"Pumpkin spices... Ask Matthew to get pumpkin spices."

"What— What are you talking about, Martha?"

"The pumpkins. We've got to make the pies. But I need more spices. The right spices. Okay? The right spices. The pumpkin pie spices. Okay?" Martha tried to rise, but Anna restrained her. "I've got to go..." Martha lay back on the floor, her face ashen and her eyes clamped shut.

"It's okay," Anna said. She feared that Martha's struggling would dislodge the new stitches. "Easy, Martha. It's okay. I'll make the pies. You rest."

"But use the right spices..."

"I will," Anna assured her.

She's delirious. How do I bring the fever down? How?

"Let's get you back into bed, okay?" Anna struggled to lift Martha, who had fallen back to sleep, but the woman was too heavy. Instead, Anna pulled the covers from the cot and drew them up over Martha. She knew she couldn't leave Martha on the floor; the chill of the ground would make her start to shiver and the shivering would make the fever go even higher.

"I'll be right back."

A few moments later, Anna and a young native man, his dark hair pulled into a thick ponytail, lifted Martha back onto her cot.

"Thanks," Anna said.

"You're welcome." The man reached out and touched Martha's face. "She's running a fever."

"I know." Her brusqueness barely skirted the edge of sarcasm. She wrung her hands. "I'm not sure what to do for her. I can't bathe her to bring down the fever."

"Why not?"

"There's no way to immerse her in warm water the way I would a child... and then dry her before she begins to shiver."

"My granny had a way to take care of our fevers."

"Your granny?

"Yeah, she was a tribe elder. My granny took care of my brother and me. We were sick lots."

"What did she do?"

"A sweat lodge—"

"A sweat lodge—but that's hot, right?"

"Yes, but she said it would chase away the bad spirits. We'd sweat them out."

"But that will drive her fever higher. She's already delirious. Besides, I can't get her to drink anything... and I don't have any intravenous supplies. Sweating without replenishing the water in her body, will make her organs shut down." She shook her head. "Do you remember any herbs your granny used?"

The man thought for a moment. "Yarrow—"

"Oh my God, yes...yarrow." Anna hit herself in the forehead with the heel of her hand. "How could I have been so stupid? We had lots growing around the compound. And Martha hung bunches in the dried goods storehouse." She gave the man a hopeful look. "Do you know what yarrow looks like? Could you find some around here?"

"I think so."

Martha groaned from the bed. She tried to get up, but Anna held her down.

"Tell Josef he's on patrol tonight," Martha mumbled. "I put his Bible on the table." Martha opened her eyes. She rolled them from side to side, trying to set a focus. She clawed at her ring finger. "My ring...who took my ring?"

"Sh..." Anna said. She draped herself across Martha in an attempt to keep her from falling out of the bed again. The young man came to her aid.

"My rings...my rings...I need my rings," Martha cried, clutching at the ring finger on one hand, and then the other.

"Sh... I'll find your rings," Anna assured her.

Finally, Martha went quiet. Anna placed her hand on Martha's chest; the woman's heart beat wildly under Anna's palm.

"We've got to get some liquids into her. Her heart is going to jump right out of her chest." She looked up at the young man. "Go. Get that yarrow."

Anna watched him leave and then she returned to her own cot. She dropped her head into her hands. "Remember, Anna. Remember. What did Martha do with yarrow?" she muttered while she forced her sleep-starved brain to perform. She smiled gratefully as the memories resurfaced.

A few minutes later, the man returned. He held a mass of gray-green, spindly plants with bushy heads and fern-like leaves. Anna jumped up and took the herbs.

"I need boiling water. I need to make tea. And rags. I'll soak the rags and wrap her head." Anna regarded the man looking at her. "Well... don't just stand there. Go!"

Between them, the yarrow tea had been administered, orally and topically. Martha now looked like a Civil War soldier with her head wrapped in wet cheesecloth. Her feet and her hands had been bathed in the tea solution, and they had managed to get her to drink some of the tea without making her choke too badly.

"Thank you," Anna said with a small smile.

"You're welcome." The man turned. "Call me if you need anything. The name's Sparrow."

"Sparrow?" Anna gave the man a once over; he was not small. She looked up, puzzled.

He laughed. "It's better than being called...*Chochmo*."

"What does that mean?"

"It's a Hopi word— Means *mud mound*."

They both laughed.

"Sparrow is short for *Sparrow-of-the-winter*. That's my real name."

Anna made a small sound of confirmation, but she still looked puzzled.

Sparrow interpreted her confusion. "Sparrows are tough. Have you seen them in the middle of winter?"

"Oh— I see. I get it," she assured him.

Sparrow smiled. "Call me if you need me." He gave a small bow as he exited the tent.

"Wait!"

Sparrow stuck his head back inside.

"Garlic, olive oil, and plastic wrap— can you get those for me, too? I remember another remedy."

Sparrow smiled again. "Give me a few minutes."

He soon returned with the requested items. "One of the guys is a chef. He carries this stuff everywhere." He handed the items to Anna. "He said to tell you he has more garlic, if you need it."

Anna prepared a salve. She crushed two fat cloves of garlic, and mixed the white flesh into a small amount of olive oil. She held a metal cup over a candle flame, warming the oil, infusing it with the power of the garlic. Soon, she poured out a small puddle of warm oil into her waiting palm; she applied it to Martha's feet, followed by plastic wrap.

"There. That makes me feel a whole lot better." Anna wiped her hands on a bit of cheesecloth. "I hope it works." She stared into the cup that still had the remnants of the garlic floating in a bit of oil. She wrinkled her brow. "Hey, I can use this on her cuts, too." She smiled enthusiastically. "The garlic will kill the infection." She turned back to the man. "You gotta leave now. I have to undress her."

Sparrow held up his hand. "No problem. Just call—" He left the tent once more.

"Wait!"

Sparrow lifted the tent flap and looked inside. He was grinning. "Maybe I should just stay."

"Have you seen Meteor?"

"No."

"When you see him, tell him I want to talk to him, okay?"

"Sure. Is that it... for now?"

Anna gave a small laugh. "Yeah— No, wait. I should nurse Gordon."

"Who's Gordon?"

"My little boy. He's with one of Meteor's friends—in the tent nearest the pond. Would you bring him to me?"

"I'm on it."

MATTHEW AWOKE with a start. He was cold. He rubbed sleep from his eyes and checked his watch; it would be dawn soon. He clambered to his knees. Old injuries stirred in his bones. He groaned. He stood and stretched. His stomach rumbled. He retrieved the bag of cookies that had fallen to the ground. He stuffed them, one by one, into his mouth. He recovered the half-eaten one and ate it, too. They were delicious this morning, and the silken sweetness of the chocolate on his tongue brought his wife to mind again.

God, where was she?

He found his canteen, unscrewed the cap, and tipped it back. He drank. Water trickled out of the corner of his mouth and onto his shirt.

The pre-dawn sky caught his eye. Cherry pinks and blood-red oranges mingled and then strayed into bands of distinct color behind wispy angel-hair clouds. He walked to the other side of the fire. He stopped in front of his would-be killer, the man he had almost executed, his old friend. He gave the sleeping man's boot a kick.

"Wake up, Virgil."

"Wh—?" Virgil opened his eyes and then squeezed them shut to clear them. He opened them again. "What?"

"Get up. We gotta talk."

Virgil pushed himself into an upright position. "Talk."

"Your men are with us. I will trust they mean what they say on the strength of your word."

"You have my word."

"Good— Now what about you? You haven't said anything—one way, or the other. Are you in...or are you out?"

"I want you to know The Man wanted me to take over your camp...but I wouldn't have any part of it. I didn't have anything to do with Josef's death, either. I was totally against killing him." Virgil looked down at his bound hands. "I'll join you. But, I have one condition."

"A condition?" Matthew smirked at his former friend's—former enemy's—audacity to set terms for his surrender. "Shoot."

"I gotta get Marion."

"Who's Marion?"

"The Man's sister," Virgil said. He paused when he caught Matthew's eyes and the question lighting them. "Well, she's not exactly his sister. More adopted really. Childhood friends. But—"

"But you have a relationship with her?"

"Yes. And he'll kill her out of spite when he finds out I've joined you."

Matthew studied the ground at his feet. "How dangerous will this rescue be? And what if she doesn't want to be rescued?"

"She'll come with me. We're close."

"Closer than she is to her... *brother*?"

"I think so... I'm pretty sure. I'm also sure he'll hurt her when he finds out. So, I gotta get to her soon."

"What're you saying? That I should send a team to get her? Or assign you and a few of your men to the task?" Matthew kicked at a piece of wood lying near his foot. "Virgil—"

"No, Matthew. You have my word. I gave it, and I meant it. There's no going back for me. He'd kill me on the spot anyway. And I won't risk anyone else's life. Just mine. I'll go get her. I'll bring her back."

Matthew widened his eyes. "So, you'll run off to find your woman, while I'm stuck here with no clue about *my* wife?" He paused. His voice hardened. "No... Here's the deal—you'll help me take back the camp. When I've found Martha, then and only then can you go after Marion. Those are my terms. Take them or leave them. No negotiation."

Virgil nodded. "I'm good with that." He motioned to his hands that were still secured with a white electrical tie. He held them out to Matthew.

Matthew reached for his knife. He gripped the blade, pulled it open, and then slipped it between Virgil's wrists. He slit the tie. He stepped back.

"On the strength of our old friendship, I trust you Virgil. Don't give me a reason not to, or I will kill you."

"I gave you my word." Virgil rubbed his wrists. He looked up and stared at Matthew. A silence passed between them. Then Matthew nodded.

Matthew began to speak, but intermittent clicks from his radio drew his attention.

~~~
~~~

A Scent on the Breeze

BRAD LIFTED his head and sniffed the air. He smiled.

"Smell that?" he asked.

"What—?" the man with the hunter's cap responded.

"That— Smells like onions."

All the men stopped and drew in a breath of air through their nostrils.

"Crap...I'm damn hungry," exclaimed the whiny guard.

Brad ignored him. "Means we're close, but the light's coming up. If they're armed, we could get shot." He motioned to the man with the radio. "Turn that thing off." Brad turned his own radio off as he spoke. "No sense telling them we're here."

"I'm so hungry," the guard repeated.

"All of us are hungry. Shut up," the man with the cut hand said.

Brad studied the map. "We've got to be close." He trailed his finger along the line the kid had drawn. He looked up and then down at the map. His other hand held a compass. "Anyone else want to look at this thing?" The man with the radio took the map.

"A copse of fir trees. A big hill. Looks like a meadow or a pond over here. Did we pass one?"

Brad shrugged.

The man with the radio took the compass. "We're going in the right direction at least. Let's just keep walking." He returned the map and compass to Brad.

"There should be some sign that they've come this way," said the man with the cut hand. "Don't you think? I mean, we're following kids. Wouldn't they have dropped something?"

"I think we strayed from the path earlier," offered another man.

A sound caught Brad's ear and he held a finger to his lips. In a moment, the other men could hear it, too.

Women's voices.

Brad smiled.

"Bingo," he said softly.

Chapter Five

Rendezvous at Ten Acres

THE FALL sky had begun to brighten. A wash of crimson hues announced the coming new day. Jonah stood up and stretched. He pushed his cap back and looked around. Some of his men were slumped in sleep, while others stood on guard, their guns cradled in their arms. The gunfire had slowed down to a mere trickle of pops and flares during the night. Now everything was silent. Small fires burned in the distance, vestiges of vehicles taken out by rocket launchers. Dark shapes of men with buckets and fire extinguishers moved quickly to suppress the flames. He scanned the Hutterites' land. The giant farm was still standing along with its barns, assorted silos, and smaller buildings. Jonah beamed with self-congratulatory joy.

We've done it—we held off The Man. No harm had come to these peaceful people, he thought. *Now what about our guys?*

Jonah lifted his radio. It had been silent for most of the night. He wondered about calling Matthew. He itched to make the call.

It couldn't hurt to call him now.

He wrestled with the idea, and set it aside.

Orders...were orders.

Jonah had learned to obey and to love the man who had welcomed him and Martha's family a year ago. He had arrived at the compound as an introverted boy-man, but now he was a man, and one of Matthew's most trusted captains. He prized that trust; a call might be construed as disobedience. He put the radio back on his belt and began to awaken his men. He jostled some by their shoulders, and roused some with small kicks. Soon all the men were standing, stretching, groaning, and muttering.

Weariness made Jonah stagger. He grabbed a fence post and steadied himself. It was time to go home. He looked longingly at the radio.

Call him?

He resisted the urge again. He began to walk.

He reached a cluster of men; they were lifting bodies, commenting, cradling some, dumping others.

A head count.

Jonah dreaded the idea. Dreaded knowing whom they were going to find among the dead. Too many of his men.

Far too many.

One of the men noticed him and waved. Jonah recognized the short, older man with the handlebar mustache—he was one of the compound's newest bachelor members—a favorite with the women, flirty and funny. His usually cheery face was grim. He wagged his head as he approached.

"Lots of ours, Jonah."

Jonah placed a hand on the man's shoulder. "But lots more of theirs?" he asked, hopefully.

"Not sure. We just got started."

Jonah squeezed his shoulder. "Carry on. I'm going to check with the other captains."

"What about Matthew? You heard anything?"

"No."

"Gonna call?"

"Maybe. I'll give it a few more minutes."

RICHARD TURNED as Meteor caught up to him. The soft morning light was not being kind to the big man's countenance. Even his blue eyes were dim and hazy.

"You look like shit, man. Get some rest."

"It's light enough. Let's get a team and go check the bodies. And then we go after Matthew."

"Matthew—? Why the rush to find Matthew?"

"Martha's in bad shape. He should be here with her."

"Oh." Richard hesitated and then added, "What about the Hutterites?"

"We'll send a team over there, too."

"And what about the other women and kids?"

"Sounds like Ruth led them to safety. They should be okay. We'll go after them later."

"When do we use the radio?" Richard asked.

"You haven't heard from anyone?"

Richard shook his head. "I've been listening for hours," he said, dangling the radio like a dead thing from one hand. Meteor wrenched the radio away. Richard's eyebrows shot up in surprise.

"We'll break the silence," Meteor said with a small growl.

Meteor pressed the *send* button. Twice. And waited.

No response.

He pressed it again. Twice. Then again, once more.

No response.

The next time he pressed the button, he held it down.

"Anyone out there? Over."

Richard and Meteor waited.

JONAH STRETCHED again, fighting against the hypnotic, womb-like fatigue lulling him, inviting him to sit down, to rest. The morning sun was warm. He removed his jacket and slung it over his shoulder. He risked closing his eyes, allowing sunlight to bathe his face.

"Sir?"

Jonah jumped. A bedraggled man stood next to him. His clothes were filthy, like he had been lying in a pool of cow manure. He had a blood-encrusted mouth and a black eye.

"You okay?" Jonah asked.

"Sure," the man said, swiping at his mouth with the back of his hand. He grinned apologetically as he surveyed his own clothing. "Did some belly crawling through the cattle enclosure."

Jonah gave a small laugh. "I can see that."

"Can we go back to camp now? The men are really tired. And we're so hungry..."

"Yeah, I know." Jonah took a long breath. "First...a perimeter check...along the far side—find our dead, gather them up, and then head for home."

"Already done," the man said.

"How bad?"

"Not too bad. Lots of dead Crazies. But only a few of us."

"How few?"

"Eighteen."

"That's more than a few. Do we have enough vehicles to take them back to camp?"

"I don't know, but the Hutterites said they'd bury them for us."

Jonah rubbed his hands over his face. "I'm so friggin' tired."

The bedraggled man said nothing. He picked at the crusted blood on his lip.

"Get someone to make a list of all the dead," Jonah added.

"Done." The man held up a small notebook. He flipped it open. "Here..."

Jonah took the book and searched the list. "Oh, damn." He closed his eyes. "I came to the compound with him and his family."

"Who?"

Jonah pointed at a name. He made a small noise in his throat. "It's not enough that we've been fighting all night—now we have to tell women that their loved ones are dead."

The bedraggled man touched his sore eye, winced, and growled. "Was this worth it?"

"You got a girlfriend?" Jonah asked.

"No."

"Me neither, but these guys do—girlfriends, wives, kids. So, for them, it was worth it."

"But I thought the women and children were being held by The Man's people."

"Last I heard they were." Jonah rolled his head, rocking it back and forth, in an attempt to relieve stiff muscles. "I'm hoping against Hell that something's changed." He reached up and massaged the back of his neck. "But...just in case...let's head back to the first camp." He breathed heavily. "It's over—when it's over."

The bedraggled man opened his mouth to speak, but clicks coming from the radio on Jonah's belt made both men stop and stare. The deep voice that followed made the pair grin.

MATTHEW AND Virgil stared at the radio. They both recognized the voice coming from the speaker.

"Meteor?" Virgil asked, his eyes narrowed and his forehead furrowed into a deep frown. "Who's he working with now?"

Matthew smiled.

"Shit! I knew it," Virgil exclaimed.

Matthew pressed the *send* button and held it.

"Rendezvous...ten acres."

JONAH'S GRIN deepened at the sound of the second man's voice. The bedraggled man stared up at him, expectantly.

"Matthew's headed back to meet with Meteor," Jonah said. "They've got a secret meeting place about an hour away from the first camp."

"Then it's okay for us to go back, too," the bedraggled man said, looking less bedraggled as the thought took hold.

"Tell the men. And tell the head man with the Hutterites that *we bury our own*. Tell him to burn the dead Crazies."

"Yes, sir."

"Oh, and be careful...just in case some of The Man's people are still lying in wait to ambush us."

The bedraggled man trotted off, a new spring in his step. "We're going back," he called, forgetting Jonah's advice. "We're done here. We're going back."

A small band of men cheered.

Jonah smiled, but the smile disappeared when he gazed down once more at the names in the small notebook. He slapped the notebook shut and shoved it into his pack. He stared at the rising sun. He didn't relish giving Martha the news.

But telling Ruth...was going to be terrible.

METEOR HEAVED a sigh of relief. He clapped Richard on the back. "He's alive. Hallelujah. The bastard made it."

"Ten acres? What does that mean?" Richard asked.

"It means we stay put. He's on his way."

"Should I tell Anna?"

"No, let her be. She's probably asleep. Let her sleep."

RUTH FLINCHED in her sleep as she morphed in and out of dreams. She had come off guard duty, and had fallen into a dead sleep—almost from the moment her head hit her pillow—not even bothering to remove her boots. Other than the soft snuffles of nursing babies, the bunker was quiet. Outside, a second shift set up watch, but the bunker had given the women a sense of security, so they chatted and snoozed. Mostly snoozed.

METEOR PACED near a low-burning campfire. The disappearing night had gone silent except for the pop and snap of burning logs and the snores of exhausted men. He glanced toward the tent where Martha lay, began to walk toward it, but changed his mind. Like a troubled wolf, he continued his pacing.

Matthew was on his way. Tell him the truth? Tell him that Brad shot her. No, he'll hold it against me for not protecting her like I promised I would. No, I can't tell him. Who else knows the truth? Anna... she knows. But she won't tell. Or will she? Remind her not to tell? No. What do I do? What?

An emotion rose inside him, hotter than any he had ever known. He clenched his hands into fists, the physical act fueling the rage in his brain.

If I find Brad... If I kill Brad? Is that it? Find Brad? Kill Brad? Or bring him back as a prisoner?

Meteor studied the parked bikes and trucks. He knew Matthew was on his way and that once he returned, his small army would return to their families. He made a quick turn in the direction of the parked vehicles.

"Meteor—"

He stopped and glanced over his shoulder. Richard was running after him.

"You need to see this," Richard called.

BRAD WAVED to his men. He pointed at a trio of women coming toward them; the women were still several feet away. They were chatting. A flock of prairie chickens exploded in a flurry of feathers out of the underbrush, making the women screech and finally giggle in relief. Brad motioned to his men, and three of his guards slipped into the trees in the direction of the women.

Brad pointed to two more women seated near them, their backs against a large spruce tree, their heads tipped forward onto their chests, with their guns draped across their laps. The panicked birds had not disturbed them. They slumbered on. The men crept forward.

"Ladies?"

Both women jerked awake and gave a small scream at the sight of the men.

"Sh..." Brad said. "No noise. You'll wake the babies." He motioned with his gun. "Get up." He looked around. The other three women were now in the custody of his guards, their arms twisted up behind their backs, their mouths covered by gags. "Is that all of you?" he asked.

The seated women nodded meekly as they were disarmed. They stood and blinked, still not fully awake. Brad motioned for them to be gagged, too. He pointed down the path with his pistol.

"Lead on," he said. "We're hungry."

The two women shuffled forward, one lagging behind the other. Brad noticed the slower one and gave her backside a swift kick. The woman gave a sharp yelp and fell to her knees. Brad leaned over her.

"Move it. I said we're hungry."

The woman cowered, expecting more pain. The second woman bent and clutched at the fallen woman's arm. She hauled her to her feet.

"C'mon. Don't make him hurt you again." She glanced at Brad as she spoke.

He was smiling.

THE KID WITH the orange hair smirked up at the two men. A thin native man was holding him by his collar, while another man stood near him, his gun trained on his chest.

"Where did you find him?" Meteor asked.

"Shadowing us," said the native man. "As we were coming back to camp with the women." A black and gray feather swung from his long, jet-black hair. "He had this with him." He showed Meteor a walkie-talkie.

"Where did you get this?" Meteor asked, taking the radio. The kid stayed silent, his look stony.

Meteor studied the boy. He knew this kid. This kid with the very bad attitude. This was the kid with the nasty dad, the dad that once attacked Martha because she was following orders and teaching the kid how to cook eggs. His father had burst into her cabin, incensed that his son was expected to do women's work, and was about to punch Martha when Meteor stopped him. The dad was hauled off, leaving both the abused kid and his abused mother screaming vulgarities, threatening Matthew, and proclaiming that the beloved man in their lives had been accused wrongly, and without a proper hearing.

After that, the boy courted trouble—getting into it was routine, as ritualistic as the morning prayers his religious father had drilled into him. Pray in the morning, steal in the afternoon, and face the music at night. He wound up in front of Matthew and the Discipline Committee on occasion. For stealing. And for attacking one of the women in the camp kitchen—she had ordered him to wash pots. The whipping did nothing more than to fuel his hatred of Matthew, and his belief that his bully father had been exiled unfairly. Revenge soon replaced outrage.

The cunning boy slipped around the compound like a tiny snake, poking his head in here and there, and all the while gathering intelligence about Matthew's plans. And about the secret second camp with the oil reserves. Then he took his knowledge to the enemy, their worst enemy:

The Man. Betrayal was this kid's talent, so telling Brad about the bunker in the woods was just a small blip in his day. Keeping the secret that he had done so, was all part of the game. The boy's eyes narrowed.

"I don't need to tell you nothin'," he said, attempting to wrench his collar out of the native man's hand. But the man held fast, jerking the boy upright.

"Start talking, kid." The man gave the boy a rough shake.

Meteor put his hand on the kid's other shoulder, and nodded to the native man.

"Let me have him for a while. I'll talk to him."

The native man released the kid's collar and backed away. The kid eyed Meteor nervously. The big man towered over him.

"Sit down with me," Meteor said, walking a short distance with his hand still on the kid's shoulder. He pointed to a log near a small fire. "Here. Sit here." When the kid resisted, Meteor exerted enough pressure to make the kid sink like a deflated balloon to the ground. "There, that's better. Now we can talk."

The kid jerked away. He shrugged his jacket into place, pulling and smoothing his crumpled collar. "I got nuthin' to say to you."

"Sure, you do," Meteor said. He clenched and unclenched his meaty hand, making sure the boy could see his fist. "I know you don't care about pain, but we need to know what you were up to. And how you got that radio. It's one of theirs, isn't it?"

"Yep."

"How'd you get it?"

"I already told you—."

"And I told you that you're going to tell me." Meteor's voice was hard and smooth like cold marble. He threw his arm around the boy's neck; his hand was still clenched into a fist. He tugged the boy closer to him. He put his mouth near the boy's ear. "Now talk to me. Tell me what they know. Or we'll make a trip into the bushes."

The kid stiffened. He still refused to speak.

Meteor began to rise, pulling the boy up with him. He turned at the sound of his name.

"Meteor," Sparrow called. "Martha's conscious. Anna said you'd want to know."

"Take him," Meteor said to Richard who was standing near them. "Keep an eye on him. He's bad news."

Richard grabbed the boy and hauled him to his feet.

Chapter Six

A Promise Made

CAMMY HAD been sleeping, her head resting on Trojan's shoulder, but after a nudge from him, she was fully awake, her almond-shaped eyes bright and searching. Trojan stopped the truck and watched smoke rising above the trees.

"Oh, my God, not a fire," Cammy said, pulling silken strands of brunette hair at the nape of her neck, and gathering them into a quick ponytail. She leaned toward the dash, to get a better look, while she twisted a yellow elastic band into her hair.

"Hope it's not too big." Trojan said, pushing himself against the steering wheel and peering toward the sky. He reached for the glove compartment and then corrected himself. "Not my truck," he mused. "I have binoculars in there."

The truck once belonged to the enemy. The pair happened across the vehicle driven by The Man's messenger, its truck bed crammed with weapons. They tricked him, stole the truck, and delivered the weapons to Matthew. The truck was now theirs.

"I don't see flames," Cammy said. She reached over and grabbed Trojan's hand, seeking his comfort. He returned her squeeze. She smiled. She liked the feel of his rough, warm hand. So much nicer than The Man's calloused hand. Trojan had told her he loved her, for the very first time, just a few hours before. The thought sent a little shiver through her belly. He had said it, and she knew he meant it. She smiled again.

So much better than The Man, she thought.

She remembered the biker leader's impassionate face, his cruelty, and she shuddered. The Man had coveted her, but he had never loved her. She clasped Trojan's hand tighter.

Life had become much brighter for the slight, pretty woman who had once been The Man's bedmate. Months before, Meteor and Trojan had kidnapped her, along with a full load of the enemy's weapons. The Man was furious over the loss of his woman, but he was more irate over the loss of his guns and ammunition. Cammy never returned to him. Instead, she was awarded to Trojan like spoils of war. Soon the two became inseparable.

"At least it's nearly daylight," Cammy said. "We'll be able to run a water brigade."

"If there's anything left to save."

"Don't say that. Let's go."

Trojan threw the truck into gear and tromped down on the accelerator, making the big truck fishtail and swerve. The truck sped up the highway. Matthew's compound and their cabin were only a few miles ahead.

MARTHA STRUGGLED up through the haze. She forced her eyes open, but the effort was futile. They closed again. She descended back into a nether world of hollow-eyed owls and evil elves. One elf sat haughtily on a naked, gnarled branch stretched across a midnight forest. His dark, slanted eyes bore into her. He never spoke, but the message in his eloquent eyes was clear: she was doomed. Martha climbed above the trees, flew actually, catching a ride on a low, thick yellow cloud—the color of bad air. It felt good to lay back and let the cool mist sweep her away—away from the haunting, accusatory eyes of the elf.

One of her struggles to regain consciousness brought about an acute awareness of pain, first the sharp stabs between her legs, and then the dull throbbing ache across her chest. She slipped back into the mists, moaning softly as she did. She dreamed again.

This time, she was calling from her cabin door. Calling for a man, a large man, with apple cheeks, a beard, and curly hair. She called louder, but her breath was sucked from her, and she collapsed to the floor. Then she was no longer in her cabin, but in the Meeting House with many men. Her mind swept in and muddied the image before she could see the details. She called out again. This time she was answered.

"Martha," a soft female voice said. "I'm here."

"Josef? Where's Josef?"

"Uh...Josef isn't here," Anna replied. Martha's repeated mention of her dead husband alarmed her. "Can you wake up?" she said softly. "Wake up, Martha. Open your eyes."

Martha slipped away again, but consciousness was calling, and she opened her eyes. "Where is he?" she mumbled. Her eyes stayed open this time.

"Martha... You've been badly injured," Anna said. She pushed an arm under Martha's head and tilted her forward. "Are you thirsty? Would you like some water?"

Martha gave a slight nod. Anna tipped a metal flask to the woman's lips. Martha took only a small sip and fell back against Anna's arm.

"Josef? He's on patrol?" Martha asked. Anna grappled for the right words that would tell Martha that her husband—her first husband—had been dead for months. Then suddenly, Martha stiffened. She cried out. "I hurt so much. What's wrong with me?"

"You were shot in the chest."

Martha expelled a small grunt. "Why'm I not dead then?" she mumbled.

"Your breastbone deflected the bullet."

"I had my vest on. Didn't I?"

"You did, but whoever shot you was close enough to shoot right through your vest." Anna paused. "Do you *know* who shot you?"

Martha went very silent in contemplation of the question. A memory rose up. Crystal clear.

"Brad," she said. "Brad shot me. I should have taken his gun, but I didn't. He shot me." That's when Martha noticed the large man in the shadows.

"Who's here? Jo—," she stopped herself. "No," she corrected herself. "Josef is dead." She seemed to slip away, but was soon back again. "Matthew? Meteor?" The man moved from the shadows into the light.

"I'm right here, sweetheart." Meteor came over. He had stepped into the tent only moments before. Now he knelt beside the camp cot and took Martha's hand in his. "Right here."

Martha gave him a small smile. "It's you...," she whispered. Her eyes gave up the fight to stay open and closed. She slept for a few moments. When she opened her eyes, Meteor was still at her side. She forced another smile. "Hi, Meteor. I hurt so much." He stroked her hand and smiled.

"I know you do, but you're going to be alright. Anna took care of you. She removed the bullet. She stitched you up."

"She's done that before," Martha said softly.

"I have some Demerol," Anna said. "Will you let me give you some?" Anna didn't want a repeat of the time when Martha had been stabbed. The older woman had berated her for administering painkillers to her without her expressed consent.

Martha nodded in concert with another very loud groan. "Go ahead." The injection was given, and Martha welcomed the cocoon of drugged bliss that enfolded her. "Where's everybody? Where's Matthew?" she murmured.

Meteor smiled. "Matthew's coming here. I broke radio silence. He's on his way." He gave Martha's hand a comforting squeeze. "He should be here soon."

Martha mumbled something and drifted away. Suddenly, she jerked awake, her hands grasped at the coarse wool blanket in an attempt to lift it. "Mary? My daughters? The other women?"

Anna pushed a small hand down on Martha's hands, calming their frantic movements.

"They're fine. Ruth and Elizabeth took everyone to the bunker."

Martha sagged back with a soft expulsion of breath. In a moment, she was deeply asleep.

Anna and Meteor exchanged looks of compassion and concern.

Anna touched his sleeve. "I'm so glad you reached Matthew. Is the main camp secured now? Is it ours again?"

"I'm not sure. There's no way to be sure...at least not until we can do a body count in the daylight."

"A body count... Simon..." Anna's voice grew very soft. Their *moving-in day*, a romantic event that had taken the place of marriages after the *Change*, hadn't been that long ago. "I miss him. Have you heard anything about Simon?"

Meteor shook his head. "Sorry." He put his hand on the young woman's shoulder. "I'm so sorry, Anna. It's been pretty rough on you."

"I'll be fine. I just want to know if my husband's dead or alive." Meteor gave her shoulder a warm squeeze.

Martha twisted in her sleep, mumbled some unintelligible words, and then cried out. "I want—"

Meteor laid his hand on her forehead to quiet her. He scowled as he drew it away. "She's really hot."

"She's fighting an infection." Anna passed Meteor a rag she had wrung out in cool water. "Here, wipe her face with this. I'll check her chest." She pulled back the soiled dressing. "That's funny. "

"What is?"

"Doesn't seem infected." Anna frowned. "What's giving her such a high fever?"

"Maybe she has other injuries? Did you check?"

Anna looked up and stared into the big man's blue eyes. She looked sheepish. "I was so worried about the bullet wound... I...." she faltered.

"Well, do it now," Meteor said, somewhat gruffly. He pulled off his coat and dropped it over the end of the cot. Something clunked as he did so.

Anna began a slow investigation of her patient. With Meteor's help, she turned Martha from side to side, examining her from her shoulders on down. Her chest was mottled in a wash of yellowed-greens, hideous purples, and shades of black. A variety of less worrisome bruises and scrapes covered her back and arms. There were a few cuts on her face, but nothing of concern.

Anna pulled up the white dress, revealing Martha's legs. She frowned. Martha's underwear was stained with blood. Anna reached for the waistband of the underpants and pulled them down. The man and woman stared at a menstrual pad hardened with dried blood, and shiny with fresh crimson blood. Anna's frown deepened.

"Her period?" she asked. She eased Martha's legs apart. A sickly sweet smell erupted into the air. "This can't be right."

Anna examined Martha's vaginal area. This time she cried out in horror. She clapped a hand to her mouth and backed away.

"Oh, God. Oh my God." Her voice quavered with emotion. She looked up at Meteor. His blue eyes were dark and his face had hardened. She knew he knew the truth before she spoke. "She's been *raped*."

"Raped," he repeated. "Raped." Meteor said the word as though he were trying to grasp its meaning.

Anna stood shell-shocked, unmoving, her hand still near her mouth. Tears filled her eyes.

Meteor leaned over Martha, stroking her hair, and mumbling words Anna could not make out. She spoke again:

"Who do you think did this to her?" Anna sobbed.

Silence.

"Meteor? Who—?"

Meteor raised his head. "We know who." His voice was low, his words barely audible.

"Brad?"

He looked back at Martha. He wiped her forehead and her face once more with the wet cloth.

"'I'll take care of Brad," he said, his voice still deep and hollow. "Keep this between us. Don't tell Matthew. He's got enough to deal with." He turned hard eyes on Anna. "Did you hear me?"

Anna nodded. "Okay, if that's what you think is best. At least until Martha can make that decision for herself." She sniffed and wiped her eyes on her sleeve.

"I do." Meteor continued wiping Martha's face. "How long do you need to clean her up? Matthew should be here soon."

Ten minutes later, Anna lay back on her cot. The sight of Martha's wounds had made her queasy. She shuddered at the thought of a man doing that to a woman. Brad's face came into her mind. She shuddered again.

"Why, Meteor? Why?"

Meteor still stood beside the bed, rinsing the rag, wringing it out, and wiping Martha's face. "Brad hated her. He's a coward. It's a coward's way," he said, his voice level and cold.

Anna controlled a sob. "It must have happened in the Meeting House. Mary said the men were being mean to her." Anna clapped a hand to her mouth again. "Oh, no, do you think Mary watched that?" Her tone was breathy with horror.

Meteor said nothing. He put the rag back into the bowl. "I'll see if Matthew is here yet."

He picked up his jacket, making another clunking sound against the cot's metal frame as he did so. He shoved his hand into a pocket and withdrew a pistol. He examined it in the lamplight. "She had this when I found her." He held it up. "It's my old gun."

"Your gun?"

"Yeah... Martha took it as a kind of trophy from me... a long time ago," he added. He sounded wistful. "It was lying under her at the bunkhouse."

"Oh," Anna said. She sat up and swung her legs over the edge of the cot.

"It hasn't been fired. It's still loaded," he observed. He put the pistol back into his pocket. "I'll be right back. Watch her."

"I suspect there's internal damage, too." Anna said. "There's not much I can do about that."

Meteor lifted the tent flap and then turned back. "Keep her alive."

"I'll do what I can, but you'd better hurry. I'm not sure she's gonna make it—" Anna began to cry again.

"Don't say that," Meteor said, his voice once more low and threatening.

Anna's tears stopped abruptly and she drew back in surprise. "I can't—"

"Don't say that. Promise me you'll keep her alive."

"I *can't* promise you that." It was almost a shout.

"Promise me!"

Anna's face contorted with the knowledge that no matter how hard she promised, this was a promise she might have to break. Nevertheless, she uttered the words, knowing Meteor needed to hear them.

"I promise."

Meteor pulled up the flap and left the tent.

Anna got up from the cot. She couldn't believe what she had seen. She remembered her own rape by bikers that had taken place months before, long before she joined Matthew's compound, long before she made Martha's acquaintance. The rape had been invasive; a terrible violation of her young body, certainly an act against her will, but it hadn't been brutal, not like this.

She pulled up Martha's dress and examined her again. Some of the ragged wounds had crusted over, some were weeping with infection, while others gaped—angry and raw. And the odor was nauseating. Anna gagged.

This is awful. I've never seen a woman ripped up this badly. Not even when giving birth.

A fury rose up inside the young woman as she washed away more sticky blood, revealing the true gravity of Martha's injuries.

Brad? Brad did all this?

Her eyes went wide.

Or were there more men? Good God! How many more men?

Martha flinched and moaned. Anna hesitated. Martha quieted. Anna continued her examination.

How am I going to fix you this time? she thought miserably. *Stitches...I have to stitch some of these.*

Anna drew the back of her hand across her forehead. A wave of fatigue made her sway. She took a deep breath and shook the dizzy spell away. She reached for her shoulder bag and the small sewing kit inside. Martha cried out again. Anna threaded a needle, but her fingers trembled. Partially from stress. Partially from exhaustion.

But mostly from rage.

She gritted her teeth to steady her hands.

MATTHEW AND VIRGIL craned their necks. They were en route to the meeting place near the pond, but the sight of smoke in the distance, in the direction of the compound, made Matthew reconsider. He picked up the radio lying on the seat next to him. He pressed the *send* button.

"Fire. Head to the main camp. Over."

A series of "Copy that" and "Roger" came from the radio. Matthew swung the truck up the main road leading to the compound.

"Who would have been stupid enough to start a fire?" Virgil asked, clutching the armrest and righting himself.

"A Crazy. They don't see the big picture. No matter how hard The Man has worked in bringing the motorcycle clubs together, they still don't see the big picture."

"This whole thing, this war suddenly seems useless. I'm glad it's over for me," Virgil said angrily.

Matthew faced him. "It's not exactly over for you yet, Virg. I expect your loyalty...and your help."

"And you'll have it... but as soon as this mess is over with, I'm gonna find Marion, and take up potato farming somewhere."

"It's a good choice. You'll have plenty of customers. But how will you stop Crazies from stealing your crops? You'll need to ally yourself with muscle."

"I'll worry about that later. Once I've had a full night's sleep...in a bed. Preferably with Marion next to me."

They neared the compound. The parking lot was still in the distance. Matthew slowed the truck and stopped on the side of the road.

"I think we should walk from here. No sense driving into an ambush and getting shot."

"I'm good with that," Virgil agreed. He hopped out of the truck. "I'll need a gun."

Matthew opened the back door and drew out handguns, holsters, and rifles.

"Here," he said, handing one of each to Virgil. "Remember which side you're on," he said with a wry grin.

"Thanks. Ammunition?"

Matthew grabbed boxes of bullets and handed them to Virgil. Virgil took them, loaded his guns, and stood expectantly.

"So, how should we do this?" Virgil asked.

"A call back to Meteor first."

METEOR AND RICHARD stared down at the radio in Richard's hand.

"He's going to the main compound instead," Richard said.

"He should be here, not there," Meteor roared. He grabbed the radio. Richard grabbed his arm.

"Hey, take it easy." Richard looked puzzled. "What's up with you?"

"Nothing. Tired."

"He's probably seeing the smoke from what's left of the women's bunkhouse."

"Our guys have that under control, don't they?" asked Meteor.

"As far as I know. None of the scouts arriving back have said otherwise. They couldn't save the bunkhouse, but they put out the fire." Richard continued, "Look, we can't see from here. Let Matthew check the compound. He'll get here in good time."

"Fine. I'll check on Martha. Anna needs a break."

Richard gave him a small smile. "You do that. You might want to get a little sleep, too."

Meteor glared at him. Richard raised his hands in surrender.

"Just a suggestion."

TROJAN BRAKED the truck, sending a spray of gravel into the air. He and Cammy leapt out and joined Matthew and Virgil. Other trucks pulled up; more men jumped out, armed and ready for instructions. Among them was the pony-tailed captain, one of Matthew's most trusted men. He sprinted up to Matthew.

"Matthew— Sounds like the women are safe. Just spoke with Richard. He says he has no idea if Brad is still in control of the camp, but he thinks he isn't. And I can't reach Jonah. We'll go in and check the buildings, help you secure the camp. I'll take a crew to the Hutterites after that."

"That'll work," Matthew said. He waited for more trucks to pull up, and more men to join him. He spoke to them as they ran up. "Break into groups. Come in from all sides. We have no idea who has control of the camp now. Assume it's The Man's people. And we might need all hands to put that fire out if it's still burning."

"Richard says he thinks the fire's under control," the pony-tailed captain added. "He left men behind to take care of it."

"We won't take any chances," Matthew said. "Let's assume The Man's people are still here."

The men grunted their understanding. They slipped into the dawn, dark shadows under the hint of a rising sun. The pony-tailed captain remained behind. Matthew turned to him.

"You go in through the front gate. Help us secure the compound, and then grab two of the teams. Head over to the Hutterites. I'll go back and meet with Meteor."

"You got it. Any word on Martha?" the captain asked.

"No. Not yet," Matthew replied.

The captain nodded and turned. "Hope you find her soon." The captain raised his hand in salute.

"Hey," Matthew called after him. "Holler if you need more fire power at the Hutterites."

"Will do. See you later."

METEOR PULLED back the tent flap and entered. Martha still lay on the camp cot, unmoving, and illuminated by a propane camp lantern set on a small table near her head. She was very pale save for a feverish blush to her cheeks. Meteor walked over and knelt beside the cot.

"Martha?" He bent low to her ear and called her name again. "Martha?" She didn't awaken. Anna came up behind him.

"She hasn't been conscious for a while now—since I cleaned her up." Anna grabbed a rag and wiped beaded sweat from Martha's face. "I'm not sure she'll make it, Meteor. I'm praying, but..." She shook her head.

"Matthew should be here soon. He's stopping at the compound to check the fire first.

"I thought the fire was under control."

"It is."

"I hope he doesn't take too long," Anna said. "You should tell—"

"Tell him what, Anna?" Meteor barked. "Tell him that his wife has been raped? Tell him that she might be dying? Tell him what?"

Anna jumped back. "Okay. Okay." Tears of hurt shone in her eyes. Meteor's outburst had taken her totally off guard.

Martha gave a small shriek that made them jump. Her eyes were open, but she wasn't seeing.

"Sh..." Anna said. She stroked her arm. "It's okay, Martha."

Martha quieted and fell back asleep. Anna turned to Meteor. "Have you...had any sleep?" she asked gently, not wanting to draw his wrath again.

"No."

Anna touched his hand, a concerned gesture filled with affection. "Don't you think you should?"

"Later— When Matthew is here. When the camp is back in his hands."

"Meteor?" Anna asked, her voice soft and tentative. "Do you... do you have special feelings for Martha?"

"We'd all miss her feisty spirit, wouldn't we?" he said dismissively.

"Yes, we would," Anna agreed. She wanted to tell him that he hadn't actually answered her question, but she thought better of it, and let it rest. Instead, she said, "I would miss her horribly."

"Then keep her alive."

"I'm doing my best. But I don't have her knowledge or her medical textbooks."

"I can get those." Meteor rose. "I'll get them after Matthew gets here."

"Uh—I'm not sure I should tell you this..." Anna waved the idea aside. "Never mind."

"Tell me what?" Meteor glowered down at her. Anna shrank away. "Tell me what?" he repeated.

"I think she was raped by more than one man..." She hesitated. "I think there might have been many men."

Meteor growled, low in his throat. Anna backed away.

"I—I'm sorry—" she said.

Meteor stared into her eyes. "Not a word to Matthew," he said. "Not...a...word!" His eyes blazed.

Anna suddenly understood. "It wasn't your fault, Meteor," she said, her voice firm.

Meteor ripped up the tent flap and strode out the door.

CAMMY AND TROJAN followed the pony-tailed captain down the main road toward the Gatehouse. The light was still too low to see well, but there were no sounds of shots being fired.

"I'm surprised there aren't any guards," Cammy whispered. She crept along behind the men, keeping low to the ground. The smell of acrid smoke hung heavily in the air and it burned their eyes. As they neared the front gate, they could see the faint embers of a razed building.

"Oh, God," Cammy said, her voice thick with emotion. "The women's bunkhouse..."

Trojan stopped her. "Don't think it."

A scuffle off to their left drew their attention. It was followed by men's voices. They peered into the gloom. The men came closer. More low conversation.

"I don't think they're with The Man," Trojan whispered. The men around him crouched and raised their guns. The strangers came into view.

"Hold it," hollered the pony-tailed captain. "Identify yourselves, or we'll shoot you."

The men froze. One of them spoke, a man with full muttonchops. "We're with Meteor."

"Prove it," the captain said.

"Prove it? How the hell am I going to prove it?" The man with the muttonchops held up his hands. "Look at me—do I look like a Crazy?"

"Yeah—you do," Trojan replied.

"Hey," the man with the muttonchops said, his voice rising in anger. "We rescued the women. We put out that fire. Would we have done that if we were with The Man?" He waited for a response.

"Okay, throw your weapons down," the captain commanded. The men obeyed.

"Are we good now?" asked the man with the muttonchops. His face was florid and sweat rolled down his cheeks.

Cammy pushed forward. She pointed to the smoke in the distance. "What happened?"

"The Man's people burned the bunkhouse."

Cammy grew pale. "Anybody—?"

"It's okay— Only one woman got hurt," the man assured her.

"Where's everyone else?" Trojan asked.

"I don't know. All I know is that we sent a bunch of women and kids over to our camp near the pond."

"The pond?" Trojan asked.

"Yeah— We set up our base camp there," the man replied.

The pony-tailed captain interrupted. "What about the Hutterites' farm? Any news from there?"

"No," the man with the muttonchops replied. "Nothing— Not a word." The man stretched and groaned. "Can I take my men back to camp now? Everyone here is tired as shit. They'll be glad you're here."

"Are you sure there are no more of The Man's people around?" the captain asked.

"Only dead ones," the man replied.

Then the question on everybody's mind: "What happened here?" Cammy asked.

A different man spoke. "Lots happened here. Brad had the camp. He took the women and kids prisoner. He had them locked in both of the women's bunkhouses, but Martha helped one group escape in the middle of the night. None of the women and kids got hurt... as far as I know. Except for Martha," the man added. "She was shot."

Cammy's eyes went wide. "Where is she? Is she alive?"

"Yeah, she's back at our camp. She's hurt pretty bad. At least that's what Meteor says."

"Where is he?" Trojan asked.

"Still back at the camp. He's the one who found Martha."

Cammy looked behind her. "Where's Matthew? He doesn't know. This is going to kill him."

"Here they are," Trojan said, watching a large group of men spill into the compound. "Hey—" Trojan waved to the men. "Over here!"

Matthew strode up. He eyed the smoldering remains of the bunkhouse. "Oh, Lord."

"It's okay," Cammy said. "He says they got everyone out." She indicated the man with the muttonchops.

Shouts of joy erupted from Matthew's men. They clapped the man on the back and shook his hand.

"So, *all* the women and kids are okay?" Matthew asked.

"No, Matthew..." Trojan said. He placed a hand on Matthew's shoulder and led him away. They held a hurried conversation and then Matthew ran off. Cammy watched him lope through the front gate and up the road. She walked over to Trojan.

"I feel for the guy," she said.

"Me, too." Trojan took Cammy's hand. "Let's go to our cabin."

"Okay." Cammy smiled. "And then a nice long sleep in our bed?"

Trojan put his arm around her shoulders and gave her a brief hug. He turned to the pony-tailed captain. "You good with us taking off? We're beat."

The captain nodded. "Go," he said with a wide smile. "We've got this."

He turned to the rest of the men under his command. "I want the single guys and Virgil's guys to stay with me. The rest of you—go to the pond area a few miles from here—that's where you'll find your wives and kids."

A rowdy corporate cheer went up, and the men rushed back to their trucks.

"Hey," he called after them. "Take this guy with you," he said motioning to Virgil. "Watch yourself," the captain cautioned Virgil. "Matthew might trust you, but I don't."

Virgil said nothing. He followed the men out the gate. The captain watched him leave.

"What about the Hutterites?" a man asked the captain. "And our people over there?"

"I think it's safe to use the radio now. Let's find out." The captain pulled the radio from his belt. He pressed the *send* button and spoke.

Jonah answered. "It's all good here. And there? Over."

"We've taken back the main camp. Over."

"We're coming home," Jonah replied. "We've got casualties. Over."

"Lots here, too. See you at Meteor's camp. Over."

The captain put the radio back on his belt. He turned to the men. "Let's identify the bodies." He shook his head. "Not the way I like to start my day, but we'd better do it, before the women get back here."

~ ~ ~

A Rerouting to Medicine Hat

THE DRIVER jumped back into the truck. He was holding two cans filled with an energy drink. They had pulled over at a highway gas station, an Esso. It was another of The Man's radio relay stations. They were halfway to Calgary. He offered a can to The Man, but he was ignored.

"He says they've heard from Brad."

The Man stroked the Persian cat and waited.

"He found out where the women are. He ordered buses. He's bringing them to the South Camps."

The Man pondered the information. "I'm not so sure I want them in the South Camps. Our hothouse in Medicine Hat might be better. Farther away. Less chance of them being found."

The driver waited for instructions. He knew better than to rush The Man. He popped the tab on one of the cans and took several swallows, his Adam's apple on his skinny neck, bobbing with each gulp.

"Go back inside. Tell them to get word to Brad. I want those women and kids re-routed to Medicine Hat."

The driver leapt from the truck. The Man called after him.

"Do you know if they have the Gatekeeper's wife?" The driver shook his head. "Ask."

The driver ran back into the gas station. A few minutes later, he returned.

"No word about her. They weren't able to reach Brad, but they'll keep on trying."

The Man nodded, gave the cat another pat, and put it back into the pet carrier. He zippered the small case closed. He leaned back against the seat, reached up, and massaged a small area on his shoulder. The old wound where Martha had shot him still ached.

"I hope Martha is part of that shipment," he said. "I want to talk to her." He pulled a cigar out of a front pocket, pulled off its cellophane wrapper, and rolled it around in his fingers, studying it. The cigar suddenly snapped in half.

"I ***need*** *to talk to her."*

Chapter Seven

A Short Reunion

THE SOUND OF truck engines roused Meteor's men. They waited and then cheered as they recognized the men heading up the path toward the pond.

"Matthew's coming!" Then, "He's here... Matthew's here."

Meteor pushed through the excited men. He strode up and gripped Matthew in a bear hug. "Man, it's good to see your ugly mug."

Matthew hugged back. "Yours, too." The two men separated. "Take me to Martha."

Meteor gave Matthew a quick, puzzled look. "You know about Martha?"

"She's here... She's shot. But she's okay? Right?" There was a high note of hope in Matthew's voice. Meteor gave his head a slow, solemn shake.

"No, buddy, she's not okay."

"Take me."

"This way." Meteor began to walk when another man caught his eye. "What the hell?" He glanced over at Matthew for confirmation. "Him?"

"Yeah. He's with us now."

Virgil joined them. "Hi Meteor."

Meteor returned his greeting with silence.

"What?" Virgil asked with mock outrage. "You can switch sides? But I can't?"

"You're dirt," Meteor said finally. "You were tight with the man... Why would I believe anything else?"

Virgil took a long breath. "Well, I'm here... I'm alive. That oughta count for something."

Meteor's eyes had narrowed. "Steer clear of me."

Virgil gave a quick nod. "Whatever you say." He stepped back. "But I'm with the Gatekeeper now... No matter what you believe."

"Yeah, sure ya are."

Virgil laughed. "Oh, I get it. You're seeing me through your liar's eyes. Just because you are a liar, you think I'm one, too."

"I lied for good people. You're lying for an asshole."

Virgil's face hardened. "We don't like each other, Meteor. That's for sure. But we're on the same side now. Give it a rest."

Meteor made a move toward Virgil, but Matthew got in between the two men before fists could swing.

"Guys...relax. Meteor, I know Virgil. I trust him. You gotta take me at my word."

Meteor backed off slightly. "I don't trust him."

"That's fine. But for now, let it be. We're all tired. Let's end the war at least for twenty-four hours. I want to see Martha."

"How is she?" Virgil asked.

Meteor glared at the tall man. "Don't you ask about her. Just don't." His anger against The Man, against Brad—simmered, white hot—like lava pulsing beneath a thin veneer. He narrowed his eyes. "Don't let me catch you anywhere near her, you got that?"

Virgil moved forward in an effort to pass the big man. A meaty palm slapped down on his chest. "Hold it. I want to know about Brad."

Virgil's eyebrows shot up in alarm. "I haven't heard from him in hours. I don't know where he is. Or even if he's alive." Meteor gave him a hard, searching look. "I mean it. Really—that's the truth."

"C'mon, Meteor," Matthew said, grabbing Meteor's shoulder. "I need to see Martha."

WOMEN'S CRIES filled the air as more trucks pulled up and men unloaded. Children's eager screeches added to the symphony of early morning joy upon recognition of the faces of their fathers, their uncles, or their older brothers. Some men had no one rushing up to greet them. Those men first hunted around, sorting through the faces of the women and children; then they asked hurried questions. Once answered, they joined a campfire, comforted that while their family members weren't there to greet them, they were safe in the secret bunker in the woods. Simon was among these men; his eyes searched the crowd, too; Anna was nowhere in sight.

"Has anyone seen Anna?" he called out. No one paid him any attention, so he called out again. "Has anyone—?" A slender native man spoke up.

"She's caring for an injured woman in the far tent." He pointed to the west. Simon's eyes followed the man's slender finger.

"Thanks," he said. He gave a quick grin. "Name's Simon. Yours?" He extended his hand in greeting.

"Sparrow." The men shook hands.

"How's my Anna doing?"

"Good. I got her some things she needed to help with Martha." He paused. "Your son is doing good, too."

"He's not my son."

"Oh. Sorry, I just assumed—"

"Oh, no... no problem..." Simon waved his hand to end the stream of conversation. "And, Martha... how is she?" The news about Martha being shot had traveled fast.

Sparrow shook his head. "I don't know. You'll have to ask your wi—uh, Anna."

Simon smiled. "She's my wife," he confirmed. "We had our *moving-in day* this summer."

"'*Moving-in day*?'"

"It's what we do now because real marriages aren't possible... so we have a moving-in day. Same difference, I guess."

"Oh," Sparrow said. "Anna's your wife... but Gordon's not your son..."

"Long story," Simon said.

"Well... I'll let you get going."

Sparrow gave a small bow and walked away. Simon sprinted in the direction of the far tent.

METEOR PULLED the canvas flap aside, allowing Matthew to enter the tent. Matthew smiled at Anna who was seated on her cot with Gordon in her lap. Anna smiled back and stood up.

"Oh, Matthew! It's so good to see you."

"You, too." he said, walking to Martha's cot.

Martha's face was turned away from him. "Martha?" he whispered. Matthew dropped to his knees, and touched her hand. "Martha?"

"She just fell back to sleep," Anna said. "She'll probably sleep for a while. She let me give her a pain shot." She grinned. "Can you believe that?" she asked brightly.

"How's she doing?"

"Hard to tell. But I've done everything I can for her."

Matthew smiled. "I know you have." He gave Martha's hand a soft kiss. "How bad is it?"

"Anna got the bullet out, and stitched her up," Meteor said.

"I think Meteor found her before she lost too much blood," Anna said, flashing a quick smile at Meteor.

Matthew turned Martha's face toward him. He pulled back in alarm. "What the—? Her face? What happened to her *face*?"

He turned Martha's face toward the light, examined it, and then looked back to Meteor. "Who did this?" His voice was low.

"Not sure," Anna said quickly. Meteor's blue eyes flashed a warning.

Matthew drew back, his hands gripped into fists at his sides. He spoke through clenched teeth, "Damn." He reached out and began to examine her arms.

Anna and Meteor exchanged looks, but said nothing.

Gordon had been nursing, but now he squirmed away. He squealed in recognition of his father. Anna tried to silence the child, but he began to bob in her lap, eager for Matthew's attention. Matthew gave Martha's hand another soft stroke and then went to Anna. He took Gordon from her arms.

"Hello, little man." He kissed the top of Gordon's head and snuggled the baby to his chest. Gordon reached up one chubby hand and began to stroke Matthew's neck. He gazed back at his mother, his wide eyes showing extreme contentment with the perfect balance of his world. Matthew cuddled him again, and then handed the child back to Anna. Gordon twisted around, his arms reaching out for Matthew, as a howl erupted from his tiny mouth. Matthew looked torn.

"I can't take him right now."

"He misses you. It's okay... I've got him." Anna took the wailing child outside. Gordon's howls grew louder.

"The kid knows what he wants," Meteor said.

A sound from the cot drew their attention. Martha was whispering. She lifted an arm above her head, flung it down onto her chest, and then cried out from the pain of contact. Meteor dashed to her side.

"Whoa, sweetheart. Settle down." Meteor moved her arm to her side. "Guess who's here?" he whispered.

Martha didn't respond; she remained asleep.

Matthew drew his hand across Martha's forehead, swiping gently at sticky tendrils of damp hair. "She's so hot."

"She's had a high fever for hours now."

"I want to see," Matthew said.

"Go ahead. But be prepared..."

Matthew drew back the blanket. A thick slab of gauze stained with darkness and held fast by surgical dressing tape greeted him. He lifted one piece of tape, gently, and then another. Finally, the gauze, with just a little tugging against the grip of crusted blood, gave way to reveal the stitched wound and the surrounding bruised flesh. Matthew drew back.

"How did this happen?" he demanded.

Meteor answered quickly. "Buddy, I wish I knew. I can tell you what I've heard...but until she comes to..." He shrugged and glanced away, not wanting to be trapped in his lie.

Matthew's eyebrows drew together in puzzlement and concentration. "Who shot her? Do you know that?"

Meteor clamped his eyes shut and turned away.

Matthew noticed the response. His eyes narrowed. "You do know—"

"Matthew, you're not going to like it... We did the best we could... We tried to get to them in time... We were taking back the camp...checking all the buildings...Martha had already saved the women and children from the new bunkhouse." He paused. "That's when I found her. At the top of the steps. In front of the door. She'd already lost a lot of blood."

"Who shot her?" Matthew held Meteor's eyes. "Who?"

"Brad."

With jaw clenched, Matthew replaced the gauze and gently drew the blanket up over Martha's chest. "He's a dead man."

"Maybe he's already dead," Meteor said. "My men might have taken him out."

"I hope that's true....but if not... when I find him..."

Matthew took Martha's hands and clasped them between his own. He bent his head and kissed her fingers. He jerked back.

"Did somebody take her rings?" He searched the small table near the cot. Martha's crystal earrings and necklace lay there, but not her rings: Josef's wedding band and his high school ring, the one he'd given her the day they had married. "She would never have taken those rings off. Somebody must have taken them."

"Why would somebody take her rings?"

"I don't know, but they did. Maybe Anna knows." Matthew rose to go, but a sound from Martha made him stop.

"Anna...?" came the breathy whisper. "Anna...?" Matthew grabbed Martha's hands.

"No, it's me, Martha." He took her hand in his. "It's me... Matthew... I'm here...open your eyes."

Martha mumbled as she struggled up out of her dream world into a conscious state.

"Come back to me," Matthew encouraged. "Wake up."

Martha's eyes opened. She closed them and reopened them. She gave a small smile.

"Hi, Matthew." She clutched at his fingers and entwined her own in his. "I'm so glad you're here."

Matthew leaned over and gave her forehead the gentlest of kisses. "God, I'm glad to see you," he said.

Martha raised an arm to embrace him, but cried out with the effort. Matthew took her arm and placed it gently alongside her body. "You can hug me later." He smiled. "Do you know how much I've missed you?"

"Me, too," Martha breathed. "Are you okay? Nothing shot off... or broken?"

"I'm fine."

She rolled her head to the side, focused, and then re-focused her eyes on the other figure in the room. She gave another small smile. "Oh, Meteor, it's you." She closed her eyes. "Did you bring me flowers?" she mumbled.

Meteor laughed—a shocking sound in the somber, dimly lit space. He stopped his laughter long enough to greet her.

"Hi! Glad you're back. How're you feeling?" he said, coming over to the cot.

Martha gave a small grunt. "Like I've been shot in the chest. Owwww..." She grinned. "Hurts almost as bad as a gun to the head."

Meteor roared again. He laughed so hard and so long that tears streamed from his eyes and dribbled down his cheeks.

Matthew looked puzzled, but smiled in appreciation. It had been too long since he'd heard his friend's familiar booming laughter.

Martha moved her head slowly so she faced Matthew again. She reached to touch his face. She spoke again:

"Jonah? Simon? Peter? They here?" She didn't wait for an answer, "And my girls... Are my girls okay? Did they make it?"

"I don't know," Matthew said, shaking his head. "But we expect we'll know soon. I put out the order for everyone to meet here."

Meteor wiped his eyes with the heels of his hands, smearing the wetness on his pants.

"Anna says Ruth took the women and children to the hidden bunker. We haven't heard from them. So, we're assuming they made it."

"And the men, Matthew... the men. Did we lose any?"

"Some," Matthew replied. "We'll do a body count. We'll know then."

"Is—the camp—ours again?" she asked, her eyes closing as she spoke the words.

"Yes."

"They're all dead..." she mumbled.

"Who?" Matthew asked.

"That's good..."

"Who do you mean, Martha?"

Matthew and Meteor waited, but there was no response—Martha had fallen back to sleep.

Matthew looked up at Meteor. "Who do you think she meant?"

Meteor shrugged. "I don't know." He glanced down at his feet to hide the guarded look in his eyes. He looked up. "You've got to meet with the men, Matthew."

Matthew stood. "I know." He tucked the blanket around Martha, and kissed her bruised cheek. "Let's go."

THE WOMEN AND children cowered near the far end of the bunker, except for the women and older girls who had been put into service to fetch and carry food. Brad and some of his men lined several of the tables; it had not taken them long to make themselves at home. Ruth sneered as they bent over their plates, greedily filling their mouths with stew atop bright green plastic forks. They drank water from yellow plastic cups. Ruth watched in disgust as the men ate her precious food and then called out for more. She mentally kicked herself.

I should have been awake. Damn.

Capturing the women had been relatively easy, since most of them—except for the guards—were asleep when Brad arrived. The gagged women, captured in the wood, were secured to a tree outside the bunker. Getting inside had been easy—Brad simply waited for the door to open. The woman exiting was grabbed and threatened. After that, the men slipped inside and began to awaken the women, one at a time, and direct them to the end of the bunker. Ruth had been deeply asleep...

...Sarah shook Ruth's shoulder.

"We're in trouble," she hissed.

"What?" Ruth asked, bleary-eyed. The man with the gun standing over her was all the answer she needed; *it was Brad.* He motioned her off her cot and over to the gathered women. Two teen girls were bound and were seated on chairs. Two men stood next to them, pistols leveled at their heads.

"Be good," Brad warned, motioning to the girls. "And nothing will happen to them."

Soon all the women and children were clustered near the back of the bunker. Babies squalled as mothers tried desperately to shush them. Older children stared at their captors with big eyes, accusatory eyes, fearful eyes, questioning eyes. Brad surveyed the group. Then he grinned.

"Well, I'll be damned," he said. "We have Martha's kin." He laughed. "Won't The Man be pleased?" He crooked his finger at little Mary, but she slipped behind Hannah, who put a protective hand on the girl's back. "What? You don't remember your old friend, Brad? We used to play together."

Ruth grimaced at the foulness of the idea—her daughter playing with this man. She stepped closer to Mary. Elizabeth came up beside her.

"A matched set!" Brad exclaimed. The guard in the hunter's cap looked puzzled. "Sisters."

The guard grunted his approval.

"We need food. Make some." Brad settled in at one of the tables. He waved his pistol at the women. "Hurry up—make some food."

Cooking pots began to clatter...

Ruth now stood quietly, her jaw clenching, watching her food get eaten. A man beside her whacked her arm. She glowered at him. She had been assigned her own personal guard—the man who had cut his hand on the trek up to capture them.

"I need this taken care of," the man said, shoving his hand at Ruth. "Got stuff here?"

Ruth nodded.

"Well?" he asked.

"Well, can I go and get the supplies?" she asked, her tone sing-songy in mock deference.

"Sure," he said with a wide grin. Elizabeth stood next to him. He encircled her waist with his good hand. Ruth watched her sister grit her teeth as he drew her into his side. Elizabeth turned to face him.

"Take your *fucking* hands off me." Her green eyes narrowed to slits, and she quivered with rage. "Now."

Ruth shot Elizabeth a warning look for using the swear word in front of the children. The man snuggled Elizabeth closer. She contorted her face when she caught the expired-meat scent of bad breath. She gagged and craned her head away from the man's face.

The man looked back at Ruth. "Go on. We'll be right here. Waiting for you."

Ruth fetched a first aid kit and dressed his wound. He grunted his satisfaction.

Elizabeth rolled her eyes, but remained silent.

Ruth turned her attentions back to the men at the table. They continued to gorge themselves. It galled her that the children, who hadn't eaten since the middle of the night—and then, only popcorn—were not at the tables eating, too. She stalked toward one of the tables. Her guard tried to stop her, swiping at her with his bandaged hand, but Brad waved her forward. She stopped in front of him, legs apart, arms folded tightly across her chest.

"The kids haven't eaten yet. They're hungry," she said firmly.

"And how is that my problem?" Brad asked.

"You won't be much of a hero in The Man's eyes if you starve your cargo." Ruth's look was caustic and her tone silken. "Even you can figure that out, can't you?"

Brad sat back, grabbed a paper napkin, wiped his mouth, and then rose from his chair. He came around the table.

The slap came fast—too fast for Ruth to duck. She fell to the floor. The women shrieked, and Elizabeth rushed forward. She reached Ruth as she was getting to her feet.

"I'm fine," Ruth said, waving away the assistance. "I'm fine." She flinched when Brad grabbed her forearm and hauled her to her feet.

"You won't be fine if you talk to me that way again." He gave her a sharp shake, narrowed his eyes, and stared into her face. "You got that?"

Ruth yanked her arm out of his grasp. "Yes, I got that." She held a hand to her burning cheek.

Brad addressed the women. "We're leaving soon." His frigid, no-nonsense tone reverberated around the bunker. "Pack up what you need. It's going to be a long walk." He appraised Ruth once more, and added quietly. "Feed the damn brats, but do it fast."

ANNA MET Matthew and Meteor a short distance from the tent. Anna's eyes flipped wide in surprise when Matthew enveloped her in a warm hug. Matthew wasn't a hugger, so the impromptu show of affection took her off guard and she froze in his arms.

"Thank you," Matthew said. "Thank you for taking care of her."

Anna pulled away. "No problem... But it's Meteor you should be thanking. He's the one who found her and carried her all the way back here."

"I know... But I wanted you to know how much I appreciate you." He motioned to the tent. "I'll be back in a bit. Should I bring anything?"

"Have you rested? Have you eaten anything?" Anna asked.

Matthew drew a trembling hand over his forehead. "Food...that's not a bad idea." He smiled. "Tell Martha I'll be back."

Anna watched the two men walk away. Sounds came from inside the tent. Anna lifted the flap and rushed in.

"Oh no," she cried. "Not again."

SIMON SHOUTED out a greeting as he watched the two men come toward him. "Matthew? Meteor?" He waved to get their attention. He was seated at a campfire—an upraised fork and a plate of food were in his hands.

"Hey, Simon. Good to see you again." The men clasped hands. "How're things at the second camp?"

"No problems there. I left a guard detail, but I doubt it'll be needed. Everything was quiet."

The two men found a log near Simon and sat down. Food was being passed around and they accepted plates of steaming baked beans, hunks of cured pork, and slices of sourdough bread. They chatted between mouthfuls. Soon other men joined them.

"I would have said hello sooner," Simon said. "I came by the tent, but...I didn't want to interrupt anything." Simon scooped at his beans with a hunk of bread. "I still haven't seen Anna."

"She's in the tent," Meteor said. "She's good. She's been taking care of Martha."

"How's she doing?" Simon asked, concern softening his voice.

"She's a fighter," Matthew said.

Simon nodded between mouthfuls. "That's for sure." He swallowed. "Did you know that Jonah's on his way back? I caught a call between him and the captain. Says they're bringing back casualties." He didn't wait for an answer. He stuffed a final piece of bread into his mouth, dropped his plate to the ground, and jumped up. "See you later." He ran to the tent.

Meteor wiped his mouth. "There's something else you need to know."

"Yes..." Matthew said.

"It's that kid with the orange hair... He showed up here with one of the man's radios."

"Is that all we know?"

"It's all he'd tell me. I got interrupted while I was questioning him." Meteor fought back a sharp stab of guilt.

How could he tell this man, his friend, that all he could think about for the past few hours was his wife? HIS wife.

"I should have asked him more...I kind of got distracted."

Matthew put an arm over Meteor's back. "C'mon. Where's the kid?"

MARTHA LAY on the floor. She tried to rise, but kept falling back to the ground. Anna rushed to her side.

"Let me help you, Martha."

"I have to pee," she said, her voice a soft squeak.

"Give me a second." Anna grabbed the washbasin from the small table, lifted the tent flap, and tossed the dirty water. She came back to Martha. "I don't have a bedpan...this will have to do." She pushed the basin beneath Martha. Its coldness drew a gasp from the woman. Anna waited. Soon she heard the sound of liquid hitting the basin.

Martha screamed.

The sound of trickling stopped.

"Oh, God," Anna said, her voice empathetic and soothing. "Oh, I know...it must burn something awful. I'm so sorry, Martha."

Martha whimpered.

"Let it go," Anna coaxed. "Then I'll give you a nice bath."

The sound of trickling resumed and then another scream. Martha's body jerked upward in response to the pain of the urine passing over her ravaged flesh.

Anna steadied the basin with one hand, while her other hand pushed down on Martha's shoulder. "It's okay. It won't hurt forever." Martha whimpered again, but this time sobs accompanied the whimpers.

Anna waited a moment and then removed the basin. She glanced down—the urine was orange, almost rust-colored, and rank. The smell made Anna gag. She left the tent.

When she came back, Martha had pulled herself up on one elbow. She was trying to get back onto the bed, but her clawing hand only resulted in pulling the blankets from the bed. Anna rushed over.

"Let me help."

Anna pulled Martha's arm around her neck, slipped an arm around Martha's waist, and lifted her. The exertion made the small woman stagger, but she managed, and soon Martha was back on the bed. "I'm going to give you a bath, okay?"

"Okay," Martha said, her voice barely above a whisper. "Thirsty," she said.

"Sorry... Of course you are." Anna held a small metal flask to Martha's lips; she tipped it and Martha took a few swallows. She began to cough.

"Owwww... It hurts so much to cough," she groaned.

"I'll bet. Let me give you a bath. Then maybe you'll want something to eat?" Anna asked. Optimism lifted her last word encouragingly.

"Not hungry. Just thirsty."

"I wish I had ice for you to suck on."

"It's okay. Give me another sip."

Anna did so. Martha coughed again. A sound from the doorway made Anna jump.

"Hello," a male voice said.

Anna turned, her eyes widened with delight, and her face beamed with pleasure. "Simon... Oh, Simon!" Anna rushed at him, throwing herself into his arms, her own arms firmly around his neck. "Oh, I've missed you."

"Me, too, baby... Me, too."

Anna began to cry.

"Hey, what're the tears for?"

Anna whispered into his neck. Words of exhaustion and frustration, punctuated by loud sobs, poured out of her.

"It's been awful. I've been trying so hard—but I'm so tired. Martha's so sick... I did what I could. But maybe it's not enough...I'm not good enough—"

Simon pulled her face up squarely with his. His eyes were warm and his smile gentle. "How can you say that? Don't you know that you're my hero?"

Anna gave him a thankful smile as the tears continued in rivulets down her cheeks.

"I love you, Anna."

"I love you, too."

Anna snuggled back into his arms. In a few moments, she pulled away. She wiped her face on her sleeve. "I've got to give Martha a bath. Would you get me some warm water?"

"Okay. And then after that can you and I get some time alone?"

"I think so. Matthew's here."

"I know. I saw him." Simon caressed her cheek. "I'll ask him to come and stay with Martha."

Simon left, returning a few minutes later with a bucket filled with warm water. He stood near Martha's cot. She was awake.

"Hi Simon. I'm glad to see you."

"Hi, yourself." He reached out and gave Martha's hand a gentle squeeze. "You'd better get well fast." He grinned. "The boys are already getting out of hand."

Martha gave a tiny grin. "I'll be up...riding their asses soon..."

"Good." Simon gave Martha's hand a final squeeze. He turned to Anna. "I'll see you later, okay?"

Anna gave him a quick kiss and shooed him away.

THE KID WITH the orange hair glared at Matthew. Meteor stood next to Matthew, his arms crossed on his chest. Matthew stared back at the kid.

"So, tell me about the radio. How did you get it?"

"I already told him," the kid said shoving a forefinger in Meteor's direction.

The slap knocked the kid off the log.

Matthew bent his fingers inward and rubbed to stop the stinging in his palm. "Don't make me ask you again."

The kid got to his knees, one hand protecting his face. His glance glowed with hatred. "Hit me all you want, you bastard. I'm not telling you a goddamned thing."

Matthew strode forward. The boy shrieked and scrambled back. Matthew reached down, grabbed him by the back of his ski jacket and the waistband of his pants, and tossed him. The boy landed with a loud *whump* and a cry of pain. Matthew advanced again. Meteor caught up.

"Whoa, Matthew," he said, placing a restraining hand on Matthew's arm.

"The little bastard knows something," Matthew growled. "He's gonna tell me." He raised his fist. The boy shrank back.

"The bunker! They know about the bunker," the kid sputtered.

"What bunker?" Meteor's eyebrows lowered and then rose in realization. "You mean the sanctuary?"

The kid nodded.

"Son-of-a-bitch," Matthew said. He dropped his arm. "How long ago?"

"Hours," the kid said.

Meteor frowned and glanced at Matthew.

"Was Brad with them?" Matthew asked.

"Who?" the kid asked, feigning innocence.

"You know who he means," Meteor said sharply. "Was he there?"

The kid shrugged. "I don't think so. Never saw him."

"How did they find out?" Meteor asked, his eyes bright with accusation. "You told them, didn't you?" The kid cowered back, but said nothing.

"Matthew?" It was Simon. He ran up. He sneered at the kid on the ground. "So, what's up with this little shit?"

"He told the man's people about the secret bunker," Meteor said.

"What...really?" Simon turned on the kid. "You asshole." Simon sneered again. "When you're done, Anna wants you to come back to the tent."

Matthew nodded. "I'll be there." He walked over to the boy. The kid scuttled out of the way. "There better not be more, kid."

"I don't know nuthin' else." The boy's reddened face contrasted with his orange hair made him look like a comic book clown.

Matthew stifled an urge to laugh. He glared at the kid instead.

"I swear!" the kid screamed. "Nuthin' else."

A HALF HOUR later, Martha was bathed, her vaginal wounds were cleansed, garlic oil had been applied, and her chest wound was neatly covered in bright squares of fresh, white gauze, secured at each corner with surgical tape. She had slipped in and out of consciousness during the bath, but she was awake now.

"There," Anna said, giving Martha's thin pillow another fluffing before settling Martha back against it. Martha closed her eyes. "Can I get you some soup?" Martha moved her head back and forth. "How about more water?" Martha shook her head again. "Matthew should be back soon." Martha was silent. "Did you hear me, Martha?"

Martha gripped Anna's hand. "Does he know?"

"Does he know what?"

"About Brad?"

"He knows Brad shot you. But the rest of it...I don't think so. Meteor and I agreed not to tell him...that you should be the one to tell him."

Martha gave a small sigh. "Thanks." She took a shallow breath, and then another. "I don't want Matthew to know. He might blame me."

Anna drew back shocked.

"Martha! You were *raped.*" Anna spoke in a loud whisper. "No woman can ever be held responsible for being raped."

Martha's eyes widened. "Wait a minute—" She looked confused. "I'm mixed up. You...you know? About the rape? How?"

"I don't know the details...but, yes, I know you were raped." Anna's voice cracked with constrained emotions. "I examined you. You're all ripped up." The words kept tumbling from her mouth. "Who did it?" And then the question she really wanted to ask: "How many were there?"

Martha gave another soft expulsion of breath. "I don't know," she said. "More than one...I don't know...I passed out."

Anna gasped. "You don't—"

"I know who was first..."

"Brad?" Anna volunteered.

Martha gave a small nod. Then she asked hesitantly, "Does...Meteor know?"

"He does."

Martha laid her head to one side and stared at the tent wall, golden in the morning sunlight. "God, I hope he doesn't tell Matthew. I feel so dirty. I'll never be clean. I'll never be clean of him. Ever." She began to weep. Anna took her hand.

"Martha, you can't believe that. You— You're reacting like thousands of other women who've been raped... You're believing a lie." Anna reached over and brushed the tears from Martha' face. "And if you believe that lie... well, then... Brad wins." She squeezed Martha's hand. "Don't let him win, Martha. Don't let him win."

"I wish Brad would have killed me."

Anna tried again.

"What? Where's the woman I learned from?" she scolded. "Where's my mentor? Where's the woman who won't take shit from anybody? Where is she?" Anna's voice rose in volume. "Don't you dare give up, Martha. Don't you dare. I'm still waiting for you to give me hell for the way I stitched you up... For the drugs I gave you." Anna was sobbing and she began to yell. "After all the work I did, Martha. After how hard I've tried to keep you alive—don't you dare give up. Don't you dare let that bastard win!"

Anna took a step back, and blinked, surprised by her own emotional fireworks. She sucked in a ragged breath, swiped at her nose with her shirtsleeve, and waited. A quiet void lay between them.

Finally, Martha spoke: "You gave me drugs?" She turned back to Anna. "Damn you." A soft smile belied the curse she'd uttered. "I'll be fine, dear. Don't you worry about me."

Anna touched the older woman's cheek, still rosy with fever. "Martha... you can't believe—"

"Go, now. Take care of Gordon." Martha reached up and squeezed Anna's hand. "He's here, isn't he?"

"Yes, he's fine."

Martha gave Anna a curious look. "I just realized something...you came back..." Martha's voice trembled with tears.

"I had to," Anna said simply. She smiled and brushed hair from Martha's eyes. "I couldn't leave you behind. Besides, Meteor and I found each other right away. I was never in any danger. But you...you could have died."

Martha drew a long breath. She gave a small huff. "You sure like taking liberties, don't you?" She chuckled. "Take care of Matthew for me, too, okay?"

"I will. But he'd rather you do that."

"Hm..." Martha murmured. She nested one of her hands inside the other, massaging the fingers on the inner hand. "Hm," she said again. "My hand hurts." She paused. "I miss my rings."

"Where are they?"

"Back at the cabin."

"I suspect you'll be back in your own bed soon. But..." Anna frowned. "Why did you take them off?"

"I didn't think I'd need them where I was going."

"You thought..." It dawned on Anna. "You thought you were going to die."

"Well, I thought there was a pretty good chance I would. And after what Brad and his men did...I didn't really care what happened to me."

"Meteor was wondering something..." Anna paused to give Martha a chance to evince curiosity. When she didn't, Anna continued. "He found his old gun... You were lying on top of it. Didn't you get a chance to fire it? I mean...before Brad shot you?"

"I did have the chance, Anna. Lots of chances."

Anna screwed up her face in confusion. "Then..." she asked, while shaking her head. "Why didn't you shoot him?"

Martha concentrated for a moment. "Something happened to me during the rape." She held up her hand as though in defense. "This will sound nuts, but I believe Jesus came for me."

"Jesus?" Anna was not unfamiliar with the man many called the Messiah. She had gone to church, she knew about God, the Bible, and about His son, the Christ child. "Jesus?" she repeated, raising her eyebrows.

"Yeah, I think he was there. I saw this bright figure and beautiful face. I wanted to follow him. So, I did." Martha shrugged and grimaced at the shooting pain. "I think maybe I was born again."

"And that's why you couldn't shoot Brad? Because it's against your religion?" Anna was truly puzzled now.

"No, it's not that. I was ready to shoot Brad... I had every intention of shooting Brad— But when I lifted the gun to do it, Jesus—God—came into my mind and told me it was wrong...that it would be murder. Something inside my heart wanted to obey him. So, I lowered the gun. That's when—"

"That's when Brad shot you."

"Yeah...I should have taken his gun away from him, but...I forgot." She nestled her head into the pillow. "A stupid mistake," she added softly.

"Maybe it doesn't matter now," Anna said hopefully. "Maybe they'll find Brad when they do the body clean-up."

"Maybe," Martha mumbled. Her eyes closed and she slumbered.

Anna lingered for the moment, making sure Martha was asleep. Finally, she left the tent.

She squinted into the morning light and scanned the campground. When she couldn't see Matthew, she wandered in the direction of people's voices.

One voice—a man's—was very loud.

And...very *angry*.

~ ~ ~

Warm Winter Woolies

THE MAN waited for the door to close. The woman stood before him, quietly appraising him, while clasping and unclasping her work-worn hands. Her cuticles were ragged and her nails were torn and dirty. The Man pulled out a small kitchen chair and sat down. He watched her fidget.

"Has that scar gotten worse?" The Man asked with pretended innocence. "It looks redder somehow."

The woman lifted her left hand to her face. She rested it on her cheek, while her fingers fiddled with a few strands of her raven black hair. Her blue eyes stared back at The Man. "No, it's the same."

"We've got a new shipment coming in," he said. "But we're not bringing them here."

"So where then?"

"Medicine Hat. There's a home down there that's more secure. Farther away."

The Man stared at the window. Autumn sunlight spilled through the venetian blinds creating shadow patterns on the wall and the floor. He snorted dismissively. "There was a day when I would have photographed that," he said.

"I know," the woman answered. "I remember."

"Yes, of course you do." The Man twisted in the chair and looked behind him. "Is this your place?"

"Yes. He gave it to me."

"Did he now? Do you have much to pack?"

"Pack? Why?" The woman eyed him with suspicion.

"You're going to prep the home in Medicine Hat for the new arrivals."

"But, I don't want to go there. I'm hap—"

"I don't recall asking you what you want..." He turned back to face her. "Gather your rosebuds. You're heading out."

"When?"

The Man checked his watch. "Right about now. Truck's waiting."

The woman stood silently for a moment. She wrestled a plastic tub from the shelf. She grabbed a pair of shoes and heaved them into the tub, so hard that one bounced out again. Shirts, jeans, and dresses followed the shoes. Soon an unruly pile of fabric spilled from the container.

"You might want to pack some warm winter woolies, too." The Man held up a hand when the woman turned on him, her lips pursed, her eyes dark with anger. "Just sayin'..."

"I'm going, but I'm not staying," she said firmly.

"You'll stay as long as I tell you to stay."

"He might have something to say about that."

"He might, but then again..."

The woman grumbled as she pulled another tub from the shelf. She filled this one with winter boots, jackets, scarves, mitts, and woolen toques.

Chapter Eight

A Long Walk and a Bus Ride

THE CHILDREN cried as they were herded out of the bunker. Once gathered outside, the armed men did a count: eighty-nine kids and forty-seven women. The men threatened violence and shouted commands, demanding that the women keep the kids quiet. The women worked frantically to quell the howls of tired, hungry, and scared children. Samuel and Mary clung in silence to their mother's coat. Ruth watched as more women came out of the hut; they were added to the count:

One hundred and twelve kids...and fifty-nine women.

"Are we ready?" Brad asked.

"I guess so," answered the man with the bandaged hand. "Do we have them all, Ruth?"

Ruth's stare was hard and she remained mute. Brad walked over.

"Are they all here?" Brad asked.

Ruth stared ahead. Anger sealed her lips, and she refused to speak.

Brad turned toward a tiny blond-haired woman with large eyes. She was fighting to maintain her grip on twin boys, barely a year old. Brad spoke to the woman. Ruth watched the woman's eyes grow wide when Brad pointed his gun at the boys. The woman spoke quickly, and gathered the twins tighter into her arms. The boys screeched.

"That's it," Brad called. "We've got all of them. The buses are on their way." He shouldered a long gun he had taken from the gun cellar. "Let's go for a walk, ladies."

Ruth walked just ahead of Brad. The forest trail was tough going. It was littered with snaking tree roots and broken branches. Many of the children stumbled and tripped, but their mothers picked them up, dusted them off, and encouraged them to continue walking. The women understood the harsh looks of the armed men and Brad's threat that if they—or their kids—couldn't keep up, they would be shot.

"*Culled*," is how he had put it.

"This is cruel," Ruth muttered. She stopped walking and turned back to Brad. "You can't do this to children."

"Sure I can," Brad replied.

"They're going to get too tired to walk. Then what are you going to do? Shoot the lot of us?"

"I might."

Ruth stood unflinching, and resolute. She remembered the slap he had landed on her earlier, but at that moment, she didn't care. Her sense of indignation birthed a fresh spurt of bravado and a bold tongue.

"No wonder my mother hated you. You are horrible."

Brad gave a hollow laugh. "If only you knew," he added.

"If only I knew what?"

"Never mind. Get moving." He pushed at her with the barrel of his gun, but Ruth held her ground.

"I'm telling you again," she said through clenched teeth. "It's too far. The kids are too little. And what about the women who are carrying kids?" She pointed at the line of women coming up behind them, some with children on their hips, some with children riding their backs—their pudgy arms clasped around their necks. The women were dripping sweat, their faces red with exertion, strands of sticky hair stuck to their faces. "See what I mean?"

Brad gave Ruth a long look, thick with exaggerated suffering. "I'm losing my patience with you. The kids or the women who fall behind will be shot. It's that simple."

"And what would The Man say about that terrible waste?" Ruth shot back. She flinched as Brad raised his hand to strike her. He smiled in satisfaction at the instinctive fear he had instilled in her. He bent near her ear.

"You won't be walking too much farther. I asked a friend of mine to have a couple of buses ready for us. Just up the road. We're almost there." He shoved her. "Now move."

"How do you know where we are?"

Brad pulled a thick wad of paper out of his pocket. He unfolded it and grinned. "You know that ugly kid with orange hair?"

Ruth blinked. Then she remembered. He was talking about the boy whose father had been evicted for attacking Martha.

Brad continued, "Looks like he has a bit of talent. He can draw a map right down to the finest detail. He's a great little spy, too. And..." He grinned widely. "...He knows who his friends are."

"I'll just bet he does," Ruth said.

"So, be a good girl and keep on walking. I promised The Man a collection of the Gatekeeper's women, and I must keep my promise," he said smugly.

"What if he's already dead?"

"Dead? The Man?" Brad laughed. "I can't imagine that. He's too careful with number ONE."

A few moments later, Elizabeth turned around.

"We're going to be dead soon, you jerk. We barely got a chance to eat," she said.

Brad sighed, a bemused expression on his face. He raised his pistol. "I don't think I can handle *two* of Martha's brats yakking at me."

Ruth shot Elizabeth a warning look. "Shh..."

"I'm sick of this," her sister said.

"Be quiet!" Ruth commanded.

"No, I've had it. I don't care anymore."

"He'll shoot you."

"Whatever!" Elizabeth pierced Brad with a stare. "Go ahead. I don't care."

Ruth watched Brad's eyes narrow at the challenge. She had seen his eyes do that before, but usually only when her mother was involved.

Her mother. He knew something about Martha.

Ruth watched Brad lower his gun. A small grin curled his lips. Something else was coming and she tensed for it.

"So, Elizabeth..." he drawled. "You don't care about yourself, but maybe you care about someone else." Brad stepped back from the procession and waited as it trudged by him. "Maybe someone littler than you." At that moment, Mary came into his line of sight. Ruth understood in a flash.

"Don't you dare!" she shouted. "Elizabeth! Shut up and keep moving." She turned to confront her sister, but Elizabeth was already walking again with the rest of the women.

Ruth turned back to Brad. He stared at her, and scratched the side of his neck with the barrel of his pistol.

"You bastard," she hissed. Her face was dark with rage and her green eyes blazed. "I hope you die the foulest of deaths."

"Move along, Ruthie."

~~~

They walked for another half hour until they came to a clearing. Brad ordered everyone to sit down. The children flopped down on their mothers' laps and stared up at the man doing the shouting—the man making their lives a misery. Some of the mothers took advantage of the stop and began nursing their babies. Brad's men watched, nudging their companions, and making ribald jokes. Brad beckoned two of his men and sent them ahead. Ten minutes later, they returned.

"Are the buses here yet?" Brad called out. His men waved him forward. "Let's go," he said.

The women mumbled protests, but got to their feet, pulling cranky children with them. They walked for a few minutes. The unmistakable screech and hiss of bus brakes could be heard in the distance. They made their way out to a gravel road. Four yellow buses were there, puffing exhaust. The doors swung open, and the women and children filed in. Two men clambered aboard each bus.

Brad stood on the side of the road. He held a hurried conversation with several men gathered around him. Ruth fiddled with the window latches and lowered the pane. She could hear Brad speaking:

"They'll come looking for them. Stay on guard for twenty-four hours. Keep out of sight. You've got food in the bunker. Don't build any fires."

"How do we get out of here?" one of the men asked.

"Take one of their vehicles," Brad said. "They won't walk all the way." The men grunted their understanding and headed back into the woods. Ruth shut the window.

What now? Where are we off to now? Will I ever see this place again?

She wondered about leaving a clue behind for Matthew to find. Nothing came to mind. She slumped back into her seat. Mary snuggled up near her, and she clasped her arm around the little girl's shoulder. From behind her, she could hear Reggie's soft mutters.

"Weggie. Weggie."
~~~

Brad signaled to the bus drivers as he boarded the lead bus. Soon they were bouncing down the country road to parts unknown. Some of the women tried to lighten the mood by singing bus-riding songs with the children. Samuel and Mary joined them.

"The wheels of the bus go round and round..."

Ruth drew her feet up to her chest, pulled her scarf over her face, and wept.

ANNA HURRIED toward the crowd. The fall morning was unusually warm, and she shrugged her down jacket off her shoulders, catching it with one hand as it fell. She snugged it around her waist and tied the arms together. She saw a man standing atop a small hill. He was speaking to the crowd. His black parka hung open; a sky-blue trucker's ball cap emblazoned with a Labatt's beer logo was clutched in his fingers.

"How do you know?" a thin, gray-haired woman called out.

"We found one of The Man's guys," he said. "He was shot, but he was still alive. He said Brad gave the order to burn the bunkhouse."

"I knew it was Brad," yelled the woman.

"It had to be him," shouted another. The crowd murmured its angry consensus. The sound made Anna recall an old Frankenstein movie she had watched as a kid, in front of their television, alongside her father and a big bowl of popcorn. The memory made her heart ache.

She missed her dad—the gifted veterinarian who had taught her much about diagnosing illness in animals, administering drugs, setting broken bones, and repairing wounds. She often did the stitching when her father's eyes had grown fatigued. She recalled the night the Crazies raided their home and her father's private clinic in search of drugs—murdering her father in the process, and then raping her. She didn't get pregnant because of the rape; the pregnancy happened later when she met Matthew while scavenging in a department store. Her baby, Gordon, had been named to honor her late father.

The man raised his cap into the air. "There's more... He said one of Matthew's guys told Brad about a secret hideaway."

Anna blanched at the news. "Oh God, no..." she murmured. "He knows..."

"What's going on?" Sparrow had come up beside her.

Anna pointed. "He's got news about the other women and kids...the ones that escaped to the bunker. And about the man who shot Martha."

A moment later, Matthew brushed past them. He took up a position beside the man who was speaking.

"What do you know for sure?" he asked.

"I know for sure that Brad knows where the first group of women and children went to hide out."

Matthew glanced to his left, toward Meteor who was standing on the edge of the crowd—he was holding the kid with the orange hair by one arm. Their eyes met, briefly. Matthew turned back to the man in the parka.

"How long ago?"

"That I don't know. Sorry."

"Where is this guy you talked to?"

"Dead. He died on the way back here."

Matthew eyed the kid. A tic started in his cheek.

"Sir?" One of Meteor's men addressed Matthew, a native man with ebony hair that hung in straight, glistening strands from beneath a wide leather headband.

"What?"

"What are your orders?"

Matthew held up a hand. The crowd quieted. He mentally ran through his options. The bunker was deep on the back property; it would take hours to reach by foot. Quads would be faster, but the noise would attract attention. Then there was Brad.

Had he already reached the women? How many men were with him? Were they heavily armed? Did they have time to set up booby traps?

Matthew looked back at the expectant faces.

"Who's rested enough to go after them? It's a long walk. You can go part of the way by quads. Volunteers?"

Anna caught a glimpse of Simon's lanky form on the far side of the crowd. She watched with horror as his hand went up. Many other hands went up, too. She recognized them as belonging to the husbands, boyfriends, fathers, and brothers of the missing women and children. Anna pushed her way through the crowd till she was standing next to Simon.

"You just got back," she whispered. "What are you doing?"

Simon looked surprised. "I'm perfectly all right. Why wouldn't I go? Martha's daughters are part of that group, aren't they? And her grandkids?" Anna nodded. "Then why wouldn't I go?"

"Okay," Anna said with a sad sigh. "Go ahead. But please stay safe."

"I will." He gave her a quick kiss and ran up to the men who had crowded around Matthew.

Anna watched as the group of men conversed, agreed on their plans, and then ran to the trucks. Engines fired up, and her Simon was gone.

"He'll be fine, Anna." Matthew had come alongside her. "He's good at his job. Smart."

"I know."

"He'll be back soon." Anna stared up at Matthew, waiting for more. "They're going back to the camp, loading up quads, and then driving to an access point we used when we stocked the bunker. They've got a map, weapons...and brains." He caught her look of misgiving. "He'll be fine. Really." He hugged her shoulders.

Meteor strode up. Richard was with him. "We're going, too, Matthew. If there's a chance of getting to Brad..."

Matthew nodded. "I'd go, but Martha—"

Meteor smiled and held out his hand. "I've got this, Matthew. Take care of her." He turned and then called over his shoulder. "The kid is tied up. I left him with one of the older guys."

Meteor and Richard walked away, got into a truck, and drove off.

Anna pulled at Matthew's sleeve to get his attention. "I should take care of Gordon. Martha is more alert now and she was talking quite a bit."

"Is she awake now?"

"No... But she will be in a few hours."

"I'll take care of her. Go." Matthew drew her close, and kissed her cheek. "It's alright. He'll be back."

~ ~ ~

The Southern Retreat

THE FIGURE leaned forward, out of the shadows and into the light. It was an older man with watery eyes, red-rimmed and sunken in a myriad of saggy creases, but bright with presence and intelligence. His eyebrows were thick with orphaned hairs that curled wildly onto his forehead. His mustache hung low over his lips—gray, thick, unruly, and in desperate need of a trim. His hair was pulled back into a ponytail, a scrawny cord comprised of the limited hairs he had gathered from around a bald spot on the top of his head—inked with a spider's web—and words of war. He cleared his throat—a deep, phlegmy sound that resulted in a fat gob of yellow spittle being spat to the floor.

"So, how's our plan going?" the old man asked.

"It's not our plan," was the curt reply. "It's my plan. And it's going fine." The Man paused. He stared at the glistening orb on the floor. "Can I get you a tissue?"

The older man snuffled, made hawking noises in his throat again, and spat once more. On the floor. "No, thanks."

The Man pulled out a straight-backed chair and settled down at a large, wooden dining room table. He placed a fabric cat carrier on the table beside him. The cat inside gave a long and insistent meow. The Man unzipped the carrier's doorway, and the Persian stepped out, one paw delicately placed after another in wary anticipation of its new environment. The cat stared at the old man, turned away, and headed back to The Man; it butted its head against his hand. The Man indulged the animal and scratched its head. The Persian began to purr. It soon sat down and began to lick its paw, rubbing the paw over its face in a scrubbing gesture.

"We had a little trouble with The Gatekeeper," The Man said.

"Really. You mean you don't control his camp?"

"Had it and lost it."

"Whose fault was that?"

"Brad."

"Where is he?"

"On his way here."

"You gonna have words with him?" the old man asked.

"I'll deal with Brad when the time is right. For now, he serves a purpose. Besides, he's bringing new stock."

"Really? Fresh? Young?"

"Over one-hundred-fifty of the Gatekeeper's women and children."

The older man pushed out his lower lip. "Impressive." He rocked back in his chair.

"We've pulled our forces back here. Our resources and storehouses in Edmonton won't take us through the winter. We were counting on the Gatekeeper's storehouses to do that, but now—"

"Ah, I see..." the older man mused. "The proverbial grasshopper fiddled while the ant worked. And then the ant proved to have bigger balls than expected." He laughed. "Was that part of your plans, too?"

"Matthew surprised me. Tougher and smarter."

"Surprised you? Even though you had been on his grounds? Even though you had Virgil, his ex-best friend? Even though you had the military guys?" The older man stopped and gave his throat another clearing, but this time didn't spit. "Where is Virgil, by the way?"

The Man hesitated before answering. "He got caught...in an attack by Matthew's men... out near the second camp."

"The camp with the oil reserves—?" the old man asked with a sound in his voice that said he already knew the answer.

"There's been no word from him. And no word from the men who went out with him. If they aren't dead, they may have been forced into surrender." He paused. "Maybe they now work for Matthew..."

"Would your guys do that?"

"They had no allegiance to me. Just to Virgil. If he's dead, I can see them crossing over... into a new camp—especially one filled with winter provisions."

The Man stroked the cat as it sauntered by, its fluffy tail twitching side-to-side, and catching him just under the nose. He brushed its tail aside. He went on:

"Most of the men have families, wives, and children—they're tired of fighting—they want to settle in for the winter."

"Tough to do when your storehouses specialize in cigars, whiskey, and women." The old man watched the cat pad across the tabletop. "What're you doing with your Edmonton women?"

"Bringing them all here."

"Wouldn't it be better to just turn them loose? Start from scratch in the spring? You won't have to feed them that way."

The Man rubbed his chin. "It's a thought. But I still think clean women have great trading value. We've got enough supplies here to feed them through the winter. And you're into talks with the mafia. They'll be looking to buy in the spring."

"The hothouses are going to be full. What are you doing about Matthew's women and kids?"

"Sending them to Medicine Hat. It's isolated and easy to protect, if necessary."

"You think the Gatekeeper will come after them?"

"I'm sure he will—but I don't know if he's alive. And if he is—he won't know where they've been taken." The Man smiled. "We've got a bit of an edge—we've got his wife's daughters and grandkids."

"Nice. And I hear you're sending one of my ladies to oversee the operation?"

"Yes, I am. Any objections?"

"Oh, no. Take her. I've got more. She's a little long in the tooth." The old man coughed again. "And how's it going with our forces? The Archangels still all you had hoped they'd be?"

The Man scowled. "Allying the clubs is a lot harder to do than anticipated. It'll get easier, though, as the resources dry up. But the independents still have too many options. MCs are warring among themselves. And many club captains are refusing to lay down their colors and patch over."

"What're you doing about that?"

"In a few months from now, we'll be living in a different world. Unless the power grid magically fixes itself—and it doesn't look like it will—the world will become a much simpler place. The independents will figure out that the only way to survive is to band together, share skills, share resources—"

"What about the clubs that haven't shown yet? What about the mafia? What about hidden pockets of survivalists like the Gatekeeper? What about military guys who have started their own armies?" The old man shook his head. "You think we'll be strong enough to stand up to them?"

"Bargaining power. That's why I must keep those women. Old diseases, especially sexual diseases, are starting to take people again. No drugs—and the drugs still around—well, very few people know what they're for. Or how to take them."

"Wasn't there a medical woman in Matthew's camp? What was her name?"

"Martha—"

"Yeah, her. Where's she at?"

The Man shrugged. "Last I heard, she had been taken by Brad."

"Brad—that can't have been good. He hated her, didn't he?"

"I told him to keep her alive and bring her to me."

The older man gave a wry grin. "Hope he treats her well." He scrubbed at his face with a thin hand corded with veins and dotted in brown liver spots. "She would be worth a whole dancehall filled with clean women, don't you think? The Gatekeeper would pay—"

The Man held up his hand and stopped him. "She's on the list of priorities. We'll deal with her after Brad gets here."

"I see..." the older man said. He coughed, cleared his throat, and sent a flurry of gob to the floor. "Damn, this chest cold. Can't seem to shake it."

"Maybe it's not a cold. Maybe it's a flu...a new version. And if it is..." The Man said, reaching behind him and grabbing a box of tissues. "Here...use one of these. And burn it." He shoved the box in the older man's direction.

The older man eyed him. "What difference does it make? If we get sick—we survive it...or we don't. It's that simple." He began to cough again. He pulled a handful of tissues from the box, held them to his mouth, coughed, and hawked into the tissue. He looked around, and failing to find anywhere to dispose of it, he shoved it into his jacket pocket.

The Man suppressed a grimace.

The old man spoke again. "Where's Marion?"

"I asked her to do something for me."

"What?"

"See if she can get into Matthew's group as a friendly."

"Why are they gonna believe her?"

"We messed her up before sending her in. Figured they'd feel sorry for her."

"She let you do that?"

"No choice," The Man said flatly.

"Like your ex?"

The Man scowled.

The older man reached into his breast pocket for a plastic bag filled with tobacco. He pulled out rolling papers, and soon fashioned a homemade cigarette. He licked the paper's edge, and popped the cigarette into his mouth, dampening the thin paper to slow the burn. With a silver flip-top lighter, he lit the cigarette's tapered end. "So, are all your troops falling back here for the winter?"

"Yes—unless Marion gives us intelligence we can act on. Like the whereabouts of one person. If she finds out where Meteor is, I'll send some guys to take him out."

"Meteor? Friendly guy, right? I met him. Thought he was with us."

"So did I." The Man waved at the cigarette smoke that had entered the air space above his head. "He played me. The next time I see him—there won't be any questions. A bullet to the brain."

The old man grunted. "And the other guys?"

"Who? Matthew? Virgil? They can wait till the spring... if they're still alive."

"And Brad?"

The Man pursed his lips. "We'll see."

Chapter Nine

A Glass of Tang

MATTHEW PULLED back the flap and entered the tent. He walked over to Martha's cot. Her chest rose and fell in time with her soft, breathy snores. He watched her for a moment, sighed, and looked at the second cot. It was empty. And so inviting. A soft rustling from Martha's bed, made him turn.

"Hi..." Martha whispered.

"Hi, yourself," Matthew said. Martha reached out her hand. He took it. "Go back to sleep," he said.

"I will, if you will." Martha gave his hand a weak squeeze.

"Give me a second."

Matthew withdrew his hand, grabbed the small camp table next to Martha's bed, and repositioned it near the tent's entrance. He grabbed Anna's cot and pulled it over. He jimmied it into position, aligning it with Martha's cot. Satisfied, he flopped down.

"Gonna take off your boots?" Martha whispered.

"Nah." He took her hand again. "I am crazy tired, Martha."

"I know." She held her husband's warm hand. "Matthew?"

"Hm..."

"I'm glad you're here."

"It's where I belong, Martha."

SIMON CREPT through the bushes, following what looked to be a pathway. It was heavily congested, making their progress very slow. The men had split into four teams. He was leading the first team, but he and his partner had gone on ahead, leaving the other four members of their team behind. He missed the convenience of his quad, but the machines could take them only so far, so they had abandoned them about a half mile into the forest. Now they struggled along on foot, breaking a trail through heavy underbrush and gnarled, slender deadwood that cracked and snapped with each footfall.

"Damn," Simon said under his breath. "We're coming in like fucking tanks."

The man with him tripped and fell headlong into a spruce tree. He swore, too. He rubbed his knee as he got up and pointed forward. "This trail sucks. How long ago did you guys use this?"

Simon shrugged. "Not sure. I helped stock the bunker a couple of times—in the spring. I don't remember it being this bad. Maybe, we aren't on the path." He checked the map. "But it looks right." A sharp crack off to their left made the pair duck.

"Might be one of our guys," his partner whispered.

"Maybe."

They crawled forward and settled in behind a rotted log draped in a blanket of curled, rust-colored leaves. They waited.

THE BUSES pulled over at a rest stop near Bowden. The women had been begging for a bathroom break. Ruth wrinkled her nose. Their bus was beginning to reek of urine. Some of the younger children had not managed to hang on and were squirming in their wet pants, plucking at the stained fabric. The rest of the children just wanted to get out.

The drivers barely had time to open the folding doors before children were running down the steps, pushing and shoving, and spilling out onto the parking lot. Mothers called to them, armed men threatened them, but brown squirrels scampering across the lot took priority. The children ran after them, squealing with delight.

Ruth watched out the window. Samuel and Mary were with the crowd chasing after the squirrels. She smiled a tiny smile.

Let them, she thought. For the moment, her children were free. *And alive*, she reminded herself.

A shriek, much louder than the other children's cries, made her turn in her seat with alarm. She relaxed and smiled as she watched Reggie running in circles, emulating the other children as they pursued the squirrels.

She shielded her eyes. Her head ached and the bright sunshine compounded the pain. She looked up at the sound of footsteps coming up the bus steps. One of the armed men reboarded the bus. He stared at her a moment before speaking.

"Hey? Aren't you getting off?" He smiled as he walked down the aisle.

Ruth didn't answer. She was puzzled by the man's kindness and the concern in his tone. Suspicion wrinkled her brow. His actions were incongruent with his tough biker exterior, the bearded face, the leather vest...and the big gun. He settled onto the seat beside her. Ruth moved over until she was flush up against the side of the bus. He put one arm along the back of the seat, and the other along the back of the seat in front of them. Ruth noticed the enclosure formed by his arms. She shifted closer to the window.

"Don't you need a break?" Bright, white teeth flashed as he smiled.

Ruth gave him a nervous grin. "No. I'm fine. Thanks." She cupped one hand over the other, in her lap, and stared out the window.

The man reached over and placed one of his hands on hers. Ruth jerked her hand away. The man persisted. "C'mon. I'm just trying to be nice." He reached for her hand again. Ruth crossed her arms. The man chuckled. He dropped his hand to her knee and squeezed. Ruth grabbed his hand and shoved it away.

"Stop it." She turned to him, her eyes ablaze. "I am *married*."

The man chuckled again. "What do I care? I think you're pretty foxy." He reached for her again, this time clamping his hand high on her thigh. Ruth gripped his wrist, pressing her nails into his flesh. She wrenched his hand off her leg and slammed it down into his lap. The man grunted with the impact of his hand on his crotch.

He grabbed a handful of her hair. Ruth screeched. He twisted her face toward him and planted his lips on hers. He wrapped his other arm around her shoulders, hugging her to him. Ruth thrashed inside his embrace. The vision of another bearded biker forcing his lips down on hers swam into her mind. But she had had help then—when Martha's friend, Amanda, swung her stone-laden handbag, knocking Ruth's attacker unconscious. Now, she was on her own. Ruth struggled harder.

The man's breath was coming faster. He dropped his hand to the waistband of her jeans, and tried to shove his fingers inside. Ruth squirmed, but the man still gripped her hair tightly. The fingers of his other hand picked feverishly at her pants' zipper. Ruth drove her hand upwards and grabbed at his throat, sinking her nails into his windpipe. The man choked and pulled away. He was breathing hard and his face was ruddy with lust. He raised his arm to strike her, but Ruth ducked. He slammed his fist into the bus window instead.

Ruth twisted around and pulled her knees into her chest. With both feet, she kicked at the man. He slid from the seat and crashed to the floor. Ruth clambered over him and ran for the door. She pounded down the steps and raced toward a group of children. She gasped for breath and turned. The man wasn't following her. Her eyes grew hot with tears, but she fought them. Mary ran up.

"We found squirrels, Mummy...lots of them."

Ruth forced a smile and smoothed her daughter's hair. "Sounds like fun." Ruth tried to quell her trembling as she took Mary's hand. "Show me."

RICHARD SHIFTED the truck into a lower gear as he traversed the primitive dirt track road. It was deeply rutted and, in some areas, completely overgrown with weeds. He spotted a clearing, shifted again, and the truck sped up.

"You sure this is the way?" Richard asked, bouncing like a jumping bean on his seat. Meteor steadied himself with a hand on the dashboard.

"I'm sure. We used it a lot in the summer. Not many people know about it though. I don't think Brad ever knew about it. It should get us there a little faster." Another pothole made the pair of men shift violently side-to-side.

They drove along for a few more minutes and then stopped when the track became impassable. Meteor got out. He examined the huge tree limbs that crisscrossed the path. Richard joined him.

"Want to try moving them?" Richard asked. His tone made it clear that he was hoping Meteor had a different plan.

"Too many of them," Meteor replied. He glanced ahead. "We'll walk from here."

They went back to the truck, retrieved their packs, weapons, ammunition, and canteens. They shouldered the gear and hustled up the path. They flushed a covey of partridges as they walked.

"Wish we were hunting," Richard said.

"Yeah, me, too."

"Why don't I take a few down? For dinner?" Richard asked. It was meant as a joke.

"Sure," Meteor said. He gripped his pistol in one hand, while the other hand rubbed his forehead.

Richard gave him a surprised glance. "Hey, where are you, man?"

"Here."

"No, you aren't. What's going on?"

"Nothing."

Meteor stared ahead. His feet kept pace with Richard, but his mind was busy picking at a memory—rolling it around, replaying it from beginning to end, and each time it played, it elicited as much pain as had the actual event. The memory played again...

Meteor told Richard that he had to go back to the camp, on the ruse that he had forgotten a compass (it was actually in his pocket). He dashed across the campground in the direction of Martha's tent. He couldn't leave without telling her.

Not again. Not this time.

This time...he would make his feelings known. This time he would tell her—that he loved her. Because this time...she might be dead before he got back to her.

He crept in through the tent opening. He nearly stumbled over a small camp table that had not been there before. He gingerly set the table aside and waited while his eyes grew accustomed to the gloom.

He studied the dark shapes on the cots. He recognized them. He heard their steady breathing. He saw the clasped hands. Hurt hit him like a punch to the gut, driving the breath from him. He stifled the rush of emotions and a resulting groan.

Meteor left the tent...

Now, Meteor clenched his fist. He pounded his thigh in an attempt to exorcise the vision, but the memory lingered, insidiously nurturing its evil like some dark cancer on his heart. He caught his foot on a hidden tree root. He was thrown off balance and he fell. His pistol disappeared into the tall weeds.

"Dammit," he exclaimed, pulling himself to his feet, brushing off dirt and leaves, and recovering his gun. He shoved it into the holster on his thigh, and stood with his fists clenched at his sides, his head down.

Richard glanced at his friend and walked by. Meteor trudged along behind. Still lost in his thoughts.

A few minutes later, Richard ran back. "I found quads. Up there," Richard said, pointing ahead.

The men ran side by side, their feet slapping the ground and their breaths coming hard. Suddenly, sounds—two sharp, whistling cracks—made them jolt to a stop. They grabbed their guns.

They waited, but the woods had gone silent—tomb-like—not even a bird twittered.

"Gunshots..." Richard whispered.

"But only two?" Meteor asked. The question was rhetorical. "That's not a battle," he added. "That's an execution."

The pair ran forward.

RUTH EYED the biker who had attacked her. He seemed disinterested now that they were back on board, headed up the highway again. She felt relieved, but she wondered if his actions were merely a foretaste of what was to come. Mary lay beside her, asleep, her soft hair spilling onto Ruth's lap.

I should braid it, she thought. A memory of Martha braiding her own hair when she was a little girl made her heart clench in sadness.

Mom? Are you okay? God, I hope so.

METEOR AND Richard had sprinted for about a half mile, when an explosion of gunfire caused them to drop low, their pistols raised. But the staccato rattling and popping was distant.

"Let's go," Meteor said.

They ran along, in a crouch, until they reached a clearing. Sunlight streamed through a break in the forest canopy, pooling on a small pond—diamonds of light glimmered and sparked as they danced off the water's surface. A half dozen ducks and a pair of geese rocketed across the water.

The gunfire petered out and finally stopped. The men looked at each other. Meteor pulled out his compass and checked the map. "We're close," he whispered. They crouched low and advanced.

"What's that?" Richard said, grabbing at Meteor's arm, and pointing with his gun.

"What's what?" Meteor responded. Richard pointed again.

Meteor turned and caught sight of something glistening in the sunlight. He moved closer. The brightness turned out to be the back of a man's head. Fresh blood glistened in his hair.

"Hope they're not ours," Meteor said.

The pair picked their way through twisted piles of deadwood. They stopped and stared. One of the men was lying on his face, a hole blasted into the back of his head. The other man lay face up, one arm flung above his head, the other arm twisted beneath him. Blood oozed from a round hole between his eyes. There were no guns in sight.

Meteor dropped to his knees beside the man lying face up. He reached out and picked up the dead man's arm. He lifted it carefully and laid it on the man's chest.

"He must have looked back after his friend was shot," he deduced. He stood up and grabbed the other man by the shoulder. He flipped him over, and jumped back as though stung.

"Oh, no," Richard said.

Meteor clamped a hand over his eyes and squeezed. "Oh...Anna..." he breathed. He squeezed harder.

Richard looked away.

RUTH STARED out the window. They had been traveling for hours and she was fatigued. She'd gotten snatches of a nap, her chin falling to her chest, and then her head jerking up again. In spite of the man's attack, she wished they were back at the rest stop. It was better there, out in the sunshine, with her children running around. She looked behind her.

Mary had joined her brother on the very backseat; she and Samuel were linked around each other like a couple of kittens.

Wilbert, Ruth thought. Mary had asked repeatedly for her gray kitten. But Wilbert was just a cat.

Why hadn't they asked about their father? Ruth slumped against the window, and wrapped herself in a bear hug. *I miss Peter.*

She decided she was glad that Mary and Samuel weren't asking about him. Their questions and their pain would have intensified her own pain too much.

Sarah slipped into the seat beside her. "Where are we?" she asked.

"Not exactly sure," Ruth said. "I fell asleep."

"Me, too," said Sarah.

Ruth studied the landscape. The open stretches of pale yellow grainfields, and the gently rolling hills made her suspect they were somewhere in southern Alberta. She tried to catch a glimpse of road signs, but they were sparse on the country highways. She guessed they were beyond Calgary, but how far beyond—she had no idea.

The hum of the bus engine and the roadside zipping along lulled her.

Ruth fell back to sleep.

MEN SWARMED toward the bunker. Several of them checked the domed enclosure after ensuring there was no one hiding inside; it was deserted.

"They're gone," a man said. He held up a tiny striped t-shirt. "But they were here." He tossed the shirt aside.

One of the men, a father of three young children, bent and took the shirt in his fingers. He fondled it, folded it, and placed it in his pack.

Several of the men shambled back and forth. “Too late,” they muttered. “We missed them.”

Meteor and Richard arrived. “We heard gunfire. Did we lose men?” Meteor asked a native man with long ebony hair.

“Yes, but we think we got all their guys. At least, Virgil thinks we did.” He motioned over his shoulder where Virgil was in conversation. Meteor appraised Virgil for a moment.

The native man then pointed to a trio of men seated on the ground. “Too late to save their women and kids though.” He tipped his chin at Richard. “Where’d you guys get to?”

“Came up a back trail.” Richard shuffled from one foot to another. “We have to go back the way we came.”

“Why?” asked the man with the long hair.

“Couple of bodies back there, too.” Richard turned to Meteor. “What now? We could try to track them, but I suspect they’re long gone. Or should we pick up the bodies and go home?”

“There’s food on the plates in the bunker,” said the man with the long hair. “It’s got to be several hours old.”

“I don’t think there’s much chance of chasing them down now.” Meteor said. “Let’s pick up the bodies.” He turned back to the men hovering near the bunker. “There’s a gun cellar in there.”

The man with the long hair shook his head. “Cleaned out. Matthew’s men checked it right away.”

Meteor gave his head a rueful shake. He located a log and sat down, groaning as he stretched out his leg. He dropped his pack in front of him and propped his elbows on his knees. Richard stood nearby and ran interference as men approached the big man with more questions.

“Let him be,” he said. “He lost a friend.”

One man pushed by—the man in the black parka who had addressed the men back at the camp. “Some of us are going after the women.” Meteor looked up. “We think he might have taken them to Devon. We’ll look there.”

Meteor stood, limping slightly. “What are you going to do about fuel?” he asked.

“We’ve decided...” the man said, waving at men clustered behind him. “We’ll take two trucks, siphon fuel out of the other trucks...take that with us.”

Meteor rubbed his thigh. “How are—”

"The other guys will quad back," the man interrupted.

"I was going to ask you how you were going to get the women and kids back to camp."

"We'll worry about that when we find them."

"It's a big province," Meteor said. "The man has an entire network of safe houses and fuel depots." He shook his head. "I don't think they stopped at Devon."

"We have nothing to go back to," the man said, his voice rising in anger. "Our wives and kids are gone." He waved an arm at the men standing near him. "We're going."

Meteor put his hand on the man's shoulder. "Take what you need. But leave enough fuel for us to get the dead back to camp."

"Agreed." The man in the parka turned. "Let's go."

"Wait a minute," a short man with close-cropped hair said. "I have a question." He stepped to the front of the group. He had the look of one steeling for a fight. "You knew they were here. Why didn't you go after them?"

Meteor pulled back as though slapped. "We knew they were here, but we didn't know they were in any danger. We didn't know Brad's men knew about the bunker till after we returned to camp. That was hours later."

"You could have gone after them," the man said accusingly.

Meteor's eyes narrowed, but he remained calm. "I told you—"

"You could have gone after them," the short man repeated, pressing his face toward Meteor. "Why didn't you go?" The short man's fists were balled at his side. Anger flamed in his eyes.

Meteor remained silent, his face dark with warning. He reached out and tried placing a calming hand on the man's shoulder, but the man slapped it away.

"You're probably still with The Man," he barked.

Meteor's fist connected with jawbone and the man fell backwards. Two men in military garb dashed forward, fists raised, but they were blocked.

"Boys, calm down." Virgil stood in front of Meteor, facing the men, his arms outstretched. "I can assure you, Meteor *isn't* with The Man."

"Who are you to be talking?" one of the military men asked. His glare was hateful. "You're The Man's boy, too."

Virgil drew himself up, feet planted apart, arms now stiff at his sides. "You're right. I was." he said, his words measured. "But I'm not now. And Meteor *never* was," he added, motioning over his shoulder.

Meteor brushed past Virgil. “I’ll take it from here.”

Meteor offered his hand to the man on the ground. The man hesitated and then grasped Meteor’s hand. With a quick pull, the man was back on his feet. Meteor brushed off the back of the man’s coat.

“I understand why you’re angry,” Meteor said. “You have every right to be, but we did what we thought was best. You gotta believe that…” The man gave a curt nod. Meteor nodded, too. “I need at least one truck to take the dead back to camp.”

“Fine,” the man said as he straightened his coat with a hunch of his shoulders.

“Help them with the fuel,” Meteor said to three younger men hovering near him. The men trotted off. Meteor turned back to the man he had hit. “Go,” he said with a tilt of his head. “You’ve got some driving to do.”

Richard joined Meteor as they watched the men depart. “I hope they find them.”

“I hope so, too, but they won’t. I know the man,” Meteor said, shaking his head. “Those women and kids are long gone.” He groaned. “Let’s get the bodies.” Meteor noticed Virgil standing alone. “Just a second.”

He walked over to Virgil and stopped in front of the tall man. Virgil eyed him warily. Meteor held out his hand. “Thank you.”

Virgil shook the proffered hand. “I can help with the dead,” he said.

Meteor gave a quick nod. “We’d appreciate that.”

SARAH TOUCHED Ruth’s shoulder. Ruth awoke, rubbed her eyes, and glanced out the window. The bus was still rattling along, but they were now in a city—or on the outskirts of one.

“I think we’re in Medicine Hat,” Sarah whispered. She pointed to the men at the front of the bus. “They were talking about stopping.”

The bus lumbered along, swung left, and then right, and finally pulled to a stop outside a low building. The women and children sat up, alert and interested in their new surroundings.

One yellow school bus was already parked, and another two buses pulled up behind them. Their brakes screeched and their drivers jumped out. The armed men began herding the women and children off the vehicles and into the building.

The sun was still bright, but it was low in the sky. Ruth guessed it was around four o’clock. She rubbed her wrist where her watch had been. Brad had taken it from her when he saw how often she checked it. “Time isn't going to mean much where you're headed," he said. Ruth trembled at the memory—the annoying sound of his laughter, and the unwelcome touch of his hand on her skin. She rose from her seat and headed back to her sleeping children.

Ruth gave Samuel and Mary a gentle shake. "C'mon. We're here." The children resisted her attempts to rouse them. She heard the men outside yelling for them to "hurry their asses up." She grabbed the children by their arms and pulled them out of their slumber. "Come on—we're getting off the bus."

"That way," a man said, pointing to the front of the building. Ruth saw a sign to her right: *Sunnyvale Senior Care Center*. She studied the exterior.

An old folks' home, she thought.

She hoped they wouldn't be imprisoned with rotting bodies. Or stuck in an environment riddled with disease. Smoke coming from a chimney was a welcome sight. Ruth knew it wasn't coming from a furnace, so someone must have set up a wood stove.

For cooking, she surmised. The thought brought her some pleasure.

Soon the home's new guests were inside. Children sniveled and mothers shushed them. Ruth was surprised to see a woman coming towards them. She didn't appear to be under anyone's influence or under any guard. Ruth studied her as she came into view... Dark hair—as black as India ink, attractive blue eyes, and a wide red mouth. It was the huge scar across her face that captured Ruth's attention.

A burn? A car accident?

The woman spoke:

"Welcome. You are The Man's property now. You'll live here. You'll be well fed and cared for. If you behave yourself, do as you're told, don't give the guards any trouble, you'll do fine here." She gave the women a small smile. "You might not be happy, but you'll be alive."

She motioned to a hall behind her. "You'll bunk in these rooms. You'll be locked in at night, so don't get any ideas. The Man isn't forgiving. Attempt to get away and you'll be shot. Does everyone understand that part?"

The women mumbled their understanding.

"The apartments are small, so a mother with two children or more can have a room to herself. The rest of you must bunk together." She waved in the opposite direction. "Through there is the kitchen and dining room. You'll have three squares a day. You'll be given work details. Don't mess up. Or you won't eat. And neither will your friends."

She paused and pointed down a hallway to the left of the entry door. "There's a large community room down there. That's where you'll spend your time—if you aren't locked in your rooms. Or you aren't in the dining room."

The women mumbled again.

"Farther up that hallway is the medical unit. There's equipment...tables and stuff, but no one here really knows what to do with it. So, if there's a doctor or a nurse in your group, especially a midwife—"

"I'm a midwife," Ruth said.

The woman studied her for a moment. "What's your name?" Ruth told her. The woman grunted her approval. "We've got a few women due in the spring," the dark-haired woman said.

Ruth nearly vomited at the thought.

Spring? This insane woman thought she was going to be there in the spring? Ruth itched to speak, but she clamped her mouth shut.

A young mother spoke up. "Our children are very hungry. I'll volunteer to cook them a meal, if you will let me." Several others offered their services, too.

"That won't be necessary," the woman said. "We were expecting you. We've got a meal ready. Find your rooms first and then go to the dining room." The women began a slow shuffle toward their rooms. "But I warn you," the woman called after them, "if you think you'll be able to escape..." She shook her head and nodded in the direction of the armed bikers at the door. "They shoot women who try to escape." She smiled a small smile, making her scar crease like a red crepe paper streamer.

Ruth frowned. *They were expecting us? All one hundred and seventy-one of us?*

Ruth followed the crowd down the hall. Doors were opened and women and children disappeared inside their new bedrooms, whittling the group down quickly and efficiently. Ruth chose a room and ushered the children inside. She closed the door. She surveyed the room, while the children claimed the beds, bouncing up and down on the mattresses.

The room was small, but not cramped. Twin beds flanked either wall of a sleeping area, while a full-sized couch and an overstuffed armchair anchored a small sitting area. The room was bright with plenty of light. Best of all, the room was clean. *A little dusty*, she noted, as dust motes flew into the air, driven up by her children's antics.

"Stop." They ceased their jumping and sat on the edge of their new beds. "Are you hungry?" They nodded.

She took their coats and hung them in a small closet. A cardboard box in the bottom of the closet caught her eye, and she stooped down. It was filled with wire coat hangers, old ties, shoes, and knick-knacks. She ran her hand through the box and smiled when she came across an old-fashioned man's wristwatch—the wind-up kind. As she picked it up, she heard the sound of tiny items rattling together. She pushed the top items aside; the bottom of the box was full of old pill bottles. She picked up one white square bottle, shook it, and tested its cap. *Childproof.* She picked up the box, shoved some items off the closet's top shelf, and put the box in their place. *No sense taking a chance on kids getting into this.*

She waved for the children to follow her out of the room.

THE DINING ROOM was a cheery place, too, and the smells emanating from the kitchen made Ruth's stomach rumble. It had been hours since she'd eaten a real meal. The children clambered up on chairs as though they were guests of a favored aunt, totally oblivious to the seriousness of their reality. Soon, the tables filled with loaves of fresh bread, pots of butter, and huge soup urns filled with steaming chili. Pitchers of orange Tang and glasses joined the food. The women and children dug in.

"Maybe I'll be able to stand this," Elizabeth said. "They're not planning to starve us. Or hurt us as long as we don't try to escape."

"But why do they want us? And why were they *ready* for us? What good are a bunch of women and little kids to them?" a teen girl asked.

"I don't know," Elizabeth said. She helped herself to a slab of bread. She searched for a table knife. Not finding one, she scooped yellow butter onto the bread, and spread it with the back of her spoon. "Right now, I'm starving and this food is delicious."

Ruth took a spoonful of chili. Elizabeth was right— The food was tasty. But it sat like lead in the bottom of her stomach.

What was going on here? Why were women expecting babies?

She took another mouthful. Then another. Her hunger silenced the little warning voice in her spirit, and she ate. She was thirsty, so she took a swig from the glass of Tang someone had poured for her—she grimaced at the sharp too-sweet flavor. A tiny voice nagged again.

What are these people up to? Ruth took a bite of her bread. *I'm too tired and too hungry,* she thought. *And this food tastes so good!*

Tomorrow. I'll figure it out, tomorrow.

Chapter Ten

When I'm Washed

MARTHA AWOKE with a start. She scanned the dim room in a panic. For the moment, nothing looked familiar.

Where am I? What time is it? What month is it?

She closed her eyes against the confusion. Her chest throbbed. Her fingers sought out the pain and encountered a large bandage. The area under the gauze itched. She scratched, but only succeeded in making herself cry out. Pain brought her back into sharp reality.

"I'm home," she said softly, recognizing her own bedroom. Her brain raced to open mental filing cabinets, helping her piece together the recent past. A face came into her mind.

Josef? No—she corrected herself—*Matthew. Josef is dead.*

Another face swam into view, this one foul, and she cringed with shame. She tried to thrust the vision of Brad's face away, willed it to vanish, but it only became clearer—more haunting, more accusatory.

Now, you'll learn— Just the way you like it, Martha.

She squeezed her eyes shut against the remembered voice, and turned her face into the pillow. Finally, she lifted her head and stared at the empty spot beside her.

Where was Matthew? A foggy recollection unfolded. He had been banished back to his old cabin and told she needed her rest—that she needed an entire bed in which to thrash around during her convalescence.

That's what I told Anna to tell him. Guilt pricked at her.

"Matthew..." The sound was ghostly even to her ears.

A small camp lamp burned on the table near her. She struggled to sit up. She had to go to the bathroom. A memory of burning pain made her grimace inwardly at the thought of relieving herself, but she had to go.

Could she make it to the pot? Where was the pot?

She pulled herself to the edge of the bed and attempted to swing her legs over. The effort made her want to vomit so she lay still, eyes closed, willing the nausea to pass. She tried again, and this time managed a sitting position, with her feet on the floor. The room spun around her and she clutched at the table for support. Her actions sent the lamp flying to the floor with a crash. She swayed, but remained sitting up. The room continued to swirl.

"Martha?"

Martha struggled to see the speaker.

Ruth? Was it Ruth?

A thin, older woman she barely recognized came into view. "Let me help you."

"I have to pee," Martha said weakly.

"Okay— I have a bedpan for you. Why don't you lie back down? I'll bring it."

"Where's everybody?" Martha groaned. "Where's Anna?"

The woman helped Martha lie back. She bent and retrieved the lamp and set it back on the table. "Anna needed a break. She asked me to watch you. She'll be back." She reached down. "Don't worry," she added. "Remember, I'm a nurse." Martha didn't remember. The *nurse* offered the bedpan. "Here."

The ordeal of urinating was exhausting, the pain excruciating. After taking a few sips of water, Martha fell back asleep. The nurse tucked the blankets around her patient, picked up the bedpan, and with a confirming glance back at Martha, she left the room.

Martha sighed in her sleep. She rolled onto her side, her left hand visible on the coverlet. The camp lamp glowed. It sparked a tiny fire in the green gemstone in the man's ring on Martha's hand. She had not noticed her rings were back on her fingers—both of them—Josef's gold wedding band and Matthew's high school ring.

She slept.

MATTHEW SAT alone in the Gatehouse. With Martha back home safely tucked in her own bed, under the care of a nurse, he could turn his attentions back to business. A plate of food sat near him on his desk. Near it sat a mug half-filled with coffee, but it was cold. He took a sip anyway, made a face, and swallowed. He pushed the cup aside. An old-fashioned hardbound journal lay open in front of him. He consulted a small notebook, running his finger down a handwritten list of names. He flipped a page in the journal, made notations, and gently closed it. He leaned forward with his elbows on the desk, his head in his hands. He stayed that way until the sound of a crying child roused him. He got up and looked out the window.

Women and children, the ones rescued from the burned bunkhouse, were still being trucked back to the compound. Terrible wails of heartbreak echoed through the camp when wives and children found out that their spouse, their father, or their brother would not be coming home. The casualties among the men who had been assigned to Matthew had been few, but the casualties among the men who had protected the Hutterites and the main compound were much greater. That list included a trusted captain, Thomas, and Martha's son-in-law, Peter. Martha didn't know. Matthew decided she was too sick to be told about his death. She was already grieving her missing daughters and grandchildren; she didn't need more misery. He glanced out the window. The sun was low and golden. He checked his watch.

Six-thirty.

Matthew pulled another thick book toward him and opened it. He thumbed through the supplies log, ran his finger down a column, scowled, and took a long breath. He flipped to another page, studied it, and frowned again. He leaned back in his chair, pulled off his cap, and scratched his head. He sniffed his armpits, and grimaced.

"I need a bath. No wonder Martha didn't want me around."

He checked his watch again. It had been several hours since Meteor, Simon, and the rest of the men had gone off in search of the missing women and children. He wondered why there had been no radio contact. He checked his radio.

Dead.

"Forgot to recharge," he muttered. He suspected most of their radios were dead. He laid the useless unit on the desk, and studied the book again.

A sharp rap on the door made Matthew look up. "Come," he said.

Two of the gate guards entered, supporting a woman between them. Her arms were draped around their necks. She was barely standing.

"What the hell happened to her?" Matthew got up and came around the desk.

"We don't know."

"Can you sit?" Matthew asked, pulling out a chair.

The woman, bruised and bloodied, was trying to make herself understood, but her words were muffled. She collapsed into the seat and slumped onto the desk, her head cradled in her arms. Matthew turned to the guards.

"Where did she come from? I don't recognize her."

"She was walking up the road. We found her a few minutes ago."

"Was anyone with her? Anyone drop her off?" Matthew asked.

"Not that we know of. Just her."

Matthew turned to the woman whose head was still down on her arms, her eyes closed.

"Who did this to you? Did a Crazy do this to you? One of The Man's people?"

She gave a faint nod.

"What's your name?"

"Marion," she said. Her voice was barely audible.

"Marion?" Matthew stepped back, a stunned look on his face, unsure he had heard her clearly. He waved the guard away and bent down to Marion's ear. "Are you his sister?" he whispered. Marion nodded again. "What are you doing here?"

"He threw me out," she said. "He nearly killed me. Please don't send me back."

With a quick purse of his lips, Matthew said, "Take her to the medical building. Find Anna—she'll know what to do. Keep her under house arrest."

Matthew bent and helped Marion to her feet. One of the guards put his arm around the woman's waist and escorted her out of the building. The first guard remained behind.

"Send Virgil to me," Matthew said.

"Virgil's not here," said the guard. He looked puzzled. "He went after the women that went to the bunker. I thought you knew that."

"Right—" Matthew gave the closed door a hard look. "Keep an eye on her."

~~~

MARION LAY on the bed, her head tilted away—a bloodied mass of honey-colored hair hid her features. The sound of the door opening and closing didn't rouse her. Anna dropped her jacket on a chair and leaned over the woman.
~~~

"Hi. I'm Anna. What's your name?"

When the woman didn't respond, Anna pushed sticky strands of hair aside to reveal the woman's face.

"Oh—" she said when she saw the cuts, the blood, and the bruising. "What happened to you?"

"Hit me..."

"Who hit you?"

"Man..."

"Are you one of The Man's women?"

"Was..." she mumbled.

"What's your name? Did you come here with somebody?" Anna looked up at the guard.

"Her name's Marion. No one else was with her."

"Okay... We'll get the details later. Right now, let me examine you."

With help, the woman sat up. Anna observed that she very pretty in spite of the damage to her face.

"Are you hurt anywhere else?" Anna asked. The woman tugged at her coat. Anna helped her remove it. "I see bruises, but no broken bones. No bleeding, except for the cuts on your face." She reached for a small medical kit tucked on a shelf, above her head. In a few minutes, the woman's wounds were cleaned and bandaged; some had needed small butterfly patches to hold their edges together, but no stitches. Anna returned the kit to the shelf and washed her hands. She pulled the chair over to the bed and sat down.

"I'll keep you here for the time being. Watch you for concussion. You'll be moved to the women's bunkhouse in a few days."

Marion's eyes were closed, but she heard Anna and she agreed. Anna leaned closer.

"Want to tell me what happened to you?"

Marion mumbled her tale, precisely constructed with just enough truth to camouflage the lies.

MATTHEW WAS standing outside the Gatehouse when the quads roared into the parking lot. They were followed by a single truck. Richard was driving; Meteor was in the seat beside him. Neither man was smiling.

Matthew walked up to meet the truck. That's when he saw Virgil riding in the truck bed—he was crouched beside a tarp-covered mound. Matthew noticed that the mound was about the size and shape of a human body. *Bodies*, he corrected himself. He steeled himself for the news.

Richard got out of the truck and waved. "I'm heading back to my people," he said. Matthew waved back.

Several men gathered around Matthew. "So?" they asked eagerly. "What happened? Did they find them?"

Meteor joined the group. He looked haggard, desolate. "It's not good, Matthew."

"Who's in the back?" Matthew asked.

Meteor told the men the story—of how they had heard shots, and then later found the bodies. He told them about finding the bunker and the weapons locker empty. He told them Brad's men were dead. And he told them about the men who decided to go in pursuit of the women. He neatly left out the part about the man he had punched in the face.

The family men swore and argued. They demanded that Matthew put together a search party. Their anger grew hotter when Matthew negated the idea.

"I told you...men are already out there searching," Meteor said in Matthew's defense. "They will have a much better chance of finding them."

The men quieted, but like a bubbling brew, they mumbled under their breaths. Matthew gave orders to have the bodies prepared for burial. Everyone agreed that Matthew would be the one to tell Anna about Simon. He pulled Meteor and Virgil aside.

"You two go to the second camp and relieve Simon's relatives of guard duty. He's got an aunt and uncle...and a couple of cousins over there. Let them come to the funeral. Take four more guys with you."

The two men agreed. He gave them a quick, apologetic look. "You guys are single—I've gotta give priority to the family men."

"We get that." Meteor said.

"You could be there for a while—you might want to take your stuff."

Virgil held up his hands. "I'm wearing my stuff."

Meteor gave Virgil a once over. "I'll loan you something. I'll be right back." When Meteor had gone, Matthew turned to Virgil.

"I—" he began, and then changed his mind. "Never mind. I'll see you later."

Virgil touched his fingertips to his cap in a tiny salute, and returned to the truck. He watched as men removed the bodies, deftly and somberly.

Matthew called after him. "Get those radios recharged."

Inside the Gatehouse, Matthew opened his logbook again. His pen trembled as he added a date in the *Deceased* column across from Simon's name. He flipped the page and did the same for Simon's comrade. He hesitated, and then turned to a fresh page. He added a new name: Marion. With a final quick stroke, Matthew dropped the pen, and sank his face into his hands.

~ ~ ~

MARTHA OPENED her eyes. This time the room was filled with light. The sounds outside the window were familiar, camp life returning to normal: screeches of children, mothers calling, cattle lowing, whinnying of horses, dogs barking, rumbling generators, crackling of fires, men in yelled conversation, and the sound of hammers on wood. Her bedclothes were soaked with sweat. She shivered when she lifted the covers, but she wanted to look outside. The nausea came again, and she fought it. She pushed herself to her feet, groaned her way through the pain, and shuffled to the window.

How long have I been sick? A week? Two weeks?

Bright sunlight made her blink. She could see horses attached to wagons—wagons filled with lumber, crates, barrels, and tools. She nodded. The Hutterites had been quick to respond and show their gratitude for all Matthew's men had done to keep them safe from The Man's attack.

The Man's attack? How long ago?

Martha tried piecing together her memories of the last days, but shook her head when she couldn't come up with a definitive answer. She touched her chest; it was still bandaged, but it didn't feel as sore. The pain between her legs had lessened, too.

She watched as several black-capped men in dark pants and jackets surveyed the sooty remains of the destroyed women's bunkhouse. Other men had begun building wooden frames.

One man pointed to another location. Martha guessed he was suggesting the spot as a good place to erect a new bunkhouse. She scanned the grounds trying to see Matthew. When she couldn't find him, she turned her eyes back to the building crew. She gasped when she recognized one of the men carrying lumber, a tall, slender man, a man she never expected to see in her courtyard... in her campground: *Virgil.*

What was he doing here? Did Matthew know? Had he tricked the Hutterites into helping him get into Matthew's camp?

Old protective instincts rose inside her and she desperately wanted to scream out, to get someone to notice the intruder—the enemy who had so boldly entered their midst. Then she saw Matthew. He was coming out of the Gatehouse with a half dozen armed men in tow.

Good, she thought. *He'll get him.*

Her mouth hung open when Matthew sauntered up to Virgil and engaged him in conversation.

"What?" she said. "Am I awake? Is this for real?"

The front door screeched and banged. Martha tottered back to her bed and sat down. She closed her eyes against the pain.

"Martha?"

"Hi Anna. I'm up. Just barely, but I'm up."

Anna came through the bedroom door. She had a pile of folded bed linens in her arms. She wasn't smiling.

"I'm glad to see you moving around. You've been sleeping hard for days." She set the linens on the foot of the bed.

"Any news on my girls?"

"No, not yet. Sorry."

"What's going on outside?" Martha asked. "Why is Virgil here?"

"You saw Virgil?" Anna stopped by the window and looked out.

"Yeah, he was talking to Matthew." Martha paused. "Why would he be talking to Matthew?"

"I guess no one has told you—Virgil's with us now. Matthew let him live. He and a bunch of his men have joined us."

"Just like that?"

Anna shrugged. "Well, it's really no different from what Trojan did—or what Meteor did when they joined us." She picked up a pillow and removed its case. She reached for a fresh pillowcase.

"Still—that's hard to believe. Where's Meteor?"

"I don't know—I haven't seen him." Anna replaced the pillow and plumped it.

"Can—" Martha paused. Anna still had not smiled and her face was grim. Martha searched her memories.

Had she forgotten something?

"Do I remember correctly? The women and children got away safely? Are they back here now?"

"No." Anna turned away, but not before Martha noticed the girl's teary eyes.

"What's wrong, Anna?"

Anna kept her back to Martha. She remained silent. Her shoulders shook slightly.

"What?" Martha prompted. "Tell me...."

Finally, Anna spoke. "Simon...he went to find them...he..." Her voice caught in her throat and she struggled not to cry.

"Simon's dead?" Martha asked. A foggy memory of someone telling her...

Oh, no. Poor Anna.

Martha struggled up from the bed. She put her arms around Anna. "I'm sorry. So sorry." She gave her a small squeeze.

Anna gave her a gentle push. "You're going to hurt yourself."

Martha let go and sat down. "Anna..." Her tone was earnest with deep concern.

Anna swiped away tears. "I'll change that dressing now."

"Never mind me. You—"

"I'm fine, Martha," Anna interrupted. "I've got to change that dressing."

Martha gave Anna's arm a sympathetic squeeze. Anna's eyes filled again. "You look so tired. You need to rest," Martha said softly.

"I will. As soon as I finish here."

"You are so strong, Anna...so very strong."

Anna helped Martha to lie back on the bed. She lifted the edges of the surgical tape and then gently pulled at the gauze firmly stuck to the bullet wound.

"Owww..."

"Sorry," Anna said. She hesitated and then pulled again. "Do you remember anything? Do you remember Matthew bringing you back here?"

Martha shook her head. "No." She paused. "But I remember asking you to tell him he couldn't sleep with me. Thanks for not telling him anything."

"You mean about the rape?" Martha nodded. "You're welcome, but I think you should tell him. He has a right to know."

"I'll never tell him," Martha blurted. "Never."

Anna let it go and continued changing the bandage. "How about your vaginal area? Is it feeling better? I've been bathing it in garlic and olive oil."

"Still burns like hell, but I think it's better."

Anna tried again. "If it's like the tears during pregnancy, you should be okay in about six weeks. Will you tell Matthew then?"

"No!" Martha said sharply. "I said *no.* Aren't you listening to me? I don't want him to ever know."

Anna stepped back, stung by the acid in Martha's tone. But she pressed on. "How will you explain your aversion to having him touch you?" she asked gently.

"What aversion?"

"Martha, you're forgetting that I've been raped, too. I know what happens in our minds. Until Simon came along..." She faltered, steadied her voice, and continued. "I didn't want any man touching me."

Martha's eyebrows lifted—a corrective look shone in her eyes. Anna blushed.

"Uh, well..." Anna stammered. "Except for that one time with Matthew."

Martha looked away. "That won't happen with me..."

Anna raised her eyebrows. "Really? Hasn't it happened already?" She waved her hand over the bed. "Do you really need this whole bed to yourself?"

Martha stared toward the window. "I need a bath."

"I'll get the water and towels. But I've gotta check on Gordon first...then I can help you."

"No— I want to bathe myself," Martha said irritably.

"You're still pretty weak—are you sure that's a good idea?"

"I want a bath—" Anna began to protest anew. "And I'll do it *myself*—" Martha's tone was brittle.

Anna gathered the dirty linens as she spoke, "I understand. I'll set up a tub for you in the kitchen. It'll take me about ten minutes to get it ready." She sounded defeated. Martha suddenly felt contrite.

"Sorry," Martha mumbled as Anna left the bedroom. She knew she had been unkind to Anna, but she was angry. So very angry. At herself. At Matthew. At Anna. At God.

At...

She closed her eyes against the memory.

Martha pushed back against her pillows with their newly changed cases. Her nose caught the scent of sun-dried fabric. She took a deep breath.

A bath. That'll wash the feelings away.

The unwelcome vision appeared again. And with it came a fresh shot of hot shame. She pushed at it, willing it to stop its berating echo.

When I'm washed, I'll feel better, she assured herself.

When I'm washed...

Martha lay still and listened to the sounds around her. Anna was clattering around in the kitchen, while chainsaws whined and buzzed outside. Martha heard the steady *bang-bang-bang* of metal on wood—as hammers rose and fell—and the happy sounds of men with a mission in animated conversation. The repetitiveness of the commonplace sounds became an irresistible lullaby and she drifted back to sleep.

~ ~ ~

A BANGING on the cabin door awoke her. The room was dim. She guessed it was early evening. A lamp burned on the table next to her head. She moved gently, not wanting to incite a painful response from any parts of her body. She sat up and peered into the gloom.

Where was Anna? She was making me a bath. Today? That was today, wasn't it? Martha gave her head a tiny shake. *Or am I mixed up? Was that yesterday?*

"Helloooo? Martha?" It was a man's voice.

"Jonah?" Martha asked—surprise and delight coloring her voice. "Hi! It's okay. Come on in." She pulled the covers up to her chin as she sat up. Jonah's face appeared in the doorway.

"They said I could visit you."

"Yes, of course. Bring a lamp in from the kitchen. It's dark in here."

Jonah returned to the room, lantern in hand. He placed it on the small table on the other side of her bed. Then he stood, quietly, head down.

"I'm so relieved to see you. How are you?" Martha asked.

Jonah didn't speak.

"What's wrong?" she asked. Martha's mind searched its depths for an answer.

What had Anna said? Someone had gone to get the women—gone to get her daughters and her grandchildren... Yes, that's what she'd said. Simon had gone...

Then she understood. "Oh, Jonah...I'm so sorry. He was your best friend..."

"I'm okay," Jonah said quickly. He slumped into a hard-backed wooden chair set against the wall. "After all we've been through... I don't think I can feel anymore. Numb— I feel numb. We've buried so many bodies. Thomas, too— we buried him. Numb." He shook his head. "I don't know Martha... I just don't know."

Martha stared at the stricken man, still so much a boy. Her heart broke for him. "Oh, Jonah... I'm so sorry..."

Jonah shrugged. "Right now, I hate this world. I hate the Change. I hate being alive." He gripped his head between his hands. "I gotta go, Martha. I gotta get out of here."

"Don't say that, Jonah. You're a good man. You're brave...and strong...and you've helped so many people. Josef loved you and so does Matthew—" Martha stopped. She had run out of platitudes and niceties.

He was right. His world sucked. Both their worlds sucked.

Jonah rose from the chair. He stooped to hug her. She touched a hand to his cheek. She frowned and felt his forehead.

"Jonah. You're sick. You have a fever."

He pulled her hand from his face. "I'm fine. Can I do anything for you before I go? Get you anything?"

"No, dear. I don't need anything." Suddenly, her eyebrows drew together in puzzlement. "What about Cammy and Trojan? Did they make it?"

"Yeah. They're good." Jonah gave a slight huff. "Trojan managed to steal another truckload of The Man's weapons."

"I'll just bet he did," Martha chuckled. She blew him a kiss. "I love you. Get some rest, Jonah."

"Love you, too."

She heard the cabin door open and close. A draft of cool air blew in and she shivered. She grabbed a blanket and drew it around her shoulders.

That poor kid. He didn't deserve this. Neither did Simon. No one did. Brad! All I had to do was shoot him.

Guilt replayed a scene in her mind, a scene she had been forced to witness a thousand times...

Brad's bloodied face in the moonlight. The glint of the gun.

Why didn't I shoot him? I could have shot him.

She closed her eyes.

If I had shot him, Simon would be alive. My girls would be here. My little Mary would be here.

She squeezed her eyes shut against a brutal wave of self-recrimination.

Why aren't I dead? I should be dead, God. Not Simon. Me! I should be dead.

She tugged the blanket closer, trying to comfort herself against the onslaught of responsibility.

They're going to hate me. And this time, they'll be right. This time, they'll be justified. I could have shot him. I should have shot him.

The voice she had heard that night—in her mind—came again.

Thou shall not kill.

"You're wrong," she cried out. "This time, God—You are wrong. I should have killed—I should have..."

Thou shall not kill.

She lowered her face into her hands, and sobbed.

Noises from outside interrupted her. She hoisted herself from the bed and stood, unsteadily, at the window. She was dressed in burgundy sweat pants, a t-shirt, and a thick zippered hooded sweatshirt.

The compound was lit by construction lamps on poles. The skeleton of the new women's bunkhouse sat eerily in the deepening gloom. Nearby was a crowd of people—angry people. They were yelling and waving their fists. She squinted and tried to make out faces. One man seemed to be the brunt of their anger. She squinted again.

Matthew. Was he in trouble?

She shuffled out of the bedroom, grunted as she pulled on a pair of boots, and opened the door. Generators hummed, but she could still hear the shouting. She shivered as she listened.

"It's our decision. They're our family. We're going after them," called out one man, his fist punching the air. He wore an orange cap and a long khaki jacket. His declaration was mirrored by a handful of other men, all equally angry and demonstrative.

"No," Matthew said. "Wait till we find out where they've been taken. Then we'll go after them."

"We've waited long enough."

"There's already one search party out there," Matthew said with a firmer edge to his voice. "Wait till they get back."

"Easy for you to say, Matthew. Your wife is here," said a younger man, a white ball cap turned backward on his head.

"My wife was shot," Matthew retorted. "It's lucky she's even alive. And I'll remind you that she got shot trying to save your wife."

"But..." The male voices of the crowd rose ever higher with reasons for why they should go after their women and children.

However, Matthew's voice proved louder.

"We...don't...have...the fuel," he said, punctuating his words as he spoke. "We'll wait." He eyed the man in the orange cap. "That's an order." He paused and added, "If you leave now, don't come back."

"And if I do?"

Matthew crossed his arms and planted his feet.

"You won't be welcome back here."

Sheree Zielke

Chapter Eleven

A Face-Pounding

JONAH SLUMPED in the wooden chair. His young face was haggard and pale. He coughed—once, twice—then he entertained a drawn out spate of coughs, lung-ripping sounds complete with warbling mucous. He cleared his throat and looked around.

The Meeting House was filled with men; most were already seated, but some stood or leaned against the wall. Jonah coughed again, this time bringing up a wad of phlegm. He pushed back from the table and headed to the door. He went outside, leaned over the railing, and spat. A thick gob of greenish slime hit the dirt. He drew a hand across his forehead, wiping sweat aside. He went back inside.

"You look like shit, man," a redheaded man observed as Jonah pulled back his chair.

"I feel like shit," Jonah said, his voice guttural. He sat down. He looked toward the front of the room where Matthew and the pony-tailed captain were chatting. Trojan and Meteor stood next to them. Jonah watched for a moment and then laid his head down on his crossed arms. Sweat dripped from his face. He coughed again. The redheaded man patted his back. Jonah lifted one shoulder, shrugging away the man's hand. "I'm fine."

More men entered the room, chairs scraped on the wooden floorboards as they took their seats.

"Is everyone here now?" the captain asked the assembled men. He nodded to Matthew. "Any time..."

"Good morning," Matthew began..."I wish the news was better—the search party got back about three hours ago." His look was grave. "We still don't know where the women and kids are." He took a breath and continued..."Men, I'm sorry—sorrier than you can know."

The room fell silent. Tears shone in his eyes. He glanced away and cleared his throat. Finally, he spoke again, his voice husky with emotion...

"We *will* find them. I promise you. But right now, we have other issues to deal with."

"We shouldn't have left the camp so weak in the first place," announced a man near the back of the room. His face was chiseled and tanned, and the ears that stuck out from under a skullcap bore copious holes; most were studded with white gemstones.

"What did you say?" The pony-tailed captain's tone threatened as his eyes searched the room. Nobody spoke out. The captain relaxed. He nodded once more to Matthew.

"It's been two weeks now—we've mourned and buried our dead, the injured are being cared for—things are getting back to normal. But...we've done an inventory. We're low on supplies. Not food so much—at least, not yet—but ammunition, and fuel. And winter's coming. You all know what that means. Fuel will be needed for the generators. Ammunition will be needed for hunting. Unfortunately, unlike wars in history, this war has not been good for our economy. Unless we are very careful with our reserves...or the power miraculously comes back on... We're in trouble."

The men glanced back and forth at one another. Helplessness and futility clouded some of their faces. They stared back at Matthew, their eyes willing him to solve the problem.

"We have limited resources of stabilized fuel left and we'll need that for scavenging runs."

"And for when we go after our women," the man at the back yelled out, rising from his chair. The pony-tailed captain stepped forward, but Matthew stayed him with a hand on his arm.

"Yes," Matthew said, looking pointedly at the man. "We're saving fuel for when we rescue your families. As soon as we find out something, we'll go after them. We'll find them—I promise."

"You can't promise that," the man shot back.

"You're right, I can't promise we'll find them...but I can promise that we'll try."

The other man opened his mouth, closed it, and sat down.

"We need to finish building the second women's bunkhouse," Matthew said. "We should have it done before the first snow falls. Have it ready for the ladies' return. We could use a few more carpenters." Hands shot up into the air. "Didn't think we'd have a problem finding volunteers," he said with a smile. His smile disappeared. "There's a flu going around the camp. Any of you sick?"

Several men looked in Jonah's direction. His head was still on his arms. He flipped up his hand. "Me," he mumbled.

"You shouldn't be here, Jonah," Matthew observed. "Go to the medical building. We'll fill you in later." Jonah groaned.

"I don't think I can move," he croaked. Men near him laughed good-naturedly at the sickly sound. He lifted his head and grinned. Then he got up and shuffled out of the building.

"I miss Simon," the captain said as an aside to Matthew. "But not as much as Jonah misses him."

"I know. You couldn't pry those two apart." Matthew cleared his throat. The room quieted.

"We've got lots of work to do before winter." Matthew laid out plans for camp clean-up, he set out work details, he assigned men and their families to the second camp, scavenging runs, and he announced a guard schedule for the Hutterites' farmland.

The pony-tailed captain tapped Matthew's shoulder and they held a brief whispered conference. Matthew turned back.

"We need scouts. Anybody up for that?" A few hands went up; they belonged to the single men, the men without ties back to the camp: Virgil's men. Matthew gave them a wry look.

"This task is for men loyal to our camp. We have to find out what The Man is up to. I don't want scouts going out and not coming back." Some of the hands lowered.

"Don't get me wrong—I'm not doubting your word—but I want scouts with a vested interest in the people here to go out. I *know* they'll be back."

The captain nodded at two men in black leather on the far side of the room. Their hands were still in the air.

"Those two..." the captain said. Matthew considered the pair.

The cousins were new, part of Meteor's army. They had decided to join the camp. It was hard to tell they were related since they looked nothing alike. They were a Mutt and Jeff pair, the shorter of the two had spiky, blond hair and expressive eyes, a pistachio green. His lanky cousin's smiling blue eyes beamed out from under dark eyebrows. His muscled body towered over his shorter cousin. Both were gregarious and well-liked. And they were single.

"Set them up," Matthew said. The captain walked away.

"As for the rest of you, you know your jobs. Go do them."

~ ~ ~

SLOWLY AND PLODDINGLY, a mundane routine returned as the people began to feel more secure. Matthew managed to make the angry men see reason—that running after their loved ones, without having any idea of where they were going, would be both ineffectual and foolhardy—and a huge waste of precious fuel.

Martha began to feel more normal, too. She hurt less, and her bullet wound had healed into a long, ridged leathery scar. She was healed below, too, and all infection had passed. She would leave her cabin to get fresh air, but for only short periods. However, in spite of her improved health, she still insisted that she needed to sleep alone. Matthew obliged, although he grew less obliging as the days passed...

"I really miss you, Martha," Matthew said one morning over breakfast. He reached across the table and took Martha's hand. "Are you sure you still aren't feeling well enough for me to sleep here?"

She gently withdrew her hand with a quick grin—more a fleeting curl of the corners of her mouth. "I miss you, too, but it's better this way." She gathered the breakfast dishes and rose from the table.

Matthew got up. He waited till she had deposited the dishes in the sink and then he pulled her into his arms. "It's been weeks, Martha. I promise I won't roll on top of you." He gave her an impish smile.

Martha caught the meaning of his smile and froze in his arms; she tried to thaw, tried to push away the feelings of revulsion at his touch, but without success, so she stood unmoving...unspeaking—her breath caught in her chest.

Matthew ducked his head and tipped her chin upwards, so he could look into her eyes. "C'mon. Give it a try. Okay?"

Martha fought against the creeping panic threatening to claim her. She remained in Matthew's arms although she wanted to scream, to run, to find solace in the sanctuary that her bedroom had become.

Should I tell him? Oh, God, help me. Should I tell him?

Matthew bent to kiss her lips, tenderly, just a soft touch. Martha held herself still, as still as she could. After all, he was her husband. This was his right.

Husband.

Suddenly, an unbidden thought screamed across her mind.

Josef. I want Josef. Josef would make things better.

Tears sprang to her eyes, and she gasped for breath. She pulled away. "No, Matthew." She couldn't bear to look at him. She could feel hurt emanating from him. "It's not you, okay? It's me. I just can't get it together. I'm sorry." She turned away, but he grabbed her by the shoulders and turned her back to him.

"What's going on? It's not your chest, is it? It's something else." His eyes searched her face for an answer, but she stared past him. "Why won't you look at me?"

"Matthew—please—"

He gave her a small shake. "Tell me. Tell me what's wrong."

Tears dribbled down her face. "It's nothing. I can't—"

"Yes, you can. Tell me."

A knock sounded on the door. Martha pulled free and swiped at her tears with her shirtsleeve. "You answer that."

She brushed by him, walked into the bedroom, and closed the door. She sat on the bed, and held her head in her hands.

"This is ridiculous. I've got to get back to being me. Time for rounds."

~ ~ ~

THE WOMEN quieted when the bunkhouse door swung open. Martha walked in. She surveyed the women who stared at her. She smiled.

"Yeah. It's really me. In the flesh," she joked. "Surprised?"

"We didn't think you were up and about already."

"Well, I am." She caught sight of a woman tucked away in a corner. She walked over. "Hi. Anna told me about you. Marion, right? How are you?"

"I'm fine. Thank you."

"Do you need anything?"

"No, everyone's been very kind to me."

A commotion from the window drew their attention.

"Hey, they're back," exclaimed a redheaded woman. She bobbed up and down, shifting from foot to foot, and trying to catch a glimpse over the heads of the taller women standing at the window.

"Who's back?" Martha called out.

"Meteor and Virgil."

"Virgil?" Marion's eyes grew bright. "Virgil? Virgil is here?"

Martha gave her a puzzled look. “You know Virgil?”

“He and I were...together,” Marion said. “It’s another reason why The Man had me beaten up— He found out about Virg and me.” She glowed with excitement. “He’s here now? With your camp?”

“Yeah. Ever since he surrendered to Matthew.”

“Virgil surrendered?” Marion asked incredulously.

“Yes— He did.”

“I can hardly wait to see him.”

“How did you end up here?” Martha asked. Suspicion colored her tone. She didn’t try to hide it.

“I got lucky,” Marion replied. “One of his—The Man’s—guys felt sorry for me.” She spoke in a rush. “He knew you’d taken in women before, so he dropped me here. Didn’t want to see me get killed.”

“Really...” Martha said. She turned toward the door. “I’ll tell him you’re here.”

“Thank you.”

“Wait a minute,” Martha said, turning back to Marion. “Virgil’s been back to the camp before this. You never ran into him?”

“I’ve been under house arrest,” she explained. “Matthew...”

Martha nodded. “Oh,” she said simply. “I’ll talk to Matthew.” She left the bunkhouse and headed across the compound to the Gatehouse.

Did Matthew know about Marion and Virgil? Why hadn’t he said something? Why was he keeping them apart?

Matthew was just leaving the Gatehouse. His eyebrows went up in surprise when he spotted Martha. Then the corners of his mouth lifted.

“Hi— You’re out and about...” His tone was playful. “You looking for me?”

“I just visited Marion.” Martha went straight to business. “Did you know that she’s with Virgil?”

Matthew’s smile faded. “Yeah, I did.”

“And you didn’t tell him that she’s here?”

“No.”

“Why not?”

“I thought I’d keep an eye on her for a while. Without him knowing about her.” He looked into Martha’s face. “He’ll understand.”

“I don’t.”

“It’s not for you to understand, Martha.” Martha’s eyes widened. “I did what I thought was best.”

"I think he should be told. Why would you keep two people apart who love each other?" Her tone was confrontational.

"Why would *you*?" Matthew replied, matching the edge in her voice.

Martha caught his meaning. "I—" she began. "She knows he's here now. Maybe it's time you told him." Martha turned on her heel and walked away.

Matthew stared after her, confused. She had given him a glimpse of the old Martha, but not quite the old Martha. She had changed.

What was it? The girls? Was she angry at him? Because he hadn't rescued them before Brad kidnapped them. Was that it? Or was there more? What was she hiding?

He stared after her, his heart hanging heavily in his chest.

Doesn't she love me anymore? Then another thought.

Is there somebody else?

The stinging thought slipped away when he caught sight of Virgil in the parking lot. Other than helping with the building of the bunkhouse, Virgil had spent most of his time assigned to guard duty at the second camp. Matthew waved to him.

It was time.

MEN SAT AROUND tables in the men's bunkhouse. They were playing cards, cleaning guns, and filling up on fresh baking. A plate of molasses colored muffins sat in a tall stack in the middle of the table. A plate of oatmeal cookies layered with raspberry jam filled another plate. The men were chatting as they ate. Meteor was with them.

"So, she had a gun, but she didn't shoot him... Why not?" asked a man with spiky dark hair. He was new to the compound. He had heard the rumours, but not necessarily the truth. He was devouring muffins as fast as he could pick them up. "I mean, if she really hated him so much—"

"I don't know. Maybe she never got the chance," Meteor responded.

The dark-haired man wolfed down another bran muffin. Bits of food fell to the table as he spoke. "Maybe she has a thing for him."

The blow came so quickly, the man had no chance to duck. Or to take back his words. Meteor's fist drove him backwards, toppling his chair and sending him down onto the floor. Muffin crumbs flew from his lips.

Men and boys scrambled to get out of the way, tipping their own chairs in haste. They stood, muffins suspended in mid-air, and stared at the man lying on the floor. Nobody moved to stop Meteor. He rubbed his fist with his other hand.

"You want some more?" He nudged the man with the toe of his boot. The man made a small coughing sound. "One more word about her from you—and I'll take you apart."

The man glanced up. He raised a hand in submission. "I got it," he said. He rolled to his side and coughed again.

"Better pick him up before he chokes," Meteor growled. He stomped out of the building.

~~~

A few hours later, Matthew caught up to Meteor. He was cleaning his pistol. Matthew sat down on the bench seat next to him. He picked up a gun part and rolled it between his fingers.

"I heard you cold-cocked one of the new members in the bunkhouse. What was that all about?" Matthew asked.

"Something he said."

"I know that much. But why the face-pounding?"

"Assholes should learn to keep their mouths shut."

Matthew remained quiet for a moment. "What's going on with you, Meteor?" He leaned in. "I know you hate Brad—we all do—but the new guy didn't know any better. He was just jawing."

Meteor took a huge breath and looked away. "Just rubbed me the wrong way, I guess."

Matthew looked puzzled. "All kinds of people have rubbed you the wrong way, but you've never gotten so angry... so fast."

"Did you hear what he said?"

"Yes—some bullshit about Martha having a thing for Brad."

"And that doesn't bother you?"

"It does, but the guy was just talking nonsense."

"Have you talked to your wife lately?"

"What do you mean?"

"Why don't you ask Martha?"

"Ask her what?"

"Nothing." Meteor picked up his gun and looked down the barrel. Satisfied with its cleanliness, he returned it to its holster. He gathered his cleaning tools into a small leather pouch and got up.

"Ask her what?" Matthew repeated.

"I think it's time for me to go, Matthew." Meteor tried to push by, but Matthew held his ground. He put his hand on Meteor's chest.
~~~

"Go? You mean leave the compound?" Matthew paused. "No, my friend. Don't go. We'll take Brad out together...you and I. Stay— I need you here." Matthew squeezed Meteor's shoulder. "I trust you. C'mon, you're my closest friend. You gotta know that."

Meteor looked up. "I think—"

"Stay. I need someone I trust to watch my back."

"Matthew, you don't know—"

"Martha needs you here," Matthew added quickly.

Meteor scrubbed his hands across his face in a rough massage. "Damn." He breathed heavily. "Sure. For Martha."

Matthew clapped his friend on the back. "Remember the meeting tomorrow."

~~~

THE MEETING HOUSE was crammed. Matthew had called for a census, and everyone was there from the newest baby to the oldest soldier. Martha stood near Matthew at the front of the room, but her eyes kept straying to the dark elliptical stains on the floor, while her mind replayed bits of the attack in sudden flashes of bold color and crystal clarity.

Pay attention.

She squeezed her eyes shut against the memory and willed the sound of Brad's voice out of her brain. A flash memory of his hot breath in her face made her shudder. She gripped the edge of the table and took a slow, controlled breath. Matthew's voice cut through the deadly haze.

"Please line up in family groups and give us your names and ages," Matthew said. "And the names of the missing. We need those, too."

It took several hours for the camp members to file by, but Matthew's census was soon completed. The women and kids were ushered out and Matthew called the men to order. He perused the logbook. "We've lost forty-three men. And we're missing one hundred and seventy-one women and kids," he said gravely.

"When do we go after them?" a man with sad dog eyes asked. Matthew gestured for the man to continue. "My wife and my three kids are gone. I need to find them. I can't live this way."

"I know," Matthew said, his tone softened with empathy. "It's been really bad for you. But I believe your wife and children are safe. They're of no value to The Man if he hurts or kills them. I believe that. But this is a big province—we need to have some idea of where they are before we go after them."
~~~

"I don't care—I can't wait anymore. We know he took them south. That's enough for me. I'm ready to go." Two other husbands and fathers chimed in; they were ready to go, too.

Matthew held up his hand. "Then go, but the snow's coming. Gas will be hard to scavenge along the way, not to mention how hard it'll be to find food. And the odds of getting killed by Crazies—they're pretty damn good. Think about it, boys."

The men grumbled, but they finally agreed that Matthew had a strong case for them staying put. At least for the time being.

"What are we doing about the kid?" asked a grandfatherly man with a mass of white curls bubbling out from under a wool cap.

"What kid?" Matthew asked.

"Orange hair. He's been jailed at my place for weeks. Should we let him go? I mean, what's the harm. It's nearly winter. Where's he gonna go?" The dog-eyed man spoke up:

"He betrayed us. He needs to die." Everyone turned to face him. "My family would be here if he'd kept his fucking mouth shut." Other men agreed.

"You can't just kill him," called out the grandfather.

"We can if the Discipline Committee decides his act was murder."

"We disbanded that committee," Matthew said.

"Well, let's band it together, right now," called out the dog-eyed man. "I'll chair it." Other men threw their hands into the air. "I'm in," a chorus of voices shouted.

"No," Matthew said. "You're sounding like a lynch mob. Let him go. He's a stupid kid. He can't do anything to hurt us now." He turned back to his notes. "Virgil's men— Some want to join us permanently."

"Sure. But what makes you think they'll stay on our side when the chips are down?" a man called out.

Virgil's men responded with angry denials, but Matthew quieted them with an upraised hand. "How about if Virgil takes that question?" Matthew nodded to the tall man leaning against the back wall, arms folded. "Virg? The floor is yours."

Virgil cleared his throat. He uncrossed his arms and moved to the front of the room. He drew his thumb and forefinger down along either side of his salt and pepper mustache.

"I know The Man. And I know Matthew. They're both strong leaders, but Matthew's system of government is better. He is more organized and...he has a stocked larder." Sarcastic laughter peppered the room. "The Man's supplies in southern Alberta are good, but here...not so good. My men know that," he said with a nod to the soldiers. "They don't want to starve over a winter. They like it here. They like the people...they like the women." That brought ribald comments and chuckles. "And most of all, they like the peace. They won't slip back over to the other side. I'll guarantee that."

"Thanks, Virgil."

Virgil began to walk away. Matthew stopped him. "One more thing you should know. Virgil's woman showed up here a couple of weeks back. She was badly beaten." The men muttered. "We've welcomed her to the camp." The men muttered some more. "She's staying with Virgil now. Her name is Marion."

Meteor had watched the proceedings without speaking. Now he spoke: "Who beat her up?"

"The Man," Virgil replied. Meteor cocked an eyebrow.

"Why did he do it? Have you asked yourself that?"

"He found out I'd surrendered, I guess. He took it out on her."

"Really. He beat her to teach *you* a lesson. That's what she told you? Why didn't he just shoot her and dump her body at the gate? Wouldn't that have been a better lesson? More his style?"

Virgil shrugged. "It's hard to know what The Man is thinking."

"Then *you'd* better do some thinking." The acid in Meteor's tone was undisguised. "How did she get here? Why is she here? What's she up to?"

Virgil went silent for a moment. "I— I trust her," he said simply. Then he added, "I'll be the first one to put a bullet into her brain if she turns out to be a traitor, okay?" His voice grew deeper. "Does that help, Meteor?"

Meteor's face darkened. "There's no way she got here by accident. She needs to be watched." He motioned towards Virgil. "By someone else. No offense, Virgil, but you are biased. Keep her in the bunkhouse."

Matthew stood silently for a moment. "He's right, Virgil. We don't know why she's here."

Virgil held up his hand. "I swear I'll keep an eye on her."

Matthew gave a curt nod. "Okay. For now." He looked down the row of seated men. "Any other business to discuss? Jonah? You're awfully quiet. You have anything to add to the meeting?"

Jonah looked up, but did not smile. Since Simon's death, he rarely smiled. The burying of his friend had been hard on him, and he tended to keep to himself. The evening's meeting was no different.

"No— Thanks. I've got nothing to say."

Trojan elbowed him. Jonah glared back.

"C'mon. Tell him." Trojan said.

Matthew waited.

"I'm leaving." Jonah said.

"What? When?" Matthew asked.

"Soon."

"Jonah, you're still sick. We're headed into winter. Where you gonna go?" Jonah shrugged. "Can we talk about this? Stay behind after the meeting." Matthew smiled encouragingly.

Jonah shrugged again.

ELIZABETH GRIMACED at a little boy playing next to her. Thick gloopy streams of green ran from the child's nose and down over his upper lip. She nearly retched when she saw him lick at the shiny goo.

"Oh, good God," she said. "Can't somebody wipe this kid's nose?" She looked around at the other women, mothers mostly, who were assembled in the home's massive front room. None of them moved to help.

Elizabeth made a face and pulled a terry cloth rag from her jeans. She waggled the cloth in front of the boy's face. "Here." When the boy ignored her, she waggled the cloth more vehemently. "Here!"

"You'll have to hold it for him," said one of the mothers, struggling to suppress a grin. Elizabeth shot her an evil look. "I'm just saying," the woman added.

Elizabeth made a face, reached down, and covered the boy's nose and mouth with the cloth. "Blow." Without stopping his play, the little boy blew into the cloth. Elizabeth shuddered at the burbling sound that came from his nose. "Here, you keep it," she said, pinching one corner of the rag between her thumb and forefinger. The boy ignored her.

"You'll have to wash it out," one of the mothers said.

"Like hell I will," Elizabeth said. "Where's his mother?"

"He doesn't have one. We take turns taking care of him. He doesn't talk much." Elizabeth stared at the boy as he continued to play with small hunks of wood and pieces of kindling. "He's three. We call him Duke." At that moment, the little boy looked up and smiled. His nose was running again.

"Oh, for heaven's sakes," Elizabeth exclaimed, reaching for his nose again. "Give it a good blow this time." The boy did as he was told. Elizabeth's eyes widened when the child clambered into her lap, snuggling his shoulder against her breasts, his head tucked under her chin.

The mothers giggled.

Elizabeth repositioned the little boy in her lap. "You've got a bony butt, kid."

THE MEN FILED out the door leaving Jonah and Matthew behind. Matthew pulled out the chair next to Jonah and sat down. "What's this all about, Jonah?"

"I'm tired."

"I understand that...but why leave now? So close to winter?"

Jonah fixed his eyes on Matthew. "Because there's nothing here for me."

"Nothing? Not even Martha. She loves you."

"I know that."

Matthew cocked his head. "I know you miss Simon, and I'm sorry for that, but are you missing someone else? One of the women?"

Jonah hung his head. "No." He sat silent for a moment. "One of the kids."

"The kids?"

"Yeah— My son."

Matthew drew back in surprise. "Your son? You have a son?"

"He's just tiny. He was born in August."

"I'm sorry, Jonah. What about his mother?"

"We aren't close anymore. But she was letting me spend time with him."

"What's his name?"

Jonah looked uncomfortable. "I asked her to call him *Josef*."

"That's a great name." Matthew smiled warmly. "If you've gotta go, then go. But we'll always be here for you." He placed a hand on Jonah's back.

Jonah hunched over and his shoulders began to shake. "He was my best friend, Matthew. My best friend." His sobs became louder. "It's not fair...it's not fair that he's dead."

"I know. I know."

Matthew sat next to Jonah and allowed his thoughts to stray to the day he had retrieved his own best friend's body. He had stopped by a creek on the side of the highway and had bathed Josef's bloodied body before taking it back to the compound. He had wept then. He remained silent now.

The door banged open and Matthew turned. The pony-tailed captain rushed in. "Matthew, I think we've finally got something." He noticed

Jonah, and noticed his distress. "Sorry, buddy. I—I didn't mean to interrupt."

"It's fine," Matthew said. He stood up and pulled the captain to the side. "What's up?"

"The cousins—the scouts— They say they've got a lead on somebody who might know something about the women. But that it might take several weeks to find him—"

"Where are they?"

"Eating in the men's bunkhouse."

"Let's go." With a quick glance back at Jonah, Matthew strode to the door.

RUTH BACKED against the far wall; she was tired, but she was prepared for a fight. The weeks spent imprisoned in the senior's home had impacted her usually calm and steady self. She was angry and she wanted out. She missed camp life, she missed her husband, and she missed her mother. The day-to-day drudgery had pushed her to an edge, and these days it took very little to set her off. She was ready to fight.

The women had been summoned before The Man. He had arrived in the middle of the night, surprising everyone, especially the women from Matthew's camp who had heard about him, but had never met him. Now a group of them stood crammed inside a large office awaiting his arrival.

A commotion outside the door, with men's voices raised in greeting, was followed by the entrance of a tall man. His jeans were grimy, but his belt buckle sparkled. His beard hung nearly to mid-chest, and his hair clung to his neck in limp, dirty hanks. The man paused just inside the room. He motioned toward the doorway.

"Ladies," he said. "Meet The Man."

Ruth and the other women stared as another man, even taller than the first man, entered. He paused, and his presence filled the room. No one spoke. He swept the room with cold, copper eyes from beneath heavy, dark eyebrows. Some of the women shrank back.

Ruth was surprised—*The Man was handsome.* She understood how Cammy could have been in a relationship with him. With his craggy features—curled, wiry silver and black hair, and his intense eyes, he resembled a rugged movie actor—the kind destined eternally for roles in Western movies—and not necessarily as the bad guy.

Ruth watched him like a mouse eyeing an owl. A path was cleared for him as he made his way to a large desk. A fat biker pulled out a leather desk chair and motioned for him to sit. The Man did so. He pushed at a few papers on his desk. Then he settled back in his chair. Finally, he spoke:

"So, show me," he said.

The women were herded before him like cattle. They were appraised. Comments were made—some kind, some not so kind, and some highly derogatory.

"Put a paper bag over that one's head in an emergency," laughed one of the men—a stocky man with a bushy beard, a completely bald head, and large, gold hoop earrings.

Several men laughed, but The Man ignored the comment and continued perusing the women. He made notes as the women were introduced by age and number of children. Finally, Ruth stood before him.

"We've saved the best for last," Brad said.

Ruth glanced over at Elizabeth who stood next to her, arms hanging at her side. Brad's hand was on the back of her neck. He gave her a little shove and she stumbled up to The Man.

"Who're these two?" The Man asked.

"Martha and Josef's brats," Brad responded.

"Really..." The Man smiled—an enigmatic curve to his lips that didn't exactly mirror internal humor. He settled back in his chair. "Same dispositions as their mother's?" He took a cigar from a wooden box on his desk.

"Not both— Just that one," Brad said, pointing at Ruth. "She always has a lot to say."

The Man regarded Ruth, flicking his eyes from the top of her head down to her laced, leather hiking boots, and then back again. He bit the end of the cigar and stuck it in his mouth. A young man in filthy oil-stained jeans dashed up, a disposable lighter in his hand. He lit the end of the cigar and waited until The Man waved him away.

"Does she have kids?" The Man asked.

"Yes... Two."

"Are they here?" He blew a thick cloud of smoke into the air.

"Yep."

"Get them." The Man watched the effect his words had upon Ruth. Her small gasp made him grin wider. "Bring them here."

"What—?" Ruth's mouth hung open in shock. "What do you want with my kids?"

The Man concerned himself with his papers.

"Answer me!" Ruth demanded.

A shocked silence gripped the room as the men and women waited for The Man's response to Ruth's outburst.

The Man did not answer, nor did he look up. Ruth sensed the danger, and she struggled to hold her tongue. As much as she ached to prod him into a confrontation, she had learned that silence was often its own reward in this inhospitable environment. She stared at him, but he continued to read, rhythmically puffing on his cigar as he turned pages.

Noises from outside the door merited The Man's attention, and he looked up. Samuel and Mary were being ushered into the room by three bearded bikers. Beards had become not so much the fashion by selection, but rather by laziness. Nearly all the men under The Man's leadership had beards or thick mustaches, and most were unkempt, making them look like they belonged in mountain caves. Ruth eyed the men as they herded her children through the doorway.

"Mom?" Samuel asked. He held Mary's hand. The little girl cowered near her older brother.

Ruth blanched. "What do you want with my kids?" Her voice trembled slightly, knowing she was on brittle ice.

Her shoulders tensed and her fists clenched as she watched The Man rise from his desk. He walked toward the children. He stooped down in front of Samuel and placed his hand on the boy's shoulder.

"Hi," he said.

"Don't talk to him," Ruth cried out.

The two children backed away at their mother's command, but they couldn't go far since their way was blocked by their bearded shepherds. The Man reached into the breast pocket of his blue, denim shirt and withdrew brightly wrapped toffees. He held out his hand.

"Do you like candy?" The children's eyes brightened. Candy was a rare treat. Ruth watched them struggle with their innocent desires as they glanced from their mother's face to the candy in The Man's hand. "Go on, it's okay," he said. "I like candy, too," He grabbed a piece, unwrapped the gold foil, and popped the toffee into his mouth. "Oh, so good."

He offered the candies again.

"No," Ruth said. "Don't."

Habit and a learned desire to please their mother kept the children's hands by their sides. They shook their heads.

"I have video games," The Man said. "Do you like playing video games?"

Samuel could no longer resist. "Yeah. Cool. Where are they?"

The Man smiled—the contented expression of a cat with a belly full of prey. "I'll show you." He held out his hand. "What's your name?"

"Samuel."

"And who is that?" The Man asked, motioning to Mary.

"My sister— Mary."

"Would she like to come, too?"

"No," Ruth cried out. "Leave my kids alone." Her voice vibrated with threatened tears.

The Man stood and faced Ruth. His unblinking eyes appraised her. Coldly. Critically. "Your kids?" He reached down and took Samuel's hand. "*My* kids now."

Ruth gritted her teeth as a chill shot through her belly. *He's going to take my kids.* She fought the gorge that rose in her throat.

"You can't take my kids."

"I can. And I have." The Man leaned forward. He tugged at his shirt and drew it aside, revealing a small, round, ragged scar. "See. You owe me." He sat back and adjusted his shirt. "Well, at least your mother owes me."

"My mother?" Then Ruth remembered... Martha had shot The Man during one of their skirmishes. "That's got nothing to do with me...or my kids!" The Man merely grinned.

Hatred bubbled up inside her—intoxicating and hot—roiling and twisting around her heart like a deadly viper—a hatred for everyone and everything that had brought her to this moment—those responsible for the power grid failing, the Crazies, Brad, The Man, and...her mother. Especially her mother. *Martha* was the reason they were at Matthew's camp in the first place. *She* was the reason her father was dead. *She* was the reason her children were now in The Man's hands.

Ruth wanted to scream, to launch herself at The Man, claw at him, hurt him, and pull her children into the safety of her arms. But she held herself in check, remembering that this man had ordered the execution of her father. She would be no good to her children if she were dead. A stony hardness like pack ice, slid across her heart. She pressed her fingernails into her palms, and steadied her breathing.

"Mommy?" Mary squeaked. The sound drew Ruth out of her black haze.

What awful things is he planning? Will he hurt them? Please, God...

As though reading her mind, The Man added, "Let's say I have a soft spot for Martha's grandkids. I will treat them as though they were my own." He motioned toward the doorway. "They'll have a good home with me." He reached to take Mary's hand, but she flinched away. He grabbed it, and she began to wail.

Ruth jumped forward, but one of the scruffy bikers stopped her.

"You be good," The Man said. "Do everything we tell you to do and you'll see them... From time to time." His words were accompanied by a tight, ominous grin. "Supervised visits... Every other Sunday."

The men guffawed at the joke. Ruth could only stare, tears spilling from her eyes.

God, please!

In an instant, a wave of comfort like thick down covered her spirit, and she knew—her children would be safe—at least for now. She forced a smile and gave a tiny wave. Samuel waved back. Mary, still crying, gave a single, confused backward glance over her shoulder as she disappeared around the corner.

Suddenly, Ruth shouted. "I expect you to be a man of your word." She waited, her heart thudding in her chest.

In a moment, The Man's face reappeared. "Earn your privileges," he said. He walked away.

Ruth's heart cracked in two. The hurt made her gasp for breath. She stared at the empty doorway.

I will not cry, she thought. *I will not cry in front of these people.*

Ruth forced her lips into a tight line as she looked over at Elizabeth. "C'mon," she said."

Elizabeth gave a small robot-like nod. She tried to pull away from Brad, but his hand still clutched her neck.

"Easy does it," he warned.

Under guard, the two women were ushered out of The Man's office. The bikers opened the doors leading to a community room, and gave both women a shove. Duke recognized Elizabeth and ran to her. He clutched her leg. At first, she didn't acknowledge the little boy. Then she bent and encircled his shoulders. She pulled the terry cloth rag out of her pocket.

"Blow your nose, little guy."

Ruth sank to her knees. Utter desolation arose in her soul. Misery cloaked her heart. Yet, at another more primal level, a new feeling grew—a power, a determination, and a strength. She trembled at its intensity. She stared at her hands, and clasped them together.

There's a way, she thought. *There's got to be a way.*

I'll find it.

By God—I'll find it.

Chapter Twelve

Eight Weeks Later

MEALS HAD become sparse affairs. The women noticed and they grumbled. The children objected, too. However, hunger has a way of softening the temperament of even the pickiest child. Soon, oatmeal flavored only with a little salt, and no sugar, became an anticipated feast. Any time of the day.

Protein was reserved for The Man and his men. The tantalizing scent of their meals regularly drew children. The captives were no longer confined to their rooms; they had the freedom to wander. So, during meal times, children hovered near the dining room entrance, their eyes wide, and their mouths open.

"What's up with the food supply?" Ruth asked. She was on kitchen duty, assisting a hefty woman who had been cooking since their arrival eight weeks ago. The woman was one of The Man's people, a loner—nobody's mother, nobody's grandmother—a no-nonsense woman with a gravelly voice. She was simply called, "Cook."

Cook smashed several cloves of garlic with the flat of the blade of a large chef's knife, pulled the papery shells away, and then chopped the garlic into tiny bits. Her pale, fleshy arms, thrust through the openings of a heavy gray shawl, quivered with the effort. The shawl was spattered with food and its fringes were soiled. Ruth frowned, wondering at the intelligence of working with open flames in a flapping shawl. Nevertheless, the woman was a wonderful cook, worked tirelessly from dawn to dusk, and never complained. Cook gave the pile of garlic one last whack and turned, knife pointed back over her shoulder.

"They say there're having problems with getting supplies to us. Snowstorms have blocked some of the roads, and no one wants to drive miles and miles by snowmobile just to get food to a bunch of women."

"I don't understand that," Ruth said. She peeled another potato and plopped it into a bowl filled with cold water. "We're valuable property to them—they've told us that over and over again. That's why they don't do us any real harm."

"I still have grains, rice, flour, oil, salt...but sugar, meat, dairy..." Cook shrugged her shoulders. "Got lots of potatoes. That's a blessing."

Ruth gave her a questioning look. "Meat? Why can't we have meat?" she scoffed. "I see deer in the front yard...every day." She turned her hands out, palms upward in emphasis. "Shoot 'em."

The woman grinned wryly. "Yeah. Sure. But I don't know how to handle meat that's not already butchered."

"No one here knows how to dress a deer?"

Cook shook her head. "I don't."

Ruth sighed. "Fine, I'll do it." A memory resurfaced. "Yes, yes..." she said under her breath.

Martha had insisted in the year leading up to the Change that her children learn to clean and butcher a wild animal. Ruth found the bloody, gory experience revolting. She had been angry with Martha for forcing the lesson on them, but now the lesson was going to come in handy—it would keep meat on their table; it might even keep them alive.

Ruth gazed out the kitchen window. She caught the flip of a short, furred tail as a doe leapt into the bushes. Three more toffee-colored animals sprinted after her. *Lots of meat*, she thought.

"Look at those little devils run. Steaks on the hoof," Ruth said.

Cook looked up briefly.

"As long as we have bullets, our larder will be full," Ruth said confidently. "Just gotta get The Man's lazy-ass men to shoot them."

"Ruth?" Elizabeth came into the room. She looked troubled.

"Hi. What's going on?"

"More of The Man's Crazies just showed up—it's an endless stream."

Ruth shrugged. "Winter should slow them down."

Elizabeth leaned over a table and rested her chin in one hand. "I wish they'd stop coming here."

"What? The new guys? They don't bother us."

"Well, maybe they don't bother you as much as they bother some of us," Elizabeth added icily. "Especially that damn Brad."

Ruth looked puzzled. She took her sister's arm and led her out of the kitchen. "What about Brad?"

"He's always cornering me. Sitting beside me. Touching me."

Ruth frowned. "So, use him...as your ticket out." It was said coldly, philosophically. "If he's that interested in you and he thinks you find him special, he might be your key to getting out of this damn place."

Elizabeth groaned. "I can't do it. I would puke on his shoes."

"Well, that's not the best way to turn a man's head, but who knows... this is a different world. Give it a try."

The two sisters looked at each and burst out laughing.

ANNA PUSHED the steaming teacup towards Martha. The two women were seated in Martha's cabin; outside the light was flat and gray. A few dogs barked. A couple of children laughed. The roar of quad engines reverberated in the distance.

"What's the date today?" Martha asked, idly. She put both hands around her teacup.

"It's mid November."

"How long have the girls been gone?"

"About eight weeks."

"And still no word..." Martha sighed loudly. "It's not fair. It's just not fair." She touched her chest. "I took a bullet... and for what? So that my daughters... my grandchildren... could be taken prisoner to someplace far away from me? Is that why I did it?" She slammed her hand down on the table. Tea sloshed out of her cup.

"Martha," Anna chided. "Stop." She reached out a hand and laid it atop Martha's hand. "You did all you could for us. You did the right thing. They're alive. We know that. And they're your daughters. They'll make it. I know they will." Tears filled her eyes. "Please stop being so hard on yourself."

Martha growled. "I wish I was dead."

"You don't mean that— You can't mean that. You don't know what might have happened to us if you hadn't come up with a plan to save us."

Martha went quiet. She blew on her tea and sipped carefully. She felt the grayness of the day slither in through the window and embed itself in her soul. Wilbert leapt onto her lap and she moved to push him off, but the little creature gripped her jeans in his claws. Martha gave in and began stroking him. His purr rumbled under her hand. The sound made memories of her beloved granddaughter return.

Where was Mary? What terrible things was she enduring? Because of me... Because I could have shot him... When I had the chance. She winced. *I could have shot him. I should have shot him.* Her hands clenched. *When I see that bastard again, I will shoot him.*

"I think I'm pregnant again," Anna said.

No response.

"Martha? Did you hear me?" Martha's eyes flickered up. "I think I'm pregnant." Anna beamed as she spoke the words.

"Whose is it?" It wasn't meant unkindly, but Simon had been dead for several weeks.

Anna ceased smiling, hurt by the blunt question. "Simon's." She blushed. "I was never with anyone else."

"Of course not—I knew that," Martha said gently. "I'm sorry for asking. I didn't mean anything by it. Stupid question."

"It's okay," Anna said hesitantly.

"When are you due?"

"Well, I haven't had a period since August. So...May, I guess."

"You guess? You've been a midwife for a year. And you guess?"

Anna looked stunned by the criticism. "I didn't mark my last period on the calendar," she added, her lower lip quivering.

"What's wrong with you? Haven't you learned anything? How can you be so stu—" Martha clapped her hand to her own mouth. Anna's crestfallen face stabbed her conscience. Heat flooded her face.

What did I say? To this girl? Of all people?

"Oh...I didn't mean that Anna. I'm sorry." She reached across the table and placed her hand on Anna's arm. "A summer baby. That'll be nice."

RUTH EMPTIED a large cast iron fry pan of bacon onto a platter. She looked around for one of the servers, but not seeing one, she wiped her hands on her apron and toted the platter into the dining room herself. Several tables were full of men who laughed as they crammed food into their mouths. A man at a far table beckoned to her, and she walked over. She could barely set the plate down before forks began stabbing at the crispy strips. She sneered at the men and looked across the room.

Samuel and Mary looked out of place, the only two children in the room, sitting next to The Man and two other men. Their plates were loaded with food. Samuel dug in, but Mary only picked at the food, pushing it around with her fork

They're getting fed better with him than with me, Ruth thought wistfully.

Mary looked up, saw Ruth, and her face broke into a wide smile.

"Mummy!" she cried, and leapt from her chair. The Man's arm swept out, caught her around the waist, and deposited her back into her chair. A warning look from him and Mary slumped down, arms folded resolutely across her chest.

Ruth did her best to smile as she called out, "Be a good girl, and eat your breakfast, Mary." She tapped her chest and held up her hand, two middle fingers bent toward her palm, her thumb, index, and pinky finger extended. Mary understood. Ruth had signed 'I love you' to her ever since she was a baby. She lifted a small hand and signed back.

The Man turned around and glowered at Ruth. "Don't you have work to do?" he called.

"What have I got to lose," she muttered and stalked over to the table.

"We need meat," she said. "The women and kids can't survive on porridge."

"And you're telling me this because..."

"There's deer all around us. Why isn't somebody killing deer?"

The Man stared for a moment before he spoke. "I'll look into it." He pushed his fork into a mound of scrambled eggs. "Can you butcher an animal?"

Ruth blinked. "What? You're trusting me with a gutting knife now?

The Man looked bemused as he pointed his fork in Mary's direction. Ruth caught his meaning.

"Of course, I can."

"Good." The Man put the eggs into his mouth.

"And?" Ruth waited, but The Man ignored her. She ruffled Samuel's hair, gave Mary's cheek a quick stroke, and walked away.

~ ~ ~

RUTH FLIPPED the page of the cookbook, studied the ingredients, and flipped the page again. Several cookbooks lay open on the rectangular table in front of her. Knitting magazines, how-to-bead books, books on baking, recipe books for quick casserole dishes, art books, expired Old Farmer's Almanacs, and poetry books lay strewn within her grasping range. She gave the books a sharp shove and put her head down on her arms.

"What's all this?" Elizabeth asked. Ruth looked up.

"I've gotta keep busy. Keep my mind off the kids. And the women need something to stimulate their brains. They're going stir-crazy. So, I'm going to set up classes. On everything..." She drew an arm across the books and magazines. "From cooking to painting. We're not locked into our rooms anymore. We might as well do things together."

"You got these out of the library?" Elizabeth pulled a craft magazine towards her, flipped a few pages, and lost interest. "You're becoming more and more like mom every day, ya know?"

"Don't remind me." Ruth heaved a long sigh. She glanced at her sister. "What do you want to teach?"

Elizabeth shrugged. "Nothing."

"Thanks for all your help."

"Just not interested."

"How about a class on survival skills... building fires, foraging, shelter building, plant identification—?"

"Nope."

Ruth sighed again. "Fine, have it your way."

"What is that supposed to mean? Just because I don't want to do things your way?"

"I'm just trying to do what's best for everybody. You included. It would be nice if you'd help me do that."

"See—just like mom."

"I'm not!" Ruth said hotly.

"You are. And I hate it." Elizabeth stood up. "Do what you want. Just leave me out of it." She stalked out of the kitchen.

Elizabeth went into the main lobby of the home's front entrance, and stopped at an upright piano set in a corner by a large stone fireplace. She pulled out the bench seat and flopped down. She opened the keyboard cover and slid it away. The keys were a mess—food debris and the sticky fingerprint smears belonging to dozens of unmonitored children marred the ivory surfaces. Elizabeth scowled.

She returned to the kitchen, got a rag, and washed down the keys. Satisfied, she sat down again, and began to play—a plinky, one-handed version of *Heart and Soul*. The sound was naïve, but it was music. The happy notes made her heart lift. And she smiled. She began to plunk with gusto. And to sing along.

"Heart and soul, I fell in love with you..."

She felt a presence beside her. She looked down. Duke placed a small hand on her thigh, and beamed up at her. "I want to pway."

"Where did you come from?" Elizabeth gathered the little boy into her lap, put her hand over his, took his tiny index finger between her own fingers, and began poking at the keys.

Several minutes passed before she noticed that others had joined them. She turned to see the faces of eager children. Their heads bobbed in unison, as one of the older boys asked, "Will you teach us to play?"

Elizabeth hesitated and then waved the children to her. She pulled music books and sheets from the bench seat. She found a folded keyboard chart with notes. She unfolded it and tucked it in behind the keys.

"This is *Middle C,"* she began. She struck the key.

Duke mimicked her action. He twisted his head and met her eyes.

"Good job," she said. She dropped a kiss on the top of his head.

He giggled and hit the note again.

~~~

THE DOOR to the cabin opened and Matthew stomped in. Snow fell from his boots, his shoulders, and his cap in soft mounds. Wilbert watched water trickle along the floorboards.

"God, I wish it would stop snowing. This is ridiculous. We can't keep the main road open." He smiled at the women staring back at him. "Hi."

"Hi, Matthew," Anna said. She picked up her teacup and placed it in the plastic tub on the counter. "I'll head out. I think Gordon will be awake now." She stopped by Martha, gave her a quick kiss, and then scooping her coat from a peg on the wall, she left.

Matthew stared at the closed door and then turned back to Martha. "I might have some good news," he said. His eyes were bright.

I love his face. Especially when he's smiling.

"What's up?" she asked. "I need some good news."

"The scouts just got back. They've figured out which direction the women and kids were taken."

"Really? Where are they?" She sat up straight, her face beaming with glad expectations. Matthew held up a hand.

"Hold on now. A contact in Red Deer told them that he heard about some yellow school buses heading down the QE II about the same time the girls went missing. Then another contact says he heard that Crazies were taking over some of the bigger senior care homes near Calgary, on both the north and south sides of the city. And filling them...with women... And kids."
~~~

"Matthew, how does that help us?" Martha said, her tone heavy with disappointment. "There must be hundreds of old folks' homes near Calgary."

"Ah, that's true, but there's only one called... *Sunnyvale.*"

"You have a name?" she asked in surprise. "How did you get a name?"

"A guy heard a guy talking about a fresh group of women being sent to a home called Sunnyvale."

She jumped up. "When...when do we go after them?"

"*We* do not go after them. *I* will go after them. *You* will stay here. Keep getting better."

"I'm well enough for a road trip, Matthew. It's not like we're going into battle."

"Arrrrgh, Martha... You drive me crazy. You aren't well enough."

"I am so."

"You aren't. And that's final."

Martha glared at him. "Fine."

Matthew wandered to the window. "They sure did a nice job on that new women's bunkhouse. It'll be good to fill it again." He turned and smiled. "We're leaving as soon as we can."

"I'm so glad. Want some supper?"

"Sounds good to me, missus."

Martha grimaced. "Missus?"

"I haven't used my last name in forever," Matthew said. He thought for a moment. "You'd be Mrs.—" Martha rose, came to him, and touched his cheek.

"I'd be Mrs. Gatekeeper."

Matthew reached for her, but Martha ducked under his hands. "Go sit down. I'll make you something to eat."

VIRGIL ROLLED over and gave Marion's butt a playful smack. She jumped.

"Ow. Why did you do that?" Virgil grinned.

"Going off with Matthew," he said.

"Why?"

"Gonna track down the missing women and kids."

"You have a lead on them?"

"Yep. They're being held in some old folks' home in southern Alberta."

"Really," Marion said. "How did you find this out?"

"Matthew—"

"How does Matthew know? The Man keeps those homes top secret."

Virgil rose up on one elbow. "Our scouts." He paused. "You know about the homes?"

"I've heard about them. Never actually saw one. Especially the ones down south."

Marion got up from their bed and pulled a thick, black bathrobe around her; it was one she had selected along with the rest of her new wardrobe from the storehouse. She opened a dresser drawer, searched around, and grabbed what she wanted. She crammed it into her pocket, and left the room.

"Where are you going?" Virgil called.

"To the outhouse. I'll be right back." The door screeched and banged on her exit.

Virgil turned over, punched his pillow into shape, and closed his eyes.

Outside, Marion checked around as she neared the outhouse. No one was in sight. The day's grayness had deepened into gloom. She pulled on the outhouse door and went inside. All the stalls were empty.

"Good," she whispered. She went back outside, looked around again, and then went behind the small, rectangular building. She reached into her pocket and pulled out a walkie-talkie. The reception would be poor, but the man she was trying to reach was only a few miles away. She had used the radio before, and it had worked then. She expected it would work just fine now. She clicked the *send* button a few times, and then waited.

"Yeah?" a male voice responded.

Marion spoke into the radio.

~~~

ANNA SHOVED open the door to the women's bunkhouse. Several women were playing cards at a small, collapsible, four-legged table. A handful of babies corralled in a makeshift playpen gurgled and swatted at building blocks, piling them up and knocking them down. Gordon was with them. He cooed at his mother. He clung to the edge of a small bench and pulled himself up on both feet. He let go, tottered, took a small step, and fell down.

Anna cried out. "Your first step!"

The other women turned as Gordon made another attempt. Another step, and he fell again. He got up and tried again. The smile on his face was
~~~

dwarfed only by his gargantuan attempt to walk. Anna rushed over. She stepped into the play area and held out her hands.

"C'mon. Come to Momma." This time Gordon took a little running start and managed three steps before crashing into his mother's arms. Anna swept him up, twirling in delight. "What a big boy. What a big boy."

Gordon beamed.

"Wait till Matthew sees," said a large girl seated near a window.

"Yes. But I wish Simon could have seen him walk." Anna hugged Gordon to her chest. "He will never see his child walk."

"*His* child?" The woman wrinkled her brow in confusion.

Anna patted her stomach.

"You're pregnant?"

Anna smiled her confirmation.

The door opened. A middle-aged woman walked in, shaking snow from a shawl she had had around her shoulders. She was shivering.

"I can't stand those outdoor toilets. Can't we rig up something more civilized for the winter? So we can be warm when we pee?"

"Ah, you'll get used to it," the girl at the window said. "We all do."

"That new chick doesn't seem to mind."

"What new chick?"

"The Man's chick—the one that Virgil is shacking up with."

"Marion?" Anna asked.

"Yeah, her," said the woman in the shawl. "She doesn't mind peeing outdoors. I just saw her. In her bathrobe. She mustn't like the smell in the outhouse, because she went in...came right back out...and then went behind the outhouse."

"Eww, in the snow?" the girl at the window said. "Did she have her radio with her?"

"Her radio?" Anna asked.

"Yeah. At least I think it's a walkie-talkie. It fell out of her coat pocket the other day."

Anna looked puzzled. "You must be mistaken. Why would she need a radio? Unless she was carrying it for Virgil."

"Why would she carry a radio for Virgil?" the large girl asked.

Anna set Gordon back into the playpen. "Watch him for me, okay?" She grabbed her coat and ran out the door.

MATTHEW PADDED to the door in his stocking feet. He turned the knob.

"Hi, Anna. What's up?" He showed her into the cabin.

"I'm not staying. I just wanted you to know that maybe you should be keeping an eye on Marion."

"Marion? Why?"

"One of the women thinks she has a radio."

"A radio?"

Martha came up behind Matthew. "You know what? That wouldn't surprise me at all. I don't trust her. Neither does Meteor."

Matthew thought for a moment. "We're leaving to find the women and kids soon."

"Really?" Anna interrupted. "That's wonderful."

Matthew turned to Martha. "Can the two of you keep an eye on her?"

"Is Virgil leaving with you, too?" Martha asked.

"Yeah. I was planning on taking him."

"We'll watch her," Martha said. "Maybe a shakedown of her cabin is in order."

"Be careful how you do it. If she's a plant and she's feeding information to The Man, she might be useful to us."

"Misinformation— Simon's specialty." Martha took a quick breath, and added, "Oh, I'm sorry, Anna. I didn't mean—"

"It's okay. He was good at that, wasn't he?" Anna said with a tiny grin. She patted her stomach. "Maybe he's passed on his deceptive abilities."

At first, Matthew didn't catch the nuance. "You're pregnant?" he asked.

Anna nodded.

Matthew caught her in a gentle all-encompassing hug. "Congratulations." He pulled back. "Gordon will have a brother."

"Or a sister," Anna said. She kissed them good night. Matthew closed the door.

"Meteor never trusted Marion," Martha said.

"I know," Matthew agreed. "He grilled Virgil at one of our meetings, but Virgil seems to think she's trustworthy."

"I'll watch her."

Matthew reached for Martha and pulled her into his arms. "So—?"

Martha extricated herself. "Um...no, Matthew." She walked to the table, sat down, and picked up a medical textbook. "I want to do some reading before I get too tired."

"Martha...it's been forever. I miss you."

She looked up, but she avoided direct eye contact. "I miss you, too."

Matthew took a long breath. "This can't go on." He shrugged his shoulders. "Either we are married, or we aren't." He sat across from her.

Martha shrugged in return. "I'm doing the best I can, Matthew. I still don't feel well enough." This time she looked into his eyes. "Please give me time," she pleaded. "Please understand."

"I just want to hold you." He reached across the table for her hand, but she withdrew it.

"I know you do. Just—not yet."

Matthew rose. "Well, at least a good night kiss then." He walked around to Martha and pulled her to her feet. He pulled her in close and tipped her head up. He touched her lips with his. Martha stood quietly, allowing the kiss to proceed. When she didn't kiss back, Matthew stopped. His look was puzzled. "It's just a kiss. You aren't ready to kiss yet, either? Martha—" he said with exasperation. "It's been weeks."

Martha put a hand on his chest and pushed at him. He didn't budge. She dropped her eyes so he couldn't see her confusion.

Rapid memories of the day in the Meeting House fired through her brain: Brad's voice in her ears, Brad inside her, Brad's scent around her, the pain, the blood, and...the shame.

She couldn't let him touch her. Let him be where Brad had been. No one would touch her that way. Not ever again.

She pushed at Matthew. "Sorry, I—I've got to sit down." This time, he stepped away. She didn't want to look up, couldn't look up. She didn't need to look up. She could feel the hurt coming from him. It broke her heart, but his hands on her, his lips on her lips had not had the desired effect. Instead, her stomach had rolled at his contact, and the feel of his rising maleness against her thigh made her panic. She fought against the desire to gasp for air, to run.

Matthew bent and took her hands in his. "I love you so much, Martha. I've never loved any woman more than I love you. Not ever. But you've got to let me in. Something else is bothering you." He squinted at her. "Tell me."

Martha stared down at their hands. She pulled her hands free, grasped his hands, and brought them to her lips. She gave each one a warm kiss. "There's nothing to tell." She gave Matthew a small smile. "Just love me, okay?"

"I will, Martha. I do. But I want to be needed by you. I need to be needed by you. Marriages fall apart when there's no communication. Talk to me."

"I am talking to you," Martha said, her voice rising in volume. "But you aren't listening. I need to be left alone. For a while. Okay? It's got nothing to do with you. It's me." She dropped her husband's hands and flopped back in her chair.

"Okay, I'll leave you alone. But I have needs, too. And one of those needs is to be with my wife." Matthew walked to the door, grabbed his coat from the hook, and pulled it on. He pulled his boots on, not bothering to lace them, and picked up his gloves, the same ones she'd gifted to him only a few short months before.

Martha's heart ached. She yearned to tell him, but a familiar voice nagged from the back of her brain.

He will despise you. He will never want to touch you again. You are damaged goods.

"Good night, Martha." Matthew closed the door behind him with a sharp bang.

"Good night, my love," she said softly.

Tears dribbled down her cheeks.

~ ~ ~

A Final Solution

THE MEN SHUFFLED around the office. The bikers looked out of place in the feminine space once occupied by the predominantly female staff responsible for the running of the Sunnyvale home. The Man had claimed the multi-cubicled room when he arrived. The windows were big and the room was bright. The men jostled each other, joking, and sharing stories. The Man's chair creaked as he swung around to face them. A cigar burned in his hand, its smoke twisting upward, and flattening out against the acoustic ceiling tiles. The room went silent.

"We haven't heard the last of the Gatekeeper," The Man said. "Got word that he knows where the women are—or thinks he does."

"How do you know?" asked a biker seated across from him. He was an older man with intelligent eyes. His thick paunch hung like a deflated waterbed over his leather belt, and a shiny, black vest hung loosely from his wide shoulders. His meaty knuckles were covered in wiry hairs and etched in tattoos. Machine grease embedded his ragged fingernails.

"Same way I know that Virgil caved—he surrendered," he growled. "My sister, Marion told us— Radio relay."

"Marion? I thought you dumped her?"

"Not exactly. I asked her to do me a favor. One of the boys dropped her near the Gatekeeper's camp—her and a radio, too."

"Oh— So, she's feeding you information from inside his camp." The Man nodded and the biker grunted. "So, what did she say?"

"That Matthew would be leaving soon— Heading our way."

"That's a long run. A lot of snow. Think he'll make it?"

The Man guffawed. "I doubt it. Too much interference." He stubbed out his cigar in a brass ashtray. "I'd be very surprised to see him here."

"But what if he does make it?"

"Bring in some more men from the South Camps."

"How many?"

"Two dozen should do it."

"They aren't gonna like that. Lots of them are settling in for the winter. They've got families now."

"I didn't ask if they were going to like it...I said— GET them."

"Sure. What about transportation? Bikes are packed away."

"Use the bigger trucks. Load up some of those new snowmobiles. Bring them, too."

"What about supplies? We're really low... Fuel. Propane. Cereal. Rice. Pasta. Sugar. Ass-wipes."

"A truckload oughta be enough."

The heavy biker gave The Man a quick puzzled glance before he spoke. "Don't go postal on me, okay?" He held out a placating hand. "But Brad and his boys brought in nearly two-hundred people, and you've got at least a dozen guys here now. We're bringing in twenty-four more, and you say a truckload of supplies will be enough?"

The Man lifted his eyes—a slow motion oozing with dark malice. The biker stood up and backed away. He gave his pants a quick hitch.

"Wait. Think about it. The men will eat the food...and the women and children will starve. Just protecting our investment. That's all I'm saying."

The Man eased back in his chair. He appraised the fat biker. "Then maybe you shouldn't be the first one at the dinner table...and the last one to leave it."

The men laughed.

The biker glanced down at his belly. "There's still too many people here. We don't have the supplies to carry them through the winter."

"So, what do you suggest?" The Man asked. The men stood mutely, looking from one to another, waiting for someone else to solve the dilemma. "Well?" The Man's voice rose with impatience.

Another biker spoke up. He was a handsome man, clean-shaven, but the layers of clothing he wore were grimy with road dirt and engine grease. Long, dark curls framed his face.

"We could eliminate the unnecessary ones. You know... like the boys... and the old bitches."

The Man looked up, his eyes bright with interest. "A final solution..." he mused, referring to Hitler's infamous plan for the genocide of the Jews. He raised his eyebrows. "Killing off superfluous grammas..." He chuckled. "Is that what this world has come to?" He glanced over at Samuel who was engrossed in a Nintendo video game. "And little boys?" He looked back at the men. "No— Little boys can be adopted. Leave the boys alone. But...as for the grammas... Do what you have to do."

A tall biker with heavy, dark eyebrows spoke up. He looked perplexed. "How do we decide which of the old women to get rid of?" His Adam's apple bobbed. "Like..." He took a breath. "Is there a cut-off age?"

The Man examined the tip of his cigar. "There's a psychological exercise called the Lifeboat. You heard of it?"

The men stared blankly, some grunted.

"Well, it goes something like this. A bunch of people are in the water, but the lifeboat holds only a limited number. So, based upon their merits, you must decide who gets into the boat. Who gets to live... Who has to die... Got it?"

The men blinked.

The Man gave a soft sigh. "Let me 'splain— Don't worry about their age. Ask yourself if they're valuable. You wouldn't want to kill an old doll who was a doctor, right? Just 'cause she's old..."

The Man sat back.

Some of the men still looked troubled by the problem. The handsome biker smiled and looked at Brad. Brad nodded.

"How soon?" Brad asked.

The Man met Brad's eyes. "I'll let you know."

Brad stepped forward. "So—while you're thinking about it, we'll just let the food run out?"

The Man rose from his chair. He picked up a revolver lying on the desk. He opened the cylinder. He snapped it shut. "I said—Brad—I'll let you know." The Man set the pistol back on the desk. "Is that clear?"

A moment passed. The other men stepped away from Brad, their eyes intent on the Man.

Brad's eyes narrowed. Then he grinned. "Yes, sir," he drawled. "Crystal."

Sheree Zielke

Chapter Thirteen

A Haunch of Deer and a Snowmobiler

RUTH GRIPPED the knife and contemplated the deer's long body suspended in front of her. She and Cook had managed to hoist it up, between two trees, on a makeshift gambrel fashioned out of a piece of rebar and rope, all the while swearing at the man who killed the deer. He had roared in with the body slung over the seat of his snowmobile. Following a quick explanation—it had run out in front of his machine and he figured it would make good eating—he sped off, refusing to help them lift the heavy body into position.

Ruth drew her arm across her forehead, wiping the sweat away. They were in a sheltered area behind the home, but the wind had picked up—she turned her face into the breeze, allowing it to blow through her hair, cooling her.

"Now what?" Cook asked.

Ruth found a hacksaw in a nearby toolshed, and sawed off the deer's legs, at the joints. Now, it was time for the skinning and gutting. She grabbed at the carcass, but it swung out of her grasp.

"Steady it, would you?" Cook stepped up and blocked the deer's sway. Ruth raised the blade and slit the hide. "Be careful in this area," she said. "If you cut the scent glands, it'll taint the meat." Cook nodded. "Give me the shoelace."

"What's it for?"

"Tying off the end of the intestine...the butthole," Ruth clarified. No poop gets on the meat when I pull out the guts."

"Eww."

Ruth continued to skin the deer, and give instructions as she proceeded. "It gets harder to pull back the skin when the deer gets cold," she said with a grunt as she gave a mighty tug on the hide. Before long, the deer had been skinned and its head removed.

"Be careful not to cut into the stomach. You've gotta pull up the skin and cut towards the hide. Protect the gut from your knife."

"Okay...I see," Cook said.

A few more slices with her knife and the deer's innards began to spill forward. Ruth pulled a small, white garbage bag over her hand and arm; she dug into the deer's body. She tugged and pulled, and grunted with the exertion. She stopped to cut surrounding membranes that were restraining the organs, and then she pulled again. Soon, a pile of entrails, the liver, heart, and the esophagus flopped to the ground.

Ruth stepped back. She staggered a bit and flexed her shoulder. "Whoa, that was hard work." She dropped the bloody bag to the ground and drew an arm across her forehead. She wore a man's flannel shirt, a blue down vest, and saggy blue jeans.

Shortly after arriving, the women had been directed to a large building near the seniors' home; she'd guessed it had been a garage. Clothing was everywhere—both men's and women's—some heaped on tables, some dumped into piles on the floor, and some still on hangers and hanging from clothing racks. Most women, except the heavier ones, found comfortable changes of clothing in their sizes, including underwear and socks. Fashion meant nothing, but that didn't stop many of the other women and teen girls from selecting skimpy dresses, tiny t-shirts, lacy bras, and form-hugging pants. Ruth had been practical, choosing only small size men's clothing. She'd found a warm parka, too. It now lay draped on a nearby white board fence.

"It'll be dark soon," Cook warned.

Ruth looked up from the deer carcass. The sun was sunk low into the horizon, a wide, dazzling half orb. Its fiery hues deepened and merged into hazy cloud layers across the horizon—fingers of bruised purples intermingled with jewel-bright orange light. A yellow snowmobile roared into the yard. A man in winter military fatigues killed the engine and jumped from the toboggan. Another three machines arrived. The men shut down their machines and joined the first man. They held a hurried conversation.

"Who are they?" Ruth asked.

"More of The Man's people," Cook said. "I haven't really gotten to know the guys that show up here. I cook for them...I clean for them...I do a few other things for them...but I barely know their names."

"Why do you stay?"

"Where am I gonna go?"

"But how can you stand it? They treat you like a slave."

Cook gave Ruth an earnest look. "The same way you're gonna stand it—if you want to survive. I've learned to lower my expectations. You will, too."

"What are they going to do with us? Do you know that?"

"Yes, I know." Cook looked sheepish. "The same thing they've done with many other women and children."

"What's that?"

"The Man is kind of like a..." She searched for the word. "...peddler...of women. He deals in women. They're a commodity—a valuable commodity—but a commodity just the same. And it's my job to make sure you are taken care of." She gave Ruth a small grin. "Makes me feel like the old witch in Hansel and Gretel—you know...the one who fattened the kids up so she could cook them in the oven."

"Nice analogy," Ruth said with a sour smile.

"Hey, you!" one of the men called out, motioning to them. "Put these machines into the hut."

"Can't you—" Ruth began. Cook stepped in front of her, cutting off her words.

"Yes— Right away," Cook called.

"We're busy," Ruth said in an angry whisper. "Can't they see we're butchering this deer?"

"Do you think they care?" Cook shot her a corrective look under raised eyebrows. "Let's go."

The women took one and then another of the snowmobiles into the hut. Both were familiar with power toboggans, and quickly had them neatly parked inside.

Ruth had not been in the Quonset hut before; she stopped to look around. Motorcycles parked for the winter sat under heavy plastic; machine parts, assorted tools, shiny silver pipes, rubber belts, thick suspension springs, studded tracks, crankshafts, and metal funnels lay scattered across long, narrow plywood tables resting on sawhorses; wooden shelves bowed under the weight of fuel cans; oil cans sat pyramided on the ground near the fuel. Snowmobiles were parked in neat orderly rows, row upon row of machines, in all sizes and colors; green

Arctic Cats stared forward—their headlights made them look like comic book villains. A memory of Peter learning to ride a Cat came to her...

He had throttled up, causing the machine to buck, and had wound up on his back in the snow. He lay like a snow slug, until she came and helped him up. The mental image made her heart ache, and a tear found its way to the corner of her eye. She swiped it away.

Another area of the hut was filled with outdoor clothing, helmets, snowmobile boots, and outdoor camping equipment. Ruth let out a low whistle. "Our guys would kill for this stuff."

Cook huffed. "The men here...already have."

Ruth cast a sidelong glance and walked toward the end of the hut.

"What're you doing?" Cook asked.

"I want to look around...see what they have—"

"Better not," Cook said. "If you get caught..."

Ruth guessed at the unspoken consequences and turned around. "We'd better finish that deer. Or the meat'll be too cold to cut up."

The women left the hut and closed the double doors. There were no locks—keyed, combination, or otherwise. Ruth made a mental note.

Dusk had fallen and the light was very low. The carcass had become almost unrecognizable in the deepening shadows. Cook gathered up the knives. The women cut the carcass down. With each grabbing a hind leg, they hauled the deer around to the kitchen door. They wrestled it through the doorway and hoisted it onto a long stainless steel preparation table.

METEOR LEANED over the truck's engine, banging, and cursing at something Martha couldn't see. She waited for him to finish. When he looked up, he smiled.

"Hi, sweetheart. How are you?"

"I'm fine," she said.

He wiped his hands on a rag and then blew into them. "Freezing," he said. Martha stepped forward. She took off her gloves and held his hands in her own. She gave them a brisk rub.

"How's that? Better?"

"No, they're still pretty cold," Meteor said, a grin twisting at the corners of his mouth.

Martha laughed. "You're bad."

"We're both bad," he said, with a wink.

Martha blushed. She looked away.

"Do you have time to talk?" she asked.

"Sure. I'm finished. It's getting too dark to see anyway. Where should we talk?"

"I don't want anybody overhearing us."

Meteor took her by the arm and led her out of the parking lot. They stopped behind the Gatehouse.

"Is here okay?" Martha glanced around and nodded. "What's up?" he asked.

"I think I'm going crazy. I'm not sleeping very well. I can't stop dreaming about the rape. I feel so guilty about not shooting Brad. I miss my girls...my grandkids." She leaned into his chest as she spoke, resting her forehead against him. He wrapped her in his arms and kissed the top of her head.

"You're not crazy. I think you're suffering from P.T.S.D."

"What?" She pulled away and looked up at him. He still held her in his arms.

"Post-traumatic stress disorder. You keep reliving that night. You're stuck. You can't move forward."

"Oh, sure. I guess that's it." She leaned against his chest again. "Matthew's making it worse."

"You love him, right?" Meteor asked—tentatively, softly.

"I love him so much."

"Then you've got to tell him. It's not right not to tell him."

"But he'll hate me."

"No, he won't." Meteor tilted her chin up, so he could look into her eyes. "Look at me. I don't hate you. And I know all about it." He paused. "Martha...I—"

"But I can't tell him. I just can't. The words won't come out of my mouth. I panic every time I think about telling him." She began to cry.

"You're worried that maybe he won't find you desirable anymore? Is that it?"

"Oh, Meteor, it's not just that. It's way more than that. I'm ashamed. Embarrassed." She swiped at her eyes.

"By what?"

"Remember the day we met?" Meteor nodded. "Well, I drove Matthew home. He called me a soldier. I was so proud of myself. A soldier, that's what he said." She covered her face with her hands. "So ashamed. What'll he think of me? Weak? Stupid? And worse, a victim." She looked up. "I can't have him looking at me like a victim, Meteor. He can't love me if I'm not strong. No one can love me if I'm not strong. Can't you see that?"

Her frenzy became volcanic; her words spewed out in a rush—like exploding lava. "And what if he thinks I did something to encourage Brad to do that to me? What if he thinks that?" she said, her voice cracked by another sob.

Meteor pulled her close again. He buried his lips in her hair. "Oh, Martha..." he murmured. "You've got it all wrong. He won't think those things."

Martha whipped her head up. "How do you know? How can you be so sure?"

"Because I'd never think those things," he said, smiling down at her. "Tell him."

"I can't!" She began to cry again.

Meteor held her, cradled close to his chest, his arms enfolding her like a great, winged bird. They stayed that way until Martha stopped crying. She pulled back and wiped her eyes.

"I think I feel better." She grinned. "As bad as you are, you are always so good for me."

"I know I am," he said with another warm smile.

Martha missed the shadow that passed over his face. She raised herself on her tiptoes and kissed him—a light kiss on the lips. "Thank you."

"Do you want to talk about...what happened to you?"

"No."

"Well, if you ever do...I'm here—"

"I know that."

Meteor reached out, running his fingers down her cheek. She pressed her face into his hand. "Any time, sweetheart. Any time." He dropped his arms to his side. "You better get going."

Martha gave his hand a departing squeeze and headed across the compound. Meteor gazed after her.

Another man stood in the shadows, watching. His hands were balled into fists. He began to walk toward Meteor, but stopped. He strode off in the other direction, his fists still clenched.

RUTH ROTATED her head trying to work out the kinks in her neck. She stretched her arms backward and arched her back. She rolled her sleeves, gave her head one last rotation, and picked up the large butcher knife. She was tired, but the meat had to be butchered.

"Let's do this."

Ruth grabbed the deer and twisted it into a better position. Cook stood near her, curiosity lighting her eyes.

"Start with the haunch," Ruth said, inserting a blade into the pink meat. "Cut into the pelvis—like this—and cut around the socket. Stay close to the bone."

"Who taught this to you?"

"Um...my mom, sort of. She hired some trapper-hunter guy to take us out and teach us."

"You've got a good memory."

"Nah, I saw our guys butcher animals on our compound, too. I just never had to do the cutting." Ruth continued to remove the legs and then the shoulders. "Yuck," she said. "Grab an old tea towel or something and wipe these hairs away. We don't want them in the meat."

Ruth continued cutting and pulling the meat away from the rib cage and the backbone. "I'm not so good at this part," she said. "And I'm not sure what all the parts are called, but I know how to get almost all the meat from the bones."

"You're doing great," Cook said with an encouraging smile. "That's a lot of meat."

"Venison," Ruth corrected. She finished her final cut and straightened, hands and blade bloodied. "Where should we store this?"

"Outside?"

"I don't think so. That'll attract predators. The wild dogs back home are a real problem. I suspect they are here, too. And if not them, then the coyotes. And the wolves." She shook her head. "Nope, not outside."

"How about if we make our own deep freeze?"

"That sounds like a plan. What did you have in mind?"

"Let's pull the electric freezer outside, line it with hard snow, and then pack snow all around it. The animals can't get in with the lid closed tightly."

"That could work," Ruth said brightly. She gave Cook a small pat on her back. "Let's get some help."

After recruiting a couple of women, the deer meat, except for one haunch, had been swaddled in a layer of plastic wrap and tin foil, and was now nested in the made-over freezer.

"Can we go now?" one of the women whined.

"Sure," Cook said. She and Ruth exchanged smiles. "What babies."

"You know what?" Ruth said. "I forgot about the intestines, and the rest of the garbage. I'm going to have to get rid of it."

"It's too dark."

"I'll take a lamp."

"You'll need help. And I can't go—I've got to start cooking."

“I’ll be fine,” Ruth said. “I left my coat out there— I have to go get it anyway.” Ruth washed her hands. She took an oil lantern from a cupboard and lit it. She left the kitchen.

Her boots squeaked along the hard-trodden, snowy pathway leading to the yard, her lantern swinging at her side. She was glad of it, since the night without yard lights was black. She suppressed a shriek when she heard a voice behind her.

“What are you doing out here?” a man’s voice asked.

Ruth jumped and turned around. “I—I gutted a deer. I’m cleaning up the entrails.” Ruth held up her lantern and peered ahead, trying to identify the speaker.

A man came forward; he was one of the men who had arrived earlier by snowmobile. He was lanky and was dressed in hunter garb, complete with a camouflage jacket and cap.

“I didn’t know you women knew how to dress game.”

Ruth shrugged. “Not all of us do— Just me.”

The man gazed at her as though weighing her potential. “Where you from?”

“Edmonton.”

“You part of the latest shipment?”

“Shipment? We aren’t cows,” she said indignantly.

The man gave a short laugh. “Yeah, well, kinda...you are.”

“If you mean am I one of the women and children kidnapped from our home near Edmonton a couple of months ago, then yes...I am part of the latest shipment. Are you happy now?”

“Don’t get snippy with me.” The man moved in. Ruth took a step backwards.

She could make out his face. Thick blond hair, with a slight curl, a clean-shaven face—that surprised her—a square jaw, high cheekbones, and oval brown eyes, with thick dark eyelashes.

“Let me give you some advice...” The man took a slow breath and spoke gently. “If you want to survive, you’ll have to be careful how you talk to the men around here. I’m different, a little more indulgent, but if you talk like that to some of the men here—”

“I know,” Ruth said angrily. “I know.”

“Well good then, just so you know.” He surveyed the mess on the ground. “Can I help you?”

“Uh, yeah.” Ruth drew her eyebrows together in surprise. “Thanks.”

He examined the rebar and rope contraption. “You want a real gambrel?”

"Yes, I do."

"I'll get one for you."

Fifteen minutes later, the deer's head, hide, and innards had been loaded on a makeshift sledge created out of a large piece of cardboard they had found near the trash bins. They wrestled with the load and dragged it out of the yard and down the hill, about five hundred yards away from the home.

"We can leave it here," the man said. "I think it's far enough away."

Ruth agreed. She waited for the man to pull the cardboard another few yards into a shallow ditch. He gave the cardboard another nudge with his foot, and then he joined her. They walked up the road, the lantern lighting their way.

"What's your name?"

"Ruth— Yours?"

"Mervyn."

"Oh."

"Oh?"

"Nothing. It's just that you don't look like a Mervyn."

"What name do I look like?"

"Um... like a Todd or a Steve or a Damien."

"Damien? You mean like the devil kid in the *Omen* movie?"

"No— I didn't mean that."

"Maybe my second name will be better. How do you like Orville?"

Ruth snickered. "Let's stick with Mervyn."

"Kidding— It's actually Benjamin."

"Ben...Benny. That's better."

"No— It's Benjamin."

After a few moments of silence, the man spoke again. "You know I have the right to pick any woman I want from your group."

"Wow...goodie for you."

"Look, I'm trying to be nice to you."

Ruth rolled her eyes. "By telling me that?"

"It's like this— I can choose you...make you my old lady."

"No, thanks. I'm married."

"You didn't let me finish. Doesn't matter if you're married. No one cares. If I choose you...it'll keep you from being passed around."

"I haven't been passed around yet. I'm not worried about it."

"You really aren't getting this, are you?" They reached the front door. He grasped the handle and pulled. Ruth walked into the home. He followed Ruth through the door. "I'll let you think about it."

"Thanks, *Mervyn*."

"I thought we'd agreed on Benjamin?"

"Bye."

Ruth strode away.

MATTHEW TWIRLED the noodles on his plate. The scent of cheese impregnated with garlic filled the kitchen. He lifted a forkful twisted with the pale pasta. He chewed without looking up.

"Why so quiet?" Martha asked.

"Sauce is delicious," he replied, his tone low and clipped.

"The Hutterites have been going out of their way to thank us. Fresh egg noodles, cheese, cream— I hope their generosity never runs out."

"They're good people...and they never lost a single soul to The Man. So, they're grateful."

They continued to eat without speaking.

Finally, Matthew tossed his fork onto his plate. Martha jumped as it clattered. He shoved his plate away and straightened in his chair. His expression was serious.

"It's time," he said.

"Time? For what?"

"For you to tell me what's going on. It's been weeks. Why can't I sleep here? With you? In *our* bed?"

Panic rose like a tidal wave. "Nothing is wrong. I—" Martha studied her plate.

"Bullshit, Martha. That's bullshit." Matthew slammed his palm to the table, making Martha jump. "Tell me what's going on."

Martha's head snapped up at Matthew's next words.

"Is it Meteor? Because he saved you? Is that it? You're in love with Meteor. You don't want me anymore."

"Oh, no! No, Matthew." She shook her head vigorously. "That's not it at all."

"You sure? It happened when you were married to Josef."

Martha's face flamed red and she sputtered. "How can you say that? How dare you say that? I've never been unfaithful to you. Not for a moment." Tears spilled from her eyes.

"I can't kiss you...I can't hold you, but Meteor can?" He glared at her. Martha's eyes were wide. "I saw you with him. Is there something you want to tell me?"

"Oh, no," Martha cried. "No, Matthew. I—uh—it's just that he—"

"He what? He was there when I wasn't?"

"No, Matthew. No. Please believe me. I love you so much. Meteor has nothing to do with this. Please believe me," she begged. "Please..."

Matthew's stare was unforgiving. "Unless you tell me what's going on, that's what I'm going to believe."

Martha gripped the edge of the table. The battle for her mind began again as it had so many times over the past weeks.

Tell him. Tell him. You can't tell him. He won't ever want to touch you again. He'll HATE you.

Matthew's chair squeaked along the floor as he rose. Martha thought he was coming to her, to comfort her. Her heart froze when she realized he was getting dressed instead. The slamming door sent a shudder through her soul. Her misery was complete.

Anna was right. Brad wins.

Martha raised her tear-streaked face upwards. She clasped her arms around her and drew her knees up to her chest. She rocked.

"Oh God...Why did you do this to me? Why? Isn't this damn life cruel enough? Why?" She cried out to the ceiling, her voice raspy and her throat swollen with emotion.

Her fingers grazed over the healed bullet wound.

I took this...and for what? My girls are gone. Mary's gone. My husband hates me. Why didn't You let me shoot him? Why?

She banged the table with her fist. "I hate You, God. I hate You. You did this. And now I'm supposed to clean up the mess."

The heat of her anger impeded the flow of tears. She looked around for a tissue. Instead, she grabbed a tea towel, swabbed at her face, and then blew her nose.

I can't do this anymore. Time for me to go. I want to be dead. I'll find Brad. He can finish the job.

Or... I'll finish Brad.

The venomous thought roared through her. With it came a headiness, a touch of the old wildness, a shadow of her former self...Martha, the *victor*...not Martha, the *victim*. She sucked in its intoxicating energy and allowed the viscous, black hatred to bubble up inside her. A vision of a dead biker with a bullet hole in his temple came to her. Only this time the face was *Brad's*. She shivered with the intensity of her hot desire.

Next time, you bastard. Next time.

She blew her nose again. As she dropped the towel to the table, a familiar sight caught her eye: Josef's Bible. It was in its usual place on the kitchen table. She reached for it, and swiped at the dust on the cover. She gave her eyes another wipe. She flipped the book open and stared down at the pages.

Bible Bingo, she thought. *Josef would laugh. Go ahead, God...talk to me. TALK to me.*

Her fingers landed on Psalm 39: 12-13. Her breath caught in her throat and her tears started anew as she read the words:

Hear my prayer, O Lord!
Listen to my cries for help
Don't ignore my tears.
For I am your guest—
A traveler passing through,
As my ancestors were before me.
Spare me so I can smile again,
Before I am gone and exist no more.

METEOR WATCHED Matthew stride across the compound. He recognized the gait—he'd seen it before; the man was angry. Matthew reached his cabin, yanked the door open, and slammed it shut. Meteor followed.

"Matthew?" Meteor called. He banged on the door. When Matthew didn't answer, he turned the handle and entered the cabin. Matthew was seated at his kitchen table, head in hands. He looked up.

"What do you want?" he growled.

"You okay?"

"Leave me alone, Meteor," he warned. "I am not in a good mood."

Meteor strode in and pulled out a chair. "Want to talk about it?"

Matthew looked up. "I've had it with her. She won't talk to me. She won't let me sleep with her. I've had it."

"But she's still—"

Matthew cut him off. "Don't *you* give me that bullshit, too, Meteor." The dark light in Matthew's eyes forced Meteor back in his chair.

"I—"

"Do you think I'm an idiot?"

"What?"

"She doesn't love me anymore. She loves *you*!"

"No, I—"

"Oh, shut-up. She's never gotten over you. Now you're her big hero."

"You've got it wrong, Matthew."

"Bullshit!" Matthew slammed his fist to the table. "I SAW the two of you together."

Meteor jumped up. His chair clattered backwards. "Whoa—Matthew, it's not—" Matthew cut him off.

"Go. Have her. She's yours. You saved her. I screwed up. I wasn't there."

Meteor stared, open-mouthed. Matthew continued his rant.

"I'm done. Our marriage is over."

Meteor stood silently as daring thoughts flitted through his mind. *You're done? I can have her? She's mine?* A tiny hope flared in his heart. Then, the memory of two people lying on cots, their hands clasped in sleep, rushed forward. The flame of hope went out.

"Listen, buddy…it's not what you think."

"Go! Get the hell out of here."

"Matthew…dammit! It's not me—" Meteor took a quick breath. "It's…Brad."

Matthew's eyes widened. "Brad? What the fuck does that asshole have to do with this?"

Meteor struggled for the words. "She should be the one to tell—"

"Tell what? Goddammit! Tell…me…what?"

Matthew was standing, his face dark with rage. His hands were clenched and raised. His breathing was rapid.

"Whoa," Meteor said. "Calm down." He motioned to the chair. "Sit down."

Matthew's didn't sit.

"We couldn't tell you."

"*We*? Who's we?" Matthew's anger reached a fever pitch. He shouted again. "My wife? My friend? Secrets? Who exactly is she married to?"

"I can't tell you."

"Can't? Or won't?"

In an instant, Matthew struck out, catching Meteor on the side of the face. Meteor staggered back. He put his hand to his jaw.

"Stop!"

Matthew came at him again. "I'm done with secrets. Done. You understand me? You lied to me."

"I didn't!"

Meteor sidestepped the next blow. He waited for an opening. He saw it. He grappled Matthew and tried holding the big man's arms at his sides. But Matthew's anger was supercharged with hurt and guilt. He wrenched one arm free. He swung again. This time, his fist caught Meteor on the side of his eye. The skin split and blood ran down Meteor's face.

"Stop!" Meteor cried out again. He swiped at the blood and ducked Matthew's next blow.

Matthew's fist went wild and he stumbled forward. Meteor grabbed Matthew again, but this time he pulled him to the ground. Matthew struggled wildly, kicking and punching, but Meteor leg-locked him and held him tightly in a clinch. Blood dribbled into his mouth, but he hung on.

"Stop, Matthew." Meteor tightened his grip. "Stop."

"Get off me!" Matthew roared. He kicked out and tried to pull free.

Meteor tightened his hold again. "Matthew—"

"Josef could stand her bullshit. I can't. I quit...I quit. I'm done."

Matthew tried to free himself again. He struggled until he was exhausted. He lay still, sucking in great gulps of air.

A quiet descended over the room.

A mental debate raged as Meteor weighed the consequences of his actions. *His silence would mean the end of Matthew's marriage.* He sighed inwardly. He couldn't let things go on like this any longer. He had the power to change things. He had to break Martha's confidence.

"Brad raped her," he said softly.

Matthew lay still. Panting.

"Did you hear what I said?" Meteor asked.

"Let me go." Matthew's voice was flat.

"You won't try to hit me again?"

"Let go."

Meteor slowly released his grip. He eyed Matthew as the man got to his feet. "Did you hear me—?"

Matthew held up a hand. "I heard you," he said, slowly descending into a chair. He closed his eyes and dropped his head into his hands. "I had no idea..."

"You couldn't have known."

"I should have guessed." Matthew opened his eyes and stared at his friend. "Oh, God...I just said awful things to her."

"She'll forgive you," Meteor said quickly. "She loves you."

"I thought you and she—"

"No—" Meteor shook his head. Blood trickled down his face.

"You're bleeding."

Meteor clambered to his knees, holding his head, blood streaming through his fingers.

"I'm sorry," Matthew said, his voice a dull monotone. He reached for a towel and handed it to Meteor. Meteor took it and pressed it to his face.

"Am I going to need stitches?"

Matthew looked at his own clothing spattered in Meteor's blood. "I think so."

Meteor picked up his toppled chair, and sat down.

Matthew dropped his eyes to the floor. "That explains everything...why she didn't want me to touch her." Meteor nodded. "But why wouldn't she tell me?" Meteor leaned forward.

"Think about it, Matthew." Matthew looked up. "She thought you'd blame her."

"What—? Why? Why would I blame her?"

"She feels like she let you down."

Matthew moaned. He clamped his hand to his forehead, and closed his eyes against the words. "Let me down? Oh, Martha... "

They stayed silent for a moment. Then Matthew took his hand from his face, and stared into Meteor's eyes. "I need to know—tell me everything."

"I'm really bleeding here, Matthew."

Matthew left the cabin. He returned with a plastic bag filled with snow. "Here."

Meteor grunted. He pushed the bag against his cut. "Think I'm gonna need Anna."

"I'll get her."

~~~

ANNA FINISHED the stitching. She cleaned her tools with alcohol and returned them to her pouch.

"So," she said, stepping back from the two men. "Is someone going to tell me what's going on?"

Matthew glanced up at Meteor, but neither man spoke.

"It's about Martha, isn't it?" Anna waited. Then it dawned on her. "Oh no— You told him, didn't you?"

"You knew, too?" Matthew said with indignant surprise. And then, "Of course, you knew..."

"Martha wanted to tell you herself. She made us promise." Anna knew it wasn't exactly the truth—that it had been Meteor who had made her promise, initially.

"I don't understand," Matthew said. "Why didn't she want me to know?"

Anna spoke gently. "She couldn't... Try to imagine being a woman and having all those guys do that to you. It made her feel *dirty*, Matthew."
~~~

Meteor looked stricken by Anna's revelation.

Matthew's eyes widened. "*All* those guys?"

Anna took a step back. "Oh...."

It took several minutes, but Matthew finally had the whole story, at least as much as Meteor and Anna knew. "They hurt her so badly," Anna told him. "I couldn't figure out why her fever was so high...and how she got one so fast. Her chest wound didn't seem infected, but she was obviously fighting an infection. I checked her out and that's when I knew—"

"Knew what?"

"She was all ripped up, Matthew. Worse than I've ever seen. Even at the most complicated birth."

Matthew said nothing as he digested the information. "Is she healed now?"

"Yeah, but she's scarred. And I'm not sure about permanent internal damage. There's no way for me to know." Anna paused. "I think she might be afraid to find out." She paused again. "And then there're the mental scars—"

"Damn— I was mean to her tonight." Matthew pushed back his chair and stood up. He reached a hand towards Meteor. "I'm really sorry."

Meteor took his hand and shook it. He pulled Matthew to him. The two bear-hugged and clapped one another's backs.

Anna smiled as she watched the two men affirm their affection for one another. Meteor pulled away.

"Listen, Matthew. It's more than that. She's deathly afraid of how you'll look at her. That you'll lose respect for her. See her as weak. Stupid. As a victim. Not a peer anymore."

Matthew shook his head. "I promise you that's not going to happen. There's nobody I respect more than her."

"Then tell her." Meteor sat down. He touched his fingers to his newly stitched wound. "Thanks, Anna." He chuckled. "You sure are getting good with that needle."

Anna smiled again. "I gotta go."

Matthew walked her to the door. He glanced back at Meteor and gave him a warm smile. "Stay here," he said. "I won't need this cabin anymore."

Meteor nodded. "Please don't tell her I told you."

"I won't. I won't say anything. I'll wait for her to tell me."

Matthew strode across the compound.

To Martha's cabin.

To his wife's cabin.
To *his* cabin.

Sheree Zielke

Chapter Fourteen

A Snowstorm and a Soldier

MARTHA JOLTED up in her bed. The sound of her name being called had awoken her. Matthew strode into the room. He still wore his heavy jacket.

"Martha," he said. "I've decided." He pulled a chair next to the bed and sat down.

"What have you decided?" she asked slowly, suspiciously. She stiffened and squeezed back against the headboard. She pushed her hair back from her eyes and waited.

"I want to sleep here with you. No pressures. Just sleep here with you. I want to wake up with you. Can we do that?" He looked hopeful. "Just that?"

"You aren't still mad at me?"

"No." He smiled and took her hand. "Not even a little bit."

Martha's shoulders relaxed and she allowed him to keep holding her hand. "What about me and Meteor?"

"I'm sorry about that," he said quickly. "I never really thought that in the first place."

She eyed him. "So, what's changed?"

He held her eyes with his. "Me— I've changed."

"Really? How did that happen?"

"I talked to Meteor."

"You talked to Meteor?" Panic crept up inside her and she withdrew her hand from his.

"We had a fight. I sort of...hit him."

Martha looked shocked. "You hit him? Are you crazy? He's the most loyal friend you have."

"I know. I know. I made a mistake. But it's good now."

"So, besides hitting him...what did you talk about?"

"About you. About how you're feeling. About the pressures you're under with the girls gone."

"Oh," Martha said flatly. "What else did you talk about?"

"Nothing," he lied. "I just want you to know that I'll be here for you. No pressures," he repeated.

"Is Meteor okay?"

"He's fine," Matthew said flippantly. "Anna stitched him up."

"He needed stitches?" Martha grimaced. "Oh, Matthew!"

Matthew lifted his hands in a helpless gesture. "What can I say?" He shot her a small, rueful grin. "I want my wife." He reached for her hand again. "Truce?"

Martha smiled and pulled back the covers. Matthew dropped his coat, kicked off his boots, and slid under the blankets.

"No rolling on top of me," Martha said, her tone severe.

Matthew slipped an arm under her pillow. "No rolling. I promise."

Martha lay back against his arm, tense and uncomfortable. She waited for him to fall asleep before gently pushing his arm back against his side. She clutched her pillow to her, and stared into the darkness.

She slipped into an uneasy slumber filled with wild dreams.

~ ~ ~

THE MORNING light was flat and gray. Martha stood at their bedroom window with a flannel blanket clutched around her. She watched snowflakes fall—a steady, lacy curtain of white.

Softly. Silently. Deadly.

With the fall of each flake, she knew she was being pushed further away from her daughters, her grandchildren.

How long before she'd see her family again? Weeks? Months? Next summer? Would she ever see them again?

A heavy, curled lip of snow slipped from the roof and splatted to the ground. It shook Martha out of her reverie. She gazed out at the sea of white, at the dark shapes of men shoveling in vain as snow quickly filled the hollows they had dug, and she sighed.

Peter would have been there. Simon would have been there. Ruth would have been there, too. If only I had...

Martha shivered and pulled the blanket tighter around her. Her mind wandered again.

Once more, she was staring into Brad's moonlit face—dark blood shadowed his mouth and nose. Martha remembered the gun in her hand—she remembered the feel of the trigger beneath her finger—she remembered the exhilaration that rose up inside her at the thought that she was about to kill her abuser...her rapist...the man who had killed Josef.

She toyed with the memory, rolling the scene around like a cat with a toy ball. Poking at it. Replaying it. Then came the words—the words she had heard that night—the words that stopped her from firing her gun:

Thou shall not kill, Martha.

The words echoed inside her head, inside her heart.

Why, God? Why? If I had shot him...if only I had shot him...they'd be here. Out there. Shoveling. Why?

Hot anger flared inside her, only to be doused by a suffocating cloud of condemnation—noxious and insidious—as it settled over her soul. Her shoulders sagged under its weight and tears burned hot in her eyes. Her thoughts flitted back to Mary and Samuel.

"Please," she whispered, "Please let them be okay. Please."

Martha saw more men join the snow-clearing crew. One of them was Meteor. She watched the big man heft snow high over his head. Wave upon wave of snow flew into the air.

Like a human snowblower, she thought.

Bend. Lift. Throw.

Meteor. How different my life might have been...

Bend. Lift. Throw.

He's changed, Martha thought.

Since the taking back of the camp, the happy-go-lucky rogue, whose blue eyes had once charmed her to the point where she had nearly cheated on Josef, had morphed into this quiet, hard working, selfless soul. Meteor's satirical quips and booming laughter no longer filled the common areas of the campground. The thought squeezed Martha's heart.

Oh, Meteor. What have I done to you? I am so sorry.

More guilt insinuated itself atop the culpability she felt over the women and children. Along with it, came thoughts of escape from the endless condemnation. Of death. But she knew she couldn't kill herself.

But God can, she thought.

No, she corrected herself. *Brad can.*

Martha made her decision.

A hot tear trickling down her cheek sealed her resolve.

RUTH RAN the blade across the long cylindrical steel—first one side and then the other, and then again. She tested the sharpness of the blade on her thumbnail. Satisfied, she set the knife down and picked up another. She began sharpening that one, too. Something clattered behind her and she jumped, half expecting to see one of her captors staring at her. She looked toward the kitchen door. Cook entered. She was carrying several slender, metal forms in her hands. Ruth smiled.

Mervyn... he'd come through with the gambrels he had promised. Then she frowned. He was so different from the rest of the men.

Almost too different.

"Here," Cook said. "Found them outside the door. It's snowing again. Didn't want to lose them in the snow."

Ruth accepted the heavy metal trusses. "I hope they bring in more deer."

Cook grunted. "Making potato pancakes today. Get some of those lazy girls in here to do the peeling." Cook hung up her coat. "On second thought, I'd rather have Sarah. That girl does the work of ten."

MATTHEW ROLLED over and pulled the covers tight under his chin. The room was cool. He had been too tired to get up in the night and stoke the fire; now he regretted it. He pushed a hand toward Martha's side of the bed. She was gone. He opened his eyes. She was standing at the window, a white fleece blanket clutched around her shoulders.

"Why are you up so early?" Matthew asked.

"You better look at this."

Matthew clambered out of bed. He grabbed a flannel shirt and pulled it over his sleeping shirt as he made his way to the window. "What's up?"

Snow had fallen heavily overnight. Several feet of white lay banked against doorways. A foot of snow topped the cabins, the shed roofs, the Gatehouse, crates, barrels, tools, equipment, and anything with a surface. Matthew looked toward the parking area; the truck cabs all wore thick marshmallow caps, too. He groaned.

"The boys have been shoveling for hours." Martha pointed to the Meeting House. "Some of them used the quads with snowblades. They've carved paths between the bunkhouses and the rest of the common areas." She craned her neck. "They've made pathways to the barns, too. They're working on the main roadway now. But it keeps coming down."

Matthew put his arms around her and rested his chin on her shoulder. He gave her ear a tiny kiss. "You know what this means?"

Martha turned to face him. "I know— It'll be harder to rescue the girls."

"Harder?" Matthew's eyebrows shot up. "Try...impossible."

"Not impossible. We have snowmobiles."

"Martha..." His voice was tinged with irritation. "It's hundreds of kilometers to Calgary. The highways will be congested with snow and abandoned vehicles." He shook his head. "Think about how much we'll have to carry in supplies—food, gas, oil, parts, extra clothing, camping gear." He sighed. "And even if we make it to Calgary...we still might not find them. And we know The Man's forces are strong down there. Virgil said so. Martha, it could mean certain death. I can't ask the men to do that."

Martha stroked her husband's grizzled cheeks. He hadn't shaved in several days and the stubble prickled her fingers. "There are men here who will go no matter how much snow falls."

"Think!" Matthew's irritation level had escalated. "How do we bring back a hundred and seventy-one women and kids? Make them walk?"

Martha blinked at the thought.

"Don't you understand what I'm getting at?" He forced his voice to soften. "I know you want to see your girls and your grandkids. So do I. But I've gotta be practical. What if we get hit by a blizzard? We'll be stranded in the middle of nowhere. We could all die."

Not all of us, she thought. *Maybe just one of us.*

Martha pressed her forehead to her husband's chest in a weary attempt to find solace. It was good to have him back in her room, in her bed. Nevertheless, she still felt tentative. He had promised her the moon last night, and she so wanted to believe him.

"Martha?"

My Mary. I'll find my Mary. I can do it. I can make it. On my own. And if I don't...

"I've got to get going," Matthew said. He gave her a quick squeeze. "I'll see how bad things are. Send out a scout...find out if the roadways are as impassable as I suspect they are."

Martha returned his hug. "I'm going out to help, too."

"Is that a good idea? What about your chest?"

"I'm fine. A little shoveling will be good for me. Gets the blood moving."

THE DAY HAD brightened, but the winter sun remained obscured by heavy overcast skies. Snow clung to everything. A flock of sparrows twittered and fluttered up in fear when Matthew approached the trees anchoring the west side of the compound. The flock corporately changed its mind, and the birds flew into a neighboring group of denuded lilac bushes.

Matthew continued checking the buildings. The cattle and the rest of the animals seemed content. Six feet of snow had to be shoveled away from the barn doors first, but their human caregivers had reached them. Now they munched on alfalfa, lowing softly, and swishing their tails. Matthew left the barn.

As he walked toward the Gatehouse, he noticed a snowmobiler in full winter gear hop aboard one of the Arctic Cats. A sledge filled with gear followed behind.

Where's he going?

Matthew guessed the Hutterites needed some help. A guard stood near the Gatehouse door, stamping his feet and blowing on fingers protruding from his fingerless gloves. Matthew approached him.

"Who just left?" Matthew asked, his hot breath puffing out in a frosty cloud in front of him.

"Don't know," the guard replied. "I just got here."

Meteor came around the side of the Gatehouse. He was dressed in full snowmobile gear, too. He pulled on heavy, long gloves. Matthew walked up to meet him.

"How's your head?"

Meteor touched the stitches. "Good." He grinned. "I've had worse."

"I'm really sorry about that."

"Things good with you and Martha again?"

"As good as they can be. I mean she still doesn't know that I know about Brad."

"Give her time. She'll tell you."

"Who just left on the snowmobile?"

"Don't know."

"I hope some of the guys aren't jumping the gun," Matthew said.

Two armed men wound their way through the parking lot toward the Gatehouse. "Hey, Matthew," one said. "What's going on?"

"What do you mean?" Matthew asked.

"Where's Martha off to?" the other man asked.

"Oh no." Matthew groaned. "Dammit. Get me one of the machines. I'll get dressed."

"I'll get her," Meteor said. He ran into the parking lot, jumped aboard another Cat. "Is the tank full?"

"Yeah. Go!" the Gatehouse guard called back.

Meteor throttled up, and the machine jumped forward with an angry whine, spraying up a fan of snow and gravel. He found the track left by Martha's machine and followed it. The sturdy machine hit drifts and bucked, but he held the throttle down.

Meteor saw Martha in the distance, bobbing and weaving through the soft snow. At one point, she slowed. It gave Meteor the advantage and he raced to catch her.

Martha slowed her machine again as he came alongside her. He motioned for her to stop. She did. Meteor jumped from his machine and marched over to Martha. He hit the kill switch. Her toboggan rumbled to silence. Martha dropped her hands into her lap.

"Where're you going, sweetheart?"

Martha looked up. "Don't stop me, Meteor. I've got to go."

"Go where?" he asked, one gloved hand resting on the handlebar of her machine.

"To get Mary. I've gotta get Mary." Tears filled Martha's eyes. "It's my fault she's out there. It's my fault. I should have shot him," she said, her eyes darting from side to side.

"You—"

"I thought God was telling me not to shoot him. So, I didn't. But I wish I would have—"

"You made a decision. You were under stress. Let it go. You did what you thought was right."

"Right?" she screamed. "Right? What's right in this screwed up world?" Tears were pouring now. "What's right? Nothing's right in this fucked-up place." She unbuckled her helmet and threw it. She jumped off the snowmobile and started to tromp ahead into the snow.

Meteor ran after her, grabbed her, and pulled her to him. She struggled, but she remained in his arms. She pulled back and stared up into his eyes. They were bright and as blue as she remembered. They ignited the old fire inside her.

"Kiss me," she said fiercely—her words were more challenge, than invitation. Meteor bent his face to hers and kissed her warmly. On the forehead. "That's not what I meant," she mumbled.

"I know," he replied. Martha pushed at him, and he let her go. He stooped and retrieved her discarded helmet. He brushed the snow away. "C'mon. Let's go home. Matthew is worried."

"Why didn't he come?"

Meteor raised his eyebrows. “Oh...he’s coming,” he said ominously.

Martha studied his face, observing the stitched cut near his eye. She pulled her glove off, and touched the puffy skin. “Looks infected. He really nailed you.”

Meteor grabbed her hand, kissed her fingers, and pointed to her machine. “Get on.”

They had just started their machines, and were putting on their helmets, when Matthew roared up. He hit the kill switch and jumped from his toboggan. Martha and Meteor turned their ignitions off, too. They got off and waited, helmets in hand.

“What are you doing, Martha? Where were you going?” Matthew grabbed her by the shoulders and gave her a small shake. Martha squirmed in his grasp, but he held her fast.

“South,” she said wearily. She looked down at her boots. “I can’t stop feeling guilty for what happened to the women.”

“Martha, listen to me—for once and for all—listen to me! You aren’t responsible. If anybody should take the blame, it should be me.”

Martha shook her head. “No, Matthew. That’s not true.”

“Then it’s not true for you either. Okay?”

Martha gave a half grin and nodded. “Okay. Not my fault.”

Matthew smiled. “Go back to our cabin. Can I trust you to do that?”

Meteor gave a short laugh. “We could always lock her in my truck.” He was referring to the R.C.M.P truck he’d scavenged nearly a year before. Its barred windows made a great jail on wheels.

Matthew laughed, too. “No— I think I can keep tabs on her.” Matthew stared into Martha’s eyes. “Right?” He glanced back at Meteor. “Thanks.”

Meteor gave a curt nod, got on his machine, secured his helmet, turned the key, and roared away.

The couple stood in silence, two lonely figures, like colored pushpins on a map, standing out against a field of endless white. No birds called, no trees creaked. Even the sound of Meteor’s toboggan had died away.

Matthew undid his helmet. He dropped it to the ground. He turned to Martha. She stood near his toboggan, arms hanging by her sides, but her jaw was set. She was ready for a fight. Her eyes told him that.

“What exactly did you think you were doing?” he demanded—his tone sharp and corrective.

“Going after the girls,” she said.

“You would have died, Martha.”

She didn't speak.

"You couldn't have—" He paused. "Is that—? Oh." His tone softened. "No, don't do this. Don't leave me. I need you here. With me. No matter what's happened. I want you with me." He grasped her by the shoulders and gave her a shake. "Don't you get that?" He growled in frustration. "Don't you get that I love you?"

Tears shone in his eyes and he struggled to stop them. One escaped and rolled down his cheek. He cleared his throat. His hands gripped her shoulders. "I love you. Just plain love you." He smiled. "I can't lose you." Another tear slipped down his face.

Martha drew a breath that quickly became a little gasp as a familiar craving stirred inside her. It had been awakened first by Meteor's eyes, but now her husband's warm smile, the feel of his familiar strong hands on her shoulders, and his tears fuelled it. She felt her heart soften as she touched the tiny trail of dampness on Matthew's face.

He does love me. He really does.

Martha smiled. "I love you, too. So much. I'm sorry, Matthew," she whispered. "But I just—"

"Martha..." He paused. "I know what happened," he blurted.

Her eyes grew wide and she stiffened. "You know?"

"It's okay. It's really okay," he said soothingly, running his hands up and down her arms.

"You know...everything?" She stepped back, her eyes wary.

"Yes. I know. Meteor told me about Brad. The other men...I understand now. I—"

Martha felt her stomach sicken as a cold chill ran through her. She took another step back. "Y—Y—You don't think I messed up?"

"Messed up? You're a hero. I can't imagine how you managed to save those women. You must have been in awful pain."

"I was."

"I'm sorry, Martha," Matthew said gently. He reached for her again. "So sorry I wasn't there for you. That I left you unprotected."

"I wasn't unprotected, Matthew. I had a gun." She violently shrugged his hands from her arms. "I just didn't fire it. He was right in front of me. I didn't shoot him." She was yelling now. "I had the chance. But I didn't take the shot. Now they're gone."

"But they got away," Matthew said.

"And he has them *again*," she shouted.

"That's *my* fault. Not yours. I should have left more men at the camp. I made the mistake. Not you. You did everything right. You were amazing."

"Like a good soldier?" she asked bitterly.

"Better." He gripped her shoulders and looked into her eyes. He smiled. "The best."

She drew a quick breath. "After what happened..." she said tentatively. "I thought if you knew...that you wouldn't want me."

Matthew gave a slight jerk. "Not want you? Why would I not want you?"

"Because of Brad...the other men—" Matthew stopped her words with a soft kiss. Martha pulled back. "You'd think I didn't do everything I could to stop them. That it was my fault. That I was stupid for not shooting him. You wouldn't respect me anymore..." A sob caught in her throat.

Matthew shook his head as he pulled her in close to his chest. "Oh, God. I never thought any such thing. I couldn't think it." He sighed. "So like us, wife. So like us. Misunderstandings...till death do us part. I love you more than I have ever loved anyone else alive." He gave her a firm squeeze.

Realization took hold.

He means it. He doesn't think I'm stupid. He doesn't hate me for what happened. He doesn't blame me.

Martha relaxed and her mental ramparts tumbled. Comfort and relief flooded her, its wake intoxicating. Her heart opened to receive the healing. She clutched her husband's hard body and pulled herself tight against him.

Oh God. Thank you. I can feel again. I can feel...

Her breath quickened. She tipped her head back and smiled. "Kiss me."

Matthew encircled her with both arms, kissing her softly, and then deeply. Martha moaned and yielded to the rush of desire. It had been so long. Waves of need engulfed her, deadening the guilt, pushing it back. She leaned into Matthew's chest, welcoming the excitement. Her heart pounded. She wanted him. She wanted to be out of her clothes. To feel his skin on hers. To hear him cry out.

"I need you," she whispered against his lips. "I need you."

Chapter Fifteen

A Whipped Cream Lesson

WOMEN BUSTLED back and forth in the camp's cookhouse. Pots banged and utensils clattered while the women and older teen girls chatted about children, womanly aches and pains, their husbands, their boyfriends or their lack of boyfriends, and their kidnapped friends. Martha had slipped in moments earlier. Now she lifted the lid on a huge pan of roasted potatoes. A tantalizing aroma hit her nose. Cloves of roasted garlic, slices of Spanish onion, generous chunks of unpeeled potatoes, butter, and salt had come together into caramelized goodness. Her stomach growled.

It was good to have a real appetite again. She smiled—a small, secret smile. *It was good to have an active marriage bed again, too.*

"What else are we having, ladies?" Martha asked, unzipping her coat. She hung it on a peg near the door. It joined a bevy of coats, jackets, shawls, and heavy sweaters already on hooks.

"Roast deer. Pickled beets. Baked squash. Apple pie. Rye bread. Blueberry pancakes," one of the older women called out. "How does that sound, Martha? Good to see you up and out," she added.

"Sounds good to me." Martha wandered over to a group of girls fussing over a burlap bag filled with potatoes. "What's wrong?" she asked.

"These potatoes are spoiled..."

"Spoiled? Why?"

One of the girls—with matchstick wrists and spindly long legs—held up an offending spud. "Look, they've gone soft. They're all wrinkled and...they're starting to sprout." She screwed up her face in disgust. "They look like aliens."

Martha took the potato. "Looks fine to me."

"Yuck— I think they should be thrown out."

Martha shook the potato in the girl's face. "Don't—and I mean, DON'T—be so quick to complain about our food. I know you're relatively new here, so I'll cut you some slack— But unless our potatoes are gray with mold, or black through and through—we'll use them. You got that?"

The girl stepped back, abashed, as the women around her tried to suppress their giggles. "We always used to throw them out at my house," the girl muttered.

Martha wanted to grin. The girl's face was as red as the rubber boots she wore. "Yes, I'm sure you did. But that was before. This is *now*. We don't waste food. As to the sprouts, break them off or rub them off— Like this." Martha gave the potato a quick scrubbing with the palm of her hand. "There. Done." She dropped the potato into the bag. "Carry on, girls."

Martha stopped at the baking table. A dozen freshly baked pies with their crusts toasted golden were a luscious temptation. She breathed in their warm scent. Her mouth watered. "Hey, are we having whipped cream with these?" she asked.

"Can't get anyone to whip the cream. You want to do it?" asked a woman measuring white flour out of a large plastic bin. She had flour in her tightly curled silver hair, and her wrinkled hands were covered in bits of white bread dough.

"Sure." Martha picked up a thick glass bowl and a wide, wire whisk. She noticed some of the younger girls eyeing her and she addressed them. "Have you girls made whipped cream before?"

"With my mom's electric mixer," one said. The rest shook their heads.

"Well, come on over. I'll show you how it's done...by hand."

Two women, kneading fat balls of puffy dough, nudged each other and grinned. "Aaaaand...she's back," one said under her breath, mimicking a race announcer. The other laughed.

Martha fetched a basin of cold water. She set the bowl into the basin. "It's easier to whip cream in a chilled bowl," she said. "Somebody get the sugar and the vanilla. Do we still have vanilla?"

"We're getting low on some of the other seasonings and flavorings, but we still have quite a few bottles of vanilla," said a redheaded woman near the ovens. Martha stared at the woman, not recognizing her.

The woman was short, middle-aged, and well proportioned in an old-fashioned burlesque sort of way. Her green eyes were wide and her face was framed in a mass of fiery red curls that had been caught up in an unruly ponytail. The woman did not notice Martha's appraisal of her.

Martha poured cold cream into the glass bowl. She added vanilla and sugar. She began to beat the cream. "Nice and fast. Take wide sweeps. You're trying to trap air in the cream." She stopped and indicated that one of the girls should take over for her. A girl did, but after a minute, she began to whine that her arm was hurting. Another girl took her place.

Five minutes—and several girls later, the cream began to thicken. "Hey, look...it's working," cried one of the girls. "That's so cool."

"Don't turn it into butter," the redhead cautioned. "Just whip it till the peaks can stand by themselves." She nodded at Martha and smiled.

Martha grunted. "Okay— It's done." She lifted the whip. "See? Peaks."

The girls congratulated themselves on their success as they poked fingers into the sweet, white concoction. "Oh, it's so good," one said.

"Leave some for the rest of us," the redhead chuckled. She was now at the pie table, rolling out circles of dough.

"Only if you leave some Meteor for us..." responded a husky woman, cheekily. Her t-shirt encased a prominent muffin top that spilled over the top of her blue jeans. "He's too young for you anyway," she teased.

The redhead didn't reply. She continued rolling pie dough.

"We need another ten cups whipped up," said the woman with the flour in her hair. "Go to it." She flopped into a chair. Martha sat next to her.

"I'm too old for this," the woman said, pushing wiry curls from her eyes.

"Yeah, but your bread is so good." Martha sniffed appreciatively as she hugged the woman—she always smelled like fresh baking.

The two women watched the dinner preparations continue. Suddenly, Martha pointed to the redhead at the pie table. "Who is she?"

"Georgie— She helps out here most days."

"When did she get here?"

"Couple months back, I think."

"She single?"

"I think so. The girls tease her a lot about Meteor." Martha said nothing. The baker gave a soft sigh. "He sure is a catch. Those eyes... Wish I was younger."

Martha slapped her knees and rose. "Time to go. I'll see you at the dinner meeting." The baker gave a small wave.

Martha gave Georgie a quick backward glance before she left the cookhouse.

MERVYN POKED his head into the kitchen. He held a rack of antlers in his hand. He smiled at Hannah.

"Got a nice one," he said, beaming. "Look— Five points on each side. Where is she?"

Hannah looked around. She shrugged her shoulders.

"Tell her it's already hung and ready."

Hannah wiped her hand on a towel. "I'll find her."

A high-pitched scream from the front room grabbed their attention. Mervyn dropped the antlers and sprinted after Hannah. She was already halfway through the dining room by the time he caught up to her.

"Is that one of the kids?" he asked.

"I think it's Reggie."

The pair burst into the front room, just in time to see Brad scoop Reggie up under his arm like a human football. He spun around. Reggie screamed, a high-pitched wail reserved for only the truly horrified.

"What are you doing?" Hannah shouted. "You're scaring him. Let him go." She rushed forward, but Mervyn held her back.

Brad spun Reggie again. Reggie screamed and struggled.

"Hey, man...what's going on?" Mervyn asked a biker lounging near the doorway.

"Brad wants the kid to speak."

"What?"

"The kid doesn't talk. Brad thinks scaring him will make him talk."

Ruth rushed up the hallway and burst into the room. Elizabeth was on her heels. Ruth stopped a few feet short of Brad. Her eyes blazed.

"*Put...him...down*!" she commanded.

Brad ceased his spinning. Reggie struggled like a fly inside a spider's web. His arms flailed and his feet thrashed. Brad dropped him to the floor. Reggie fell with a small thud and scuttled away. Like a wild animal, he sought solace behind one of the big armchairs. Hannah went to him. The boy's whimpers and staccato shrieks filled the room.

Onlookers crowded in. Ruth stood, legs apart, eyes still blazing, her arms ramrod stiff at her sides. Brad whipped around to face her.

His face was red from the exertion of swinging Reggie around, but the color had deepened. It was now almost purple. The roomful of people held their breaths as they waited for Brad's reaction to Ruth's correction. Ruth's stare never wavered.

"What did you say? What did you dare to say? To me?"

Ruth's lips pressed together. A tic—like a countdown—began in her cheek. She was trembling. Her fists were tight at her sides. She stared into Brad's eyes. "He's AU-TI-STIC," she explained, her tone steel cold. Her voice vibrated slightly. "He can't speak."

Brad smiled—a forced wooden movement at the corners of his mouth. "Take her. Outside." He crooked his fingers at two bikers as he spoke. "To the hut." He smiled again.

Mervyn recognized the smile. He stepped forward, but Elizabeth had already slipped in between Brad and Ruth.

"Ruth," she scolded. "He didn't know. It's no big deal." She looked back at Brad and smiled. Then she looked back at Ruth. "He was just trying to get him to talk. Nothing so wrong with that. I mean Reggie can be pretty annoying." She reached back and touched Brad's arm in a reassuring way. "We all wish he could talk. Right? You never know...maybe he will talk after this." Elizabeth shot Ruth a warning look. "You really should apologize."

Ruth closed her eyes, and steadied her breathing.

"Apologize," Elizabeth advised again. Ruth looked up. Her face was still dark, but the storm had passed. Elizabeth's look intensified. "Apologize," she said a bit louder, a bit more insistently.

"I'm sorry," Ruth muttered in a low, steady monotone. "I thought you were hurting him."

The room waited in a hushed silence. The two bikers stood nearby waiting for Brad's next command. Mervyn stiffened. He tried to read Brad's face, but it was a closed mask.

He's enjoying this, Mervyn thought. *She's in trouble.*

Mervyn opened his mouth to speak, but Brad abruptly pushed Elizabeth aside. He and Ruth were once more face-to-face. He leaned in.

"Remember your place here, woman. Don't ever tell me what to do again." The palm of Brad's hand caught Ruth's cheek, and she stumbled backward. Elizabeth sucked in her breath, but she remained near Brad. Other women rushed in to help Ruth up from the floor.

Brad rubbed his palms together. He nodded to the bikers. "Let's go," he said. He turned back to Elizabeth and smiled. "Later, doll."

Mervyn let out his breath.

~~~
~~~

THE MEETING HOUSE hummed with the sounds of contented people—people acting normally, people embracing the prospect of tantalizing food and warm human interaction, people who had forgotten about the Change, forgotten about their missing loved ones, forgotten about their woes—if only for an afternoon. Pots, rectangular pans, and bowls heaped high with steaming goodness filled long tables set along a far wall. Someone had draped the tables in red and white checked, plastic gingham, giving the room a festive air.

Martha allowed the warmth of the room to infuse her. The big room with its camp lanterns, dripping candles, and good smells had taken on a new look, and she welcomed it with a smile. She searched the floor again just as she always did, looking for the dark stains. She couldn't see them, but she knew they were there. She was sure of it. As she studied the floorboards, she wondered who had cleaned up the blood. She decided that Anna had done it, since no one had mentioned the bloody floor to her. She looked up and watched as people settled at tables.

Cliques formed. Virgil's men—most hadn't found female companionship—kept to themselves. Martha wasn't sure how she felt about the new compound members—to her, they were still interlopers—but they had done her no harm. And Matthew seemed to trust them.

Older teens, teasing and shoving, claimed three tables at the back of the room. Young mothers, with their babies, clustered around a table nearer to the door. Several men sat with their wives or girlfriends, choosing family over their battle buddies. Virgil, Marion, Anna, baby Gordon, Meteor, and Jonah shared a table, including the pony-tailed captain who was on R&R leave from the second camp. Two chairs sat empty for her and Matthew.

The door opened and Matthew stepped into the room. Martha walked to him, pulled off his ball cap, and kissed him. The kiss lingered. Soft hoots and catcalls erupted. Matthew smiled as he pulled away.

"Later," he said softly, reaching under her long sweater and squeezing her behind.

Martha moved against him and murmured. "I can't wait."

"Well, you'll just have to," Matthew replied, his tone husky and promising. He linked fingers with Martha. "C'mon. I'm starving." They joined the line at the food table.

People filed by, scooping and piling food onto their plates, and stopping every so often to pop a bite-sized morsel into their mouths. Children scooted in and around the adults' legs, screaming and laughing, and avoiding their parents' attempts to control them.

"Where's the Discipline Committee when you need it?" the pony-tailed captain said with a wry grin, cringing as another child screeched. His tablemates laughed. The camp members knew he was an avowed bachelor—he liked children, but he didn't want any. He coveted his supply of condoms, and refused relationships with women who were interested in procreating. "Bloody ankle-biters," he growled.

Meteor clapped him on the back. "Oh, c'mon...the right woman will come your way...and then you'll want enough kids to make your own baseball team." The captain gave him a sour look. "I mean look at this little guy—" Meteor reached across and took Gordon from Anna's lap. "Want to hold him?"

The captain flushed. "No, thanks." Everyone laughed again.

Gordon wrapped his arms around Meteor's neck and began to bounce in Meteor's lap.

"Ow— Not there little buddy," Meteor said with an exaggerated squeak.

The pony-tailed captain roared. "See what I mean?"

The rest of the table joined in his mirth while Meteor gingerly returned Gordon to his mother.

"Hey," called out a man from a neighboring table. "Do we even have a Discipline Committee anymore?"

"And what happened to the Morals and Ethics committee?" asked a woman seated next to him.

Matthew had taken a seat at the table. He looked up from his plate and shrugged. "Maybe it's not necessary anymore. It was always more Brad and Vince's thing anyway."

"Any word about Brad?" asked the man.

Meteor fielded the question. "No. And any conversation about him is now over." He tilted his head slightly toward Martha. The man read the subtle message and returned to his food.

"Where are Trojan and Cammy?" Jonah asked.

"Well, on the subject of kids—" Martha said.

"Trojan forgot what his name stands for, huh?" the pony-tailed captain chortled.

Jonah looked blank and then it dawned on him. "She's pregnant?"

"The morning sickness is taking its toll," Martha added.

"Yep...first the puking, then the pooping, then the screaming—" the captain said.

Somebody threw a bread roll at the captain. It bounced off his head. Everyone laughed.

People lined up at the food tables again, this time for thick slabs of bronzed pie oozing purple juice. Dollops of whipped cream made satisfying plops as they landed atop the flaky crusts. Even the children quieted for a few minutes as forkful after forkful of the fragrant dessert made its way into eager mouths.

"Matthew?"

Matthew looked up to identify the speaker. It was one of the younger men—a regular on the night patrol. "I'm listening," Matthew said, forking pie into his mouth. "Damn," he cursed, as hot berry syrup burned his mouth.

"I think we need a special hunting crew," he said.

"For?" Matthew mumbled. He was still coping with the heat in his mouth.

"The wild dogs are getting pretty bad. We're seeing more and more of them near the Hutterites. They've already attacked the livestock. It's only going to get worse."

Jonah spoke: "I saw a big pack near the west border of our compound."

"I'd be happy to help with that, Matthew," Virgil said. "Good target practice. My guys would enjoy it."

"I think some of the dogs are interbreeds." The young man gave them an earnest look. "Wolf crosses, maybe."

"Not good," Anna said. "Wolf instincts for killing, but they're not as afraid of humans."

"I had a wolf once," Meteor said. "When I was a kid."

"Really?" Anna turned bright eyes on him. "How did you get him?"

"My dad trapped a bitch. My brother and I found her den. There were two pups, but one had already died. I took the other one."

"That's so cool. What happened to him?"

"I raised him like a pet dog. But by the time he was about a year old...when the wolves would howl at night... he'd answer. After a while, wolves began visiting our cabin. My dad didn't like that. And it made Mom afraid for our chickens. He told me to get rid of him." Meteor took a breath. "He meant that I should shoot him, but I couldn't do it. I took him several miles into the bush and let him go. I'd see him every so often when I was hunting, but he never came back to our cabin." He sighed. "He was the best pet I ever had."

"Oh, I'm sorry, Meteor." Anna touched his hand. He smiled at her.

"I learned how to imitate him. Want to hear?"

Anna nodded.

Meteor tipped back his head and howled. The room fell into a shocked silence.

"What the hell was that?" a man called out from a distant table.

"Meteor," Jonah replied. "He's part wolf."

"Oh, well then...that's okay then," the man said.

The room filled with laughter once more.

Anna spoke again. "Your eyes should be copper like a wolf's eyes."

Martha glanced up. Meteor was smiling and his eyes sparkled in the candlelight.

No, she thought. *I like them blue.*

Just the way they are.

ELIZABETH SAT with her head in her hands. She listened as Ruth—cool and collected—instructed a class on native plants—as though nothing had happened only hours before. Only a faint red mark from Brad's hand was evidence that her sister had done something dangerous. Ruth showed the women pictures she'd taken from a book in the home's library, and then described each plant's food and medicinal values. Stinging nettle, fireweed, fiddleheads, sorrel, buckthorn, lamb's quarter... the list droned on. Elizabeth clapped her hands over her ears.

"I've got to get out of here. I can't take this anymore."

A young woman sitting near her stroked her back. She was one of the girls dumped at Matthew's camp by Crazies months earlier; she had been pregnant then. She whispered consolation into Elizabeth's ear.

"It's okay. You can do it. We're all doing it." Elizabeth jerked away.

"How would you know?" she demanded. "You're used to this crap. You were one of their girlfriends."

The girl straightened, stung by the attack. "I—uh... I was a virgin when they found me. They kidnapped me from my parent's farm." She stomped off to the other side of the room.

Ruth saw the heated exchange. She shook her head. "Girls... c'mon. No fighting. We need each other." She rubbed her eyes. "We've got to stick together. All of us have family that we want to get back to. All of us are tired. And we're sick of this place. But we're alive."

"So, you're good with him taking your kids, then?" asked a thin woman, her tone as dark as her choppy hair.

"No, of course, I'm not," Ruth spat. "But I don't think he'll hurt them. And as long as I'm alive... and I have both my hands... and my brain... then, I have a chance. And so do you. So, everyone should quit whining. If you want out... then find a way out. That's what I'm going to do."

"You know what we're here for, don't you?" asked the thin woman. "You know what he plans for our daughters, don't you?"

"Yes, I do," Ruth responded. "I know very well what his plans are for us. But that doesn't mean he'll succeed."

A short, chubby girl seated at a collapsible table near the window piped up. "So, what should we do? Anybody have any ideas?"

"Or maybe we should be asking, 'What would Martha do?'" piped up Sarah. She was working on a crafts project with a group of children in the far corner. She got up and came over to Ruth.

"I wonder if she's even alive," mused the chubby girl.

"Well one thing's for certain," offered Sarah. "If she's alive, she's probably figuring out some way to find us. The least we can do...from our end..." She smiled at Ruth. "...is try to figure out a way to get back home."

"We'll never get out of here," the chubby girl whined.

Ruth sighed, dropped the pictures she was holding, and walked to a wall of windows. She shielded her eyes from the glare as she stared through the glass. The late day light was still bright; it reflected off an endless expanse of white snow, hurting her eyes. She touched her cheek; it still burned. She shuddered at the thought of what might have happened.

I'll have to be more careful.

She thanked Elizabeth again, in her heart.

She's amazing. Thank you for her, God.

Men on skates raced around a makeshift rink, slapping at the ice, cheering with arms and sticks raised high in the air when a puck found a goal. Very cold temperatures and a huge dump of snow enabled the men to form a bank around a rectangular section of the parking lot. She had watched the process as bikers flooded the cement, pail by pail, again and again, until they had perfected their manmade pond. Somebody had managed to secure arena-sized hockey goals with white netting. Another enterprising soul had even painted a red line and two blue lines on the ice, approximating the lines on a huge rink.

Ruth gave a small huff.

It was so bizarre.

She was watching something so Canadian, so normal, and yet, she was imprisoned under anything but normal circumstances.

It's going to be a very long winter, she thought.

Another cheer from the men on skates.

I've got to find a way out.

One of the skaters swung his stick at his opponent. A brawl broke out and men tumbled to the ice in a flurry of skate blades, hockey sticks, and fists. One man stood up, his face smeared in blood. Ruth looked on, dispassionately.

He'll be expecting me to fix that.

Ruth's head snapped around as the doors sprang open. Two armed men strode in. They walked over to two older teens sitting quietly at a far table. Each man grabbed one of the girls. They screamed as their upper arms were gripped and they were dragged through the room and into the hallway. The other women did nothing; they had already learned that to interfere was to risk a beating. They sat in silence and watched the abduction of the shrieking girls. Ruth stared at her hands.

That could have been me, she thought with a little shot of panic.

"You know what they're doing, right?" asked the thin woman again. The woman's voice was sharp with hysteria.

Ruth listened, but she didn't look up.

"You know what they're doing with them. You know—" The woman coughed and sputtered. "You know it won't be long before they start coming after the younger girls, too." She glared around the room, willing someone to dispute her claim. None did. Ruth sat quietly, head down, and shoulders slumped.

It wasn't fair. None of it.

The girls' cries still echoed through the building. Ruth clenched her fists.

I'll find a way. They will never take little Mary from me.

She closed her eyes against an unbidden vision.

Never.

MATTHEW CALLED the meeting to order. The aroma of their communal dinner still hung in the air, intermingled with the scent of burning candles and wood smoke from the stove in the corner of the room.

"What's our highest priority?"

One of the older women in charge of the kitchen spoke up, "We're running short on sugar, some seasonings, coffee is almost gone, tea is low, and I can't remember what lemon juice looks like."

Matthew nodded. "Noted," he said. "Anyone else?"

Virgil answered. "Ammunition is running low for some of the weapons. I suggest we gather those guns and dole them out with the remaining ammo and use them only for target practice."

"Agreed."

Jonah was next. “Fuel, Matthew—fuel is a big problem. We’ve got oil, but the fuel...”

“How bad is it?”

Jonah shook his head. “Pretty bad. We’ve gotta get rid of some of the vehicles. Keep the ones that carry more than four people. Use them. Dump the gas pigs.” He sighed. “We should have done that ages ago.”

“You’re right, Jonah. By the way, I’m glad to see you’re still here. Thanks for staying.” Matthew smiled. Jonah nodded.

Matthew turned to an older man—an elder, who was seated at the end of the table. “Take care of this. Let the members know we’ll be choosing what vehicles stay on the lot.”

“And our missing women and kids?” another man asked. “What about them?”

“We’re snowed in,” Matthew replied. “We don’t have a choice—”

“We should have gone after them right after they went missing,” the man said, his voice trembling with restrained anger.

Matthew lost his temper. His fist slammed the table. Everyone jumped.

“I’m going to tell you this one more time. After that—the subject is closed.” He took a breath. “We couldn’t go after them—we had no idea where they were taken. This is a big province. And while we were on our wild goose chase, The Man could have walked right back into here...and taken over.”

The man stood up. “We still—”

“Then we’d have lost *all* our women and kids.”

Martha watched her husband, fury blazing from his eyes. She wondered about his heart. *Was it strong?* She realized she knew nothing about his health. *What was this stress doing to him?* The idea of his death made her cringe inwardly. She wanted to grab him, hold him, and lead him back to their bed. Instead, she stood up. All eyes turned toward her.

“Both my daughters and my two grandchildren are among the missing. I want to go after them as badly as the rest of you do, but I know Matthew’s right. We can’t go after them now. We must believe they’re okay, wherever they are. They’re of no value to The Man if they’re injured or killed.” She paused. She glanced back at Matthew. His eyes shone with affection. Warmth filled her and she continued to speak. “Pray for them. That’s how I’m getting by.”

“Pray for their safe return,” Matthew said, echoing his wife’s sentiment. “That’s what Josef would have done.”

Chapter Sixteen

A Chip off the Old Grandma

BRIGHT JANUARY sunshine embraced the backyard, dusting the undulating snow canvas with millions of twinkling ice diamonds. The women were gathered in the home's community room. Ruth stared out the window. She eyed a spruce tree entwined with snow-covered Christmas light bulbs—a vestige of life before the Change. Ruth turned and looked around the room. Red and green crepe streamers had been draped and taped to the walls. *Christmas*, she thought.

The special day had since come and gone. The women had made what attempts they could to make the occasion a festive one for the children, by decorating the community room, baking cookies, and singing Christmas songs. They even encouraged the kids to make presents for each other and for their mothers. But Santa never came, and Christmas morning slipped by as just another day.

"We'll never get out of here," Elizabeth said as she crossed off another day on a handmade calendar. "Look how long we've been here. It's almost four months." She growled. "There's no way out. Every time I turn around, there's another man telling me what to do. They own us."

"That's where you're wrong. You give those men way more credence than they deserve." Ruth spoke from her vantage point at a window overlooking the parking lot. She was watching men play hockey again.

Elizabeth made a small, derisive sound. "I'm giving these men—these bikers—our jailers—more credence than they deserve? I'm giving Brad more credence—?"

"Men are just big boys. They never grow up." Ruth turned to her sister. "Stop giving them so much power in your own mind. Remember Corrie ten Boom... What did she say? 'Learn to see great things great... and small things small.' These men are small things... see them as that."

"So, that's how you feel about Peter, too?" Elizabeth asked in a tone, both sour and unkind.

Ruth shot her a look. "You know what I mean. Why're you being so damn bitchy?"

"Gee, I wonder... Could it be because these guys can walk in, take any one of us they want, and then treat us like whores? Could that be it?"

"Elizabeth," Ruth said, a stern sharpness in her voice. "Quit feeling sorry for yourself. You're in good health, you eat well, none of these men have done any harm to you so far... and *your* children haven't been taken from you—" Ruth faltered.

Elizabeth cut off her own heated retort and squeezed up next to Ruth. "Sorry, Ruthie." She put a comforting arm around her sister's shoulders. "Sorry. I forgot. I'm worried about the kids, too. But I don't think I can take much more of this forced servitude."

"Then curry favor. Use them like they're using us."

Elizabeth sputtered, "Curry their favor? I can barely stand the sight of their ugly faces. And Brad—" She shivered with revulsion. "In fact, when we get out of here, I'm turning lesbian."

"Elizabeth!" Ruth gave her sister a hard look. "Don't say things like that."

Elizabeth laughed and dropped her arm to her side. "My hatred for them is the only thing keeping me alive. But it's killing me, too."

"Then stop hating them... Start taking control."

"Oh, really. That's what you're going to do? When they're raping you? When they're passing you around? You got away lucky, you know?"

Ruth went very quiet, remembering the Reggie incident.

Maybe Elizabeth was right.

Brad's attack and kidnapping of the women and children in her charge had come as a complete surprise. There was no time to plan a resistance. But she'd kept them all alive. Hadn't she?

That had to count for something, didn't it? But for what? For what? So they could live here like indentured servants, or worse...as prostitutes?

The men outside cheered. Ruth glanced out to see an outraged goalie waving his stick in the air. Suddenly, the door to the community room crashed open. The sisters jumped at the sound. Two armed men stormed in. From down the hallway came the cries of a child. Ruth's gut went cold.

It was Mary.

A third biker came through the doorway with little Mary in tow. The child howled at the top of her lungs. "Mommmmeeeeeeee!"

The biker gave Mary a small shove. "Take this brat!" he said.

Mary stumbled to the floor, but clambered to her knees. She turned to the biker and screamed. "I hate you! You are a bad man." The little girl was up on her feet now and she ran at him, her little hands pummeling him. The man raised a hand in an attempt to protect himself from his tiny attacker.

"No!" Ruth cried. She rushed across the room to stop her daughter's attack, but she was too late—one of Mary's fists found the man's crotch.

"Uhhh..." the biker groaned as he bent double. Ruth reached Mary who was still flailing at the man. She grabbed the little girl in a bear hug. Mary fought the restraint, but soon realized she was in friendly arms and stopped struggling. She collapsed against her mother's chest and sobbed. The bikers waited a moment for their comrade to recover and then the three of them—the injured man bent double between them—left the room, locking the door behind them.

A brief silence. The women waited to be sure the men had gone and then they let out a collective *whoop*.

"Mary," one of them exclaimed, "You're our hero." Mary's sobbing abated and she peeked over her mother's shoulder, whimpering and snuffling. Women crowded around her, petting her and pawing her, and showering her head with kisses, and her actions with praise.

"Way to go, Mary. That'll teach that bad man not to mess with you."

"What a kid," another woman said. "Her grandma would be so proud."

Ruth held out a hand in an effort to shush the women. "Stop." She said the word, but inside she secretly rejoiced and applauded her daughter's courage. She lifted Mary from the floor and carried her to a far table. She set her down. The other women crowded around.

Mary, her face tear-stained and her nose bubbling with snot, had begun to smile. One of the women held out a tissue. Ruth took it.

"Blow your nose, sweetie..." she said, holding the tissue in place, "...and then tell Mommy what happened." Ruth looked up and caught Elizabeth's eye. Elizabeth was smiling and nodding. Ruth smiled back.

Mary blew her nose.

She told her story.

IT DIDN'T TAKE long for the roomful of women to understand that Mary had managed a coup d'état. An uprising of sorts. A tiny revolution. And all in the name of Martha. Mary had been playing in The Man's office when Brad and a couple of his cohorts walked in. She recognized them instantly…

"They're bad men. They were mean to my Nana," Mary said, pointing to Brad and the three bikers with him. "They hit my Nana. I saw them." Her blue eyes flashed with righteous indignation.

"They hurt your Nana? How?" asked The Man, his tone saccharine-sweet and lilting. He looked up at Brad as he spoke. "Come over here. Tell Daddy what happened." He held out his arms to Mary. She trotted closer, but stopped within a few feet of him. She placed her chubby hands on her hips.

"He hit her and made her fall down. I saw him," she said, lifting one hand and pointing a finger at Brad. "He made her throw up, too. I saw him." She pointed at the men next to Brad. "They were squeezing her neck, too. I saw them."

"Did they now… Did you see them do anything else to your Nana?" The Man exchanged bemused looks with a fat-bellied man sitting near him.

"My friends and me were crying. They took us away. I wanted to help my Nana, but they pushed us outside," she sputtered.

The Man stared at Brad.

Brad's face was blank, but his eyes flitted down to his hands and then back up again. He glanced at the men standing with him, as though seeking their support. The men shifted uncomfortably from foot to foot. They said nothing.

"I told Brad not to hurt your Nana," The Man said. "So, he wouldn't have hurt her. Right, Brad?"

Mary exploded. "He DID hurt her. I saw it. He's a bad man." She began to wail.

The Man wagged his head and chuckled. "Mary… Stop crying. Come here," he said, leaning forward in his chair towards her. Mary jumped back.

"You're a bad man, too. You *stoled* me away from my mommy," she shrieked. "I hate you!"

The Man reached to grab her, but Mary evaded him. Her screams escalated. Some of the men grimaced and covered their ears.

"Mary, stop it!" The Man commanded.

Mary's face contorted and she screeched louder.

"Send her back to her mother!" The Man bellowed.

Two men moved toward the little girl. Mary went into full terror alert and let loose with a firehouse alarm.

"Noooooo!"

She launched herself at The Man—kicking, clawing, and biting. Outrage fueled her tiny fists and The Man's eyes popped wide when she caught him on the side of his face. He jumped up, his hand curling into a fist.

"You little..."

"Whoa," the fat-bellied man said, stepping in front of Mary. "You could kill her."

"Then get her out of my sight," The Man said, his eyes narrowing and his mouth compressing into a tight line. "Or I will kill her..."

Ruth stroked her daughter's hair as the little girl wriggled into her lap, nestling closely and absorbing the affection she had missed.

"Then they brought me to you," Mary said, gulping for breath.

"Did The Man ever hurt you?"

"No. He gived us lots of toys. And Barbies."

Ruth listened as Mary continued to recount her time with The Man. She breathed a sigh of relief—her children's time with The Man sounded more like an endless Christmas morning than a prison term.

"What about Samuel? Is he okay?"

Mary bobbed her head. "Oh, he's okay. He likes being there. But not me... I like it here."

"Even though you don't have lots of toys and dolls to play with?"

"I like it *here*," she repeatedly stubbornly.

"I like you here, too," Ruth said.

"Don't want to go 'way from you again."

Ruth's heart sank. She knew Mary was awaiting a promise that she'd never be "stoled" again. But Ruth didn't make promises she couldn't keep, so she ignored Mary's words. She hugged her instead.

In a few moments, Mary slid from her mother's lap and ran off to play with children in the far corner of the room. Ruth's smile followed her, but her glad face hid a heart filled with dread. She knew she couldn't stop The Man from taking Mary away from her again. Desolation swept over her.

Maybe Elizabeth was right. Maybe there was nothing they could do. Maybe they would never see their home again.

Sorrow filled her and she turned back to the window. The men were still playing hockey. Shouting and laughing.

They would be prisoners forever.

A hockey player fell to the ice. He got back up, hopping on one leg, while he grabbed at his shin. *What a baby!* She knew he would soon be around to get his injury patched up.

Just like a little boy. They're just little boys...

The words she had quoted at her sister rang in her mind.

"Small things small..." A strength rose inside her at the thought.

I can manage a bunch of little boys.

THE HUTTERITES welcomed the camp women with much excitement and fussing. They waved Martha and Anna, and the rest of the women into their big kitchen with mingled cries of warm greetings and offers to assist with the removal of outer clothing. A woman offered to help Marion with her thick, down parka, but Marion refused, and kept the coat with her.

"Please come in. Sit," said a large woman, whose chubby cheeks dwarfed her wide smile.

The women padded across the wooden floor, in their sock feet, and sat down on long wooden benches at a huge table. Plates stacked with fresh sweet rolls, aromatic cinnamon buns, lemon squares, oatmeal cookies, sugar cookies, chocolate brownies, and small loaves of sourdough bread were arranged up the center of the table. Nearby, slabs of yellow butter, and jar after jar of berry preserves and jewel tone jellies—pink, amber, and cranberry red—awaited the guests.

"We're so happy you are here. Please help yourself," the woman said with a wave of her ample arm across the table indicating the baked goods.

"We're glad the snow stopped long enough for us to get here," Martha said.

"How are you?" the woman asked. She feather-tapped Martha's chest with two fingers.

"I'm fine. Still achy, but I feel okay."

Martha and Anna sat next to Marion. The woman fidgeted and glanced around like a nervous cat. She finally shrugged off her coat and hung it over the bench seat between her and Anna.

"Please," the friendly Hutterite woman said, motioning again toward the overflowing plates. "Help yourself. Eat your fill...then we'll get to the toilet paper lesson."

"Toilet paper lesson?" Marion's face darkened. "We're here to make *toilet paper*?"

"We can't find toilet paper anymore," Anna said. "And the personal rag thing is just so unsanitary."

"The Man always had toilet paper," Marion grumbled. Anna drew back, surprised.

"Well he might have had toilet paper, but he also beat you, didn't he?" Anna whispered.

"No."

"I'm confused."

"He never touched me," Marion said firmly, ending their conversation.

One of the Hutterite women held out a fresh plate stacked high with fat cinnamon buns. Marion selected one. When the plate came by again, she grabbed a second one. Anna watched Marion scour her pockets with one hand, while her other hand gripped the sticky bun.

"What are you looking for?" Anna asked.

"A napkin or something. I want to take a bun with me." Marion used her free hand to pat her sweater pockets.

"Have you checked your coat pockets?" Anna reached down and picked up Marion's coat as she spoke. Something hard banged the bench. Anna looked surprised. She began to investigate, but Marion grabbed the coat.

"Leave my things alone." Marion glared at Anna who let go of the coat, but not before her hand slid over one of the pockets, and across the hard, rectangular mass inside. Their eyes connected. Anna's eyes were steely with accusation.

Marion stuffed her coat under the bench seat.

She said nothing.

~~~

ELIZABETH'S HEAD snapped up as two men entered her room. She was used to being interrupted, but not this late at night. Something about the two men alarmed her. Her heart pounded. She stood up. One man, wearing an orange do-rag emblazoned with a grinning skull, stepped forward. He tilted his head back toward the open doorway.

"Let's go," he said.

Elizabeth held a warning finger to her lips and pointed at the bed where a tiny form lay asleep. "What do you want?" she whispered.
~~~

"I said..." The man in the do-rag walked closer until he stood directly in front of her. He leaned into her face till their noses almost touched. "Let's go."

Elizabeth didn't argue. She knew better. With a backward glance, she let the man take her arm and lead her out the door. "Where are we going?" she asked as she was hustled down the hallway.

"You've got a date."

"A what?" Elizabeth tried to yank her arm away, but the man held it fast. She trotted along beside him. They reached the end of the hallway and turned the corner. Her eyes widened.

They were headed toward the men's sleeping quarters.

Elizabeth's heartbeat quickened. They stopped outside a door near the end of the hall. Music filtered through the door. The man in the do-rag knocked.

"It's open," said a man's voice. Elizabeth paled at the sound of the voice.

Oh, no, she thought.

The man in the do-rag turned the handle. When she hesitated, he shoved her into the room. Elizabeth stumbled against an overstuffed chair. When she had righted herself, she stared in shock at the scene.

Candles lit the room, their tiny flames casting flickering shadows against the walls. The window was heavily curtained and the bed was neatly made up, its pillows plumped, and the coverlet drawn back. She swallowed—hard—and backed against the chair.

"Hello, Elizabeth," Brad said. "I thought you'd enjoy a special dinner." He waved his arm in front of him. "It's a treat for you— To thank you for sticking up for me."

He was standing near a small oval table. It was dressed in a white lace tablecloth and fine china. Silverware sparkled and wineglasses beckoned, half-filled with a blood-red wine.

Elizabeth struggled to speak. "I—I—I'm not really hungry."

"Oh, come on now. Look," Brad said, lifting the cover on a casserole dish. The aroma of a meat dish hit Elizabeth's nose, and her stomach clenched. She gritted her teeth and forced her voice to stay low and controlled.

"It smells wonderful, Brad. But I'm really not hungry." She paused, and struggled for something to say. "I haven't been feeling well."

Brad set the lid back on its dish, and walked over to her. He took her chin between his fingers and examined her face. Elizabeth resisted a shudder, but she lost the battle.

"Are you cold?"

"Yes," Elizabeth said quickly. "I think I have the flu."

"Oh, that's too bad. Well, come in. Sit down. Have a little wine with me."

Elizabeth balked, but when he took her hand, she relented.

They walked over to a small couch, and she sat down. Brad retrieved the glasses of wine from the table, and joined her. He offered her one of the glasses.

"Here. It's a nice merlot."

Elizabeth took a sip. She squeezed out a tiny smile. "Yes, it's nice. Thank you." She gave a little cough and used the opportunity to move away from Brad. He relaxed, stretching his legs out in front of him, and laying his arm along the puffy, upholstered couch back. Elizabeth hugged the armrest, keeping herself at an angle, her knees in Brad's direction.

"I like you, Elizabeth. You've got style." Brad leaned toward her, dropping his hand to her shoulder. Elizabeth shrugged it off. "Oh, come on now...we've known each other for a long time. We can be friends."

He slid over, and snuggled next to her, his arm wrapped around her shoulders. "Let's toast to a friendship," he said, raising his glass to hers.

Elizabeth forced a grin and raised her glass to her lips. She trembled, sending a bit of wine trickling from the corner of her mouth. Brad scooped up the dribble with his index finger. He eyed her as he brought his finger to his mouth, and licked away the wine. Elizabeth took a quick breath and turned away to hide another shudder.

Brad turned her face back to his. "I don't want to force you into anything, Lizzy. Can I call you Lizzy?"

"No— I prefer Elizabeth."

"But I like Lizzy," he cajoled. "Just for me, okay?"

"Sure," she said, grinning mechanically. *Curry their favor.* Her sister's words illuminated in her mind like a neon marquis. "Just for you." Brad ran his fingers down her cheek and across her lips. Elizabeth held her breath.

"So, what do you say? Friends? With benefits?" Brad added with an encouraging grin. He leaned in and attempted to kiss her. Elizabeth pulled away and shrank back into the couch.

"I'm really tired. This is not a good night for me."

Brad eyed her suspiciously. "Do you think you'll feel better tomorrow?"

"I don't know," Elizabeth said. "But I sure hope so," she added brightly. *Start taking control.* She leapt from the couch and raised her glass. "Here's to feeling better tomorrow." She tossed back the wine, walked to the table, and poured more.

Brad came up behind her and slipped his hands around her waist. Elizabeth stiffened. He ran his hands up her ribcage, hesitated, and then reached for her breasts. Elizabeth held her breath. His hands closed over her breasts and began to knead them, his fingers searching for the nipples beneath the fabric of her clothing. Elizabeth used her elbows to shove at his hands, spilling her wine in the process.

"Oh, I'm so sorry," she said, pulling free from Brad. She grabbed a paper napkin and swabbed at the spilled wine.

"Never mind that," Brad said, taking the napkin from her. He turned her to face him. "I think we could be good together, Lizzy..."

Elizabeth looked away. "Maybe," she said. "But I need to know some things first."

"What things?" Elizabeth turned back to face him, her eyes steady.

"Did you kill my father?"

ANNA STARED at them, her eyes large and earnest.

"She's got a radio."

"Are you sure?"

"Pretty sure. I felt it. In her coat pocket."

Matthew turned to Martha. "Did you see anything?"

Martha shook her head.

"I'm serious, Matthew. She *has* a radio."

Matthew pursed his lips. "Why didn't you tell us earlier?"

"I was second guessing myself. I didn't want to get her into trouble, but I thought about it. And I'm pretty sure."

"I'll take it up with Virgil in the morning."

"I'll take it up with her, right now," Martha said, rising from her chair. Matthew put a restraining hand on her arm, and she sat down.

"In the morning," he repeated.

~~~

THE DOOR to Ruth's bedroom creaked. She sat up. Elizabeth stood there, silhouetted by the dim light of the lantern she was holding. Ruth gasped.

"What?—What's going on?" she whispered.

"Brad..."

"Brad? What do you mean?"

"He sent them to get me. He wanted to talk to me."
~~~

Ruth looked thoroughly puzzled. She jumped up and grabbed Elizabeth by the hand; she drew her past the beds, one of which held a sleeping Mary, and towards the couch. "Come. Sit." She paused. "Did he hurt you?"

Elizabeth shook her head. "No."

"Then I don't understand. What happened?"

"He wanted me to party with him. He had his room all laid out sort of romantically... candles... You know what I mean. He even had music playing. I wanted to puke, but—"

"But..."

"I remembered what you said to me."

"What I said—?"

"About using him."

"Oh-h-h... that." Ruth looked relieved. "So what happened?"

Elizabeth gave a quick grin. "So—I played him."

"You did?"

"He thinks I want to be his girlfriend. Well, his *old lady*."

"Do I really want to know any more?" Ruth looked slightly alarmed.

"It's okay. He tried, but nothing happened."

Ruth sat back. "Whew. You better be careful. We both know Brad has issues with women. And he killed Cindy. We're pretty sure of that."

"I asked him about that. He says he didn't."

"Yeah, right," Ruth said, sarcasm as thick as molasses coated her tone.

"I don't believe him, either, but I let him think that I did."

"Good move." Ruth said. "Wait a minute," she hissed, "does he honestly think you are just going to ignore the fact that he murdered our father?"

Elizabeth shrugged. "I asked him that, too. He says he didn't."

"And you let him believe that you...believed him?"

"Exactly."

"This is deadly dangerous. If he gets involved with you...has feelings for you...and you make him jealous—" Ruth paused for effect. "He'll kill you, too."

"Well, for the first time in weeks, I feel like I've got some control back. Besides..." Elizabeth said, "I'd rather be doing something than sitting around here like some obedient—dog." She spat the last word.

Ruth smiled. "Now who's starting to sound like mom?" Elizabeth shrugged. "What are you going to do when he pushes you to have sex with him?"

"I'll put him off with some story. Venereal disease, maybe. Or maybe I'll fake being terrified." Elizabeth shrugged again. "I don't know. I'll figure out something."

"God help you," Ruth said. "Try not to be alone with him, okay?"

Elizabeth smiled. "I have a little ace up my sleeve."

"What's that?"

"Duke. He stays with me now."

"That would make you like his...mother?"

"Nah. Older sister."

"Okay, if you say so." She hugged Elizabeth. "Please be careful."

~ ~ ~

Two Birds with One Bullet

THE MAN swiveled in his chair. A camp lantern burned brightly on the window ledge behind his head. A half-empty glass of Scotch and a smoldering cigar sat near his hand. "What do you want?"

Brad smiled—a long slow smile. "I figured I'd make friends with Martha's kid... Elizabeth."

"Friends?" The Man asked.

"Yeah— I'm claiming her. She seems to like me. And she knows a lot about Matthew's compounds—"

"She seems to like you?" The Man looked at him quizzically. He leaned forward over the desk. "She's Martha's kid. You shot her father. Why in hell should she like you?"

Brad stroked his chin. "I'm not bad-looking. I know how to treat a woman."

The Man snorted. "Like how you treated Martha?"

Brad's head snapped up. "What do you mean?"

"You think I'm stupid? I know you went against my orders. I know what you did to her."

"I—"

"Don't—" The Man said. "Don't bullshit me. Bullshit her kid if you want to, but it's a really bad idea to bullshit me. Understand?"

Brad gave a curt nod. He glanced out the window. "What're your plans for this lot?"

"We're keeping them here until spring."

"And then...?"

"We ship them into Calgary. Our trading partners will be set up by then."

"You gonna trade all of them?"

"You mean will I trade Elizabeth?" Brad didn't answer. "I'll trade any of them that I damn well please. And I'll start with Elizabeth."

Brad eyes flashed. "What—? I've earned the right to choose a woman. I captured them. They wouldn't even be here if it wasn't for me—"

"Wasn't for you? If it wasn't for you—" The Man spat. "We'd have Matthew's camp. We'd have his damn wife— And the rest of the women."

"You weren't there!" Brad hissed. "Where were you exactly? Oh—oh, right... You retreated."

The Man rose from his chair. He slapped the desk, the sound like a gunshot. "One more word Brad— Just one." The Man's eyes were dark. "I am The Man. Don't...test me again."

Brad raised his hands in surrender. He left the room.

The Man sipped his Scotch, took a puff on his cigar, and rocked back in his chair. Something occurred to him, and he emptied his hands. He opened a drawer in the desk and pulled out a thick journal. He flipped a few pages, searched the entries, stopped at one, and circled it:

***Elizabeth**.*

The door opened. It was the fat-bellied man. The Man returned the book, and closed the drawer. He picked up his glass.

"Did you tell him?" the fat man asked.

"What?"

"That you're sending him east?"

"No, I've changed my mind. I'm going to keep him here for a while longer." The Man pulled a jar of colored candies across the desk; he lifted the lid, studied the colored orbs, and chose two green ones. He popped them into his mouth. "He just told me he's got a thing for Martha's daughter, Elizabeth. That might work in our favor."

The fat man grunted.

"Anything else?" The Man asked.

"Nope. Heading to bed." The fat man banged the door shut.

The Man picked up a revolver lying on his desk, spun the cylinder, and lifted the gun to his eye. He peered down the sight. He smiled.

Brad and Elizabeth. He would send both of them east. But only after he had used Elizabeth for his own purposes. She might be the key to taking Matthew down. And...Martha.

Once and for all.

He opened the jar of candies again. He chose two red ones.

Two birds with one bullet.

He smiled as he chewed.

Chapter Seventeen

A Howling in the Dark

MARION DROPPED into a chair at the kitchen table. She bent and unzipped her boots, flinging them against the wall. She shrugged her coat from her shoulders and stared up at Virgil. Virgil picked up a pot of tea, two mugs, and joined her. He poured their tea and then sat down.

"Tea...I've never drunk so much tea in my life." He sighed—a great, long exaggerated sigh. "I miss Scotch—he always had great Scotch."

"I miss my house," Marion said. "This place is more like a dog kennel." She kicked at a chair opposite her. She lifted her hands. "Look at my hands." Virgil did so, but said nothing. "They're all chapped." Virgil still said nothing. "She had us making TOILET paper." Virgil hid a grin. "I have *lots* of toilet paper in *my* house." Marion shoved out her lower lip. "I hate it here."

"Had a nice time at the Hutterites, did you?" Virgil sipped his tea.

"God, how can anyone stand to dress the way they do? So...dull and horrible."

"Maybe so—but does it really matter how they dress? Because of them, we live really well here. There's not a lot left to scavenge in the city anymore. You're remembering the way things were last year—things are different now. The world is running out of stuff."

"Yeah, but my house..." Marion whined.

"Your house? You mean the house The Man gave you? What are you talking about? Stop going on about your house. It's not yours anymore. This—this is your house now. Besides, those generators and all that fuel you used last year? Not possible now. Fuel's too hard to find. So, stop bitching and start appreciating. You're here. You're warm. You're alive. And you aren't under his thumb. Isn't that what you wanted?"

"Yeah...sure. If you say so."

Virgil took another sip of tea. "That's it—that's all you've got to say?"

Marion gave him a sharp look. "What? What else is there to say? How grateful I am that the Gatekeeper took me in? How thrilled I am to have camp duties? How delighted I am to be making fucking *toilet paper*?"

"No," Virgil said. "I thought you'd say how glad you are that you're here with me." He picked up his cup, went to the sink, placed his cup in the washbasin, and turned. "Are you happy to be here with me?"

"Of course, I am—you know that," Marion cajoled. "It's just that I was used to a different life."

"A spoiled life, you mean."

"So what! I was special to The Man...and he took care of me."

"And just what did he expect of you?" Virgil asked, his tone hedged with sarcasm.

"Not that!" Marion stood. She stormed into the bedroom and slammed the door.

Virgil went after her, reached for the doorknob, thought better of it, and went to the coat rack instead. "I'm going out," he called over his shoulder.

"Good— Go," Marion shouted back.

JONAH DEALT a new hand. He, Trojan, several of the camp captains, and some of Virgil's men sat around a table in the men's bunkhouse. A game of poker was in the works and the ante was piled with bets: a small switchblade knife, a disposable razor, two boxes of wooden matches, a half-smoked cigar, a girlie magazine, and several papers scrawled with promised actions like, "I will take your graveyard shift for one night."

"I'll see your cigar and raise you this leather pouch," Jonah said.

"Well, I'll see all your stuff and raise you this bottle of gin," Trojan said, tossing a tiny bottle of Beefeater's gin into the pool.

"Where did you get that?" asked a thin man with bushy eyebrows and a ragged scar on one cheek.

"Oh, I have my ways," Trojan said with a wide smile.

All the men looked up when the door opened. Virgil stepped inside.

"Hey, Virg," they called out. "Come play."

Virgil slung his coat over a chair. He looked at the betting pot. "Gin? No Scotch?"

"Ask Trojan," Jonah said. "It's his bet."

Virgil looked at Trojan and smiled.

Trojan shook his head. "I'll never tell."

Jonah dealt another round. "Ante up," he said. Virgil threw in a small pocketknife. Another man followed with a corkscrew.

"What the hell is that good for?" Trojan asked. "You think I got a wine cellar?"

"It's all I got," the man replied.

The hand ended with the man with the corkscrew taking the pot.

"Not fair," Trojan said. "We need to go out again. We need more stuff to bet with." Jonah dealt again.

"Anybody up for an adventure?" Virgil asked, gathering his cards to him.

"Like what?" asked one of Virgil's men—he had been doing poorly at the poker game, and was sitting out the round.

"Let's scavenge The Man's clubhouses."

The man's mouth hung open. "You're kidding, right?"

One of the camp captains, who had been part of the raid on the west side clubhouse the previous spring, spoke up. "Is that such a good idea?"

"It's a great idea. The Man had plans to retreat to the South Camps, if he didn't capture this compound. He didn't have enough supplies to make it through the winter. So, I'm sure he's gone." Virgil fanned his cards. "What d'ya say, boys?" he asked with a nod in the direction of his men. "Good Scotch. Maybe even some cigars. Ammo. Some nice trinkets for the ladies..."

"That sounds like fun..." said a man with curly red hair. He was one of Virgil's men who had surrendered to Matthew in the fall. "But Matthew might have something to say about that."

Jonah grunted. "Yeah— You'd better take this up with Matthew first. Or there'll be hell to pay. I guarantee it."

"Of course, I'll talk to Matthew about it—but first I wanted to see if anyone else was interested."

A rumble of eager agreement came from the men around the tables. The card game continued. More bets, more hands, more bluffing, and soon Trojan was scooping up a pile of winnings, including his bottle of gin.

"Thanks, guys. That's it for me."

"What? You're leaving? You aren't gonna give us a chance to win our stuff back?" the man with the bushy eyebrows asked.

Trojan gave the men a mock serious look. He placed a hand to his chest. "I have a woman with child back at the cabin. She needs my attention." He rose and jammed his winnings into his pockets. "And this chocolate bar," he said, holding up a miniature Milky Way. "It needs my attention, too. See you around, boys."

"That guy is so damn lucky," the curly redhead said. "We shouldn't let him play anymore."

"Good luck telling Trojan not to play," Jonah said with a laugh. "He'll find a way to get what he wants— He always does."

Virgil stared down at his empty hands. "Nobody here has any Scotch?"

One of the camp captains smiled. He wore a hunter cap with its flaps turned up—it made him look dull and slow.

"Well..." the captain drawled.

"You do?" Virgil leaned over, hope brightening his eyes. "Would you consider sharing?"

"What do you have in exchange?"

Virgil reached into a breast pocket and removed a fat cigar. He held it aloft. "Well?"

"You got yourself a deal. Get some glasses." The captain grabbed his coat and left the cabin.

It took the captain a few minutes, but soon he was back—puffing and his face was grim. "You guys are needed outside. One of the women says she saw a pack of dogs near the barns." The men stood and checked their side arms. Virgil held up a hand.

"Hold it. You'd better make sure every shot counts. You know how low we are on ammunition." To the captain he said with a smile, "Don't forget—we have an appointment—you and I."

The captain pulled a small bottle of Glenfiddich from his coat pocket and gave Virgil a friendly salute.

MATTHEW WATCHED through the window as the men descended the steps of the bunkhouse. He could see they were on a mission.

"Where the heck are they off to?" Matthew stared for a moment longer, and then grabbed his gun and jacket. Martha came out of the bedroom. She had a blanket clutched around her shoulders.

"Where are you going?"

"Not sure. Just going to see what the guys are up to." He gave her a quick kiss and ran out the door.

Matthew loped across the yard. The night was dark and cold, but the moon was bright. He reached the men as they rounded the corner toward the barns. "Where're you guys going?" he shouted.

"Wild dog hunt," Jonah said. "One of the women said she saw a big pack out this way."

Virgil stepped alongside them. "I've already warned them about conserving bullets."

"Good," Matthew said. He took a dark woolen toque from his pocket and pulled it onto his head, snugging it down over his ears. "Damn, it's cold."

A howl pierced the night. Then another. And another. The men walked toward the sound, their boots crunching on the crisp snow beneath their feet.

"Wait," Jonah whispered. "There's somebody up there."

"Where?"

"Near the barn."

The men looked in the direction Jonah had pointed. A solo figure was silhouetted in the moonlight. A tall figure. A big man. His head was thrown back, his mouth open.

He was howling.

"Who is that?" Virgil asked.

Jonah snickered. "It's Meteor."

"What the hell is he doing?"

Meteor turned as the group of men approached him. He held a finger to his lips.

"What are you doing?" Matthew asked in a gruff whisper.

"I'm getting their attention."

"Why?" Jonah asked.

"Easier to hunt them if I bring them to me." He patted the rifle slung from his shoulder.

Jonah shook his head. "Meteor, you never fail to amaze me. I thought you were kidding. I didn't think you could actually speak to wolves."

"Sh..." Meteor said. He pointed to a spot about fifty yards in the distance where dark shapes shifted and blended. "There— Look."

"Shit," the captain with the Scotch said. "That's a huge pack."

"What's the plan?" Virgil asked. "Break into groups? Try to surround them?"

"No," Meteor said. "Let's wait for them to come to us."

"Makes me wonder why they're here," Matthew whispered. "Isn't there enough game for them deeper in the woods? Seems strange they'd chance human encounters."

"Like Anna said—they're probably interbreeding—*coydogs* or *wolfdogs*—they don't fear us if they're hungry," Meteor said. "I don't think they're after us anyway—they're after the cows and horses." He paused. "But I've never seen a pack so big."

Silence.

Jonah spoke up. "Where are our dogs? Why aren't they barking?"

"Not really our dogs anymore," Meteor said. "They might hang out here, but they don't get steady food from us anymore. So, they're probably running in a pack, too."

Another howl sliced through the dark. Then another. And another. Until an entire chorus of howls began.

"They're looking for pack members," Meteor said. "Or trying to scare off rivals."

The men watched dark shapes slinking around in the darkness ahead. None of the shapes answered the distant howls.

"Do you think they'll attack us...or run?" Jonah asked.

"Not sure," Meteor answered. "But we're about to find out." He pointed as the black shapes thinned out and disappeared into the gloom. "They're coming up behind us. Watch your backs."

RUTH JUMPED at the unexpected sound. She was alone in the community room. She was staring out the window. The darkness was inky black, but moonlight illuminated the fir trees near the home.

"Hi," a male voice said. "You alone here?"

Panic rose in Ruth's chest—she was supposed to be in her bedroom, but after Elizabeth's disturbing visit, she couldn't go back to sleep. She covered her mouth with her hand. Then she relaxed—it was Mervyn.

"Hi," he repeated from where he stood in the doorway.

She held a hand to her chest. "You nearly gave me a heart attack," she whispered.

"That wouldn't be good," Mervyn said as he walked toward her. He smiled. "I looked for you at dinner. Where were you?"

"Not feeling so good."

"Can't sleep?"

"No."

"How's little Reggie?"

"Fine." Ruth gave him a little smile. "Thanks for asking. It's nice to know that someone cares."

"How about some fresh air?

"Fresh air?"

"Yeah— Want to go for a snowmobile ride?"

Ruth smiled at the thought. She remembered times at Matthew's camp when she and Peter, and a group of friends would go out night riding. They would stop along the trail, start a fire, and have a cookout. She remembered the stillness and the intense brightness of the stars. But mostly the deep, almost heavenly quiet— It had spoken to her soul.

"Yes, I'd like that."

"Got a suit?" Ruth shook her head. "I'll find one for you."

Before long, Ruth was dressed and the pair headed to the Quonset hut. Mervyn grabbed a lantern and lit their way to the machines. "This one is good," he said. "It's got lots of fuel."

"Just one?" Ruth asked. She looked disappointed.

Mervyn smiled. "Oh, the lady wants her own machine." He shook his head. "Yes, we'd better stick to one." He pulled off his glove and started the engine. "Don't want to piss off The Man," he said above the motor's rumble.

"You won't upset him by taking this one out?"

"No— I'll just say I was scouting. He'll be okay with that."

"With a woman?"

Mervyn laughed. "He won't know that part."

He ran the machine out of the hut, turned, and patted the seat behind him. "C'mon."

Ruth straddled the seat and grasped his sides. She could feel the hardness of his body through his snowsuit and heat rushed through her. She blinked in surprise.

"Where are we going?" she asked.

"You'll see."

Mervyn pressed down the thumb throttle and the machine roared ahead, its headlight jouncing up and down across the trees as it passed.

Ruth closed her eyes and yielded to the power of the machine. Wind infused with tiny ice darts stung her cheeks and her eyes, and she leaned into the man's back for protection. The machine hit a drift and jolted upwards, nearly unseating her. Mervyn slowed down. He reached back and grabbed her arm, pulling it tighter around his waist.

Ruth didn't resist. She shivered.

MARTHA OPENED the cabin door and stepped onto the landing. She was wearing only a hooded, zippered sweatshirt over flannel pajamas. She hugged herself as she peered into the darkness. Matthew had reduced the number of construction lights and generator set-ups to conserve on fuel, so it was difficult to see very far—even in the clear moonlight.

"Where the heck did they go?" Her frosty breath hung in the air. She took a step forward and squinted into the darkness. A sound to her right captured her attention.

A growl? Is that a growl?

The sound came again, but this time another accompanied it. The hairs on the back of Martha's neck rose and she backed against the cabin door. Her hand fumbled for the knob. She wanted to scream, but her throat closed. The growls grew louder. There were more of them. Her hand found the knob. She turned it and pushed, throwing herself backward into the cabin. She kicked at the door to shut it, but not before she saw the faces.

And the teeth.

Chapter Eighteen

A Snowmobile Ride

MARTHA HEARD a sharp yelp as a creature slammed against the closing door. She threw her body against the door, praying it would remain closed. She gasped for breath as her heart pounded in her chest. Then her eyes grew wide at a new noise. A scratching, scrabbling sound—swift and repetitive.

Were they trying to dig their way in?

Martha stared down at the narrow opening where the door met the floor. She imagined the sharp curves of the digging, insistent claws, and the intense desire of the single-minded beast who owned them.

What do I do now?

Another thought took hold.

The men? Where are they? Where is Matthew?

MERVYN CROUCHED, knees slightly bent, as he leaned into a curve. Ruth followed his lean. The snowmobile whined as it bogged down in a deep drift, but with more throttle, it was soon out of the gully and headed into an open field. Ruth could see the dark shapes of giant, round hay bales dotting the field—shadowy memories of life before the Change. When the power disappeared, many farmers didn't clear their hay fields, choosing to concentrate on human food storage instead. Mervyn slowed as he wove between them. Across the way, a dim line of reedy poplar trees stood sentry.

There must be a river down there, Ruth thought.

Mervyn crossed the field and entered the woods. He slowed again, this time to wend his way through the trees. Ruth noticed that the narrow path bore the packed-down, laddered tracks of other snowmobiles.

He's been here before.

Mervyn crested a small ridge and then with a moment of careful hesitancy, he headed the machine downhill. Soon they were on another open expanse that led away in both directions, with short banks on either side. Ruth could see the crisscrossing of many narrow snowmobile tracks cut into the snow. Mervyn turned to the left, chose a track to follow, and gunned the engine.

Ruth studied the night sky. The stars were huge, so bright, and there were so many of them. Many times, she'd heard people comment on the beauty of the night sky after the Change—as if the power they had lost on the earth had been redirected up into the heavens. She sighed. How many times she'd seen these skies while nestled in Peter's arms. Tears came into her eyes, but she blinked them away, not wanting them to freeze on her eyelashes.

No crying. Peter's at the camp—you're here. Live with it.

She closed her eyes and mentally slammed the emotional gate protecting her heart.

Stay strong. Don't think about him. Or you'll go crazy.

The snowmobile forged forward, its metal track throwing up snow, while its headlight bobbed up and down. Suddenly, other headlights appeared. Ruth counted them. At least eight machines. They were coming toward them.

Mervyn slowed and followed a trail to the right, up the bank, and into a treed yard. Ruth could see the silhouettes of a house, a barn, and a bevy of smaller sheds. As they drew closer to the house, she saw it was lit up. Silhouettes of people filled the windows. Mervyn slowed the engine and entered a small field near the house. Their machine joined a flock of snowmobiles—all shapes, sizes, and colors—angled haphazardly in the thick snow around the yard. He parked, and turned off the engine. He jumped off and removed his helmet. He motioned for Ruth to do the same. He held out his hand to her as she stood up.

"Ow, my butt's sore." She gave a small giggle. "I'm not used to that. It's been a while since I was on the back of a machine. At least when I'm driving, I don't have to sit."

Mervyn smiled. "Want to drive back?" Ruth beamed with surprise.

"Okay! I'd like that." She turned and pointed to the house. "Who are these people?"

"Ah, people from all over. We sort of found each other. We get together—have parties."

"Are these The Man's people?"

"Some."

"Does he know? Does he come here?"

Mervyn held a finger to his lips, and grinned. "The Man doesn't know everything—he only thinks he does."

Ruth grinned. "I see." She hesitated when Mervyn took her hand and pulled her toward the house. "Wait. Is it safe for me to be here?"

"You're with me. You'll be fine." He grinned. "Just give me a big kiss every so often, so that they know you're with me."

Ruth pulled her hand from his. Her face was stern. "I told you I'm married."

"I know. I heard you the first time. But if the guys here don't think you're taken..." He let Ruth fill in the blank.

"Maybe we should just go back," she said sullenly. The joy of the moment had vanished, engulfed by her miserable reality.

She wasn't free to do this. She could get caught. And...punished.

Mervyn shook his head. "It's okay...really...trust me."

He took her hand again and she walked with him toward the house. He waved and hollered out greetings as more men with women passengers zoomed into the yard.

"Are those...The Man's women?"

Mervyn shook his head. "Don't know who they are. There's lots of independents around here. Bikers. Farmers. Survivalists—lots of those." He shrugged. "We like getting together. No turf wars here." He smiled. "Just partying."

"Who owns the house?"

"Hell if I know...owners are probably dead."

He pulled on her hand again and led her up the steps to a wide wraparound porch. He tapped on the door. An eye peered at them through a tiny peephole.

"Hey, it's our boy, Mervyn." The door swung open. Their greeter was a middle-aged man with a thick, dark beard and black horn-rimmed glasses. His dark hair stood up, choppy and off-kilter. "Hi'ya brother. How are you?" He clapped Mervyn on the back. "Who's your friend?"

"*Deerhunter*," Mervyn said with a warning squeeze of Ruth's hand. Ruth blinked with surprise at the name. She said nothing.

The man reached over and pulled Ruth into a bear hug. Ruth stiffened, but she allowed the man to hug her. She gave him a quick, shy smile when he let her go. He smiled back and waved them inside.

The big rectangular room was bustling with people. Camp lanterns adorned the windowsills, while dozens of thick candles burned on silver platters and dinner plates on every flat surface in the room, including a wooden staircase leading up to the second floor. Their scents intermingled, giving the room a warm, homey aroma—as if mom was baking apple pies down the hall and dad was smoking his cigar in the family room. Ruth liked the feeling, the familiarity of it. She let herself be led into the room.

ANIMALS RUSHED in from behind. The men had only the slightest warning. Their guns were out, but the dogs were moving too fast. The dogs had the advantage—they could see in the dark. The sounds of bodies hitting bodies and the grunts and expulsions of air as the men went down were soon replaced by the angry, sharp barks and threatening growls of dogs.

"Shoot them!" one man screamed. A shot rang out and then another. A yelp of pain. Another shot. A man screamed. Two more shots. Another dog yelped. "It's got me—" More shots.

Matthew kicked at the dogs attacking him. He heard the smack of a bullet, and one of the dogs dropped to the ground at his feet. Another dog still clung to his coat sleeve, its feet braced, its teethed bared. He raised his hand, his glove was gone, and blood trickled down his fingers. He steadied his pistol and pulled the trigger. The dog dropped and lay still. Meteor rushed up.

"You okay?"

"Yeah...I think so. But it bit me." Matthew held up his hand. Meteor swept a small flashlight back and forth across the small puncture wounds. "It looks bad, but I can't see very well. Let's get you back to the cabin."

Jonah rushed up. "What the hell was that? They were so fast, I could hardly shoot."

Matthew closed his eyes against the throbbing pain. "Did we kill most of them?"

"I don't think so." Jonah motioned behind him. "After we started shooting—the dogs ran that way. Some of the guys went after them."

The redheaded captain limped into view. "Crap—I'm really bleeding." He waved his gun in the air. "But I nailed the little bastards."

Jonah glanced around. "Where's Virgil?"

"Here," Virgil said as he came out of the shadows. He was dragging one of the dogs behind him. "Take a look at this animal, Meteor. What breed is it?"

Meteor gave Virgil a guarded look, but he bent down. "It's a coydog." He stood up. "I'll bet most of the domestic dogs—especially the smaller ones—are dead. Food for the bigger dogs, most likely. But the bigger bitches—the German shepherds, the huskies, the labs, and the Dobermans—are cross-breeding." He nudged the body of the dead dog. "This one's a husky cross."

"What'll we do? Poison them?" Jonah asked. "If there's that many out there—so nearby—they're gonna be a big problem. Maybe even in the daylight."

Virgil agreed. "Poison might be best. At least on the perimeters of our compound and the Hutterites' land."

"I'm thinking the Hutterites will refuse," Matthew said. Blood oozed down his hand and dripped in dark droplets to the snow.

"Well, at least let's poison the ones near us," Jonah urged.

"Wish we could get our hands on some wolf pups," Meteor said.

"Why?" Jonah asked.

"They're loyal...and smaller dogs are afraid of them. If we had wolves howling around here, we wouldn't have to worry about packs of roving dogs attacking at night."

"Well, that's fine for later...but it doesn't do anything to solve our problem, right now," Matthew said. He held up his bleeding hand. "Let's talk about this back at the Meeting House. I've gotta get back to the cabin."

The men rounded the corner and started across the compound. The sound of snarling and snuffling in the distance made them reach for their guns once again.

"Holy shit," Jonah said. "They're outside your cabin, Matthew."

"Don't shoot at the cabin. I don't know where Martha is. Scare the dogs, instead."

Virgil nodded at Meteor and Jonah. "We'll go around to the rear—pick off the dogs when they run." Matthew stared after the men, his own pistol raised, and his other hand dripping blood.

MARTHA SAT frozen against the door. She heard the shots, but the scratching hadn't subsided. She envisioned a hole being dug under the door, and a dog with slavering jaws pushing its way underneath. The thought made her shudder and she crawled away in haste. She stared at the door, her eyes wide, as the claws continued their digging. Her eyes sought wildly.

A gun? Where's my gun?

She hadn't thought about a gun ever since returning to the compound. She jumped up and grabbed for the fry pan, but it was full of simmering meat and potatoes. She grabbed a butcher knife instead.

Suddenly, the sound of men's voices yelling and then the answering pops of handgun fire. The scrabbling at her door ceased. More gunfire and a distant yelp. Martha crept over to the door and pressed her ear against it; the sounds were gone.

A pounding of boots on the steps, and she barely managed to get out of the way before the door crashed open. Matthew stormed in. Jonah was right behind him.

"Martha?"

She stared at him, her mouth open, the knife clutched in her hand.

"Are you okay?" Matthew asked.

"I'm fine." She dropped the knife and grabbed his bleeding arm. "What happened? The dogs did this?"

"Not the ones outside here. A different pack."

Martha looked at Jonah. "You okay?"

"Yeah, I'm fine."

The pair helped Matthew remove his coat.

"It's bad, Matthew," Martha said. "It'll need stitches. Let's get this bleeding stopped." Martha grabbed a towel and handed it to Jonah. "Fill this with snow." He ran out the door and, in a few moments, returned with a snow compress. Martha pressed the towel to Matthew's wound. She looked up. "Do you think they were rabid?" she asked gravely.

"God, I hope not," Matthew said. "Man...that hurts."

"We don't have rabies vaccine," Martha reminded him.

"I know. So, let's hope for the best."

Martha got soap and water and began cleaning the punctures.

Matthew looked up at Jonah. "We've got a few more guys out there that'll need attention, too."

"I'll get Anna." Jonah left the cabin again.

Martha returned the cold compress to Matthew's arm and gave it a firm push. "Hold this—"

"What are you doing?"

"Reading." She pulled a home remedy first aid book from her shelf. "Dog bites..." She read and then gave a tiny chuckle. "Oh my, you guys aren't going to like this..."

"Like what?"

"It says I should apply a chili pepper paste."

"Is that as bad as hot salt water?" Matthew asked with a grin.

"Worse."

"Well, if it has to be done..."

"Says it'll make it heal faster. No infection. And it'll kill the rabies virus."

"Well, then...let's get it done."

Martha gave Matthew a serious look. "You'll need to lie down for this, dear husband."

MERVYN STOOD on the far side of the room, laughing and talking with a group of men—all young, all about his age. Ruth smiled politely as two women tried engaging her in conversation. The women were older, silvery hair, cropped short—their faces reddened and wind-ravaged. She guessed they were seasoned snowmobilers—and bikers, too.

"Did you drive here, girlie," one of them asked. "Or did you get the bitch seat?"

"Uh—I rode behind," Ruth said.

"Trudy and I got our own machines. Ski-Doos. No bitch seat for us," the woman said with a loud, gravelly laugh.

"Where are you from?" the other woman asked. "And how come they call you...*Deerhunter*?"

"Yeah— Where did that name come from?" the second woman asked. "It's a cool name."

"I—uh—I'm good at cleaning deer." Ruth shrugged. "Just a nickname."

"So, you and your man took one of the farmhouses out here?"

"Uh—no. We're—uh—"

Mervyn slipped in beside Ruth. He put his arm around her waist. "C'mon, I want to show you something." Ruth sighed with relief. She linked her arm through his and walked to the door.

"What is it?" she asked.

"Nothing," he said with a grin. He bent and whispered in her ear, "Just thought you might want to get away from them."

Ruth grinned. "Thanks. You're right."

Mervyn held out a handful of small cookies, overbrowned on the bottoms. She chose one, bit down, and made a face.

"Somebody isn't used to baking in a wood stove." She held the cookie gingerly and then frowned. "Deerhunter?" she whispered. "Where did that come from?"

Mervyn shrugged and dropped the cookies he was holding onto a small table. "Just seemed to fit. You don't mind, do you?"

Ruth shrugged and grinned. "No, I kinda like it." She looked down at her watch—a man's watch, the old-fashioned wind-up kind—one she had found in the box in the closet in her room. She was careful about keeping it wound. "It's late— I should get back to the home."

Mervyn nodded. "Okay. I've done my business here. Let's go."

"Business?" He ignored her question.

They reached the power toboggans. Mervyn started the machine and with a flourish, he directed her into the driver's seat. Ruth straddled the seat, and then pointed behind her.

"Bitch seat," she said with a wide grin. Mervyn threw back his head and laughed. Ruth liked the sound. He settled in behind her.

"Can you find your way back?"

"I think so," she called above the sound of the engine.

"Okay— Go."

Ruth maneuvered the machine across the farmyard, and down onto the frozen river. She hesitated and then gave the thumb lever a firm push. The machine leapt forward. She bent her knees and leaned into the curves. Mervyn's hands clamped onto her hips and he put his weight into the turns, too.

Ruth traversed the bank, wound her way back through the trees, and burst out onto the hay field. A group of dark shapes ran across the track and she yanked on the handlebars. The machine swerved off the trail and hit a small hummock. The skis went up in the air, and both she and Mervyn flew off into the snow. Ruth fell with a loud *whump*. Her lip split as her face hit ice-encrusted snow. She rolled onto her back and groaned.

Mervyn ran after the machine, jumped on, turned it around, and drove back to Ruth. He pointed the headlight at her. He jumped off and ran to her.

"You okay?" He slipped his hand under her head and lifted her up.

"Ow, my mouth." Blood ran down her chin.

"Oh, boy." Mervyn pulled off his glove, grabbed a handful of snow, and pressed it to her lip. "Here...this'll help."

Ruth sat up and rubbed the side of her face. "Oh, this is gonna hurt."

Mervyn examined her cheek. "A little road rash. It's scraped, but not deep." He pulled his hand away from her mouth. The snow was drenched in blood. "Let's see if that's stopped bleeding." He tipped her face toward the light. "Looks like it's stopped."

Ruth watched him, her eyes grateful—both for the gentle caring and for the touch of his hand on her face. She pressed her face into his palm and closed her eyes. Mervyn traced the contours of her face with his thumb. He bent and kissed her eyelid. Ruth jerked back in surprise.

"It's okay," he said. "Just a little kiss. Nothing more." He gave her a warm grin. "You're married."

Ruth took a cleansing breath and released it in a soft huff of relief. "We better get going." She cupped her gloved hand over his hand and gave it a quick squeeze.

Mervyn got up, and pulled her to her feet. He grinned. "I'll drive, Mario..."

Ruth giggled. "Ow," she said, touching her lip. "Don't make me laugh."

She trudged through the thigh deep snow and clambered onto the seat. Mervyn grabbed her arms and pulled them around his waist. Ruth turned her head to the side to protect her sore lip and cheek, and then rested her forehead against Mervyn's back. He drove the machine back onto a hardened track and headed for the home. Ruth noticed that he slowed for bumps. The sweetness touched her heart.

The pair parked the snowmobile inside the hut and then made their way into the home. Mervyn held the door for Ruth.

"How's your lip now?"

"I think it'll be okay. It's not bleeding anymore." Ruth kicked off her boots. She unzipped her suit, pulled out her arms, sat on a chair, and pulled at the legs. "Where did this come from?" she said holding the suit toward him.

"Keep it," Mervyn said. "We've got lots in the shed.

Ruth threw the suit over her arm, grabbed her boots, and began to walk down the hallway. She stopped, ran back, gave Mervyn a peck on the cheek, and a soft smile. "Thank you."

Mervyn smiled.

Ruth turned and fled down the hallway.

She pushed open the door to her bedroom. It was dark. She grabbed a small battery powered lantern and flicked the switch. She gasped and staggered back against the wall. She dropped her gear to the floor.

A man in the shadows leaned forward.

"Had fun, did we, Ruth?" The Man was seated on the end of Mary's bed. "I don't remember giving you permission to go off on a midnight jaunt. Did I?" He shook his head. "No, I don't believe I did."

The Man stood and walked toward Ruth. "Where were you?"

Ruth took a step back. "I—I—I couldn't sleep. I went out for a ride."

"A ride? We're taking out snowmobiles now?"

She thought quickly. "Looking for...uh—more deer."

The Man smiled, but his eyes remained shadowed. "I'm sure you were." He motioned to Mary. "You shouldn't leave a little girl all alone at night. You never know what might happen to her."

Ruth blanched and stepped back. "I—uh—"

The Man walked past her. He reached the door and turned the knob. "By the way, Samuel and I will be moving to Calgary for the rest of the winter."

"No! Oh, please...no...don't take him," Ruth clutched at The Man's sleeve. He glared at the offending hand. "Don't take him— I'm begging you."

"Good night, Ruth." He walked out and closed the door before she could utter another word.

"Bastard," she mumbled. "You, bastard."

Ruth sank into a chair. She touched her cheek. The scraped side of her face was raw and stinging, and her split lip pulsed. She got up and sat next to Mary who slumbered peacefully under a heavy down comforter. She gripped a handful of Mary's blanket and squeezed. Her heart sank.

Mary murmured in her sleep. Ruth tucked the blanket around the little girl's shoulders, and then lay down in her own bed. A tear ran down her face.

Why, God? Why don't You help us? You can help us!

The thoughts raging inside her brain made her head ache. She put her hand to her forehead and massaged her temples between her thumb and fingers. More tears dripped.

"Small things small..." The words sprang to her mind. She took a deep, shuddering breath.

"I'll find a way," she whispered.

Another hot tear crawled down her cheek. It found its way to her cut lip, stinging when it hit. She licked at it, tasting the salt. A memory bolted up.

The kiss.

She remembered the gentle look on Mervyn's face as he cared for her, the gentleness of his lips on her eyelid. She remembered the feel of his body, the strain of his muscles under her hands as he maneuvered the snowmobile across the field. Then she remembered her excited response.

She gave a little gasp.

Is that why? Payment for my adultery? I'm sorry, God.

Shame rose inside her. She squeezed her eyes shut, willing the vision to disappear.

"No more of that," she whispered resolutely into the dark.

Exhaustion overtook her.

Ruth fell asleep.

Chapter Nineteen

Puke on the Boots

PALE LIGHT was beginning to dawn. Pastel hues coated the sky outside their bedroom window. The pair lay naked under the covers, snuggled close for warmth. Matthew's eyes were open when Martha turned to him.

"Hi. How're you feeling this morning?" Martha reached over and pushed the covers off Matthew's injured arm. "I'll bet that'll be festering soon."

"Maybe not. Dogs are supposed to have clean saliva."

"I think that's an old soldier's tale. I asked Meteor to check the bodies for rabies. He said he would." She gave Matthew a quick kiss and began to roll away.

"Hey, where're you going?"

"To research rabies."

"Anna would probably know all about that. Why not leave it to her?"

Martha pulled away. "I'd just feel better—"

"Stop." Matthew grabbed her shoulder and pulled her back down on the bed. "Stay. Let the world take care of itself for a while. Stay with me."

Martha smiled and touched his cheek. She ran her finger across the scar on his lip. "You never told me how you got that."

"Yes, I did— Hockey." Matthew reached up and ran his own finger down her throat, between her breasts, and along the bullet wound scar. "Does it still bother you?"

"It's sensitive. It twinges now and then...the scar tissue pulling..."

Matthew bent his head and kissed the ridged, red flesh. He moved his mouth to her breast and onto a nipple.

"Stop..." Martha gave his head a gentle push. "Not now."

"Why not?" He continued his advance.

"I haven't even gone pee yet," she said with a playful slap.

Matthew rolled over. "Me neither." He threw back the covers. "See?"

Martha laughed at the sight. "Oh boy. Can't keep a good man down."

They both laughed.

"I really have to get things done." She gave Matthew an earnest look. "And you, mister—you need some hot salt water on that arm." She grinned—a wicked grin. "I owe you for all the times you held *me* down for salt water treatments."

"I think you got your revenge with that bloody chili pepper crap. Da-a-a-mn...that hurt." Matthew sighed loudly as he pointed to his crotch. "So—what am I going to do about this?"

"Oh—I'm sure you can think of something." Martha smiled.

Matthew reached out and cupped her face in one hand. "But my darling wife, that's what I have you for."

"Matthew...infection— I'm worried about your arm. You know how bad infections can be. Especially without antibiotics."

He still cupped her face. "Yes, I know. I was worried about you, too. But you survived without them." He paused, and then added softly, "You never really told me what happened that day... Will you ever tell me?"

"No."

Matthew's eyes darkened. "What he did— He'll pay for. I promise you that, Martha. I promise you."

She smiled, but it was more in solidarity than genuine delight in his words. "It's history now. I'm healed."

Sure you are, Martha, she chided herself. *Sure you are.*

She turned away as she spoke, so Matthew couldn't see the truth in her eyes while her mouth spoke the lies.

"I've forgotten most of it now." Brad's face came into her memory, and she closed her eyes.

Sure, you have.

She moved again to the edge of the bed, but Matthew caught hold of her. "I'm sorry," he said softly. "That was stupid of me. I shouldn't have brought that up." He grinned hopefully, and then he added with exaggerated enthusiasm. "Look—my arm. It's infecting as we speak. Quick—get the salt water."

Martha burst out laughing. She rolled on top of him and kissed him—hard and deep. Matthew responded. In every way.

"That's more like it," he growled, pushing her onto her back.

"Your arm—"

"Forget my arm."

They didn't notice the rising sun, they didn't notice the light rays spill into the room, and they didn't hear the knock on the door.

RUTH SLUMPED down into a big armchair. All around her, women and children chattered and laughed. They often gathered in the home's front room because of the camaraderie induced by the massive wood-burning fireplace. However, the recent Arctic temperatures made this day's gathering imperative. Most of them hadn't slept through the night. Even with doubled-up, down sleeping bags, woolen blankets, and extra clothing, sleeping in the bedrooms was a chilly adventure. The fire had already been burning for several hours.

Ruth watched the logs glow, tumble, and spit cinders. One fiery bit flew through the air and landed on the carpet. A woman jumped up and swatted at the tiny spark. The women didn't like being held prisoner in the home, but to lose their only shelter to fire, in sub-zero temperatures—that thought was too horrific to bear—even for the lazy ones. So, each woman took her turn at cinder-babysitting without complaint.

Mothers, wearing big flannel shirts, fleece-lined vests, sweaters, and shawls clutched firmly about them, chatted as their children played. Babies in cloth diapers and doubled-up sleepers rolled about on a bed mattress placed a safe distance from the fireplace. One mother had the good sense to snag a mattress from an unused bed; it kept the babies up off the cold floor. Smaller children played nearby with makeshift toys—rocks, pieces of wood ruggedly carved into tiny animals, stand-up people cut from magazines and pasted to cardboard, plastic spoons and bowls, sock dolls with yarn hair, and a pile of dress-up clothing. Older kids teased and laughed, or griped as they struggled with ill-fitting snowsuits and boots. However, nothing was stopping them from going outside. Mary trudged over to Ruth, a scarf in her hand.

"Mommy? Tie this?" Ruth leaned forward and took the scarf.

"It's really cold out. You sure you want to go outside?" Mary responded with little girl enthusiasm.

"The snow is so big. We can roll down the hills."

Ruth began wrapping the scarf. She stopped before covering Mary's mouth.

"Did you see anyone in our room, last night?" Mary shook her head. "Are you sure?" Mary shook her head again. "Good." Ruth completed mummy wrapping her daughter's face. "Keep your mitts on. If they come off, you come back inside. Otherwise, your hands will get chapped. Okay?"

"Okay, mommy."

Ruth watched as Mary ran for the door. She stumbled and tripped, but one of the older girls bent and lifted her to her feet. As they headed out the door, another child burst into the room. Ruth's heart leapt.

Samuel.

She waited for him to rush over and greet her. He didn't. Instead, he gave a quick glance her way and then ran after the other children. Ruth noticed that his clothing—his snow jacket and pants, his boots, his mitts—were all in his size. She struggled with her emotions.

He's got nice, warm clothes. He's being well cared for. He's better off...

But her heart soured at the next thought. And the next.

The Man has taken my son. Taken his love from me.

"Samuel..." she called quickly. But she was too late—Samuel had disappeared from view.

MARTHA FINISHED wrapping Matthew's arm in fresh gauze. She knew the salt water would work its magic, so long as the dogs weren't rabid. She banished that thought.

"There you go." Martha took the basin of salt water to the sink. She didn't throw it out. With the frigid temperatures, it was too hard to get fresh water; she'd boil this water and use it again.

"I should see how the other guys are," Matthew said.

"Ask Meteor about the dogs," she reminded him.

"I will." Matthew reached for his boots. He took his coat and gingerly pushed his sore arm into a sleeve.

"That's pretty bloody," Martha observed. "Ripped up, too. You should go to the storehouse and get a new jacket."

"I will." Matthew did up his coat, pulled on a pair of gloves, and then he kissed her. "Repeat performance tonight?" His eyes were twinkling.

"Not so fast, buddy. You might be foaming at the mouth by tonight." She straightened his collar. "And I'm not into making it with mad dogs."

"It could be fun."

She chuckled. "Go away."

Matthew reached for the door. "It's time for that inventory of our supplies. Want to help with the food supplies?"

"Sure... Right now?"

Voices outside drew their attention. And a pounding on the door.

"Matthew? Martha?" It was Meteor. "You in there?" Matthew swung the door open. Meteor was there with about a half dozen men flanking him.

"We've got to do something about the dogs. The Hutterites' patrol came back in and said the Hutterites have lost stock on the back pasture."

"How many?"

"Too many." Meteor looked grim. "Nearly two dozen head. The Hutterites figure the dogs have been picking them off for weeks."

"What?" Matthew was astounded. "Didn't our patrols see anything?"

"That's a hell of a big field, Matthew. The Hutterites are panicking—they lost a lot of pregnant cows. They can't afford to lose more."

"Why didn't someone come get me sooner?"

A man at the back spoke up. "We did— I knocked, but nobody answered."

Matthew flushed slightly. "I must have been sleeping. Where's Virgil? I need to talk to him."

"He's already gone," Meteor said. "He went through the guns and ammo—divvied them up. He armed his guys and left."

"On toboggans?"

Meteor nodded.

Martha piped up. "Did you get a chance to examine the dogs' bodies?"

"Yeah...as best I could. They froze up pretty fast. I put one in the barn. I'll get Anna to take a look."

"But could you tell anything? Were they sick?" Martha asked.

"I don't think they're rabid. Just hungry," Meteor replied.

"Did Virgil suggest sending out another hunting party?" Matthew asked. "In the other direction?"

"No, not that I know of. He left before I could talk to him."

"Who's on patrol tonight?"

"Jonah and his crew."

"They're good." Matthew rubbed his arm.

"Sore?" Meteor asked.

"Yep, but I'll live. We'll leave the dogs to Virgil then. Right now, I need help with inventory." He nodded to the men standing behind Meteor. "Get your crews and meet me at the Gatehouse. I'll give you your assignments then."

The men walked away, their boots squeaking across the hard-packed snow. Martha watched them disappear along paths bordered by white snow banks, some as high as their shoulders.

Please God, no more snow. She closed the door.

Wilbert brushed along her ankle. Martha looked down. The gray cat was small, still very kittenish, but he was healthy. Martha made sure of that.

Mary will be so happy to see him when she gets back.

The thought delighted her, but then reality set in.

I might never see her again.

Martha hunched her shoulders and closed her eyes, protecting herself from the pain. The cat bumped up against her ankles again. Its purring—soft staccato rumbles—reached Martha's ears. She scooped him from the floor.

"Hello, little one." She rubbed behind one of his ears as he leaned his furry head into her hand. "Are you hungry?" She stared out the window. Men were gathering outside the Gatehouse. "It's a good thing you're a housecat, Wilbert. Those dogs would make a quick meal of you." She gave the cat another cuddle. "And speaking of meals— I'm starving."

Martha considered eggs sitting in a wire basket—three of them.

No, I'll leave those for Matthew.

"Hm..." She opened a cupboard door, and shrieked. A small, brown creature streaked across the shelf and disappeared. Wilbert leapt to the counter, tail whipping slowly side to side. He had seen the movement, too. Now he waited.

"Dammit," Martha cursed. "Bloody mice." Then she brightened. "Hey, Wilbert...you just might be old enough to catch yourself a little fast food—a *Quarter Mouser*." Martha howled at her own joke.

Wilbert waited and then sat down. He stared at Martha expectantly.

"Nope, you can get your own lunch, buddy boy." The cat lifted a paw and gave it a dainty lick.

"That's it," Martha said. "Prepare for the feast."

The cat blinked and went on with its bath.

Suddenly, a thought dawned on Martha. "You!" she cried out. "It was you the dogs smelled."

Wilbert switched to his other paw, licked it, and swiped at his face.

She chuckled. "Good old food chain..."

ELIZABETH PLOPPED down on the arm of Ruth's chair. Ruth was asleep. She nudged her. Ruth awoke and stretched. They gazed out the window where the children were running and leaping into the snow. The sun was bright and their shrieks were loud.

"They look like they're having fun." When Ruth didn't respond, Elizabeth asked another question. "What's on for today?"

Ruth shrugged.

"You going outside with the kids?"

"No."

"What's wrong?"

"Nothing."

"Really? Sure seems like there's something wrong." She squinted at Ruth. "Whoa— What happened to your face?"

"I fell outside. It's nothing." Ruth waved Elizabeth's concern away and stared out the big picture window. "Look at that."

Both women watched as a group of men came out of the Quonset hut. When they got closer to the children, they began to play with them—tossing snow, running with them, leaping into snowdrifts, and laughing. Ruth noticed that one of them was Mervyn. He fell to the ground, allowing the boys to tumble on top of him. He staggered to his feet with boys clinging to him like leeches; he pulled at them, tossing them into the snow. They got up and ran back at him. Samuel ran at him, too. Ruth couldn't stop the smile that creased her face.

"The kids really seem to like him," Elizabeth said. "That's Mervyn, right?"

"Yeah," Ruth said softly.

Elizabeth studied her sister. "I think he's sort of got a thing for you. He sure hangs around you a lot."

"Samuel likes him—that's for sure," Ruth said, diverting Elizabeth's observation. Their conversation was suddenly interrupted by men coming out of the dining room.

Brad and The Man led the group. They stopped by the front door. The women eyed them warily. None of them spoke. Brad gave Elizabeth a wink. She forced a smile, peppermint sweet. The Man appraised the women and then turned back to the men.

"What's the word from the scouts?" he asked.

A biker in a dirty green parka and ripped snow pants answered: "The big trucks are pushing through just fine. One of our guys from the South Camps made it here." He pointed to a truck parked higher up on the main road. "He said the drive wasn't that bad."

The Man pulled on his coat, did it up, pulled on his gloves, and pointed toward the door. Another man opened it, and the men walked outside. The Man motioned toward Mervyn and Samuel. One of the men walked over, scooped Samuel up by the back of his jacket, and carried him over to The Man. The Man reached down, took Samuel's hand, and they walked toward the trucks.

"No!" Ruth cried.

Elizabeth stared at her in alarm. "What's the matter?"

"Samuel— He's taking Samuel."

"But he always takes Samuel."

"No. You don't understand— He's taking him to Calgary."

"How do you know?"

"He told me last night. When I got back—"

"When you got back?"

Ruth ignored the question. "He's taking him. I've gotta stop him." She jumped from the chair.

Elizabeth grabbed her arm. "Are you crazy? You run out there now and he will shoot you. You want him to do that in front of the kids?"

Ruth threw herself back into her chair. She clutched her head in her hands. "Dammit. I hate this place." She growled in frustration.

The front door opened. Mervyn walked in.

"What's going on?" he asked.

"The Man took off with her son." Elizabeth said.

"That little guy is her son?"

Elizabeth nodded.

"Sorry to hear that." Mervyn squatted down in front of Ruth. "Can I be of some help?" he whispered.

"Sure," Ruth mumbled. "Get Samuel back." Tears shone in her eyes.

"Where are they going?" he asked.

"He said he's taking him to Calgary." Ruth paused and added bitterly. "As punishment for last night."

"Punishment?" Elizabeth asked. Mervyn glanced up.

"She was out with me on the snowmobile last night." Mervyn touched Ruth's shoulder. "How did he find out?"

"He was waiting in my room."

Mervyn stood up.

"I'll see what I can find out." He dashed out the door.

"What were you two talking about?" Elizabeth got down in front of her sister and looked up into her face. "Tell me—"

"He asked me to go for a ride last night. That's all. The Man found out."

"You went off...without permission?" Elizabeth looked impressed. "You rebel, you."

"Yeah...and look what it's gotten me..." Ruth clasped her hands together and squeezed till her fingertips turned pale. "I've lost my son."

"Maybe not," Elizabeth said with a grin. She pointed to the window. "Look."

Ruth jumped up and stared out the front window. Mervyn loped back to the home. He pulled on the door and came inside. He gave the sisters a wide smile.

"Not going," he mouthed.

A few moments later, The Man came back into the home with Samuel trotting next to him. He directed Samuel over to Ruth with a firm push. Samuel was crying. Ruth jumped up and grabbed the weeping boy. The Man left the building.

"What's wrong, sweetheart? What happened?" Ruth asked with alarm. Mervyn gave her a sly smile.

"What happened?" Ruth repeated.

"Seems Samuel had a little stomach upset." Mervyn chuckled. "Puked all over The Man's boots." He grinned widely. "I suspect it was from being thrown around by me when we were playing."

"And—?"

Mervyn gave her a mischievous grin as he tousled Samuel's hair. "I suggested the kid might have the flu—that he'd be throwing up all over inside the truck. That seemed to do the trick."

Ruth's warm smile lit her eyes. "Thank you," she said. She pulled Samuel into a cuddle on her lap. He came willingly.

"See you later." Mervyn shot Ruth a conspiratorial wink and strode into the dining room.

Ruth luxuriated in the warmth of feelings that rose up inside her. She hugged Samuel close.

Moments later, The Man returned—his entourage followed. He stood near the front of the room and cast his eyes across the women.

"Her, her, and her," he said. The three women—in their early twenties—squealed in terror as the bikers came to get them.

Elizabeth stood up. "What's going on?"

The Man turned cold eyes on her. He waggled a finger in her face. "Not another word..."

Ruth held her breath. She pushed herself back into her chair in an attempt to disappear, and not draw The Man's attention—hoping and praying he wouldn't change his mind about Samuel.

Please go. Please go.

"Where to?" asked the man in the green parka.

"Truck," The Man said. He eyed the struggling, crying women. "Vacation time is over. Time to get to work."

The Man turned back to the other women. They regarded him—breathlessly, eyes wide—silently willing him not to pick them. He grinned—a controlled action that curled the corners of his lips upward, slowly, like a snake swallowing a frog.

"Don't get too cozy. Your time is coming."

Chapter Twenty

From the Frying Pan into the Fire

METEOR AND Anna stared down at the dog. Its tongue hung crookedly from its stiffened body; white frost blanketed its fur. Anna pushed at the animal with her foot and moved it into a pool of sunlight streaming in through the barn window.

"What do you think? Meteor asked.

"You say the dogs attacked as a pack?"

"Yeah. It was as if they planned what they were doing. They rushed in and surrounded us."

"Did they hesitate...or rush at you as soon as they saw you?"

"No— They took some time to attack us."

"Hm...a rabid dog would have rushed at you instantly. There's something called *furious rabies*. It's a late stage in the rabies cycle. That's what we'd call a "mad dog." A dog like that is in a hyper state. It would attack immediately. Wouldn't stop to consider options. Sounds like these dogs were thinking just fine." Anna pushed at the dog's mouth. "And there would be foam around the mouth. I don't see any. It would be frozen on the muzzle if there was some."

"So, you think our guys are safe then?"

"I suspect so...but I'm no vet." Anna sighed. "My dad would have known." She yielded to an emotional moment in honor of her late father. "He was so smart."

"You're pretty smart, yourself," Meteor said. He gave her shoulders a quick, affirming squeeze. "Your dad would be proud of you." Anna smiled and continued speaking.

"Incubation periods are very different. Dad said rabies can take up to a year to show up."

"A year?"

"Yes. And I know this much—if the men begin to fear water—then we'll know."

"Fear water? Really?"

"That's when they'll start acting crazy."

"I really hope it doesn't come to that," Meteor said.

"I could be wrong— I'm just going from memory."

"What'll we tell them?"

"That I think the dogs *weren't* rabid," Anna said. "We'll watch them— We'll deal with the problem *if* it becomes reality. Otherwise, why scare them unnecessarily."

"Agreed," Meteor said. "Words of a wise woman." He squeezed her shoulder again.

Anna groaned and arched her back. "You mean a very pregnant woman."

"How you doing?"

"Mercifully, the morning sickness didn't last long. But the backaches and the leg cramps— What joy."

"I give good back and foot massages," Meteor said, his blue eyes warm and caring.

Anna gave a little chuckle. "Now wouldn't that make for some great camp gossip?"

"Ah, who cares..."

Anna laughed again. "I know of at least one redhead who would care."

Meteor grunted. "Her. She's been after me for weeks."

"No interest?"

"No, not really."

"Is there anyone special?"

Meteor gave her a serious look. "You already know the answer to that."

Anna touched his hand. "I'm sorry. It must be really hard on you."

"I should get this dog out of here," Meteor said quickly.

SILENCE LAY across the room like a suffocating quilt, stifling and dense. The women sat rigidly, not daring to speak—still fearing a return of The Man. Only the gurgles and playful shrieks of the babies and the younger children broke the awkward stillness. Elizabeth risked the first words:

"Where did he take them?"

"I don't know," Ruth said. Samuel was still cuddled on her lap. "I'm guessing to the South Camps."

The women had heard terrible rumors about the South Camps—a place where women were enslaved and prostituted...to the highest bidder.

"I wouldn't survive the Camps," Elizabeth said. "Brad is beginning to look better by the second."

"Don't be so sure that he'll be able to stand in the way if The Man decides to transfer you, too."

Elizabeth grimaced and shuddered. "Then I'll kill myself."

"Don't say that!" Ruth said. "You don't mean it."

"I do," Elizabeth said firmly.

Ruth took her sister's hand. "Help me find a way out of here," she said in a gruff whisper. "Focus on our escape...instead."

Elizabeth gazed out the window. "Oh crap— He's coming back."

METEOR STEPPED back and wiped his arm across his brow. He sweated heavily in spite of the cold. It had taken him nearly ten minutes to dig the large fire pit out of the snow. Matthew had decided that getting rid of the dogs was more important than doing inventory, so he assigned the task to Meteor. He shrugged off his coat, and searched his pocket for a butane lighter. He found it, flicked it, and flicked it again, but it didn't flame up. He shook it, and then tossed it into the pit. He checked another pocket and retrieved a small box of wooden matches.

It took a few attempts, but Meteor got a fire going. He waited for the flames to grow, and then he threw a dead dog into the fire. He stood and watched the dog's body smoke as its hair curled with the heat. He was part way across the yard in the direction of the other dog bodies, when he heard his name called. He turned back. At first, he couldn't see the speaker.

"What?"

"Can I help you?" A woman rounded a snow bank.

The redhead.

"Hi, Georgie," Meteor said cordially. "How are you today?"

"I'm good." The woman gave him a wide smile that showed evenly spaced, white teeth. Her red hair escaped in wild tendrils out from under her fur-trimmed hood. "I heard about the dog attack last night. Can I help?"

"I need more wood."

"I can do that. Take it from the regular wood shed?"

"Yeah. Use one of the kids' toboggans to haul the logs." Meteor grinned. "Better still—grab one of the kids and get them to pull it."

Georgie smiled. "Good idea."

"We'll need quite a bit."

"I know," Georgie said brightly. She touched his arm. "Leave it to me."

"I'm going to get the rest of the bodies."

THE MAN SHOOK snow from his shoulders as he walked back through the doors. The women stared like frightened rabbits, clutching their children to them, waiting for the axe to fall.

"Where is she?" The Man demanded. He walked into the dining room. "Cook!" he yelled. "Where are you?"

The women let out a collective sigh of relief.

In a few moments, he was back. Cook was with him. The Man walked over to Ruth. She blanched.

Oh God, what now?

"Cook says you're doing all the butchering. You hunting, too?"

"Uh—" Ruth looked puzzled.

Had he forgotten their conversation last night? She had told him she was out hunting deer. And he knew she could butcher a deer. She had told him that ages ago, too.

"Is that what you were up to last night?"

Ruth could hardly believe her good luck. He didn't seem perturbed—just forgetful. She grabbed the opportunity and nodded eagerly. Ruth pointed to her lip. "I had an accident."

"You were driving?" The Man asked.

Ruth panicked. "I was—"

Mervyn cut off her words. "She was with me."

"So, I heard," The Man said softly. "Hunting in the dark?"

"Flashlight. You can see their eyes. And they freeze. Easier to shoot," Mervyn said. "She drives...I shoot."

There was a brief pause as The Man stared at Mervyn. Mervyn returned his gaze, unflinchingly. The Man turned back to Ruth.

"We need meat for the South Camps."

Oh, no. Dread filled Ruth. *Don't take me there.*

"I want a truckload of meat ready by next week."

Thank you, God.

Ruth relaxed and let her breath out slowly. "We can do that."

The Man motioned to Mervyn. "Put together a team—some of the younger guys. Get these women...deer. Lots of deer."

Mervyn nodded.

"I'll be back in five days. I'll expect that meat ready to go." The Man looked pointedly at Ruth. "You got that?"

"Yes. You'll have the meat as long as your men bring us the deer."

"*Five* days," he said. "That meat had better be ready." He walked through the home's front doors, a small entourage of bikers trailing alongside him.

Ruth slumped down. She took a deep breath. "Oh, God," she said. "I thought he was going to take me, too."

Elizabeth got up and walked to the window. "I think he's gone now."

"I wonder who he left in charge."

"Oh, damn," Elizabeth said. "Three guesses and the first two don't count."

Brad walked through the doors. He smiled at Elizabeth. She pulled out the required response—she smiled back.

"Things will be different around here for a few days," he said, pausing to address the women. He walked into the dining room. A small band of armed men joined him.

"Oh, God," Ruth breathed. "From the frying pan into the fire." Elizabeth perched on the arm of the chair.

"We'll see about that," Elizabeth muttered. "We'll just see about that."

VIRGIL STOMPED his feet on the wooden landing and shook the snow from his shoulders before opening the cabin door. Marion was seated at the table with a down coat pulled tightly around her. She had been crying.

"What's the matter?" Virgil asked.

"You know what's wrong. I hate it here."

"So, what would you have me do about that?"

"I don't know." She blew her nose on a rag. "Where were you?"

"Killing wild dogs."

"Oh."

Virgil sat in a chair and pulled off his boots. He dropped them to the floor. "I'm beat. I'm going back to bed for a while." He rubbed the back of his neck. "Did you make anything to eat?"

Marion gave him a vicious look. “I am not your cook. You want something—make it yourself.”

Virgil gave her a stern look. “Marion, I don’t know what delusions you’re under, but this has got to stop.”

He reached across the table to take her hand. She pulled her hands away and dropped them into her lap. She stared at him sullenly.

“I don’t cook.” She burst into tears. “I hate cooking. I hate this place. I want my own house.”

“Marion—you don’t have a choice—”

“I do— I do have a choice. He promised me I wouldn’t have to stay here long—” Her eyes went wide with the realization of what she had just said.

“What—? What did you say?”

She babbled on, almost feverishly. “The Man told me he’d kill me if I didn’t tell him everything that was going on here. I did for a while—but the battery died ages ago.”

“Battery—?”

Virgil stood up. He stormed into the bedroom. Sounds of rummaging and things being thrown to the floor. He returned with the radio in his hand.

“You stupid bitch.”

“But I did it for us.”

“For us?” He shook his head. “No Marion, you did it for you.”

“But Virgil—I didn’t know what else to do. He said he’d kill me if I didn’t do what he said.” She began to screech. “Besides, The Man is more powerful than Matthew. He has thousands of men—all over the province. He’s going to come after this compound again. You know that. If he thinks I’m still loyal to him...” She clutched at him, her eyes frenzied. “C’mon. If we stay loyal to him—”

Virgil shook off her hand. “WE? WE? You’re crazy. And so is he.” He reached for his boots and pulled them on. He stood. “They knew, you know. They knew...”

Marion turned white. “Wh—what’re you doing? Where’re you going?”

Virgil picked up his coat and gloves. “Something I should have done months ago.” Virgil slammed the door behind him.

“Good, I’m glad, you son-of-a-bitch. I’m glad,” she screamed after him.

Virgil glanced back at the door and then walked toward the Gatehouse.

"Goddammit," he muttered.

MERVYN MOTIONED to Ruth. She lifted Samuel from her lap. He joined some of the other children in play near the fireplace. She got up from the chair and followed Mervyn down the hall. He turned suddenly and hugged her.

"Good thinking on your feet."

"Thanks. I thought so, too." Ruth gave a little giggle. Then she grew serious. "But now there's Brad."

"Yeah, he might be tougher to handle, but I think he'll leave us alone."

"Us?"

Mervyn shrugged. "We'll be spending a lot of time together, getting those deer ready."

"Oh."

"What did you think I meant?" Mervyn asked with a crooked grin.

"Uh—nothing."

"Maybe you meant this?" He pulled her to him and kissed her.

Ruth struggled, but Mervyn held her close, tightly, until she yielded to the pressure of his lips. His kiss became more forceful, more searching, and she moaned. A vision of Peter swept across her mind, and she stiffened. She pushed against his chest and turned her head away.

"Stop. Please stop."

Mervyn pulled back. "Okay. For now. But it's a different world, Ruth. You might never see your husband again."

Ruth slapped him. The blow snapped his head to the side. He looked back at her, surprised hurt in his eyes.

"Hit me all you want," he said. "But it's not going to change the facts."

"That was a cruel thing to say."

"Cruel...or truthful?"

"Leave me alone," Ruth said.

She pushed by him.

TROJAN HELD Cammy close—the tiny woman was shivering. She had caught the camp flu and the vomiting was violent. He refused to leave her even when word got to him that Matthew wanted help doing inventory.

"Feeling better now?" he asked.

Cammy didn't answer. She gave a small groan instead. She leaned forward. Trojan held her hair, while she bent over the slop bucket, her stomach heaving. Moments later, she rested against his chest, weak and trembling like an aspen leaf on a tree.

Trojan reached down and caressed her belly, now swollen with six months of growing baby. A tiny bump moved and jerked under his hands.

"Woo-hoo— He just kicked me," he said with undisguised delight.

Cammy looked at him tiredly and bent forward over the slop bucket.

MARTHA STARED out the window again. More snow had begun to fall. A cold sun shrouded over by a curtain of January gray beamed dully through the frost.

A hot pocket in the sky, she thought.

Within moments the sun shrank from a perfect round coin to just a small wedge of weak light. She watched as men and women hoisted shovels heaped with puffy snow. She wanted to join them, but her chest hurt; the shoveling would only make it worse.

One man came near the window—the pony-tailed captain. Martha tapped on the glass; he looked up. His mustache hung with a dozen tiny icicles, and frost covered his eyebrows and his beard. His ponytail was tucked up under a hunter's cap—its furred earflaps, covered in white frost, drooped like a dachshund's ears. The captain gave her a two-fingered salute and a smile, and then returned to his shoveling.

A memory flashed into Martha's mind of Josef shoveling snow, of Josef smiling up at her, his mustache covered in frost and hung with ice. She grinned. Josef had wanted to kiss her, but she held him off, and blew him an air kiss instead. They had both laughed.

Was it only a year ago?

It had been a long time since she entertained memories of her late husband and she clutched at the memory, fondling it like a rare gem, turning it, and examining its facets...

She remembered how Josef looked standing in the snow, his boots muddy, his curly hair frosted in white flakes, and the crotch of his jeans (which never fit him right) sagging halfway to his knees. She remembered his ready smile, his apple cheeks, and his twinkling, green eyes.

He really did look like Santa sometimes, she thought. She smiled again.

He had been a good man, a wonderful father, and a devoted husband. A feeling surfaced, one she hadn't felt in months. The thought tore at her heart.

I miss Josef.

A fumbling at the cabin door startled her and she swiped at the tears on her cheeks. Matthew burst through the door. Martha busied herself at the sink, her head low and her eyes shielded. It would be too hard to explain her tears.

"We're missing stock!" he said. He was furious. "Somebody has been stealing from the storehouses."

Chapter Twenty-One

Dealing with Marion

METEOR ADDED another log to the blaze. Anna had examined more of the dead dogs and stuck to her initial diagnoses that the dogs were not rabid. The smell of burning hair and flesh rose into the winter air. Meteor wondered if the dogs would have made good eating. He pushed the thought aside. He would have to be starving before he'd eat a dog—too much like eating a friend. His mind went back to his idea of finding another wolf pup... like Charlie—the wolf he'd raised from a cub. He stared into the flames.

"That's some stink."

"Huh?"

Georgie stood next to him, hood thrown back, red hair spilling down onto her shoulders. The top of her head wore a lacy cover of snowflakes. She held her hand over her nose.

"If they were diseased, that'll burn off any threat. But it sure reeks."

"The smell might help to keep the rest away, too," Meteor conjectured. He crouched and warmed his hands near the flames. Huge snowflakes drifted down and fizzled on the fire. He looked up and sighed. "Do we really need all this snow?"

Georgie knelt beside him. "I don't think so, but who knows...maybe Mother Nature has a plan."

Meteor pushed at a log with a long stick. He shrugged.

"Want something warm to drink?" Georgie asked.

"Like?"

"I have some chocolate squirreled away. I call it my *bad day survival chocolate,*" she said with a grin. "I can make cocoa—real cocoa." Her eyes gleamed with invitation.

Meteor smiled at her, warily. He shook his head. "No, thanks."

"Oh, c'mon," she said. "It'll do you good." She rested her hand on his arm. "C'mon."

Meteor smiled and gently lifted her hand from his sleeve. "Thanks, but no. Not now."

Georgie looked crestfallen, but she didn't give up. "Look, you have to eat. Let me make you some lunch. Where's the harm in that?"

Meteor pondered her offer. "Can you make that lunch to go?"

"To go? Why?"

"I want to take one of the snowmobiles out—see if I can track down the wolves I heard last night."

"You *want* to go looking for wolves?" She was flabbergasted. "Whatever for?"

"I want to find their dens. So I'll know where to look in the spring. I want a wolf pup. I had one when I was a kid."

"Sounds fascinating. What did you name it?"

Meteor told her about Charlie.

"So...ever since Charlie," Meteor concluded, "I've wanted another wolf pup."

"Want some company?" Georgie asked with a tiny, hopeful grin. "You know...when you go out looking."

Meteor took a big breath. "You just don't give up, do you?"

"Never."

"Okay, you win. Cocoa. Lunch. Then let's go hunting."

MATTHEW TWIRLED the pen in his hand. He sighed. Virgil sat across from him, waiting. Matthew leaned back in his chair, reached up a hand, and rubbed his forehead.

"Shoot," Matthew said.

Virgil tossed the radio onto the desk. The two men stared at it.

"You were right about Marion," Virgil said. "She can't have been much use to him, though. She says the battery has been dead for a while."

"Damn— Anna told us she had a radio. I forgot all about it. The dogs..." Matthew sat forward. "How much did she tell The Man?"

Virgil shrugged. "It couldn't have been much. I didn't really ask her for details though." Matthew sat quietly. Virgil shook his head. "I'm sorry." "What do you want me to do?"

Matthew drew a long breath. "Well, we aren't murderers—we can't toss her out in the middle of winter."

"So, what should we do with her?"

"There's always the Discipline Committee—we could resurrect that. Or take her before the elders— Let them decide what to do with her."

"Okay, if that's your decision...that's what'll happen."

"Did you have another idea?" Matthew asked.

"Stick her back in a bunkhouse."

"Not a bad idea. The women will exert their own kind of discipline on her. They won't put up with any of her bullshit."

"She's not going to like it, but she'll see that the alternatives could be much worse."

"You sure you've gotten all the equipment The Man gave her?"

Virgil shrugged. "I think all she had was this." He poked at the walkie-talkie.

"Well, I'll leave it to you then." Matthew met Virgil's eyes and added gently. "I'm sorry it didn't work out, Virg. I really am."

Virgil looked away.

Matthew changed the subject. "I've got more problems," he said, flipping a page in the logbook.

"What's going on?"

"Somebody's been stealing from the storehouses." He scratched his head. "Can't figure it out. They're locked. I trust everyone who has the combination."

Virgil thought a moment. "Lots of new people here, Matthew."

"I know. I barely know most of them." He tapped the book with his pen.

"What are they taking?"

"What d'ya think?" Matthew's tone was sharp. "Flour, sugar, salt, tea, coffee, medical supplies, matches, fire-starter bricks... The kinds of things you'd take if you were stocking a survival larder."

"You're looking at me like you suspect me of something."

"No, not you—"

Virgil's face darkened. "You mean my men."

Matthew raised his eyebrows and tilted his head. "It's possible, isn't it?"

"I trust them," Virgil said heatedly.

"You trusted Marion, too."

"I'll do some checking." A muscle in Virgil's jaw twitched. "If I find out something, I'll deal with it." He shoved the chair back and stood. "You have my word."

"Okay— I'll hold you to it." Matthew settled back in his chair. "What's up for tonight? You going after more dogs?"

Virgil strode over to the window. "If we can. The snow is really coming down again."

"Well, at least now that the patrols know what's happening, they'll be more watchful."

"The Hutterites were really upset," Virgil said.

"I'll bet they were— Losing pregnant cows is a serious loss. To them. And to us."

Virgil walked toward the door.

"Can I ask you something?" Matthew said.

"Sure."

"Why in hell did you join up with The Man? You could have run your own army. Taken him out yourself." Matthew wagged his head in disbelief. "I just don't get it."

"You have no idea about the capacity of his troops. They were growing exponentially when I was his confidante. His South Camps are huge. And he's got people down there who are very loyal."

"Like who?"

"Thousands of men that he's set up...on their own lands, their own fiefdoms. His ex-wife, Scar. And some old guy...I think he's a relation to The Man...he's gotta be in his seventies—ex-military, probably mafia, too." Virgil returned to his chair and sat down.

"Mafia?" Matthew's eyes widened as he leaned forward. "How did the mafia get into this?"

"Think about it. Tight knit groups survive in chaos. What's tighter, better organized, and more disciplined than a motorcycle club?"

"Mafia," Matthew confirmed.

"The Man was already in negotiations with eastern reps. He found out the mafia had taken control of eastern Canada—Montreal, Toronto, Ottawa—the big cities. They tried chasing the clubs into the country. But the clubs fought back—tried to hold their ground. Eastern bikers say the bloodshed was fierce. The Man didn't want another army interfering with his plans, so he sent an ambassador to parlay with the mob bosses. The guy made it there...and back. Alive."

"What saved him from being killed?"

"The Man offered women."

"What? They don't have women down east?"

"You don't get it...The Man was way ahead of the game. Right after the Change, he began corralling women, pulling them out of circulation—and the younger the better."

"Oh, wait— I know what you're talking about—*clean* women—Meteor told me...before the battle."

"And—it hasn't happened here yet—but in the east they were hit by a terrible epidemic. Cholera. Killed lots of people. Lots of women. Young ones."

"I'm starting to get a better picture of his scheme. I don't like it, but I feel better about our women and kids. He won't harm them or let them be harmed— They're an investment."

"Yeah, but he's crazy, too. He has a real thing for Hitler. Kept a copy of *Mein Kampf* in his office."

"Hitler? How does he figure into his plans?"

Virgil lifted his palms upwards. "World domination, I guess," he said with a sneer.

Matthew laughed. "Not exactly the most successful role model."

"The Man has ego issues— He thinks he's smarter than other world leaders. That he's going to succeed where others in history failed."

"Well, he's not done too well so far."

"With you, but that's not true down south. He rules down there. Everyone is afraid of him. And everyone kowtows to him." Virgil leaned forward. "Your camp was key to his plans. It's well designed...sits in close proximity to the Hutterites, has a constant food supply—he saw it as the perfect place to set up his North Camps." Virgil chuckled wryly. "You screwed things up, Matthew."

"Come on, there's got to be other compounds like ours..."

"Sure, but not as well organized. They tried, but they didn't survive the attacks. You did something many others couldn't do." Virgil paused and gave Matthew an earnest look. "I respect you, buddy."

"Thanks."

Virgil shook his head, slowly. "But you have no idea what's coming. He'll be back as soon as the snow is gone, and he'll have thousands of troops. We've got to get ready for that."

"We?" Matthew smiled.

"Okay—I'll say it—I'm glad to be here. Glad to be your friend again. We'll let Deena be water under the bridge." Virgil got up, and held out his hand. "We're solid."

Matthew took his hand and shook it. His mind skipped back to a memory of Deena, the slight, pretty woman they had both dated in high school. She had nearly married Virgil, but at the last minute, she indulged a change of heart. She canceled the wedding and moved in with Matthew. They lived together till the day she died.

"I'm glad, too. And if it helps any to know it—I think she loved you right up till the end."

"Bone cancer was a bad way to go," Virgil said softly.

"It was."

Virgil turned back to the door. "Time to give Marion the bad news." He smiled. "I hope she doesn't have a gun."

"Want somebody to go with you?"

Virgil huffed. "I think I can handle this, Matthew. Thanks." He put his hand on the doorknob. "Oh, wait. There's something else—I think it'd be a hell of a good idea to head into Edmonton and scavenge The Man's clubhouses."

"What?" Matthew laughed. "Why would we do that?"

Virgil held up his hand. "Hear me out— His supplies were too low to take him through winter. So, I doubt he stayed. I also doubt that he packed up everything and took it with him." He paused, lifted his eyebrows, and titled his head in conspiratorial encouragement. "Three clubhouses, Matthew. I'm sure they'd be worth a visit. He kept good Scotch..." He grinned widely. "I talked to the men. The guys are ready to go."

"I'll think about it," Matthew said. He grinned back.

Virgil left the Gatehouse. Matthew returned to his accounting.

He flipped the pages, and growled. Unlike the previous winter—because of the current year's endless snow—their regular scavenging runs had been curtailed. Now with the stealing... Maybe a visit to The Man's clubhouses was a good idea. Besides, the men needed an adventure—they needed to get the adrenaline flowing again.

Matthew decided— As soon as the weather allowed, he would go. He raised his eyebrows in contemplation of one unpleasant task ahead of him— Martha was going to give him a fight when he told her she would not be going.

He sighed and closed the book.

THE WOMEN huddled together, their hoods up, hands shoved into pockets, some clutching at the necks of their parkas in an effort to keep out the bone-chilling breeze. They watched Ruth work—some with great enthusiasm, some with disgust—as she demonstrated the skinning of a deer. Sweat poured down Ruth's forehead as she tugged a knife through the hide. Her dark hair—she had thrown back her hood—was coated in a blanket of heavy snowflakes. She grunted in exertion, expelling her breath in a white crystalline cloud.

"Don't damage the bowels, whatever you do," she said. "Run your fingers down, like this, and pull the hide away as you cut." She turned back to her students. "Anyone ready to try?" Two women stepped up and she guided them through the cuts. "That's not bad," she said, stepping back and eyeing the naked carcass. "Okay, two of you get this one down and take it into the kitchen. Cook will teach you how to cut it up." She glanced toward the sound of toboggans coming up through the yard. "The rest of you can help me with the fresh deer."

The snowmobiles pulled up. Mervyn was driving the lead machine. He stopped the engine and jumped off. Two deer lay in a sled attached to the rear of his machine. The other men pulled up; they had deer, too. The men wrestled the deer out of the sleds and soon had them hanging from the steel gambrels Mervyn had provided.

Mervyn watched as Ruth gave instructions to the women. When she stopped talking, he approached her. "Can I talk to you?" he asked.

"I'm busy." She kept walking.

"Please."

Ruth gave him an unpleasant look, but she followed him a short distance away from the hanging deer carcasses.

"What do you want?" she asked curtly.

"I'm sorry. Okay? I'm sorry. It was a terrible thing for me to say. I get that. Please, let's get past this."

Ruth eyed him. "Don't ever kiss me again."

"Fine— I won't."

"And don't talk about my husband again, either."

"Agreed." He stooped and stared into her stormy face. "Friends again?"

"Okay— But remember what I said."

Mervyn held up a hand. "I will. Scout's honor."

"How many more deer are coming in today?" asked Ruth, getting back to business.

"That's it. I figured they'd freeze up before you could get to them if we bring in too many."

"You're right. Thanks." She turned away, but he grabbed her arm.

"I'm here—give me a job."

"A job?"

"Yeah," he said with a wide smile. "I'm happy to help you."

Ruth cocked her head. "Are you sure you're one of The Man's men? You sure don't act like it." She grinned and added sternly, "Well, except for earlier."

"I am as much as I want...or need to be," Mervyn said. "Now, what should I do?" He swept an arm across his body in an exaggerated bow. "I am your servant."

Ruth burst out laughing.

VIRGIL ENTERED the cabin. Marion was nowhere in sight. He called out, but she didn't answer. He walked across the kitchen to the bedroom without removing his boots. Marion was seated on the bed. She turned to face him.

"Marion..."

She held up a hand. "I already know. I was just waiting for you to come back." She began to cry. "I am so sorry. I'm so mixed up. So confused." Virgil did not go to her. "I'll go." She rose from the bed, still weeping, grabbed a satchel, and brushed by Virgil. She hesitated. "I really am very sorry."

"Wait." Virgil caught her by the arm. "Where do you think you're going?"

"I've been thrown out, haven't I? That's why you went to see Matthew. To get me evicted..."

"Yes, I did, but no one expects you to go off in the middle of winter. You're staying here."

"I am?" Marion looked hopeful.

"But you'll be staying in a bunkhouse."

Marion's face fell. "Of course."

She pulled away and walked over to the dresser, opened the drawer, and began removing clothing. Tears dripped from her eyes.

Virgil sighed. He walked over and turned her to face him. He took her chin in his hand. "You could have made this work."

"No, Virgil...I don't think so. I don't fit in here."

"Let me help you with your things."

"Please don't— I'll do it myself."

Marion finished filling her bag. She shrugged on her down coat, and gathered a handful of scarves and sweaters from hooks by the door. Virgil picked up a pair of gloves and handed them to her.

"By the way," he said. "Matthew asked if you had any more of The Man's equipment."

"What kind of a Mata Hari would I be if I told you that?" She gave Virgil a tired look. "No, Virgil—nothing else—just the radio you took."

Virgil held the door for her.

METEOR FIRED up the snowmobile. Georgie slipped onto the seat and waited.

"We'd better get back," he shouted over the sound of the engine. "It'll be getting dark soon."

Georgie smiled.

"Sorry about the wild goose chase," he said. "I really thought we'd find something."

"Another time," she said with an encouraging smile.

Meteor gave her cheek a gentle stroke. "Thanks for the lunch."

"Another time?" she repeated.

"Another time."

MATTHEW AND MARTHA stood in their kitchen. Matthew held Martha in a firm hug. She hugged him back. He finally pulled away and slumped down at the kitchen table.

"We've gotta get more supplies," he said. "I've changed the locks on the storehouses."

"There's a lot missing?" Martha asked.

"Too much. With the stealing. And we aren't replenishing our stocks like we once could."

"Finite supply...no one is making any more."

Matthew grinned wryly. "Glad you girls learned how to make toilet paper."

"Oh, yes..." Martha said with a satirical lilt in her voice. "One of my life's greatest accomplishments."

Matthew gave a small laugh and then he grew serious. "We might need the bunker supplies."

"That's not such a good idea...to deplete emergency rations," Martha said. "This isn't an emergency yet."

Matthew stroked his chin. "There's another option— Virgil suggested we go to Edmonton and scavenge The Man's clubhouses."

"That sounds like a plan," Martha said, picking up a pan from the hotplate. She scooped a seasoned mix of deer meat and potatoes onto a plate. She brought it to the table. Matthew accepted the plate, but he didn't start eating. Martha gave him a quizzical glance. "What?" she asked.

Matthew looked perplexed. "I tell you about a scavenger mission. And you don't jump on it?" He raised his eyebrows. He got up and grabbed Martha by the shoulders. "You don't want to go?"

"I do—I always want to go—you know that...but I'm tired, Matthew." She rested her head on his chest. Matthew kissed her hair.

For the moment, he wished she had argued with him, like the old days. For the moment, his heart yearned for the old Martha—the feisty and combative woman he had fallen in love with. He held her close. He held his hatred for Brad even closer.

Brad had stolen something from her. Matthew wanted to get it back. He ached to make Brad pay. Visions of the man dying an agonizing death brought a heady rush. He would welcome the chance for a shot—a fist in the mouth—a bullet in the brain. Brad's days were numbered. He would see to it. But for now, his wife needed his attention.

"Martha, if you decide that you'd like to go with us, then I want you to go. Okay?" He whispered into her hair. "Like the old days—you and me—and a truck."

Martha looked up. "There is something I would like— I would like to go back to your house," she said, referring to Matthew's family farmhouse with the barn, the hidden tunnel, and the secret war room. "That would be nice."

"*Our* house," he corrected. "I'd like that, too."

Chapter Twenty-Two

Getting Rid of the Dead Weight

RUTH SWIPED at the misty cloud of condensation formed by her breath on her bedroom window. She peered into the gloomy, overcast morning. The falling snow looked more like falling rain, pouring down in a thick curtain of soundless white. She sighed and sat down on the edge of her bed. Samuel and Mary's beds were already empty. The children were long gone in search of their breakfast. Ruth rubbed her eyes, stretched, and groaned as her neck cracked and sore muscles complained. She checked her watch. It was just past nine o'clock.

She grabbed her hiking boots from the floor. A whiff of her socks made her wrinkle her nose. She grabbed another pair from a box under the bed—they weren't clean, but they didn't stink. She tugged on one boot and then the other. She tied one, reached for the second boot, but instead of tying the lace, she groaned again, and flopped back on the bed. She closed her eyes and entered into the swirl of exhaustion that swamped her head.

Just a little more sleep. I won't be missed. Just a few more minutes.

They had butchered deer for three days, and the truck larders were getting full—they had adapted Cook's freezer idea and lined three truck boxes with thin slabs of hardened snow; they packed in the meat, pulled the truck beds' covers closed, and piled more snow atop that. Ruth's back ached, but Mervyn insisted on getting more deer—for their own larder. She reluctantly yielded to his good sense. In spite of the additional help from the women she had tutored in the art of skinning and gutting deer, she didn't crawl into bed until almost five o'clock that morning.

Ruth sat up at the sound of her name. She tied her boot, pushed her arms into her parka, and did up the zipper. She left the room. She turned when she heard her name again— Elizabeth called to her from down the hall.

"There's nothing more I can do for her," Elizabeth said with a scowl. "She's all yours now."

"Oh, God...is she ready?" Ruth raised her arms and arched her back. "Are you sure?"

"I'm guessing so. Hollering and swearing. Nobody wants to stay in the room with her. She's horrible."

"She's so young...and it's her first. We've gotta cut her some slack."

Elizabeth made an unpleasant sound in her throat. "Please...be my guest."

"What about the deer?"

"You've trained enough women...they can handle it," Elizabeth responded.

"But they need supervision..."

Another unpleasant sound. "I'll do it. Just don't make me go back to that witch."

Ruth chuckled and closed her eyes at the thought of Elizabeth managing the other women.

You are better off telling a stiff, cold deer what to do, she thought.

Elizabeth started down the hallway.

"Wait— Might be better to ask Sarah," Ruth said gently. "She's gotten good at butchering."

And telling people what to do. They'll listen to Sarah.

Elizabeth agreed.

Ruth went back into her room. She unzipped and pulled off her coat. She grabbed a hooded sweatshirt and a heavy wool sweater and pulled those over her flannel shirt. Fatigue made her shiver in the coolness of the room—their rooms were like stone tombs in spite of propane heaters. She left the bedroom.

It wasn't hard to locate the pregnant girl—her howls echoed down the hallway. For the moment, Ruth wished for her mother's presence, Martha's steady no-nonsense hand on the situation. She missed Anna, too. It had been ages since she thought of her birthing partner—the girl was a natural midwife with endless patience when it came to new mothers in the grips of a labor pain.

What's happened to Anna? Did she make it?

A man's laugh coming from the community room caught her attention. The door to the room was ajar. She gave the door a small push and peered into the room. Brad was seated at one of the tables; two of his Crazies reclined nearby—elbows on the counter, their boots crossed at the ankles. Ruth recognized one of the men as a guard who had ushered her into the women's bunkhouse, months ago—during the attack on the compound. She guessed that he must have arrived in the night, since she hadn't seen him there before.

"Supplies are way too low," the guard said. "The South Camps can't spare any more. The Man says it's time to get rid of the dead weight. Said you'd know what he meant."

Ruth suppressed a gasp. She froze—her eyes wide with shock.

Dead weight? Who?

Brad spoke and uncannily provided the answer to her unspoken question. "The old broads— We'll get rid of them."

"All of them?" a fourth, unidentified man asked.

"Unless they cook," Brad clarified. "Or they do something else useful—" He bent his head toward the high-pitched screeches of the laboring woman down the hall. "Like handling that shit."

"How soon?" the third man asked.

"Soon. Before The Man gets back here," the guard answered.

"So, how do we do this?" asked one of the men.

An eerie silence followed. Ruth held her breath.

"It might be a good idea to take them somewhere. No sense spooking the rest of the herd," the guard said.

Ruth's ears burned and she trembled with anger.

The herd? Cattle? We're cattle?

"Who should do it?" the fourth man asked.

"You two can handle it," Brad said. "Get a couple of the young guys to help, too. It'll toughen them up."

"We're on it."

Ruth began to slink away when she heard Brad speak again. She pressed her ear near the opening.

"Get rid of that retard, too."

"Who?" the guard asked.

"The kid that barely talks," Brad explained.

Ruth's breath caught in her chest.

Reggie? Brad wanted Reggie dead? They were going to kill Reggie!

Hardness crept into her spirit like a rush of winter wind. With it came a steadfast resolve, a power, and a determined courage that infused her from tongue to toe. She stood erect.

Over my dead body! You will NOT touch that little boy.

Ruth slipped away and ran down the hall—in the opposite direction from the birthing room. She burst into the kitchen—her eyes were evergreen dark and wild. Cook and Hannah turned to her. Hannah was making bread dough; the cook was hacking at a side of deer.

"What the heck is going on?" Hannah asked. Ruth grabbed the older woman by the arm.

"Come with me. Now!"

Hannah pulled her arm from Ruth's grasp. "Wait. Why?"

"Come with me. Now!"

Hannah gave a quick backward glance at the cook, and then followed Ruth into the dining area. Cook watched them leave and turned back to the deer. She looked up when the backdoor squeaked. Mervyn and one of the women lugged in another deer carcass.

"Here you go," he said, dumping the deer's denuded body with a loud thump onto the stainless steel prep table. "This one's a little messy. Sorry. One of the girls got a little carried away with the knife."

"Did someone wash out the cavity?" Cook asked.

"Yeah, as best as we could. It's pretty cold out there." Mervyn dropped down into a chair. "That's a lot of meat. We've filled three truck beds. And we've started on a fourth."

"How many more?"

"I don't know. I'll have to ask Ruth." Mervyn craned his neck around. "Where is she? I haven't seen her all morning. Slacking off, huh?" he said with a wide grin.

Cook tipped her head toward the dining room. "In there. She's all fired up about something. She's got Hannah with her." Mervyn jumped from his chair and strode out of the kitchen.

Ruth and Hannah were in a huddled conversation at the far side of the dining room. Ruth's hands and arms flew up and down in emphasis. Hannah stood, arms drooping at her sides, her jaw hanging down. Mervyn crossed the room.

"What's going on, Ruth?"

Ruth ceased talking. She gave Mervyn a quick appraisal. "I don't think I can tell you."

"Tell me what?"

"You're one of them, Mervyn. I don't know if I can trust you."

Mervyn's eyebrows shot up. "What? Are you kidding me?" He gripped Ruth's shoulders, and pulled her face close to his. "Ruth, you can trust me. And you know it."

Ruth's lip trembled and her eyes grew shiny with tears. "They're going to *kill* Reggie, Mervyn."

"What?" Mervyn squinted at her. "Are you sure?"

"I just overheard Brad talking with a guard from the South Camps," Ruth said in a heated whisper. "He said we're short on food...they can't spare any...The Man says to kill them. The older women. And...*Reggie*." She swallowed to clear the swelling of emotion threatening to choke her.

Mervyn glanced at Hannah. The woman stood stone silent, like a captured deer—her face pale, her eyes large. Tears ran down her face.

"No— This is *not* going to happen." Mervyn stared down into Ruth's eyes. "Leave this to me. I'll take care of it. I promise." He gave her shoulders an encouraging squeeze. "Okay?"

"Okay," Ruth said softly. The three turned toward the sound of men's voices outside the dining room. "It's them," Ruth said.

"Get Hannah out of here," Mervyn said in a hurried whisper. He gave Ruth a little push. "Go!"

Ruth grabbed Hannah's arm again and rushed her back into the kitchen. Once inside, they stopped and peered around the doorjamb. Mervyn sauntered over to the dining room entrance, just in time to intercept two men.

"Hey, guys. You hungry?"

One of the men glanced at his watch. It was the guard Ruth had recognized earlier. "Yeah, I could go for some chow."

"Me, too," the other man agreed.

"C'mon," Mervyn said with a wide smile. "I was just heading into the kitchen myself. Why don't you guys have a seat? I'll find out what's on the menu. Want pie?"

"That sounds good."

"I'll be right back," Mervyn said.

The two men settled into chairs and leaned back. One pulled out the remnants of a cigar. He lit it and passed it to the other man. The air above their heads filled with tendrils of white smoke.

"Girls!" Mervyn shouted. "Rustle up some food to feed these guys. And make damn sure there's pie." He stopped near Ruth and hissed, "While they're eating, I'll find out what's going on."

Ruth and Hannah filled plates with sliced venison, thick slabs of sourdough bread, crimson beet pickles, and slices of white onion. One of them cut wide wedges of pumpkin pie they had made from canned pie filling. Hannah went into the far corner of the pantry and retrieved a bowl of whipped cream. The small, unheated area of the kitchen made a perfect refrigerator. She swirled on a generous dollop of thick, sweet cream. A pinch of nutmeg, and the feast was ready.

Mervyn nodded at Ruth. "Help me carry these out." To Hannah, he said, "Stay out of sight, until I find out more."

"I will," Hannah said breathlessly. "You can count on it."

Mervyn and Ruth deposited the plates of food in front of the men. They ignored Ruth and dug in. Mervyn sat down. He picked up two pieces of bread, slices of meat, and began making a sandwich. He looked up at Ruth.

"So, is that baby born yet?"

"Oh, I—" Ruth sprinted out of the room. She had completely forgotten about the impending birth. The men didn't look up.

Mervyn took a large bite of his sandwich. He stared out the window, checked the kitchen door, and then turned his attention back to the men who were still shoveling food into their mouths, bits of bread and meat falling to their plates as they chewed.

Mervyn groaned. "I wish we could go back to the South Camps. It's pretty dull here." He waited. Neither man responded. He tried again. "So, what's up for today? Anything interesting happening?"

"Something you can help us with," mumbled the guard.

"What's that?"

The guard looked around. "Can't really talk about it here."

"Why? There's no one here."

The man grunted his agreement. "Brad wants us to knock off some of the dead weight."

"What dead weight?"

The guard motioned to his food. "He says it'll be easier to feed everyone if we get rid of some of the women."

"Get rid of—you mean waste them?" Mervyn's face was a palette of cool neutrality.

"Yeah." The guard lifted a forkful of pie slathered in whipped cream to his lips. "Kill them."

"Who?"

"The old women."

"How old is old?" Mervyn asked. He took a small bite of his sandwich and chewed.

"Ugly and saggy, I guess," the other man said with a laugh. "Like that Hannah."

"The cook is old. Is she on the hit list, too?" Mervyn asked.

"No, not Cook. She stays." The guard burped and wiped his mouth with the back of his hand. "Unless you know how to make a fuckin' pie."

Mervyn gave a hollow laugh. "Not me."

"We're supposed to get rid of that idiot kid, too," the second man said.

"What kid?"

"The retard that doesn't talk."

"Why?"

"Brad said."

"What about the other kids? The babies?"

"No, Brad says not to touch the kids. The Man says they'll be useful."

Mervyn fidgeted with his fork. He pushed his pie plate across the table. "One of you want this?" He stood up.

"Where ya goin'?" asked the other man.

"Somebody's got to shoot deer to keep your fat faces filled." He shot them a teasing grin.

"Better you, than us," the guard said as he pulled Mervyn's pie plate over. He began eating again.

Mervyn left the dining room. He followed the howls coming from the birthing room down the hall. He stopped at the door and knocked. A woman opened the door.

"What do you want?"

"Ruth," he said.

"She's busy."

"Tell her I need to speak to her."

The woman shut the door. In a moment, Ruth appeared. She slipped out of the room and closed the door behind her.

"What did you find out?" she whispered.

"You were right— Old women. And Reggie. But the other kids are safe."

"What are we going to do?"

"Can you leave here for a few minutes?"

Ruth listened to another screech come from inside the room. "She's not quite ready yet...but the baby's head should be crowning soon. Tell me what you want."

"Find Reggie. Dress him...in oversized clothes. Make him look bigger. Bring him around to the kitchen door. I'll tell Hannah to get dressed, too."

"You're going to take him away? In broad daylight? Where?"

"Remember the farmhouse?" Ruth nodded. "I have friends there who will help us. But hurry. The guys think I'm going back out to hunt deer."

Ruth's eyes filled with questions, and she began to speak, but Mervyn interrupted her with a warning look. "I can't save them all, Ruth. You know that."

"I know," Ruth said softly.

"You'd better get going," Mervyn warned, checking his watch.

"I've got to send Reggie's things with him...he needs his Veggie Tales stuff."

"We don't have much time."

Ruth held Mervyn's eyes in determination. "He *needs* those things."

"Okay. But you've got only a few minutes. I'm getting ready now. I'll be waiting by the kitchen."

"I'll be there," she said firmly.

"Oh...and make sure Reggie's wearing something Brad would recognize." Ruth looked puzzled. Mervyn gave her a crooked grin. "I have an idea," he said.

"Okay." Ruth went back into the bedroom.

Mervyn loped down the hallway.

Ten minutes later, Ruth appeared at the back door, with Reggie in tow. Hannah greeted them. She was dressed in full snowmobile gear. She had a large shoulder bag clutched to her chest; it was bulging.

"Food," she whispered.

"Where's Cook?" Ruth asked. They had not taken the older woman into their confidences.

"She's still not feeling well," Hannah said. "I told her we'd take care of the lunches. She went to her room."

"Good. I don't trust her not to say anything."

Snowmobiles revved and whined outside. Ruth studied Reggie. He looked ridiculous in a huge gray snowsuit, massive black boots, and a yellow helmet. It was hard to tell his age or his sex in the get-up. Except for the canvas bag filled with Veggie Tales books and toys, he could be mistaken for one of the hunters—at least from a distance.

Ruth gave Reggie a quick hug and a squeeze. "Be a good boy," she said. She gave Hannah a firm hug, too. "Go with God."

Hannah squeezed back. "We'll be fine." She pulled away and smiled. "Thank you." She pulled her helmet over her head. "Don't forget to make the lunches." She held out a hand to Reggie. "C'mon, sweetheart." Reggie took her hand.

Mervyn opened the kitchen door. "Now," he said. "Quick. Let's get them out of here." He looked at Hannah. "You can drive a machine?"

"Easy."

"Good. Let's go." Mervyn turned back to Ruth. He raised a gloved hand and touched her cheek. "Do what you have to do. I've got this." He bent, gave her forehead a small kiss, and then ran toward the waiting snowmobiles.

Hannah and Reggie were already onboard one of the machines. Reggie was seated behind Hannah. He was examining the snowmobile, twisting this way and that, trying to peer through his helmet.

"That won't do," Mervyn said. He grabbed the boy and sat him on his machine, on the seat in front of him. He signaled to Hannah and the two machines roared away.

Ruth watched them disappear into the field. She breathed a sigh of relief and scurried back through the kitchen.

MATTHEW RUBBED his temples and listened to the two young women standing in front of him. They had intercepted him on his way back to the cabin. The women were not happy about having Marion—*the traitor bitch*—moved into their bunkhouse. Word of her subterfuge had spread quickly around the camp. Matthew continued rubbing his head.

"Ladies," he said. "We have no choice. We aren't going to throw her out. She has nowhere to go. In the spring, we'll help her relocate. But for now, you'll just have to be patient."

His words incited a fresh string of heated complaints from the women. Matthew closed his eyes against the sound.

"Can I help?" Matthew turned and grinned with relief when he saw Martha.

"I'll let my wife take this," he said, squeezing Martha's hand. "I'm beat. See you later."

Martha turned to the women. "You've got an issue with Marion moving in? Well, guess what? I once had an issue with you moving in, too. And not that long ago," she said, pointing to a redhead, the taller of the pair. "Remember, way back...when you showed up pregnant? We didn't send you away."

"We don't trust her," the redhead said hotly.

"I didn't trust you either," Martha said. "Make the best of it. Surely you can handle her."

"You want us to *handle* her, Martha? Like how you *handled* Brad?"

"What?" Martha's mouth hung open in surprise.

"Everyone wants to know, you know. Everyone's talking. Why didn't you shoot him?" the redhead asked. "He killed your husband. If he had killed my husband, I would have shot him. And then cut off his balls, too."

Martha's eyes flashed with dark anger. She advanced on the redhead, stopped in front of her, and glared up into her face.

"Watch yourself, missy. Or you'll be the one looking for a new home."

RUTH COLLAPSED into one of the big armchairs in the home's front room. She drew her arm across her forehead. The birth had been grueling, for both mother and midwife. The baby would crown and then slip away. Ruth was used to first births and reluctant first-time mothers, but each one seemed more difficult than the last. She had finally convinced the woman to stop screaming and start working. The woman listened to Ruth's advice and within twenty minutes, a new baby boy was born.

Ruth closed her eyes and drifted into sleep. The sound of jabbering men at the front door shocked her awake. She jumped, and clutched her chest. Her heart pounded. She turned. Several men walked in; Brad was one of them.

"Where are the young guys?" Brad asked.

"Hunting deer," said a woman.

"Still?" He turned at the sound of snowmobiles whining in the distance. Ruth watched them arrive, appearing and disappearing as they bobbed in and out of snowdrift valleys.

The drivers zoomed up to the home, braked, cut the engines, and jumped from the machines. Deer carcasses filled a sled attached to one of the toboggans—its driver pulled off his helmet. Ruth recognized Mervyn and her heart leapt.

No sign of Hannah or Reggie.

The hunters laughed and joked as they made their way to the front doors. They entered the home, guns and helmets in hand. They stamped their boots and shrugged off their outer clothing. Women sitting nearby knew what to do—they gathered the men's snow gear, shook off the snow, and arranged items near the fireplace to dry. Mervyn came in behind them. He searched the room, espied Ruth, and gave her a tiny wink.

Mervyn strode over to the guard he had had lunch with earlier; the man was standing with Brad near the dining room. Mervyn handed the guard something balled up in his hand. The guard looked puzzled. Then he shook out the item. Ruth nearly screamed.

Reggie's shirt! Covered in blood.

The guard lowered his eyebrows at Mervyn. "What the fuck—?"

Brad reached over and took the shirt. He turned it so that *Bob, the tomato* and *Larry, the cucumber* faced him. "It's the kid's shirt," he said.

"What kid?" the guard began. Then realization struck him. He eyed Mervyn. "What did you do?"

"You told me at lunchtime that we had to start eliminations," Mervyn said in a conspiratorial whisper. "I was going out hunting anyway. I thought I'd kill two birds with one stone—save you the trouble." Mervyn screwed up his face. "It's what you told me to do, isn't it?"

"Yeah—sure," the guard blustered. "I just didn't think we were doing it today."

Brad stared at Mervyn. Mervyn returned the stare—a goofy expectation of praise lighting his eyes. Brad snorted, and shoved the shirt into his jacket pocket. He walked away.

Mervyn clapped the guard on the back. "What's for supper? I'm starving. I shouldn't have given you my pie." He laughed. The guard returned the friendly greeting and the men went into the dining room.

Elizabeth slipped in beside Ruth. "Was that Reggie's shirt?" she whispered. Ruth didn't speak. "What's going on?"

Ruth still said nothing.

Elizabeth's eyes grew wide. She covered her mouth with her hand.

Ruth remained silent.

~ ~ ~

The Deserters

THE TWO MEN studied the logbooks on the large dining table. Both wore woolen greatcoats; the coats hung open, their hems swaying around the men's calves as they moved. Tattered bits of lining and loose threads still clung to the ragged openings where sleeves had once been attached to the shoulders. The men turned pages, made notes, and turned more pages. The Man picked up a map of Canada. With one index finger, he traced a path between cities and towns circled in red. Some of the cities had hand drawn blue stars next to them. He made another note, and then returned to his musings and page turning. The older man next to him clucked his tongue as he reviewed entries.

"Spring is coming soon," the older man said. "It's a good thing. We need to trade women soon."

"We can move the Gatekeeper's women east from Sunnyvale. There's no reason to bring them here first." The door opened and the two men looked up.

"What?" The Man asked. Scar stood there. She looked perplexed.

"It's getting harder and harder to feed all these women. When are we getting more food?"

"I've got meat coming up from Medicine Hat. Lots of deer down there and Ruth knows how to butcher."

"When?"

The Man said nothing.

"When is the meat coming?" Scar repeated. "We are bloody low on food."

"Ration the food tighter," the older man suggested. "Won't hurt the women to lose a little weight."

"The women!" Scar said with exasperation. "It's not the women. It's the men. They eat like pigs. Like we have a magic pantry. And they don't do any hunting," she blurted, her anger rising. She looked from the old man to The Man. "Well?"

"I'm leaving soon," The Man said, returning his gaze to the maps. "I'll send the deer meat back. But in the meantime, squeeze the Hutterites for more food."

"We've done that," Scar said, her voice bitter with barely constrained resentment. "Don't you think we've done that?"

"Lower your voice," The Man said with a dip of his eyebrows.

Scar did so. "Please tell the men to start helping out." Scar glanced from one man to the other. "Or we will starve."

"Too bad you didn't manage to take out the Gatekeeper," the old man said with a snide edge in his voice. "Sounds like he's got quite a system."

The Man narrowed his eyes. "For all his systems and all his plans, we still have his women."

"And his wife's daughters," Scar added.

"When do I get to meet them?" the old man asked.

"Maybe never," The Man answered. "They'll be part of the eastern shipment."

"You're kidding me, right? You aren't about to give away that kind of bargaining power, are you?" The older man took a sip of the amber liquid glowing in the crystal highball glass in his hand.

"Brad has claimed the younger one. Elizabeth."

"Really. Just like that?" Scar asked.

"I decided it might work in our favor. We'll see what happens." The Man shrugged. "I might ship them as a pair, envoys to the east. Not a big loss—if something goes wrong with our dealings with the mafia." The Man gave the knuckles on his right hand a brief rub. "Besides," he said, looking pointedly at Scar, "I'll remind you that it's none of your business."

"It is my business. You asked me to set up Sunnyvale and I did it. Now I am in charge of making sure your stock is kept in good health. I can't do that without food. Either we reduce the numbers here, or you get us more food."

"I sent a messenger to Brad. Told him to begin eliminations— The older women of no value."

Scar blinked. "Well, that's fine for there...what about here?"

"Eliminations can start here, too," The Man said. The old man coughed. The pair looked his way.

"Matthew hasn't come after his women yet," the older man said. "Why not bring the women here? I mean the ones that can be bartered. It might be a way to get Matthew to give up his compound."

"For a few women?" Scar asked, aghast at the notion.

"Martha's daughters," the old man said.

"Grandchildren," The Man said. "We have them, too."

The older man shook his head, slowly and ominously. "I think the Gatekeeper is coming after his women. And soon. Get those other women traded now. The snow will be gone in a month or so. Pull them back here. Sort them. Send a caravan to the east. Put Brad in charge. But get them the hell out of here. Before it's too late."

"And me?" Scar asked.

"You just keep doing what you are you told to do," The Man said. "And you will stay here."

The old man coughed again, cleared his throat, and spat into his hand. He smeared the sputum on a grimy rag he pulled from his pocket. "What about Drumheller?" he asked.

The Man sat down and reached for a glass. He sniffed and took a long sip. He let out a long sound of satisfaction as the liquid slid down his throat. "Drumheller is ours. We have amassed our ammunition near the city. Any women and children that weren't killed in the siege are here now."

"Exactly," Scar said. "Just what I have been saying. You keep adding mouths to feed, but without hunters, farmers...we can't feed them." Scar's voice rose again. "It's one thing to execute these women, but starving them is a horrible idea." Her cheeks had grown rosy. She took a breath. "Do something."

The Man looked up, a slow motion that caused a dark shadow to encase the left side of his face. "One more time, Scar...and you will join the eastern caravan." He stopped and waited. "Do you understand me?"

Scar ran a hand across the damaged side of her face. She dropped her eyes. "Understood." She left the room.

"She's right," the older man said. "You've got a bunch of lazy-ass shits who can't grasp the future. Have you checked our fuel supplies lately?"

"I hear they're still in good shape."

"Really?" the older man said. "Do some checking yourself. Do you think your Archangels are honoring you? Think again. These aren't trained soldiers. Feed them, or they'll desert you."

"I have strongholds all over the province, into B.C, and Saskatchewan. I have most of Montana covered, too."

The older man got up, grasping the armrest of the chair to steady himself as he rose. He stood erect and appraised The Man. "You might be my brother's son, Hezekiah, but sometimes I don't think you have his brains. That man knew how to run a congregation...he knew how to make people believe."

The Man said nothing.

The older man bent forward at the waist, grabbed the small of his back, and groaned. "Sure could use some pain pills."

The Man sat silently, swirling the liquid in his glass. He watched the older man shuffle to the door. The older man clucked his tongue as he reached for the door handle.

"You've got a good thing here, but you'd better do some rethinking." He coughed again. "Your dad would know what to do."

"But he didn't know how to stay alive, did he, Uncle?" The words oozed from The Man's mouth, darkly, like molten lava from a crater.

The older man paused and turned back. "No, I gotta say...you have him beat there. Yes, indeed. You have him beat there."

The old man gave The Man a quick glance, a wry grin, and then gave the door a push. He left the room.

The Man waited. A moment passed.

"Scar!" he yelled. The woman was back in the room instantly.

"What?"

"Have you heard anything about the men guarding our weapons in Drumheller?"

Scar shook her head and sighed. "I've heard through the grapevine that they're deserting." She shrugged. "Can you blame them? Food is so scarce and they want to be with their families. Better hope nobody goes after that stronghold. At least nobody with any strength."

The Man took another long swallow. He grimaced as the alcoholic heat hit his belly. He placed the glass on a side table and leaned back into his chair. He closed his eyes.

Scar came over and stood near him. "You're tired." She reached out and drew her fingers lightly across his forehead. "I'm sorry I gave you a hard time."

She gasped in pain when he slapped her hand away.

"I'm going to Medicine Hat. I'll put the women into your charge."

"The women?"

"Martha's daughters. I'll bring them here. Then we're going north. As soon as the snow clears...I'm going after the Gatekeeper. I don't think he'll refuse when his wife's kids are at stake."

"What about Ruth's children?"

"I'll keep them here. As a back-up plan."

Scar backed away, rubbing her sore hand. "I'll get you some supper."

The Man looked away as she walked to the door. Then he called after her. "Uncle wants pain pills. See if you can find any."

"I will." She placed her hand on the door handle. "Oh, one more thing. There's a rumor about one of the guys—a young guy from the States—going into business for himself."

The Man leaned forward. His eyes flashed. "What?"

"Just a rumor. Thought you should know. You might want to look into it." Scar looked away and then back at him again. "I still care about you, you know."

"Get my supper."

Sheree Zielke

Chapter Twenty-Three

A Guy with a Fu Manchu Mustache

MERVYN HELD up his hand and interrupted their conversation. He listened to hear if anyone was coming. Ruth stopped speaking and listened, too. They were just outside the kitchen door. It was early morning. The sky was resplendent in rich salmon tones, and the wind was calm. Birds twittered in the distance, and someone banged pots and pans around inside the kitchen, but no one else was in sight. Mervyn let out his breath.

"It's okay," he said.

"Where are they?" Ruth hissed.

"They're fine," Mervyn whispered back.

"Why was Reggie's shirt covered in blood?"

"Deer blood looks the same as human blood," he said with a grin.

"Where are they?" Ruth asked again.

"The farmhouse— I told you that's where I'd take them."

"Was Reggie okay when you dropped him off?"

"Remember the two women you met when you were there?"

"Yeah."

"They're...*partners*. Pretty cool chicks. One of them's a pastor...the other is a mountain guide from Jasper—I know her from my guide days. We'd see each other at conventions. They were there when I got there. I told them the problem. They said it wasn't a problem."

"You trust them? What if they tell?" Ruth voice rose an octave in panic.

"They won't. They know about The Man. They don't like him. Reggie and Hannah are safe."

"What about the other machine that Hannah rode?"

"I couldn't figure out a way to bring it back from the farmhouse without arousing suspicion, so I left it there."

"What if somebody notices that it's gone?"

"I'll figure out something."

Ruth stood quietly for a few moments. "Somebody will notice the missing machine. We could go out together— I could bring it back."

"You don't think somebody would notice that? You—coming back on a machine—alone?"

"Yeah, I guess you're right. But I'm still worried."

"Machines are disposable these days. We've dumped bikes that have broken down. It won't seem that odd if I tell them that. Besides, these guys don't care much about the day-to-day operation of this place. Most of them just want to go back to the South Camps."

"Still makes me nervous," Ruth said. "Brad might ask."

"If he does, I'll deal. But I really don't think it's going to be a problem." He lifted Ruth's chin and peered into her face. "So, stop worrying, okay?"

Cook came to the door. She pushed it open and came outside. She wiped a hand across her brow where sweat had beaded up. "Are we done with deer now?"

Mervyn glanced up. "We've filled five truck beds. If we keep one of the truck loads for ourselves, will that take us through the rest of the winter?"

Cook thought about it. "It might. What about rabbits? Lots of rabbits running around. We could supplement with rabbits."

"That's a good idea." Mervyn glanced at Ruth. "Can you skin a rabbit, too?"

Ruth screwed up her face. "I don't like that idea. They're too much like pets. But, yes—if I can skin a deer...I can skin a rabbit."

"Let's go hunting rabbits today," he said brightly.

"I don't know about that."

"Why not? The Man's not here."

"Brad will have something to say about me taking off."

"Maybe. We'll see." Mervyn scrutinized her face. "Did he hit you again?" Ruth shook her head.

Cook coughed—a wet, soggy sound, deep in her chest. "I can't shake this damn cold." She coughed again. "I need help with breakfast. Hannah hasn't shown up. She usually helps me. Is she sick, too?"

Ruth shrugged. "I don't know." She cast a furtive glance at Mervyn. "I'll give you a hand." Ruth opened the kitchen door. The cook coughed again, cleared her throat, and spat. She followed Ruth into the kitchen.

More women wandered into the kitchen while the cook and Ruth prepared flapjacks and Saskatoon berry syrup. Three women put out plates and cutlery.

"Do we still have butter?" one of them asked. Ruth pointed to the cold pantry. The woman followed her finger and soon returned with bowls of pale, yellow butter. Ruth often wondered where the dairy supplies were coming from—she guessed there was a harried farmer nearby that was supplying The Man—much against his will. Regardless of the circumstances, she was glad to see butter, milk, and eggs.

"Where's Hannah?" asked one of the older women gathering coffee cups. "She's always here in the morning."

"I don't know," Ruth replied. "She might not be feeling well."

Men arrived in the dining room. Ruth peeked out—a dozen or so. Brad was not with them.

"Hey," one of the men yelled. "We're hungry. Get the damn food in here."

Ruth grabbed platters piled high with warm griddlecakes. She scurried into the dining room. Another woman followed her with pitchers of hot berry syrup.

Several children hung near the doorway to the dining room, their eyes locked on the plates of hotcakes. The men forked a half dozen of the circular cakes onto their plates, smeared them with generous portions of butter, splashed them with the thick, purple syrup, and then began to eat. The children watched, their eyes growing wider with each forkful the men lifted to their mouths. Only the smallest children dared enter the room until the men were done eating. The bravest ones learned that their patience would be rewarded.

As soon as the men had filled their bellies, they would crook their fingers, and invite the children to their tables. They would refill their plates and push them towards the hungry children. The children attacked the food like ravenous puppies. Oversized pieces did not slow them down—they simply scooped and crammed the food into their mouths. Like they were doing today. The sight made the men chuckle.

Brad arrived. The men stopped laughing. He pulled out a chair and sat down. He waved a hand in the air and a woman ran from the dining room. In a moment, she was back with a plate filled with fresh hotcakes. She set it down in front of him. Another woman, with silvery hair streaked with white and twisted into a bun at the nape of her neck, scooped up a pitcher of syrup and a bowl of butter; those were pushed within his reaching distance, too. Brad began to eat and then hesitated.

"How old are you?" he asked.

"Fifty-three," the woman replied.

"Stick around," Brad said. He resumed eating.

MARTHA SHRUGGED on her coat and pushed her arms into the sleeves. She wrapped a scarf around her head and throat. She wasn't looking forward to going outside this early in the day, but it was her turn to attend to the two milk cows the camp owned. Only a few people in the compound knew how to hand-milk a cow and she was one of them. She turned the door handle and opened the cabin's door. A huge bank of snow blocked her way. She grabbed a broom and swept it down the steps and into the yard.

So much snow.

Martha wondered if the snow would interfere with Matthew's plans to go scavenging. She searched inside herself for the old fire of desire, the need to go adventuring, the excitement of treasure hunting, but it wasn't there. She watched men with shovels clear the paths they had cut into the snow the day before. Other men riding ATVs fixed with snow blades cleared a runway up the main road heading away from the Gatehouse. If they cleared enough, and it didn't snow again, they might be able to get into Edmonton. Martha checked herself again.

No— Still nothing.

She made her way to the barn, lifted the latch, and opened the door. The overpowering reek of ammonia stopped her in her tracks, and she gasped for air. She took very small breaths, allowing her lungs to get used to the chemical aroma.

"Why do cows have to smell so bad?" she muttered.

Martha pulled a wooden milking stool from a peg on the wall, took a wide-mouthed aluminum pail from a shelf, and pushed in beside one of the cows. The Holstein cow took one lazy step over, just far enough to allow Martha to squeeze in, place her stool, and sit down.

"Don't over exert yourself, cow," she said.

She gave it another push, and then pushed her head against the cow's leg. She reached for the udder, swollen and distended with milk. The teats had already begun dripping. With both hands working, Martha pulled and squeezed and soon the pail began to fill with warm, frothy milk. The cow's calf bawled at her from a small enclosure.

"Yours is coming," she said. "Hang on..."

Martha turned her head at the sound of squeaks coming from the other side of the barn. Tiny faces soon popped up on the other side of a straw bale. Five pairs of dark eyes watched her, while five pairs of furry ears twitched. The wild kittens knew this human could be trusted, and they scampered from their hiding place. They sat a few feet from Martha, expectantly. Martha complied. She had played this game before.

She bent a teat to one side, pulled it, and squeezed. A stream of warm milk arced into the air and landed on one of the kitten's faces. The kitten opened its mouth and began to lap at the stream. The other kittens bowled it over and soon all the kittens were bathing in the spray of milk. Martha laughed at them, and then returned to her milking. The kittens, realizing their treat had ended, sat down, licking and pawing milk from their fur. Martha gave a soft sigh. The laughter had felt good.

The barn door opened and a cool breeze wafted in.

"Martha?" a female voice asked. "Oh my God, I can't breathe," the woman said, gasping for breath.

Martha looked up. "I'm over here."

Georgie's mouth was muffled by her scarf. "How can you breathe in here?"

"You get used to it. Take short breaths—till you can stand the smell."

Georgie dropped her scarf from her face. She gave Martha a hopeful grin. "I would like to help out with the barn chores—if that would be alright with you."

"Sure. What can you do?"

"Not much. I'm a city girl. But I can learn." She smiled. "I'd like to be more of an outdoorsy girl."

"Really?"

"I'm good at gardening." Georgie waited. "And Meteor taught me how to look for signs of wolf dens."

"Did he now?" Martha stopped milking. "And what else has Meteor taught you?" The brittleness in her voice surprised even her.

"Oh, not much yet. But he says we can go out again." Georgie gave a self-conscious laugh. "I really like him. He's so gorgeous. And those eyes."

Martha pushed her head into the cow's leg—a little too firmly—the cow gave a quick kick.

"So...can I?"

"Can you what?"

"Learn to do what you're doing?"

Martha felt something familiar rise inside her, but she held it at bay. "Sure. Come over here. I'll teach you how to milk a cow."

THE WOMEN poured coffee. Two men picked up their steaming cups and joined Brad at his table. One was the guard he'd been conversing with the day prior.

"What's up for today?" the guard asked. Brad ignored him and continued to eat. The guard looked at his watch. "The Man should be back here in a couple of days."

"And—?" Brad asked.

"Do you still want us to do the culling?"

"Why not?"

The guard stared at his coffee cup. He began to examine his thumbnail. "The guys aren't real keen on it," he said.

Brad looked up. "Mervyn didn't seem to have a problem."

"He's weird," the guard said.

"Where is he, by the way?" Brad asked. He took another three hotcakes and covered them in syrup.

"Don't know. Haven't seen him yet. But he goes out hunting pretty early sometimes."

"Where are we at with the deer meat?"

"Don't know."

Brad looked up. "Well, find out."

The guard grunted his assent and pushed himself up from the table. He went into the kitchen.

Brad looked across at the second man, an oddity among the Crazies with his neatly manicured Fu Manchu mustache that hung down, pencil-thin on either side of his mouth. The facial hair had earned him the nickname, *Fuma.*

"You have a problem with culling?" Brad asked.

Fuma gave his head a vehement shake. "Nope. Not at all."

"Good. Then I'll expect you guys will get it done."

"But—"

"But what?"

"The guys want *you* to pick the women." Fuma grimaced. "We don't want to make a mistake and piss off The Man."

Brad pushed back his plate. "When all the women are here, I'll point out the ones you should do." Brad motioned to the older woman he had spoken to earlier. "She's on the list," he said.

The guard returned from the kitchen. He flopped down into a chair and grabbed his coffee cup. "They've filled four truck beds. Kind of smart. They turned them into freezers. They used snow as insulation."

"He should be happy with that." Brad waved a hand above his head. "We're done. Get the rest of the women in here."

Brad's men stood near the doorway and watched as the women chattered, serving children, and then dishing up their own plates. Ruth and Cook stood near the kitchen door; they watched the food go down.

"Not much more Saskatoon syrup," the cook said, stifling a cough in the crook of her arm. "We're nearly out of the berries I canned." She coughed again, a low, phlegmy noise.

"Too bad. The kids really love it. Not to mention the vitamins."

The back door opened and the sound of stamping boots could be heard. The two women turned to see Mervyn. He brushed by them and took a seat at one of the kids' tables. He stole a plate from one of the little boys; the child made a terrible face and grabbed his plate. Mervyn pulled back with an exaggerated look of surprise; it made the children giggle. The sound drew Brad's attention.

"Those kids have no idea who's playing with them, do they?" Brad chuckled. He looked around the room. "Where's the tall broad? The old one? Who always works in the kitchen?"

In concert, the men near Brad muttered their lack of information.

"Well, when you find her—she's on the list." Brad cocked his head to one side and butted his chin toward a chubby, older woman with gray hair. "Her, too," he said. "And her. And her. And her," he added, indicating all the women with gray or silver hair.

"But that one cooks," Fuma said, pointing to the chubby woman.

"Stop pointing, you idiot." Brad shot him a look. "Then not that one."

"How do you want this to go down?"

"Tell the women that some of them are being moved to the South Camps. That they need older women down there to help with things."

"What things?" asked a younger man with freckles and cropped dark hair.

"Make something up," Brad growled.

"When do you want us to do this?"

"Today." Brad turned to Fuma. "You're in charge. And I don't want this leaking out, scaring the women— Understand?"

"What do we say about the missing kid?"

"Kid?"

"The one Mervyn got rid of? The retard..."

Brad looked across the room where Mervyn continued to tease the children. "Talk to him. Let him come up with some kind of story. I don't know. Maybe the kid wandered off in the middle of the night. Froze to death."

From across the dining room, Ruth watched Brad speak to his men.

"Huh?" Ruth said. Cook was speaking to her. "What?"

"Where's Reggie?" Cook asked.

Ruth glanced around the room. "I don't know. Maybe with Hannah. Maybe they're both sick."

The cook stretched. "I've gotta start prepping lunch." She coughed and groaned. "I'm too old for this."

"No," Ruth said. "You're not. Trust me—you are not *too old*."

"Well, old or not...it's too much work for just me. I am so damn sick," Cook complained. "And Hannah's not here to help."

"Sarah will help..." Ruth said, absently. She was watching the men.

Fuma walked over to Mervyn's table. He shooed two children out of a chair, and then he sat down. "Brad says you've got to come up with a story."

"For?"

"You know—the kid you offed."

"Oh, that." Mervyn continued stuffing pieces of pancakes into his mouth. "I'll think about it." He chewed. "Maybe it's best not to say anything at all. That way the women will think he just wandered off."

"Maybe." Fuma sat for a moment. "Have you seen the tall woman? Hannah?"

Mervyn looked surprised. "I told you guys yesterday that I got two birds with one stone."

"You did her, too?" Fuma looked genuinely surprised at the concept.

"Yeah, at the same time I did the kid."

"Where're the bodies?" Fuma whispered.

"Probably eaten by wild dogs or coyotes by now."

Fuma shook his head. "We're taking more women away today," he said slowly. He paused, but Mervyn didn't look up. "Want to help?"

Mervyn shook his head. "No— I had my fill yesterday. Besides, I'm tired. I've been hunting deer every day. I want to sleep today."

Fuma rose. He clapped Mervyn on the back. "Okay, brother. Later."

Ruth watched the camaraderie between Mervyn and Fuma. She suppressed a sudden shiver; Mervyn didn't seem to be in any kind of trouble, but still she wondered what he had said. An announcement from Brad quieted the room. He told them that some of the women were needed to *help out* at the South Camps. He pointed out four women; they were hustled out of the dining room by two guards. The women were screaming and crying. The rest of the women simply stared.

"And—" Brad added. His eyes swept the room, landing intermittently on the younger, prettier women, their eyes filled with worry. "We're a little bored. It's time for some fun." Brad's men looked up eagerly. "I think we should have a beauty contest," he said.

Hearty shouts of approval filled the room.

"A what?" Cook asked.

"Oh, my God..." Ruth said.

"A wet t-shirt contest," Brad continued. The women groaned in unison, while the men applauded and pounded their tables. Brad pushed back his chair. "Tonight," he added. He called an older man to his table.

Ruth watched the man join Brad. He was neatly dressed in a white denim shirt, a heavy wool sweater, and blue jeans. Instead of boots, he wore moccasins laced to his knees. His stringy hair was thinning on top, and pink flesh, the color of a newborn mouse, shone through the sparse hairs. The two spoke, and the man smiled. He turned and faced the room.

"I will be the pageant coordinator," he announced. "Sign up with me, ladies," he said with an enthusiasm that made Ruth's stomach sick. She glanced at Mervyn. He was shaking his head.

Brad clapped the older man on the back, and left the room.

Mervyn left, too.

In the front room, Fuma and the two guards urged the women to dress in their outdoor clothes. Under threat of being backhanded, the women stopped screaming, but they were still crying. Mervyn sauntered up to the men. He stopped near Fuma, who turned to him.

"You sure you don't want this job?" Fuma asked.

"Who's going?" Mervyn asked.

"Just me and him," Fuma said, indicating the shorter guard. "We'll cram the women into the back of a truck. Drive a ways up the road. Do 'em. And then come back."

Mervyn checked his watch. "Have you thought about that plan?"

"Why?"

"You leave here for about twenty minutes...and come back with an empty truck...what do you think the women will do? I thought Brad said not to scare the rest of them. He doesn't want to deal with a bunch of crazy, screaming chicks. You should stay out there for at least three hours."

Fuma sighed. "I guess you're right."

The guard herded the wailing women through the door. Fuma and Mervyn followed.

"Shut-up, or I'll shoot you right now." The guard pulled his pistol and held it to the head of one of the women. The woman struggled to stop her weeping.

"I'm really not into this," Fuma whispered. "One of them reminds me of my grandma." He grabbed Mervyn's arm. "Do this, okay?"

"I already told you—I'm beat. I need sleep."

Fuma helped load the women into the backseat. They closed the door and the guard jumped into the driver's seat. He motioned for Fuma to come, too. Fuma gave Mervyn a long, pleading look. Mervyn leaned over and spoke into his ear.

"Look—if you really can't stomach doing this...then take them all the way to the South Camps. The bottom line is that they'll be gone. Who'll know?" Fuma pointed to the guard in the front seat. Mervyn shrugged. "Well...then have fun shooting your grandma..."

Fuma pulled open the passenger door and got in.

Suddenly, the driver's door opened. The guard jerked around to see Mervyn standing there, motioning to the steering wheel.

"Fuma and I have some catching up to do. I'll drive," Mervyn said.

The guard jumped out. He looked relieved. "Thanks."

Mervyn grabbed hold of the guard's coat and pulled him close. "We've got to make it seem like we've taken them to the South Camps," he whispered. "Don't expect to see us for several hours. Otherwise, we'll spook the other women. And Brad said not to do that. Okay?"

The guard nodded.

Mervyn leapt into the truck, started the engine, and drove off.

"Thanks," Fuma said. He turned around. The women were whimpering and sobbing. "Easy ladies. It's not so bad in the South Camps."

Mervyn hid a small grin.

Chapter Twenty-Four

An Exorcism via Wine Bottle

MARTHA EXAMINED the bite on Matthew's arm. The skin around the punctures was still puffy and red. Scabs surrounded the ragged holes; they were crusty with weeping pus.

"Well, your body is doing what it's supposed to be doing. Doesn't look any worse. But I'm still worried. More hot salt water..."

Matthew flipped the pages of the journal on the table in front of him. He flinched when the hot salt water hit his arm. "Shit, that's hot." He gritted his teeth. "I'm taking a team out tomorrow. Snow has been cleared. Scout says the roads are passable."

"Why do you have to go?" Martha asked, an accusatory lilt in her voice. "There're enough people here—younger than you—who would be perfectly happy to go scavenging."

Matthew's head jerked up. "Is that Martha speaking? The Martha I know?"

"What are you talking about?"

"You don't want to go scavenging?"

"Too much to do here."

Matthew reached across the table and touched her arm. "Really—?" His face matched the surprise in his voice.

"I just think we'd better stick closer to camp. The younger ones have more energy." She flipped one hand into the air. "Let them go."

Matthew turned back to his journal. "I can't believe my ears."

"Besides, Cammy's baby will be coming soon. And without Ruth—" Martha paused to quell the emotions that arose with the mention of her daughter's name. She took a breath. "Without Ruth to help out, Anna might need a hand."

Matthew said nothing.

"This is going to sting…" Martha coated the wound in a thin sheen of golden honey.

"Honey?"

"Antibacterial agent…something like that. It works." Martha bandaged Matthew's arm. "I have a kitchen meeting to attend. I'll find out who wants to go scavenging." She gathered up her equipment and left the table. Matthew watched her go.

"You're sure about this?" he asked again.

Martha shot him a firm *I-already-answered-that-question* look.

"I'm still going scavenging," he said. "I'm curious. I want to see how The Man lived. See his stuff. Learn something about him."

"Could be fun."

"And you're still not interested?"

"No," Martha said. This time her tone was peeved. "I said, N*o*. I meant, N*o*."

"Okay."

Martha kissed the top of his head. "I'll see you later." She paused at the door. "And speaking of supplies…don't leave sugar cubes at the back of the cupboard. Too much temptation for midnight visitors." She pointed to the open cupboard. Wilbert sat nearby, one paw lifted into the air, his tongue flicking delicately along the gray fur.

Matthew laughed. "I suspect he's made short work of them."

"Yeah, like those dogs wanted to do to him the other night. I think they were after him."

"Maybe we shouldn't be keeping him inside. Put him into the barn instead."

Martha's eyes blazed. "He's Mary's cat. He stays here till Mary comes back for him."

"Whoa. Okay," Matthew said soothingly. "Just a suggestion."

"Keep those suggestions to yourself."

"Sorry. But if he's attracting—"

Martha narrowed her eyes.

"Okay, never mind." Wilbert padded over and sat at Matthew's feet. Green feline eyes stared up at him. "Look at that little bugger." Matthew laughed again. "It's like he knows we're talking about him." Matthew scooped up the cat and scratched behind its ears. "I never was a cat person, but this guy, I like. Attitude." Wilbert began to purr. "Wish those dogs had gotten you. Not me," Matthew whispered. The cat purred.

Outside, a woman screamed.

Matthew shoved the cat to the floor. He jumped up. Martha followed him to the window. "I can't see what's going on," he said.

Martha pointed to the right. "I think it's Marion. I'll go—"

Martha left the cabin.

The screams continued.

THE WOMEN were gathered in Sunnyvale's front room. Many still wore boots and coats, while others crowded around the fireplace. Children played nearby. No one had seen any sign of Hannah or Reggie, even though they had been searching for the past two days.

"We've looked everywhere," Sarah said. Several of the women agreed. "Why would the two of them just disappear?"

Ruth struggled to portray concern. "I don't know."

"Maybe they were taken to the South Camps, too," Sarah suggested.

"I'm worried sick," Ruth said.

Elizabeth stood near the doorway, her arms crossed. "Sounds fishy to me."

"Did they go for a walk? And no one noticed?" a teen girl asked.

"Why would they take Reggie?" a young mother asked.

"I don't know," Ruth said, twisting her hands in mock nervousness. "There's got to be some reasonable explanation."

Elizabeth eyed her sister. Ruth gave a tiny shake of her head. Elizabeth caught the movement.

"I really like Hannah. I miss her," Sarah said. "And Reggie was so sweet. I couldn't stand it if something had happened to them."

"We've done all the searching we can," Elizabeth said flatly. "Let's get on with our work."

"Well, I need at least three more helpers on regular duty in the mornings. The cook is too sick. So, who's that gonna be?" Sarah asked.

Nobody volunteered.

"That's fine." Sarah pointed. "You, you, and you. Breakfast help. Every day. Six A.M.—"

"Not me," the teen girl whined. "I hate cooking."

"Too bad," Sarah said sharply. "And you'd better be there. Or I'll know the reason why."

"You're as bad as Martha," the girl said.

Sarah marched over and slapped the girl, a stinging blow that snapped her head to the side. Ruth's eyes widened. "Be glad you're alive. Be glad you've got something to cook. Be glad you haven't been taken to the South Camps. Be glad of Martha."

The teen whimpered and held her burning cheek in her hand.

Elizabeth held back a grin. She and Ruth exchanged a look.

Their mother was in their midst.

MARTHA RAN across the compound toward the cookhouse. Two women were struggling; one was still screaming. Marion had a woman by the hair and she was pulling her across the field. Martha stepped between them.

"Stop it!" Martha gave Marion a shove, but Marion would not release her grip on the other woman's hair.

Young men began to gather. They leaned on their shovels and hooted their encouragement. "Cat fight," one of them called. "Let them fight..." another one said.

"Marion!" Martha commanded. The woman paid no attention, intent on dragging her quarry across the yard. Martha tried separating the combatants again. The boys continued to hoot.

The other woman screamed again, louder, more high-pitched. She hit and scratched at Marion's hand. She kicked out at the tall woman's legs. Her feet never connected with Marion, but they caught one of Martha's shins. Martha launched herself at Marion. The tall blonde stumbled backwards, releasing the screaming woman as she fell. Martha stood over the pair, one hand rubbing her sore leg.

The boys booed.

"What the hell is wrong with you guys?" Martha asked.

The screaming woman dropped to her knees. Now she was wailing. The younger men elbowed each other. One yelled out, "Should have let 'em fight, Martha."

Marion got up—her face was a furious shade of red. "I'm gonna kill that bitch. If she says one more word to me..."

"About what?" Martha demanded. She still rubbed her shin.

"About him!"

"Him who?"

"You know who," Marion shouted. She vibrated with anger.

"You gotta calm down. Or you'll get yourself kicked out." Martha grabbed the woman's shoulder. "Understand me?"

Marion began to cry. "I hate it here. Hate it. I want to go..."

"Go where? Where are you going to go...in the middle of winter? Huh? Where?"

"Home—no—I don't know—I just wanna be dead."

"C'mon. Let's go." Martha took Marion by the arm. Marion pulled away. Martha grabbed at her arm again. "We'll talk somewhere."

"What about me?" asked the woman on the ground. "She hurt me."

Martha turned. "Any cuts? Any blood? Any broken bones?"

"No," the woman said weakly.

"Good," Martha said. "You'll survive." She took Marion by the arm again. "Let's go to the Meeting House. We'll have privacy there." Marion balked. "C'mon. I might be your last chance at a friend here." She tugged on Marion's arm. "Come on," she said again, her tone forceful.

One of the boys came over and helped the crying woman to her feet. The woman swiped at her face with her coat sleeve. "I hate you, you bitch. Don't come near me again."

Martha grabbed Marion before she could launch another attack. "Let's go." The two women walked to the Meeting House.

The boys went back to shoveling.

ELIZABETH CLOSED the door to Ruth's room. She flopped down on the bed, and pulled her heavy sweater tight around her. Ruth sat next to her.

"What's going on?" Elizabeth asked. "Spill."

"Sh..." Ruth said, pointing at the door. Ruth got up, checked down the hallway, and then came back to the bed. "They're okay," she whispered.

"They are? How— How do you know? Where are they?"

"Mervyn saved them."

"Mervyn?"

"I heard Brad planning to kill them. I told Mervyn. He took them to a safe place."

"You trust him?" Elizabeth was aghast. "He's one of them!"

"No—he's good. He's my friend." Elizabeth's expression remained unconvinced. Ruth pressed on. "Really...he is."

"That *was* Reggie's shirt I saw. Covered in blood. Wasn't it?"

"Yes—but that wasn't his blood. Deer blood," Ruth whispered.

"Where are they?"

"With Mervyn's friends."

"He has friends who aren't with The Man?" Ruth nodded. "Then why the hell doesn't he help all of us get the fuck out of here?"

Ruth's eyebrows shot up. Elizabeth rarely swore.

"He can't. We'd all die. Two—he could save. But not almost two hundred of us..."

Elizabeth pushed out her lower lip. "Spring isn't that far away. There are fewer of us now that some of the older women were taken to the South Camps." She paused and drew her eyebrows together. "Or were they?"

"They were supposed to die, too, but Mervyn stepped in." A sound outside in the hallway made them jump. "Shh— Mervyn will get killed if they find out," Ruth whispered.

They waited. Everything was quiet again.

"I think we should start making plans for the spring," Elizabeth said softly. "With his help—"

"Elizabeth...you're talking about nearly two hundred people escaping. Brad and The Man aren't stupid. They'd be after us in a flash. The kids can't walk very fast. They'd catch us in no time."

"Maybe all of us shouldn't go then."

Ruth blinked. "What? What are you saying?"

More noise in the hallway.

Elizabeth jumped off the bed. "Later."

MARION SAT sullenly, her hands resting on the table, her mouth pursed into silence. She'd been that way for nearly ten minutes. Martha sighed and got up.

"Fine...have it your way," Martha said. She walked across the room and pulled on the door.

"I wasn't his whore," Marion blurted.

"Whose whore? Brad's?"

Marion strangled a laugh. "Brad? That asshole?" She unfolded a rag in her hand, searched for a dry spot, and blew her nose. "The Man."

"I know. You're his sister."

"Not a real sister. But *never* one of his whores—I'd never allow that."

"Don't sweat it. People believe what they want to believe. Especially in confined spaces."

"Yeah, but they don't know the whole story—"

Martha came back and sat down. "So...talk..."

Marion rambled on about The Man, about her house, about Virgil, about toilet paper...Martha's attention wandered. Sunlight poured in through the Meeting House window. It glinted off the woman's rich hair. A shaft of light caught Martha's eye, and she followed it to the floor. The beam marked the spot—the spot where she had lain in shock.

After Brad... After his men...

The bloodstains were muted, but Martha could see them. Or, she imagined she could. She pointed to the floor.

"See there?" Martha said, interrupting Marion's tirade. Marion turned to look. "There. That spot. There on the floor."

Marion squinted. "What about it?"

"That's where Brad left me to die—"

"What?" Marion gave the floor another look. She couldn't see anything remarkable. "What happened?"

"The day before they took this camp...Brad and his men captured me. They raped me in here. Half to death. Then left me here. Without any clothes."

"I'm sorry..." Marion gave her head a small shake. "You know, I'm pretty sure The Man told him not to harm you."

"Sure he did."

Marion shrugged. "Maybe he didn't. Who knows? But I am sorry."

"Thanks."

The two women let the minutes tick by.

"Do you drink?" Martha blurted.

"Yeah, but not hard stuff. Makes me ill."

"How about wine?"

"Wine is good. Red is best. An Australian shiraz."

"A what?"

"Or a smooth merlot. Right now, I'd polish off a whole bottle. By myself."

"Do you get hung-over?" Martha asked.

"Oooh, yeah..."

Martha laughed. *The two of them could get drunk together*, she thought. Enemy with enemy. Thoroughly soused. Here. In this room. They could groan together in a hung-over stupor in the morning. An exorcism of sorts.

"Wait here. I'll be right back." Martha slammed the door behind her.

ELIZABETH HURRIED down the hallway. A group of women blocked her path. They were arguing. "What's your problem?" she asked. A couple of older teen girls turned to face her.

"You haven't heard?"

"Heard what?" Elizabeth asked.

"Brad says we have to participate in a beauty pageant."

"With a wet t-shirt contest," another girl added.

Elizabeth huffed softly and shook her head. "Oh, God...what's next?"
MERVYN WAS WAITING near the kitchen door. He grabbed Ruth's arm and pulled her around to the back. Ruth clutched at her chest.

"You scared the hell out of me." She smiled at him. "Is something wrong?"

"No. Everybody is well and happy." Mervyn winked.

Ruth glanced over her shoulder. "You checked on them?" she whispered.

"Yep—this morning. The gay chicks love Reggie. And I think he really likes them. Hannah seems happy, too. She was talking religion with the pastor."

"What about the other women?"

"What do you think?"

"You took them there, too? I thought you were taking them to the South Camps."

Mervyn smiled.

"Oh, thank you, Mervyn. Thank you." Ruth threw her arms around his neck and gave him a full kiss on the mouth. Mervyn allowed the kiss and then pulled away.

"Whoa. What's with the double standard? I'm not allowed to kiss you—but you can kiss me?" Ruth grinned crookedly. "I don't think that's fair, do you?" he asked, pulling her to him.

Ruth felt her stomach twist. He covered her mouth with his, forcefully and warm. His mouth felt good and she struggled to find something inside her to resist the sudden rush of emotions.

Such a good man. How I wish...

She pulled back. "No..." she breathed. "I can't. I want to. It's not right."

"It's okay. That will do me for now." He pushed the hair from her face. "But some day..."

The kitchen door creaked and the two moved apart. Mervyn bolted toward the Quonset hut. Ruth took a breath, composed herself, touched her burning cheeks, and luxuriated in the moment. She didn't want to let it go...not just yet.

"Ruth?" It was Sarah. "The girls are really upset about that beauty pageant. Would you talk to them?"

MARTHA AND MARION howled till the tears came. Everything was funny by the time they had reached the second bottle of wine. Martha had presented first one bottle and then another with a waiter's flair, dug into the cork of the first bottle, and twisted it free. Both women engaged the scent coming from the bottle—like a rare perfume, of the most expensive kind—although the wine was only a relatively cheap California cabernet sauvignon. And they were drinking from coffee mugs.

"Where did you get this?"

"Scavenging. About a year ago."

"You've kept it this long?"

Martha shrugged. "Josef didn't drink. Matthew prefers the hard stuff. We have a beer now and then."

"Why today?"

"I dunno. Felt like celebrating." Martha lifted her coffee cup and took another drink. She entered into the warm burn as it hit her stomach.

"You scavenged this?"

"Yep."

"Is it fun?"

"What?"

"To go scavenging?"

Martha looked appalled. "You've *never* gone scaven-ghing? Not once in sh-hree years?" She was slurring her words now, but Marion nodded attentively. Martha leaned in close. "Do you like sh—shopping?"

"Duh..."

"Well then you'd LOVE scaven—ghing. All the fun of shopping and no checkout." Martha got up and mimed picking up items. "This, this, this. Not this." She dropped the invisible offending item to the floor. Then she walked by an imaginary cash counter. "On my card, please. I have no limit. The sky is the limit. Just sh—sharge it up—" Her voice squeaked on the final word.

Marion laughed and hung crookedly in her chair. She grabbed at her cup, but only succeeded in knocking it over. "Whoopsie." Burgundy liquid spilled across the table. She righted her cup. "More, please."

Martha tipped the bottle and sloshed more into Marion's cup. "Some for you. And...some...for...me."

The women raised their cups and clunked them together. "Here's to losing your scaven—ghing cherry," Martha said.

The ribald comment made Marion giggle and blush.

They drank.

"Soooo...When do we go?" Marion asked.

"A—S—A—P."

Martha glanced at the floorboards again. Through bleary eyes, she could still see the stain. She grabbed the wine bottle, got up, walked over, and spilled the wine at her feet.

"What are you doing?" Marion cried in stunned amazement.

"Washing out the damn blood." Martha tipped the bottle again, and pushed the burgundy pool of liquid around with the toe of her boot. "There," she said. "Gone."

The room now reeked of spilled wine. Martha tottered back to the table, and fell heavily into her chair. Marion held up her cup.

"Here's to pouring good wine on bad memories."

The two women clinked cups again, and drank.

ELIZABETH CAUGHT up to Brad. He was playing poker with some of the men in the community room. He was shuffling a pack of cards when she arrived. She watched him deal a round. Men shoved bets into the pot. She stood quietly, her arms folded, and waited to speak to him. She needed to speak to him. She had just been privy to a meeting between Ruth and the younger women angry over Brad's plan for a beauty pageant...

..."So what do we do?" asked one of the women, a pretty brunette in her early twenties. "I don't want to look sexy for those assholes."

"I know," Ruth said. "I'm not sure how we can get out of this one." Ruth looked at Elizabeth. "Any thoughts?"

Elizabeth shook her head.

"What if they try to have sex with us after?" wailed one of the other girls.

"I know...I know..." Ruth said. She held up her hand. "Anybody have any ideas?"

"At least when The Man was here, they left us alone," said the pretty brunette.

"The Man told him to leave us alone," said Elizabeth.

"Brad doesn't care," the second girl said. "He's crazy. He thinks he owns the place."

"And us," the brunette said.

The group of girls waited for Ruth to solve their dilemma. But all she did was shake her head. "I don't know. I just— I can't think of—"

Elizabeth gave a loud growl of annoyance. "Oh, for heaven's sakes. I'll do something." She stalked from the room, leaving the women standing with their mouths hanging open...

Now, Elizabeth waited. She wasn't sure how she would manage to change Brad's mind, but she was going to try. One of the men noticed her standing near the doorway.

"What do you want?" the man asked. He was dark haired and dark skinned. Elizabeth squirmed as his coffee-colored eyes appraised her, but she hid her discomfort.

"Brad..." she said, ignoring the man. "Can I speak to you?"

The dark-eyed man gave Brad a knowing look. Brad didn't look up. He continued to study the fanned cards in his hand. He reached for a burning cigar, took a puff, blew out the smoke, and returned the glowing cigar to a glass ashtray. "I'll call," he said.

Elizabeth waited. The hand ended. Brad lost. He pushed up from the table, stubbed out his cigar, and walked over to Elizabeth.

"I don't remember calling for you," he said.

"You didn't. I just wanted to talk to you." Elizabeth took a quick breath. "I didn't mean to interrupt your game. I'm sorry."

Brad shrugged. He looked back at the men. "Save my seat," he said. "I'll be back."

"A quickie?" one of the men quipped, grinning widely.

Brad shot the man a look that stopped his grin. "I don't do quickies," he replied, as he reached for Elizabeth's shoulder. He turned her around and they left the room.

Once outside the room, Brad stopped short and slammed Elizabeth against a wall. "Just for the record, don't come calling for me."

Elizabeth's eyes flipped wide in surprise. Brad's eyes were hard and his fist had clenched. He raised it.

"I—uh...sorry...I..."

Brad relaxed. He smoothed away a lock of hair from her cheek.

"No problem. Just remember for next time." He put his hands on either side of Elizabeth, palms flush with the wall. He leaned in toward her. "What did you want?"

"I thought we could spend some time together tonight."

"Tonight? Sure, but after the beauty pageant." He grinned. "Want to take part? You could win, you know."

Elizabeth struggled to keep her stomach from churning. The thought of parading around in front of Brad and his Crazies in an effort to garner their approval was nauseating. "No. Thanks. That's not for me."

"But what if I say it is for you? Then what?"

Elizabeth stood silently for a moment. "Then, I would do it." She held his eyes. "But would you really want me to do that? Some of the other guys might get interested in me..." She let Brad figure out the rest of her thought.

He dropped his hands to his sides. His face darkened. "Are you telling me that other guys are interested in you? Have they touched—?"

"No, but, it could happen..."

"Maybe we should do something about that," Brad said, his eyes narrowing.

"Do something?"

"Maybe you and I should go."

"Wh—where?" Elizabeth stammered.

"South Camps. I have a nice apartment back there. None of the guys there will bother you."

Elizabeth felt her heartbeat quicken as panic rose inside her. She fought to contain the fear. "Sure, if you think that would be best." She forced a smile. "That might be nice." She held her lips in a curve that she hoped would pass for a sweet smile. "I'm tired of the routine here. Screaming kids...nothing to do. A change of scenery might be nice."

Brad eyed her suspiciously. "You mean you *want* to go with me?"

Elizabeth glanced down at the floor and then back up again. She shrugged. "As long as you still want me." She smiled again, a tiny hopeful smile.

Brad's eyes softened and he smiled.

He bought it, she thought with a thrill of victory.

He leaned in and kissed her. "Now we're talking," he said softly. He put his hands on her waist and then pushed them up under her shirt.

"Not here," she said, with a coy giggle. "Later." She wriggled out of his grasp.

Brad reached for her, and closed his fist in her hair. He drew her face toward him—the action was firm, but not cruel. "After the pageant," he whispered. He bent to kiss her again, but Elizabeth pulled back.

"Oh, I think you should know that quite a few of the girls are sick. A wet t-shirt contest might make them very sick. They could die." She looked up at him—her green eyes wide and innocent.

Brad stepped back. He ran one hand through his hair. He thought a moment. "Hm, maybe you have something there."

Elizabeth nodded with exaggerated sincerity.

"What about you? Are you sick?" he asked.

"Haven't been feeling well. A little cough. Otherwise, I'm fine."

I think tonight I will be very sick, she thought.

She fought a grin as she cleared her throat. She lifted one hand and massaged her neck. "My glands are a little swollen and my throat has been sore." Elizabeth threw her arms around Brad's neck and made as if to kiss him. Brad leaned back.

"I don't want what you guys have," he said, pulling her arms from around his neck.

"I'm sure I'll be fine," Elizabeth said with a bright smile. "But some of those other girls are really sick. Especially the younger ones," she added adamantly. "I think some of the women might be dying already," she lied.

Brad gave her a puzzled look.

"The Man will be back here in a couple of days... You know how he feels about the women, especially the younger ones..." Elizabeth trailed off, hoping her words had created enough concern in Brad's mind.

A man walked out of the community room. "Hey," he said. "You coming back?"

"Yeah— Right there." Brad patted Elizabeth's rear. "I'll see you later." He went back into the room.

Elizabeth let out a huge breath. She smiled.

"That should put an end to any stupid contest," she murmured.

But what have I gotten myself into? A fresh wave of fear slammed into her. *What have I done this time?*

THE MEETING HOUSE door opened. Two men walked in. They gave the two women a quizzical stare. Jonah came closer. Trojan was with him.

"Martha?" Jonah asked.

"Hi, sh-wheet boy," Martha replied.

"Whew...you girls havin' a good time?" Trojan waved at the air in front of his face. "What ya drinkin'?"

"Little old wine drinkers us..." Martha sang in tune with the old Dean Martin song.

"Uh, we've got a meeting happening here right away. Want some help getting back to your cabin?" Jonah asked as a grin twisted his mouth.

"Okey-dokey." Martha tried to stand, but fell back into her chair.

Trojan stifled a laugh. "You are gonna have one hell of a hangover, girls."

Marion leaned over and in a conspiratorial whisper asked, "They're cute. Are they taken?"

Martha laughed. "Get out of here. Jonah's young enough to be your kid."

"What about the other guy?" Marion asked, eyeing Trojan.

"Cammy— I'm with Cammy," Trojan said, quickly and clearly, having overheard Marion's question.

Jonah pulled Marion's arm around his neck. "C'mon, old girl. I'll get you home."

"Old girl? Who you calling an old girl?"

Trojan helped Martha to the door. The foursome stumbled down the steps. "Geez, Martha—when you cut loose—"

Matthew met them halfway to the cabin. "What the hell?" He took hold of Martha. "Are you drunk? Is she drunk?" he asked incredulously.

Trojan and Jonah grinned, their eyebrows raised.

"Hi'ya, Matthew. Guess what?"

"What, Martha?"

"Marion is coming...shcaven—ghing...with us."

"She is? With us? You're coming now?"

"Yup." Martha swayed and Matthew caught her. "Matthew?"

"What?"

"I don't feel so good." Matthew chuckled. "I'm gonna be si-i-i-ck."

"Oh, boy— I'll take her from here," Matthew said. "Thanks."

"We'll take care of Marion," Jonah said with a wry smile. The two men slipped her long arms around their necks. "Man, she's heavier than she looks."

Trojan laughed. "That's 'cause she's passed out." They continued toward the women's bunkhouse. "She's not with Virgil anymore," Trojan added. He paused and waited for a response. "She's not half-bad looking, Jonah."

"Too old—"

"I don't know about that. With age comes experience. If you know what I mean..."

"Too old, Trojan," Jonah said gruffly. They clambered up the bunkhouse steps and knocked on the door. A redheaded woman answered.

"Trojan!" she said. "They're looking for you."

"What?"

"Cammy needs you."

Trojan shoved Marion at Jonah. "She's all yours, buddy."

Marion stirred and awoke. She looked at Jonah. "Oh, no..."

Purple vomit splashed over his boots.

RUTH LEFT the kitchen. She pulled up short when she saw Brad. He was sitting in a big armchair in the front room. Elizabeth sat next to him. Like a modern Mona Lisa, her expression was puzzling. Ruth fought to hide her confusion. Brad motioned to her and she walked over.

"I didn't want you to be surprised," Brad said. "Elizabeth is going with me when I leave for the South Camps."

"What?" Ruth tried to read her sister's face, but Elizabeth's eyes gave nothing away.

Was she part of this? Had Brad forced her?

Brad laughed. "It's okay. We get along better than your mother and I did."

Elizabeth smiled, but it was an empty, wooden action.

A small group of bikers came into the room. They stopped in front of Brad. "So, when's the contest?" one of them asked, leering at Elizabeth.

"No contest," Brad said flatly. "Too cold..."

"What? But you said—"

"And now I'm saying, NO contest. Am I making myself clear?"

Ruth exchanged a quick look with Elizabeth.

Elizabeth smiled again, but this time her eyes twinkled.

MATTHEW ATTEMPTED to help Martha undress. She flopped back on the bed, her boots still on her feet, her jeans part way down her legs. She groaned.

"Are you going to be sick again," Matthew asked, searching the room for a bucket.

"I don't think so," Martha replied thickly. Matthew watched her face contort. "Maybe..."

"Hang on," Matthew said. "I'll get—" But he was too late. Martha rolled to the edge of the bed and threw up on the floor.

"Sorry..." She lay back on the pillows and threw her arm over her forehead. "Ohhh...everything's spinning."

In a moment, she was asleep. Matthew stared at his wife and then down at the floor. He shook his head. "Oh, Martha," he said softly.

He fetched a rag and a bucket of water, and returned to the bedroom. In a few minutes, the vomit was cleaned up. He tossed the water outside, and wiped his hands on a towel. He went back into the bedroom. Martha was snoring softly.

Matthew sat on the edge of the bed and unlaced her boots. One by one, he dropped them to the floor. He pulled off her jeans, and then drew the covers up over his unconscious wife. He smiled.

She said she was going scavenging.

RUTH SLAMMED Elizabeth's bedroom door. She stood, fuming, her hands on her hips, feet planted apart. Elizabeth was standing at the mirror, brushing her hair. She turned.

"What's up?" Elizabeth asked, her tone light and innocent.

"Are you crazy?" Ruth's voice was low and controlled. "What are you doing? Have you forgotten he killed our father? Hates our mother? Betrayed Matthew and the camp? Kidnapped us?" Ruth sucked in a breath. "Have you forgotten all that?"

"No, I haven't forgotten." Elizabeth sat on the edge of her bed.

"Then what are you doing going with him?"

"Keep your friends close. Enemies closer."

"That's ridiculous. He's a murderer."

"I know."

"Then what—?"

"We've got to get out of here before it's too late. You said yourself that there's so many us...it'll be too hard for all of us to get away. Especially with Brad and The Man breathing down our necks. If I stick close to Brad, I might find out things useful to us."

"When I said curry his favor, I didn't mean for you to get into—" Ruth's eyes went wide. "You haven't gone to bed with him?" She paused. "Is that how you got him to change his mind about the t-shirt contest?"

Elizabeth pulled the hairbrush through her hair. She grimaced when she hit a knot. She tugged at it with her fingers. "No, I told him the girls were sick—and they might get sicker. Besides, he thinks I'm a virgin."

"Well, that's the truth. Isn't it?"

Elizabeth continued brushing her hair. "Let's just say...I know more than he thinks I know."

"You aren't seriously thinking of sleeping with him!"

Elizabeth touched her stomach. "Think I'm starting my period. Headache. A little cramping."

"Answer my question."

"Drop it, Ruth."

"No."

"Look...if Brad wanted to have sex with me...with you...with any one of us...he could. Right? Who would stop him? This way—I've got some control. If sex enters the picture... Well, I'll deal with that bridge when I come to it."

"Don't do it, Elizabeth. You'll hate yourself forever."

"I might hate myself forever if I don't."

"Don't. Just don't." Ruth checked her watch. "I've got to go. She gave Elizabeth a firm look. "We'll talk more about this later."

"Sure." Elizabeth said. "Uh, Ruth..." She motioned toward the small mound in a sleeping bag on the bed. "Duke— I can't take him with me. Will you—?"

"Oh for heaven's sakes, of course. But it won't come to that." Ruth left the room. Elizabeth watched the door close.

She turned and stared into the ornate, oval mirror. "Mirror, mirror..." she whispered. She rubbed her lower belly and groaned. "Damn..." Then she brightened.

At least I've got a good reason to keep Brad off me.

Chapter Twenty-Five

A Dilemma, a Hangover, and a Miscarriage

MARTHA LEANED on the barn door. She was woozy, her head ached, and her stomach was doing flips. She took a deep breath and pushed back from the door. The morning was overcast, but the frigid temperatures had abated. It had warmed up enough to ignore a scarf and hat. She smelled the air. Still smelled like winter. She reached for the handle.

"Martha?" She recognized the voice.

"Hi, Meteor." She forced a smile past the throb in her head.

Meteor chuckled. "Not feeling so good, huh?" He pulled the door open and ushered her inside. They both gasped for breath. "You sure you want to do this?"

"Nobody to take my place. Cows need milking."

"I didn't know you like to drink."

"Seemed like a good idea at the time," Martha said.

Meteor took a small wooden three-legged stool from a peg. "Sit." He took another stool and grabbed a pail. "Move over, girl," he said, giving the cow's hindquarters a push with his shoulder. He sat down. "Haven't sat like this in a long time. Tough on the old war wounds." He stretched out the leg that had taken a bullet the year before. Soon, the sound of liquid spurts rhythmically hitting metal, echoed through the barn.

"You rascal— You can milk a cow?" Martha asked.

Meteor laughed—one of his hearty happy-go-lucky laughs—a sound Martha had grown to love. A sound she missed. "Yep."

Martha moved her stool in closer. She motioned to the far wall. "You'll have visitors right away."

As if on cue, the wild kittens scampered over the straw bales and across the floor. They sat down in an untidy row, about two feet away. Their eyes shone with anticipation. Martha grinned as Meteor filled the tiny mouths with the creamy spray.

"You've done this before, too."

"I lived in a cabin with my folks when I was young. We had cows, and chickens, and goats, and pigs. All kinds of animals...my brother and I would find them and bring 'em home." He gave the cow's teat another squeeze—the kittens lapped greedily at the milk spray. "I miss having a pet," he added.

"Like a wolf pup?"

"Yeah. How do you know about that?"

"Georgie."

"Oh." Meteor went back to milking.

Martha examined her fingers. "You getting serious?"

The milk streams ceased. Meteor pulled his head away from the cow. "Serious?" He wiped sweat from his brow. "Do you really want to know?"

"Yes."

"No, Martha. I'm not getting serious. Georgie is fun. She's lively. She's interesting. She likes me. And..." he raised his eyebrows. "She's available."

"You mean...unlike me?"

Meteor didn't answer. The milk streams resumed.

"It's been a long time since you bashed me across the head," Martha said lightly. The laugh she hoped for never came. "I'm sorry, Meteor," she said softly. "I never meant to hurt you."

Meteor pulled a hand from one teat and held it up. "Don't, Martha. It won't change anything. You're married to one of my best friends. And that's where it has to end."

"I just wanted you to know..."

"You wanted me to know what? Something that would ease my heart? Ease your heart?" The cow shifted and gave a small kick at the bucket. "Easy, girl." Meteor began milking again.

"Meteor, it breaks my heart to know you're hurting. Please know that."

Meteor sat back on the stool and regarded her. "Martha—how does me knowing that...help me?" He paused and then answered his own question. "It can't. It doesn't. It hurts every time I see the two of you together." He shrugged. "What is...just is..."

Martha hung her head and searched for something to say. Something that wouldn't sound trite or platitudinous. When she couldn't think of anything, she changed the subject.

"Can I tell you something?"

Meteor laughed again—the sound warmed Martha's heart. "What's ever stopped you before?"

"I am so unhappy. I don't think I've ever felt this unhappy before. I'm glad to be back with Matthew, but I just can't get over the guilt. I wake up, but then I just want to go back to sleep. I feel like I'm stuck inside this suffocating gray cloud, and I can't get out. I am so worried about the girls. And my Mary..."

Meteor sat silently for so long that Martha began to worry. "Meteor...?"

Meteor picked up the milk pail, and got up. He walked over to Martha, set the pail on the floor, and pulled her to her feet. With his hands on her shoulders, his blue eyes held hers.

"Martha, you've been through a lot. You have nothing to feel guilty for."

"But the girls...and my grandkids..."

"We'll get them back," Meteor said. "I promise you."

"But..."

"I promise. Now let it go, okay?"

Martha sighed as he pulled her into a hug. She leaned into his chest, once more taken with the instant rush of emotions that his presence wrought inside her. His scent. His warmth. His touch. The rest of the world, her troubles, and her guilt ceased to exist. She relaxed into the stolen moment.

Her head jerked up at the strident creak of the barn door. Light spilled onto the wooden floorboards.

"Oh, this smell is so awful..." a woman's voice said.

Martha stepped away from Meteor. Meteor turned toward the speaker, his arms hanging at his sides. They watched a backlit silhouette enter the barn. It soon became recognizable—a woman. Georgie.

"Hi, Mar— Meteor?" Georgie raised her eyes above the scarf covering her face. "What are you doing here?" she mumbled.

"Milking cows." Meteor picked up the pail and went back to the cow.

"Thanks," Martha said to Meteor. "I'm going home. This headache..."

Georgie stepped aside as Martha brushed by.

"Hope you feel better soon," Georgie called. She sat on Martha's stool, and put her chin into her hands. "Did I interrupt something?"

Milk streams splashed into the pail.

MERVYN EXAMINED the engine. Fuma stood nearby. The smoke from a thin cigar spiraled toward the ceiling of the Quonset hut. Mervyn wiggled hoses and checked the spark plugs. He removed them.

"Hm, this one is dry." He replaced it. "But this one...wet." He wiped it on a rag and thrust it back into the engine.

"Need new spark plugs?"

"No, the carb needs a tune-up. We're not dumping the fuel in spring—fuel's too short. Don't want to waste it. And fuel stabilizer is tough to find. It's gunking up the works." He wiped his fingers on a grimy rag. "I'll clean it later."

"Do you think anyone knows what we did?" Fuma asked.

Mervyn faced him. "Not unless you told 'em."

Fuma shook his head. "Something I don't understand..."

"What's that?"

"How could you just kill that kid and that other woman?" He dragged on his cigar. "Doesn't sound right."

"You do what ya gotta do."

"I don't think you're a killer, Mervyn."

"That makes two of us." Mervyn gave him a sly smile.

Fuma blew smoke into the air. "You didn't kill them, did you?"

Mervyn placed tools into a red toolbox. "You'll never know, will you?" He wiped his hands again and tossed the rag. "Just like The Man will never know what you did."

Fuma raised his eyebrows and smiled. "Understood."

Mervyn glanced at his watch. "Weren't we supposed to have a meeting?"

"Right. Let's go."

The two men entered the office, once more crowded with men. The Man's chair was empty. Brad was nowhere in sight. Fuma and Mervyn took a spot against the far wall. They scanned the room and watched as others chatted. Two bikers started up a conversation near them.

"I liked it better back in the Edmonton clubhouses," said a man with an unruly head of carrot-red curls. His freckles were so abundant that his face was patched like a calico cat. He had a deep vertical crease between his eyebrows. His eyes were bright and earnest. "We had great parties."

"We got good parties in the South Camps," said the other man. His mustache had grown well over his upper lip, and his eyebrows were wild with long tendrils of wiry hairs. "But the most fun is running the territory. Keepin' the suppliers in line."

"Yeh— we did that, too—in the Edmonton area. But there was one guy we couldn't control. Still can't. Even though we've got a bunch of his women and kids."

"Gatekeeper?"

"Yeah."

"That'll change in the spring."

"Why?"

"South Camps are getting stronger and stronger. The Man will move an army out of there once the snow's gone."

"That's his plan?"

"Yep— The Gatekeeper's going down."

"Brad'll be glad to hear that," said the man with the curly red hair.

"Why?"

"He used to be with their camp. He's got a hate-on for the Gatekeeper...and his wife...has had for a long time." The man laughed. "He showed her a good time. He...and a bunch of our guys."

"Kill her?"

"Don't think so. But they all took a turn. That's what one guy told me."

"Probably she would have been better off dead after that."

"Two of her daughters and her grandkids are here," the redhead said.

The door opened and Brad strode into the room. "Gentlemen..." He sat in The Man's chair. "He's on his way back."

MARTHA STRETCHED. Her head still ached, and she was desperately thirsty, but her stomach wasn't rolling. She got out of bed and pulled on her jeans. She was about to go into the kitchen, when she spied her trunk. Late afternoon sunlight bathed the case in warm, golden rays. She bent over and lifted the lid.

Her white dress lay on top. It was no longer white, and no longer a whole dress, but it was there. It was always there. She touched it, tracing the stiffened bloodstains. She knew the bodice had been cut away, and that the dress was filthy, but something had kept her from throwing it out—

something she couldn't quite determine. All she knew was that when she touched the dress, looked at it—she felt...something. A memory of that night flashed into her brain. The dress. The crystal jewellery. The gun.

The gun? Where was Meteor's gun?

She slammed the lid. She finger-combed her hair, wincing when they caught knots. She slammed her feet into her boots, grabbed her coat, donning it as she ran down the steps. She sped toward the men's bunkhouse.

"Hi, Martha," Jonah said. "Feeling better?" he asked with a grin.

"Is Meteor here?"

"No. He left this morning. Haven't seen him since."

Martha ran to the Gatehouse. She burst through the door. The room was empty. One of the gate guards came rushing in behind her.

"Martha? Do you need something?"

"Meteor. Have you seen him?"

"Tobogganing. Left a couple of hours ago."

"Oh."

"Can I help?"

"No. It's nothing." She cleared her throat. "I'll see him when he gets back."

"Matthew is at the munitions storehouse. If you're looking—"

"No."

THE DINING ROOM bustled with activity. The scent of roasted venison with pan-browned potatoes, garlic, and onions wafted through the air, making stomachs growl. Sarah had marinated four deer roasts in bottled Italian salad dressing, and then roasted them in wood burning ovens set up near the kitchen. Sarah drained the drippings into big saucepans seated atop propane burners. The women added flour to the tangy salad dressing marinade and then dumped the mixture into the bubbling broth. They whisked it into thick, rich gravy.

Children once more gathered by the dining room door—large, hungry eyes capturing the scene of tables laden with plates, loaves of fresh bread and butter. The men hacked slices from the bread and slathered them in butter. They leaned their bodies indulgently to the side to allow women to set down steaming plates piled high with the meat and potatoes. The children watched.

"I didn't think I'd like deer this much," Fuma told Mervyn as the two chewed their way through their suppers.

"I hope we got enough. We packed a truck bed with meat for our use, but the other four trucks are headed to the South Camps."

"They'll be happy to get the meat."

"I wonder who Brad is sending."

"He's taking one of the trucks himself," Fuma said.

"He is?"

"Yeah— Ruth's sister is going, too."

"What?"

"Elizabeth." Fuma wrinkled his forehead. "Does that surprise you?"

Mervyn shrugged. He kept eating. He glanced around the room as he ate. Finally, Fuma called him on it.

"Who are you looking for?"

"Just wondering how many people the cook expects to feed with this meat," Mervyn replied.

Fuma looked back at the children. "They look hungry." He pushed back from the table and motioned to two of the youngest children. They scampered over and climbed into chairs near him. He took two plates, filled them with food—he cut the meat, fastidiously into small bite-sized pieces, and then set the plates in front of the kids. Mervyn watched with great interest. Fuma noticed.

"I am the oldest of five kids. Had to do this all the time for my brothers."

Mervyn gave up his seat to another child hovering near his elbow. "Here's another little bird. I'll leave it to you. I have some things to take care of." He left the dining room.

Mervyn glanced back over his shoulder, and seeing that nobody was watching, he left the home. He ran around to the back of the kitchen, and slipped inside. He saw Sarah and motioned to her.

"Where's Ruth?"

"She was here. Look outside. Maybe she went back to the ovens."

Mervyn searched around, but didn't see her. He went back into the kitchen. "Tell Ruth I need to talk to her about the deer," he said to Sarah. He ran out the door.

A moment later, Ruth walked in. "Have you seen Mervyn?"

Sarah laughed. "What is it with you two?"

"What?"

"Mervyn was just here looking for *you*."

"Where did he go?" Sarah pointed.

Ruth ran out the door.

MARTHA PUSHED her reading glasses up on her face. The words had stopped making sense, and her head still throbbed. She rubbed her hands across her face. Matthew was due in for supper, but she hadn't prepared anything.

Send him to the cookhouse, she thought.

Snowmobiles buzzed outside. Martha peered through the window. She could see several headlights coming up the main roadway.

Meteor is back.

She heard boots on the stairs. She waited for Matthew to come through the door, but instead someone knocked.

"Martha?" The door opened and Anna came in. "Sorry, didn't mean to disturb you, but I think Cammy might be miscarrying. Can you help?"

"Oh, God." Martha grabbed a textbook from the shelf, clutched at her coat, and ran out the door. "She's only about six months, right?"

She kept pace with Anna as they neared a far cabin. Trojan opened the door. Martha felt a pang in her heart; she'd never seen him look so stressed.

"Trojan, would you do me a favor?" Martha asked.

"Sure."

"Find Matthew and take him to the cookhouse." Martha smiled sheepishly. "I didn't make any supper."

The women watched Trojan leave.

"He needed a mission," Martha explained. "Now let's see about you, Cammy."

Martha studied the pretty woman's ashen face. Cammy had gotten very thin, waif-like, with big doe eyes underscored by dark shadowy hollows. Martha knew she had been sick for several weeks with the flu. She wondered if she would be strong enough to give birth.

"What's going on?" Martha asked gently.

"I started getting cramps a few days ago. Just twinges. Then I started bleeding. A little."

MERVYN STOPPED when he heard his name called. Ruth called again. He motioned to her and pointed to the Quonset hut. Once inside, they checked the building, but it was dark and deserted. They huddled into a corner, and talked by the light of a small flashlight.

"Do you know anything about what happened to your mother when your camp was attacked?" Mervyn asked.

Ruth had told him about their exodus in the middle of the night, and of Brad's capture of them the next morning, but she had not said very much about Martha.

"I know she was hurt. Mary saw her in the Meeting House with Brad and some of his Crazies."

"How hurt?"

"Her face was bruised—" Ruth paused. "Why are you asking me this?"

Mervyn stared into her eyes. "Steady yourself."

"For—?"

"Your mother was...raped. By Brad and some of the men here."

The blood drained from Ruth's face and she sank to the seat of a nearby snowmobile.

"I— I'm sorry. Couldn't think of a better way to tell you—"

Ruth held up a hand. "That explains everything. She was so secretive that night. And her face..." She froze. "Oh my God, I wonder if she's still alive. She would have been horribly hurt." She began to cry.

"Don't do that," Mervyn said. "There's nothing you can do for your mother. But what about your sister?"

"My sister?"

"Elizabeth is going with Brad to Calgary."

"I know, but that's not for a while." Ruth stifled a sob.

"In a day or two— He's taking a truckload of meat back. And he's taking her."

"Oh, no...he's—"

"Can you stop her?"

"I don't think I can," Ruth said, snuffling into her sleeve. "She's got it in her head that she can act like a sort of...spy."

"Why?"

Ruth searched Mervyn's face for veracity. "Can I really trust you?"

Mervyn sighed. "You know you can."

"Okay— We're going to escape in the spring."

"That's crazy. How're you planning—?"

"I know— We can't get everyone out, but we can get some of us out."

"If you do that, he'll kill the rest."

"No, he won't. We're too valuable."

"If The Man gets angry—" Mervyn shook his head slowly from side to side. "He will have his revenge. He'll kill you." He paused. "I can't let that happen." He tipped her chin up. "I love you, Ruth."

"No. Don't—" She looked away.

"It's okay— I know the deal." Mervyn took a breath. "Tell you what—you keep me in the loop and I'll help you get away. Okay?"

Ruth stared at him.

"Okay?" he repeated, his voice more forceful.

Ruth nodded.

"The Man will be back here in a couple of days. We'll figure something out before then. Don't worry."

Ruth nodded again.

CAMMY LAY in silence on the bed, while Martha studied the textbook in her lap. Martha scratched her head. She flipped a page. She looked up at Anna.

"Homeopathic remedy. We've gotta give her herbs that will induce a miscarriage."

"What?" Anna asked.

Martha held up a hand. "If the fetus is healthy, it should have an opposite effect. It'll stop the cramping. And the bleeding. And it says here that the herbs will make Cammy stronger."

"That's a big IF— Herbs are dangerous during pregnancy."

Martha shoved the book at Anna. "Here. You read. Maybe I'm missing something."

Finally, Anna looked up. She waited for Cammy to look at her. "She's right. Will you trust us?"

"Okay," Cammy said softly.

Martha stood up. "I'll make the mixture. Don't tell Trojan. It'll just upset him. Instead talk to him about how much you want this baby." She stopped. "You do *want* this baby, right?" Cammy nodded vigorously. "Okay, the herbs must be taken every two hours till the cramping stops."

"What if the cramping doesn't stop?" Cammy asked.

"The baby will miscarry," Martha said gently. "But you'll get better, faster."

Anna reached over and stroked Cammy's hand. "I'll stay with you."

"Start a massage, Anna."

"What kind?"

Martha put her hands into the air. "I don't know—anything that'll calm her. And think positive thoughts."

METEOR CALLED out as Martha left the cabin. "What's up? You were looking for me?"

"I'm in a hurry right now."

"What did you want?"

"I wondered what happened to my gun— I mean your gun. I had it that night."

"I know. I found it."

"Do you still have it?"

"Of course."

"Can I have it back?"

Meteor smiled. "Going scavenging?"

"Yes. Can I have it?"

"We'll see."

"It's mine," Martha called over her shoulder as she dashed for her cabin. "I won it—fair and square. Remember? I want it back."

Meteor watched her go. He reached into his holster and pulled the pistol. He caressed it. It still had her blood on it.

"I know you do, sweetheart."

~~~

A Random Act

SCAR WATCHED the two men as they dug into bowls of oatmeal infused with cinnamon, brown sugar, and dried blueberries. A plate piled high with sourdough bread, toasted golden brown and spread with butter, sat in front of them alongside cups of dark coffee. The older man spoke first.

"They're deserting their posts. Just as I thought."

"So the rumours go," countered The Man.

"I told you. You need to rally your men. You need a show of force. And soon. Or they'll lose faith in you. And splinter off. Form their own units..." The old man coughed and wagged his head. "It's a natural science. Nothing to keep them loyal to you. And then you will have new enemies. After that, it will only be a matter of time before your kingdom falls."

"They're loyal. Maybe the odd one is falling away, but the rest are loyal."

"You sure about that? Have you checked?"

"It's been tough with all the snow, but I have regular communications from runners."

"You have to make a move on the North. A show of strength. It will rally them around you again."
~~~

"Our resources must be meted out, Uncle. We can't go on a whim. We have to know we'll gain ground. And we will. This time, there will be no mistakes."

"I wonder if the Gatekeeper's resources are as low as ours—"

The Man's fist slammed to the table making the plates and bowls rattle. "Goddammit! Enough!"

The old man continued spooning oatmeal into his waiting mouth as though he had not heard the outburst.

"Bring up the Gatekeeper's name again, Uncle—"

The old man reached for a piece of toast, unruffled by the threat. "Easy there, nephew...save that shit for the enemy. I'm just saying I suspect everyone's fuel and ammunition stocks are getting low."

"I'm going to Medicine Hat. Then I'm going north. We'll load up at the Drumheller munitions base. Matthew won't know what hit him. He expects us to wait till late spring, but we'll strike early. I ***will*** *take the Gatekeeper's camp. That's a promise."*

The Man grabbed his coffee cup and took a swig. The liquid burned his tongue and he spat it to the floor. He slammed the cup to the table, sloshing coffee onto the wooden surface, shoved back his chair, stood, and strode out of the room. Scar and the old man exchanged glances.

"He's changed—lost something," Scar said quietly. "Something's gone out of him. He never got so ruffled before."

"Self-proclaimed lords don't like being questioned or second-guessed. He'll be fine. He is his father's son."

"What happened to his father?"

"Killed. Murdered. No one knows who did it...a crazy parishioner...a random act. But I have my suspicions."

"You do?"

"Yes, I do." The old man pushed back from the table. "My brother had many enemies...some closer to him than others."

"You think—?"

The old man did not respond. He left the room.

Scar picked up The Man's coffee cup and cradled it in her hands. She rested her lips on the cup's rim where The Man's lips had been. She blew at the steaming liquid and took a sip.

Chapter Twenty-Six

The Correction

THE WOMEN WANDERED back and forth in the home's front room, glancing up nervously at the windows, and impatiently snapping at their children. They did not look forward to The Man's return. They dreaded it, worried they would be among the next to be sent off to the South Camps. Nevertheless, they watched along with their captors while the trucks pulled up on the front drive.

Ruth sighed. She hoped their meat freezers would appease The Man. They had worked so hard. He couldn't find fault with what she had done. Brad came out of the dining hall. Elizabeth was with him. Ruth remembered their previous night's conversation. She had told Elizabeth about their mother's rape, but nothing Ruth said could convince her sister not to get involved with Brad...

..."Are you really going with him?" Ruth asked.

"Yes, I am."

"Stay here...please! We can escape together."

Elizabeth was adamant. "We're prisoners here. Slaves. I can get much more done on the outside. Find out some things. Maybe even get word back to our people somehow."

"At what cost?"

"I'll do what I gotta do."

"Including selling your soul?"

"Don't be so dramatic. I know the truth about him. That gives me an edge. I'm a good actress. And I know how to survive."

"You might get killed."

"Or...he might get killed. Ever think of that?"

"What? By you? You've never killed anyone. What makes you think you could kill him?"

"I don't mean just pick up a gun and blow his brains out. I can't *murder* him," Elizabeth said emphatically. "I meant if the time was right. If I was pushed into a corner and had no other choice—"

"Mom killed a man once," Ruth blurted.

"What?"

"One of the guys back on the compound told Peter. When they were out scavenging—the time she took off by herself. Remember? The weird guys on the farm?"

"The ones who hunted people?"

"Yeah. Mom was captured by some old guy. She killed him."

"How?"

"Scissors in the neck."

Elizabeth shuddered. "Ugh. Really?"

"I wouldn't make that up."

Elizabeth pushed out her lower lip. "Maybe I do have it in me. Like mother, like daughter." Ruth reached out and clutched Elizabeth's hand.

"Please, Elizabeth, don't go."

"Just pretend I'm going off to college."

"*College*?" Ruth's stunned look made Elizabeth laugh.

"Sure, I'll major in Negotiations with Crazies, with a minor in Best Ways to Kill an Asshole."

Ruth laughed, too.

The laughter had felt good.

There was no laughter now—only dread as The Man burst through the doors. He said nothing to anyone and strode through the front room on the way to his office. A cat meowed from inside the pet carrier he swung from one hand. Brad and the rest of the men followed. Mervyn caught Ruth's eye as he passed by. He winked.

Ruth went to the fireplace. She clapped her hands.

"Ladies, I need your attention..." The women waited. "Elizabeth will be leaving us. She's going with Brad when he leaves."

Mumbles of disbelief rose from the assembled women.

Elizabeth interrupted them. "I think it's better if I go with him. He likes me. And I like him." Ruth heard the words, but she knew they must have tasted like sour milk in her sister's mouth. "Actually, it'll be nice to get away from here after all the months I've been cooped up."

Duke sidled up and insinuated himself beneath Elizabeth's arm. He smiled. Elizabeth bent and hugged him. "You be a good boy for Auntie Ruth, okay?"

The little boy glanced back and forth between the two sisters. His face crumpled and tears filled his eyes.

"Oh, now...stop that Duke," Elizabeth said.

Ruth reached out and took Duke's hand. He ignored her, and shoved up closer to Elizabeth. Elizabeth shot Ruth a pleading look.

"He'll be okay," Ruth said. "That reminds me... Is anyone interested in taking over piano lessons?" An older teen responded that she would like to teach. "Okay, it's your job now." Ruth looked across the room. "We need more kitchen help, too. Any volunteers?" There were no takers.

Sarah stepped up. "No problem. Let me pick." Ruth held up a hand.

"Look," Ruth said. "We have so many people to feed. With Hannah gone..."

"Any word about her?" asked one of the young mothers.

"We have no idea. Best guess is that they took her and Reggie to the South Camps," Ruth said. "Anyway...with her gone and Cook not feeling well, we need more help in the kitchen."

"Cook's still not feeling well?" asked another woman.

"No," Ruth said. "She can't shake her cold, or flu, or whatever it is."

"We're so lucky that none of us have been really sick. An epidemic would be really bad. We're so isolated out here," the woman added.

"Keep your fingers crossed. Anyway...I'll take over the cooking for now, but I want two other women helping out."

Two women raised their hands.

"Good... now—"

Raised voices, the meaty sounds of fists on flesh, and the sounds of bodies being thrown against furniture made the women freeze. They stared with wide eyes down the hall. Fear grabbed Ruth, its icy fingers constricting her throat. She tried to swallow.

Mervyn? Had they found out? Oh, please, God...

More slamming noises and then a door opened. Men poured into the hallway. Ruth went white.

Oh, shit. Oh, shit. Don't let it be Mervyn.

MATTHEW POURED coffee into two cups. He handed one to Martha. She leaned over and breathed in the strong, nutty scent.

"You look tired," he said.

"Thanks." Martha sniffed at her coffee again. "Wonder how long it'll be before we can't get coffee anymore."

"Soon. We'll run out of our stocks in a few months." Matthew sipped his own coffee. "How's Cammy?"

"Don't know yet. But she's pretty weak."

"How are you?"

"Better." Martha blew at the steam and took a sip from her cup. "No tolerance for alcohol anymore, I guess."

"Did you ever have any?"

"Yeah. I did. Tailgate parties. I could hold four beers before things got too stupid."

Matthew chuckled. "Wow...four..." He reached over and squeezed her hand. "You still going scavenging with me?"

Martha looked up. "Did I say that?"

"Yeah, you did. No backing out now. What one says in a drunken stupor, one must honor."

"Oh... I forgot," she said as a smile of remembered drunkenness creased her face. "Marion's going, too. I actually like her. Go figure."

Matthew laughed again. "I understand she did in Jonah's boots."

"Good. Then I wasn't alone." Martha blew at the steam and took a sip of her coffee. "I don't know what got into me—sharing a bottle of wine with her..."

"A *bottle*? Try *two* bottles," Matthew corrected her.

"Oh, I won't be doing that ever again...in the foreseeable future." She paused and then smiled sadly. "Know what I miss, Matthew?"

"Uh-uh."

"Booking a plane trip. To New York. Or London. Or Hawaii." She pondered the memory. "I'll never get to see those places again, will I?"

"Probably not, unless something miraculous happens."

"That's too sad to think about."

"Well, wife...I can't show you Europe, but I can show you inside The Man's world. How about it? Still want to come?"

"Do you think the roads will be safe to travel?"

"I think we've got a break in the weather. We only need a day."

"No camping?"

Matthew gave her a firm look. "No camping. Makes you do funny things."

Martha blushed when she realized he was referring to her near intimate misses with Meteor. "It was your fault."

"My fault? How was it my fault?"

"You didn't want me."

"You were married to Josef."

"Only the first time."

"Well, the second time...you pissed me off."

"Aw, but you aren't pissed at me now, right?"

"Why?" Matthew asked with a lift of his eyebrows. "What did you have in mind—?" He grinned.

A knocking at the door interrupted them. Matthew opened the door. It was Anna. She looked troubled.

"Martha? Would you check Cammy?" Anna asked.

"Did the bleeding stop?"

"No."

"Is she in pain?"

"Pretty bad."

"She's miscarrying. Did you keep giving her the herbs?"

Anna's face fell. "Trojan wouldn't let me."

"Dammit." Martha's fist banged the table. "He should have stayed out of it."

Matthew gave Martha a stern look. "He has a right to say something. She's his woman—"

"But he's no doctor—"

"Neither are you," Matthew chided her.

"Maybe not, but I know a whole lot more than he does."

"I know you do, but he *loves* Cammy...and you don't."

Martha glowered at Matthew. "I'll be right over," she said to Anna.

"Okay, I'll head back," Anna said, closing the door behind her.

Martha took her medical textbook and opened it to the section on miscarriages. She grabbed a book on herbal remedies and opened it, too. She read for a moment.

"I hope the baby miscarries cleanly. No way I can do a D&C." She stopped and looked up. "Whatever happened to that abortionist?"

"This is the first you've noticed he's gone?" Matthew looked truly puzzled. "He left the camp months ago, before the attack. Took his wife and two kids. Something about not being welcome. I knew it had something to do with you and your kitten fiasco."

"You knew about that?"

Matthew scowled. "Of course, I knew. But I had other things on my mind at the time."

"I remembered the pink blanket," she blurted.

"What?"

"After Brad raped me..." Martha said softly. "I had no clothes. The pink blanket that I used to cover the kittens was there. I used that. To cover me."

Matthew regarded his wife in silence. Then he pulled her to her feet and enveloped her in his arms.

"Thank you for telling me, Martha. Even that little bit." He kissed her warmly. When he pulled away, there were tears in his eyes. "Thank you for trusting me."

Martha hugged him tightly.

THE WOMEN held their breaths. The shouting and banging had to mean bad news for somebody. Men came down the hallway dragging two other men between them. Their faces were bloodied. Ruth guessed they had lost consciousness. She tried to catch a glimpse of their faces. Suddenly, she saw Mervyn toward the back of the crowd. Relief flooded her, and she shot him a questioning look. He gave a tiny shrug as he passed by. He followed the men through the door.

The women watched through the front window; children crowded up to the window, too. They watched as the beaten men were thrown to the ground. Other men pulled pistols. When it dawned on the mothers that they were about to witness an execution, they pulled their children away. Samuel was one of the kids with his nose glued to the windowpane.

"Samuel," Ruth said sharply. "Get away from there."

It was too late. Shots rang out and the prone bodies jerked with the impact of each bullet. The women clasped hands over their mouths and suppressed their screams.

Elizabeth came up behind Ruth. "Stupid guys."

"What?"

"Brad said something about them stealing from the South Camps."

"Stealing? They were executed for stealing?" Ruth asked.

"Young girls."

"Who are they? I couldn't see their faces."

"Two of the new guys that came down from the South Camps."

"What did they do exactly?"

"Stealing young girls and selling them is punishable by death."

"You got all that from Brad?"

"No, just some of it. But because they think I'm his old lady..." She grimaced. "The term makes me want to vomit, but it means they talk around me." Elizabeth continued:

"I'm getting to know him a little better. I know what motivates him. He thinks women live to make him happy. I'm being cautious—I don't do anything to make him upset. But I can find a softer side to him if I believe his bullshit and praise him for his decisions. You can't know how many times he has assured me that he didn't have anything to do with Dad's death."

"And you believe him?"

"No, of course not. But I'm getting good at snowing him."

Ruth scowled. "Don't get caught."

"Not I—for I am like the wind..." Elizabeth countered with a theatrical sweep of her arm.

Ruth shook her head.

The women watched as the dead bodies were dragged away. The other men returned to the home. Brad and The Man, deep in conversation, followed them. Brad smiled at Elizabeth on his way back to The Man's office. They disappeared down the hallway.

"I wonder why The Man has never taken a woman," Ruth mused. "He could take any one of us. Why hasn't he?"

"Ee-Dee?" Elizabeth suggested.

"Huh?"

"You remember those TV commercials—for the guys who couldn't get it up? Erectile Dysfunction."

"Oh— Now I know what you mean. Then he couldn't be the father of Cindy's twins," Ruth said. She pointed. "Speaking of the little devils."

Two little boys with whitish blond hair and blue eyes tottered around the room. *Hellions*, was their title among the women. They were toddling terrors having just learned to walk. No one wanted to babysit them. One desperate woman took two ropes—tied their ends to her ankle and the other ends around the boys' waists. Other mothers protested what they deemed as brutality, but when it came their turn to babysit, they saw the light, and quickly employed the technique. The little boys had a penchant for biting and hitting, too, and very often, a mother would rescue a screaming child from one of their attacks. Ruth watched as one of the twins clamped a chubby hand onto the head of a girl sitting quietly near the fire— He grasped a hank of hair, and pulled. The girl screamed in pain. The little boy didn't let go.

Elizabeth chuckled. "Well, on second thought..."

The sisters laughed.

Ruth checked her watch. "I have to start working on supper. Will you check Cook? We've been taking food to her, but she isn't eating much."

"Elizabeth!" It was Brad's voice.

Elizabeth's head snapped up. "The mawh-ster calls." Elizabeth got up, dropped a shoulder, and mimicked the walk of a hunchback in a monster movie. "Coming..."

Ruth laughed again. "Stay out of trouble, sister," she warned.

TROJAN STOOD at the bedroom doorway, feet planted firmly apart and arms crossed. He still refused to let Martha administer the herbal concoction. Martha fully understood why Anna had come to get her. She had tried repeatedly to explain how the herbs worked, but he turned a deaf ear to all her coaxing. She sighed.

"Trojan, nature will take its course. The herbs will help her, one way or the other."

"No."

"Goddammit, Trojan. She'll miscarry for sure. But this way—"

"No!" Trojan's face was stony.

"Fine." Martha turned back to Cammy. "Before the Change, spotting was treated with drugs and bed rest. How do you feel about another couple of months on your back?"

"I'll do it if I have to," Cammy replied in a tiny voice.

"How're the cramps?"

"Some really hurt."

Martha pursed her mouth and wagged her head. "I don't think you can hang onto the baby. I'm sorry." She turned back to Trojan. "She's gotta go through the natural process—just like she was delivering a full-term baby. It'll probably be born alive." She saw the pain that darkened Trojan's face. She spoke gently. "We have no way to care for a baby that small. I want both of you to be prepared for that. Okay?"

Cammy began to cry. "Trojan, please...the herbs might work."

Trojan sank down on the bed beside her. He put his arm around Cammy and looked up at Martha. His eyes were confrontational. "The herbs won't harm her?"

"No— They'll make her stronger."

"But they might make the baby miscarry?"

Both Anna and Martha gave small nods. "If the baby is not viable, it will miscarry. But if the baby is healthy, it will hang in there. And Cammy will be stronger for the birth."

Trojan sat silently. He stared at his boots. Finally, he raised his head. "Okay."

ELIZABETH DID NOT show up for the evening meal. Ruth was busy with preparations and serving, so she pushed concern from her mind. However, once the children were settled and fed, she handed off her duties to one of the other women, and raced off to find her sister. She found Elizabeth in her room, under the covers.

"Elizabeth?"

No response.

"Elizabeth?" The room was dimly lit, but Ruth could see her sister was shivering. She perched on the edge of the bed and put her hand on Elizabeth's shoulder. "Are you okay?"

"Fine," Elizabeth mumbled. She kept her back to Ruth.

"Lizzy?" Ruth rarely used the babyish name. "What's wrong?"

Elizabeth rolled over. Her hair covered her face. Ruth pushed the dark strands aside. She gasped. "Oh, my God. What happened?"

Elizabeth spoke through a fat lip. She licked delicately at a crack that still oozed blood. "I pushed my luck. I pissed him off."

"Brad hit you?" Ruth growled. "That son-of-a—"

"No— The Man," Elizabeth corrected quickly.

"What did you do?"

"I gave him an opinion." Elizabeth touched her lip. "Ow... He really back-handed me."

"An opinion on what?"

"Running his hothouses."

"Oh. What about Brad? He just stood there and watched?"

"Pretty much," Elizabeth mumbled through her thickened lip.

"I'll get snow."

A short time later, with Elizabeth sitting up, a cold compress to her lip, Ruth continued her questioning. "I have to know. What was the discussion?"

"Moving us to the South Camps."

"And—?"

"He wants to move us soon. He says it's too hard running this home. He says he's got more homes ready in the Calgary area. They're gonna start trading us soon, too."

"With who?"

"You'll never believe it—"

"Who?" Ruth repeated.

"The mafia."

"What?" Ruth said, her voice incredulous. "This just gets more nuts."

"I know."

"I'm glad you're getting this information...but next time— Shut up."

"Yeah, right," Elizabeth said. "Next time I'll shut up. Like that's going to happen. You and I both know better. We came from the wrong woman. We can't shut up."

Ruth touched her sister's hand. "Were you afraid?"

"Oddly...no. I just opened my mouth and there it was... He hit me so fast— I never saw it coming."

"You're lucky he only hit you once."

Elizabeth sighed. "There's more...Brad and I are leaving right away."

A silence fell between them.

Suddenly, Ruth clutched Elizabeth's hand with both of her hands. "It's a bad idea! Please don't go. Don't go!" Ruth's voice squeaked through a throat constricted by emotion. Her eyes filled with tears. "We'll find a way to get out of here. Together."

"It's too late, Ruth," Elizabeth said gently, pulling her hand away and reaching up to touch Ruth's face. "You know that."

Ruth shook her head, unable to speak. Tears trickled down her face. She squeezed her eyes shut against the thoughts...the terrible thoughts.

I'll never see her again...if she goes with him. It will be the last time I will see my sister alive. Ruth grabbed Elizabeth and pulled her into a tight hug.

God, please... Please, Father....please...keep her safe.

METEOR ROLLED over, gently, so as not to disturb the sleeping woman beside him. Her thick red hair splayed across the pillow, some of it was caught beneath his arm. He moved slowly to free himself and got up from the bed. He stood in front of a small mirror. He rubbed his hand over his cheeks and chin, and the forest of salt and pepper whiskers that grew there. He had not shaved in several days. He looked back at Georgie.

Meteor pulled on his jeans, grabbed a sweater, and pulled it over his head. He watched Georgie while he dressed, but she did not stir. He let out his breath in a soft sigh.

Martha was not going to like this.

He padded out of the bedroom into the kitchen and sat down. He contemplated a cup of coffee, but changed his mind. He got up and went to the window. Afternoon sunshine glanced off high snow banks, off their icy crusts, shooting fiery diamonds across his vision. Children dressed in snow gear, climbed and tumbled on one of the largest banks. Meteor grinned.

Nothing stopped kids. Nothing.

He remembered playing with his brother that way, at home, on their small farm, while his parents watched. He remembered their laughter, as they held hands, encouraging him and his brother in their antics.

Children...

A sound behind him made him turn around. Georgie was standing there, in her sock feet, a blanket gripped around her shoulders. She was wearing a heavy flannel shirt overtop an insulated undershirt. The gray waffle weave of the shirt showed through where the top buttons of her flannel shirt were undone. Meteor smiled. Georgie sidled up beside him, grabbing one of his arms and pulling it around her shoulders.

"They look like they're having fun." Georgie cocked her head at him. "You like kids?"

Meteor nodded.

"Why don't you have any?" Georgie's hand flew to her mouth. "Or...maybe you do?"

"No— No kids."

"Why not?"

Meteor was silent. Georgie waited. Children's laughter bubbled up from outside. Finally, Meteor shrugged and spoke:

"I would have had children. I almost got married."

"What happened?" Georgie asked.

"She was my high school sweetheart."

"And?"

Meteor remained silent.

"Did she have an abortion?"

"No— Nothing like that."

"You don't have to tell me if you don't want to, but I am interested." Georgie gave him an encouraging smile. Meteor stared out the window. The two stood in silence for a moment.

"She was a neighbor kid. We grew up together. We used to hunt frogs together, and then later...we fished together. And...well..." He shrugged. "We fell in love."

"But what happened? Why didn't you get married?"

"Died. She was killed. In a car accident. One summer night. She was eighteen." He gave a huge sigh and went on, "After that... I just didn't ever want to feel like that again."

But you do, the tiny voice inside his head chided. *Martha...*

He groaned, lifted his arms, and ran roughened hands across his face and through his hair.

Georgie gave him a puzzled glance. "No one? You never loved anyone at all after that?" She asked the question as though in full anticipation of a different, more truthful answer.

"No one," he said firmly. He pulled away. Georgie hugged her blanket tighter.

Meteor sat down at the table. He didn't know what had drawn him to Martha, and why it had bound him so steadfastly to her. There was no understanding his love for her, but he knew it was real. And he knew it was destroying him.

Eating his soul.

Georgie gazed at him, her eyes soft and warm. Inviting.

Maybe it was time. Time to change his life. Start a new life. Somewhere else. Away from here.

Meteor rubbed his hands over his grizzled countenance again.

Away from her, he thought.

Even as the words flitted through his mind, Meteor knew he would not leave Martha. She was part of him, part of his being, part of his very essence. He knew he would stay. He would protect Martha till the end.

The end. Whatever that meant.

Georgie stretched, and smiled. The blanket fell open. Her checkered flannel shirt rose up her bare thighs. Meteor appraised her legs, and then, catching her eyes, he returned the smile.

"Want some coffee?" he asked. "Or, maybe..."

MERVYN HELD Ruth in his arms, her back was nestled against his chest. They were seated on a snowmobile inside the Quonset hut. He rested his chin on her head. "Don't worry. Your sister's tough. And she's right— She *is* getting inside information." He gave a rueful chuckle. "Took a fat lip, but she's getting it."

Ruth twisted around and looked into his face. "She could get hurt worse, next time."

"Maybe there won't be a next time," Mervyn countered. "She's smart. She learns fast."

"But she won't be here when we find a good time to escape."

Mervyn took her by the shoulders. "It's war, Ruth. I know she's your sister, but shit happens. You're just gonna have to let it go."

"I can't leave without her."

Mervyn bent his face to hers. "You *can*...and you *will*. You have two children to protect. Elizabeth will take care of herself. Besides..." he added with tiny kiss on the end of Ruth's nose. "I will be around to look out for her. Just like I looked out for Reggie...and for Hannah..."

Mervyn stared into her eyes. Ruth could feel his warm breath on her face, but she didn't pull away. He lowered his head to hers and kissed her. Softly. Ruth made a small sound deep in her throat. Mervyn pulled her to him, kissing her harder. He reached up under her layers of clothing and gripped her naked back. His hands were cool. Ruth shivered.

This isn't right.

Then another thought inserted itself—as blatantly and as brightly as a red barn in a field of yellow canola.

I'm so lonely. So tired.

Hot blood rushed to her face as Mervyn's hands encircled her ribs, his thumbs brushing the undersides of her breasts. She gave a sharp gasp. Her breathing quickened.

This feels...so good... I need to feel again.

She relaxed into Mervyn's searching hands. His fingers reached higher. She shivered. Mervyn kissed her again, deeply, fully, and with purpose.

"I want you," he mumbled against her lips.

The river rushed in.

Ruth let it take her.

~~~

A Very Bad Idea

ELIZABETH HUDDLED on her side of the truck. With each passing mile, her trepidation grew. Now her stomach was in knots. She took slow breaths to quell her rising fears. Brad reached for her arm, grasped it, and attempted to pull her next to him. Elizabeth resisted.

"I'm not a truck dog," she said. "I don't ride in the middle."

Brad glanced at her. His face grew stony. He gripped her arm harder.

"Ouch. Stop it." Elizabeth plucked at Brad's fingers and tried removing them from her arm, but he maintained his grip.
~~~

"Sit beside me," Brad said, his voice low and heavy with warning.

"I'd rather sit here."

Elizabeth jerked forward when Brad slammed on the brakes. She turned to him, eyes wide. Brad rammed the truck into park. He twisted in his seat and glared at her.

"Get something straight," Brad said. His eyes were dark and the anger in his voice made Elizabeth shrink back against the door. "You will do as I say, when I say it. Understand?" Elizabeth said nothing. "You might have been a princess back home, but here you are my bitch. And you will obey me." Elizabeth thought quickly.

"I get motion sickness," she blurted. "I can't sit in the middle seat." The lies came quickly, and more easily. "Never could. Even as a kid. I can open the window if I feel sick...if I sit here." She waited.

Brad grunted. He put his hands on the steering wheel and gripped it tightly. Elizabeth watched his knuckles whiten. Tendrils of terror zipped through her and her throat closed as she tried to swallow again. She struggled for something to say.

"Besides..." she finally said with pseudo lightness in her voice. "You'll have me beside you all the time soon. Right? Won't we have a bedroom together?" Elizabeth hoped her smile didn't look too wooden. She released her breath slowly as Brad pushed the truck into gear.

"I have my own apartment in the South Camps. As far as I know, you'll be staying with me. As long as The Man doesn't tell me otherwise." Elizabeth couldn't resist.

"You mean he can take me away from you? Just like that?"

Brad nodded.

"You won't let that happen, will you?" Elizabeth reached over and patted his hand.

Brad guffawed—a disagreeable sound that caught Elizabeth by surprise. As if burnt, she pulled her hand back.

"If The Man says you jump, you'd better jump. You speak when you are spoken to...and you do as he says." Brad looked at her. "Didn't your fat lip teach you that?"

Elizabeth touched her mouth. She nodded and turned to look out the window. She took another deep breath as her stomach resumed its roiling. Maybe she ***was*** *going to be sick. She rolled down the window. "How much further?" she asked.*

"Another hour or so," Brad replied.

Elizabeth fought against tears. She leaned her face into the wind and sucked in the fresh air. Ruth was right, she thought. This was a bad idea. The words rocketed around in her skull, mocking her, repeating like an evil mantra.

A bad idea...

Brad pulled up outside an upscale multi-storey seniors' home. It was similar to the home in Medicine Hat, but much larger. Trucks and power toboggans were scattered every which way, on the driveway, the lawn, and the street. Brad jumped out, walked around to Elizabeth's side of the truck, opened the door, and hauled her out. Elizabeth stumbled, caught herself, and followed Brad into the home's large front entrance.

It had begun snowing again, and fresh snowflakes clung to their hair and clothing. Brad removed his jacket, and dropped it into the waiting hands of a woman who came to greet them.

"Scar..." he said. "Meet Elizabeth—Elizabeth, meet Scar."

"We already know each other," Elizabeth said, with a curt bob of her head. Scar grunted and jerked her head to the right, motioning for Elizabeth to follow her.

"Come with me," Scar said, handing Brad's coat to another woman standing nearby.

"No," Brad said. "She's with me—"

Scar looked surprised, but said nothing.

Brad pointed to the door. "There's a truck out there full of deer meat. Take care of it." Scar left the room.

Elizabeth pulled off her outer clothing and looked around the room. Women and men lounged around a huge fireplace. Some were playing board games, some were rolling dice, some had playing cards fanned in their hands, while others were amusing themselves with ribald stories. Elizabeth's ears burned at some of the tales and the words being used by the women.

She searched the room and looked behind her; she looked puzzled—there were no children in sight. She was about to ask Brad a question when he grabbed her by the elbow and directed her forward, through another set of double doors, and down a dark hallway.

"Where are we going?"

"My room," Brad said. Fear curdled in Elizabeth's belly. She knew this moment had to come; she had managed to put him off for weeks back in Sunnyvale. She suspected he was not going to be put off much longer.

"Can we get something to eat?" Her eyes were hopeful, her tone sweet. She placed a hand on his arm. "That was a long drive. I'll bet you are hungry."

Brad grunted, but continued down the hall. He stopped in front of a door. Words had been scraped into the wood: Do NOT Disturb! Elizabeth held her breath. She didn't want to see what lay beyond the door. Not at all. Brad turned the handle and walked in. S

The room was dark. He fumbled around and lit two propane lanterns. Elizabeth relaxed. The room looked normal with its humble double bed, a small loveseat, two armchairs, a small four-seater kitchen table, and four folding chairs. Candles surrounded her— each one secured upright on glass ashtrays or delicate china plates, cemented into a puddle of their own, once molten, hardened wax.

"You sure have a thing for candles," Elizabeth said cheerily. She hung her coat in an open closet. She turned back to Brad. "Now, how about a sandwich?" Her mouth went dry. Brad was staring at her in a way she had not seen before. She forced her tongue to move. "We'll have a much better time together after some food." She ran a finger up his sleeve. "Don't you think?"

"Sure." Brad opened the door and ushered her into the hallway.

Brad led Elizabeth through a wide set of double doors. They turned left and entered a large dining room. The scent of past meals hung in the air. Elizabeth wrinkled her nose. The aroma was unfamiliar, and slightly unpleasant. Like spoiled meat. Her stomach did a little roll.

Brad yelled at two women who were standing near a doorway that Elizabeth guessed led to a kitchen. "Food." He pulled out a chair, and then another; he patted the seat of the second chair. "Sit."

Elizabeth sat.

"So?" a female voice said. Elizabeth jumped. It was Scar. "Does she have some sort of special status? Or is she expected to work like the rest us?"

Brad glanced up. "She takes orders from me," he said.

"I manage the women here," Scar said, her tone peevish. "I think you know that. I don't want the other women getting ideas if she is allowed to lounge around here like some princess."

Brad's chair scraped angrily across the floor as he stood. He grabbed Scar's shoulder and pulled her to him, nose to nose. She blinked as he spoke.

"And I manage things here," Brad said. "Including you!" He gave her a push. "Get us some food. Did you take care of the deer meat?"

"Yes," Scar said crossly. She rubbed her shoulder as she walked away.

"I've always wondered what happened to her face..." Elizabeth whispered.

Brad shrugged. "Ask her yourself."

In a few minutes, food arrived. Elizabeth surveyed the plates: undercooked, pale scrambled eggs, bacon strips, and toast. She picked at a piece of bacon, crisp and shiny. She took a bite. It tasted okay. She finished the bacon. She tried to eat the eggs, but uncooked strings of mucous made her feel ill. She took a piece of hard toast and gnawed at a corner. It was surprisingly tasty, her hunger kicked in, and she gobbled it down.

Scar set down cups of coffee and a sugar bowl. "Go easy," she warned. "We're running low."

Brad took a heaping spoonful of sugar and stirred it into his cup, tasted the brew, and then stirred in another. He smacked his lips, and sat back, rubbing his belly.

"Report," Brad demanded, addressing Scar. Scar glanced at Elizabeth and shot him a cautionary look. Brad sat forward. "I told you Elizabeth's with me—my old lady. Aren't you?" Brad wrapped his hand around the back of Elizabeth's neck and pulled her next to him. Elizabeth gave a small nervous laugh as she straightened in her chair. She unwrapped Brad's fingers from her neck as she spoke:

"I would be glad to help out," Elizabeth said to Scar, in an attempt to ease the tension between them. "Just tell me where I'm needed."

Brad's hand clamped back down on the back of her neck. The other hand swept under Elizabeth's chin, bringing her face up level with his.

"Are you hard of hearing?" Elizabeth opened her mouth, but nothing came out. "I said you take orders from me. Not her," he said, looking at Scar. Elizabeth pried his hands off her face.

"Okay, okay," she said, cajolingly. "I get it. Orders come from you."

"That's very good, Elizabeth. And right now, you are ordered back to our room."

Elizabeth's stomach flipped. She wished she had ignored the bacon, too. It was threatening to come back up. She thought quickly.

"No bath?" she asked with a sweet, practiced smile.

"Hot water," Brad said to Scar. "We'll use the bathtub in my room." Scar turned to go. "Fresh towels, too," he called after her. "Nice ones. Those Egyptian cotton ones. From the storehouse." Brad turned back to Elizabeth. "Will there be anything else, your majesty?"

Elizabeth recognized the tone. Brad was nearing the end of his patience. "No, that's more than perfect," she said. "Thank you."

Brad got up; he had forgotten about the report he had demanded. He held out his hand to Elizabeth and she accepted it. She nodded to Scar who smirked back at her.

Elizabeth dragged her feet as they walked to Brad's room. Her mind twisted with plans, excuses, and ways to escape the inevitable. Fear erupted inside her. She came up with one story after another, but none was satisfactory. She tried to quell her trembling as realization settled over her—as thick and as absolute as wet cement.

In a few minutes, Brad was going to know she had lied to him—

She was no virgin.

Elizabeth tried to make the bath last, but with Brad in the bathroom, eyeing her every move, it was difficult to bathe, and enjoyment was out of the question. She waited for Brad to leave the room; then she took the opportunity to tend to her privates. She soaped and rinsed. Just as she finished, Brad walked in. He was totally naked. Elizabeth blushed and looked away.

"My turn he said," holding out a towel. Elizabeth had no choice. She stepped out and clutched the towel around her. The temperature in the room, in spite of a small propane heater, was frigid. She chattered as she rubbed her skin.

Brad stepped into the tub. He handed her a bar of soap and a sea sponge. Elizabeth took it. She knew what was expected. She had done this before.

Elizabeth worked up a lather on Brad's back, rinsed, and then moved to his chest. Something occurred to her, and she let her hand wander down his stomach. She immersed her hand under the water and caught hold of him. Brad looked surprised, but he didn't resist. He raised his hips out of the tub.

Elizabeth used the soap for lubricant and began a slow massage. Brad responded. His breathing quickened and he closed his eyes. Elizabeth increased her speed. Brad's breathing got faster.

Suddenly, he grabbed her by the back of her head, his fingers twisted in her hair. Elizabeth gasped and stopped stroking him. Brad grabbed her hand and put it back into position.

"Faster," he said. Elizabeth sped up. He gripped her hair tighter and tighter in keeping with the motion of her hand.

Brad stopped breathing for a single moment, and then discharged in a loud roar of release. Elizabeth waited. Brad finally relaxed and lay back in the tub, panting, eyes closed. Elizabeth washed her hand, stood, and left the bathroom.

She caught sight of herself in a small mirror. Her eyes were underscored in smoky dark rings. Her face was pale. She rummaged around for clean clothing, and then remembered that her clothes were still in a bag on the truck. She pulled on her dirty clothing, found another sweater in a drawer, and pulled that on, too. She climbed onto the bed, and waited.

Her head hurt and she rubbed the sore spots. Brad had pulled her hair before. He had a thing for hair, she guessed. Maybe it was all he needed. He would be satisfied. She hoped. Because having him inside her... That was unthinkable.

Brad came out of the bathroom with a towel clutched around him.

"What's with all the clothes?" he asked.

"I thought... It's cold in here," she said.

"Undress. I want to see you naked," Brad said.

"It's too cold." Elizabeth kept her voice level and soft. She began to shiver. "I think I might be coming down with something."

"Those clothes are coming off. One way or the other." Brad was now standing beside the bed. He reached for her.

"Okay. Fine. But bring the heater in here."

Brad returned to the bathroom.

Elizabeth stood up. She glanced in the mirror again. The green eyes looking back at her reminded her of her sister's eyes—haunted and lonely. She shuddered.

Ruth had been right...coming with Brad was a bad idea.

A very bad idea.

Chapter Twenty-Seven

The Fish Incubator

MERVYN STRODE through the dining room. Early March sunshine streamed in through the windows, turning the breakfast tables golden. The scent of morning coffee permeated the air. Men gave him a quick morning wave. "Hey, Merv." Mervyn acknowledged them with a clipped greeting, and walked straight through to the kitchen. Ruth was busy beating eggs.

"Ruth," Mervyn hissed. She gave him a startled look.

"What?" she whispered back. She added baking soda to sour milk and then combined everything with flour—beige and speckled with grain husks—in a huge stainless steel bowl. She picked up a whisk, poured the frothy, beaten eggs into the bowl, and began to stir.

"I've got to talk to you— Soon."

Ruth checked her watch. Two women entered the kitchen.

"More deer meat?" Ruth said, her voice overly loud. "I think we have enough for now." She shot Mervyn a conspiratorial look, and went back to whisking the batter.

The two women puttered around, picking up platters, rinsing bowls, and chattering, oblivious to Ruth and Mervyn. They finally left.

"In about an hour? Our usual spot?" Mervyn asked.

"Okay...but what's up?"

"Not now." Mervyn left through the back door.

TROJAN SAT on the end of the bed, in a pool of soft light diffused by an airy curtain hung daintily over the cabin's small bedroom window. He stared at his hands. The night had been a hard one. Especially for Cammy. She lay exhausted, coddled in fresh, white sheets that Anna had put on the bed. She snored softly.

"Can I get you something?" Anna whispered to Trojan. "You should get some rest now."

"No, I want to stay awake...in case she needs me."

Martha called out from the kitchen. "She's gonna need your help, Trojan. But later...when she's awake. Really, it's best if you sleep now." She came around the corner with a cup of tea. "Here," she said. "It's herbal—it'll help you sleep."

"I don't drink that stuff," he mumbled.

"You will drink it," Martha corrected him. "I was right about the other herbs, wasn't I?"

Trojan grinned, eyes glazed. The lack of sleep over the past forty-eight hours had reduced him to a zombie-like state, his face pasty, and his eyes dark hollows. Anna put her hand on his shoulder.

"C'mon, Daddy. Your little girl is going to need lots of care."

The trio looked over at a small cubicle. It had been fabricated from a fish aquarium that one of the members had squirreled away in a U-Haul—one of those just-can't-do-without possessions that they had packed up when they fled their home. Martha put out the call in search of some such device after Cammy went into full labor.

Martha posed the problem of saving the life of a premature baby to the camp geeks. One of the boys, an awkward older teen from the St. Albert area, eagerly applied himself. He polled the camp and quickly amassed everything he needed to build the incubator, just like the ones he had made to incubate eggs and chicks on his father's farm. Martha applauded the boy for his ingenuity, but it wasn't until they put the small glass box into use that she truly appreciated his brilliance.

The tiny infant was tightly wrapped in soft flannel; a miniature, minty green woolen cap hugged her head. Her face was wrinkly and was covered in soft hair. "Lanugo," Anna had said. "Common in preemie babies." The baby was a good color, and she had given a little cry to assure everyone that she was breathing on her own. Battery powered heat lamps glowed soft red all around the aquarium.

Martha walked over and peered through the glass. The infant trembled in her sleep and gave a tiny cry.

"How are we going to feed you, little one?"

Anna joined her. "She's a good size," she said. "I think Cammy was off on her dates. I'd guess she's pretty close to full term."

"I hope so— I hope she'll be strong enough to suckle." Martha turned back to the bed. She chuckled. "I see he took our advice." Trojan was flopped back on the bed, sound asleep next to Cammy, his arm thrown protectively across her. "Which shift do you want?" Martha asked.

Anna put a hand on her belly. "If it's all the same to you, I—"

Martha smiled and touched Anna's cheek. "Go— Ask Matthew to round up one of the other girls we've been training. Have a good sleep." Martha gave Anna a quick hug, and mumbled into her ear, "I miss my daughters so much, but you make my heart glad—"

Suddenly, Martha stopped hugging and pulled away.

Anna pushed her eyebrows together in confusion. "What?"

"In all this time... I never..." Martha rubbed at her eyes. "I never... thanked you. For coming back..." She hugged Anna again. "Thank you."

The baby cried again, but this time the sound was lasting.

"She's crying," Anna said, her eyes bright with tears. "She's crying."

RUTH CHECKED around, assured herself that no one was in sight, and then ran for the Quonset hut. She looked behind her again. She waited to make sure no one was following her. She slipped inside the hut.

"Mervyn?"

"Here..." Mervyn's voice came from across the dusky room.

Ruth wound her way through the toboggans to the far corner where Mervyn was working on an engine. He was standing under the light emitted from a large square flashlight that had been jury-rigged from a slender pole above his head. He held a spark plug in one hand, a dirty rag in the other. Mervyn turned and welcomed her with a wide smile.

"Anybody see you come in here?" he asked.

"No— Why did you need to see me?"

"We've gotta move our plans ahead. We can't wait for the spring."

"Why?"

"The Man—

"What? He wants more deer meat?"

"No— It's you guys. He's gonna move all the women...probably in the next few days." Mervyn's eyes became very serious. "Ruth...in Calgary, he's going to split you up. I think some of you are sold."

"Oh, God." Ruth said. "Snow— There's still too much snow. How are we going to get away—?"

"The same way you got here—"

"Buses?" Ruth's tone was high and incredulous. "How on earth are we going to manage that? Who's gonna drive?"

"I have help—"

"Hey, bus driver, speed up a little bit..." The sound of a strange man's voice singing the familiar school bus ditty made Ruth shriek. She shrank back against Mervyn, her heart hammering in her chest.

Fuma stepped out of the shadows. He smiled—a movement that caused his mustache to dance. "I drive a mean semi. I can drive a school bus."

Ruth stuttered with confusion. "Wh—wh—what's going on? He knows?" She was aghast.

Had Mervyn betrayed her?

"He's solid. I trust him."

"Wh—?"

"It's really okay. Trust me. No worries."

Fuma joined them. He nodded at Ruth. "Hi, Ruth."

Ruth still eyed him with suspicion. She turned back to Mervyn.

"How're you going to load over one hundred women and kids onto buses? Right under The Man's eyes? And then just drive off?" she asked.

"He knows I'm a mechanic. I'll tell him the buses need to be checked because they've been sitting so long. Fuma and I will run two of the buses...to a spot about a half mile from here. All you have to do is find some way to get all the women and kids down to us. It'll be cramped, but it's our only way—"

Ruth sputtered. "How in hell do you expect me to do that? What do I tell The Man?"

Mervyn shrugged. They both looked at Fuma for help. He shrugged, too.

"Oh, my God," Ruth groaned in frustration.

"We either try this or—" Mervyn said.

"I know!" Ruth said impatiently. "But give me some plan... some way to do this." She paused. "And what about Elizabeth? How do we get her?" She glanced back and forth between the two men, in a frantic search for an answer. Elizabeth had been gone from the home for days. There had been no word on her sister's well-being...or her whereabouts. Ruth had tried not to think about Elizabeth, but now she *had* to think about her. Leaving Elizabeth behind would be too painful.

"I'm working on finding out about her, Ruth. It's hard to do without arousing suspicion."

Ruth flopped down on a snowmobile's padded seat. "I don't have a clue. Not a clue."

The trio sat in silence.

Suddenly, Ruth brightened. "I cook. They trust me. I know drugs. Maybe there're enough sleep drugs to drug all of them." She looked hopefully at the two men. They looked doubtful.

"How will you drug over two dozen men?" Fuma asked. "I don't think so."

"Well then, what?"

Mervyn stroked his upper lip. "A party—" he mused.

"A party?" Ruth asked.

Fuma smiled. "A party," he confirmed. "With plenty of booze."

MARTHA LIFTED the top from the incubator. She reached in and picked up the baby. The infant barely filled both her hands. The tiny rosebud mouth opened and closed, emitting little squeaks of need. Martha knew the baby required the colostrum that would be seeping from Cammy's breasts.

But could she suckle?

"Should I wake her?" Anna asked. She had returned to the cabin, following a short nap. Martha consented.

Anna tapped Cammy's arm. Cammy opened her eyes. She reached out. Martha tucked the baby into Cammy's waiting arms.

"Oh, there you are," Cammy cooed. "She's so pretty, isn't she?" Cammy's eyes shone with first love. Both Anna and Martha nodded their agreement that this was the most beautiful baby that had ever been born—just as they had affirmed dozens of other new mothers over the past year and a half.

"You've got to try to nurse her," Anna said softly.

"Okay." Cammy pushed the covers down and lifted her t-shirt. Her breasts were full, but not engorged. She looked up expectantly. Eagerly.

"You don't understand," Anna said. "She might not have the strength to suck. But she has to get your first milk...it'll give her immunities." Cammy listened as Anna added, "Even if she can suck, she might not be able to swallow."

Anna helped Cammy sit up, while Martha held the baby.

"Have you thought of a name yet?" Martha asked, placing the baby into Cammy's arms.

"I thought you knew," Cammy said. "Her name is Ruth." She smiled at Trojan. He was still asleep on the far side of the bed. "Trojan's idea."

Emotion flowed over Martha. She didn't speak. Couldn't speak.

Your namesake, Ruth. You have a namesake. Will you ever meet her?

"Let's give this a go," Anna said. She grunted as she knelt on the floor beside the bed, her own pregnant belly pressing up against the mattress. "You've got to hold her so she doesn't choke from the milk running down her windpipe. Like this..." Anna turned the baby so its front touched Cammy's chest. "Now press down on your breast so the nipple comes up, but the flesh stays away from her nose." Anna demonstrated.

Cammy took over. She struggled and changed positions. The baby's cries had become more insistent. "It's not working," Cammy said, panic infusing her voice.

"C'mon, Little Ruth," Anna coaxed. The baby tried, but couldn't latch on. Cammy tried again and again, without success. Frustration swept over mother and baby, and they both cried.

"I can't do this," Cammy sobbed. Anna and Martha exchanged looks.

"I have an idea." Anna grasped the edge of the bed and hauled herself to her feet. She pulled up a nearby chair and sat down. "My nipples are softer and not so distended. Little Ruth doesn't know the difference, but she has to learn to suck." She pulled open her shirt and held out her arms. "Give her to me."

Martha suppressed a grin at Anna's impetuousness. The girl was all business, her arms out, and her eyes expectant.

Sounds like me, Martha thought with an inner chuckle.

Cammy looked bewildered and clutched the baby to her. Little Ruth squeaked.

"It's really okay, Cammy," Martha said, her tone comforting, but firm. She squeezed Cammy's arm. "She knows what she's doing." Martha took the infant and gave her to Anna. Anna cuddled the baby.

"You'll need to express some colostrum...into a bag," Anna said. Then I can drizzle that into her mouth...a little at a time..."

"I'm on it," Martha said.

In a few minutes, Cammy had managed to express a few tablespoons of the cloudy liquid into a small sandwich bag. Trojan had awoken and now watched the procedure. He grinned widely at the sight of two women with naked breasts.

"What're you doing?"

"Go back to sleep, Trojan," Martha said.

"Not on your life." Trojan's eyes were bright with interest.

Martha burst out laughing. The grinning ape of a man was so Trojan, the old Trojan. She wanted to hug him. "You're an ass."

Cammy glowered at him. Trojan kept right on grinning.

Martha used a pin to make a tiny hole in one corner of the baggie. She pinched it closed. "Okay, Anna. I'm ready. Do your thing."

Anna's experience showed as she directed the new infant to her nipple. The baby rooted around, snuffling, and searching. After only a few failed attempts, the baby's sucking reflex kicked in, and Little Ruth latched on. Anna's face lit up.

"Oh..." she said. "I'd forgotten how good this feels..."

Martha laughed again. She held the baggie near the baby's mouth and let the liquid drip down Anna's breast. The baby seemed content.

"Where did you learn that?" Cammy asked, amazement in her voice.

"Adoptive mothers want to feel what it's like to nurse a baby," Anna said. "They hook up tubes that run alongside their nipple. The tubes are connected to pouches of breast milk. As the baby sucks, the milk runs into their mouths. Like this." Anna cuddled the little girl. "Seems to work. Isn't that right, little one?"

The baby ceased suckling. Martha reached into the swaddling blanket and gave ten tiny toes a little tickle. The baby began to nurse again.

"Can I try now?" Cammy asked.

Anna chuckled. "Not so sure I want her to stop." She touched the soft head. "But I'll have one of my own soon." She eased the baby's mouth from her breast with a soft popping sound. The baby began to fuss. Cammy shot Martha a nervous glance.

"Relax," Martha said. "Little Ruth knows how now. You'll be fine."

MEN'S LAUGHTER boomed outside the hut—the sounds were getting louder. Mervyn motioned to Fuma. He ran to the side of the hut facing the home. He touched something and Ruth saw a shaft of light dart to the floor. Fuma bent and put his eye to an opening. His hand waved them to silence.

"I've got to get food together," Ruth whispered into Mervyn's ear. "We can't go without food."

"Get everyone to carry their own."

"That's not the problem. I've gotta decide which of the women to take into my confidence."

Fuma flapped his hand furiously in a request for silence.

"What about Sarah?" Mervyn whispered.

"Her for sure, but I'm not sure who else to tell." Ruth watched as Fuma motioned to the door.

"Shit! They're coming in." Mervyn grabbed his greasy rag and picked up another spark plug.

"What about me?" Ruth asked.

"Just play along."

Fuma rushed over and grabbed a rag, too. He and Mervyn launched into a discussion about internal combustion and clogged carburetors.

Ruth stood up as several men entered the hut. They walked across the room. She paled when she recognized one of the men. He was the same man who had attacked her on the bus months earlier.

"I fix engines, sweetheart," Mervyn said suddenly, loudly enough for the men to hear. "I don't build refrigerators."

Ruth picked up on the theme. "But the meat has to be kept cold. Isn't there some way to hook up a generator or something...to sort of make a fridge? The snow's melting fast."

Mervyn howled with laughter. "Women!"

Fuma laughed, too.

"Better get back to your pancakes," Mervyn said. "Cause you sure as shit don't know nuthin' about motors." He cast a patronizing look Ruth's way. "Besides, there're plenty of deer." The other men had reached them.

"So, don't be getting your panties in a twist." Mervyn laughed again and then nudged Fuma. "Let *me* do that for you."

The men laughed along.

Ruth's face blazed crimson with embarrassment. "I—uh—I've got to go." She tried to brush by the other men, but they blocked her way. "Excuse me," she said.

One of the bikers reached out and grabbed her breast under her heavy shirt. "Woo, nice tits."

Ruth recognized him as the same man who had assaulted her on the bus. Up to this point, she had managed to evade his advances. Now she was trapped. Ruth slapped at his hand.

"You pig!"

The man's face darkened. He grabbed her by the hair. "What did you call me?" He reached between her legs and grabbed her crotch. Ruth cried out and pushed at his arm.

"Better watch yourself there, buddy," Mervyn called over his shoulder. "The Man said no touching the merchandise. It's sold."

The biker grabbed Ruth by the arm and gave her a shake. "Watch yourself, bitch. I don't care what The Man says—you better show me respect."

Ruth met his angry stare through narrowed eyes. He raised a hand, and she flinched back. She bumped into Mervyn who was standing behind her. He gave Ruth a gentle push to the side. He threw an arm around the man's shoulders.

"Hey— Don't hurt the cook. I want to eat." He grinned. "What do you need, brother?"

The man glared at Ruth as she scurried past him. She slammed into the hut's door, pushed it open, and burst into the fresh air. Her face still burned. She marched back to the kitchen.

I'll figure this out. You filthy pig. She shuddered. *I'll figure this out.*

She burst into the kitchen. "Sarah!"

Sarah met her midway across the dining room. "Did you hear?"

"Hear what?"

"Cook is dead."

"Oh, no. God, I hope it isn't catching— We won't know it's an epidemic until it's too late."

"We wrapped her body in a sheet," Sarah said.

"Get it out of here."

"And do what with it?" Sarah asked.

"Burn it."

~ ~ ~

A Replacement

ELIZABETH CURLED into a fetal ball on the bed. Her stomach hurt and her head pounded. Sweat soaked her clothes. Brad stood over her. He poked at her.

"No," Elizabeth said, her voice barely audible.

"Get up," he said. "You've been lying around for days."

"I'm really sick." Elizabeth shivered. "I think I'm dying."

"You're not dying, Lizzy." Brad reached down, grabbed her arm, and pulled her off the bed. "You're just lazy."

Elizabeth stumbled against him, tried to steady herself, but collapsed to the floor. "I think I might have what Cook has," she mumbled.

Brad grabbed her and hoisted her up again. He pushed her back to the bed. "I'll send someone in," he growled.

He turned and walked out the door.

Elizabeth tried to stop her teeth from chattering. The effort made her nauseous. She curled back into a ball and let sleep take her.

Dream after dream rolled by—winding paths choked with squirming vegetation; jammed guns with strangely pulsing bullets; flying people with golden eyes and flapping hands; grotesque children with teeth smeared in blood; a windstorm with a swirling vortex of pink dust; a black car with no fenders; a skittering stampede of spiders with hairy legs and curled silvery fangs. Like an endless circus with ring upon ring of activity, Elizabeth's visions erupted and collided, overlapping one another—a kaleidoscope of never-never land.

She cried out, but there was no one there to hear her.

~~~

"She's sick," Brad said. "Is anyone else sick?"

He stirred sugar into the coffee cup sitting in front of him. He sipped, made a face, and plopped another spoonful of sugar into the cup.

"Better go easy on the sugar," Scar advised. She rolled her eyes, knowing her warning would go unheeded.

"I asked if anyone else was sick." Brad gave Scar a pointed, corrective stare. Scar turned her back on him and busied herself with paperwork. She spoke with her head turned away.

"We've already lost a few people to illness. A flu...it's not an epidemic though. Just a few have died...the rest of us got better." She turned. "If you're worried about Elizabeth—"

"I'm not."

"Okay, but what I was going to say is that she's young and strong...she'll make it."

Brad grunted.

"Do you need anything?" Scar asked. "I have to check on things in the kitchen."

"I want another bedroom."

Scar tapped her pile of papers together on their edges. "No problem. I will clear one for you. Anything else?"

"A healthy woman. Someone with experience."

"Experience?"

"Knows how to fuck...is that clear enough for you?"

Scar pushed her chair back and got up. "Any age in particular?"

"Young."

"I'll see what I can do. But The Man might have something to say about that. He's getting ready to trade a shipment of women. He's locked them down pretty tight. Doesn't want them touched."

"But he's not here, is he?" Brad asked sarcastically. "So, that makes me the boss."

"Not the boss of me," Scar said cautiously.
~~~

Brad stared at her. A smile broke across his lips. He got up.

"What happened to your face? You like it rough?" Scar looked puzzled. Brad moved toward her. Her eyes grew wide as his intentions dawned on her. She gulped and took a step backwards.

"I'm sure I can find someone," Scar blurted. "The Man will never know." Brad was now directly in front of her. "I'll never tell," she vowed.

Brad smiled again as he reached for her chin. He turned her face from side to side. Scar flinched as his fingers dug into her flesh. She tried to pull away, but he held her fast.

"You might do just fine," he said. Scar grabbed at his hand.

"I—you can't—I—"

Brad reached behind her head and twisted one hand into her dark hair. He yanked her head back. Scar gave a little yelp of pain.

"Let me go!"

With his free hand, Brad ripped at the front of her shirt, sending buttons flying, but her heavy undershirts blocked his way. His eyes were hazy and dark, but his look was clear. Scar drew back a fist and landed it on the side of Brad's mouth. His head jerked. In a flash, he grabbed her offending hand, bending it backwards at the wrist. Scar cried out and dropped to her knees. Brad slapped her—a sharp crack. Scar screamed and raised her hands to protect her face from another blow.

Brad unbuckled his pants. Scar glanced up at the familiar sound. She cringed and tried to scuttle away, but Brad grabbed her.

"Get to work, you ugly whore—" Brad clutched Scar's hair and pulled her face forward. Scar tried to squirm free from his grasp, but Brad tightened his grip. "And don't you dare bite me—" He gave her hair a sharp yank. "Or it'll be the last thing you do, bitch!"

Scar closed her eyes.

Brad's coffee steamed on the table behind him.

On the other side of the home, Elizabeth dreamed on.

Chapter Twenty-Eight

Shutting Down the Sunnyvale Hothouse

THE MAN stroked the Persian on his lap. Warm morning sunlight streamed in through the wide office windows. Water dripped in a steady stream from unseen eaves to the snow banks below. The cat purred and lifted its backside as The Man's hand slipped over its head and down its back. The Man was holding court again. The men were attentive. Some were eager. He was announcing a closure of the Sunnyvale hothouse and a return to the South Camps. That made some of the men very happy.

"Damn," Fuma said. "It's about time. I've got a chick back home with tits out to here and a pussy that'll swallow you whole—"

"Sure you do, ya putz," said the man with the big belly. "She's probably banging your boyfriend, right now."

Fuma made a move, but Mervyn stopped him. The other men laughed.

Another man spoke up. "Everything's dry here. It's time to par-tay!"

The Man cleared his throat. The room went silent. "We're not taking much. The leftover meat. The contents of this office. Tell the women they can take as much as they can carry. And no more. Same with the kids. Take half our fuel reserves. Anything of value..."

"What about the toboggans?" the fat man asked.

"We'll leave them. We might need this place again someday."

"What's the plan for the women? Still moving them out on the buses?" the man with the red curls asked. He and two other men—both dressed in biker jean jackets and leather vests—lounged in office chairs nearby. Mervyn spoke up:

“You might want to give those engines a check. Those mothers haven’t run in months. Bound to be problems.”

The fat man waited for The Man to respond. When he didn’t, he turned to Mervyn. “Who’s got that kind of experience?” He looked around the room. The other men muttered their lack of expertise.

Fuma spoke up. “Mervyn and I’ll do it. We know those big boys. Give us a few days.”

Mervyn held his breath. The Man could spoil their plans with a single word. Mervyn decided to up the ante.

“A-a-ah…what’s the worst that could happen? If one of them breaks down, that’s only about forty women and kids. Make ’em walk. Most of them will survive.” He sighed loudly. “Just hope only one bus breaks down.” He paused. “If they do, you’re shit out of luck— I can’t fix it on the road. No tools.”

The Man drew on his cigar, releasing the smoke into the air. “How many buses can we do with?”

“At least three,” the fat man said. “The rest of us are in trucks. Some of us can ride in on toboggans.”

“How much time to do a maintenance check?” The Man asked, turning to Mervyn.

“A couple of days. We’ll take them on a test drive, too. We’ll know damn quick if they’re ready to rock.”

“Okay,” The Man puffed again—the end of his cigar glowed. “They must be ready by next week. We’ll leave Monday…mid-morning.”

Almost a week.

Mervyn lowered his shoulders and breathed. “We can deliver,” he said brightly.

“As for the rest of you assholes…” The Man glanced across the assembly. “Some of you can leave now.” A cheer went up. “Tomorrow morning.” He motioned to a man wearing a cowboy hat. “Give me the hat.”

The men filled the hat with their names. All of them except for Fuma and Mervyn.

“How many men will we need to get us back there?” The Man asked.

The fat man counted on his fingers. “Trucks, bus drivers, guards.” He scratched his belly. “Maybe a dozen, fifteen.”

The fat man began to draw names. Fuma and Mervyn exchanged glances. The Man called an end to the lottery when the eighteenth name was drawn.

Mervyn hid a smile. Just seventeen men left behind; that included him, Fuma, and The Man.

Things were looking up.

THE SCAVENGING crew was ready. It was more than ready. Cabin fever had set in. The mission they had planned earlier had never materialized—Martha didn't want to leave Cammy alone, and Matthew didn't want to leave Martha behind—so their plans had been tabled. But the snow had stopped, the weather had warmed, and Little Ruth was thriving. It was time to go.

Martha looked out the window. The sunshine glancing off the snowdrifts made her squint. Big puddles of dirty, gray water dotted the compound. Children jumped and screeched, sending muddy sprays into the air, up their pant legs, and into their friends' faces. Martha grinned.

"Hurry up, Matthew."

"Oh, listen to you—" Matthew said from the bedroom. "Keep your shorts on. I'll be there in a minute."

"I'm going to the parking lot." Martha grabbed her blue plastic scavenging sacks and headed out the door. She stopped in mid-step. Something tugged at her. A memory. Then it came to her.

Josef. My vest. My gun. He would never let me go scavenging without my vest and gun.

She hadn't seen her Browning pistol since the day in the Meeting House when Brad took it from her. And her vest was long gone. She kept walking. Matthew would have vests for them in the trucks.

Men and women had begun to gather just outside the Gatehouse. The mood was jubilant, almost party-like. It felt good and Martha entered into the high spirits. She was in mid-laugh when she saw Meteor come out of one of the cabins. The laugh froze on her lips and her heart pinched when she saw Georgie following behind him. Hurt pressed into her.

Let it be, Martha. You have no right. Let him go.

She turned away. Jonah came up behind her.

"Marion's not coming with us," he said.

"Why?" Martha asked.

"Says she's not feeling well."

Martha nodded. "Should I check on her?"

"No. I just saw her. She's okay. I don't think she likes the idea of going to The Man's clubhouses. That's all."

Martha studied Jonah for a moment. "You— Are you seeing Marion now?"

Jonah glanced away. "Sort of."

"Oh— She's kind of old for you, isn't she?"

Jonah shrugged. He shuffled his feet and stared down at the ground. "I like her."

"Okay. Just wondering." Martha smiled—a warm gesture. She touched Jonah's arm. "Be careful, Jonah. She's damaged."

"Aren't we all?" he asked, his tone defensive.

Martha gave him a small apologetic smile. "Yeah, you're right."

MERVYN GRABBED Ruth as she stepped through the kitchen door. She stifled a small shriek. He held a finger to his lips and pulled her to the side of the building.

"It's all worked out," Mervyn said, his eyes twinkling. "And better than we expected."

"Why?"

"We've got more time. He wants us to have the buses ready to leave Monday morning." Mervyn glanced over Ruth's shoulder to ensure nobody had happened along. He pulled her deeper into the shadows. "Fuma and I are in charge of taking care of the buses. Field test them, too."

"That's wonderful."

"There's more...most of the men are leaving tomorrow. Fewer guys to deal with." He smiled. "I think we might have a chance." He gave Ruth a warm kiss. She clung to him, and then gave him a gentle push.

"Mervyn?" she asked softly. "What happens to us? If I go home...what happens to me and you?" There was a plaintive sound in her voice.

Mervyn's face grew somber. "I don't want to think about that, okay?" He held her hands in his—his thumbs caressed the soft skin below her knuckles. "I'm a big boy. I understood the risks."

Ruth withdrew a hand and ran it down the side of his face. "You have such a wonderful spirit. The woman that gets you will be very lucky." She ran a finger across his lips. "And I know she'll love you with every beat of her heart."

Mervyn kissed her again.

"What can I give you?" she asked suddenly. She blushed and looked down at her feet. "...To show you how much you mean to me?" She glanced back up at him.

Mervyn questioned her with his eyes. Then her meaning became clear. "Oh...I'd like that—very much—you know I would...but you wouldn't be able to live with yourself afterwards." He gazed into her eyes. "No, the time for that was in the hut, but we stopped then— And I'm glad we did. Besides..." He smiled warmly. "Just hearing that from you— That's enough for me." He kissed her again.

The kitchen door opened. "Ruth?" Sarah called.

Mervyn bolted away.

THE SMALLER trucks dodged around snowdrifts, while the bigger trucks rammed through them. Matthew's crew stopped to shovel only once and that was when one of the less experienced drivers panicked through a skid, and wound up backwards in a ditch.

"The highways aren't so bad," Matthew said to Martha when he got back into the cab. "But I'm dreading the city streets." The snow had begun to melt under the insistent caress of spring breezes. But without snowplows and constant snow removal, the drifts were dense and huge. "We might be in for a lot of shoveling."

Martha rolled down the window. "The air smells good."

Matthew fought his way through another drift. "You excited?"

"Not sure. I haven't scavenged in Edmonton for a very long time. We used to do it regularly when we stayed with Amanda."

"Amanda? Do I know her?"

"No. She and I were friends for about a year after the Change."

"Why didn't she come with you when you came to the compound?"

Martha shrugged. "She liked living in Edmonton. She was tough." She chuckled.

"What?" Matthew asked. He gave her a bemused look in anticipation of the thing that had made her laugh.

"One time, we were stopped by this drunk Crazy outside a church. Amanda hit him in the head with her shoulder bag. He dropped like a stone. Then she showed us the inside of her bag. She had a big brick in it. We laughed so hard, we cried."

"What happened to the biker? Weren't there other guys with him?"

"Yes."

"And...?" Matthew prompted.

"We got away." Martha leaned out the window. The memories of a biker's face covered in blood, a hole in the side of his head, his blood sprayed on her gun, her hand, and her sleeve...had all but faded. She didn't want them back.

What if I tell him? Would it be so bad? I need to tell someone. No, he might think.... But maybe I should tell. What'll he think of me then?

Martha closed her eyes and breathed deeply, expelling the unpleasant memory, bit by bit, with each rise and fall of her chest.

Another time. I'll tell him another time.

FUMA AND MERVYN leaned against the side of the Quonset hut. Fuma drew on a thin cigar, sending pungent spirals up toward blue sky. "When should we get started on those buses?"

"We don't need that much time," Mervyn said. "Tomorrow, we fire up the buses and pick the two best ones. We'll siphon fuel from the others."

"That fuel is probably going to be a problem. Might be a better idea to drain all the old fuel and fill up with fresh..."

"But the fuel in the tanks might not have been stabilized. Let's just fire them up and see how they run. We might get lucky."

Fuma smoked quietly. "You know—if those ladies don't show up—we're dead. The Man'll have it all figured out in two seconds."

"I know. Are you a praying man?"

"No."

Mervyn chuckled. "Might be a good time to start."

"How are we working this, anyway?"

"We'll get everyone used to us taking the buses for a run. After a day or two, they won't pay any attention at all. Later this week, we'll take two snowmobiles a half mile up the road... We'll hide one. Come back on the other one. Then on Sunday night, late...we'll run the two buses up the road, leave them there, and come back on the snowmobile."

Mervyn watched as several bikers wandered near them. He smiled and waved. He bent, scooped snow into his gloves, formed a snowball, and threw it. It connected with the back of one man's head.

The mock battle was on. Older children saw the action and they formed snowballs, too. In a short while, men and children were soaking wet, but they were laughing.

Ruth watched through the window. She swiped at a tear.

God, I'm going to miss him.

MATTHEW'S CREW fought their way down the snow-clogged city streets. The going was very slow, but they persevered and were soon headed in the direction of The Man's main clubhouse. Virgil was in the lead. He swung his truck around a corner, traveled a few hundred feet, and slammed on the brakes.

"What the hell—!" Matthew said.

Matthew watched as Virgil jumped from the truck. He shoved the truck into park and opened his door. Martha sat forward.

"Are you kidding me?" Matthew said, grabbing his door handle. Matthew and Martha got out of the truck and joined Virgil. They gaped at the sight ahead of them.

The clubhouse looked like something out of an end-of-the-world movie. Jagged black peaks of unburned building poked up through the snow, and scorched girders—like broken Tinker Toys—bowed to the ground as silent testimony to the explosion that had ravaged the clubhouse.

"Holy shit!" Virgil said. "He's really gone."

"Do you think he had it torched?" Matthew asked.

Virgil nodded. "Oh, yeah. He didn't want it used by the likes of you, or me—"

"Or me," Meteor said with a chuckle. The big man came up behind them.

"Think there's anything left?" Matthew asked.

Virgil shrugged. "Let's find out." He glanced at Martha. "Maybe not a good idea for all of us to be wandering around this mess. It could still be booby-trapped."

Martha cocked her head. "I can take—" Matthew interrupted her with a hand on her shoulder.

"Go back to the truck, Martha. Give us a chance to scout the place. It looks too torn up to be of any good to us anyway."

Martha returned to the truck and waited while the men poked through the ruins. She remembered the last time she was there—when she had shot The Man—and had nearly shot Meteor. She didn't know at the time he was secretly allied to Matthew.

I nearly shot you. Silly bastard.

She smiled. Because of Meteor, Matthew was alive. She welcomed the thrill of a passionate memory. They were good together again. An unexpected shot of joy suffused her. She closed her eyes and breathed. Her prayer came in a rush of feeling.

Thank you, God. Thank you. Thank you for my husband. Thank you for Meteor. Thank you for all of them. Please help us find the girls. Please.

Martha leaned out the truck's window. The men had disappeared inside a part of the building that was still standing. She pushed open the truck door and wandered into the parking lot. A voice called after her.

"Martha—we're supposed to stay in the trucks." It was Georgie. Martha gave the words a dismissive snort as she surveyed the devastation.

"Wow," she muttered. "That must have been some blast."

Debris was everywhere. Spindly metal legs of office furniture stuck up out of the snow, a couch cushion—its stuffing blown out exposing coiled springs—lay atop a small shed, jagged sheets of drywall and metal studs lay clumped like jigsaw puzzle pieces in the middle of the street. Martha spotted a large desk. It lay near the sidewalk. She walked over.

The desk would have been handsome once—thick, made of oak, like a teacher's desk from the forties. Martha inspected it. Georgie ran over to join her.

"Are we gonna get in trouble for getting out of the trucks?" Georgie asked breathlessly.

Martha gave her a sour look. "Who gives a shit..."

Georgie looked anxious, but she didn't leave. Martha continued her investigation. The desk had landed on its drawers.

"Here, help me push this."

"Oh, dear God," Georgie said, puffing with exertion. "It's so heavy."

"Just want to check the drawers." The women managed to tilt the desk backwards into the snow. "Now dig," Martha said.

They scooped wet snow until they had cleared a pathway for the drawers on one side. Martha was dripping with sweat and she drew her arm across her forehead.

"We should be able to get into them now."

She pulled on the top drawer. It was jammed. She pulled again. The drawer released, sending her backwards into a pile of snow-covered tires.

She sat up and grabbed at her chest. "Shit!"

"What's wrong?" Georgie asked.

"The scar burns like hell sometimes."

Georgie offered her hand, but Martha ignored her and crawled to the desk. The drawer hung open, its contents spilled into the snow. A clear plastic box caught Martha's eye.

"What the heck?" She showed Georgie the contents.

"Mickey Mouse toys?" Georgie asked. She took the box from Martha and touched the colorful figurines.

More things had fallen from the drawer, including an artist's sketchpad. Martha picked it up, and turned the pages.

"This looks like the drawing of a compound." She gasped. "Holy crap—it's our compound." She continued to flip pages. She stopped. "But this one isn't." She studied the cursive writing running up the side of the map. "I think this says *southern Alberta*—" She continued reading. "Hothouses?"

"What does that mean?" Georgie asked.

"Grow ops? Greenhouses?" Martha guessed. "I don't know." She flipped another page. "Oh, my God."

"What?"

"Women! They're places for keeping women. Old folks' homes! Just like the girls stayed in...here in Edmonton. Look."

The two women perused the highly stylized map of Alberta with roadways, cities, towns, and buildings—drawings similar to the line art in a child's coloring book. Long, narrow rectangular blocks dotted the map—arrows connected them to a list of words down the right side of the page. They read through a long list of seniors' homes: *Bow River Senior Care, Good Shepherd Care Centre, Beth Lane Nursing Home, Good Hope Retirement Village...* One name had a big red circle around it.

Sunnyvale Care Center.

"Son-of-a-bitch!" Martha checked the map again. "They're in Medicine Hat!"

RUTH'S BEDROOM was crowded with a dozen women; Sarah was among them. She had sworn them to secrecy. Now she told them Mervyn's plan. Not all of them were impressed; some were thoroughly unimpressed.

"That's insane," one of the younger mothers said. Her hair was clipped short—almost a brush cut, but not quite. She ran her hand through the bristles in a nervous gesture. "We'll never get away with it. The Man's not gonna let us just walk out of here." Her reluctance was echoed by several other women.

"Mervyn's bringing in liquor," Ruth explained. "He's going to get the bikers drunk."

"Even then...what about the kids?" the woman countered. "How are we supposed to get them to walk down a road in the middle of the night? There's still so much snow." Sarah spoke up:

"Would you rather see your children taken away from you when we get to the South Camps? He's planning to split us up, you know." Sarah's expression was a determined one—she would make her point. "We don't have a choice. We do this now—or we will never have another chance to escape." Sarah glanced back at Ruth. Ruth picked up the dialogue:

"It will take complete cooperation from you. Do not tell your kids. Tell them the night before that we're going to do something special. That it's a surprise. Make them understand they must be quiet." Ruth sucked in a quick breath. "Dress them in their outdoor clothes. Keep boots, mitts, and hats ready and by the door. You'll have less than a minute to get them up, dressed, and out the front door. Mothers, pack what you need—diapers, changes of clothing..."

"What about food?" the young mother asked.

"Two or three of you will help us bake bread and cook meat. A couple of you can bake cookies. Sarah and I will package the lunches just before we leave."

"One more thing..." Sarah added. "Fuma is helping us. Don't get friendly with him...or you'll raise suspicions."

MATTHEW DIDN'T smile when Martha ran up to greet him. She shook the sketchbook in his face.

"Look what we found. Look what we found!" Martha repeated. Matthew glowered at her.

"I thought I asked you to stay in the truck."

Martha waved his observation aside. "But we know where they are." She was almost screeching with excitement. "Look!" She opened the book. Virgil peered over Matthew's shoulder.

"I've never seen this before," Virgil said. "But that's The Man's handwriting. Don't know who drew the map."

Martha couldn't contain herself any longer, and the men were taking far too long to comprehend the treasure in her hands. "It tells us where they are." She pointed to the circled name.

"How do you know? There're lots of homes here," Matthew said.

"Read!"

- *66 rooms*
- *Kitchen and dining room*
- *Quonset hut*
- *Near river*
- *Heaters*
- *Supplies*
- *Dry foods*
- *Ammunition*
- *Fuel*
- *Winter clothes — women/kids*
- *Boots*
- *Snowmobiles*
- *Guards transfer from South Camps*
- *Honey farm*

The notes were scrawled near the Sunnyvale listing, in a hurried pen—like a grocery list—or like someone planning a camping trip, or scouting out a new home.

"Martha..." Matthew said, shaking his head. "The Man has lots of women...with kids, I suspect. That's a long way to go on speculation."

"But it's *Sunnyvale*!" Martha emphasized.

"It's his handwriting, Matthew," Virgil confirmed. "Where did you find this?" Georgie pointed to the toppled desk. "That's his desk." He looked back at the sketchbook. "I'm guessing it was his back-up plan. Makes sense. He scouted senior homes all over the place. He thought they made the perfect prisons, especially the ones that were kind of isolated. This place would be perfect. Far from rescuers." Virgil paused. "I think she's right."

Martha waited, her eyes bright with anticipation. "The roads aren't so bad anymore. The big trucks can make it, Matthew," she encouraged.

"Martha..." he said gently, "How do we get that many people back here?"

Martha sputtered. "I don't know. But there's bound to be some vehicles down there we can use."

Matthew sighed. "*We*? Martha—if we do this, those of us who go, might never return. It's a huge risk."

"We've got to try!"

Virgil put his hand on Martha's shoulder. She backed off, pulling her shoulder out from beneath his hand. Virgil gave her a small grin of understanding.

"I'll go," he said. "I owe you..."

"I don't trust you," Martha spat. "You'll just switch back to The Man."

"No— That's not gonna happen," Virgil assured her. "He'd shoot me on sight." Meteor spoke up:

"I'll go, too. And...I know the husbands and fathers of those missing women and kids will be onboard in a red second."

"But I—"

"Your part in this is over, Martha," Meteor said with a warm smile. "We'll handle this. Okay?" Martha took a quick breath. "Really, sweetheart. You've done enough." Meteor put his arm around Martha's shoulders and squeezed.

Georgie looked unhappy, but she said nothing.

Matthew took Martha's arm and led her back to the truck. The rest of the men and women returned to their vehicles.

"Matthew?" Virgil called out. "What about the second clubhouse? It's not that far from here."

Matthew hesitated. "How far?"

"Thirty blocks."

"We don't have time!" Martha's hands were tight fists at her sides. "We know where they are— Let's get them!"

"It's the roads, Martha," Matthew said. "It'll be slow going. I suspect we're looking at a two or three-day trip if we allow for accidents and unforeseen events. But the weather's been mild. Give it one more day to melt. And let's hope this Chinook has hit southern Alberta, too." He was referring to the warm wind that would blow across the province in the winter and early spring months. "Besides, this needs planning. The trucks must be loaded with fuel, guns, ammo, food, camping supplies. And we're short on supplies. This is an opportunity to get some. Let's do that." He motioned to the men, and circled a finger in the air.

"But Matthew—"

"C'mon, Martha..." Matthew said firmly. He opened the truck's door and pointed. "Let's go."

~ ~ ~

A Scarred Alliance

ELIZABETH AWOKE and scanned the room. The light coming through the window was bright. She guessed it was morning. Her mouth was dry and her tongue felt thick. She was desperately thirsty. She glanced around and spied a pitcher on the small table. She eased herself out of the bed, unwrapping herself from a pile of blankets and a thick sleeping bag. She caught a whiff of herself and wrinkled her nose. She went to the table and picked up the pitcher—it was empty. She looked around for something else to drink. There was nothing.

She went to the door and tried the doorknob. Her eyes widened in surprise when it turned easily. Brad had taken to locking her into his room, letting her out for meals, and having her accompany him when it suited him. She wondered what had happened to him since he had not come back the night before. She entertained a tiny shot of joy at having spent the night alone, free of his attentions, but she worried about what might have changed overnight. He might have been annoyed enough to replace her with someone else. Then what? She shook away the thought and pulled the door open.

She stepped into the hallway. It was quiet. A wave of dizziness swept over her, and she leaned against the closed door. She was still sick, but not as bad as the day before. She wondered what would happen if Brad caught her out of the room, but her thirst was greater than her sense of danger. She shuffled down the hall toward the dining room.

"Where's Brad?"

Elizabeth gave a little gasp. She turned and saw a woman standing in the doorway of a room off to her right. She recognized Scar.

"I have no idea where he is. He didn't come back to the room last night."

"I know. He slept here."

"With you?"

Scar ignored the question. She stepped forward. "What's the matter with you?" Scar asked. "He said you were sick."

"Flu, I think. Cook in Sunnyvale had it, too. I'm feeling better now."

"Really handy that," Scar said, her voice tinny with sarcasm.

"What?" Elizabeth asked, confused.

"You get sick. And the rest of us get to do your dirty work..."

"What?" Elizabeth tried to swallow, but her mouth was too dry. "I have to get something to drink," she added.

"Kitchen," Scar said. "C'mon."

The pair walked into the wide main hallway connecting all parts of the home. The light was brighter here. Elizabeth looked at Scar.

"What did you mean?"

Scar faced Elizabeth. The purple bruise on the opposite side of her scarred face made Elizabeth do a double take.

"What happened to you?"

"Brad," Scar said.

"I'm sorry."

"Yeah, sure ya are. The sympathy is pouring out of you."

"No, I mean it."

"Forget it."

"What happened?"

"What do ya think? Can't you see? He hit me."

"I know," Elizabeth said softly. "But why? Aren't you...sort of...special? Protected?"

Scar sneered. "Yeah, that's me—'protected,'" she said as they entered the dining room.

Several of the tables were filled with women. About a dozen children ran from one side of the room to the other, giggling and screaming. Pain knifed through Elizabeth's head. She covered her ears.

"God— Make it stop."

Scar laughed. "You got kids?"

"No...and I don't want any." The sight of Duke's little face made her heart ache, but she pushed the memory aside.

They went into the kitchen. Scar poured water from a large bottle into a mug. Elizabeth clutched the mug and drank without stopping. Water trickled from the corners of her mouth and down her neck.

"You smell," Scar said.

"I know. I don't have any more clean clothes."

"We've got clothes. Lots of clothes."

"Can I have more water?"

"Sure. Food? You hungry?"

"Not right now," Elizabeth said. She emptied the mug again. "That's better. Thanks." She touched her face. "I think my fever is coming back." She handed the cup to Scar.

"I don't want it. Keep it. C'mon, I'll take you to the clothing room."

Scar led Elizabeth into a workout room. Gym equipment now served as clothing racks. Small tables were piled with blue jeans, t-shirts, bras, panties, and sweaters. Baskets overflowing with socks, mitts, and scarves lined a far wall. "Take what you want," she said. "Clothing isn't hard to get. Shoes...boots—that's a little tougher. But check over there."

"I don't need boots. Just clothes."

A middle-aged woman with three pre-school children came into the room. She held a baby in her arms. The baby was writhing and whining. She walked over to Scar and offered her the baby.

"I got stuck caring for this brat. I already have three," the woman said with a nod at the other children. "I don't need another."

Scar shrugged. "Don't look at me. Take it to the nursery."

"The nursery's full. The women won't take another one."

Scar shrugged again. "Get one of the other mothers to take it."

"No one wants it." The baby began to cry.

Elizabeth held her fingers to her temples. "Where's its mother?" she asked as blades of pain stabbed into her head.

"Gone. With the last shipment," Scar responded.

"Why? Wouldn't it make more sense to keep a baby with its mother?" The thought caused Elizabeth to worry about the women back in Sunnyvale. Were they going to be split from their kids, too?

"She was more valuable to The Man in trade," Scar said. "She bought him a tanker of diesel fuel." The baby began to screech.

"Shut it up," Scar said.

"You shut it up," the woman retorted. She set the baby on the floor and left the room; like ducklings, the older children toddled behind.

Scar bent down. She picked up the screaming baby. The child quieted for a moment as it regarded her. "Don't even know your name, kid. But I think you're a boy." The baby began to cry again. Scar rocked him and the baby calmed down. He twisted around and placed a chubby hand on Scar's face. He suddenly gave her a sloppy wet kiss on her lips.

"Yuck," Scar said, wiping the slobber from her mouth. But she was smiling. The baby leaned against her chest. Scar buried her nose in his hair. "I love the smell of a baby's hair." The baby gurgled. "I couldn't keep my baby."

"Your baby?" Elizabeth asked, surprised by the revelation. "Why not?"

"He wouldn't let me."

"Who wouldn't let you?"

"Hurry up... Pick some clothes. I've gotta get this kid fed."

Elizabeth made quick selections and followed Scar out of the room. "Are you going to name him?"

"Nah. 'Kid' will do."

"What's your real name?"

Scar didn't answer. She went into the kitchen, and with the baby perched on one hip, she put together a bowl of oatmeal, sweetened with corn syrup. Kid tried to put his fingers into the bowl, but Scar pushed his hands away. She sat down, plopped Kid onto the table in front of her, and began spooning the oatmeal into his mouth. The baby ate ravenously. Scar fed him until the bowl was empty. She turned back to Elizabeth.

"My name is Luella, but most people just call me Scar." She touched the side of her face.

"How did that happen?"

Scar ignored the question. She wiped the baby's mouth with a rag.

"What happened to your baby?" Elizabeth asked.

Scar lifted Kid onto her lap and handed him a spoon. He began to pound the table. Elizabeth grimaced. Scar smiled and tried to wrestle the spoon out of the baby's hand. He wouldn't give it up. She put the little boy on the floor. Kid shoved the spoon into his mouth, drooling as he stared up at them. Scar sat back in her chair. She took a deep breath.

"I was married to Heze— The Man," she corrected herself. "For a few years. After his first wife was killed—murdered. They didn't know who did it. His little boy was killed, too. We met at church. I liked him...I was lonely. So... I married him." Scar picked at a ragged cuticle, found a hangnail, bit at it, spat, and then continued her story:

"He didn't want any more kids, but I did. I quit taking the pill and got pregnant. Really fast. He was pissed, but he doesn't believe in abortion...so, I stayed pregnant. The day the baby came, he was there. We were in our house. He didn't let me go to the hospital. A midwife was there, too. As soon as the baby was born, he grabbed it...and took it away. I don't even know if it was a boy or a girl. He told the midwife he would tell me as a surprise." Scar gave a small snort. "He surprised me alright. I never saw my baby again." She touched her face. "I cried and everything, but he wouldn't listen. I finally fell asleep. I woke up. I smelled gas...my hair was on fire. It burned down my throat and arm, too. See." She pulled back her shirt to show her collar and the top of her left arm.

Elizabeth drew back in disgust. "That's terrible. What an awful thing. I'm so sorry..." Elizabeth reached out and placed a comforting hand on Scar's arm, but the woman jerked away.

"Ah, it's nothing now. Just history."

"You must hate him."

Scar shrugged. "I asked for it, I guess."

Elizabeth was aghast. "No one asks for what he did to you."

Scar pulled up the shirtsleeve on her other arm and revealed an ugly red oval, the same kind of scar Elizabeth had seen on Meteor's arm.

"This one hurt, too. And it doesn't mean nothing either." She dropped her sleeve. "History— All history."

Elizabeth looked perplexed. "Do you still love him? The Man?"

"We're divorced now. But, yeah— I guess I do." Scar grimaced. "Why else would I stay with him? Put up with the shit that goes on here..."

"Shit like Brad?" Elizabeth suggested.

"Yeah, shit like Brad." Scar turned to Elizabeth and studied her face. "I'm surprised you aren't bruised up. How come? Brad likes things rough."

Elizabeth shrugged.

Scar cocked her head to one side. "Are you two...is he fucking you?"

Elizabeth sat back in her chair. She blushed.

"That's what he meant!" Scar blurted. Scar's eyes blazed and her scar flushed scarlet. "You bitch...you won't put out...so he comes after me."

"You?" Elizabeth asked incredulously. She stood up.

"He went after me, you stupid bitch!" She touched her bruised cheek. "You think I want that pig touching me?" she sputtered. "You think I want him..." She grabbed a quick breath. "Because he can't get it from you?" Scar rose and pushed her face into Elizabeth's face. "You're his bitch...you better start putting out—"

"Whoa...wait! I didn't make him come after you. I'm sorry. I'm really sorry. But I don't want him touching me either." Elizabeth paled as the words left her lips. A sudden silence fell between them.

"I thought you were his old lady..." Scar drawled.

"I m-m-mean..." Elizabeth stammered. "I just meant—"

"I heard you," Scar said. "I know what you meant..." Scar grinned. It was not friendly.

Elizabeth covered her face with her hands. "Oh, crap—forget what I said. I'm not feeling well. I don't know what I'm saying."

"Sure you do. You know exactly what you're saying." Scar leaned over and swiped at the drool on the baby's chin. She picked up the little boy and turned back to Elizabeth. Elizabeth stood quietly and waited for the ball to drop.

"So, if you don't like Brad, and you aren't his old lady, what are you really doing here?"

Elizabeth looked down at her hands and then up again. "I—I like Brad—I just don't want to sleep with him."

"You're lying. Don't lie to me." Scar grinned again. "I wonder what Brad will say when I tell him what you said."

Elizabeth's head snapped up, her eyes bright with anger. "I'm not afraid of you," she hissed. The force of her words made Scar step back. "And don't you ever threaten me again."

Scar stood motionless, mouth slightly ajar.

"Tell Brad anything you want," Elizabeth continued. "And I'll tell him you're a liar. I wonder which one of us he'll believe."

Elizabeth moved toward the door, but Scar blocked her way. "Get back to your room!"

"I'm hungry. I'll go back to my room when I'm damned good and ready to go back," Elizabeth said. Her hands went to her hips. She was slightly taller than the older woman, and she glared down into Scar's face. "Get out of my way." Elizabeth gave Scar a firm push as she brushed by her.

"You are in for such trouble," Scar threatened. Elizabeth stopped and swung around to face her.

"Really? You think so? Brad kind of likes me. Does he like you? I know what he does to people he doesn't like." She paused for effect. "He kills them."

Scar jerked. "He won't kill me."

"Oh, no? Don't count on it. He killed Cindy. He killed my father."

"Your father?"

"Yeah— You weren't privy to that little detail?"

Scar stood quietly. "I'm sorry."

"Sure you are. Get out of my way." Scar reached for Elizabeth's arm. "Don't touch me!" Elizabeth said.

"I'm sorry...I'm sorry." Scar said quickly. Her tone had softened.

Elizabeth turned back. She studied Scar's eyes. Then she gave a small nod. "I'm hungry."

The baby whined and Scar repositioned him on her hip. "You'll find fresh bread in the side cupboard, butter in the cooler, and honey in the cupboard beside the sink."

Elizabeth gave Scar a puzzled look. The bristling firecracker had fizzled out. "That's it? You're not going to tell Brad?"

Scar shook her head. "I'm tired of all this. I haven't had a female friend in nearly three years. Maybe it's time." Elizabeth eyed her with suspicion. Scar looked back at her with earnest eyes. "Really. I mean it."

"We didn't get a chance to know you when we got to Sunnyvale, since you left almost as soon as we got there."

"I was just there to set things up—get you guys settled in. The Man wanted me back here." Scar rested her chin on the baby's head. "I'm tired," she said again.

Elizabeth sat down. "You really mean it? You want to be friends?

"Yeah— I do." Scar stroked Kid's face as he snuggled against her. "Truce?" She grinned. This time it was a friendly expression. "I'll keep Brad off you, if you keep him off me."

Elizabeth laughed. "How do you propose we do that?"

It was Scar's turn to laugh. "Kill him."

Elizabeth rolled her eyes. "Yeah, right...I gotta eat something first." She got up. "Can't plan murder on an empty stomach."

Scar smiled—a soft action that brightened her blue eyes. In that moment, Elizabeth saw past the damaged face, saw the girl behind the scar— Pretty. Innocent. Vulnerable.

Elizabeth felt a tug in her heart.

She smiled back.

Chapter Twenty-Nine

The Escape

WOMEN WHISPERED in their rooms and, every so often, darted across the hall to each other's rooms, slipping through the dark like wispy wraiths. They were told to stay awake, awaiting Ruth's alert. She had also told them there would be a party that night. She advised precautions. Even with The Man's warnings against touching the women, intoxicated men were easily tempted. The women hustled their children into beds, closed their doors, and waited. Now they listened to the sounds of boisterous men reveling in an orgy of alcohol. Mervyn and Fuma had made sure there was plenty to drink.

Earlier that day, Mervyn traded two snowmobiles and fuel with friends at the farmhouse for a case of Smirnoff vodka and a case of Captain Morgan's dark rum—welcome rarities among the men. Hard liquor had become scarce. Ruth and Sarah camouflaged their bagged lunch preparations by making food for the partying bikers. Now, Ruth stood near the dining room door with a plate of sandwiches. Mervyn held up his hand to stop her. A bald man with thick forearms and a huge gut was weaving his way across the room, a bottle held high in his hand. He slung one beefy arm around Mervyn's neck.

"Damn, Merv—youse iss really a good guy. Good-sidea," the biker slurred. He tipped back a bottle of vodka, took a long drink, exhaled loudly, and wiped his mouth with the back of his hand. "Here-sa go—have-sa drink."

"No, you enjoy it," Mervyn said with a wide grin. "I'm on the wagon. I'm driving a busload of women and kids tomorrow. Don't want our valuable cargo to land ass-end-up in a ditch." He pounded the man on the back. "I'll make up the difference when we get back to the South Camps."

"Thass good...youse shure a good guy..."

The heavy biker fell back against a couch—he bounced off like a water-filled balloon and landed on the floor. He lay there with his arms outstretched. The bottle rolled away from his fingers, spilling its contents. Another man saw the travesty and rescued the bottle, tipping it to his lips, and draining the last of the vodka. Mervyn walked over to Ruth.

"The Man isn't here. He isn't drinking," Ruth whispered.

"He never drinks with the rest of us," Mervyn replied.

"I'd still like to try to drug him."

"How?"

"I don't know," Ruth said. She watched the drunken men reeling around the front room. Somebody had set up a sound system and old rock and roll blared from the speakers. Some of the men linked arms and jigged around the room, tripping and falling, and laughing raucously.

"It's a good thing the kids aren't trying to sleep. They are so loud."

Two more men caught sight of Ruth and made a beeline across the room toward her. Lust shone in their eyes. Mervyn took the plate of sandwiches and shooed Ruth back into the safety of the kitchen.

Mervyn and Fuma watched the men go down, one by one. Soon they were all snoring. The reek of exhaled alcohol hung in the air like the sweet smell of death. Empty bottles, cups, and glasses littered the room. Empty sacks of potato chips lay strewn about. Somebody had dug into a private reserve and shared his crunchy treasure. Sarah and Ruth surveyed the scene from the dining room. Mervyn gave them the go-ahead and they navigated over and between the bodies blocking their path. The women were nearly past the front room when a familiar voice stopped them in their tracks. The hairs on the backs of their necks rose.

"Where are you two going?" The Man asked.

Ruth turned. She gave her most obliging and desperate look. "Cleaning up the mess— Before the kids get up." She motioned to the debris. "They could get hurt."

The Man came closer. He eyed the two women without saying a word. Ruth dropped her eyes to the floor. Sarah grabbed a waste bucket and began retrieving garbage.

"Well, go ahead then. Don't let me stop you," he said finally. He looked up at Mervyn and Fuma. "And what about you two? How come you guys aren't out cold?"

"We didn't think you'd appreciate a couple of drunks driving your ladies around," Fuma said with a yawn.

"Just heading off to bed," Mervyn added.

The Man grunted. "Good plan." He checked his watch. He turned back to Ruth. "I desire hot chocolate. Make me some."

Ruth blanched. "I—I—uh—have to make it from scratch. I think I still have some cocoa powder. Let me check."

"I'll go with you," The Man said. Ruth shot Mervyn a nervous glance. He dipped his head—an almost imperceptible motion.

"Now," The Man said, grabbing Ruth by the arm and pushing her toward the dining room.

Ruth scurried into the kitchen. The Man followed her. She turned on a propane burner, took milk from the cold storage, and selected a tin of Fry's cocoa from a shelf above the work counter.

"There's not much sugar left," she called over her shoulder. "I can use icing sugar. That should work." She heaped dry ingredients into the cold milk and whisked them together. "I have an idea," she said, turning to The Man. She smiled—a small conspiratorial gesture accompanied by a tiny wink. "A little real chocolate would be perfect— I'll be right back."

Ruth ran down the hall to her bedroom. She opened the door and tiptoed in. Samuel and Mary were sound asleep in their snow clothes; their boots, hats, and gloves lay neatly on her bed. She pulled a big box from the closet's top shelf. Under the hangers and old ties, she found what she was looking for. She shoved a bottle into her pocket. She ran back to the kitchen.

"I'll have it ready in about five minutes," Ruth called. The Man had seated himself at a table in the dining room. His Persian cat was curled in his lap. "If you want..." she offered. "I'll bring it to your room."

Ruth peered through the door. The Man glanced at his watch. He yawned. "Good idea. I'll leave the door open."

Ruth leaned against the counter, relieved. She took a long breath and willed her heart to slow down. She reached into her pocket and removed the bottle.

MATTHEW PULLED Martha close to him. They had shed their clothing, enough to be intimate, but not too much since the room was cold. He traced the curve of her breasts in the light of the camp lantern.

"You have beautiful breasts," he said.

Martha laughed self-consciously. "Maybe once. They're saggy now."

"They're perfect," Matthew said, lowering his mouth to a nipple.

"Matthew," Martha said pushing at his head. "Stop. Once in a night is enough for old folks like us."

Matthew looked up and grinned. "Wanna go again?"

Martha laughed. "C'mon," she said, giggling. "Enough. You have to get up early. I want you well rested when you go after the girls."

Matthew rose up on one elbow. "I'll be fine." His fingers trailed up her leg, to the softness between her thighs.

"Matthew, stop," Martha said, but her protestations had weakened.

"Just once more," he said. "You know...for the road..."

Martha burst out laughing. She slid down the bed so she could kiss him. "Okay, for the road..."

RUTH AND SARAH worked quietly. By the soft glow of camp lanterns, they packaged sliced meat into sandwich bags. Thick bread slices smeared with butter went face-to-face into another baggie, and oatmeal cookies into another. Large rubber tubs sat open against the wall, waiting to be filled with the lunches. Mervyn was going to load the tubs onto the buses. Ruth expected him and Fuma very soon.

"Hurry, Sarah," Ruth whispered.

"I'm going as fast as I can." Sarah held up her hand. "I nearly hacked off one of my fingers."

"You okay?"

"Yeah. I'll live. Someone might find their meat extra tasty though," Sarah said with a rueful laugh. The women heard a noise. They ceased their chatter.

The back door opened slowly, with only a tiny creak. Mervyn walked in. "Are they ready?"

Ruth pointed to the wall. "We'll have to get water along the way," she said. "Melt snow. I've packed a few gallon jugs, but that's all I've got."

"It'll be fine. Have you figured out how to get everyone to us?"

"The men are still passed out, right?" Ruth asked.

"Out like lights."

"And The Man?"

"Don't know. I haven't seen him since we talked to him."

Ruth grinned. "Well, I suspect that he's having a good snooze. I slipped a little something into his hot chocolate." She held up an empty pill bottle.

Mervyn laughed—a quick muted sound. "Good for you, girl. Do you think you gave him enough?" Ruth shrugged.

"There were only four capsules left in the bottle."

"We'll have to chance it." Mervyn checked his watch. "The buses are up the road, about a half mile, okay?" He took her face in his hands. "It's not too cold, but it's dark. Be careful. I'll be watching for you." He kissed her. She kissed him back.

Sarah raised her eyebrows.

Fuma came to the door. "I'm ready. Got those containers?"

Sarah tucked the last of the cookie bags into the tubs and closed the lids. "They're all yours."

Mervyn checked his watch again. "Okay, we'll give you two hours. If you don't show up, we'll come back."

He and Fuma grabbed the heavy tubs and lugged them out the door. Sarah turned to Ruth as the snowmobiles whined and buzzed into the distance.

"How long?" Sarah asked.

"What?"

"How long has that been going on?"

Ruth blushed. "Not long. We've been friends for almost the whole time we've been here. He's been so good to me— To us."

"What about Peter?"

Ruth checked her watch. "We'd better go."

Sarah touched her arm. "It's okay— I understand." Suddenly, something occurred to her. "Wait a minute— He took Hannah and Reggie away, didn't he?"

Ruth smiled.

Ruth and Sarah crept down the dark hallway. The rest of the women had been told to have the children ready to leave—dressed in their warm clothing, so that the little ones didn't have to be awakened. They opened doors—one after the other. The head count began as women and children slipped down the hallway, boots in hand. They tiptoed around the sleeping men and scurried out the door into the night. No one spoke. By the grace of God, not one baby cried. The next door held the twin boys and the woman who had been saddled with caring for them. Ruth held her breath.

Please God. Please. Seal their mouths like you sealed the mouths of the lions in Daniel's cave.

For a fleeting moment, Ruth wished she had drugged the little devils. She quickly rejected the thought and chided herself for thinking it.

She looked down the hallway. Fear made her stomach tremble. They were so close to The Man's room.

Had she managed to do it? Was he drugged?

Sarah continued opening doors, counting as the rooms emptied. Ruth ushered women and children toward the front room, holding a finger to her mouth to quiet them as they fled. She reached to open another door when a small sound made her freeze.

She leaned against the door, holding her breath, and stared down the dark hallway—toward The Man's room. She watched as a shadow emerged from the room. A small shadow.

What the—?

The figure moved soundlessly down the hallway toward her. Its head was down, studying something. Ruth stepped out. "Samuel," she hissed. "What are you doing?"

"I wanted my Nintendo. The Man said it was mine. I wanted it."

Ruth looked wildly behind him, expecting The Man to walk out of the bedroom, too. He did not. "How did you get in there?"

Samuel held up a room key. "It's mine. He gave it to me," he whispered defensively.

Ruth gathered him to her in a possessive hug and whispered in his ear. "It's okay. I have to get Mary up. Where are your boots?"

"In the room."

"C'mon," Ruth said, dragging him to their bedroom door.

Mary left the room, groggy, but obedient. She was a veteran at remaining silent during midnight walks. She clutched a sock doll and let Samuel take her hand. Sarah ran down the hallway to meet them.

"I've got them all, except for—" Sarah motioned to the room with the toddler boys.

"Take Samuel and Mary. I'll get the boys." Ruth grabbed Samuel by his jacket. "Give me your key." Samuel gave her a suspicious look. "Give me the key," she repeated. "You can have it back after. I promise."

Samuel began to object, saw the look in his mother's eyes, reached into his pocket, and obediently handed her the key. Ruth twisted the key in her fingers as she watched her children follow Sarah.

Ruth slipped the key into her pocket, walked a few feet, turned a door handle, and crept into the twin's room.

No sound from the boys.

A woman sat on the edge of the bed. She looked up and smiled. Her young face was haggard with fear, chiseled by the dark shadows cast by a small camp lantern. She motioned behind her. The two sleeping toddlers were bundled and ready for transit. Ruth took one—he whimpered and snuggled into her shoulder. The woman took the other. They made their way down the hallway to the front room. Sarah was waiting by the front door. Samuel and Mary stood next to her. Sarah was checking a handwritten list of names.

"That's it...that's everyone," Sarah whispered. "Let's go." A moan and mumbling made them freeze.

"Mommy—?"

Ruth put her hand over Mary's mouth. "Sh..." Ruth hissed.

They waited. The room went silent. Ruth released Mary.

"Get them out of here." She pushed Samuel to follow Sarah. "Oh, my God...little Duke," Ruth said with alarm.

"I already got him," Sarah whispered. "Don't worry."

Ruth sighed with relief. "Go," she said to Sarah. "Don't wait for me. I'll catch up. There's one more thing I have to do."

Sarah's eyes blazed and her tone was severe. "What are you talking about? Come with us. Now!"

"No. Listen to me," Ruth said in a hurried whisper. "Don't worry about me. Get my children to safety." She reached up and took Sarah's face in her hands. "I mean it. Don't wait for me. If I'm not right behind you, then leave."

Sarah eyed her friend.

"Drive away! I mean it."

"We can't leave without you," Sarah hissed back.

"Yes, you can. I'll take a snowmobile. Mervyn left one for me to use," Ruth lied. One of the men mumbled and groaned. Ruth pointed at the door and mouthed, *GO*!

Sarah ran.

Ruth watched the children disappear from sight. The sound of another man groaning nearby made her heart leap. She raced down the hallway. She reached into her jeans and clutched the key in trembling fingers.

Please, God. Please. Let him be asleep.

THE BUSES' engines were fired up. Thick exhaust fumes pumped into the night. Fuma and Mervyn paced nervously. They looked up the road, but couldn't see much in the distance. Mervyn checked his watch. Then checked it again.

"They'll be here soon. God...let them be here soon," he prayed.

"I'm doing a little of that praying stuff myself," Fuma confided. "Half a mile— How long does it take a little kid to walk half a mile?"

"I don't know. Fifteen minutes," Mervyn said hopefully.

The two men shuffled from foot to foot.

RUTH FUMBLED with the key, but finally unlocked the door. She pushed her way into the dark bedroom and tiptoed across the room. A slice of moonlight slipped between the venetian blinds. She could hear The Man's steady breathing. Deep, low, not quite a snore. She could see the hazy shape of a body under the bedcovers.

Ruth ran to the right side of the room. She had seen the array of guns when she delivered the cocoa earlier. She felt around, but it was too dark. She reached into her pocket and pulled out a tiny flashlight. She cupped the lens and switched it on. A sound from the bed made her heart stop, and she closed her hand over the beam. Her flesh glowed red.

Just breathing...he's just breathing.

Ruth released the beam and swept it over the assembled weaponry. She knew what she was after. She found it—a Micro-Uzi with a folded shoulder stock. She checked the Uzi's magazine; it was full. She looked around. Boxes of ammunition sat in neat piles under the window. Next to them, she found extra magazines—*the right size*, she thought with relief. Some had been doubled up to each other with thick elastic bands—she grabbed two pair. A web belt with clips caught her eye. She grabbed it, too.

She swept the light over a bedside table. She caught the cocoa mug in the beam; the mug was still three-quarters full. The sight troubled her. The Man moved in the bed. She doused the light.

Ruth tiptoed to the door, opened it, and slipped into the hallway. She peered ahead. There was no movement.

Her own winter gear was still in her room. She ran in, dressed herself, and then hooked the sling belt to the gun. The gun was familiar to her; Matthew had trained all the women to use machine guns. Now she was glad of it. She reacquainted herself with the grip safety. She pulled back the cocking bolt and loaded the gun. She threw the belt over her head. Noises coming from the hallway drew her attention.

Somebody was awake.

She packed the extra gun magazines into a canvas bag and slung it over her shoulder. She pressed her ear to the door. More voices.

Dear God.

SARAH SCOOPED Mary into her arms. She shooed Samuel along ahead of her. Many of the women and children were already out of sight. She turned and looked back. There was no sign of Ruth. She ran on, with Samuel scurrying ahead of her.

"Where's Mommy?" Mary asked.

Sarah desperately wanted to shush her, but she remembered what the child had been through, what she had seen over the past months.

"Mommy is coming later," she said gently. Sarah's tone made Mary cry. The little girl's heartbreak brought tears to Sarah's eyes, too. "It's really okay, sweetheart. Don't cry."

Sarah hugged Mary tighter as she ran.

RUTH WRACKED her brain for ways to get out of her room without being seen, but she could come up with only one solution.

Break a window.

She grabbed a pillow from the bed, covered her window, and rammed the butt of the Uzi into it. The glass cracked, but didn't break. The voices were getting louder, and there were more of them. She rammed the window again. This time the glass burst free. Cold air swept into the room. She used the gun to tap out jagged pieces. She covered the sill in a heavy sleeping bag, and crawled through the window. She dropped into waist-deep snow.

Ruth began to slog her way through the drift. She knew the women and children were only a few minutes away. She could catch up to them if she ran. She struggled through the deep, compacted snow. The exertion and the weight of the gun made her gasp for breath. She was sucking in huge lungfuls of air by the time she reached the front of the home. She turned and ran up the driveway, keeping to the shadows on the right side of the road. Noises from behind her caused her to stop and turn.

Horror made the hairs on her arm stand on end.

The Man's bikers were tumbling through the front doors.

MERVYN CHECKED his watch again. There was still no sign of the women and children.

"I can't stand this," he said.

"Do you want to drive up the road a ways, and see if we can find them?" Fuma asked.

Mervyn paced forward and then backward. He looked up the road again. *Still no sign.* "How long has it been?"

"Only a few minutes since the last time you asked me. They'll get here," Fuma said.

Mervyn glanced at his watch again.

"How did you get that name?" Fuma asked, in an attempt to distract Mervyn.

"What?"

"Your name—it's weird. Where did it come from?"

Mervyn rolled his eyes. "My mother was Welsh," he said irritably. "I was named after a 9th century king."

"A king...that's cool. Want to know my real name?" Fuma asked.

Mervyn ignored the question, looking at his watch once more. "Oh, hell...let's drive up the road—"

"Wait— I think I see someone."

The two men ran forward. A woman appeared with two children in tow, then another, and finally a tiny crowd emerged from the gloom.

"Oh, thank God." Mervyn clapped Fuma on the back. "They made it."

They loaded the buses. Sarah boarded Mervyn's bus with her checklist. "That's everybody on my list," she said. Fuma grunted his acknowledgement and started down the steps, heading for his own bus.

"Hold it," Mervyn said. "Ruth's kids are here. Where's she?"

"Sh-sh-she said she'd be right behind us," Sarah said.

Mervyn ran to the back of the bus and looked out the window. "I don't see her. What happened? Why isn't she with you?"

"She said she had something to do. She said not to wait for her. That you left a snowmobile for her and that she'd catch up to us."

"A snowmobile? I never—" He looked at Fuma. Fuma shrugged. "Oh no..." Mervyn said. "I'm not leaving her behind."

"I thought you'd say that," Sarah said with a quick smile.

Mervyn stood at the front of the bus. "Ladies, anyone know how to drive a bus?" None of the women responded. Sarah threw herself into the driver's seat. She gripped the steering wheel. "Teach me. I'm a fast learner."

"I'll check the other bus," Fuma said. A minute later, he returned with a middle-aged woman. "She says she can drive."

Mervyn and Fuma held a hurried conversation. Sarah sat near the pair, listening.

"Go as far and as fast as you can. I'll find Ruth," Mervyn said. "We'll do the run by toboggan if we have to."

"Should we have a meeting place?" Fuma asked.

Mervyn shook his head. "Never mind that. Get these women and kids back to where they belong. Use the main highway, but switch to secondary roads before you reach Calgary. Don't use the QE2."

"You know you're dead if you get caught back there..."

"I can't leave her behind. I won't leave her behind."

"I know, buddy. I know..."

The two men hugged for a brief moment. Fuma boarded his bus, shoved it into gear, and pulled it onto the road. He signaled to the other driver. She nodded and her bus rolled forward.

Mervyn watched the buses rumble into the night. Satisfied, he ran to the snowmobiles he and Fuma had concealed under tarps earlier.

RUTH KNEW the gun's range. She crept in closer to the home. She got on her knees and lowered herself into the ditch, kicking at the snow that impeded her. She snapped the gun's shoulder stock into place. She closed her hand over the grip safety and positioned her trigger finger. She had a clear view of the front doors. More men came through the doors. Panic made her palms sweat and her mouth go dry.

They were shouting. They knew!

Terror rose like a tidal wave across her soul. She fought the urge to run. She mumbled a prayer, raised the gun, and jammed the stock into the pocket between her chest wall and shoulder. She gripped the underside of the gun with her other hand. She pressed down on the safety. She fired.

Ruth sprayed in short bursts. The sound surprised the men. They were too slow in responding. Many cried out and fell. Some just fell. Ruth waited, watched for movement, and fired again.

A wild giddiness erupted inside her. It was followed by a silken calm, as thick and as hard as granite. Suddenly, she remembered a video game Peter had played before the Change—*Call of Duty*. The bikers were no longer living, breathing humans—they had become computer-generated targets—nameless and faceless in the dark.

Unreal.

More men pushed through the front doors. Ruth pulled the trigger again. She heard their computer-generated *oofs* and *uhs* as the bullets struck. She watched as shadowy bulges on the ground writhed, and then went still.

Another staccato spray took out one of the home's large plate glass windows. Two men threw themselves at the new opening, scrambling to get back inside. Light from the front room's camp lanterns outlined their bodies, turning them into perfect silhouettes. Ruth peered down the gun's sights, and held her breath.

First-person shooter, she thought. She fired.

The dark human-shaped figures dropped. She fired again.

Six hundred rounds a minute, she thought distantly.

Mechanically, she discarded the empty clip, and jammed in a full magazine. She fired again.

Unreal.

MERVYN RIPPED the tarp off one of the snowmobiles. He started the engine, and pulled on his gloves.

"Please, God..." he prayed. "Let me get there in time."

He pushed down on the thumb throttle.

~~~

His Wife's Daughter

ELIZABETH SAT next to Brad. She kept her eyes down, her thoughts shadowed. She shifted and squeezed her eyes shut. New bruises on her back, on her inner thighs, and on her arms were Brad's homecoming gifts. He had heard she had been out and about. Without permission. Upon returning to their room, the punishment came swiftly. No damage to her face. He made sure of that. But the rest of her, the parts covered by pant legs and long sleeves—they were fair game. Elizabeth shifted in her chair, and relieved the pressure on her back. She looked across the room at Scar. The two women exchanged quick covert glances. The men continued talking.

"The fuel reserves are low," said a man with white blond hair plaited into tight braids. "The Man will have to make some decisions. Start strict rationing...or come up with another kind of fuel."

"Some of the science geeks are working on alternative fuels," Brad said. He tapped a lit cigar on a wide glass ashtray.

"It better happen soon," The Man's uncle said. "I sure as hell am not turning cowboy and parking my bony ass on a horse." A bearded man on the other side of the table laughed—a genuine sound of amusement. The uncle smiled, too.

"We've got full arsenals," the uncle continued. "But no soldiers to carry the guns. Not sure what Hezekiah is going to do about that. He gave out land parcels as rewards, but now the boys are settled in, fat and
~~~

happy into their fiefdoms. They don't want to fight anymore." The uncle shrugged his shoulders and sipped Scotch from the chubby crystal glass in his hand. "And why should they? They've got everything they need."

"For now," Brad added. "For now. But they'll get bored. They'll come looking for action."

"Might be too late by then," the man with the braids said. "What's taking The Man so long to get back here anyway?"

The uncle took another long sip and then looked up at Brad. "How long did he say he'd be down there?"

"A few weeks. I'm not sure."

"What about the Gatekeeper's supplies?" the blond man asked.

Brad shrugged. "I know what he had. Don't know what's left."

"Does she know?" the bearded man asked, indicating Elizabeth. "Well?" asked the man.

"I—I—uh...it's been a long time since I was back home," Elizabeth replied. "I don't know." Brad's hand circled the back of her neck. Elizabeth stiffened as he squeezed.

"You sure you don't know anything else? Maybe about secret storage tanks?"

Elizabeth tried to pull away, but Brad's fingers dug in tighter. "Ow— I told you...I don't know."

Brad released Elizabeth's neck and got up. He walked to the window, looked out into the darkness. He turned back to the group. "I brought her here so we'd have some bargaining power."

"Is she really that valuable to the Gatekeeper?"

"His wife's daughter."

"His wife?" the bearded man asked. "Is that the same one you fucked?"

Elizabeth's eyes shot up.

Brad was leaning against the wall, his arms crossed, his cigar nestled in his fingers. He blew a plume of smoke into the air above his head. "How did you hear about it?" he asked.

"Some of the guys were talking. They said you messed her up."

Elizabeth held her breath.

"She had it coming."

"She survived, right?"

Brad nodded.

"Sounds like one tough bitch," the bearded man said. He appraised Elizabeth. "And now you're doing her daughter." He laughed. "Nicely done." He got up and walked toward Elizabeth. "Any good?"

"So-so. You want a go?" Brad asked.

Elizabeth's face drained of color. She stole another look at Scar. Scar's face was unreadable.

"Sure, if you're offering. My old lady isn't a good looker like this one." The bearded man drew a finger down the side of Elizabeth's face. She flinched back and shuddered.

God...NO! She squeezed her eyes shut.

"Back off, brother. I'm not tired of old Lizzy yet."

Brad came back and seated himself next to Elizabeth. He threw a possessive arm around her shoulder. He grabbed her chin, twisted her face toward him, and kissed her hard and full on the mouth. The pressure made her cry out.

"Get a room," the uncle said. The men laughed. The bearded man returned to his seat.

Elizabeth sought out Scar's eyes; this time they were empathetic. Scar gave her a tiny nod.

The uncle leaned forward and slapped the table. Elizabeth and Scar jumped at the sudden sound.

"If Hezekiah doesn't get back here soon, I'll make some decisions. The mafia is waiting for a fresh batch of women. We'll ship them, and then we'll parlay a deal with the Gatekeeper. Enough pissing around. Right, Brad? You've had enough pissing around, too, haven't you?" The uncle shot Brad an enigmatic look.

"You want to go ahead...without waiting for The Man?" Brad smiled. "He might have something to say about that."

"Yeah, he might," the uncle said. "But then...I understand you don't much care."

"Why do you say that?"

The uncle pursed his lips, raised his hands to his head, and combed them through his thinning hair. "Things I've heard."

"Then you've also heard that I'm running things here? While he's away...of course," Brad added. The bearded man and the blond man exchanged looks. Brad caught the exchange. "You two got a problem with that?" He rose from the chair.

"Hell, no, buddy. If that's what The Man said, then that's how it's gonna be," said the bearded man with a conciliatory smile. The blond man agreed. The uncle said nothing.

Silence settled over the room.

"Scar, get us some more to drink," the uncle said.

"We're running low," Scar said. "Hezeki—"

"I know," the uncle said. "It'll be fine. I'll deal with The Man. Now be a good girl and fetch me another bottle."

Scar rose. "I need help moving boxes," she said. "Can she help me?" she asked, pointing at Elizabeth.

"Go," Brad said. "But get your ass back here. Quick. Or I'll come looking for you. And you know what that'll mean."

Elizabeth jumped from her chair and hurried in Scar's direction. The two women left the room, slamming the door behind them.

"That son-of-a-bitch," Elizabeth muttered as they scurried along the hallway.

"Did you know?" Scar asked.

"About my mother?" Elizabeth nodded. "Yes."

"Still want to plan that murder?" Scar asked. "Hezekiah should be back soon. We might not get another chance."

"I've never wanted to kill anyone before. Not ever in my life," said Elizabeth. "But I want to kill him."

"I know the feeling," Scar said. They turned down a narrow hallway.

"Do you want to leave here?" Elizabeth whispered.

"Leave?"

"Yeah. Let's escape. Let's go to Edmonton..."

Scar shook her head. "I don't think so. Nothing there for me."

"What's here for you?"

Scar smiled.

"Oh—Hezekiah," Elizabeth said. She wagged her head. "Love is so insane, isn't it?"

"You've been in love?"

"Nope. Never."

"Not even Brad?"

"Gross!" Elizabeth glowered at her.

Scar burst out laughing. "Sorry."

Scar opened a door. A flight of stairs led down. "Grab a flashlight."

Elizabeth saw several hung from nails on the wall. She took one and switched it on. They carefully descended a second set of steps.

At the bottom, Elizabeth shone her light over the room. Boxes upon boxes were piled high. Plastic tubs—pink, blue, white, and green—layered a wall, stacked like giant toy bricks.

"What's in those?" she asked, playing her light beam over the tubs.

"Dried foods."

"Do you store guns and ammunition down here, too?"

"No, not here. The Man has a storehouse off the premises. He's pretty damn careful about his arsenal. Not just anybody gets access to that."

"Do you have access?"

"No— Brad does."

"Of course, he does."

Elizabeth followed Scar and helped her wrestle aside several heavy boxes. They found the liquor, removed two bottles, and then buried the liquor stash again.

"The Man is going to be pissed when he sees how low we're getting on his drink of choice," Scar said, clucking her tongue.

"When is he coming back?"

"Not sure. I'm surprised he's been gone this long." Elizabeth grabbed Scar's shoulder. Scar whirled around. "What?"

"I've got to get out of here." Elizabeth took a breath. "I'm going to make a run for it." She paused again. "Will you help me?"

"How?"

"Get me a truck, gassed up, some supplies. A gun and ammunition."

Scar pondered the request. "I know where The Man keeps his personal weapons. I might be able to steal one of those. The truck shouldn't be too hard. The hard part is sneaking you out of the home."

"But you'll help me? For sure?"

Scar smiled. "Yes. You'll probably get yourself killed in the process, but I'll help you."

"Come with me," Elizabeth coaxed.

"No— I'll stay here."

"But Brad—"

"The Man will be back soon. Brad will quit as soon as Hezekiah gets back here."

"But what happens if he doesn't quit?"

"He will," Scar said. She began her way back up the steps. "C'mon, we've been gone way too long."

Chapter Thirty

The Leverage

RUTH SANK into the snow. She held still, so very still that she could hear the pounding of her heart as it made great, hurried thumps against her ribs. She studied the front door. No movement except for the undulations of the dark shapes moaning on the ground. Like fat slugs, they wriggled, lifted their heads, and fell back again.

First-person shooter.

A sound to her right startled her. Ruth sank even lower, willing the snow bed to suck her in—down...down...down—enveloping her in its sodden mass. She waited.

Ruth checked her watch. Ten minutes had passed and nothing had changed. Things were quiet. Deathly still. Even the bullet-ridden men no longer moved.

Did I kill all of them?

No one was coming out the front door.

No, she corrected herself. *The Man's drugged. I never got him. He's still in bed.*

Another sound. She held her breath again.

Nothing.

She shivered.

What do I do now? I can't stay here all night. How many men are left?

She tried remembering what Mervyn had told her.

Seventeen? Or was it fifteen? More? She guessed at the number of men she had shot.

Ten? Twelve? She knew she would have to get up and count the bodies if she wanted an answer.

Suddenly, Ruth was very tired. The gun was too heavy. Her head on her neck was too heavy. She wanted to sleep. She began to pray.

Father, get me out of here.

A faraway sound reached her ears.

A snowmobile?

Ruth pushed farther down into the ditch.

Stupid, she thought. *Stupid. Some of them weren't partying. They were out on toboggans.*

She waited. The sound stopped. Vanished. In a breath. The silence of the night was perfect again. She returned her focus to the bikers.

How many are left? I've got to know.

She crawled from her snow pit and shimmied along the ground up the driveway. Still no movement from inside the home.

I'll go back in—through my window.

A shadow passed in front of the blown out front room window. She froze.

What now?

She wished for Mervyn, his calm presence, his warm hands. A spurt of anger made her pound the ground with her fist.

I hate this. Why did you put me here, God? Why?

She heard the crisp crunch and squeak of footsteps on snow. The sound came from somewhere behind her. She threw herself into the ditch, clutching the Uzi to her chest as she rolled. She settled into the snow, and peered up toward the road. Like a startled deer, she froze in position, her eyes wide and searching.

Is this it for me? Am I going to die? She thought of her children. *I'm ready to die. Please, please take care of them.*

Ruth hugged the Uzi. She waited.

More footsteps. Running.

Ruth brightened.

The runner was alone.

She raised the Uzi and pointed it toward the sound of the steps. Her hand pressed down on the grip safety. The runner had slowed, but he was nearby. She held her breath. She waited.

The shadowy figure moved through the gloom. She could hear his breath coming quick in his chest. He was almost in her sights. Suddenly, a yell came from inside the home. Ruth gasped. The running figure dropped to the ground. Out of her sight. When he rose again, he was about twenty feet away. She raised her gun again, and settled the narrow metal stock into her shoulder pocket. More commotion came from the home's front room. Two men were yelling. Ruth crouched and watched the front doors

"What the hell happened?" asked a man. He sounded groggy.

The Man! He was awake. Maybe he'll come outside.

"Don't know," another man answered. "I was sleeping. The machine gun fire woke me."

"Where're the rest?" The Man demanded.

Ruth couldn't hear the mumbled reply.

A movement to her right.

The mysterious figure was near her now, parallel to her. He was crouched—the form of a pistol was in his hand. He turned. Ruth studied his silhouette.

Mervyn? Ruth suppressed a squeal of relief. She clamped her hand over her mouth. *What if it's not him?*

The figure crept closer. Overhead, a lazy moon rolled out from under a misty cloud cover. Moonlight fell across the man's face.

"Mervyn..." Ruth hissed. He didn't respond. "Mervyn!" She risked saying it louder. The men inside were still yelling. The dark figure turned.

"Ruth?" Mervyn whispered harshly. "Where are you?"

"Down here."

Mervyn headed toward the sound of Ruth's voice.

"Oh, my God. Are you okay?" Without waiting for an answer, he grabbed her in a hug and connected with the Uzi. He stood back, flabbergasted. "Where the heck did you get that?"

"Long story. Tell you later."

"Are you okay?"

"I'm fine. Scared half to death. But fine."

"Bring me up to date. Where is everybody?"

"I can't tell for sure— But I think I got maybe a dozen guys." She motioned toward the front of the home. "I got them as they came through the doors."

"You didn't get The Man— I heard him yelling."

"I know. He was next on my list."

Mervyn lifted his eyebrows. "You were going after The Man?"

"I thought he was still asleep."

"You were going to kill him in his sleep?"

"I—I—I never gave it that much thought."

"Well...there're two of us now. Let's find out how many are left."

Ruth tugged his sleeve. "Where're the kids?"

"All fine. All on a bus. Headed home."

"Thank, God." She settled the Uzi across her chest. "Let's go."

"No. You stay here. I'll go. Cover me." He paused. "Where did you learn to shoot that thing?"

"Matthew...he made all of us learn how to use guns. All guns."

"I'm impressed," he whispered. He sprinted up the ditch into the shadows.

Ruth trained her eyes on the front of the home. She watched Mervyn stoop and crawl as he inspected the bodies. He slipped under the big window, and peered over the sill. He ducked back down, circled around, and was soon back at her side.

"Ten men down."

"How many does that leave?

"Four...plus The Man."

"What should we do?"

"We can run. I have a snowmobile hidden up the road. The second one is a little farther away. But we'd be better off in a truck."

"I agree. So, what do we do?"

"I hate to say this but..."

"I know...we have to take down the other four guys."

"And The Man."

"We can get in through my bedroom window. I broke it."

"Let's go."

They clambered up and over the windowsill. They stood in the darkened room, listening for voices. "You didn't happen to steal a pistol, too?" Mervyn whispered.

Ruth shook her head.

"Damn— We'll make do with mine." The bedroom door was slightly ajar. He leaned his ear up to the opening. "I can hear them."

"Where?"

"I think they're in the dining room."

"Mervyn, I'm scared. I don't think I can do this. It was different out in the snow. I was far away from them. This is scaring the shit of out me."

He gave her forehead a quick kiss. "Me, too." He pulled the door open. "C'mon."

They slipped into the hallway. They could see the light from camp lanterns up the hall. No men were in sight.

"What about his room?" Ruth whispered. She pointed.

Mervyn shook his head. "He's awake— There's no way to surprise him."

"But maybe you could pretend— He doesn't know you helped us."

Mervyn thought about her suggestion. "You might be right. But he's gonna wonder where I was."

"He doesn't know the buses are missing. He can't know. Nobody knows. I shot all the guys who came outside," she whispered hurriedly.

"Okay— I'll do it." He pointed to the dark shadows several feet down the hallway. "Over there. Stay there."

Ruth did as instructed. In a moment, she vanished from his sight.

"Sir—?" He tapped softly on The Man's door.

No answer.

He tried the knob. It turned. He pushed the door forward. "Sir—?" He entered the room.

A man yelled from the front room. "What the fuck? They're all dead. What the—?" Ruth guessed that somebody had gone outside and had examined the bodies. "Who shot them?" the man asked.

"You'd better find out—and find out fast!" Ruth recognized The Man's voice. She shuddered with relief. He wasn't in his bedroom.

"Where did all the women go?" asked another man. "It's the middle of the night. They've got little kids with them."

"Well, they didn't just disappear. Find them."

"The shooter might still be outside."

"I want some answers," The Man demanded. "Now! Or, I'll shoot you myself."

Ruth wondered about the whereabouts of the fourth and fifth man. Her question was answered nearly as quickly as she thought it—they were coming up from the other end of the hallway. The men were noisily checking the rooms, slamming doors open, sweeping the rooms with a large flashlight, and stomping on to the next room.

She reached for the doorknob behind her, twisted it, and pushed backwards into the room. She flipped back the hanging bedcovers, and slid beneath the bed. Her shoulder bag got caught and she struggled to free it. She gave up. She waited.

The door slammed open. Light glanced briefly over the beds; it came to rest at the end of the bed near her head.

Please...Ruth prayed.

The light went out. The men moved off down the hallway.

"There's no sign of them anywhere," called one of the men.

"So, where the fuck did they go?" the other man asked. "How do a bunch of women and kids take off in the middle of the night? In winter?"

"There's only one way," The Man replied. Ruth shivered. He was nearby.

"You mean buses?"

"Yeah, I mean buses. Where're our bus drivers?"

"Mervyn and Fuma? Haven't seen them."

Silence.

"Those sons of bitches—they helped them," The Man said. Ruth's blood ran cold. "Get my truck ready. We'll go after them. They can't have gone very far." Ruth heard the men agree and leave.

Where's Mervyn?

She rolled out from under the bed. Her bag was still snagged, and the bed squeaked as she got up. Her stomach sank. Fear froze her to the spot.

Did they hear?

She listened, not daring to breathe. The silence was more frightening than the men's voices.

Move, Ruth. Move...or die.

She took a deep breath, and stepped forward.

A creak outside in the hallway.

She scurried into the corner behind the door, and held her breath.

Another creak.

She licked her lips, and took a quick shallow breath. Inside her gloves, her palms were greasy with sweat. She gripped the Uzi. She knew it was not the gun for close combat...but it would have to do. Her ears throbbed with the pounding of her heart.

Please...

The tension and lack of oxygen made her feel faint. She risked a long, deep breath, and willed her heart to slow its pace. The door still hadn't been pushed open.

Was he gone?

Just as she decided to move, the door opened slightly. A bolt of cold fear shot through her, and she tasted metal. She squeezed her eyes shut.

No...please...

"Sir—?"

Ruth's eyes popped open.

Mervyn! He was out in the hallway.

"I'm surprised to see you," answered The Man.

"Why would that be?"

"Ruth got to you, didn't she?"

"Sir—?" Mervyn asked innocently.

"I know about the buses," The Man said.

"The buses, yes...I went out to get them ready. Where are they?"

"You went outside? To find the buses?"

"Of course."

"Not a scratch on you?" The Man asked.

Ruth heard a small skirmish.

"I wouldn't do that," Mervyn said.

"You going to shoot me? I've still got loyal men. You didn't get all of them."

"I know...I counted the bodies," Mervyn said. "And just for the record—I didn't kill them."

"Oh?" The Man sounded slightly amused.

"Ruth did," Mervyn said.

The Man chuckled—a cold, hollow sound devoid of mirth, and thick with malice. "Her mother shot me, her daughter drugged me." He chuckled again. "And Elizabeth is with Brad." He paused for effect. "What a family..."

"Turn around," Mervyn commanded.

"Do what you will..." The Man taunted. "Those women won't make it far. A message had already been relayed. Brad's been told. He'll find them. And they'll be re-routed to the South Camps. Fuma won't be so lucky."

"I said turn around," Mervyn repeated.

Suddenly, Ruth heard the sound of bodies colliding, a scuffle, and grunting as men struck at each other. Ruth bolted out of the room.

The Man had Mervyn in a clinch, his legs wrapped around Mervyn's thighs, and one arm wrapped around Mervyn's throat. Mervyn's face was red and he was struggling for breath. Ruth jammed the muzzle of the Uzi into The Man's cheek.

"Let him go, you bastard! Let him go now. Or I will kill you."

The Man released his grip and fell back on the floor. His face wore a strange expression—a mixture of awe and surprise.

Mervyn coughed and got to his feet. He looked around, located his pistol, and picked it up.

"We've gotta hurry, Ruth," he croaked. "If a message really did get sent... Won't be long before they come looking for us."

Ruth stared at The Man. "Get up." She prodded him with the gun. The Man sat up. Ruth backed off, ensuring herself an adequate shooting distance. "I have never killed a man before, but I killed many tonight. One more won't make a difference to me." She looked at Mervyn. "You okay?"

"Yeah." His voice was still raspy from the chokehold.

"Do you have something to tie him with?"

"Tie him?"

"We'll need a hostage— Leverage for when we meet Brad."

Mervyn searched his own pockets and found nothing.

"Check his," Ruth said.

The Man smiled, reached into his pocket, and pulled out electrical ties. Mervyn secured The Man's hands together at his wrists.

They pulled The Man to his feet and shoved him into a bedroom. Ruth grabbed an abandoned mitten from the floor and shoved it into The Man's mouth. She pushed him back on the bed.

"Give me your Uzi," Mervyn said. "Take this..." They exchanged guns. "I hate to do this..." Mervyn said as he ran out the door.

Ruth turned back to The Man. "Don't move," she said. She stuck him in the chest with Mervyn's pistol. "I don't care whether you live or die. So, don't tempt me."

The Man stared at her.

The angry chatter of a machine gun broke the silence. Voices. More shooting. Then silence. Someone ran down the hall.

"Ruth—!" Mervyn dashed into the room. "Let's go."

Moments later, Mervyn was behind the wheel of The Man's truck. Ruth was in the passenger seat. The Man was bound in the backseat, a woolen mitten hanging from his mouth. They raced up the highway away from the home. The big truck rode high off the ground, so their progress was consistent, in spite of snowdrifts.

"Do you know what direction they went?" Ruth asked.

"Fuma will stick to the main highways until just before Calgary. I told him we'd catch up."

"How far ahead do you think they are?"

"Hour...hour and a half— But they're traveling slower than us."

"What about Brad? Do you think he'll have time to intercept them? Before we reach them?"

Mervyn shrugged. "I don't know. I hope not. The South Camps cover a huge area. It'll be difficult finding them if he finds them first."

Ruth leaned forward, her face in her hands.

"Drive faster," she mumbled.

A Memory of Dad

ELIZABETH JOLTED awake. Somebody was in the room. She sensed it wasn't Brad. Her heart pounded and she held her breath.

"Elizabeth?" a voice whispered. "Elizabeth, wake up."

It was Scar.

"I'm awake." Elizabeth pushed the bedding aside and swung her legs over the edge of the bed. "What time is it?" She tried to see her watch.

Scar grabbed her arm. "Middle of the night. Let's go."

"Go? Where?"

"You wanted to go home?" Elizabeth nodded. "Well, hurry up."

"Why now?"

"I just heard a bunch of the guys talking about a relay radio message they got. Apparently, the women from Sunnyvale have escaped. Thought you'd want to go, too."

"What? Ruth got away?" Elizabeth burst from the bed. She grabbed a pair of jeans, pulled them on, and zippered them.

"Better pray for them," Scar said quickly. "A team is going after them right now." Elizabeth continued to dress.

"Ruth made it. She made it— Oh, hallelujah. I knew she would. Are you coming, too? Did you change your mind?" Elizabeth tried to whisper, but in her excitement, her voice grew louder.

"Sh!" Scar reached into a coat pocket and pulled something out. She pressed the object into Elizabeth's hand. It was a gun.

"You got one!" Elizabeth hissed. "Good for you." She gave Scar a quick hug.

"Here's a box of ammo, too."

"Thanks." Elizabeth did up her boots. "What about a truck? And supplies?"

Scar bent and picked up a backpack she had carried in with her. "It's the best I could do. A couple days worth of rations. You might be able to find food on the way. And I've got a truck in mind."

Elizabeth pulled a heavy sweater over her head. Her hair sparked and crackled with static electricity. "Are you coming?" she asked again.

"Not sure. Maybe. C'mon. Let's get you out of here."

Elizabeth thrust her arms into her parka's sleeves. She grabbed mitts, a woolen toque, and a scarf from a shelf in the closet. "Okay, I'm good. Let's go."

The two women crept from the room and made their way down the dark hallway. They could hear voices coming from far away—from the direction of the front room.

"We'll use the side door," Scar said, grabbing Elizabeth's arm. "This way." The women began to run. Men's voices stopped them in their tracks.

"What now?" Elizabeth asked. "Go back?"

"Run!"

The women ran back to the room, went inside, and closed the door. They leaned against the door, panting, their hearts hammering in their ears. The men's voices grew louder. One of the voices belonged to Brad.

"Get a few more guys. Start those trucks. You can kiss your asses good-bye if those women get away."

"Those women... He means Ruth," Elizabeth whispered excitedly. The voices got closer. "Shit! What now?"

"Hide."

"There's nowhere to hide in here."

Scar thought for a moment. "I'll take care of it."

Scar pushed Elizabeth behind her and opened the door. She stepped into the hallway.

"What the hell are you doing here?" Elizabeth cringed at the sound of Brad's voice. She held her breath.

"Looking for you," Scar said.

"Well, you found me. What do you want?"

"A new girl showed up. Thought you might be interested."

"Showed up? In the middle of the night?"

"I told you I'd find you another girl. With experience."

"Where is she?"

"I put her in a room in the west wing. Second floor. Two fifty-two."

A small silence ensued. Brad finally grunted. "Save her for me. We've got trouble."

"What's up?" Scar asked.

"The women from Sunnyvale. They've escaped."

Elizabeth counted her heartbeats. Seven... eight... nine... ten... eleven... The door opened.

"C'mon," Scar whispered. "He's gone. Let's go." Elizabeth hurried out the door and ran after Scar.

The pair reached the side door, pushed it open, and fled into the night. The air was cold, but not bitterly cold. Elizabeth pulled her toque down over her ears.

"Scar!" Elizabeth hissed. "The men are going after Ruth. Maybe we can stop them."

"Are you crazy?" Scar shot back. "Forget it. Just get yourself out of here."

Moonlight illuminated the yard. Elizabeth saw trucks and snowmobiles sitting like hulking beasts in their shadowy cloaks. Some trucks had hoods mounded in fresh snow. Others were clear of snow; Elizabeth guessed they had been recently driven. Some of the trucks were running, huge plumes of exhaust swirled up into the darkness.

"Which one?" Elizabeth asked. "Which truck?"

Scar pointed to an unseen spot in the distance. She pulled Elizabeth closer and spoke into her ear. "There's a truck high up on the driveway, near the street. It's red. It's one of The Man's. It's usually tanked up. I'm not real sure, but it's a good bet. And it might be your only chance to get out of here."

"Thanks. I appreciate this, Scar."

"Don't thank me yet. You still have to start that truck."

"Keys?"

"Should be in the ignition. They usually are."

"You coming with me?"

Scar took a quick breath. "I'll stay. I'm used to this place. It's home to me."

"I get that." Elizabeth smiled. "God bless you."

"You, too. Now get going." They hugged quickly.

Elizabeth began to walk away, but turned suddenly. "Wait a minute. That girl you told Brad about...she doesn't exist. What's going to happen to you when he finds out you lied to him? And helped me escape?" Elizabeth gave Scar an earnest look. "Scar, he'll kill you. Come with me."

"I can't—"

"Come with me," Elizabeth pleaded. "Or you're dead."

A commotion in the parking lot drew their attention. Scar clutched at Elizabeth and pulled her down to the ground.

"Get those trucks moving now!" a man's voice called. Truck engines began to rumble and trucks began to roll.

"You want to make a run for the truck now?" Scar asked.

"You've got to come with me, Scar!" Elizabeth whispered urgently. "Come with me."

Scar looked back over her shoulder, thought a moment, and then nodded. "Okay— Let's go."

They ran.

A truck's headlights came on just as they passed, spotlighting Elizabeth. She ducked back into the shadows. She panted. She squeezed her eyes tight and covered them with her hand. She willed herself to sink into the snow, become one with the snow, invisible in a white womb of peace and quiet, safe from the danger. She heard a man speak.

"What the hell? There's a woman out here," the man exclaimed.

"Anyone you recognize?" asked another man.

"Yeah— Brad's old lady."

"Where did she go?"

Elizabeth and Scar didn't wait to hear the answer. They sprinted from vehicle to vehicle—crouching low as they ran, and keeping to the shadows. They stopped when they heard voices again—one of the voices belonged to Brad!

"Oh, shit! What now?" Elizabeth asked. Her hand found the gun Scar had given to her earlier. "I never checked. Is the gun loaded?"

"I didn't load it. Sorry."

Elizabeth pulled out the gun, popped the magazine, and checked it.

Empty!

She fumbled around in her pockets for the box of cartridges. In her haste to leave, she had forgotten where she had put them. Finally, she located the box. She set it on the ground, and opened it. She whipped off her mitts, and grabbed several bullets. She tried loading the magazine, but her fingers were trembling. The bullets slipped from her fingers and fell into the snow. She tried again. This time she managed to load three bullets. She heard Brad's voice again—he was nearby. She closed the box and shoved it into her pocket. She slammed the magazine into the gun and flipped the safety.

"Where do you think she went?" asked Brad.

"I don't know," answered a man.

"When I find that little bitch—"

Scar clutched Elizabeth's sleeve and pulled her close. She whispered in her ear. "I'll try to draw him away. You make a run for it. Don't start the truck. Hide somewhere. Wait for a couple of hours."

"But maybe it's the best time to go," Elizabeth countered. "I'll drive out when the other trucks leave."

"Okay, but give me a minute."

"Don't go, Scar. He'll kill you if he sees you out here. He'll figure it out—"

Elizabeth's words were too late; she could just make out Scar's shape as she headed in the direction of Brad's voice. Elizabeth squeezed her eyes tight, and waited for the inevitable conclusion she knew had to come.

"Brad?" Elizabeth heard Scar ask.

"Where is she, Scar?"

"I don't know."

The sound of a slap, as sharp as the crack of a whip, reverberated through the darkness.

"Where is she?" she heard Brad ask again.

"I told you, I don't—" Another crack echoed through the night. This time, Scar cried out.

Elizabeth winced at the sound and gripped the gun.

What? What? What do I do? What would Mom do? Her dead father came into her mind— What would Dad do?

Tears pricked her eyes. She had not thought of Josef in a long while—the man Brad had brutally murdered. A swift vision of Josef bent over his Bible at the kitchen table burst into her brain. Then came a memory of him reading to her—from the Psalms—his voice low and comforting:

> *"Oh, how I wish I had wings like a dove;*
> *Then I would fly away and rest!*
> *I would fly far away to the quiet of the wilderness.*
> *How quickly I would escape—*
> *Far away from this wild storm of hatred."*

A cloak of calm surrounded her, enveloped her soul, bringing with it a clarity of mind. Elizabeth smiled softly. Josef had made her memorize the passage: Psalm 55:6-8. She had argued with him that memorizing Bible verses was a stupid idea. Old-fashioned and useless. Her smile widened.

Thanks, Dad.

Elizabeth rose and followed the sound of Brad's voice. She pointed the gun ahead of her. Her hand was steady. She came around a large truck and spotted Scar lying on the ground—she wasn't moving. Elizabeth watched as Brad drew back his foot and kicked out. Scar grunted and tried to get up. Brad kicked her again.

"I know you know," he said. "Where is she?" He pulled his foot back again.

"Right here, Brad. I'm right here." Brad's head jerked up at the sound of Elizabeth's voice. "Let her be— I'm the one you want."

Scar groaned. "Elizabeth... No!"

"What are you doing outside?" Brad demanded. "I never gave you permission to be out here."

"I don't need your permission to be out here," Elizabeth retorted.

"How's that?" Brad asked. His tone was mocking.

"Because I'm not your bitch anymore. I never was." Elizabeth stepped forward, her gun leveled on Brad's chest. "I've always hated you, you pig. You killed my father. You raped my mother. And the things you've done to me..." Elizabeth stepped closer.

Brad backed up. "I told you— I never killed your dad."

"Liar," Elizabeth said hotly. "No more lies— I'm sick of your lies." Elizabeth stopped near Scar. "Can you get up, Scar?" Scar clambered to her feet. "Go. I'll be right behind you."

"Elizabeth?" Scar began.

"I'm good," Elizabeth said. "Go."

Scar scurried away. Elizabeth watched her disappear. Brad made a move, but Elizabeth caught his action and leveled the pistol on him.

"Stay where you are," she said.

"Or what? You'll shoot me?" Brad laughed. "Your mother had her chance. She didn't shoot me. Why should I believe you'll shoot me?"

"Because I am not my mother."

"The parking lot is full of guys. You shoot me, and they'll be on you in a second."

"I'll take that chance. Now, walk."

"And if I don't?"

"Then I will shoot you here."

Brad turned his head toward the sound of another gunning truck engine. "You won't make it..."

"Shut up. If you want to live...then walk."

"Where do you think you're going?"

"Back to Edmonton. You're coming, too...as my prisoner." Brad laughed again. "I mean it, Brad. Many people back home will want to see you again."

"Like your mother," Brad asked sarcastically.

"Especially my mother." Elizabeth motioned with the gun. "Move."

Brad started walking. Suddenly, he flung himself to the side, and rolled away into the darkness behind a large truck. Elizabeth fired off a shot in surprise, but to no avail. The bullet went wild, and pinged off some unseen metallic thing. She crouched down and berated herself for letting Brad get away. She waited. A movement off to her left made her grip her gun tighter. She held her position.

Silence.

Elizabeth wondered about making a run for the truck. Just getting in and driving away. They might have a chance, camouflaged by the noise from the other trucks. She slipped alongside a nearby truck, keeping to the shadows. Snow crunched beneath her boot and she grimaced. She heard the slow, steady footfall of boots squeaking across the snow just a few feet away. She risked moving and slipped around to the front of the truck that was concealing her. She peered into the darkness, but could see nothing. She bent low and ran.

The sound of steps behind her got louder. She turned and fired. The steps faltered, but there was no sound of a body hitting the ground.

Damn! Another wasted shot.

Elizabeth melted into the shadows of another truck. The sound of steps continued. They were closer now. She tried to see who was coming after her, willing her eyes to see in the dark, but failed. Then she remembered...

One shot, she thought. I have only one shot left. Better make it count.

A large figure came into view. Elizabeth raised the pistol, and fired. The figure grunted and dropped to the ground. She held her breath and waited for the lump to move; it didn't stir. She stepped from the shadows, but froze when she felt a presence come up behind her. Fear made her stomach sick. The voice made her shudder. She closed her eyes.

"Wrong guy," Brad said stepping into view, a gun in his hand. "We could have been good together—you and I. But you are too much like your mother."

"How's that?" Elizabeth asked softly, meeting Brad's eyes.

"Neither one of you knows her place."

"Maybe not, Brad...but we both know a loser when we see one."

Elizabeth never heard the shot. She fell backward against a truck, and slumped into the snow. She reached up and touched a spreading dark patch on her chest. Her fingers came away wet.

"Oh," she said softly, holding her hand up to her face. She blinked. She dropped her hand to her lap. She slid down onto her back.

Elizabeth gazed up into the night sky—her eyes dreamy and unconcerned. The stars were brilliant, a vast quilt of twinkling lights. A gauzy cloud of gray drifted in, dimming their luminance. She panicked and struggled. She tried focusing her eyes, but the effort was too much.

So...this is what it feels like to die, she thought—as the night sky and its blanket of stars faded into darkness.

See you soon, Dad.

A void opened, welcoming her into its blackened depths, pulling her down...down...down.

Elizabeth gave a little gasp. She closed her eyes.

Brad stared for a moment, and nudged her with his foot. "So long, Lizzy. Stupid bitch." He turned and ran.

A few yards away, Brad bumped into a small group of men. They looked at him expectantly.

"Who got shot?" one of them asked.

"One of the guys— I don't know who," Brad growled. "But Elizabeth won't be a problem anymore." The men looked confused. "Did you see Scar?" Brad asked.

"No— Why?" asked a man dressed in a heavy gray parka with a fur-trimmed hood.

"I'm going to kill that bitch when I find her."

"Wh—what's going on?" the man in the parka asked.

Before Brad could reply, another man ran up. Fog puffed from his mouth. "Are we going? The trucks are ready. C'mon."

Brad checked his watch. He squinted into the dark. "Dammit!" he muttered. "We've already lost too much time. Let's go after those bloody women. And hope we're not too late." He jumped into a truck.

~~~

A dark shape huddled near a truck, crouched low, clutching her coat to her chest, the other hand over her mouth muting the sounds of grief. A tear trickled down her cheek.

"I'm sorry, Elizabeth," Scar whispered to the woman on the ground. "So sorry." Another shimmering tear—sparked with the light of a star—dropped to the snow.
~~~

Chapter Thirty-One

A Day Trip to Drumheller

RUTH AND MERVYN had driven for nearly two hours before they saw the lights—far off in the distance—the highly distinguishable pattern of the red taillights of a school bus. The bus was stopped. Ruth jerked forward.

"There's only one bus!" She gaped at Mervyn. "Where's the other bus?"

Mervyn placed a hand over hers. "Don't jump to conclusions."

He sped up, got within range of the bus, and braked. The bus looked deserted—as though people had left in a hurry. He and Ruth dashed out of the truck. Mervyn stopped her.

"Stay here. Watch him," he said.

Ruth returned to the truck. She gave The Man a warning glance and got back into her seat.

Mervyn aimed his pistol forward as he investigated the perimeter of the bus. The lights were on and the door was ajar. He edged around and pointed his pistol through the hinged doors. He blanched at the sight of the man in the driver's seat. He wrenched the folding doors open.

Fuma's body hung crookedly from the seat; his head was matted in blood. Blood spray was everywhere—on the gearshift, the window, the dashboard, the floorboards, and in the door well. Mervyn could see a hole in the side window made by the bullet that had killed his friend. Fuma's eyes were open.

Mervyn boarded the bus. He knelt and closed Fuma's eyes with a gentle touch of his fingers. "Sorry, buddy."

He rose and walked toward the back of the bus, checking the seats.

Not a soul.

He spotted a sock doll on the floor. He stooped and picked it up. Its white fabric face was muddied. He brushed at it. He returned to the truck, opened the passenger door, and handed the doll to Ruth.

"Mary's..." Ruth buried her face in the doll. She fought tears, but they spilled onto her cheeks in spite of her efforts.

"I've got to get Fuma," Mervyn said. His face was grim.

"Is he...?"

Mervyn shook his head.

Ruth drew a ragged breath. "Where are the kids?"

Mervyn reached out and squeezed her hand. "My best guess is that whoever took them decided handling a single bus was easier. So, he's crammed them into the other bus."

~ ~ ~

Ten minutes later, they were back on the road; Fuma's body was rolled into a tarp in the truck bed. "I couldn't leave him behind," Mervyn explained.

"I know," Ruth said softly. "I wouldn't have wanted you to. He was wonderful to us." She stared ahead. "How long till we catch up to them?"

"I don't know, Ruth— It's a school bus. It can't go as fast as we can."

Mervyn drove on. Finally, he said, "Take out his gag."

Ruth kneeled in her seat, and leaned into the backseat. She grabbed a corner of the mitten, and pulled it free. The Man spat.

"You'll never find them," The Man said. "Brad knows his stuff."

Ruth shot The Man a piercing stare, wishing she could burn his eyes out of his head with the heat of her glare. "We got you. We'll find them. And we'll take Brad down, too." She paused for effect. "I promise you that."

"Ruth— Look!"

Ruth swung around. Mervyn was pointing to something up ahead. She squinted into the dark.

Taillights.

BRAD LED the pack—two trucks in front of the bus, and two behind. He kept reminding his driver to slow down so he could keep the bus in sight, but soon they were too far up the highway. They had lost sight of the bus once more. He told his driver to pull over and wait.

Brad swiped at his brow. He wiped sweat on his jeans. He released his breath in a loud, relieved sigh. "God, I'm glad we found them."

The trip down the highway, wending their way through an obstacle course of abandoned vehicles and snowdrifts—in the dark—had been nerve-wracking. He relaxed against the seat and breathed deeply.

"I would never have guessed that Fuma planned this... Never." Brad thought for a moment. He pursed his mouth. "Nah...he wasn't alone. Somebody else was in on this." The driver nodded. "But I wonder who..." Brad picked up a canteen and took a swig of water. "Doesn't matter now. We've got them..."

RUTH LEANED forward, her chest shoved tightly against the truck's dashboard. Tiny, red taillights moved in and out of her field of vision. Disappearing, and then reappearing, but growing brighter and larger with each reappearance. Darkness still enveloped their truck like a desperate, silent womb. Mervyn had turned off the truck's headlights; he was navigating with parking lights. Ruth glanced back. The Man, lit eerily by the cab lights, reclined against the seat, like Hollywood royalty—a demure smile pulling at the corners of his lips. Ruth considered shoving the mitten back into his mouth as an excuse to slap the smile from his face.

"Let me run something by you," Mervyn said.

"Oh, yes, do...I'm all ears, Mervyn," The Man coaxed in a giddy schoolgirl tone.

"Shut up," Mervyn warned. "Or I'll let her shoot you."

"My pleasure," Ruth said. Her hand tightened around Mervyn's pistol.

The Man's eyes lifted in surprise. "You going to shoot me, Ruth? In cold blood? What happened to my value as a hostage?"

"We know where the bus is. We don't have any use for you now."

Mervyn reached over and placed a gloved hand on Ruth's forearm. "Easy there, girl. We still need him."

"What for?" Ruth never wavered—her eyes remained fixed on The Man's face, the gun pointed at his head.

I have every right to pull this trigger, she thought. *For the murder of my father. The rape of my mother. The misery—*

"As a decoy." Mervyn tightened his grip on her arm. "Besides...you don't want to mess up the inside of his truck." Ruth lowered the gun.

"You know the Archangels will hunt you down and kill you," The Man retorted.

"I wouldn't be so sure of that," Mervyn said, glancing in the rearview mirror. "You only *think* you have control. If the power came back on tomorrow, the club would cease to exist. Vanish into thin air. And you...you would become someone's target. Probably of a pissed-off one-percenter. Wouldn't that be the perfect irony?"

The Man's eyes were cold. Mervyn gave him a quick grin.

"I think we'll turn you over to the Gatekeeper. Would that suit you?"

The Man glared back at him.

Ruth listened to the exchange with intense interest, but curiosity took hold. "What did you want to run by me?" Mervyn swerved past a large snowdrift, wrestled the truck out of a small skid, and spoke:

"No one knows I'm helping you. None of the women would have told Brad. Fuma sure as hell wouldn't have said anything. That means that me driving up in The Man's truck...will look perfectly normal." Mervyn glanced in the rearview mirror again. The Man appeared to be asleep. "Especially if he's riding shotgun." Mervyn stopped the truck. "Switch places with him."

"This is nuts," Ruth said. "He'll run."

"Then you'll get your chance to shoot him. We can still make it look like he's alive—at least long enough to fool Brad."

"I don't think he cares if we kill him," Ruth said.

"Sure he does. He doesn't want somebody else killing him. He wants to do that himself. Suicide—like his Nazi hero. Right, buddy?" Mervyn turned and poked The Man's leg.

"His hero? Who's that?" Ruth asked.

"Hitler."

"I guess that makes sense. Sunnyvale felt like a concentration camp."

Mervyn opened the door and leapt from the truck. Ruth got out, too.

"Keep the gun on him. I've got to get more guns from the back." Mervyn pulled a flashlight from his belt, switched it on, and climbed into the truck bed. He flipped up a tarp, scrabbled around, and then held up two more pistols.

The Man didn't put up a fight. He got into the front seat as directed. Mervyn took a rope and looped it around The Man's chest, fastening him and his arms to the seat.

"There. He can't do any signaling."

Ruth got into the backseat.

"Keep out of sight," Mervyn said. He thought for a moment. "Hold out your hands." He pulled an electrical tie from his pocket and loosely secured both her wrists together. "Can you get your hands in and out of that?" Ruth nodded. "If I need to, I'll make it look like you're my prisoner. It could get you onto the bus."

Ruth looked skeptical.

"We don't have a choice," Mervyn said. "We've got to get onto that bus. And I've got to stop Brad and however many guys he has with him."

"Did you bring machine guns? He had lots in his room," Ruth said, motioning to The Man.

"We're good for guns."

"Give me the Uzi."

"You can't shoot it in here— You'll blow our ears off."

"I won't. Give it to me."

~~~

They had driven another mile or so before the taillights became large again. They squinted into the gloom. Judging the exact number of vehicles was impossible, but there were several sets of taillights.

"*In your strength, I can crush an army*," Mervyn muttered.

"What did you say?" Ruth asked. She leaned forward between the seats.

"A line from a Psalm."

"Are you Christian?"

"Kind of."

"How can you be *kind of* a Christian?"

"I was raised Pentecostal. But I wasn't into speaking in tongues. Sounded like made-up babble to me, so I left. My dad was pissed, but my mom told him I could make up my own mind."

"So, what do you believe?"

"I believe in God." He jerked the wheel to the side, sending The Man's head against the side window with a loud smack. Mervyn grinned as the tall man grunted.

"What about Jesus?" Ruth prompted from the backseat.

"Yep."

"Are you born again?"

"If you mean did I have some sort of weird encounter with Jesus— then, no." He leaned into the wheel and studied the shadowed, rutted road. "I like the Bible, I like believing in God, I understand what Jesus did, but I don't like the Christian label. Too much evil done under that brand name."
~~~

Mervyn glanced at The Man who sat bleary-eyed, still blinking the drugged sleep from his eyes, and rubbing his head. "Wouldn't you agree, Hezekiah?"

Ruth sputtered. "Hezah... Wait— What? He's a Christian?"

"I suppose so. More like a Christian sect, though. My family knew his family. That's how I hooked up with him. We went to his father's cell church for a while. His dad—I mean his *daddy* was a preacher. My mom called it quits when his daddy brought in a tub of rattlers one day—she was having no part of snake-handling. My dad and I didn't mind as much—we've handled lots of snakes—but only when necessary. His daddy told people they could pick up a snake, get bitten—and the Lord would save them. My dad told him it was a crock. He reported him. The RCMP ended his snake services."

"A Christian? You're a Christian?" Ruth asked. She stared wide-eyed at The Man, but he didn't turn to look at her. "Are you completely nuts?"

The Man remained silent.

"Okay," Mervyn said. The bright red taillights of a school bus blazed out of the darkness; they were sandwiched between at least four other vehicles. "Time to put our plan—as puny as it is—into action."

Ruth's hands grew slick with sweat. She pulled off her gloves and wiped her palms on her jeans. The electrical tie hung like an oversized bracelet off one arm. She fingered the Uzi. She tried to remember the sound, the feel of bullets leaving its barrel, its recoil against her shoulder, but all she could see was a blurry, slow motion movie of silent, dark shapes—arms flailing, bodies falling.

Third-person shooter.

"Here we go," Mervyn muttered. "Lord, help us." He blasted the horn.

Ruth's heart jumped. Fear, fueled by the fizz of adrenaline, rose like a tidal wave inside her. Her heart pounded madly, so wildly that it made her head ache. She sank down and peeked between the seats, through the front window. They had almost caught up to the rear vehicle, a big pickup truck. Mervyn laid on the horn again. The truck slowed and stopped; the rest of the vehicles continued moving forward.

"This is crazy. This is just crazy," Mervyn muttered. "How do I do this, God?" Mervyn carefully slowed his truck.

The Man chuckled. "If we both pray, won't our prayers cancel each other out?"

"Yuk it up, buddy, 'cause your happy days are coming to an end." Mervyn thrust the gearshift into *Park*. "Don't do anything dumb," he warned. "If I'm dead, then you're dead, too." He opened the door. "Keep that gun on him, Ruth." He leapt out, and ran up to the driver's side of the truck in front of them.

Ruth craned her neck to peer over the dashboard and out the window. She saw Mervyn tap on the driver's window and then start up an animated conversation. Out of the corner of her eye, she caught movement. The Man had changed the position of his feet.

Why?

He moved his feet again, drawing them closer to the seat and twisting his body slightly. A quick calculation.

The gearshift!

"Don't!" she commanded. "Just don't."

She pushed the barrel of the machine gun against his ribs. She tried to catch his eyes, tried to anticipate his move. A slight shift in his gaze was all the warning she had as he brought up his right foot. In an instant, his foot was aloft. Ruth launched forward and tried to stop his foot with her hand. She cried out when his boot connected with her outstretched fingers.

"Dammit!" She jammed the butt of the gun into his ribs.

The Man gasped. He struggled for breath.

"Stop...or I'll hit you in the head," Ruth threatened. "And I mean it."

Ruth shook out her hand, and then stuffed her bruised fingers into her armpit. She rocked with the pain. The Man made small hitching sounds as he chased his breath.

Mervyn was still chatting with the driver of the other truck. Suddenly, he turned away.

Was he coming back?

A man got out of the passenger side of the truck and walked around to Mervyn. Ruth panicked.

He's bringing someone back here?

Blood whooshed in her ears. She watched as the pair made their way around the side of her truck. She could hear voices, but no words. She risked a look through the back window.

At first, she saw two men, but after a moment, she saw only one. She saw the tarp fly back, more movement, and then the tarp was pulled down. Then Mervyn ran past her window, back to the other truck. This time, the driver got out. The pair chatted amicably. They walked to the back, and the scenario repeated itself. A minute later, Mervyn ran past the window again. He jumped into the second truck, shoved it into gear, and pulled it over to the side of the road. Its lights went out. A few moments later, Mervyn jumped back into their truck. He pushed the truck into gear.

"Switch-o—change-o," he said. "Let's hope nobody noticed."

"What did you do?" Ruth looked from the back of their truck to the deserted truck on the side of the road. "Did you kill them?"

"No. Just knocked them out. I know those guys. Good old boys. Like to party. I'll give them a chance. Wake them up in about a half hour, and then let them walk back to their truck." He stepped on the gas. "We've got a bus to catch."

~ ~ ~

After dumping the two men further up the highway, Mervyn continued his pursuit of the women and children. It didn't take them long to catch up. The roadway was flatter and they could see two trucks in the lead, far in the distance, then the school bus, and then a third truck. He sped up.

"You planning to do the same thing you did to the other two guys?" Ruth asked.

"Gonna try."

"Oh, boy..." she said, her thought trailing away, unfinished. "Oh, turn off the ignition when you get out."

"Why?"

"He tried kicking the gearshift." She held up her fingers—her index finger was slightly crooked and bruised. "I stopped him."

Mervyn glanced at her hand and then back to the gearshift. "The gearshift is locked. More likely he was going after the horn." He examined Ruth's fingers. "Sorry about that."

"I'll survive," Ruth said. She glanced at The Man. "But if he tries something like that again, I am going to bash him in the head." She prodded The Man. "You hear me?"

The Man stared ahead.

They caught up to the next truck, and Mervyn went through the same process as before. Ruth heaved a sigh of relief when he hopped back into the cab. The other truck was now parked, lights out, on the side of the road.

"Like shooting fish in a barrel," he said.

"What's the next move?"

"The guys in the front trucks are probably not even watching what's going on behind them. I'd guess they're waiting for an attack from the front. I'm going to pull alongside the bus and see who's driving. If it's one of the women, I'll get her to pull over, and I'll get on the bus. If it's a guy, I'll send you out as my prisoner. He'll buy my story about adding you to the busload. Will you be able to fake being tied up?"

Ruth slipped her hand back and forth through the electrical tie. "Yeah, no problem."

"I'm guessing there'll be two guys—one driving, one keeping an eye on the women. I doubt they're watching through the back window."

"What if they have a radio?"

"Don't worry about it. We'll handle it." He glanced back at Ruth. "You ready?"

"Yeah, let's do this."

Ruth hunkered down again.

~ ~ ~

The bus came into view. The driver slowed, swerved, and then sped up again on the clear stretches of pavement. Ruth could see the outlines of heads and bodies bouncing and jogging in rhythm to the ruts and snowdrifts on the road.

"God, they must be so cramped in there," she said.

"I'm not going to use the horn this time," Mervyn said.

He caught up and pulled alongside the left side of the bus. He motioned to the driver—it was the woman they had assigned earlier to drive the second bus. She recognized The Man and slowed immediately. A moment later, a man with a long beard looked through the side window. He signaled his recognition of The Man, and the bus came to a halt.

Mervyn stopped the truck. "Watch him." He got out and loped around the front of the bus. Ruth lost sight of him. The wait was almost unbearable. She wanted desperately to rush to her children. But she remained low, and hidden, her gun jammed into The Man's ribs.

Suddenly, Mervyn appeared. Two men marched ahead of him. Mervyn followed, his gun drawn and pointed at their backs. Ruth sat up. Mervyn banged on her window.

"Help me," Mervyn said.

Ruth jumped from the truck and ran around to the back.

"We don't have much time," Mervyn cautioned. "If we don't keep moving, the guys up ahead are going to get suspicious." He threw electrical ties to her. "Tie them." Ruth did as instructed.

"Guys, I don't want to kill you, but I will," Mervyn said. "If you want to live, get into the backseat and stay quiet." The men obeyed. "Ruth, get that bus moving. I'll follow behind. I'll signal left or right, when I want you to turn."

Ruth ran to the bus. A huge cheer went up when she boarded. Sarah hugged her. "Oh, you made it. Thank, God." Sarah embraced her again.

"Go!" Ruth said to the driver. "Before they get suspicious." The bus rocked, creaked, and rumbled forward.

"Mommy," Mary screamed. Samuel clambered across bodies with his sister in close pursuit. Ruth grabbed her children and hugged them. Sarah stood nearby.

"Are you okay?" Sarah asked.

"Fine."

"How did you manage to get this far?"

"Mervyn. We have The Man, too."

"I know. I saw. How did you do that?"

"Long story— Fuma's dead."

"I thought so. Brad wouldn't let him get off the bus. He herded all of us out and crammed us in here. Good thing some of the kids are so small. But the roads are horrible."

"Brad—?" Ruth asked. "He's in one of the front trucks? Was Elizabeth with him?" Sarah shook her head. Ruth's face clouded with disappointment. "Oh... Is anybody hurt?"

"No— They didn't do a thing to us. We were surprised that he didn't put on a different driver."

"Well, he put two armed guards on board. That should have done the trick."

Ruth called for silence. "Those of you at the back— Watch the signal lights on Mervyn's truck."

"That's The Man's truck," Samuel corrected her.

"It's Mervyn's truck now, sweetheart." Ruth ruffled his hair. "Holler if he signals, okay?" The passengers at the back agreed.

Ruth searched for a spot to sit, but there was none. She sat in the door well instead. "You're doing great," she said to the bus driver. "Didn't know you could drive a bus— You holding up okay?"

"Tired, scared...like everyone else. But it's the story of our lives, right?"

"Hopefully, not for much longer. I want to go home."

"What's the plan from here?"

"I think when we get closer to Calgary...Mervyn is going to get us to detour to a secondary highway. He'll probably park and try to take down anyone who pursues us. That's my best guess."

"What happened to the guys in the other trucks?"

"He fooled them. Four were dropped off miles back, and two are in his backseat."

"Do you think we have a chance to get home today?" the bus driver asked.

"I doubt it. The roads— Remember all the abandoned cars we saw on our way down to Sunnyvale? And now there's snow."

They traveled several miles up the highway. The dark had receded and it was easier to see ahead. The bus driver skirted many a small disaster—high drifts, abandoned vehicles, broken tree branches, dead animals, and a semi truck jack-knifed across the road that nearly blocked the entire highway. The driver wriggled the bus through the small opening.

"Signal!" one of the teen girls hollered from the back.

Ruth jumped up, jamming her sore fingers against a support pole. "Ow...damn. Which way?"

"Right— I mean, left."

"Which one?" Ruth asked impatiently.

"Right," two more women said at once.

The driver slowed the bus and studied the turn-off. "This'll take us off the Trans-Canada. Looks like he wants us to cut up towards Drumheller." The driver eased the bus to the right. "It's not Edmonton, but at least it's a fair-sized city." She gave a small chuckle. "The kids will like the dinosaurs."

"We probably would have been better off turning earlier...on #56. It's a direct route," Ruth said, looking up from a bedraggled road map she had found in a compartment near the driver.

The driver shrugged.

"Is he following us?" Ruth called.

"Yes," several voices shouted.

"I wonder how much time we have before Brad realizes what's happened," Ruth said.

"Maybe that's why Mervyn had us take this highway..." the driver said. She slowed for a large drift, changed gears, inched around it, and then eased back onto open pavement. "He thinks Brad will expect us to stick to the major roads." The driver slowed again for debris, skirted it, and drove on.

"But this way will be a much longer drive," Ruth complained.

"I'll go as fast as I can."

The driver stepped on the accelerator.

~~~

Several miles passed. White-tailed deer, foraging in grain fields, looked up. They watched the long, yellow stranger growl by, flicked their ears, and returned to their high fiber breakfasts.

"It'll be light soon," Ruth said. "Look at that pretty sky."

Apricot hues filled the eastern sky, sending soft coral light falling like fairy rays on the faces of sleeping children and their exhausted mothers. Ruth surveyed the group—crammed three and four to a seat. Some of the older children lined the floor, their heads cushioned on rolled jackets; others sat erect, staring ahead like pasty-faced owls. Nobody spoke.

A tiny shot of hope filled her heart. She smiled. She stood and stretched. She placed her hand on the driver's shoulder. "Are you going to need a break?"

"Sweetheart, I will drive this thing till my eyeballs fall out of my head."

Ruth settled down on the top step in the door well. She had just begun to relax when a cry came from the back. She jumped up.

"Something's wrong!" Sarah said. She pointed to one of the owl-eyed children, a tall, skinny girl who was gesticulating madly.

"Look!" the girl screamed.
~~~

Chapter Thirty-Two

The Bright Red Scarf

RUTH LEAPT up and clambered down the aisle, clutching seat backs to vault over small sleeping bodies lying on the floor. She reached the back window and stared. Her mouth went dry.

"Stop the bus!" she screamed. "Stop! Let me off." She raced up to the front, trying to avoid tripping on the children who were carpeting the aisle. Mary and Samuel stared after their mother with wide eyes.

The driver stopped the bus and opened the doors.

Ruth grabbed the Uzi, slung her shoulder bag across her chest, and turned to the driver.

"Go— Get my children home! It's up to you now."

Ruth stomped down the stairs. She heard the hinged doors slap shut. The bus motored forward.

Ruth ran for the ditch.

METEOR TWISTED his truck's steering wheel, recovered from the skid, and drove on. He squinted into the rising sun. Snowbanks, compressed by the recent warm temperatures, glistened—their thin ice veneers reflecting golden morning light. He glanced into the rearview mirror. Six other trucks were keeping a steady pace behind him. He looked forward. Matthew's truck was barely visible. He stepped on the accelerator. He didn't want to fall behind. Medicine Hat was still many hours away.

Vast expanses of pastureland, covered in pristine blankets of white, stretched out on either side of the road. Light diamonds danced like fire sprites in the sunlight. Meteor reached for a pair of sunglasses and pulled them on. Smoke from a faraway chimney spiraled into the air, announcing the presence of another human or group of humans. Meteor mused as to their identities:

A family? A bunch of Crazies? A lonely old woman? A lonely old man?

Overhead, birds changed direction and swooped down, settling in low shrubs that ran along a farmer's field.

"Sparrows..."

"What?" Meteor asked, jolted from his thoughts.

"Sparrows...that flock of birds."

Meteor turned to face the man riding shotgun beside him. "Oh, your namesake." He grinned.

Sparrow had joined their camp in the late fall, a few months after the battle. He was a good fit—well liked by the men, admired by the boys, and sought after by the girls. However, he spent most of his time with Anna.

Anna had taken Simon's loss hard, especially with the impending birth of Simon's baby. She closed herself off to all but her closest friends, and would have nothing to do with any of the men who showed interest in her. Nevertheless, Sparrow was seen with her frequently. More and more, Sparrow managed to bring her out of her shell...and to make her laugh. Meteor's thoughts switched to the women in his life.

Martha. Georgie.

The two women were so unlike one another, and while he preferred Martha's fire and her wild spirit, he needed Georgie's adoration and her sweetness. It had been a long time since he had been with only one woman. So, he had decided. As soon as they got back from this rescue mission...

"I'm thinking of announcing a moving-in day," Meteor said.

"Georgie?" Sparrow asked.

"Yep."

"Congratulations."

"And you? Any plans?"

Sparrow smiled.

MATTHEW ARCHED his back and stretched an arm behind his head. Jonah stared out the side window. Three more men rode in the truck's backseat. A map, spread out between Matthew and Jonah, showed the province's major roadways, the secondary highways, and the little-known backroads. They had plotted a course the night before, concentrating on the quickest route with the most passable roads. They had considered taking highway #14 to Viking, dropping south on #36, and taking that all the way down to the Trans-Canada #1 highway, but Matthew nixed it as too iffy, too much open space, and too few towns to scavenge should they get into trouble. Now, they were headed south on #21 in the direction of New Norway.

The going was slower than before the Change, but the roads were good, and if the weather remained kind, they would be in the vicinity of Three Hills in only a couple of hours. From there, it would be only about an hour to the Trans-Canada. Matthew suspected the super highway would be completely blown clear of snow, and they would be able to make better time to Medicine Hat.

A sign on the right side of the road pointed to the Edmonton airport, but the road was clogged with snow and debris. A red pickup truck lay on its side in the ditch, half hidden by snow. Matthew craned his neck. "Don't see any bodies... Do you?"

Jonah shook his head.

A long row of round hay bales, curled slightly like a giant child's play beads, lay in sleepy silence on a farmer's field. A farmyard filled with small red sheds and ribbed silver silos sat nearby. Jonah pointed at an adjoining pasture where a herd of horses milled around a small pond. The pond was gray with ice, but a dark patch near the edge shimmered in the sunlight.

"People living there," Jonah said. "Someone's broken the ice." He scoffed as they passed a sign still advising a *Total Fire Ban*. "Thanks for telling us."

The trucks passed by old homesteads—the weathered-gray buildings leaned into the snow, their slat boards rotted or missing; their empty windows stared like blind eyes revealing nothing of their history. Old farm machinery—non-computerized, ancient artifacts of the past, stuck out of the snow like alien insects—their rusted metal legs and arms reaching for the sky.

Matthew grunted. "See those old things? We'll probably be using those soon."

"You think the tractors will still run?"

"Tractors?" Matthew asked incredulously. "We'll be hitching plows to horses."

"Oh," Jonah said. "I don't ride."

Matthew gave a short laugh. "You will soon. If you want to get around."

Jonah did not respond.

A lone coyote, its forelegs spread wide, looked up to watch the trucks pass by. The animal lost interest and shoved his nose deep into the snow.

"What's he doing?" Jonah asked with a little laugh.

"Chasing mice, I suspect."

The radio squawked.

"Things still looking good up there? Over." It was the pony-tailed captain.

"Still clear," Jonah replied.

"Copy that."

Jonah put the radio back on his belt. He glanced at Matthew. "I'm glad to be on the road again. I miss Simon," he added softly.

"Me, too," Matthew said. "Good man."

The men in the backseat agreed.

RUTH CLUTCHED the Uzi to stop it from banging against her chest as she ran down the embankment. She stumbled when soggy snow sucked at her boots. She crouched down and waited. She couldn't tell how much trouble Mervyn was in, but she had seen the truck swerve and lurch crookedly to a halt, half in and half out of the ditch, stopped by a pile of snow. She prayed that Mervyn would jump out, unharmed. The doors began to open. The two men, the ones Mervyn had taken prisoner from the bus, jumped to the ground. She watched the men struggle with their bonds.

No sign of Mervyn. Ruth raised the gun. *Where are you?*

She willed Mervyn to step from the truck.

The two men were speaking excitedly, although she couldn't make out what they were saying. However, she could guess what they were doing. One was trying to pull a knife from a pouch on the other's belt. She peered down the gun sights.

First-person shooter.

One of the men looked up and shouted. Ruth's head whipped up.

Did they see me? She slipped down the bank. Then she saw what had gotten their attention.

The driver's door pushed open, and Mervyn fell to the ground. Meanwhile, one of the men managed to free the knife from the other man's pouch. He flipped it open and frantically sawed at the tight, plastic band around the first man's wrists.

Ruth sighted the gun, pressed the grip safety, and fired. The man with the knife slumped to the ground. The other man, his wrists now free, ducked and ran behind the truck. Ruth scrambled out of the ditch.

"Mervyn!" she screamed. "Behind you."

Ruth reached the other side of the road just in time to see their former prisoner grab Mervyn by the throat. He hauled him to his feet. She could see blood streaming down Mervyn's face. It spilled down the front of his parka.

"I'll break his neck," the man called out. "Put down your gun."

Ruth's world transitioned into slow motion.

Shooting one meant shooting both. Giving up meant her death, too. Unacceptable. Please, make him too tough to kill...

"Kill him, and I'll kill you in a second." Ruth raised her gun as she spoke. "Let him go, and you can live. Make your choice." Ruth dropped to one knee. "You've got to the count of three."

Ruth planted the gun against her shoulder, and peered down the barrel. A rock steadiness overtook her, and she settled the gun's sights over the man's chest.

The man hesitated, and then abruptly, he released Mervyn. He stepped back, and raised his hands.

"On your stomach," Ruth commanded. The man obeyed.

She ran to Mervyn and pulled him into a sitting position. The other man pushed up from the ground. Ruth caught the movement. "Down!" He dropped back down again.

Mervyn groaned. He touched his eye. Blood ran profusely from a gaping cut near his eyebrow.

"Wasn't expecting it," he mumbled. "Not sure what they hit me with."

Ruth opened her coat and tore a strip from her flannel shirt. She wadded the fabric and shoved it against the wound.

"It's a big cut." She stood up. "I'll get snow."

She rose, and pointed the gun at the man on the ground.

"Stay!"

METEOR STEERED around abandoned vehicles littering the highway—Fords, Toyotas, Pontiacs, Dodges, big cars, little cars, pickup trucks, SUVs. Victims of winter's frigid embrace, the vehicles sat entombed in snow and in silence, immobilized in hibernation, waiting for a driver that would never come. Off to their right, an abandoned Esso station, its doors and windows smashed, poked out of snowdrifts. Vehicles lay strewn across its parking lot, too.

"Can I ask you something?" Sparrow blurted.

"Sure."

"Why do you stay with Matthew? I know you, Meteor...this life isn't you. What's keeping you at the camp?"

Meteor shrugged. "The Change— I guess it changed me, too."

The radio interrupted them.

"Everyone good back there?" they heard Jonah ask. "Over."

"Some engine trouble back here," said a man from a truck in the rear. "I don't think we're gonna make it. Over."

Radio silence.

Then Jonah's voice: "Matthew says we're pulling over at Bashaw."

RUTH CHECKED the snow compress. The blood flow had slowed, but the wound still gaped. Mervyn, one hand pushing on the bloody rag, pulled himself unsteadily to his feet. The driver's door still hung open. He grabbed the steering wheel and tried hoisting himself into the truck. Ruth stopped him.

"You're kidding me, right? You can't drive." Mervyn paused and then agreed. Ruth helped him lean against the front of the truck. "Give me a second." She backed off, ensuring she had room to use the Uzi.

"Get up," she called to the man on the ground. "Now, start walking." The man obeyed, and headed back up the road in the direction they had come. Ruth watched him go. When he was several yards away, she ran back to Mervyn.

"I'll get you into the truck. Just hang on." She reached for the pistol hanging in his holster. "Good thing, he didn't get this."

She heard a noise and checked around the truck. The man she had sent away was nowhere in sight. "Damn..." she muttered. She swung open the passenger door. The Man still sat there, trussed up like a calf at a rodeo. He grinned.

"What now, Ruth? You in over your head?"

"Shut up." She looked down the road. "I'm deciding what to do with your ass." She still couldn't see the other man. An argument began in her head.

What now? Shoot him? Keep him? Dump him? God, what do I do?

Another man made her decision for her.

MATTHEW'S MEN stretched as they left their vehicles. Two mechanics ran over to the ailing truck. The hood was raised, and the men went to work. Ten minutes later, one of them found Matthew.

"No good. We'll have to leave that one behind. Thermostat...it'll take too long to fix."

"But you can fix it?" Matthew asked.

"Sure, if I can pull one from another truck—"

"Lots of trucks around here," Matthew said. "There's a UFA and an Esso over there," he said, pointing up the road. A second mechanic joined them.

"So?" the man asked, wiping grease from his hands on an orange rag.

"You two stay," Matthew said. "We'll take some of the supplies from your truck."

"That means you won't have a mechanic with you," the first mechanic said.

Matthew rubbed his chin with one hand. "You're right...you stay. He goes with us," he said, motioning to the second mechanic. "If you get the truck fixed, go back to the camp. If not, wait for us. We'll pick you up later."

Matthew turned and hollered at a group of men standing near the ditch. "Trojan!"

"You want me to stay behind?" Trojan sputtered after hearing Matthew's orders. He was clearly unhappy with the decision.

"You've got a new baby," Matthew said. "Fix the truck and go back."

Trojan scowled.

Seven trucks pulled away. Trojan and the mechanic watched them leave. Trojan stared at the offending engine.

"Like hell," he said. "I never get left behind. Let's get this fucker fixed."

RUTH FELT the man's presence before she saw him. Instinct made her duck and whirl around. His fist went wide and connected with the doorframe, instead of her head. She raised Mervyn's pistol and fired. The man clutched at his shoulder and dropped to his knees beside his dead friend.

Terror and shock rippled through Ruth—they melded into rage. She stood over the injured man, her gun hand shaking. She screamed:

"Why did you do that? I wouldn't have shot you, you idiot!" The man groaned and rocked forward. "You asshole!" She kicked at him. "Why? Why did you make me do that?" She trembled violently.

Ruth preferred the cocoon of looking down the gun barrel from a distance, seeing her quarry as shapes; she didn't want to see faces—she didn't want to know they had faces. Laughter coming from inside the truck made her redirect her fury.

"Shut the fuck up!" Ruth said, turning abruptly. She drew back her fist and punched The Man in the mouth. His head rocked back against the headrest and his lip split. Blood trickled down his chin.

"You— It's because of you that I have to do this shit. I hate it. I hate you. I hate all of it." Ruth raised her arms and screamed at the sky. She began to cry.

Mervyn came around the side of the truck. He kicked the bleeding, injured man out of the way, and reached for Ruth. She was still screaming:

"No more! I can't take any more!" She swiped at her tears and wrestled her way out of Mervyn's arms. "This son-of-a-bitch is not going to control our lives any longer."

She bent and grabbed the switchblade that had fallen to the ground earlier. She pushed by Mervyn. He tried to stop her.

"Whoa, Ruth." Ruth glared at him. Mervyn stepped aside.

Ruth hovered over The Man. She raised the knife.

"I want to drive this into your heart. I want you to hurt the way you've hurt others. I hate you with everything inside me. I want you dead." Her eyes blazed. "But I don't murder people. You do. I don't steal children. I don't turn women into whores. You do that!" Spittle flew from her lips.

The Man said nothing, but he shrank back into his seat.

"I want you dead. So badly—" The knife quivered in her hand.

Suddenly, Ruth stopped yelling and a calm settled over her. Her breathing slowed and she lowered the knife, but as she did, she leaned into The Man's face. Her tone was icy cool.

"Just give me a reason, you bastard. Just give me a reason..."

The Man eyed her. "I wish some of my men had your spirit."

"Don't talk to me. You are a devil. Whatever your *daddy* was—he was *no* Christian. Your soul is black."

"But I believe—"

"Don't tell me what you believe...I don't want to know what you believe. And I'll tell you this—you are headed for the hottest spot in Hell."

"Ruth—?" Mervyn said softly. "We've got to go...we have to catch that bus...before..."

"Get in," she said.

"What about him?" Mervyn asked, motioning to the man she had shot.

"Leave him. He made his bed— Let him lie in it."

Mervyn raised his eyebrows, but said nothing.

Ruth helped Mervyn into the backseat and closed the door. She gripped the front passenger door, but before she closed it, she spoke:

"The only reason I'm keeping you alive, is because I think Matthew should have the right to decide what'll happen to you. But believe me...I'll happily bring back a dead body." She poked The Man hard in the chest. "You got that?"

The Man grinned, a condescending gesture that Ruth missed because she had slammed the door.

Ruth got into the driver's seat, put the truck into gear, and pulled back onto the road. Her knuckles were white, and her jaw was set. She rammed the truck through a large pile of snow, skidding, and nearly toppling the vehicle. Mervyn reached over and touched her shoulder.

"Ruth— Just a little slower. You're gonna kill us."

Ruth eased off on the gas pedal. She took a shuddering breath. "I forgot about your cut. Sorry." She slowed and stopped the truck. She turned to The Man.

"First aid kit?"

"Under the backseat," he said.

JONAH STUDIED the map, sighed, and then lowered it to his lap. He rubbed his eyes and yawned. He had grown bored with the scenery—the endless rolling fields that paralleled the highway, the steady parade of barns—red barns, white barns, gray barns, even one green barn—farm equipment, roadside shrubs, and marshlands textured in reedy bulrushes and cattails. And crows. So many crows.

Jonah looked back at the map. "We should have cut over at Bashaw and taken #53...cut down #56...through Stettler. That would have taken us through Drumheller." He traced the roadway with his finger. "I've never been there. I heard they have hoodoos there. Never seen hoodoos. You?"

"Yeah, a few times," Matthew said.

"Are they cool?"

"Yep. People who visit them don't believe they're real...like someone carved them and put them there."

"So they look like statues?"

"Not exactly. They're massive pillars of eroded rock capped with a mushroom top. You can see the layers of hardened sediment that formed them. Very prehistoric looking." Matthew rubbed his head. "The natives believed hoodoos would come to life at night to protect them from their enemies."

Jonah's eyes brightened. "I'd sure like to see them some day."

"They've got dinosaurs all over town, too," Matthew continued. "Bright colors. Like Dino in the Flintstones cartoon—you know that cartoon? Cutesy, but fun. Kids like them. But the best thing is the giant T-rex at the tourist center."

Jonah picked up the map. "Next big town is Delburne," he observed eagerly. "Drumheller's not far from there."

Matthew checked his watch. He glanced out the window. The highways were relatively clear, thanks to prairie winds that had blown them free of snow. "We're making good time."

They passed by the Nevis gas plant. "Make a note of that," Matthew said. "We'll come back here and check it out."

Jonah agreed and began watching the scenery again.

Suddenly he laughed and pointed. Some creative soul had designed a freestanding, life-sized metal silhouette in the shape of a cowboy on horseback—a small herd of flat metal cattle grazed ahead of him.

They made their way across the Red Deer River—the bridge was wide and clear. Jonah leaned in close to his window to study a campground off to their right. RVs and trailers, of all shapes and sizes, could be seen through the trees. Smoke curled out of the smokestack of a large cookhouse, but there were no signs of people.

More marshlands. More iced-over ponds. More fields. More fence posts. More power poles. A rest stop announcing *Alberta's History* got Jonah's attention. He pointed at two tiny buildings.

"I like being a guy," he quipped. "We don't need no stinkin' rest stops."

Matthew chuckled.

TROJAN CLAPPED the mechanic on the back. The man slammed the truck hood, wiped his hands on a rag, pushed back his cap, and wiped the sweat from his forehead with his shirtsleeve. They had gotten rid of their jackets nearly an hour before.

"Not bad, hey?" The mechanic checked his watch. "Record time."

"Let's go."

"Which way?"

Trojan grinned. "To the party, of course. But not #21— Let's take #56 instead. We might beat them there."

MATTHEW SIGNALED and turned right at a sign indicating Delburne and Three Hills. Crows flew overhead. Several sat on the side of the road, tearing at a white object. One flew off with something that looked like a rabbit's leg hanging from its beak. The thought made Matthew hungry. They had begun to eat rabbit stew back on the compound, and he liked it.

"I've gotta take a leak," Jonah said.

"I thought you didn't need no stinkin' rest stops," Matthew reminded him with a crooked grin.

"I don't. I can piss anywhere."

"We'll stop in Delburne."

Soon they saw a sign for the *Village of Delburne*. Matthew signaled and turned left. The rest of the trucks followed. They drove down a gentle, winding road into the town. They passed a campground filled with tent trailers and RVs. On the left, they saw a quaint old diner advertising 100% Alberta beef burgers. Next was a playground lined with empty picnic tables and colorful climbing toys. Father up, they saw a sidewalk sign promoting a *Strawberry Social* at the gospel church. But the town was dead silent.

Nothing. Nobody. Not a soul.

Were they all dead? Or were they in hiding?

Matthew drove by the small Anthony Henday museum, several boarded up businesses, a small, white United church, a bakery boasting *Cakes by Asheena*, and a *Doggie* spa—all without seeing any signs of people. He turned the truck around, went back up the main street, parked, and got out. The rest of the trucks pulled over, too. The men gathered.

"Take a break, guys," Matthew said. "Twenty minutes." Someone brought out water bottles and bags of cookies. Matthew grabbed a bottle and several cookies, and walked off. Jonah saw him leave and ran after him.

They turned down a side street and found a yard filled with antique vehicles and rusted farm machinery. Matthew stopped to admire an old Ford coupe. Its back fender was rusted, but the body and all its windows were intact.

"Somebody took good care of her," Matthew said. He finished a cookie and walked around the car.

A glint, a flash of bright red color caught his eye, and he turned. A small sports car was parked near a long building. It was nearly hidden, but its candy apple finish stood out against the reddish-brown paint covering the building.

"Wow," Jonah said. "Look at that. What is it?"

"An Austin Healey." Matthew walked over and ran his hand over the tiny car's silken finish. "Where's your owner?" he asked as though the car was capable of answering.

A small sound from inside the building made both men drop their hands to the guns on their hips. They backed away, keeping their eyes on the door. Another sound made the pair duck down.

The door creaked and opened a crack. A moment later, a man's head appeared. The man checked right and left, and then he walked toward the sports car.

He was elderly, with richly weathered skin—almost walnut in color. Heavy eyebrows crowned clear, copper eyes; thick wrinkles crisscrossed his forehead and clean-shaven face. His short-cropped silver hair was covered by a hunter green ball cap. He was dressed in dark brown pants, a long-sleeved shirt, and a Scottish plaid vest, in greens and browns. The man pulled on brown leather driving gloves, rubbed his hands together, and checked the tilt of his cap in a side view mirror. Matthew suppressed a chuckle as the man stepped back to admire his ensemble, clapped his hands together, and then pulled the driver's door open.

"Hey, buddy," Matthew said. The man yelped and looked wildly around him. "It's okay. We won't hurt you. Just keep those nice gloves where we can see them."

"I—I don't have anything of value," the man stammered. He held his hands in the air above his head.

"We don't want anything," Matthew assured him. "Just want to talk to you."

"Where did you guys come from?" the man asked. His eyes flitted nervously between Matthew and Jonah, and the guns on their hips.

"Edmonton. What's your name?" Matthew asked.

"Stewart. They call me Stew, for short." The man bobbed his head in greeting.

"I'm Matthew. This is Jonah. Is this your town?"

"No. Just passing through. I knew the guy who used to live here. Bought my foreign car parts from him."

"Where do you live?"

"Here and there."

"You've been driving around in this all winter?" Matthew asked, his voice heavy with doubt.

"No. Just pulled her out a week ago. The snow melted enough to take her for a run."

"So, where do you live?"

"I used to live in Drumheller. I live mostly in Big Valley now." The man paused and regarded them for a moment. "You guys are sure far from home."

"We're headed to Medicine Hat."

"You're not going through Drumheller, are you?" the man asked. He didn't wait for an answer. "That place is cursed."

"Cursed?" Jonah asked. "What do you mean?"

"Long story, but you should stay away from there."

"Why?"

"Taken over."

"By who?"

"You ever heard of The Man?"

Jonah rolled his eyes. "Yeah, we know The Man."

"You his friends?" Fear lit the man's eyes and he glanced at their guns again.

"No," Matthew said, shaking his head. "We are most assuredly NOT his friends."

Matthew checked his watch. "We've got to go." He pointed up the street. "We're heading off. Our men are waiting for us. Do you want to join us?"

The man gave his head a firm shake. "No, thanks. I do just fine on my own." He opened the car door and slipped inside.

"Good luck," Matthew said. "Stay safe."

"You, too," the older man answered. "And stay away from Drumheller. The Man made life miserable for everybody who lived there. Kidnapped the women and children. Killed the men."

"Is everyone gone?" Jonah asked.

"Not sure. All I know is that the town belongs to The Man. And I want no part of him. So, I stay away. And you should, too."

The man started the car's engine, revved it, threw the car into gear, and sped off. Matthew and Jonah watched as the man raised a gloved hand and waved good-bye.

"All by himself," Jonah said. "How does he survive?"

"I don't know," Matthew said. "But he's doing something right." Matthew began walking back to the main street. "I wonder if Martha is right about Medicine Hat. Maybe the women and kids were taken to Drumheller."

"It's a possibility," Jonah said. They continued to walk. "It's a good possibility," he repeated.

"The guy was so adamant about us not going there..." Matthew mused. "I wonder..." His thought trailed off.

"You know we could still bump over on #590 and head towards Big Valley," Jonah said. "Drop down from there on #56. Might be faster. Highway #56 runs straight into the Trans-Canada."

"And will that take us through Drumheller?" Matthew asked with a grin.

Jonah gave a sheepish chuckle. “Yeah.”

“Tell the men,” Matthew said. “You’ll see your hoodoos...and the biggest dinosaur in the world.” He clapped Jonah on the back. “Let’s find out what The Man is up to.”

THE BUS DRIVER got out of the bus, leaving the folding doors ajar. She squinted. The sunlight reflecting off snow banking the highway was so brilliant that it hurt her eyes. She pulled over at an intersection; a left turn would take her to #21 and north to Edmonton; a right turn would take her to #56 and north to Drumheller. She glanced at her watch. She sighed. They weren’t making good time. In some spots, the poor highway had slowed them down to a crawl.

She rotated around, her boots crunching on the dirty pavement. She looked back down the road to see if Mervyn and Ruth were coming, but the road was barren of everything except for a few magpies that swooped and soared, their indigo blue feathers ablaze in the sunlight. One of the mothers walked up to her.

“The kids really need a break,” the woman said. “Can’t we stop here for a little while? For a bathroom break, at least? But longer than the other breaks?” They had stopped along the way for quick pee breaks, but once the kids did their business, they were herded immediately back on board. “Give them a chance to run around for a bit,” the mother added.

The bus driver took a deep breath of the earthy, spring air. “Yes,” she said. “Twenty minutes. That’ll give Ruth and Mervyn a chance to catch up to us.”

MATTHEW’S TRUCKS passed by the Big Valley turn-off, and turned right, heading south to Drumheller. The highway was dotted with piles of rotting snow and wide puddles of gray water, but overall the roadway was clear, thanks to prairie winds. The highway was arrow straight, and Matthew could see for miles, up to the horizon. He pressed down on the accelerator.

“Might as well make up some time.”

Jonah opened his window and leaned into the breeze. “It feels like spring.”

The scenery began to change: the marshes were more numerous, with greater expanses of open water; the rolling hills were now dotted with scrub brush; the snow cover on the fields was spotty, allowing the prickly yellow remnants of old crops to poke through.

They whipped by a *Rowleywood* sign. Jonah gave Matthew a questioning look.

"Rowley...it's a kind of old west ghost town," Matthew said. "They drive an old steam train into it out of Stettler. Actors rob the train. That sort of thing."

They passed by a small power station, its cables adorned with white ceramic insulators that glistened in the sunlight.

"Well, there's a pile of useless junk," Jonah observed.

THE BUS DRIVER checked her watch. Twenty minutes had passed. Children ran every which way, screaming with delight at having been released from their yellow prison. Mothers faced the sun, their eyes closed, reveling in the warmth of the rays and their first hours as free people again. The driver checked the road, in all three directions.

Nothing.

"Time to go," she said. The children protested, but they obeyed their mothers. Soon everyone was back on board.

"Which way?" Sarah asked.

"I'm nervous. If I go west...there aren't a lot of towns through that way. And if we run into trouble..."

"So, you think going through Drumheller is the best idea?" The driver nodded. "Then let's go."

The bus swung right. Suddenly, it stopped. The doors swung open. Sarah ran out with a bright red scarf in her hand. She charged into the ditch and up the other side. On a fencepost, she tied the scarf into a big red bow. She got back on the bus, cheeks flushed.

"There— Now they'll know which way we turned."

RUTH TRIED to make up for lost time, but it had taken several minutes to dress Mervyn's cut. He was dozing on the backseat. She desperately hoped he didn't have a concussion, but she would deal with that later. Her damaged finger throbbed and now her knuckles were turning purple, too. She glanced at The Man. He had remained very quiet, moving only to touch his lip—he dabbed at it with a chunk of gauze that Ruth had given to him.

"You made a small tactical error back there," he said.

"I thought I told you to shut up."

"My men have radios."

"Are you trying to make me throw you out of this truck?"

"Just sayin'..."

Ruth checked the rearview mirror. There were no signs of any other vehicles, and no dust in the distance. "We'll be fine," she said.

Ruth stopped at the T-intersection. She leaned over the steering wheel. They had discussed this. The bus driver had assumed that Mervyn wanted them to go through Drumheller. Signs indicated the city of dinosaurs was to the right. But highway #21 was to the left. Ruth hesitated. Then she saw the scarf.

"Thank you," she said swinging the truck to the right.

The Man chuckled softly. Ruth shot him a dirty look.

"What now?" she asked sharply.

"The scarf."

Chapter Thirty-Three

Something Divine

HOT SUNSHINE streamed in through the windows. The children shed their outer clothing like butterflies emerging from cocoons. Many were groggy and dozed across their mothers' laps, or in the aisle. The windows were down, and a sweet, early spring breeze filled the bus. Sarah passed out the lunches. She was grateful that Brad's men had listened to her when she had asked them to collect the tubs from the other bus. The tubs took precious seating room, but there would be enough food—if carefully doled out—for several days. She gazed at the passing scenery from her vantage point in the door well. Still so much snow, especially in the ditches, but the drifts lining the road were ragged and dirty—cratered by the hot sun. She saw a farm in the distance with a barn and a house. No smoke poured from the chimney, and there was no activity in the yard.

Strange, she thought. *No people. Not a soul.*

"I wonder if we'll see people in Drumheller," Sarah said.

"I'm sure we will. It's a fair-sized city," the bus driver answered. She gave a huge yawn and stretched out an arm.

Sarah looked concerned. "Do you need a nap?"

"In Drumheller— We'll find a motel. I'll sleep then."

"It would be nice to see people," Sarah continued.

"Not so sure they'll think it'll be so nice to see—" The driver gave a little gasp. "Oh my God! What's that? It's not—"

Sarah cried out in alarm. "Oh no—"

The sunny day had lost its charm.

RUTH YAWNED and the truck careened slightly. Mervyn stirred in the backseat.

"Uhhh..." he groaned.

"You're awake," Ruth said, looking into the rearview mirror. "How're you feeling?"

"Better— Pass the water..." Ruth handed back a canteen. "Can we stop?" he asked.

"Stop?" Ruth asked.

"Bathroom..."

"Oh, sure," Ruth said with a grin. "Sorry."

"Me, too," The Man said.

Ruth glanced at him. For just a moment, she wanted to tell him he could just pee in his pants, but then she remembered the scent of urine from her kids' peed pants, and she quelled the impulse. She pulled over.

"Are we on #21?" Mervyn asked.

"No, we're headed to #56—"

"We're headed to Drumheller?" Mervyn was aghast.

"Yes— Sarah and I figured you wanted us to go that way. Didn't you?"

Mervyn's face was intense. He swung open the back door.

"We've got to catch that bus."

"Why? What's the big deal?"

"Just not the best place for them to go. I'll tell you later." He jumped out of the truck. "I'll be right back."

A few minutes later, after giving The Man a chance to relieve himself, too, they were back on the road.

"No one following us..." Mervyn observed. "They've had time to catch us. Wonder where they are."

"Maybe Brad went looking for us, but he missed taking the highway we took."

"I hope so, but they've got to be looking for us." Mervyn rolled his head around on his neck and groaned again. "Gotta shake this headache."

"Look in the first aid kit— I think I saw Tylenol."

"Any signs of the bus yet?" Mervyn asked, pawing through bandages, rolled gauze, and tubes of medicinal ointments. "Found it."

Ruth sighed. "If that scarf was a real clue, we should be almost caught up to them." She yawned again.

"Want me to drive?" Mervyn asked.

"No, I'll make it."

JONAH TWISTED the map around. His finger followed their route. They had just crossed over #9, heading due south to Drumheller. He yawned loudly. They had been on the road since 7 A.M.—it was almost 11 o'clock. He yawned again and tapped the map.

"The *Tie-rell* dinosaur museum is there," Jonah noted enthusiastically.

"That's *Teer-rill*," Matthew corrected him. "I think it'll be closed for the season," he said with a grin twisting at the corners of his lips.

"Oh, funny..."

Matthew gave a small chuckle. "Can't do both. It's either the hoodoos...or the museum." Matthew checked the rearview mirror, assured himself that the trucks were still following behind, and sped up. "Besides the museum's not much to see from the road." Matthew skirted a massive puddle. "We'll need a break. Might as well be in the hoodoos. Tell the men."

Matthew stared out the window. Ponds, ponds, and more ponds—many were still iced over, but some shimmered with patches of open water. A pair of Canada geese stood sentry over their silvery, rippling turf. Undulating hills, a collage of yellow stubble and white snow, stretched to the horizon. Fence posts lined either sides of the highway—some stood staunchly erect, while others leaned haphazardly, some nearly parallel to the ground. An arc of fence posts dotted a gently rising hummock like cloves on a ham roast. All were linked by a trio of long strands of dark barbed wire.

Lots of fences. No people, Matthew thought. He wondered how many people had survived. If a census was taken, how many would there be?

In the millions? Still in the billions?

He doubted that. He suspected the world numbers—he assumed the power was down around the globe—were vastly reduced. Especially in the big cities. He mentally scoffed.

Take down the power grid and watch sophisticated, modern day, enlightened humans bumble about like bewildered bed bugs. With no clue of how to take care of themselves.

Matthew watched a flock of dark, feathered bodies streak across the highway. "Look at all the crows," he said, pointing to the sleek, black birds settling into the bushes. "We never used to see so many crows together in one place. The Change hasn't bothered them. They haven't just survived—they've thrived."

"Carrion," Jonah suggested. "Probably lots of dead things lying around with no one to bury them."

As if in confirmation of his theory, they came upon a small Dodge van—its hatch was open. Nearby, heaps of colorful clothing poked through snow. Crows pecked at the material. One grabbed a piece of something in his bill, and a feathered squabble broke out. The bird holding the treasure flew off, and landed a few feet away. The losers began excavating their own stringy portions. The men realized the clothing contained rotting flesh.

"Oh, God," Matthew said. "They must have died in early winter. The snow's melted. Their bodies are exposed. A feast for the crows."

SARAH'S EYES went wide as she leaned in to take a better look. She recognized the trucks—two of them. *Brad's trucks.* They were angled across the highway, bumper to bumper, blocking their path. The bus driver slowed down and was about to stop when Sarah spoke—low and determined:

"Don't stop."

Sarah turned to the women and older children who stared ahead in horrified silence. Only the babies and toddlers continued to squeal and laugh. "Get down. Protect your heads. And hold onto the babies."

The women responded immediately.

Sarah turned back to the driver. "Ram them," she said. "With everything we've got."

"That might kill us."

"This is a big machine. We can push them out of the way."

"But what if they shoot us?"

"They won't shoot us," Sarah said firmly. "Drive."

She settled in between the front seat and the metal door well, and awaited the impact.

Men lounging against the trucks suddenly jumped to attention as the bus bore down on them. Like startled rabbits, they shifted from foot to foot, trying to determine their next move. Finally, they sprinted. The drivers shoved their vehicles into gear in an attempt to clear the road. But the bus was coming fast. Too fast.

The heavy vehicle roared into the V-channel formed by the truck bumpers. It clipped both trucks, sending them sideways, one halfway into the ditch; the other now faced in the opposite direction, its rear bumper dangling. The bus rocked unsteadily upon impact, but the driver clung to the wheel—she steadied the huge machine, and drove on.

A loud cheer went up. Whoops and screeches filled the bus as the children responded to the driver's success. The bus driver looked into the rearview mirror and smiled. A big smile.

"You're good," Sarah said, admiration shining in her eyes. "That was awesome!"

"We aren't out of the woods yet," the driver said, motioning to the mirror. The men were scrambling, attempting to get the trucks back onto the road. "I don't think we're far from Drumheller now, but— How in hell do we lose them?"

A cry from behind distracted them. It came from a boy about seven years old.

"The giant dinosaur... Let's climb inside the head of the big T-rex!" he exclaimed. Other children, familiar with the popular tourist attraction, cheered the idea.

Sarah looked at the children in disbelief. "Kids... It's always about play." She turned back to the driver. "Should we try a side road?"

The driver veered around a small snowdrift, making Sarah sway backwards and clutch a support bar.

"Check the map again," the driver said. "A secondary highway should be okay, but not a gravel road. It'll be too greasy with this hot sun and melted snow. We'll slide into a ditch."

"If we go right, that will take us to #10...that goes into Drumheller." Sarah studied the map again. "Not sure about that connecting road though. Might be pretty rough." She looked behind her through the bus's back window. "Still clear back there."

The driver checked the rearview mirror, too, and nodded. "Maybe we should just barrel straight ahead. Take our chances. This highway has been nice and clear so far. They would be able to see our tire tracks when we turn off anyway."

"What if we pull over somewhere and hide? Let them pass, instead of trying to outrun them?"

"That's a good idea," the driver agreed. "But all I see are fields and one big long stretch of highway. Do you see any towns coming up?"

"Maybe this one— Dalum. It's at the junction."

The driver looked ahead at the open roadway and pressed down on the accelerator. "Dalum or bust."

MATTHEW'S EARS popped as he led his convoy into the deep valley leading toward Drumheller—Alberta's *City of Dinosaurs*. In spite of the immediacy of their mission, he couldn't help but admire and wonder at the eerie landscape of gnarled trees and scrubby vegetation that surrounded them. Glaciated hills, with their layered evidence of millions of years of sedimentary deposits and wind erosion, menaced like brooding sentries on either side of the twisting roadway. Matthew pointed as they passed by a weathered sign advertising the *Canadian Badlands Passion Play*. Jonah tried to contain his glee when they passed the *Welcome to Drumheller* sign flanked by a Dijon mustard-colored Tyrannosaurus Rex, but the little boy in him was not to be repressed.

"A T-rex! Get out of here," Jonah laughed.

"See...campy...like the Flintstones," Matthew said.

"Is the other one bigger?"

"Oh, yeah—much bigger. You'll see him in a minute."

They pulled by *Dino's RV Nest* with its small, lime green brontosaurus. A green overhead sign with a downward pointing arrow indicated that the downtown was straight ahead. The north *Dinosaur Trail* was off to their right.

Matthew slowed the truck, but continued forward; the men in the backseat had the windows down, and their guns trained on the empty streets. Jonah had pulled his pistol, too.

"It's quiet," one of them said.

Nothing. No people. Not a soul.

A bright blue sign indicated the *Royal Tyrrell Museum* was to the right, only six kilometers away. Matthew ignored the sign and drove forward past a Travelodge motel. A stubby, white water tower, emblazoned with the word, *Drumheller*, stood on slender metal legs in the distance.

Suddenly, Jonah shouted. Matthew slammed on the brakes. The truck skidded to a halt.

"I see it. I see the head," Jonah said, pointing to the green and yellow head of a giant dinosaur peering over the bushes. Matthew smiled indulgently. He started forward, but as he rounded the curve leading to a concrete bridge spanning the Red Deer River, he slammed on the brakes again.

"Whoa," Matthew said. "Look at that."

The men behind him nervously shouldered their guns, while he and Jonah gaped at the mass of building materials, tree branches, picnic tables, and vehicles blocking access to the bridge. Across the bridge and to their left, towered the world's largest dinosaur—a giant, steel Tyrannosaurus Rex—its great mouth filled with pointy, white teeth.

"What the hell has been going on here?" Matthew asked as he leaned forward.

Jonah glanced from the barricade to the dinosaur, and then back again. "Looks like the town banded together to keep somebody out."

"They've done a good job," said one of the men from the backseat. "Where is everyone? This is a big town. They can't all be gone. They can't all be dead."

Matthew opened the truck door and got out. He walked back and forth along the barricade. Virgil and Meteor drove up and joined him. The pony-tailed captain arrived right behind them.

"It's so quiet," Meteor said. "You'd think there'd be somebody here."

"This is one of the cities The Man went after last year," Virgil said. "I never spent time in the South Camps, but I knew this city was a major holdout. The Man had some work to do to take it over."

"Why aren't we under attack then?" Meteor asked.

Virgil pursed his mouth. "I don't know."

The men stared at the barricade, and then back up the street.

Not a sound.

"What do we do now?" Jonah asked. Matthew grabbed the map.

"We'll retrace our steps." He gave Jonah an apologetic smile. "The hoodoos will have to wait. Sorry."

"I'm good— I got to see the biggest dinosaur in the world."

"The museum's not far from here," Matthew said. "It's secluded off the main road. It'll be safe to rest there."

Matthew wheeled the truck around. He turned left, before the *Dinosaur RV Campground*, and headed toward the museum.

The rest of the trucks followed.

THE BUS DRIVER slowed at the small, white road sign. *Dalum,* it read. She changed gears. The bus jerked and rumbled forward. The driver pointed. Sarah craned her neck. She could see buildings ahead. A large white building, the *Dalum Community Hall*, appeared on the right. Kitty-corner from that was a stone church—stark and handsome with its white walls and black roof tiles. On their left, a white gas station—its sole fuel pump pulled from its moorings—sat next to a small, corrugated-steel building. Behind that, up a steep hill, the pair could see a domed machine shed, its front doors long gone, and gaping holes in its curved walls.

"Do you think you could pull up there?" Sarah asked, indicating the dilapidated shed.

"No way the bus will make it up that hill," the driver replied. "Maybe we could pull in behind the church."

The driver stopped just short of the intersection. A sign gave them the option to turn right to East Coulee. The two women studied the churchyard instead.

The large, fenced area was cluttered with trailers, campers, and tents of all shapes and colors. Most of the tents were collapsed under dense blobs of melted snow. There were no fires burning, nor were there any people in sight. The church doors were open, held ajar by a small bank of snow.

"Wow, looks like lots of people took sanctuary here," Sarah said. "Probably right after the Change." She heaved a big sigh. "But nobody lives here now."

"We had better make a decision soon," the driver reminded Sarah. "We could try driving straight up #56."

"Give it a go. The highway has been great so far." Sarah looked behind. "Still no sign of the trucks."

The driver pushed the bus into gear—it screeched, jerked, rolled forward, and stalled.

"C'mon, baby," the driver said to the bus. "We've still got a ways to go." Sarah looked alarmed. "It's okay. She'll go. Just having a little hissy-fit." The driver started the bus again, and this time the bus accelerated up the road.

They had not gone far before they spotted trouble. A big rig truck was jack-knifed across the highway. Around it were several other cars and trucks. The telltale signs of a huge explosion marked the ditch and the fields on either side of the pavement. The road was scorched and black, as were the vehicles. The children crowded up to the front of the bus to get a better look.

"Oh, gross," one exclaimed. "Look at that!"

Several children and some of the women echoed the child's revulsion at the sight of a man's body, torn in half, lying across the hood of a small truck. More and more children cried out as they surveyed the wreckage in front of them. More bodies, and parts of bodies, could be seen in the ditch and in the field, sticking out of the snow, every which way, like broken puppets.

"That's enough," Sarah said. "We can't go this way. Let's turn around."

The driver stopped at the intersection again. There was still no sign of Brad's trucks. "So, which way?" she asked.

"I don't know anything about East Coulee. Let's go west. Maybe avoid Drumheller altogether," Sarah said, pointing to the map. "Then go straight up to Edmonton." She regarded the driver. "It's gonna be a long drive. Can you make it? Or do you need a rest?"

The driver waved Sarah's concerns aside, pushed the bus into gear, and swung the big vehicle to the right.

"Here we go," she said. "Come hell or high water."

Sarah kissed her fingers and held them up to the church as they motored by.

RUTH PUSHED the truck's accelerator down hard. She was determined to catch up to the bus. Debris on the road ahead caused her to ease up, and apply the brakes. Mervyn leaned between the seats.

"What's up?"

"Doesn't that look strange to you?" Ruth asked. They were nearing a major intersection. Bits of a vehicle littered the road—a piece of fender, a chunk of fiberglass, red glass from a broken taillight. "That looks like a fresh accident. Not one that's been there for months."

"I agree," The Man said.

"No one asked you," Ruth replied icily.

"Stop, Ruth," Mervyn said. "I'll take a look."

Mervyn jumped out. He was back in a minute.

"It's fresh." He held up a piece of glass. "Look at this." A dark yellow smear was etched across the glass.

"The bus hit them?" Ruth asked incredulously. She looked around. "So, where's the bus?"

"Up ahead," Mervyn said, pointing to tire tracks that led to the left. "Brad must have backtracked and gone straight up #56. That means he's chasing the bus— Right into Drumheller." Mervyn shook his head. "Not good..."

The Man suddenly laughed—a raucous sound. "It's like watching Keystone Kops." Ruth glared at him. He raised his eyebrows. "Don't mind me," he snickered. "Carry on."

"You won't be laughing once I turn you over to Matthew," Ruth said.

The Man laughed again, but this time, not as long.

Ruth turned back to Mervyn. "What's up with Drumheller?"

"Yeah, Mervyn..." The Man said. "Why don't you tell her about Drumheller..."

Ruth's eyes went wide. "What? Tell me what?"

"Bad things happened there," Mervyn said. "Just hurry."

MATTHEW DROVE the truck into the museum parking lot. The place looked deserted—ominously so. A few minutes later, men left the trucks; some ran up the long wooden stairway that led to the valley viewing platform; a few others wandered past life-sized dinosaur statues on their way to the museum's front doors.

"Fifteen minutes, guys," Matthew called after the departing men. He and Jonah pulled a cooler from the back of the truck. Jonah waited expectantly. Matthew smiled. "Go— See it, if you want. Be careful. There might be squatters living in there."

Jonah tapped his pistol, grinned, and ran off.

Matthew grabbed a small collapsible stool from the truck, opened it, and sat down. He turned his face up to the sun and let its rays warm his skin.

Sunshine on my shoulders...

Matthew hummed the tune that he had heard Martha sing hundreds of times. He smiled and shook his head. She had put up a fight over this trip, but she finally saw reason in his decision to make her stay behind, and she reluctantly agreed. Matthew felt his heart grow warm as he remembered their time together—making love, laughing together, and finally making love again.

My wife, he thought with a rush of emotion.

Martha had changed his life—she and her family—her children and her grandchildren. Before the Change, Matthew had kept mostly to himself, preferring the solitude of his compound; now, because of Martha, he was running around the province with an army of men, getting into gun battles, and nearly getting himself killed. He suspected this time was going to include dodging bullets, too.

Matthew bumped his cap back from his eyes, and rubbed sweat from his forehead. He opened his jacket. His fingers brushed across the necklace he now wore—a brushed steel cross on a thick silver chain. It had once belonged to Josef—a gift from Martha. It was his now.

Matthew's thoughts strayed to Josef. His murdered friend was so unlike his other friends, but someone he had held in high esteem. He often missed Josef, sometimes more than he missed his boyhood friends. Something about the peacefulness that accompanied the man. He remembered watching Josef pull his old Bible from his canvas bag while they were on patrol together. In the evening, after supper. Frequently.

Calm, steady Josef. Maybe there was something to that Bible of his...

"So, old man...?"

Matthew looked up and shielded his eyes against the noonday sun. "Hi, Meteor. You want something to eat?" Matthew pointed to the food chest. "Lots there."

"No...not hungry." Meteor checked his watch and squatted next to Matthew. "Think we'll find them today?"

"Hope so..."

"It's peaceful here. So quiet. I like the sound of the breeze." Meteor closed his eyes, leaned his head back, and breathed deeply.

"I'm thinking about that barricade," Matthew said. "Might be faster to take it down, than to backtrack."

"We could do it." Meteor agreed. His radio crackled; he pulled it from his belt.

"Where are you guys? Over," a familiar voice asked.

Matthew wrinkled his brow.

Meteor pressed the *Send* button. "Trojan? Where are ya, buddy? Over."

"Hey, Meteor. We're coming south on #56. Where are you guys? Over."

"Drumheller. By the museum. Over."

"I know that place. We're thinking of heading down #9, and then cutting down #36 to the Trans-Canada. We can meet up in Medicine Hat. Does that work for you? Over."

Meteor grinned, a quick knowing grin. He looked to Matthew for a response. Matthew took the radio.

"Thought I told you to go home, Trojan. Over."

"Never paid my parking tickets either, sir," Trojan quipped. "The truck's better than good. Besides, you need us. Over."

Matthew pulled a map from his pocket. He looked at it and then back up at Meteor.

"Let's do it." He pressed the *Send* button. "Change of plans. Come straight into town. Meet us at the main bridge." He checked his watch. "Twenty minutes."

"Copy that."

Matthew handed the radio back to Meteor.

"Move out," Matthew said.

RUTH SWERVED to avoid an upended compact car, its tires all but invisible under a cushion of snow. Wet tire tracks stretched into the distance; the water between their narrow treads glistened in the sunshine. Ruth rolled down her window.

"You sure you don't want me to drive?" Mervyn asked.

"I'm fine," Ruth said with a shortness of temper she never intended. "Sorry. Kind of grumpy."

The Man opened his mouth to speak, but Ruth shot him a look before he could say anything.

"We're getting close to crossroads here," Mervyn said. "We can go right or left—either way will take us into Drumheller."

"The tire tracks are easy to see. And they're still wet, so they must be new."

Mervyn laughed softly. He reached up and squeezed her shoulder. "Talking like the deerhunter I know."

"Thanks."

"Slow down," he said. "We're close..."

MATTHEW'S MEN formed an assembly line at the bridge and with much huffing and grunting, they managed to clear a path for the trucks. Trojan and the mechanic showed up just as they were moving the last vehicle. Some of the men teased them about their perfect timing and ability to avoid work. Matthew called for silence. The group stood quietly and listened.

No movement. Not a sound. Not even the chirp of a bird. Whoever had built the barricade was no longer around to watch them take it down.

Matthew motioned the men back to the trucks. They wended their way across the bridge. Matthew followed the *Hoodoo Trail* for a short distance, and then pulled into the parking lot of the Greentree Mall. He picked up the map.

"I'm getting nervous," he said. "We should have seen people by now." Jonah nodded. "We've got two choices— Three actually. I'm going to send scouts."

"Which way?" Jonah asked. "Highway #10 would take us past the hoodoos...but it looks like a complicated run...before we get back to a major highway. South on #9 might be better."

Several men had gathered outside Matthew's driver side window.

"What's up?" the pony-tailed captain asked. Trojan and Meteor stood nearby.

"I think Trojan had a better idea of taking #9 to #36," Matthew said. Trojan beamed and elbowed the captain. "If the town set up more barriers, I'm guessing they'll be close to the city. I'll send out a couple of scouts. If they run into barricades, we'll have no choice but to turn around."

"Makes sense," the captain replied. "Can we risk the time?"

"We risk a lot less fuel if only two trucks go out."

"Right." The captain waved to two younger men dressed in military fatigues. The men ran over. "Grab radios," he said. "We'll explain."

Matthew held a quick conference with the two scouts. A few moments later, the scouts ran off with maps and radios in hand.

"How long?" Meteor asked.

"I figure twenty minutes out...twenty minutes back should do it." Matthew checked his watch. "We're still making good time."

The two men wandered up the street. Suddenly, Meteor pointed and laughed. "Hey, look—a Walmart. And no Martha." Matthew laughed, too.

Trojan joined them. "What's so funny?"

"Déjà vu," Meteor said, pointing at the familiar blue sign with the white star. "Does it bring back memories of Hinton?"

"Yeah, my tooth is still loose, asshole," Trojan said. Then he brightened. "Hey, I could find some new baby clothes." He ran to his truck. "Anybody else want to go to Walmart?"

"Twenty minutes," Matthew called after him.

Virgil walked over. He stood near Matthew and Meteor, surveying the silent city. "This doesn't feel right, Matthew."

"This place is creepy," said the pony-tailed captain who sauntered over, a half-eaten sandwich in his hand. He took a bite and chewed.

Meteor agreed. "It feels strange—sort of like a Stephen King novel. Too quiet. Where're the people? You'd think there'd be people...maybe a dog..."

"I'm glad there're no dogs," Matthew said, indicating the healed bite wound on his arm. "I've had my fill of dogs. Thanks."

Sparrow joined them.

"No sparrows," the young man said. "Not a single sparrow."

"Why do you say that?" asked Virgil.

"Very rare not to see sparrows. Kind of a harbinger of bad things. Like having birds fly at your window."

"Maybe we shouldn't have let the guys split up," Virgil said.

The pony-tailed captain nodded his head, vigorously, and mumbled an agreement.

"They haven't gone far," Meteor said. "They'd hear a warning shot." He grinned. "Let the ladies do their shopping."

THE DRIVER pushed the bus forward as fast as she could, but the road was a misery of melting snow and mud, and the pavement, what there was of it, was heavily pocked with potholes. The bus bumped along, sending the riders halfway to the ceiling, and back down again. A few close calls, when she slowed and swerved to get around abandoned vehicles, made the riders suck in a quick breath.

"No trucks following us," Sarah said, squinting toward the back of the bus. "Maybe you did some damage to their steering thing-a-ma-jigs when you hit them." The driver nodded.

Sarah nearly pitched into the front window as the driver braked for another pothole. "Maybe you could slow down just a bit," Sarah suggested. They hit another bump—it sent Sarah tumbling into the door well. "Ouch!"

"You okay?" the driver asked as Sarah pulled herself back up, rubbing the back of her head.

"This road is awful. Maybe we should have gone the other way."

The driver gave a huge sigh. "We're committed now. Let's hope Brad goes east."

"They'll see our tire tracks," Sarah said. She sat down. "I wonder where Ruth and Mervyn are," she added glumly.

A baby began screeching. Sarah covered her ears.

They reached a dead end. Sarah stood up. The road ahead had deteriorated even further; they had no choice except to turn right.

The driver eased the bus over compacted drifts of dirty snow as she made the turn. Once more, the riders shot up from their seats like human popping corn. However, the kids had begun to enjoy the carnival ride—they added exaggerated groans and giggles to each bounce. Their joy, in spite of their circumstances, made Sarah and the driver smile. Sarah glanced behind.

Still no sign of their pursuers.

"Go, girl...it's all good," Sarah encouraged the driver.

A clear stretch of good road opened up before them, and the driver pressed down on the gas pedal. She had just achieved a rolling pace, when she saw it. A truck about a half mile away.

It was headed toward them.

"Now what?" the driver asked, her voice constricted with fear.

Sarah gripped the metal support bar. She said nothing.

RUTH EASED the truck to the right. The tracks were undeniable—three sets—all were heading west. They had noticed the tracks heading forward on #56, and had first followed them; they saw the semi and the bodies in the snow, and quickly turned back around.

"We must be really close now," Mervyn said.

Ruth wasn't listening. She gripped the wheel in both hands. She had forgotten how stiff and sore her right hand was. Now, a new force, a new energy had overtaken her. She was close to her children. She could feel it. That—and something more.

Something she couldn't quite put her finger on.

Something divine?

THE TRUCK HAD stopped; sunlight glanced off its hood. Like a bird of prey, it sat waiting for its quarry. Sarah and the driver peered ahead as the bus inched forward.

"It's not Brad's men, is it?" asked the driver.

"They're behind us, aren't they?" Sarah asked.

"Could they have swung around?" the driver asked. Sarah glanced at the map.

"I don't see how. It can't be them."

"What do we do?" the driver asked.

The driver slowed and brought the bus to a screeching halt. She looked back at the women and children. Everyone was silent, having seen the truck. They waited expectantly.

The driver scratched her head. "I can't turn around here. We'll end up in the ditch." She searched Sarah's face for an answer.

"Open the doors," Sarah blurted.

"What?"

"I'm going out. You stay here."

The driver gave Sarah a disbelieving look, but she opened the doors. Sarah stepped out and began to walk up the road toward the truck.

In response, the truck moved forward. Slowly, it drew nearer and nearer to the walking woman. Suddenly, the truck stopped; the driver's door opened.

The bus driver sucked in her breath as a man stepped out of the truck. "Sarah!" she screamed, but Sarah didn't pay any attention.

Sarah was running.

Forward.

Women and children crowded to the front of the bus and watched the drama unfold. They watched in amazement as Sarah ran into the arms of the truck driver.

"He's ours!" one of the women cried. Women and children tumbled from the bus, and ran to greet the man, screaming and cheering.

Like a Hollywood star, Matthew's scout stood awkwardly, his arms akimbo, overwhelmed by the human energy that flew at him.

The bus driver smiled. She breathed a long sigh of relief. Suddenly, something caught her eye. She leaned on the horn. She jumped from the bus and screamed.

"Get back here! They're coming. Back on the bus now." Then to the truck driver, "Get your truck turned around. Or we're all dead."

The bus driver was breathing hard as the women and children raced back; they clambered onto the bus. The truck driver did a speedy three-point turn and was soon headed in the opposite direction. The bus driver changed gears, and the bus rattled up the road. Sarah, clutching one of the bus's metal support poles, stood next to the driver. She was breathless with a combination of fear...and exhilaration.

"Did you recognize him?" she asked excitedly. Her cheeks were bright with color. "He's one of the boys from camp. He says they were coming to rescue us. Matthew is back in Drumheller...with a bunch of men. They've come to take us home."

The bus driver said nothing. She was intent on the road ahead.

Sarah glanced through the bus's back window. She could see two trucks in the distance. They were closing the gap.

"Drive, girl...like you've never driven before."

"I am," the bus driver said. "Believe me...I am."

THE SCOUT raced back up the road, his tires spitting up a shower of small rocks. He checked his rearview mirror. The bus was following close behind, rocking from side to side on the uneven pavement. He couldn't see anything past the bus. He hit the intersection and turned right. He grabbed the radio.

"Scout One requests assistance. Over."

"Go," Meteor said.

"They're with me. In the bus. Coming behind. We need help... Over."

Matthew grabbed the radio from Meteor's hand. "What? Who's coming? Over."

"...the women and kids! Their bus is behind me. Someone's chasing them. Over."

"What's your twenty? Over."

"Highway #9. Heading back into the city. Over."

"The women and kids?" Meteor looked stunned. "What the hell?"

"On our way," Matthew said. "Over." He shoved the radio back at Meteor.

Trojan ran up. His arms were filled with little girls' dresses, stockings, and frilly panties—most were massively too big for a new baby, but his face shone with conquest. "Look," he said.

"The women and kids are coming here!" Meteor said.

"What?"

"By bus," Matthew said. "They're in trouble. Let's go." He signaled to Jonah who jumped into the truck. "Tell the rest."

Jonah spoke into the radio.

Trojan raced back to his truck. "Rescue mission," he yelled. He opened a large tub stored in the truck bed and jammed the baby clothing inside. He jumped into the driver's seat and started the engine. The mechanic jumped into the passenger seat and slammed the door.

"The ladies are coming," Trojan said. A huge smile lit up his face.

"We found them?" the mechanic asked, his voice rising in amazement.

"No, it sounds like they found us," Trojan replied as he sped after the rest of the trucks.

Sheree Zielke

Chapter Thirty-Four

Something Rotten in the Town of Wayne

SIX TRUCKS left the Hoodoo Trail and sped up the highway, past Fred and Barney's restaurant, and past the Jurassic hotel. Just outside of the city, Matthew's lead truck stopped. He jumped down from the cab. He held his walkie-talkie up to his ear. He waved the men over to him. The other drivers slammed on their brakes, jumped out, and ran up to him. Some held radios, too.

"The Man must be here!" the pony-tailed captain said.

Matthew held his radio aloft. The men listened to the voice of the second scout:

"...they're close behind me...I hid and watched...there's an army barracks...it's guarded...they saw me...trying to run...heading to Wayne...don't think I'm gonna make it...*Static*...munitions and barracks in Rose...*Static*...right side...Outlaws...*Static*..."

"What?" Matthew asked, jamming his thumb down on the *Send* button. "Say again... Dammit!" It was no use since the scout continued to speak.

"...chasing me...*Static*...over the seventh bridge...I'll try to find a place to hide...*Static*..."

"What? What bridge?" Jonah asked. The voice continued from the radio.

"...another bridge...they're shooting at me...*Static*...I see the Wayne sign."

"The women!" the pony-tailed captain exclaimed. "He'll have to take care of himself."

Matthew tossed the radio to Jonah. "Let's go!"

"Split up?" asked the captain.

"Three and three," Matthew said, running for the truck. "I'll lead three ahead to meet the bus. You keep three back here. Sniper fire."

Three trucks sped up the highway.

The scout on the radio continued his breathless report...

"...in Wayne...main road ends here...gravel road...*Static*...oh, God...so many...can't believe this..." The scout's voice cracked in horror. "...really fucked up..."

The sounds of gunfire and the radio went dead.

Matthew accelerated the truck forward, grabbed the radio from Jonah, and pressed the *Send* button.

"We copy. Get out of there. Women and kids are coming by bus. We're heading out #9 to meet them. Over."

The scout's voice came on again. It vibrated with revulsion...

"...bodies...arms...legs...heads...all sticking up out of the snow." The scout didn't break to allow Matthew to respond. "I—I—I've never seen anything like this...think they're all men...there's so many...field's full of them...you copy?" The radio went quiet.

Matthew glanced at Jonah. The scout's voice came over the radio again.

"...Oh, man...the field is covered with bodies...*Static*...it's a mass grave...like a Nazi death camp..."

The sound of more gunfire.

The radio went dead again.

"Come back, kid...get out of there," Matthew yelled.

The radio remained silent.

RUTH LEANED forward into the steering wheel. She slowed and squinted. She rubbed her eyes. Mervyn leaned between the seats.

"Can you see how many there are?" Mervyn asked.

"I think just two."

"Can you see the bus?"

"I did. But I lost it. Oh, wait...there it is."

Far in the distance, the yellow bus stood out plainly against the dowdy fields of dry grass and snow. The bus turned right.

"I see the trucks now," Mervyn said. "Hey—they've stopped."

THE BUS ROCKED dangerously, sending kids and mothers flying out of their seats as the driver rounded the corner onto the highway. She heard cries of pain from the back. She gave an *I'm-so-sorry* glance into the rearview mirror, and changed gears. The bus growled, but soon they were cruising up the pavement. She glanced into the side mirrors, but could see no sign of the trucks. Ahead, the scout's truck was nearly out of sight. She raced to catch up.

MATTHEW'S TRUCKS veered to the side of the highway as the scout's truck approached. The scout shot by. Moments later, lumbering like a maddened yellow elephant, the bus appeared. The men waited. The bus roared by. They could see the heads of women and children bouncing up and down in their seats. When no other vehicles appeared, Matthew's trucks wheeled around, and sped after the bus. Matthew pulled up behind the bus and honked his horn.

"Who is that?" Jonah asked. He could see a woman's face pressed to the glass in the exit door. She was waving at them.

Matthew pulled around the left side of the bus; he accelerated so he was parallel to the driver, and honked again. The bus driver looked wildly at him—once, twice, and then again—before recognizing him with a wide smile. The bus slowed and stopped. The driver opened her window.

"Jonah? Matthew? Is that really you?" She gave them a wide grin.

A repeated chunking sound erupted from the side of the bus as windows were lowered. Women and children's faces filled the open rectangles. A huge cheer went up.

"We're saved!" The children whooped and jumped up and down on the seats. Women cried and hugged their babies.

The driver shot Jonah a desperate look. She pointed back over her shoulder. "We can't stop. Brad and his men are chasing us."

"There's no one following you now," Jonah said. He held a hurried conversation with Matthew, and then turned back to the driver. "We'll go back the way you came. You keep heading into Drumheller. We left three sniper units there. You're safe now." Jonah shot her a quick grin. "How many were following you?"

"Two trucks. Brad's men. I think Brad was with them. I crashed into them," the driver added jubilantly.

"Go," Jonah said. "We'll catch up to you in town."

Matthew turned the truck around and sped up the highway. The other two trucks followed.

BRAD WHEELED his truck around. He headed back in the direction from which they had come. The other truck followed. Brad pulled over. The second truck did the same. They jumped out.

"What're we doing?" asked the driver of the second vehicle. He tugged at a jean vest pulled snuggly over a hunter's jacket.

"Let them go," Brad said. "That was one of Matthew's trucks. I don't know how many men he has with him. We'll go back. We know Mervyn and Ruth are still behind us. And—" he added with a twisted grin, "I suspect they still have The Man. Rescuing him wouldn't hurt our reputation."

The other driver nodded.

"Besides, we know the back way into Drumheller. Let's go to the Rosedale compound. Tell them what's going on," Brad said, getting back into his truck. "Won't Matthew be surprised," he muttered as he shoved the truck into gear.

"Look ahead," said the man sitting in the passenger seat next to him. He pulled out his pistol. "There's a truck up there."

RUTH AND MERVYN watched in surprise as Brad's trucks came back into view.

"What's he doing?" Ruth asked.

"Coming back for us—"

The Man laughed. "A fly in your ointment, Mervyn?"

Mervyn ignored the sarcastic prodding.

"Now we gamble," Mervyn continued. "Do we believe Brad knows about us? If he sees this truck...with The Man...will he believe I'm still on his side?"

The Man made a dismissive sound.

"He'll recognize the truck," Ruth said. "But will he believe you? I seriously doubt it. And what about me?"

"Okay, let's assume he knows I helped you escape...we are in one truck, and they are in two trucks. We have a couple of pistols—"

"And a machine gun," Ruth reminded him.

"Bottom line...they probably have way more fire power. So, we have to retreat. Or they'll kill us."

"They wouldn't shoot the truck," Ruth said firmly. "They might accidentally shoot The Man."

"Maybe so. But only if they know he's in here." Mervyn paused. "So, what do we do?"

"Oh, Ruth...what do we do now?" The Man asked with his breathless, schoolgirl enthusiasm.

The pair ignored him.

"What about using me?" Ruth blurted. "Like you planned before?"

"I think it's too late for that. Remember the guy you shot? The one we left behind? I never checked him for a radio. Did you?"

Ruth shook her head. She glanced at The Man. He wore a wide, smug smile. "Told you," he said.

"Then they know we're together," Ruth said. "And that we have The Man. They won't fire on us. If we stay in the truck...we should be okay."

"No, I suspect they'll still shoot," Mervyn said.

"Then what? What do we do?" Ruth wrenched at the steering wheel in frustration. The act hurt her damaged hand. "I want my kids. God— Tell us what to do!" She turned—her eyes were emerald bright with crazy anger. "Let's fire on them."

"Ruth, if they know, we'll just waste ammunition."

"Then what should we do?" Ruth asked, her tone high-pitched in annoyance. "Turn around? What about my kids?"

Mervyn studied the Uzi. "How many clips do you have left?"

"Two, I think. They're in my bag."

Ruth pulled the shoulder sack over her head and handed it to Mervyn. He slipped the bag over his head.

"I've got an idea. I'll get out," he said.

"You'll get out?" Ruth asked, horrified. "They'll kill you."

The Man grinned in agreement.

"They've seen us by now. They're coming for us. Back up...so we're out of sight...enough for me to get out without being seen."

"And then what?"

"Just do it. When I get out, you back up. And wait. Draw them to you...past me."

Ruth reversed the truck, stepped down on the gas pedal, and navigated backwards until they were hidden behind a curve. Mervyn jumped out, the Uzi slung across his chest. He threw himself down behind a small rise covered in spindly vegetation. He waved Ruth away. She drove backward another hundred yards. She clambered up on top of the cab's roof, and peered down the road.

"They're coming," she yelled.

She watched as the trucks began to move, more quickly now, directly towards them. She felt sure that Mervyn was right—

Brad knew.

She shivered in spite of the heat of the bright midday sunshine. She willed the trucks to come closer. She could hear the motors now, gunning in the distance, running at top speed. Only minutes away now. She jumped back into the truck.

The Man sat, staring out the side window, dispassionately, as though out for a Sunday drive. He gave Ruth a languid look as she spoke:

"I could be dead soon— I have to know," she said. "Why are you so awful? Why? Did somebody hurt you? Did something happen to you to make you what you are?"

The Man gazed out the window and then looked back at Ruth. "Hmm...I kind of like you, so I'll indulge you, Ruth. Just this once." He grinned—a cold, humorless curl of his lips. "My father helped me decide who I wanted to be. I watched him run our lives like he ran his church...his congregation of *sheeples*...and the town council. What he wanted, he took. What he wanted, he got. Everything and everybody."

He paused, considering his next words. "What the hell— They say confession is good for the soul."

Ruth glanced nervously through the window. The trucks had slowed down.

"He wanted my wife, too," The Man continued. "I didn't know she let him have her. Then one day, my wife told me that I was actually raising my brother—my father's child. I remember that day."

"What?" Ruth tore her eyes away from the windshield to question The Man. "What?" she asked again.

"I took them all to the barn. My ridiculous mother, too. 'A new colt,' I said." His voice had grown low and introspective.

Goosebumps rose on Ruth's arms.

"None of them left the barn," The Man confided.

"You murdered them?" Ruth asked softly.

"Eliminated them," he said flatly. "Like so much vermin."

Ruth stared back at The Man. "You're lying. I don't believe you."

"Ask Marion," he said.

"Marion? Who's Marion?"

"My sister. Oh—you've never met her. She's in your camp now." Ruth looked puzzled. "At least, last I heard, she was there."

"Did you go to prison?"

"No. Nobody else knows besides Marion. Except now, for you." The Man steadied his gaze on her.

Ruth had never stared into The Man's eyes before, but she did now. Their oily, enigmatic blackness filled her soul with horror, sucking her toward him like a magnet. She shuddered.

"I've never met anyone so evil," she whispered.

I shall fear no evil.

The sound of engines snapped her out of her trance. She looked out the window. The trucks raced up the road toward them. They stopped. Six bikers jumped out. They all carried machine guns. They pointed them at the truck. Fear bubbled up inside Ruth, making her light-headed, almost giddy.

"I wonder what Heaven is like," she said softly.

"Me, too," The Man said.

"You'll never know," Ruth said dreamily. She watched the bikers advance on the truck, their guns pointed forward.

"Get out of the truck," one of the men yelled.

"I'm a little tied up," The Man called back.

"Shut up," Ruth said.

"Oh, now you want me to shut up."

"Shut up or I will shoot you." She aimed Mervyn's pistol at his lower ribs while keeping her eyes on the advancing men.

The sound of gunfire made Ruth jump. The men were about fifty feet away when the bullets struck. They fell to the ground—nameless, faceless lumps of clothing.

Third person shooter.

The Man never flinched.

The gunfire ceased.

Silence.

Ruth searched the road. Her eyes returned to the lumps of clothing on the ground. Nothing moved.

Where was Mervyn?

She sighed and smiled when she saw Mervyn's head pop up. He gave her a small wave. She reached for the door handle, but a movement caught her eye. She gasped.

Another man. Down on one knee. Partially hidden behind the first truck. He was drawing a bead on something. On someone...

Someone—

Mervyn was standing— His back was to the man with the gun.

"No!" Ruth screamed.

She rammed the truck into gear and stomped down on the accelerator. The truck fishtailed as it closed the short distance. A shot rang out. The shooter ran out from behind the truck, raised the gun, and aimed again.

"No!" Ruth screamed again.

The shooter turned, but he didn't run. He stood, transfixed, as the truck bore down on him. He pointed his gun at the truck. Ruth saw the man's face.

Brad!

Anger shot through her veins.

Brad!

The past three years streamed through her mind—a wild, crashing river of turbulent emotions: the fear, the degradation, the death, the inhumanity, the violence, the loneliness, and the hate. Her father's face, her sister's face, her mother's face, Reggie's face. Now...Mervyn's face...

Ruth held the wheel steady and ducked sideways as a bullet crashed through the glass. She felt the truck hit a mass, and rattle across it. She sat up and fought the wheel to keep the truck from flying off the road. She braked and swerved. The truck came to a halt. The engine hummed.

Ruth lifted her hands from the wheel— They were shaking. She clutched them into fists. She didn't want to look, but curiosity won out, and she glanced in the rearview mirror. She gasped.

Brad was getting up!

She watched in horror. Unbelieving. Blood streamed from Brad's face. He waved a pistol.

He's alive?

Her face grew hard, her green eyes, bright and wild.

"No more!" she yelled.

Ruth fought with the gearshift. She stared into the rearview mirror. "That was for my father...and my mother...and my sister—" she growled through gritted teeth.

She stomped on the gas pedal. "This is for me!"

The truck sped backwards.

Suddenly, Ruth cried out in pain as The Man's booted feet caught her right hand. The truck swerved and careened sideways into a ditch. It struck a small snow bank, jolted, and came to a stop.

Ruth slammed the truck into *Park*. She leaned her head on the steering wheel, and gasped for breath. She shuddered uncontrollably. Her stomach twisted and nausea swept over her.

She pushed the door open, fell out of the truck, and retched. Tears joined her vomit. She stayed on her knees, crying and shaking. She didn't care if Brad came back to life. She didn't care if he walked up and put a pistol to her head. She didn't care. She just wanted it over. All of it. She was done.

"Ruth?"

She jerked her head up.

Mervyn was standing there. He was clutching his arm. His shirtsleeve was soaked in blood.

"I...can't. No more!" Ruth collapsed to the ground. "No more!" Mervyn knelt beside her. He put a hand on her back.

"It's over, sweetheart. He's still alive, but he's hurt. Badly."

Ruth wept.

Mervyn touched her back again. "Ruth, you gotta get up. There're more trucks coming." He helped her to her feet. "Do you recognize them?" She wiped her nose on her sleeve and watched as three trucks came into view. She held her breath.

It wasn't possible. But there was no mistaking the luminescent markings.

"Yes," she said, snuffling. She walked forward, woodenly. "They're friendlies."

Fatigue and a constant state of alertness combined with profound relief into a heavenly concoction of escape. Ruth leaned into the intoxicating wooziness and allowed the grasping hand of unconsciousness to claim her.

She slipped to the ground.

RUTH AWOKE a few minutes later. She was lying in a backseat—her head was in Mervyn's lap. Somebody had bound his arm, but blood still seeped through a makeshift bandage. Mervyn's head was against the headrest, his eyes were closed. Ruth reached over and squeezed his hand. He opened his eyes, looked down at her, and squeezed back. He smiled. Ruth moved and groaned. Her head pounded.

"How are you doing, Ruth?" a voice asked gently. Ruth recognized the speaker and smiled.

"Matthew..." She sighed softly. "It's good to see you."

"You, too," Matthew said. He reached back and squeezed her knee. "Are you okay?"

"Pretty groggy."

"Sure am glad to see you. Your mom has been worried sick about you." The truck hit a pothole—Ruth groaned again.

"Headache. Bad one," she said. "Where are my kids?"

"Were they on the bus?"

"Yes— Is everyone okay?"

"Let's find out." He picked up the radio. "Matthew to Meteor. Over."

"I read. Over."

"Are the women and kids okay?"

"Yes. Bruised...scraped up from the bus ride. But okay."

"Anything going on? Over."

"No. Quiet here. Over."

"I have Ruth with me."

"Hello, Ruth! I've got such a big hug waiting for you. Over."

Ruth smiled at Meteor's outburst.

"We have prisoners, too," Matthew said. "Over."

"Who?"

"Two people that you've been waiting to see for a very long time..."

Jonah pulled in behind Matthew. He was driving The Man's truck. The men crowded around. Some of them recognized The Man seated in the passenger seat, and they cheered.

Matthew shot Meteor a cryptic smile as he motioned to the truck behind him. "Take a look," he said. Meteor walked over and peered into the truck's backseat.

"Holy shit!" Meteor exclaimed. "You got him." He opened the back door. "What happened to him?"

"Ruth happened to him," Matthew said. His eyes followed Ruth as she made her way between the trucks toward the bus.

Ruth pushed through the crowd. She glanced around, and soon located Mary and Samuel. The children ran at her. She hugged them to her. Mervyn stood nearby and smiled at the tender reunion.

Moments later, Meteor, Trojan, and the pony-tailed captain gave Ruth warm hugs of greeting.

"Man, are we glad to see you," Trojan said.

"You're my hero," Meteor said, motioning to the truck holding Brad.

"I don't want to talk about that," Ruth said quickly.

"I understand," Meteor said. "But you caught The Man, too." He clapped his hand to her shoulder in admiration.

"Mervyn did that," Ruth corrected him. She smiled and put her hand on Mervyn's uninjured arm. Meteor appraised Mervyn and smiled.

"You going to introduce us to your new friend?"

"This is Mervyn, everybody," Ruth said. "He helped us escape. We couldn't have made it without him."

The men crowded around Mervyn, slapping his back, and congratulating him. His squeezed his eyes shut against the jolts of pain when they grabbed his injured arm.

Meteor and Ruth walked away a few feet, and stood apart from the group. Meteor wrapped his arm around her shoulders and pulled her to him in another warm embrace, this one longer lasting.

"I meant it," he said. "You are my hero." He paused. "You're a lot like your mom, you know?"

"I am not like my mother," Ruth said tiredly.

"But you are...and what's wrong with that?" Meteor turned Ruth to face him. His blue eyes were intent and earnest. "You have her courage, her instincts, her wisdom, her strength..." Meteor paused. "Your mother is a wonderful woman. You should be proud to be like her."

"Thanks," Ruth said, but her tone was hollow. "I'm so tired. My head is woozy...it feels like I have a river running through my ears. I need to eat. I'll see you later, okay?"

She turned as several women approached her. With arms flying and hands talking, she answered their questions. Meteor smiled.

So like Martha. Always in charge. A younger, stronger version, but she was a reflection of her mother...a mirror...

Martha's mirror...

Meteor touched his hip. His hand found a gun, but not *that* gun—he had left his Colt pistol at home. He had kept it ever since the night he retrieved it from beneath Martha's body. A strange loneliness crept into his being. Meteor wished he had the gun with him now.

~~~

Matthew pulled the pony-tailed captain aside. "What now? Did I miss anything? Any word from the other scout?" The captain gave a solemn shake of his head. "That's what I thought."

"Why aren't they attacking us?" the captain asked.

"Maybe they haven't guessed there are more of us here." Virgil joined them. "What do you make of this, Virg?"

"I wasn't privy to a lot of what went on down this way, but I know The Man was knocking over towns here. If people didn't let him walk in and take over—take their supplies—their women—he'd let the Crazies kill them." He shrugged. "If the scout was right, maybe there is a stronghold here. It would be a good place to have one."
~~~

“I can’t shake the feeling that something’s coming.” Matthew pulled off his cap and ran a hand through his hair. “But it would be good to go home. Without a gun battle.”

“Sounds like Ruth did enough of that for all of us,” Virgil said. They watched the happy crowd, greet, share stories, and laugh. “From what the women have told us about Sunnyvale, your stepdaughter is pretty amazing.”

“Can’t figure out how she managed,” Matthew said.

“Good training,” the captain said.

“No, it’s more than that...”

“Bloodlines,” the captain added with a grin.

Matthew returned the smile. He paused. “Elizabeth’s not here. Ruth said she left with Brad. She hasn’t heard from her since.”

“Should we tell Ruth about Peter?” the captain asked.

“Save it,” Matthew said. “She doesn’t need another emotional blow, right now.”

“I agree. What’re your plans for The Man?”

“Take him back to the camp. Let the camp decide. If they say he should be executed, then that’s what we’ll do.” Matthew ducked his head up and down, as he searched the crowd.

“Who are you looking for?” the captain asked.

“Meteor.”

“What about Brad?” Virgil asked. “Want me to deal with him?”

“No,” Matthew said. “That’s why I’m looking for Meteor. I think we’ll give him the honor.”

“I’ll find him,” Virgil said. He walked away.

Matthew checked his watch. He looked up at the captain. “I hate to say it, but we are going to have to desert the scout. We have to get these women and kids out of here. I don’t want them subjected to any more danger. Especially Ruth. That’s our priority. Getting them home.”

“The many is greater than the one,” the captain said, rhetorically. “I’ll get right on it.”

Ruth took a first aid kit from Matthew’s truck. Mervyn sat on the ground. She stooped down as he pulled back his shirt.

“Looks like the bullet went straight through.”

She tried opening the first aid kid, but her injured hand was too swollen. She grimaced and gave up. “I wonder if it’s broken,” she said, staring at the ugly black and purple bruise that covered most of her knuckles. She nestled her sore hand in the crook of her opposite elbow. “I can't do this with one hand. There's another guy here who's good with field wounds. I'll get him."

She rose, but Mervyn pulled her down. "Wait— I need to talk to you."

"No, I don't want to talk."

"You have to."

Ruth sank down beside him.

"I know you're leaving in a few minutes. I know you're going back to your husband. And I'm good with that. But I want you to know how much I—"

"Don't—" Ruth said, pressing her fingers to his lips. "Please, don't. It'll be hard enough, as it is."

Mervyn placed his hand over hers and squeezed it. "Okay." He smiled. "But you'll call me...if you ever get lonely?"

"Sure..." Ruth turned her face away. "I'll get the medic."

Jonah hunkered down beside Mervyn. He watched as the medic dressed the bullet wound.

"Could have been worse, huh?"

"You're gonna do fine," the medic said. "Keep it clean. How about this cut? Pretty deep. Could use some stitches."

Mervyn agreed.

The medic finished his doctoring, picked up the first aid kit, and walked away.

Jonah held out his hand. "I'm Jonah." The two men shook hands. "There's a lot I want to ask you. Wanna ride back with me?"

"I'm not going with you guys."

Jonah looked surprised. "Why not?"

"My family's down south. I've got to get back to them. Find out if any of them are still alive."

"Oh." Jonah paused. "Do you know anything about the pile of bodies near Wayne?"

"You guys know about that?"

Jonah nodded. "Our scout told us. We think he's dead. Shot."

"We don't talk about that much. Kind of a failed experiment."

"A what?" Jonah asked.

"From what I hear, there weren't that many people left here...five hundred or so. I wasn't with The Man's camp then, but I heard about it. He set up a base here, and forced the townspeople to work for him. There's a huge stockpile of explosives, you know—in a small village just up the road.

At least there was. Maybe it's gone now. Anyway, the people were more or less slaves. His men would bring in the weapons, the ammunition, the explosives...what have you...and the people would check it, stockpile it, match ammo to guns, clean weapons...that sort of thing."

Mervyn grimaced and shifted his arm into a more comfortable position. "I haven't eaten a thing. I'm starving. Would you mind if we continued this conversation after I get some food?"

"Wait— What about the barracks?" Jonah asked. "The scout said something about a barracks..."

"That's the base...just up the road...in Rosedale."

"Rose...we heard him say *Rose*—" Jonah said eagerly.

"The Man took over an industrial yard there. Not sure about the manpower though." Mervyn's look was pleading. "I really need to eat."

"Here, I'll help you," Jonah said.

The pair walked across the parking lot toward the bus. Somebody had found chairs. They sat down. Meteor joined them. He plopped down on a collapsible campstool next to them. Sheets of plywood and electrical spools had been converted into tables. Food lined the tables, a mixture of camp provisions brought in by Matthew's crew and leftover lunches that Sarah and Ruth had made the day before.

"I hear you've got quite a story to tell," Meteor said with a smile.

"Well, I'd tell you, but then I'd have to kill you," Mervyn replied.

Meteor's smile faded.

"Kidding..." Mervyn said. "Sorry— I'm really punchy. Not a lot of sleep in the past forty-eight hours. My head feels like it's full of cotton candy."

"No problem, kid. Eat. Get some rest. You can tell me on the drive home. Ride with us."

Mervyn looked at Jonah and grinned. "Don't remember the last time I was this popular. No, as I told Jonah—it's Jonah, right?" Jonah nodded. "I'm headed back south. Family."

"Understood," Meteor said. "But we want to pick your brains. And you need sleep. Come with us back to the camp. Get healed up. Fed. Rested. Then we'll outfit you with everything you need for a trip back. Whad'ya say?" Meteor's blue eyes were bright and warm with invitation.

"I don't think so. But, thanks..." A woman handed Mervyn a sandwich. He grabbed it, and bit down. "Now..." he mumbled. "I just want to eat."

Meteor grabbed a sandwich, too. Matthew and Virgil joined them.

"We sent out sentries," Matthew said. "We've got a little time to get everyone fed, and then we'll get back on the road." He turned to Mervyn. "Tell us what you know."

Mervyn scowled and lowered his sandwich. He filled them in.

Virgil looked at Matthew. "If that storehouse is as full of explosives as he says it is—" He shook his head. "Bad news for all of us."

"I know," Matthew said, holding up his hand. "We don't have the muscle to take them on now. But we know about it— We'll make it a priority *after* we get the women and kids back home. Besides, they won't have a leader much longer. Without The Man, I think his men will fall apart...faction off. If they haven't already begun to do so."

Virgil shook his head. "Matthew, The Man's not alone. There's another man. A relative. If you really want to take down their forces...you have to either capture...or destroy those weapons. *Today.*"

Matthew went quiet for a moment. "Let's get the women and kids out of here first."

Jonah walked over. "Brad's conscious."

"Is he talking?" Meteor asked. He stood up along with the other men.

"Yep."

"What should we do with him?" Matthew looked at Meteor as he spoke.

"Me? You want me to take care of him?" Meteor asked with surprise. "How about a little lead poisoning?"

"Let's talk to him first," the pony-tailed captain suggested. He began to walk.

Meteor was already three strides ahead of him.

Chapter Thirty-Five

Yahweh Strengthens

THE SUN began its ritual late afternoon descent over the Badlands, bathing the city in a rich golden glow. Following a conversation with Meteor, Matthew had relocated the vehicles and their picnic to the Drumheller tourist center. They had decided to tie up one loose end before leaving the city. Now, an anticipatory atmosphere was in high gear—children teased and ran, mothers watched from benches, teen girls sought the attentions of young men, and everyone shared news back and forth about the compound and about Sunnyvale. Glances toward a group of men in conference near the squat tourist building confirmed that the event would soon take place.

Two men left the group and joined the women and children gathered on a small patch of lawn. The pony-tailed captain pointed to his watch. Matthew called for attention.

"Ladies, do you think you can stand another three or four hours cramped up on that thing?" Matthew asked, pointing to the bus. Sarah spoke up:

"We're not leaving, Matthew. Not till we see this thing done." She crossed her arms.

"I understand. But what about the children?"

"I'll take the kids," Ruth said. "I don't want to watch. And I don't want Mary and Samuel watching either."

"But, Mom..." Samuel said. "I want to watch. This is gonna be great." Samuel beamed at Matthew.

"You'll do as I say," Ruth corrected her son. However, she was too late—Samuel had already run off with a pack of chattering children. "Stop them from climbing that thing," Ruth called out to the men standing at the base of the huge Tyrannosaurus Rex. The men gave a helpless lift of their shoulders as the children split up and ran past them, screaming and giggling. Ruth sighed. She tipped her head back and looked up.

The huge green and yellow prehistoric creature towered over the people on the parking lot. With one foot forward, its short, clawed forearms raised, and its gaping jaws—the dinosaur menaced convincingly.

Like a monster in a fifties B-movie.

Ruth shuddered. Before the Change, the giant stylized T-rex would have been nothing more than a clever, albeit tacky, tourist attraction. Now it was to be a gallows. She watched the preparations.

Two men were already in the beast's head. A rope dangled down between the dinosaur's jaws; a truck tire was attached. The men pulled on the rope, but the tire caught on the creature's pointed, white teeth. They untangled it, and threw it again. The tire plunged down, drawing the rope taut. It swung back and forth, ticking like a pendulum on a grandfather clock.

Ruth swayed as wooziness filled her head.

Sleep...I need sleep.

She steadied herself and watched as Matthew joined a group of men standing near the dinosaur. They waited while Jonah drove up and parked the truck. Meteor strode over, opened the back door, and yanked a man's bloodied body from the backseat.

Brad.

Meteor dropped the body from his arms. Brad fell to the ground. Ruth shuddered again. The memory of the thumps and soft thuds as her truck rolled over Brad made her stomach sick.

Brad tried to rise, but Meteor pulled back, and landed a kick to his chest. Brad cried out and slumped backwards. Meteor raised his foot again, but Matthew intervened. Ruth couldn't hear what Matthew was saying, but she could see Meteor scowl. He backed off. Slowly. Grudgingly.

Ruth wanted Meteor to kick Brad again, willed him to do so. But the kick might have killed Brad, and that would have been far too kind a death. The men had decided that only an execution would be fitting—only an execution by their hands would begin to appease the hatred in their hearts. The style of execution had been Meteor's suggestion; the site had been Matthew's idea.

Now, Matthew spoke to the pony-tailed captain. The captain ran off. In a few moments, he was back with a another man.

"I've got him," he called as The Man stumbled out in front of him.

Ruth watched The Man walk forward. She wondered again about what he had told her. About his father. About his wife. About his...son...well, not his...

Was all that really true? she thought. A stab of pity touched her heart, but she raked it aside when she remembered the end of The Man's story.

He had murdered them all in cold blood. Including a little boy.

Her heart grew hard once more.

We are responsible for our own lives, no matter what has happened to us, no matter what has been done to us. He made his bed...

Ruth looked up when she heard a man up in the dinosaur's mouth yell.

"We're ready."

Matthew looked up and acknowledged the speaker with a wave of his hand. He then motioned to Brad. Two men picked him up and supported him between them, his arms around their shoulders. Brad screamed out. Ruth guessed that one—if not both—of his arms was broken. The men didn't release their grip.

Ruth searched the crowd. She spotted Meteor. He was standing near the truck, his arms folded across his chest, his legs planted firmly apart. She watched his chest rise, repeatedly, as he drew in deep breaths through his nose. He watched the proceedings from under lowered eyebrows.

He's so angry, she thought. She glanced over at Matthew. *And he's so calm.*

Ruth felt herself tunneling away from the impending event. Like watching hairy spiders through glass, she was mesmerized by the men's actions, but she was glad to be on her side of the glass. Sleep clutched at her consciousness, her eyes drooped, and she swayed.

Mervyn came to stand beside her. She felt his strong hand slide up her back, to the nape of her neck, where it began a gentle massage. It made her shiver. She leaned against him.

Matthew climbed atop the hood of a truck. He stood, very tall, his chin lifted and his eyes forward. He said nothing, at first. Everyone grew silent. Even the children understood and ceased their noisy play. Matthew looked down at his hands for a moment, and then raised his head. He looked over at Meteor, gave him a small nod, and then he spoke:

"I'm calling the Discipline Committee together. Especially for you, Brad. Since you had such a love for it. We have enough elders here for a tribunal," he said. He motioned to the men holding Brad. "Bring him here."

I don't want to watch this, Ruth thought. But she couldn't tear her eyes away.

The men hauled Brad to a position in front of Matthew. In response, the captain gave The Man a push until he was standing about ten feet away from Brad. Women and children crowded around. Ruth scanned the crowd for Mary and Samuel. They were front and center in the group circling Brad.

"Want me to get them?" Mervyn asked, reading her mind.

"No," Ruth said sharply. "They've already seen so much. They might as well see this, too. Maybe they'll learn something from it." She rubbed her hand across her forehead.

"And you?" he asked.

"I'm fine."

Matthew spoke again: "Brad, you've been brought before a council of your peers to answer for your crimes. You have done great harm to the people of our camp. You are a traitor. A murderer. A rapist. How do you answer to these charges?"

A few seconds of dead silence covered the parking lot as everyone waited for Brad to speak.

He said nothing.

"Do you have anything to say before sentence is carried out?" Matthew asked.

Brad remained silent. Ruth wondered if he had passed out.

"Does anyone have any questions of this man?" Matthew called out.

Something ignited inside Ruth. She burst out of her shadowy tunnel. "I do," she said.

Matthew acknowledged her with a nod.

She shrugged away Mervyn's hand, and strode forward. She stopped directly in front of Brad.

"Where's my sister?"

Brad didn't respond.

"Where's *my* sister?" she repeated. Her tone was steady—dark and bitter.

Brad raised his head, but remained silent.

Ruth stared at his hair matted in blood, the bloodstains on the front of his shirt, his jeans, and the deep cuts on his face. Suddenly, she reached over, grabbed a handful of his bloody hair, whipped his head up, and stared into his eyes.

"Where's Elizabeth?" She gave his head a yank. "You owe me that much, you bastard. Tell me where she is." Ruth's eyes glittered.

Finally, Brad's lips moved.

"Dead," he croaked. His mouth creased into something akin to a smile. "Dead— I shot her."

The fist came quickly. Brad's head snapped back and bloody saliva flew from his lips. Ruth cradled her damaged hand against her chest.

"You deserve to die," Ruth spat. Tears spilled down her cheeks. She backed away. "You're going to rot in hell!"

Mervyn came up behind her and took Ruth by the arm. At first, she tried to pull away, but she yielded as he enfolded her in his arms. Her sobs echoed across the parking lot. Sarah collapsed to the ground, and wept softly. Children—their eyes wide—began to snuffle as they comprehended that something else bad had happened in their world.

A long silence ensued, broken only by the sound of crying. A minute later, Matthew spoke again:

"What is your verdict?" he asked the men assembled near him. "Is this man guilty of the charges as stated?"

A chorus of *ayes* lifted into the air.

Matthew nodded and turned back to Brad. "Murder is punishable by death. You will be hanged by the neck till you are dead."

A strange wariness, a hum, a palpable excitement crept over the crowd. The women and children parted and made a pathway as the men dragged Brad forward toward the dinosaur. Then, the women and children moved back, seeking a better vantage point. They had stopped their snuffling, their crying, and now stood frozen in anticipation.

A few minutes later, they saw Brad again as he was lifted over the safety glass enclosure inside the dinosaur's gaping jaws. They waited, breaths held, and watched—entranced by the sight.

No one spoke.

Matthew raised his hand. A man inside the dinosaur's head waved back. Matthew nodded.

Brad flew into the air. He soared for a moment, and then plunged down. The rope around his neck went tight—his body jerked back up, and then down again. The women and children shrieked; some covered their mouths; some covered their eyes as Brad's body danced on the end of the rope—his arms and legs convulsing in death, his eyes bulging.

Ruth stole a look through swollen eyes. She watched Brad's body twitch and swing. She watched. But she felt nothing.

Not horror. Not relief. Not joy.

Nothing.

She glanced at The Man. He stood impassively, eyeing the body as it swung. A few more small jerks and Brad's body hung still. The Man's face changed.

How strange, Ruth thought. *He looks...contented. Did he hate Brad, too?*

The Man turned his head away, as though suddenly bored. The pony-tailed captain grabbed his arm and led him back to the truck. The Man gave no resistance.

Meteor still stood near a truck, arms folded, his eyes glued to the body. He gave Ruth a slight nod, before he lowered his arms and walked over to Matthew.

Matthew met him part way. The two men clasped hands. They said nothing, but Ruth could see the confirmation that passed between them—the silent message was clear.

It is done. And rightly so.

THE WOMEN AND children filed up the steps. The bus driver was the last to board. Matthew stopped her with a hand on her shoulder.

"I'll get one of the men to drive." She began to protest. "Take a rest. You done good." He smiled warmly.

She relented, stepped inside, and took an available seat. Matthew circled a hand above his head.

Three trucks pulled onto the road—Jonah took the lead position with Sparrow riding shotgun. Jonah leaned out the driver's window and shouted at Mervyn.

"Sure you don't want to come?"

Mervyn grinned and waved him on. He turned his attentions back to Ruth. They were standing near the second truck. Trojan sat in the driver's seat. Her children were already in the backseat. Mervyn caught hold of her hands.

"I don't know what to say..."

"Say nothing," she said.

"I might never see you again."

"Please don't do this, Mervyn. *Please*...have mercy on me—" Ruth's voice cracked. She swiped at her eyes.

Mervyn reached up and pulled a necklace from around his neck. It was a dark wooden cross on a leather thong. "Here— I've never taken it off. It's yours now." He pressed it into her hand.

Ruth clamped her fingers over the necklace. "I don't—" She hesitated, and then thought of something. "Ow," she said, as she used her damaged hand to pull her gold wedding band from her finger. She handed the ring to Mervyn. "It's all I have."

"I can't take this—"

"Take it," she said through a throat swollen with tears. "Remember me."

Mervyn gave her undamaged hand a warm squeeze. She returned his squeeze and tried to pull her hand away. But he held it fast.

"You know I'd kiss you if I could," he said.

Warmth flooded Ruth as she remembered their last kiss. "Me, too," she whispered. She gave his hand a final squeeze.

Ruth wrenched the truck door open and slid in. She turned and checked the backseat—her children were slumped over in sleep, but they were belted in. Duke was wedged in firmly between them. He was awake; his big brown eyes regarded her. Ruth smiled.

"Go to sleep, little guy," she said gently. Duke popped his thumb into his mouth and closed his eyes.

Ruth faced forward as Trojan started the engine. Mervyn still stood near her window, but she wouldn't look at him.

Couldn't look at him.

"All set?" Trojan asked.

"Go," she said.

Please go. Now. Hurry.

Ruth's hand throbbed and she hugged it to her chest. She held her breath against the rush of emotions that welled inside her as the truck moved forward.

Halfway across the bridge, Ruth looked back. She stared at the handful of men still standing on the parking lot. She knew Mervyn was among them, but she couldn't see him. Her gaze swept over the perpendicular human-shaped thing swinging gently like a stone pendulum in the breeze. She watched, hypnotized. Matthew had commanded that Brad's body would stay there—as a warning.

Right to left. Left to right. Right to left...

Ruth tore her eyes away.

Elizabeth was dead.

A wave of emotion swelled in her chest. Ruth squeezed her eyes shut tight against it. Disbelief took its place.

Maybe she wasn't really dead. Brad was a liar. Maybe he lied. Yes, maybe he lied.

She stared at her hand, swollen and purple.

Elizabeth.

Numbness crept over her. She felt her eyes grow heavy.

I need to sleep.

She took a quick breath and tried to clear her mind. She turned to Trojan. "So, you're a new daddy," she said. She tried forcing her lips into a tight smile, but was unsuccessful. "How wonderful..."

Ruth drifted as Trojan spoke. Her head drooped forward, her chin on her chest.

She slept.

Matthew, Virgil, and the pony-tailed captain watched the bus rumble away, up the street, and over the bridge. They stood in silence as the small convoy disappeared from view. A tiny breeze caught a pile of paper cups left on a picnic table and sent them tumbling to the ground. They made a soft chucking sound when they hit the pavement, spiraling into the street.

"What do we do about the other scout?" the captain asked grimly.

"I think it's a pretty good bet that he's dead," Virgil said.

"We'd better get going," Matthew said.

"What about the explosives?" the captain asked. "You want a team to check it out? Rosedale is only a few minutes away."

"No," Matthew said. His tone was abrupt. "We're lucky that no one has come after us. Let's get out of here. Brad's dead, and we've got The Man..."

"But those explosives trouble me," the captain said. "There might not be a better chance to take them out."

Matthew shook his head again. "No, not now. Let's go home. We're not ready for another war."

"Okay, but—"

Matthew clapped his hand on the captain's back. "Look, we could try to get our hands on those munitions, but..."

"Or we could destroy them," Meteor interjected. Matthew looked over his shoulder.

"You, too?" he asked Meteor with a grin. "You guys got a death wish?"

Matthew sat at a picnic table. "Not this time," he said. "Too few of us. But we'll be back." He picked up a plastic bag. It still held three cookies. He took one and bit into it.

The captain persisted, his voice insistent. "You know as well as I do that we've got to do something about those explosives—"

Matthew held up a hand. He sighed. "Give me a minute."

Nearby, Meteor and Mervyn leaned up against The Man's truck. The Man sat on the ground, trussed, hands and feet bound. Meteor cleared his throat. "Well, that's one down. One to go." He nudged The Man's foot as he spoke. "Your time is coming."

The Man scowled at him.

Meteor laughed. "What do you say, Mervyn? Two hangings in one day?"

Mervyn said nothing. He twisted a small gold ring around the pinky finger of his right hand. Meteor threw an arm around the younger man's shoulders.

"I don't get it— Why didn't you go with her?"

"What?"

"You know what..." Meteor said with a crooked grin.

"We knew we'd be parting. We expected it."

Meteor gave a soft snort. "Man, I had the chance once to go after a woman I loved—"

"What happened?"

"She was in love with somebody else...so, I let her go."

"Well, then you know *my* situation."

"Your situation. Who's Ruth in love with?"

"Her husband!" Mervyn's voice was brittle with irritation.

"She doesn't— Oh, wait. Neither of you know— Peter died," Meteor said.

"He did?" Meteor had Mervyn's full attention. "How?"

"During the takeover of the camp. He was assigned to the Hutterites farm. He caught some shrapnel. He died the night Ruth escaped." Meteor clapped Mervyn on the shoulder. "Go— They haven't gone far."

"She's not married..." Mervyn let the thought seep into his heart. It produced a smile.

"Go!" Meteor said again.

Mervyn shook his head. "I've got something to do first." He beamed.

Meteor glanced down at The Man. "Yeah...me, too." He looked back at Mervyn. "Don't take too long, buddy." He smiled—a warm, meaningful curve to his lips. "The good ones get taken fast."

"I won't." Mervyn's smile widened.

Meteor shrugged out of his coat and slung it over his shoulder. He was wearing a short-sleeved, navy t-shirt that exposed thick, sinewy arms, and a large oval scar; it was ragged with ridged tissue and still colored an angry red.

Mervyn caught sight of the scar. His smile faded. "What's that?" He eyed Meteor with suspicion. He took a step away. "You with him?"

Meteor rubbed his hand over the scarlet patch of skin. "Only when it suits me, kid...only when it suits me." He nodded toward Mervyn's arm. "Where's yours?"

"Never took one. I came in later—after the Vulcan color-cleansing. Hezekiah knew better than to try and push that on me. We've known each other for far too long."

"Humph." Meteor pulled his coat back on and patted his pockets.

"What are you looking for?" Mervyn asked.

"I was going to offer you a cigar—"

"No thanks. I don't smoke."

"Why did you turn?" Meteor asked suddenly.

"Why *didn't* you turn?" Mervyn parried. He had heard about Meteor's double agent role from Ruth.

Meteor grinned. "Fair enough."

Matthew, Virgil, and the pony-tailed captain came over and stood in front of The Man.

"It's time," Matthew said, nudging The Man with his boot.

"You going to kill me here?" The Man asked.

"No. We're taking you back to the compound."

"Leave him to me, Matthew," Meteor said. "You don't want to take this piece of shit back to the compound."

"He'll go before a tribunal," Matthew said—his words clear and measured. "The whole camp will have the honor of that decision. I think it'll be a healing thing. For all of us."

"Okay, have it your way— At least let me have the honor of driving him." Meteor flashed a wide smile.

Matthew shrugged. "Go ahead."

Meteor wrestled The Man to his feet, opened the truck's passenger door, and shoved him into the front seat. He grabbed a roll of gaffing tape and lashed The Man, arms at his side, to the seat. Meteor inspected his work, and smiled his appreciation.

Mervyn walked up and stood beside him. He caught Meteor's eye and he winked. "Want some help?"

Meteor grinned. "Mervyn's riding with me," he hollered. He opened the driver's side door. He paused. "Give me a minute," he said to Mervyn.

Mervyn watched Meteor run off.

When Meteor came back, he had a dark, green canvas bag swaying from his hand—the bag bulged.

Mervyn gave Meteor a quizzical look.

"Treats..." Meteor said with a grin. He placed the bag into the truck bed.

Mervyn watched as Meteor walked around the side of the truck to where Matthew stood. He threw his arm around Matthew's shoulders.

"You have a good trip back, my friend." Meteor looked at Virgil. "Make sure he doesn't hang around here. Take him home."

Virgil gave a curt nod.

Meteor got into the truck and started the engine. Suddenly, he gunned the motor and shot out onto the street—up the Hoodoo Trail, in the opposite direction, toward Wayne. The truck's wheels slid across the pavement leaving behind a large, black S-curve. His action caught the men off guard. They stared after the truck, puzzled looks on their faces.

"What the hell's he doing?" asked the pony-tailed captain.

"Go after him?" Virgil asked, heading for his truck.

"No— Let him go." Matthew said with a big sigh. He picked up his radio. "Meteor? Meteor? Do you copy? Over."

"Loud and clear."

"What the hell are you doing? Where are you going? Over."

"I've got this, Matthew. Over."

"Get back here. Over."

"Go home, Matthew..."

The three men heard a scrabbling sound.

"Go after him?" Virgil asked again.

"No— Let's wait..." Matthew said, drawing out the last word as one exercising monumental patience—for the umpteenth time. "He's Meteor. Who knows what he's up to..."

Matthew pushed his radio's *Send* button. He clicked his tongue. His brow furrowed. "I can't reach him. The bastard's locked it into a *Send* position." Matthew's eyes darkened.

The three men stood with the radio between them. Over the roar of the truck's engine and the sounds of the road, they heard Meteor's voice:

"Let's find those explosives, shall we?"

"Dammit!" Matthew said. He thumbed the *Send* button again. "Goddammit!"

"Kid, you know where they are, right?" Meteor's deep voice asked.

"Just up the road," they heard Mervyn reply. "About five minutes from here...in Rosedale. There's a saloon there. Outlaws..."

"Ah-ha! Hear that, Matthew? Outlaws! I know you're listening." Meteor paused. "Matthew...I've got to do this," he said, his voice taking on a serious tone. "It's the only way..."

"Goddammit, Meteor," Matthew said to the radio, his voice rising in hot anger. "Get back here."

The road noises resumed.

"So, your real name is Hezekiah," Meteor said. "Kind of a stylin' name for an asshole. How'd you come by it?"

"My father," they heard The Man say. A long pause ensued before The Man added, "It means *Yahweh strengthens.*"

"Hebrew for God," Meteor said. "Gave you some sort of divine complex, did it? I thought 'the man' was kind of contrived."

Road noises.

"How did you get that name anyway?" Meteor asked.

"I just did."

"I'm curious. What's going on in your South Camps? Anyone gonna step into your shoes?"

"There's one who will."

"How strong are your forces?"

"Over five-thousand...and growing...now that we're affiliated with the eastern Mafia—"

"Mafia? You're connected to the Mafia?" Meteor grunted. "You're quite the guy. Oh, I mean...*The Man...*" Meteor laughed at his own joke.

The three men in Drumheller shook their heads and smiled, in spite of themselves.

More road sounds.

"That's it. Just up ahead. See those buildings?" they heard Mervyn ask. "Turn here, or the guards will see you. I think you can see the compound from just down that street."

Crunching of gravel and the sound of the truck's engine.

"We're in Rosedale, Matthew." It was Meteor's voice. "We're perpendicular to the base. I'll be right back." The truck door screeched.

"C'mon, Mervyn," they heard Meteor say. "Let's you and I take a walk. Check things out."

Sounds of booted feet crunching on gravel.

"It's up there," they heard Mervyn call out.

"I can see it, Matthew. Big Archangel's logo. Like a bull's eye." Meteor laughed, his big booming laugh.

Crunching of gravel.

"Okay, I see a few men," Meteor said. "Just a few. They're armed. Big guns." He paused. "Oh...some really big guns."

Scrabbling sounds.

"There's a big bunker. I'm gonna guess that's where the explosives are..."

More scrabbling sounds.

"They can't see me from here," Meteor said.

The three men stared at the radio. Helplessly.

About five minutes later, the truck door squeaked again.

"Got anything you want to say to Matthew? Before we take our little trip?" the men heard Meteor ask.

Silence.

"Sorry, Matthew...the man's not talking to you." Meteor laughed. "Oh, I almost forgot something." They heard the truck door screech open.

More scrabbling sounds.

The truck door banged shut. Meteor spoke again:

"Okay, kid...time for me to roll. Get out of here, and don't forget what I told you."

The men heard Mervyn mutter something in response. A door banged again.

"We found Mervyn a dandy little truck," Meteor said. "You should see him in a few minutes."

Crackling of a plastic wrapper.

"I think this momentous occasion calls for a cigar, don't you, Hezekiah? One for you and...one for me."

A pause.

"Oh, you can't hold yours. He can't hold his, guys." Meteor laughed. "Here...we'll just stick this into that big mouth of yours."

The sound of a match being struck.

The Man coughed.

"Hey, don't do that...it's one of yours, ya know. We found them in your clubhouse. You left them behind. With some good Scotch, too. Right, Virgil?"

Virgil gave Matthew a sheepish look. Matthew raised his eyebrows.

"Matthew, my friend...it's time," Meteor said. "Old Hezekiah and I have some wrongs to right. And you know...and I know...the explosives have to go. And since his boys don't know how to play nice, I'm gonna take away their toys."

Matthew closed his eyes.

Silence.

"Virgil, I didn't like you...but you're okay," Meteor said, his tone light and friendly. "And Pony-tail...always liked you just fine."

The three men nodded at the radio.

Matthew folded his hands and bowed his head.

The Man spat the lit cigar from his mouth. It dropped to the floorboards. "You really think this will change anything, Meteor?" The Man asked. "You think killing me will stop the inevitable?"

"Relax and enjoy your cigar, Hezekiah." Meteor bent, retrieved the cigar, wiped the wet end against his jeans, and stuck it back into The Man's mouth. "You've had your chance. Now it's my turn." Meteor's tone became very serious.

"Because of you, Hezekiah, too many people have died. Some were friends of mine. You remember Josef? Brad might have pulled the trigger, but you ordered his execution. And Simon. And Peter. And Elizabeth...they're all dead because of you. And then there's your plan to merchandise women—"

"It's a smart plan," The Man retorted. "They're valuable—"

"But they were our women. *Ours*. Do you understand that word?"

Silence.

"And what about your *sister*? That's a hell of a way to treat a sister. She's doing very well with us, by the way."

Silence.

"Then there's a dear friend of mine. Remember Martha? Do you know what happened to her?"

"I know," The Man said. "But Brad acted on his own. I didn't want her harmed."

"He didn't just shoot her, you know? He and a bunch of your goons raped her. Did you know that?" Meteor's tone hardened. "Ripped her up so badly, she nearly died. But she didn't die. She survived. And then along comes her daughter..." Meteor laughed—a humorless, cold sound. "Kind of poetic justice, don't you think? That you're sitting here because of Martha's kid? Beaten out by a broad..." Meteor laughed again—a genuine sound of amusement this time.

The Man laughed, too, a caustic sound. "How long have you had a thing for another man's wife? That oughta earn you a hot spot in Hell."

Virgil and the captain glanced at Matthew, but he didn't look up. The voices continued.

"She beaned me with a gun the first time we met," Meteor chuckled. *A small pause.* "I probably loved her from the moment I saw her," he added softly.

"Lusting after another man's wife breaks the Seventh Commandment," The Man lectured.

Silence.

"We don't choose who we love," Meteor said. It was almost gentle. "Just happens sometimes."

Silence.

"You're headed to Hell, Meteor—just like I am."

"If you say so, Hezekiah."

"I do."

"Shall we test your theory?" Meteor asked.

The Man didn't answer.

Sounds of scrabbling.

"See these?" Meteor asked. "These grenades will help get things started. We'll stick one between your legs. We'll put one here on the seat between us. Ten seconds later, this truck will be the handy-dandy detonator that takes out your base...and those explosives. Now that's a smart plan, don't you agree?"

"Means you'll die with me," The Man noted wryly. "You sure you want to do this?"

"I've lived a full life. I'm ready to go," Meteor said. "And...I'm good with my Maker. Are you?"

Silence.

"It's time, guys," Meteor said. His voice grew soft. "Matthew? Tell her—" *Pause.* "I don't have to tell you what to tell her..."

"Don't do it, Meteor," Matthew murmured. His voice sank to a thick whisper. "Don't do it..."

Silence.

Matthew, Virgil, and the captain held their breaths.

"We're off..." Meteor said.

The truck's engine roared. Crackling and spitting filled the air as rocks chattered against the truck. They heard Meteor yell above the racket:

"This is gonna make one big boom. But when ya gotta go—ya gotta go. Say good night, Hezekiah."

Several seconds of road noise, more scrabbling sounds, a screeching sound, the rattle of gunfire, and then...a loud crash.

The radio went dead.

Silence.

The three men jumped as a massive explosion rocked the ground. To the southeast, the sky turned color—deep oranges and reds. Thick, twisted pillars of gray clouds, capped in darkness, mushroomed up with each explosion. The three men watched in silence.

Explosion after explosion shook the ground. The sky shimmered and flared—now light, now dark—with each blast. Balls of frenzied fire shot upward, blazing arcs across the prairie sky.

"Like meteors," Virgil murmured.

Matthew bowed his head. He shielded his eyes with his hand. He turned and walked away.

"Appropriate," the pony-tailed captain said.

"How so?" Virgil asked.

"Badlands."

Chapter Thirty-Six

A Dying Snowflake

THE TRUCKS roared up the highway. The warm day had melted much of the snow. Other than slowing down a bit to accommodate the lumbering bus and maneuvering around lake-sized puddles, their ride home was uneventful. Ruth fell in and out of sleep. When she awoke, she immediately thought of Mervyn. She considered asking Trojan to turn back, but they were too far down the road to turn around.

"You're awfully quiet, Ruth," Trojan observed. "Are you sick?"

"Yes and no," she said. "My hand is really sore." She glanced back. The children were still asleep. She estimated they were about an hour and a half away from the camp. "I was running on adrenaline for so long...my body feels like it's floating in space."

Trojan slowed the truck and nosed by a fallen tree limb. "You're amazing," he said. "A man couldn't have done what you did."

Ruth made a small noise of dismissal. "A scared woman is capable of a great deal...very capable."

"Can I ask you about Brad?"

"No."

"Okay. How about the guys back at the home?"

"No," Ruth said sharply, and then softened her tone. "At least not now, Trojan."

"I guess finding out—"

"I said NO! What part of that don't you understand?"

Trojan pulled back as though she had struck him. "Sorry," he mumbled.

"I'm sorry, Trojan...I'm sorry." In desperate need for solace, Ruth crossed her arms and hugged them to her chest. "It was like a bad dream. I don't want to live through it again. Especially now that I know about Elizabeth..." She choked.

"I understand. But you'll have to talk to somebody," he said gently. "Lots of guys have trouble after they've been through a war."

"I will. I promise." Ruth drifted back into her own thoughts.

Elizabeth was dead. Brad was dead. Her children were safe. And they were headed home. That's all that matters, she told herself.

Yet even as the thought flitted through her brain, she knew it wasn't true. It would never be true again.

How will I do this? How will I keep this secret? I already miss him so much.

Ruth turned back to Trojan. "Update me on the compound." She leaned her head back against the seat, closed her eyes, and listened.

Ruth learned that the women and children in the second bunkhouse had all made it out alive, but that Simon had been killed while trying to rescue her group. That thought made her very sad, and her heart went out to Anna, whom she learned was carrying Simon's baby. She learned that Meteor had saved her mother's life; that Matthew had defeated Virgil's forces; that Virgil and his men had joined the camp; that the second women's bunkhouse had been rebuilt; and that Brad had been a traitor all along. Her mind tried to skirt around that information since it brought back images of Brad, a bleeding Brad, rising on the road behind her truck.

Ruth remained quiet, so quiet, that Trojan stopped speaking, guessing she had fallen asleep. She wasn't asleep.

Ruth was imagining Peter's face and how happy he would be when he saw her. A memory of Mervyn overshadowed the vision. She pushed it away, tried to fight it, but finally relented to its seducing coercion. She stroked the cross now hanging around her neck.

A PURPLE duskiness had settled over the fields. Ruth saw the twinkle of camp lights through the trees. A heavy discomfort rose in her chest again, and she tried to shake it.

How will I be with Peter? It's been so long. How do I keep Mervyn out of my mind?

She knew she didn't have an answer, so she sighed—a great, long sigh.

"Almost there," Trojan said.

Martha came into Ruth's mind again. So did Meteor and their last conversation. So many people—over the past months—had told her how much she was like her mother. At first, she had hated the comparison, but she had come to accept that while she was not like her mother, she had *traits* like her mother. She was at peace with that. She wondered how Martha would respond to the news about Brad.

And about Elizabeth.

The first two trucks were already parked, their occupants unloaded. The bus was coming to a stop; Ruth and Trojan pulled up in the rear. Hundreds of camp members were at the gate—men, women, and children.

Women and children.

The thought made Ruth's heart glad. "How did they know?" Ruth asked.

"Lead truck would have radioed in," Trojan said.

Ruth opened her door as a huge cheer went up. "Wow..." She shrank back, a little abashed.

"You're a hero," Trojan said as he helped the children out of the truck. He offered her his arm. "C'mon."

The crowd parted as a woman strode through. Martha marched up to Ruth and enfolded her in her arms.

"Oh my God, it's good to see you. So good..."

Ruth hugged her back. "Good to see you, too, Mom."

Ruth pulled away and looked into her mother's face. "Brad's dead, Mom. I know what he did to you. He's dead. You don't have to think about him anymore."

Martha's eyes opened wide in surprise. "He is? How?"

Ruth gazed into the distance. "I drove over him. With a truck. He didn't die, but Matthew took him prisoner. And then...well...we hung him."

"He's dead... You drove over him. Then we're even," Martha said.

Ruth looked back at her mother, stunned. "What?"

"You stopped a man who hurt me. Well...I once stopped a man who hurt you."

Ruth looked puzzled. "What?"

"Remember that day with Amanda? The drunk biker who kissed you outside the church?" Ruth nodded. "I shot him."

"You did?"

"I did." Martha's words poured out of her. "It was awful. I could barely live with myself. I never told anybody. Not even your father."

Ruth gasped in realization. “That’s why you hated gun practices...” She gave a soft snort. “Like mother, like daughter...”

The two women hugged again.

“Guess what?” Ruth said. “We also got The Man.”

“Did you have something to do with that, too?”

Ruth grinned. “Yeah— But I had help.”

“Is...he dead?”

“No. They’re bringing him back here. We get to vote on what happens to him.”

Mary ran up and encircled her grandmother’s leg. “Nana!”

Martha scooped up the little girl. “You got so big!” Martha said as she hugged the little girl in a super-sized squish.

“Nana! I can’t breathe.”

The crowd laughed. They rushed forward and surrounded the new arrivals.

“Where’s Matthew?” Martha asked, while she unwrapped her granddaughter from her neck. Mary switched her affections and leapt at Trojan who picked up the little girl and swung her into the air.

“They stayed behind,” Trojan said. “They’re coming. Him, Virgil, the captain...Meteor.” He checked his watch. “I’m surprised they’re not here yet.”

Martha craned her neck around. “Where’s Elizabeth?”

Ruth fielded the question. She spoke quickly.

“Sh—she didn’t make it, Mom. Brad...”

Martha’s mouth hung open. “Not two children.” She began to cry.

Ruth’s face registered panic. “What? Two children? Nehemiah?”

My brother? Was he back? He left the camp ages ago.

Trojan shook his head. “No—” He set Mary on the ground and put a hand on Ruth’s shoulder. “She means...Peter.”

“Peter?” Ruth cocked her head. “What’s wrong with Peter?” She scanned the crowd, looking for her husband’s face. Suddenly, it dawned on her— Peter was not in the crowd. “What? Where is he?”

“I’m sorry,” Trojan said gently. “Shrapnel. At the Hutterites. I’m so sorry.”

Ruth’s eyes grew wide. “No! I don’t believe you. You’re lying to me.” She tore across the compound in the direction of their RV. Others watched her as she ran, calling out the name of her dead husband.

Anna stood several feet away with Cammy, who held Little Ruth cuddled to her chest. They watched Ruth run past them.

"I feel so sorry for her," Cammy said. She snuggled the baby closer to her chest.

"Me, too," Anna said. "It's gonna be so hard for her..." Anna looked back at the crowd, saw someone, and smiled. She waved. Sparrow walked toward her. He returned her smile.

"How many didn't come back?" Anna asked. She already knew that Elizabeth was gone; one of the women from the bus had told her.

"The ladies say that The Man pulled several of the teen girls, some of the older women, including Hannah, and the autistic kid," Sparrow told her.

"Reggie? Were they killed?" Cammy asked with alarm.

"Don't know for sure. The women say Mervyn might have managed to save some of them."

"Mervyn?"Anna asked.

"Yeah, one of The Man's guys. He turned...decided to help the women escape. Sounds like he got real close to Ruth, too."

Anna looked past Sparrow's shoulder. "Where is he?"

"Said he had to go back to his family. We invited him to come. But he—"

"That's too bad. Ruth needs a close friend, right now."

"I'm glad to see you," Sparrow said. He touched Anna's cheek. Anna leaned her face into his cupped hand.

Trojan came up beside Cammy and wrapped his arm around her waist. He pulled back on the flannel blanket covering his daughter's face.

"Is she doing okay?"

"She's fine," Cammy answered. "She's really eating well." She stroked Trojan's cheek. "You need a shave."

"I just need to lie down with you," he said, touching her face. "You look tired."

"I am."

"Are you feeling okay?" Trojan searched her eyes for truth.

"Much better now that you're back safe and sound." She grinned. "Are the rest right behind you?"

"Should be. They debated checking out a munitions dump, but Matthew nixed that idea. Not enough manpower."

"Hope Matthew gets back here soon. She needs him," Cammy said, motioning to Martha.

Trojan clutched Cammy to him. Right now, I need you."

~ ~ ~

THE SUPPER was not the celebration some had hoped it would be—too many missing faces. In addition, Matthew and the other men had not yet returned. Martha sat quietly at one of the long tables. She wasn't hungry, but she didn't want to be alone. Her eyes were swollen.

Elizabeth.

Anna sat next to Martha, and Sparrow sat next to her. Gordon toddled around between the tables. He had begun to walk almost immediately after his first birthday, and he was a crowd pleaser. He was welcomed wherever his tiny travels took him. He now stood by Martha, one chubby hand clutching at her jacket for support, the other shoved into his mouth, drool streaming down his chin. Martha couldn't help herself—she bent and picked him up.

"He's really a great kid," Martha said to Anna. She bumped her chin in the direction of Anna's stomach. "You still feel okay?"

Anna touched her stomach. "The baby is active."

Martha glanced over at Sparrow. "And him?"

"He's good." Anna blushed. She leaned in to Martha's ear. "I think I'll be announcing another moving-in day soon."

Martha gave her a warm smile, but it was short-lived. Several more people entered the room; Georgie was with them. She looked pale. She was holding her stomach.

"I think she's expecting," Anna whispered. "She's been throwing up."

Martha said nothing.

A cry went up outside. "They're here!"

Tables and chairs screeched and boots pounded over the wooden floorboards as chattering people ran out to meet the men.

Martha waited, and let the people rush by her. She followed the group outside, and stood alone on the Meeting House steps. From there, she watched the excited crowd.

"Hey, it's a new truck," she heard one of the teen boys say. He pointed to the last truck pulling up to the Gatehouse. It parked in a pool of light cast by a large construction lamp mounted on a pole.

"That's one of The Man's trucks," Sarah called triumphantly. "They've brought back The Man, too."

Martha walked down the steps. She clutched at the stair rail to take the weight off her sore leg. The old knife wound ached, as it sometimes did, like her chest scar. Brad had left his mark.

But he was gone. He would never hurt her again.

The thought brought her comfort, but a vision of Elizabeth filled her mind again, and she felt the tears rise. She swiped at her eyes, and looked across the compound.

Three men got out of the last truck. They strode side-by-side toward the waiting crowd. She could barely see Matthew in the dim light, chatting with his men. She smiled. He was already giving instructions.

Suddenly, she sensed that something was wrong. Trojan and Jonah broke from the pack and rushed up to the men. They held a whispered conversation. When it was over, the two men hung their heads.

Martha gulped.

Everyone was too quiet.

A razor edge of fear cut through her. Her mouth went dry. She felt dizzy and she grabbed the stair railing again to keep herself from stumbling. She squinted.

Was that Matthew? Maybe it wasn't.

She raced across the compound. She breathed a sigh of relief when she recognized her husband. He walked towards her, flanked by Virgil and the pony-tailed captain. Jonah and Trojan trailed behind them.

A sound caught her attention—it was Georgie. She was crying. Martha tensed again.

Matthew reached her. His face was somber. Martha's eyes searched wildly.

Then she knew.

"Martha, I'm sorry..." Matthew said. He took her gently by the shoulders. "He..."

"No." Martha held up her hand. She wanted no further words. A weight as thick and as hushed as the grayest fog settled over her.

Choking. Squeezing. Suffocating.

"He said to tell you—" Matthew continued, but Martha pulled away.

"No..." she breathed. The word sank softly like a dying snowflake into the abyss that had opened in her heart. She turned and walked away.

Matthew let her.

Silent.

Soundless.

Secret.

For it had to be.

Sheree Zielke

Epilogue

Deerhunter

TWO WEEKS passed, and with the sunny, spring days went most of the snow. Warm breezes reduced the massive snow piles to wide, gray pools of kid joy. Martha leaned on her elbows, staring out her kitchen window, and enjoying the sun on her face as she watched the children play—stomping and splashing through puddles, soaking their pants, their friends, their mothers. Martha smiled—the children had survived the last six months; they had come through seeming quite unscathed. Now they were back to being normal children—all of them, except for one child...

Samuel ran across the compound, hollering at the top of his lungs. He was in the middle of one of his mock gun battles. He let out another whoop and waved his pistol in the air.

"I'm gonna kill you guys when I catch you. You filthy bastards." Martha blanched.

Filthy bastards?

She considered running out and correcting him, but she knew better. He had been corrected before about the words he was now using, by his mother, but her admonitions resulted in a hollow agreement and flippant retorts of, "Okay...sure, mom," and a secret sneer—one that Martha recognized—and it chilled her.

Samuel's time with The Man had put an edge into the little boy's soul—a kind of brittleness, a wariness, and more importantly...a coldness. He had not seemed at all affected by his father's death, and only slightly troubled by The Man's death, remarking that *one who lives by the sword, shall die by the sword.* That observation, so out of place for his age, surprised and concerned Ruth and Martha, but he was young, and they agreed he would grow out of it.

Samuel pretended to fire his pistol at three other boys running for cover behind a pile of dirt. The gun was a real weapon—devoid of its magazine and bullets—but it was real, since it was not only politically correct for children to play war games in this new world; it was necessary—for their survival. Martha sighed and turned back to her granddaughter who was on the floor with the cat.

"Here you go, Wilbert. C'mon, catch it." Mary was teasing the gray cat with an elastic hair band tied to a length of yarn. She dangled it out of the cat's reach, dropped it down, and just before the cat could catch it, she swung it away. Her little girl giggles filled the room. Martha smiled.

Mary didn't talk about the past six months, except for once, when she asked Martha about the scar on her chest. "Does it hurt, Nana?" she asked, pulling a tiny finger across the corded scar.

"A little—sometimes," Martha had told her. "If I turn too fast." The answer had placated Mary, and she had switched the conversation to news of a fresh batch of barn kittens.

Martha's mind wandered to her daughters. She missed Elizabeth, but it was Ruth who troubled her. Ruth had retreated into her RV, and rarely socialized with the rest of the camp. Everyone knew about the part she had played in the women's and children's escape, and the curious would coax her to tell them about the night of the escape—the killing of the bikers, the capture of The Man—but mostly they wanted to know about Brad's death. Ruth refused to say anything about it.

Martha understood.

Martha looked past the children to the Gatehouse. Matthew was there, doing what her husband did best: organizing and assigning. Jonah was there, too. So was Virgil, the pony-tailed captain, and Trojan—smiling and laughing—old friends and trusted brothers-in-arms. All of them were there.

No— Not all of them.

Smiling blue eyes and a mischievous grin flashed into her memory. Her heart clutched in pain. She had not cried over Meteor's death; she had not allowed herself to do so, feeling it was an act of disloyalty, a terrible treason, a great betrayal to cry over another man with her beloved husband nearby. She wouldn't cry now either.

She clenched her hands and shoved her nails into her palms. She squeezed tight as she retreated into the familiar steel coolness that had become her constant companion—a deadly stillness that forced her tears deeper into her soul.

Silent. Soundless...

The camp had rejoiced at the news of The Man's death, but news of Meteor's *sacrifice* (no one called it a 'suicide') had left a pallor, a grayness, and a deep sadness that robbed them of their jubilance. It affected all of them, Matthew included. But he never spoke of Meteor. He knew better.

Another high-pitched war cry echoed across the compound. More pretend gunfire. More pretend deaths. Samuel ran near her window. Martha saw the gun in his hand.

Memories surfaced again. One particular memory—a man with blue eyes, near a campfire... The image roared through her brain and along with it came a kaleidoscope of exquisite emotions—so intense, so painful, she couldn't breathe.

Martha clutched her fists tighter and willed the vision, the pain, to stop. She remembered something Amanda had said, so long ago:

"The time will come when the missing stops, and the forgetting begins."

Really? Really? Will I ever stop missing him?

Martha squeezed her eyes shut tight.

Let him go. Let him go, she screamed inside her mind. *But I need to speak. I need to tell. But who was there to tell? Who can I tell?*

She fought an urge to cry out. Instead, she gritted her teeth. Like a drowning kitten, her heart clawed its way back to the frozen emotions that had protected her since his death.

No, dear Amanda, you were wrong. I have not forgotten you—

I will NEVER forget him.

Another memory flashed... It curled the corners of her mouth in a sudden smile. *Their first meeting...* He had bashed her in the head with his gun to stop her from laughing.

His gun. Was it still here? Did he have it with him when he...? It would be so good to hold his gun.

"Mary— Nana has to check something. Feed Wilbert. I'll be back in a few minutes. Then we'll go look at the new kittens."

Mary beamed. "Okay, Nana."

Martha kissed the top of Mary's head before dashing out the door.

Meteor's cabin wasn't far; it was Matthew's old cabin. Martha tapped on the door. When no one answered, she turned the knob and went inside.

The cabin was so silent, so strange in its stillness. She stood quietly like one at a graveside, afraid to speak, afraid to trouble the spirits, afraid to touch the misty gate. Like a morning dream, the silence reached up and enfolded her, claiming her, drawing her into its web of memories.

She turned slowly and looked around.

Meteor's jacket hung from a hook, a pair of his boots sat on the floor below, a pen and notepad lay on the table. She reached over, but didn't touch. She drew back her hand.

Martha went into the bedroom. The bed was neatly made. Women's clothing hung over the back of a chair.

Georgie.

Long stalks of pussy willows burst from an empty Scotch bottle seated on a table near the bed. The sight made Martha grin. She remembered the day they raided The Man's second west side clubhouse, and the look of victory on Meteor and Virgil's faces when they emerged, clutching a case of Scotch and two large humidors filled with cigars. Martha ran her hand over the pussy willows, their softness tickling her fingertips. She turned to a tall dresser.

She reached for the top drawer, but stopped. It felt too much like opening a casket. Finally, she pulled the drawer open. She looked inside—a few t-shirts, some underwear, a booty of mismatched socks, and a dark turtleneck sweater.

She picked up the sweater and held it to her face. It still smelled of him. She inhaled deeply. She flipped the sweater across her back and tied the arms at her neck, in a college boy style. She opened another drawer. Then another. More clothes, papers, knick-knacks, boxes of ammo, a bottle of cologne—she opened that and sniffed. The scent made her shiver. She recapped the bottle and continued her search.

She pulled the bottom drawer open. How-to books, survival books, gun magazines, and an old Bible.

A Bible?

She blinked and picked it up.

A Bible? Was he a believer?

They had never discussed religion. Or God. Or Jesus. She flipped it open. His handwriting filled the margins. A notation at the front of the book indicated it had been given to him as a confirmation present. Martha closed the Bible and returned it to the drawer.

She was about to shut the drawer, and then changed her mind. She reached for the Bible again, but as she did, something caught her eye. A rag stained in patches of burgundy peeked out from under the magazines. She pushed the copies aside to reveal a large package wrapped in a bloodstained cloth.

She gasped. She recognized the material. It was a piece of her dress. Meteor and Anna had cut a swatch from her dress—the white dress she had worn that night—the night Brad shot her—the night Meteor had saved her.

He kept this?

Martha began to cry, a steady stream of hot droplets, but she never noticed. She picked up the packet—it was heavy. She began to unwrap it.

The blood-encrusted fabric cracked, sending rust-red flakes to the floor. The bloodstains grew bright where her tears fell. She lifted a final flap of fabric and revealed the contents. Her heart burst open, and she stood—transfixed—as she stared down at the item in her hand.

His gun. Their gun.

She dropped the cloth to the floor, and turned the gun over in her hand. She clutched it to her chest, and sank to her knees.

"God...help me," she begged.

Memories flooded back again, but this time she had no resources to stop them, no steel guard to keep them at bay.

She saw him standing...his big arms extended wide in welcome from across a fire pit...milk hitting a kitten's whiskers...rich, booming laughter...bright, blue eyes...and a deep voice crooning in her ear...

"...but she breaks just like a little girl..."

Realization struck hard.

I'll never see you again.

The dam broke.

~ ~ ~

RUTH PICKED at the food on her plate. She lifted a forkful of scrambled eggs to her mouth, and then dropped the fork. Egg bits scattered across the table. She shoved her plate away, crossed her arms on the table, and put her head down.

Living on the compound, without Peter, was proving to be physically and emotionally exhausting. She could barely drag herself from her bed in the mornings. Sleep was short, and when she did sleep, she was tormented by endless dreams of blood, and shooting, and faces—so many faces of people who didn't exist in her life anymore—her father, Peter, Elizabeth, Simon, Meteor, and...

...Mervyn.

She touched the thick leather cord around her neck. She had worn Mervyn's gift to her since the night they arrived back at camp. She stroked the smooth wood of the cross.

I was a widow, Mervyn. I was already a widow. I didn't know. I'm so sorry.

Tears trickled down her cheeks and splashed to the tabletop.

Somebody knocked on the door.

"Go away," she mumbled.

"Ruth?" It was Jonah.

"Oh, damn...what?" she said, wiping her face on a tea towel. She checked her pockets, eyed the towel, and then blew her nose in it, too. She opened the RV door. The late morning sun struck her hard in the face and she blinked. She shielded her eyes. "What is it?"

"Somebody's arrived. Matthew wants you at the Gatehouse."

"Why me?"

"He thinks the guy might be one of the Crazies from the South Camps."

"Oh, for God's sakes...ask one of the other women."

"No, Matthew said you have to come," Jonah said stubbornly. Ruth heaved a sigh. She followed Jonah across the compound.

A crowd of people had gathered near the Gatehouse. Jonah led her through the assembly. Ruth gave them a queer look—they were smiling. Jonah pointed to the Gatehouse door. Ruth was about to climb the steps when she heard a giggle, a sound she recognized. She looked toward the parking lot.

A little boy came around one of the trucks, his head in the clouds, his eyes settling nowhere, giggling at something that only he could see. His Veggie Tales bag was slung across his chest.

"Reggie!" Ruth cried. "Reggie!" She ran to him and clutched him in a bear hug, kissing the top of his head. Reggie giggled again.

"Weggie," he said. "Weggie."

Ruth turned back to the Gatehouse. Jonah was standing next to Matthew. Hannah was standing next to them. They were smiling.

"Oh my God, Hannah!" Ruth rushed over and grasped the woman in a warm embrace. "Oh, I'm so glad to see you." She pulled back. "You brought Reggie back? By yourself?"

Hannah shook her head. "No, I had help." She looked over Ruth's shoulder. Ruth turned around.

A man was walking toward her.

Ruth's hand flew to her mouth. Her eyes grew bright with tears.

The man reached her. He was smiling—a warm smile—the same smile he had worn the day they had said good-bye. He raised his hand to her cheek. A gold band twinkled on his pinky finger.

"Hi, Deerhunter."

"Mervyn! You came..."

The pair gripped each other in a complete embrace. After a moment, Ruth pulled away.

"I'm not married," she said softly.

"I know," Mervyn said. He smiled again, and kissed her forehead. "That's why I'm here."

Ruth clutched him to her. "I'm so happy to see you."

This time Mervyn pulled away.

"Where's Martha?" he asked.

"Why?"

"I have a message for her."

~~~
~~~

Sheree Zielke

Author's Notes

THE PENNING of a novel's first draft is easy; it is the editing that is hard—a seemingly endless, fastidious, stressful, and time-consuming job that can make a writer feel very alone. Fortunately, I am never alone.

I wrote the first draft of *Martha's Mirror* in six weeks. However, a first draft is as close to being a finished book as a fetus is to being an adult human. The first draft is only the skeleton of the book. It takes edits—so many of them—to turn a bunch of spindly ideas into a book. However, as the book's author, I am too close to the subject and I cannot see all the problems, or worse, I see the issues, but choose to ignore them. Thank God for editors.

I am blessed to have people in my life like David, Rob, and Susan who—apart from being dear to me—exhibit unsurpassed editorial abilities. Then there are the readers who surprise me with their editorial abilities, too. Like Paula, Paul, and Denise.

As hard as it is to address all edits from so many different perspectives, I am deeply indebted to those who give so much time to ensuring my novels make for a "cracking good read." (One of my readers said that...I liked the sound of it.)

Aside from typos and grammatical errors, they catch continuity problems, character motivational issues, character voice inconsistencies, the "What the...?" plotline holes, and the over usage of words and phrases (Rob loves his word "alerts"—ask him about *snort*.)

My editors keep this author honest. If I have gotten tired and want to blow off plot details with a few lines, I am gently asked to go back and write an actual scene, giving credence to a line I have oft quoted myself: "Show, don't tell."

I do not accept all their edits; some things just are. Like the names of my characters. (I write this with great affection to Susan who cannot abide the name, Mervyn.) The truth is my characters name themselves. There are several names in my books that I really dislike, but those are their names. End of discussion.

Some edits deal with reader perception; these edits are harder to honor, so I seek a consensus from among the other editors. Oftentimes, a reader/editor points out exactly the thing that was nagging at me. I know the book gets better when I acquiesce—and fix the problem.

Thank you, to all of you...my editors, my readers, and my fans. I am humbled by your care and interest in my wild imaginings.

Sheree Zielke

Because of your support, I might have a trilogy in me after all.

About the Author

SHEREE ZIELKE resides in Edmonton, Alberta, Canada. She was born in Winnipeg, Manitoba, but spent her formative years outside the city, on a farm near Beausejour. Sheree credits her time as a farm girl for the successes in her life.

"I learned about hard work and diligence. I learned about disappointments and I learned about escape. And I learned about believing in myself, against all odds."

Sheree teaches digital cameras as a profession. Her photography can be seen on Flickr.com. One of her images won the Royale Tissue 2011 Canada Collection (Alberta/BC region).

For many years, Sheree has written for newspapers, magazines, and radio stations. She is an incurable adventurer, whose travels have taken her around the world, including New Zealand, the Amazon, Europe, and South Africa. She also took in the 2010 Sturgis Motorcycle Rally where she met and interviewed Hells Angels' chief, Sonny Barger.

Sheree is always ready to take advantage of a publicity opportunity; she became known as the "Crazy Canadian," during the celebration of the royal marriage between Kate and Prince William, in April 2011. She slept on the cobblestones across the street from Westminster Abbey where she became a media favourite.

"I'm a romance novelist. How could I not be at the romantic event of the century?"

Sheree is mother to three grown children, and Nana to nine grandchildren. She lives with her comedy actor/magician husband, David Thiel.

For the record, she hates having her name mispronounced. It is the first thing her students learn about her. *"I don't answer to Sherry."*

Martha's Mirror is Sheree's second novel.

Email Sheree: shereezielke@shaw.ca
Photography by Sheree: www.flickr.com/photos/97705796@N00
Martha's Vine book website: www.marthasvine.com

About the Artist

I MET HIM as TheWalkinMan.

Well—I have never actually "met" him. We are Flickr.com buddies, photographers, who happened across each other online, and who enjoyed each other's work. We have met many times through our images, but never in person. This is our third collaboration together.

His mundane name is Fred SanFilipo. But to me, he will forever remain...TheWalkinMan.

TheWalkinMan intrigued my imagination with his name and his images, but then he impacted my life. I learned from his work, from his attitudes, and from his extreme talent. My eye began to see things a bit differently through my camera lens; I began to process my images differently—with more flair, with more abandon. I even got the courage to try self-portraits. I learned a great deal from TheWalkinMan.

Then, in keeping with my impetuous nature, I asked Fred if he would do the jacket art for my first novel, *Martha's Vine*. Because we had worked so well together before, I believed that Fred would be the one to interpret my written words with a graphic image.

And he did. Admirably so.

So, it would make sense that a sequel be fronted with Fred’s magnificent art, too. I sent him a first draft of *Martha’s Mirror*, and let him be. Once more, Fred interpreted my words with his vision. And what a vision.

Instead of using himself as a model (as he did for *Martha’s Vine*), he enlisted the help of Emily Elizabeth Wise (see next page). Fred did the photography, the post-processing, and the cover layout.

Once more, I think it’s perfect!

I am honored to have TheWalkinMan's work on a second novel, but I am more honored to call him my friend.

Fred SanFilipo is a long-time upstate New York regular. Fred closed the doors on a successful 20 year design and marketing firm a few years ago in quest of the quieter pace and lifestyle of a freelance designer. He lives in the city of Rochester on Lake Ontario.

About the Model

I NEVER have a set-in-stone idea of what my main characters look like other than striking traits like blue eyes (all the females know to whom I am referring). I believe the description of a main character is best left to the reader's imagination. So, Ruth—this Ruth—came as a total surprise to me—a very pleasant surprise.

The model's name is Emily Elizabeth Wise. She is 23-years old and lives in New York State. She met the cover artist, Fred SanFilipo, at a coffee shop, where she works.

She is a college student with a sweeping appreciation for life. Her eclectic interests include people, music, art, alchemy, hiking, plants, New Mexico, magic, and aliens.

Besides having captivating, expressive features, Emily is also an adventurer—very appropriate for the strong-willed woman she is portraying.

Thank you, Emily. Your lovely face has added a special dimension to the saga of Martha.

Emily can be found on *Facebook*.

Sheree Zielke

CPSIA information can be obtained at www.ICGtesting.com
Printed in the USA
LVOW092056251111

256488LV00001B/3/P